HANNIBAL
ENEMY OF ROME

Ben Kane was born in Kenya and raised there and in Ireland. He qualified as a veterinary surgeon at University College Dublin, and worked in Ireland and the UK for several years. After that he travelled extensively, indulging his passion for seeing the world and learning more about ancient history. Seven continents and more than 65 countries later, he decided to settle down, for a while at least. While working in Northumberland in 2001–2002, his love of ancient history was fuelled by visits to Hadrian's Wall. He naively decided to write bestselling Roman novels, a plan which came to fruition after several years of working full time at two jobs – being a vet and writing. Retrospectively, this was an unsurprising development, because since his childhood, Ben has been fascinated by Rome, and particularly its armies. He now lives in North Somerset with his wife and family, where he has sensibly given up veterinary medicine to write full time. To find out more about Ben and his books visit: www.benkane.net.

HANNIBAL
ENEMY OF ROME
BEN KANE

arrow books

Published by Arrow 2012

10 9 8 7 6 5 4 3 2

First published in Great Britain in 2011 by Preface Publishing

20 Vauxhall Bridge Road
London, SW1V 2SA

An imprint of The Random House Group Limited

www.randomhouse.co.uk

Addresses for companies within The Random House Group Limited
can be found at www.randomhouse.co.uk

The Random House Group Limited Reg. No. 954009

A CIP catalogue record for this book is available from the British Library

ISBN 978 1 84809 229 7

The Random House Group Limited supports The Forest Stewardship Council (FSC®),
the leading international forest certification organisation. Our books carrying the FSC label are
printed on FSC® certified paper. FSC is the only forest certification scheme endorsed by the leading
environmental organisations, including Greenpeace. Our paper procurement policy can be found at
www.randomhouse.co.uk/environment

Typeset in Fournier MT by Palimpsest Book Production Limited,
Falkirk, Stirlingshire
Printed and bound by CPI Group (UK) Ltd, Croydon CR0 4YY

For Ferdia and Pippa, my wonderful children.

GAUL

Alps

Rhodanus

Taurasia Placentia **CISALPINE**
        Padus
       Genua **GAUL**

Pyrenees

Massilia

Iberus

Pisae

ITALI

IBERIA

Tagus

CORSICA

Rom

Saguntum •

Balearic Islands

SARDINIA

• Gades

New Carthage

M A R E

NUMIDIA

Carthage •

SIC

CARTHAGE

N

0   100   200   300   400   500

Miles

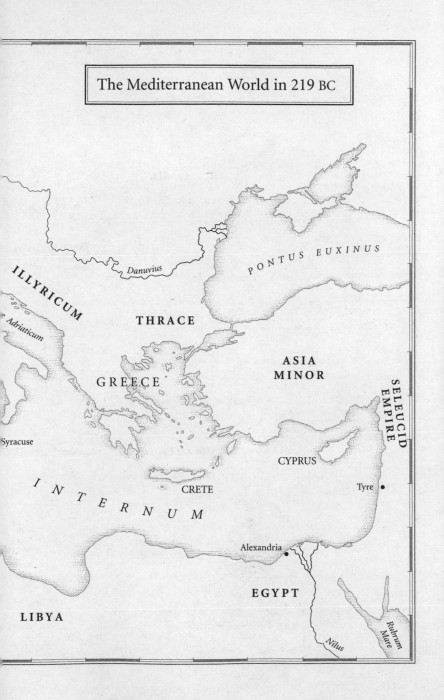

The Mediterranean World in 219 BC

ILLYRICUM

e Adriaticum

THRACE

Danuvius

PONTUS EUXINUS

GREECE

ASIA MINOR

SELEUCID EMPIRE

Syracuse

CYPRUS

INTERNUM

CRETE

Tyre •

Alexandria •

EGYPT

LIBYA

Nilus

Rubrum Mare

Chapter I: Hanno

Carthage, spring

'Hanno!' His father's voice echoed off the painted stucco walls. 'It's time to go.'

Stepping carefully over the gutter that carried liquid waste out to the soakaway in the street, Hanno looked back. He was torn between his duty and the urgent gestures of his friend, Suniaton. The political meetings his father had recently insisted he attend bored him to tears. Each one he'd been to followed exactly the same path. A group of self-important, bearded elders, clearly fond of the sound of their own voices, made interminable speeches about how Hannibal Barca's actions in Iberia were exceeding the remit granted to him. Malchus – his father – and his closest allies, who supported Hannibal, said little or nothing until the greybeards had fallen silent, when they would stand forth one by one. Invariably, Malchus spoke last of all. His words seldom varied. Hannibal, who had been commander in Iberia for just three years, was doing an outstanding job in cementing Carthage's hold over the wild native tribes, forming a disciplined army and, most importantly, filling the city's coffers with the silver from his mines. Who else was pursuing such heroic and worthy endeavours while simultaneously enriching Carthage? In defending the tribes who had been attacked by Saguntum, a city allied to Rome, he was merely reinforcing their people's sovereignty in Iberia. On these grounds, the young Barca should be left to his own devices.

Hanno knew that what motivated the politicians was fear, partly assuaged by the thought of Hannibal's forces, and greed, partly satisfied by the shiploads of precious metal from Iberia. Malchus' carefully chosen words therefore normally swayed the Senate in Hannibal's favour, but only after endless hours of debate. The interminable politicking made Hanno want to scream, and to tell the old fools what he really thought of them. Of course he would never shame his father in that manner, but nor could he face yet another day stuck indoors. The idea of a fishing trip held too much appeal.

One of Hannibal's messengers regularly came to bring his father news from Iberia, and had visited not a week since. The night-time rendezvous were supposed to be a secret, but Hanno had soon come to recognise the cloaked, sallow-skinned officer. Sapho and Bostar, his older brothers, had been allowed to stand in on the meetings for some time. Swearing Hanno to secrecy, Bostar had filled him in afterwards. Now, if he was able, Hanno simply eavesdropped. In a nutshell, Hannibal had charged Malchus and his allies with the task of ensuring that the politicians continued to back his actions. A showdown with the city of Saguntum was imminent, but conflict with Rome, Carthage's old enemy, was some way off yet.

The deep, gravelly voice called out again, echoing down the corridor that led to the central courtyard. There was a hint of annoyance in it now. 'Hanno? We'll be late.'

Hanno froze. He wasn't afraid of the dressing down his father would deliver later, more of the disappointed look in his eyes. A scion of one of Carthage's oldest families, Malchus led by example, and expected his three sons to do the same. At seventeen, Hanno was the youngest. He was also the one who most often failed to meet these exacting standards. For some reason, Malchus expected more of him than he did of Sapho and Bostar. At least that's how it seemed to Hanno. Yet farming, the traditional source of their wealth, interested him little. Warfare, his father's preferred vocation, and Hanno's great fascination, was barred to him still, thanks to his youth. His brothers would be sailing for Iberia any day. There, no doubt, they would cover themselves in glory in the taking of Saguntum. Frustration and resentment filled Hanno. All he could do was practise his riding and weapons skills. Life as ordained by his father was so boring, he thought, choosing to ignore Malchus' oft-repeated statement: 'Be patient. All good things come to those who wait.'

'Come on!' urged Suniaton, thumping Hanno on the arm. His gold earrings jingled as he jerked his head in the direction of the harbour. 'The fishermen found huge shoals of tunny in the bay at dawn. With Melqart's blessing, the fish won't have moved far. We'll catch dozens. Think of the money to be made!' His voice dropped to a whisper. 'I've taken an amphora of wine from Father's cellar. We can share it on the boat.'

Unable to resist his friend's offer, Hanno blocked his ears to Malchus' voice, which was coming closer. Tunny was one of the most prized fish in the Mediterranean. If the shoals were close to shore, this was an opportunity too good to miss. Stepping into the rutted street, he glanced once more at the symbol etched into the stone slab before the flat-roofed house's entrance. An inverted triangle topped by a flat line and then a circle, it represented his people's pre-eminent deity. Few dwellings were without it. Hanno asked Tanit's forgiveness for disobeying his father's wishes, but his excitement was such that he forgot to ask for the mother goddess's protection.

'Hanno!' His father's voice was very near now.

Without further ado, the two young men darted off into the crowd. Both their families dwelled near the top of Byrsa Hill. At the summit, reached by a monumental staircase of sixty steps, was an immense temple dedicated to Eshmoun, the god of fertility, health and well-being. Suniaton lived with his family in the sprawling complex behind the shrine, where his father served as a priest. Named in honour of the deity, Eshmuniaton – abbreviated to Suniaton or simply Suni – was Hanno's oldest and closest friend. The pair had scarcely spent a day out of each other's company since they were old enough to walk.

The rest of the neighbourhood was primarily residential. Byrsa was one of the richer quarters, as its wide, straight thoroughfares and right-angled intersections proved. The majority of the city's winding streets were no more than ten paces across, but here they averaged more than twice this width. In addition to wealthy merchants and senior army officers, the suffetes – judges – and many elders also called the area home. For this reason, Hanno ran with his gaze directed at the packed earth and the regular soakaway holes beneath his feet. Plenty of people knew who he was. The last thing he wanted was to be stopped and challenged by one of Malchus' numerous political opponents. To be dragged back home by the ear would be embarrassing and bring dishonour to his family.

As long as they didn't catch anyone's eye, he and his friend would pass unnoticed. Bare-headed and wearing tight-fitting red woollen singlets, with a central white stripe and a distinctive wide neckband, and breeches that reached to the knee, the pair looked no different to other well-to-do youths. Their garb was far more practical than the long straight wool tunics and conical felt hats favoured by most adult men, and more comfortable than the ornate jacket and pleated apron worn by those of Cypriot extraction. Sheathed daggers hung from simple leather straps thrown over their shoulders. Suniaton carried a bulging pack on his back.

Although people said that they could pass for brothers, Hanno couldn't see it most of the time. While he was tall and athletic, Suniaton was short and squat. Naturally, they both had tightly curled black hair and a dark complexion, but there the resemblance ended. Hanno's face was thin, with a straight nose and high cheekbones, while his friend's round visage and snub nose were complemented by a jutting chin. They did both have green eyes, Hanno conceded. That feature, unusual among the brown-eyed Carthaginians, was probably why they were thought to be siblings.

A step ahead of him, Suniaton nearly collided with a carpenter carrying several long cypress planks. Rather than apologise, he thumbed his nose and sprinted towards the citadel walls, now only a hundred paces away. Stifling his desire to finish the job by tipping over the angry tradesman, Hanno dodged past too, a grin splitting his face. Another similarity he and Suniaton shared was an impudent nature, quite at odds with the serious manner of most of their countrymen. It frequently got both of them in trouble, and was a constant source of irritation to their fathers.

A moment later, they passed under the immense ramparts, which were thirty paces deep and nearly the same in height. Like the outer defences, the wall was constructed from great quadrilateral blocks of sandstone. Frequent coats of whitewash ensured that the sunlight bounced off the stone, magnifying its size. Topped by a wide walkway and with regular towers, the fortifications were truly awe-inspiring. Yet the citadel was only a small part of the whole. Hanno never tired of looking down on the expanse of the sea wall that came into view as he emerged from under the gateway's shadow. Running down from the north along the city's perimeter, it swept southeast to the twin harbours, curling protectively around them before heading west. On the steep northern and eastern sides, and to the south, where the sea gave its added protection, one wall was deemed sufficient, but on the western, landward side of the peninsula, three defences had been constructed: a wide trench backed by an earthen bank, and then a huge rampart. The walls, which were in total over 180 stades in length, also contained sections with two-tiered living quarters. These could hold many thousands of troops, cavalry and their mounts, and hundreds of war elephants.

Home to nearly a quarter of a million people, the city also

demanded attention. Directly below lay the Agora, the large open space bordered by government buildings and countless shops. It was the area where residents gathered to do business, demonstrate, take the evening air, and vote. Beyond it lay the unique ports: the huge outer, rectangular merchant harbour, and the inner, circular naval docks with its small, central island. The first contained hundreds of berths for trading ships, while the second could hold more than ten-score triremes and quinqueremes in specially constructed covered sheds. To the west of the ports was the old shrine of Baal Hammon, no longer as important as it had previously been, but still venerated by many. To the east lay the Choma, the huge man-made landing stage where fishing smacks and small vessels tied up. It was also their destination.

Hanno was immensely proud of his home. He had no idea what Rome, Carthage's old enemy, looked like, but he doubted it matched his city's grandeur. He had no desire to compare Carthage with the Republic's capital, though. The only view he ever wanted of Rome was when it fell – to a victorious Carthaginian army – before seeing it burned to the ground. As Hamilcar Barca, Hannibal's father, had inculcated a hatred of all things Roman in his sons, so had Malchus in Hanno and his brothers. Like Hamilcar, Malchus had served in the first war against the Republic, fighting in Sicily for ten long, thankless years.

Unsurprisingly, Hanno and his siblings knew the details of every land skirmish and naval battle in the conflict, which had actually lasted for more than a generation. The cost to Carthage in loss of life, territory and wealth had been huge, but the city's wounds ran far deeper. Her pride had been trampled in the mud by the defeat, and this ignominy was repeated just three years after the war's conclusion. Carthage had been unilaterally forced by Rome to give up Sardinia, as well as paying more indemnities. The shabby act proved beyond doubt, Malchus would regularly rant, that all Romans were treacherous dogs, without honour. Hanno agreed, and looked forward to the day hostilities were reopened once more. Given the depth of anger still present in Carthage towards Rome, conflict was inevitable, and it would originate in Iberia. Soon.

Suniaton turned. 'Have you eaten?'

Hanno shrugged. 'Some bread and honey when I got up.'

'Me too. That was hours ago, though.' Suniaton grinned and patted his belly. 'Best get a few supplies.'

'Good idea,' Hanno replied. They kept clay gourds of water in their little boat with their fishing gear, but no food. Sunset, when they would return, was a long way off.

The streets descending Byrsa Hill did not follow the regular layout of the summit, instead radiating out like so many tributaries of a meandering river. There were far more shops and businesses visible now: bakers, butchers and stalls selling freshly caught fish, fruit and vegetables stood beside silver- and coppersmiths, perfume merchants and glass blowers. Women sat outside their doors, working at their looms, or gossiping over their purchases. Slaves carried rich men past in litters or swept the ground in front of shops. Dye-makers' premises were everywhere, their abundance due to the Carthaginian skill in harvesting the local *Murex* shellfish and pounding its flesh to yield a purple dye that commanded premium prices all over the Mediterranean. Children ran hither and thither, playing catch and chasing each other up and down the regular sets of stairs that broke the street's steep descent. Deep in conversation, a trio of well-dressed men strolled past. Recognising them as elders, who were probably on their way to the very meeting he was supposed to be attending, Hanno took a sudden interest in the array of terracotta outside a potter's workshop.

Dozens of figures — large and small — were ranked on low tables. Hanno recognised every deity in the Carthaginian pantheon. There sat a regal, crowned Baal Hammon, the protector of Carthage, on his throne; beside him Tanit was depicted in the Egyptian manner: a shapely woman's body in a well-cut dress, but with the head of a lioness. A smiling Astarte clutched a tambourine. Her consort, Melqart, known as the 'King of the City', was, among other things, the god of the sea. Various brightly coloured figures depicted him emerging from crashing waves riding a fearful-looking monster and clutching a trident in one fist. Baal Saphon, the god of storm and war, sat astride a fine charger, wearing a helmet with a long, flowing crest. Also on display was a selection of hideous, grinning painted masks – tattooed, bejewelled demons and spirits of the underworld – tomb offerings designed to ward off evil.

Hanno shivered, remembering his mother's funeral three years before. Since her death of a fever his father, never the most warm of men, had become a grim and forbidding presence who lived only to gain his revenge on Rome. For all his youth, Hanno knew that Malchus was portraying a controlled mask to the world. He must still be grieving, as surely as he and his brothers were. Arishat, Hanno's mother, had been the light to Malchus' dark, the laughter to his gravitas, the softness to his strength. The centre of the family, she had been taken from them in two horrific days and nights. Harangued by an inconsolable Malchus, the best surgeons in Carthage had toiled over her to no avail. Every last detail of her final hours was engraved in Hanno's memory. The cups of blood drained from her in a vain attempt to cool her raging temperature. Her gaunt, fevered face. The sweat-soaked sheets. His brothers trying not to cry, and failing. And lastly, her still form on the bed, tinier than she had ever been in life. Malchus kneeling alongside, great sobs racking his muscular frame. That was the only time Hanno had ever seen his father weep. The incident had never been mentioned since, nor had his mother. He swallowed hard and, checking that the elders had passed by, moved on. It hurt too much to think about such things.

Suniaton, who had not noticed Hanno's distress, paused to buy some bread, almonds and figs. Keen to lift his sombre mood,

Hanno eyed the blacksmith's forge off to one side. Wisps of smoke rose from its roughly built chimney, and the air was rich with the smells of charcoal, burning wood and oil. Harsh metallic sounds reached his ears. In the recesses of the open-fronted establishment, he glimpsed a figure in a leather apron using a pair of tongs to carefully lift a piece of glowing metal from the anvil. There was a loud hiss as the sword blade was plunged into a vat of cold water. Hanno felt his feet begin to move.

Suniaton blocked his path. 'We've got better things to do. Like making money,' he cried, shoving forward a bulging bag of almonds. 'Carry that.'

'No! You'll eat them all anyway.' Hanno pushed his friend out of the way with a grin. It was a standing joke between them that his favourite pastime was getting covered in ash and grime while Suniaton would rather plan his next meal. He was so busy laughing that he didn't see the approaching group of soldiers – a dozen Libyan spearmen – until it was too late. With a thump, Hanno collided with the first man's large, round shield.

This was no street urchin, and the spearman bit back an instinctive curse. 'Mind your step,' he cried.

Catching sight of two Carthaginian officers in the soldiers' midst, Hanno cursed. It was Sapho and Bostar. Both were dressed in their finest uniforms. Bell-shaped helmets with thick rims and yellow-feathered crests covered their heads. Layered linen *pteryges* hung below their polished bronze cuirasses to cover the groin, and contoured greaves protected their lower legs. No doubt they too were on their way to the meeting. Muttering an apology to the spearman, Hanno backed away, looking at the ground in an attempt not to be recognised.

Oblivious to Sapho and Bostar's presence, Suniaton was snorting with amusement at Hanno's collision. 'Come on,' he urged. 'We don't want to get there too late.'

'Hanno!' Bostar's voice was genial.

He pretended not to hear.

'Hanno! Come back!' barked a deeper, more commanding voice, that of Sapho.

Unwillingly, Hanno turned.

Suniaton tried to sidle away, but he had also been spotted.

'Eshmuniaton! Get over here,' Sapho ordered.

With a miserable expression, Suniaton shuffled to his friend's side.

Hanno's brothers shouldered their way forward to stand before them.

'Sapho. Bostar,' Hanno said with a false smile. 'What a surprise.'

'Is it?' Sapho demanded, his thick eyebrows meeting in a frown. A short, compact man with a serious manner like Malchus, he was twenty-two. Young to be a mid-ranking officer, but like Bostar, his ability had shone through during his training. 'We're all supposed to be heading to listen to the elders. Why aren't you with Father?'

Flushing, Hanno looked down. Damn it, he thought. In Sapho's eyes, duty to Carthage was all-important. In a single moment, their chances of a day on the boat had vanished.

Sapho gave Suniaton a hard stare, taking in his pack and the provisions in his hands. 'Because the pair of you were skiving off, that's why! Fishing, no doubt?'

Suniaton scuffed a toe in the dirt.

'Cat got your tongue?' Sapho asked acidly.

Hanno moved in front of his friend. 'We were going to catch some tunny, yes,' he admitted.

Sapho's scowl grew deeper. 'And that's more important than listening to the Council of Elders?'

As usual, his brother's high-handed attitude rankled with Hanno. This type of lecture was all too common. Most often, it felt as if Sapho was trying to be their father. Unsurprisingly, Hanno resented this. 'It's not as if the greybeards will say anything that hasn't been said a thousand times before,' he retorted. 'Just about every one is full of hot air.'

Suniaton sniggered. 'Like someone else not too far away.' He saw Hanno's warning look and fell silent.

Sapho's jaw clenched. 'You pair of impudent—' he began.

Bostar's lips twitched, and he lifted a hand to Sapho's shoulder. 'Peace,' he said. 'Hanno has a point. The elders *are* rather fond of the sound of their own voices.'

Hanno and Suniaton tried to hide their smiles.

Sapho missed Bostar's amusement, but he lapsed into a glowering silence. He was acutely aware, and resentful, that he was not the senior officer present. Although Sapho was a year older, Bostar had been promoted before him.

'It's not as if this meeting will be a matter of life and death,' Bostar continued reasonably. His wink – unseen by Sapho – told Hanno that all hope was not lost. He slyly returned the gesture. Like Hanno, Bostar resembled their mother, Arishat, with a thin face and piercing green eyes. Where Sapho's nose was broad, his was long and narrow. Rangy and athletic, his long black hair was tied in a ponytail, which emerged from under his helmet. Hanno had far more in common with the gentle Bostar than he did with Sapho. Currently, his feelings for his eldest brother often verged on dislike. 'Does our father know where you are?'

'No,' admitted Hanno.

Bostar turned to Suniaton. 'I would assume, therefore, that Bodesmun is also in the dark?'

'Of course he is,' Sapho butted in, eager to regain control. 'As usual where these two are concerned.'

Bostar ignored his brother's outburst. 'Well?'

'Father thinks I'm at home, studying,' Suniaton revealed.

Sapho's expression grew a shade more self-righteous. 'Let's see what Bodesmun and Father have to say when they discover what you were both really up to. We have enough time to do that before the Council meets.' He jerked a thumb at the spearmen. 'Get in amongst them.'

Hanno scowled, but there was little point arguing. Sapho was in a particularly zealous mood. 'Come on,' he muttered to Suniaton. 'The shoals will be there another day.'

Before they could move a step, Bostar spoke. 'I don't see why they shouldn't go fishing.'

Hanno and Suniaton stared at each other, amazed.

Sapho's brows rose. 'What do you mean?'

'Such activities will shortly be impossible for both of us, and we'll miss them.' Bostar made a face. 'That same day will come for Hanno soon enough. Let him have his fun while he can.'

Hanno's heart leaped; the gravity of Bostar's words was lost on him.

Sapho's face grew thoughtful. After a moment, though, his sanctimonious frown returned. 'Duty is duty,' he declared.

'Lighten up, Sapho. You're twenty-two, not fifty-two!' Bostar threw a glance at the spearmen, who were uniformly grinning. 'Who would notice Hanno's absence apart from us and Father? And you're not Suni's keeper any more than I am.'

Sapho's lips thinned at the teasing, but he relented. The idea of Bostar pulling rank on him was too much to bear. 'Father won't be happy,' he said gruffly, 'but I suppose you're right.'

Hanno could hardly believe what he was hearing. 'Thank you!' His cry was echoed by Suniaton.

'Go on, before I change my mind,' Sapho warned.

The friends didn't need any further prompting. With a grateful look at Bostar, who threw them another wink, the pair disappeared into the crowd. Broad grins creased both their faces. They would still be held to account, thought Hanno, but not until that evening. Visions of a boat full of tunny filled his mind once more.

'Sapho's a serious one, isn't he?' Suniaton commented.

'You know how he is,' Hanno replied. 'In his eyes, things like fishing are a waste of time.'

Suniaton nudged him. 'Just as well I didn't tell him what I was thinking, then.' He grinned at Hanno's enquiring look. 'That it would do him good to relax more – perhaps by going fishing!'

12

Hanno's mouth opened with shock, before he laughed. 'Thank the gods you didn't say that! There's no way he would have let us go.'

Smiling with relief, the friends continued their journey. Soon they had reached the Agora. Its four sides, each a stade in length, were made up of grand porticoes and covered walkways. The beating heart of the city, it was home to the building where the Council of Elders met, as well as government offices, a library, numerous temples and shops. It was also where, on summer evenings, the better-off young men and women would gather in groups, a safe distance apart, to eye each other up. Socialising with the opposite sex was frowned upon, and chaperones for the girls were never far away. Despite this, inventive methods to approach the object of one's desire were constantly being invented. Of recent months, this had become one of the friends' favourite pastimes. Fishing beat it still, but not by much, thought Hanno wistfully, scanning the crowds for any sign of attractive female flesh.

Instead of gaggles of coy young beauties, though, the Agora was full of serious-looking politicians, merchants and high-ranking soldiers. They were heading for one place. The central edifice, within the hallowed walls of which more than three hundred elders met on a regular basis as, for nearly half a millennium, their predecessors had done. Overseen by the two suffetes – the rulers elected every year – they, the most important men in Carthage, decided everything from trading policy to negotiations with foreign states. Their range of powers did not end there. The Council of Elders also had the power to declare war and peace, even though it no longer appointed the army's generals. Since the war with Rome, that had been left to the people. The only pre-requisites for candidature of the council were citizenship, wealth, an age of thirty or more, and the demonstration of ability, whether in the agricultural, mercantile, or military fields.

Ordinary citizens could participate in politics via the Assembly of the People, which congregated once a year, by the order of the suffetes, in the Agora. During times of great crisis, it was permitted to gather spontaneously and debate the issues of the day. While its powers were limited, they included electing the suffetes and the generals. Hanno was looking forward to the next meeting, which would be the first he'd attend as an adult, entitled to vote. Although Hannibal's enormous public popularity guaranteed his reappointment as the commander-in-chief of Carthage's forces in Iberia, Hanno wanted to show his support for the Barca clan. It was the only way he could at the moment. Despite his requests, Malchus would not let him join Hannibal's army, as Sapho and Bostar had done after their mother's death. Instead, he had to finish his education. There was no point fighting his father on this. Once Malchus had spoken, he never went back on a decision.

Following Carthaginian tradition, Hanno had largely fended for himself from the age of fourteen, although he continued to sleep at home. He'd worked in a forge, among other places, and thus earned enough to live on without committing any crimes or shameful acts. This was similar to, but not as harsh, as the Spartan way. He had also taken classes in Greek, Iberian and Latin. Hanno did not especially enjoy languages, but he had come to accept that such a skill would prove useful among the polyglot of nationalities that formed the Carthaginian army. His people did not take naturally to war, so they hired mercenaries, or enlisted their subjects, to fight on their behalf. Libyans, Iberians, Gauls and Balearic tribesmen were among those who brought their differing qualities to Carthage's forces.

Hanno's favourite subject was military matters. Malchus himself taught him the history of war, from the battles of Xenophon and Thermopylae to the victories won by Alexander of Macedon. Central to his father's lessons were the intricate details of tactics and planning. Particular attention was paid to Carthaginian defeats in the war with Rome, and the reasons for

14

them. 'We lost because of our leaders' lack of determination. All they thought about was how to contain the conflict, not win it. How to minimise cost, not disregard it in the total pursuit of victory,' Malchus had thundered during one memorable lesson. 'The Romans are motherless curs, but by all the gods, they possess strength of purpose. Whenever they lost a battle, they recruited more men, and rebuilt their ships. They did not give up. When the public purse was empty, their leaders willingly spent their own wealth. Their damn Republic means everything to them. Yet who in Carthage offered to send us the supplies and soldiers we needed so badly in Sicily? My father, the Barcas, and a handful of others. No one else.' He'd barked a short, angry laugh. 'Why should I be surprised? Our ancestors were traders, not soldiers. To gain our rightful revenge, we must follow Hannibal. He's a natural soldier and a born leader – as his father was. Carthage never gave Hamilcar the chance to beat Rome, but we can offer it to his son. When the time is right.'

A red-faced, portly senator shoved past with a curse. Startled, Hanno recognised Hostus, one of his father's most implacable enemies. The self-important politician was in such a hurry that he didn't even notice whom he'd collided with. Hanno hawked and spat, although he was careful not to do it in Hostus' direction. He and his windbag friends complained endlessly about Hannibal, yet were content to accept the shiploads of silver sent from his mines in Iberia. Lining their own pockets with a proportion of this wealth, they had no desire to confront Rome again. Hanno, on the other hand, was more than prepared to lay down his life fighting their old enemy, but the fruit of revenge wasn't ripe. Hannibal was preparing himself in Iberia, and that was good enough. For now, they had to wait.

The pair skirted the edge of the Agora, avoiding the worst of the crowds. Around the back of the Senate, the buildings soon became a great deal less grand, looking as shabby as one would expect close to a port. Nonetheless, the slum stood in stark contrast to the splendour just a short walk away. There were few businesses, and the single- or twin-roomed houses were miserable affairs made of mud bricks, all apparently on the point of collapse. The iron-hard ruts in the street were more than a handspan deep, threatening to break their ankles if they tripped. No work parties to fill in the holes with sand here, thought Hanno, thinking of Byrsa Hill. He felt even more grateful for his elevated position in life.

Snot-nosed, scrawny children wearing little more than rags swarmed in, clamouring for a coin or a crust, while their lank-haired, pregnant mothers gazed at them with eyes deadened by a life of misery. Half-dressed girls posed provocatively in some doorways, their rouged cheeks and lips unable to conceal the fact that they were barely out of childhood. Unshaven, ill-clad men lounged around, rolling sheep tail bones in the dirt for a few worn coins. They stared suspiciously, but none dared hinder the friends' progress. At night it might be a different matter, but already they were under the shadow of the great wall, with its smartly turned-out sentries marching to and fro along the battlements. Although common, lawlessness was punished where possible by the authorities, and a shout of distress would bring help clattering down one of the many sets of stairs.

The tang of salt grew strong in the air. Gulls keened overhead, and the shouts of sailors could be heard from the ports. Feeling his excitement grow, Hanno charged down a narrow alleyway, and up the stone steps at the end of it. Suniaton was right behind him. It was a steep climb, but they were both fit, and reached the top without breaking sweat. A red concrete walkway extended the entire width of the wall – thirty paces – just as it did for the entire length of the defensive perimeter. Strongly built towers were positioned every fifty steps or so. The soldiers visible were garrisoned in the barracks, which were built at intervals below the ramparts.

The nearest sentries, a quartet of Libyan spearmen, glanced

idly at the pair but, seeing nothing of concern, looked away. In peacetime, citizens were allowed on the wall during the hours of daylight. Perfunctorily checking the turquoise sea below their section, the junior officer fell back to gossiping with his men. Hanno trotted past, admiring the soldiers' massive round shields, which were even larger than those used by the Greeks. Although fashioned from wood, they were covered in goatskin, and rimmed with bronze. The same demonic face was painted on each, and denoted their unit.

Trumpets blared one after another from the naval port, and Suniaton jostled past. 'Quick,' he shouted. 'They might be launching a quinquereme!'

Hanno chased eagerly after his friend. The view from the walkway into the circular harbour was second to none. In a masterful feat of engineering, the Carthaginian warships were invisible from all other positions. Protected from unfriendly eyes on the seaward side by the city wall, they were concealed from the moored merchant vessels by the naval port's slender entrance, which was only just wider than a quinquereme, the largest type of warship.

Hanno scowled as they reached a good vantage point. Instead of the imposing sight of a warship sliding backwards into the water, he saw a purple-cloaked admiral strutting along the jetty that led from the periphery of the circular docks to the central island, where the navy's headquarters were. Another fanfare of trumpets sounded, making sure that every man in the place knew who was arriving. 'What has he got to swagger about?' Hanno muttered. Malchus reserved much of his anger for the incompetent Carthaginian fleet, so he had learned to feel the same way. Carthage's days as a superpower of the sea were long gone, their fleet smashed into so much driftwood by Rome during the two nations' bitter struggle over Sicily. Remarkably, the Romans had been a non-seafaring race before the conflict. Undeterred by this major disadvantage, they had learned the skills of naval warfare,

BEN KANE

adding a few tricks of their own in the process. Since her defeat, Carthage had done little to reclaim the waves.

Hanno sighed. Truly, all their hopes lay on the land, with Hannibal.

Some time later, Hanno had forgotten all his worries. Half a mile offshore, their little boat was positioned directly over a mass of tunny. The shoal's location had not been hard to determine, thanks to the roiling water created by the large silver fish as they hunted sardines. Small boats dotted the location and clouds of seabirds swooped and dived overhead, attracted by the prospect of food. Suniaton's source had been telling the truth, and neither youth had been able to stop grinning since their arrival. Their task was simple: one rowed, the other lowered their net into the sea. Although they had seen better days, the plaited strands were still capable of landing a catch. Pieces of wood along the top of the net helped it to float, while tiny lumps of lead pulled its lower edge down into the water. Their first throw had netted nearly a dozen tunny, each one longer than a man's forearm. Subsequent attempts were just as successful, and now the bottom of the boat was calf-deep in fish. Any more, and they would risk overloading their craft.

'A good morning's work,' pronounced Suniaton.

'Morning?' challenged Hanno, squinting at the sun. 'We've been here less than an hour. It couldn't have been easier, eh?'

Suniaton regarded him solemnly. 'Don't put yourself down. I think our efforts deserve a toast.' With a flourish, he produced a small amphora from his pack.

Hannibal laughed; Suniaton was incorrigible.

Encouraged, Suniaton went on talking as if he were serving guests at an important banquet. 'Not the most expensive wine in Father's collection, I recall, but a palatable one nonetheless.' Using his knife, he prised off the wax seal and removed the lid. Raising the amphora to his lips, he gulped a large mouthful. 'Acceptable,' he declared, handing over the clay vessel.

18

'Philistine. Sip it slowly.' Hanno took a small swig and rolled it around his mouth as Malchus had taught him. The red wine had a light and fruity flavour, but little undertone. 'It needs a few more years, I think.'

'Now who's being pompous?' Suniaton kicked a tunny at him. 'Shut up and drink!'

Grinning, Hanno obeyed, taking more this time.

'Don't finish it,' cried Suniaton.

Despite his protest, the amphora was quickly drained. At once the ravenous pair launched into the bread, nuts and fruit that Suniaton had bought. With their bellies full, and their work done, it was the most natural thing in the world to lie back and close their eyes. Unaccustomed to consuming much wine, before long they were both snoring.

It was the cold wind on his face that woke Hanno. Why was the boat moving so much? he wondered vaguely. He shivered, feeling quite chilled. Opening gummy eyes, he took in a prone Suniaton opposite, still clutching the empty amphora. At his feet, the heaps of blank-eyed fish, their bodies already rigid. Looking up, Hanno felt a pang of fear. Instead of the usual clear sky, all he could see were towering banks of blue-black clouds. They were pouring in from the northwest. He blinked, refusing to believe what he was seeing. How could the weather have changed so fast? Mockingly, the first spatters of rain hit Hanno's upturned cheeks an instant later. Scanning the choppy waters, he could see no sign of the fishing craft that had surrounded theirs earlier. Nor could he see the land. Real alarm seized him.

He leaned over and shook Suniaton. 'Wake up!'

The only response was an irritated grunt.

'Suni!' This time, Hanno slapped his friend across the face.

'Hey!' Suniaton cried, sitting up. 'What's that for?'

Hanno didn't answer. 'Where in the name of the gods are we?' he shouted.

All semblance of drunkenness fell away as Suniaton turned his head from side to side. 'Sacred Tanit above,' he breathed. 'How long were we asleep?'

'I don't know,' Hanno growled. 'A long time.' He pointed to the west, where the sun's light was just visible behind the storm clouds. Its position told them that it was late in the afternoon. He stood, taking great care not to capsize the boat. Focusing on the horizon, where the sky met the threatening sea, he spent long moments trying to make out the familiar walls of Carthage, or the craggy promontory that lay to the north of the city.

'Well?' Suniaton could not keep the fear from his voice.

Hanno sat down heavily. 'I can't see a thing. We're fifteen or twenty stades from shore. Maybe more.'

What little colour there had been in Suniaton's face drained away. Instinctively, he clutched at the hollow gold tube that hung from a thong around his neck. Decorated with a lion's head at one end, it contained tiny parchments covered with protective spells and prayers to the gods. Hanno wore a similar one. With great effort, he refrained from copying his friend. 'We'll row back,' he announced.

'In these seas?' screeched Suniaton. 'Are you mad?'

Hanno glared back. 'What other choice have we? To jump in?'

His friend looked down. Both were more confident in the water than most, but they had never swum long distances, especially in conditions as bad as these.

Seizing the oars from the floor, Hanno placed them in the iron rowlocks. He turned the boat's rounded bow towards the west and began to row. Instantly, he knew that his attempt was doomed to fail. The power surging at him was more potent than anything he'd ever felt in his life. It felt like a raging, out-of-control beast, with the howling wind providing its terrifying voice. Ignoring his gut feeling, Hanno concentrated on each stroke with fierce intensity. Lean back. Drag the oars through the water. Lift them free.

Bend forward, pushing the handles between his knees. Over and over he repeated the process, ignoring his pounding head and dry mouth, and cursing their foolishness in drinking all of the wine. If I had listened to my father, I'd still be at home, he thought bitterly. Safe on dry land.

Finally, when the muscles in his arms were trembling with exhaustion, Hanno stopped. Without looking up, he knew that their position would have changed little. For every three strokes' progress, the current carried them at least two further out to sea. 'Well?' he shouted. 'Can you see anything?'

'No,' Suniaton replied grimly. 'Move over. It's my turn, and this is our best chance.'

Our last chance, Hanno thought, gazing at the darkening sky.

Gingerly, they exchanged places on the little wooden thwarts that were the boat's only fittings. Thanks to the mass of slippery fish underfoot, it was even more difficult than usual. While his friend laboured at the oars, Hanno strained for a glimpse of land over the waves. Neither spoke. There was no point. The rain was now drumming down on their backs, combining with the wind's noise to form a shrieking cacophony that made normal speech impossible. Only the sturdy construction of their boat had prevented them from capsizing thus far.

At length, his energy spent, Suniaton shipped the oars. He looked at Hanno. There was a glimmer of hope in his eyes.

Hanno shook his head once.

'It's supposed to be the summer!' Suniaton cried. 'Gales like this shouldn't happen without warning.'

'There would have been signs,' Hanno snapped back. 'Why do you think there are no other boats out here? They must have headed for the shore when the wind began to get up.'

Suniaton flushed and hung his head. 'I'm sorry,' he muttered. 'It's my fault. I should never have taken Father's wine.'

Hanno gripped his friend's knee. 'Don't blame yourself. You didn't force me to drink it. That was my choice.'

Suniaton managed a half-smile. That was, until he looked down. 'No!'

Hanno followed his gaze and saw the tunny floating around his feet. They were shipping water, and enough of it to warrant immediate action. Trying not to panic, he began throwing the precious fish overboard. Survival was far more important than money. With the floor clear, he soon found a loose nail in one of the planks. Removing one of his sandals, he used the iron-studded sole to hammer the nail partially home, thereby reducing the influx of seawater. Fortunately, there was a small bucket on board, containing spare pieces of lead for the net. Grabbing it, Hanno began bailing hard. To his immense relief, it didn't take long before he'd reduced the water to an acceptable level.

A loud rumble of thunder overhead nearly deafened him.

Suniaton moaned with fear, and Hanno jerked upright.

The sky overhead was now a menacing black colour, and in the depths of the clouds a flickering yellow-white colour presaged lightning. The waves were being whipped into a frenzy by the wind, which was growing stronger by the moment. The storm was approaching its peak. More water slopped into the boat, and Hanno redoubled his efforts with the bucket. Any chance of rowing back to Carthage was long gone. They were going one direction. East. Into the middle of the Mediterranean. He tried not to let his panic show.

'What's going to happen to us?' Suniaton asked plaintively.

Realising that his friend was seeking reassurance, Hanno tried to think of an optimistic answer, but couldn't. The only outcome possible was an early meeting for them both with Melqart, the marine god.

In his palace at the bottom of the sea.

Chapter II: Quintus

Near Capua, Campania

Quintus woke soon after dawn, when the first rays of sunlight crept through the window. Never one to linger in bed, the sixteen-year-old threw off his blanket. Wearing only a *licium*, or linen undergarment, he padded to the small shrine in the far corner of his room. Excitement coursed through him. Today he would lead a bear hunt for the first time. It was not long until his birthday, and Fabricius, his father, wanted him to mark his transition to manhood in fitting fashion. 'Assuming the toga is all well and good,' he'd said the night before, 'but you have Oscan blood in your veins too. What better way to prove one's courage than by killing the biggest predator in Italy?'

Quintus knelt before the altar. Closing his eyes, he sent up his usual prayers requesting that he and his family remain healthy and prosperous. Then he added several more. That he would be able to find a bear's trail, and not lose it. That his courage would not fail him when it came to confronting the beast. That his spear thrust would be swift and true.

'Don't worry, brother,' came a voice from behind him. 'Today will go well.'

Surprised, Quintus turned to regard his sister, who was peering around the half-open door. Aurelia was almost three years younger than he, and loved her sleep. 'You're up early,' he said with an indulgent smile.

She yawned, running a hand through her dense black hair, a longer version of his own. Sharing straight noses, slightly pointed chins and grey eyes, they were clearly siblings. 'I couldn't sleep, thinking about your hunt.'

'Are you worried for me?' he teased, glad to be distracted from his own concerns.

Aurelia came a little further into the room. 'Of course not. Well, a little. I've prayed to Diana, though. She will guide you,' she declared solemnly.

'I know,' Quintus replied, expressing a confidence that he did not entirely feel. Bowing to the figures on the altar, he rose. Ducking his head into the bronze ewer that stood by the bed, he rubbed the water from his face and shoulders with a piece of linen. 'I'll tell you all about it this evening.' He shrugged on a short-sleeved tunic, and then sat to lace up his sandals.

She frowned. 'I want to see it for myself.'

'Women don't go hunting.'

'It's so unfair,' she protested.

'Many things are unfair,' Quintus answered. 'You have to accept that.'

'But you taught me how to use a sling.'

'Maybe that wasn't such a good idea,' Quintus muttered. Much to his surprise, Aurelia had proved to be a deadly shot, which had naturally redoubled her desire to partake of forbidden activities. 'We've managed to keep our secrets safe so far, but imagine Mother's reaction if she found out.'

'You're on the brink of womanhood,' said Aurelia, mimicking Atia, their mother. 'Such behaviour does not befit a young lady. It must come to an immediate end.'

'Precisely,' Quintus replied, ignoring her scowl. 'Never mind what she'd say if she knew you were riding a horse.' He didn't want to lose his favourite companion, but this matter was beyond his control. 'That's how life is for women.'

'Cooking. Weaving. Taking care of the garden. Supervising the slaves. It's so boring,' Aurelia retorted hotly. 'Not like hunting or learning to use a sword.'

'It's not as if you're strong enough to wield something like a spear anyway.'

'Isn't it?' Aurelia rolled up one sleeve of her nightdress and flexed her biceps. She smiled at his surprise. 'I've been lifting stones like you do.'

'Eh?' Quintus' jaw dropped further. Keen to get as fit as possible, he'd been doing extra training in the woods above the villa. He'd clearly failed to conceal his tracks. 'You've been spying on me? And copying me?'

She grinned with delight. 'Of course. Once my lessons and duties are over, it's easy enough to slip away without being noticed.'

Quintus shook his head. 'Determined, aren't you?' Persuading her to give it all up would be harder than he had thought. He was glad that the duty wouldn't fall to him. Guiltily, Quintus remembered hearing his parents talking about how it would soon be time to find her a husband. He knew how Aurelia would take that announcement. Badly.

'I know that it can't go on for ever,' she declared gloomily. 'They'll be looking to marry me off shortly, no doubt.'

Quintus hid his shock. Even if Aurelia hadn't heard that particular conversation, it wasn't surprising that she was aware of what would happen. Maybe he could help, then, rather than pretending it would never come to pass? 'There's a lot to be said for arranged marriages,' he ventured. It was true. Most nobles arranged unions for their children that were mutually beneficial to both parties. It was how the country ran. 'They can be very happy.'

Aurelia gave him a scornful look. 'Do you expect me to believe that? Anyway, our parents married for love. Why shouldn't I?'

'Their situation was unusual. It's not likely to happen to you,' he countered. 'Besides, Father would keep your interests at heart, not just those of the family.'

'Will I be happy, though?'

'With the help of the gods, yes. Which is more than might happen to me,' he added, trying to lighten the mood. 'I could end up with an old hag who makes my life a misery!' Quintus was glad, though, to be male. No doubt he would eventually wed, but there would be no unseemly rush to marry him off. Meanwhile, his adolescent libido was being satisfied by Elira, a striking slave girl from Illyricum. She was part of the household, and slept on the floor of the atrium, which facilitated sneaking her into his room at night. Quintus had been bedding her for two months, ever since he'd realised that her sultry looks were being directed at him. As far as he was aware, no one else had any idea of their relationship.

Finally, she smiled. 'You're far too handsome for that to happen.'

He laughed off her compliment. 'Time for breakfast,' he announced, continuing to move away from the awkward subject of marriage.

To his relief, Aurelia nodded. 'You'll need a decent meal to give you energy for the hunt.'

A knot of tension formed in Quintus' belly, and what appetite he'd had vanished. He would have to eat something, though, even if it was only for appearance's sake.

Leaving Aurelia chatting to Julius, the avuncular slave who ran the kitchen, Quintus sloped out of the door. He had barely eaten, and he hoped that Aurelia hadn't noticed. A few steps into the peristyle, or courtyard, he met Elira. She was carrying a basket of vegetables and herbs from the villa's garden. As usual, she gave him a look full of desire. It was wasted on Quintus this morning. He gave her a reflex smile and brushed past.

'Quintus!'

He jumped. The voice was one of the most recognisable on the estate. Atia, his mother. Quintus could see no one, which meant that she was probably in the atrium, the family's primary living space. He hurried past the pattering fountain in the centre of the colonnaded courtyard, and into the cool of the *tablinum*, the reception room that led to the atrium, and thence the hallway.

'She's a good-looking girl.'

Quintus spun to find his mother standing in the shadows by the doors, a good vantage point to look into the peristyle. 'W-what?' he stammered.

'Nothing wrong with bedding a slave, of course,' she said, approaching. As always, Quintus was struck by her immense poise and beauty. Oscan nobility through and through, Atia was short and slim and took great care with her appearance. A dusting of ochre reddened her high cheekbones. Her eyebrows and the rims of her eyelids had been finely marked out with ash. A dark red *stola*, or long tunic, belted at the waist, was complemented by a cream shawl. Her long raven-black hair was pinned back by ivory pins, and topped by a diadem. 'But don't make it so frequent. It gives them ideas above their station.'

Quintus' face coloured. He'd never discussed sex with his mother, let alone had his activities commented upon. Somehow, he wasn't surprised that it was she who had brought it up, though, rather than his father. Fabricius was a soldier, but as he often liked to say, his wife had only been prevented from being one by virtue of her sex. Much of the time, Atia was sterner than he was. 'How did you know?'

Her grey eyes fixed him to the spot. 'I've heard you at night. One would have to be deaf not to.'

'Oh,' Quintus whispered. He didn't know where to look. Mortified, he studied the richly patterned mosaic beneath his feet, wishing it would open up and swallow him. He'd thought they'd been so discreet.

'Get over it. You're not the first noble's son to plough the furrow with a pretty slave girl.'

'No, Mother.'

She waved her hands dismissively. 'Your father did the same when he was younger. Everyone does.'

Quintus was stunned by his mother's sudden openness. It must be part of becoming a man, he thought. 'I see.'

'You should be safe enough with Elira. She is clean,' Atia announced briskly. 'But choose new bed companions carefully. When visiting a brothel, make it an expensive one. It's very easy to pick up disease.'

Quintus' mouth opened and closed. He didn't ask how his mother knew that Elira was clean. As Atia's *ornatrix*, the Illyrian had to help dress her each morning. No doubt she'd been grilled as soon as Atia had become aware of her involvement with him. 'Yes, Mother.'

'Ready for the hunt?'

He twisted beneath her penetrating scrutiny, wondering if she could see his fear. 'I think so.'

To his relief, his mother made no comment. 'Have you prayed to the gods?' she asked.

'Yes.'

'Let us do it again.'

They made their way into the atrium, which was lit by a rectangular hole in the ceiling. A downward-sloping roof allowed rainwater to fall into the centre of the room, where it landed in a specially built pool. The walls were painted in rich colours, depicting rows of columns that led on to other, imaginary chambers. The effect made the space seem even bigger. This was the central living area of the large villa, and off it were their bedrooms, Fabricius' office, and a quartet of storerooms. A shrine was situated in one of the corners nearest to the garden.

There a small stone altar was decorated with statues of Jupiter, Mars, or Mamers as the Oscans called him, and Diana. Guttering flames issued from the flat, circular oil lamps sitting before each. Effigies of the family's ancestors hung on the wall above. Most were Fabricius' ancestors: Romans, the warlike people who had conquered Campania just over a century before, but, in a real testament to his father's respect for his wife, some were Atia's forebears: Oscan nobility who had lived in the area for many generations. Naturally, Quintus was fiercely proud of both heritages.

They knelt side by side in the dim light, each making their silent requests of the deities.

Quintus repeated the prayers he'd made in his room. They eased his fear somewhat, but could not dispel it. By the time he had finished, his embarrassment about Elira had subsided. He was still discomfited, however, to find his mother's eyes upon him as he rose.

'Your ancestors will be watching over you,' she murmured. 'To help with the hunt. To guide your spear. Do not forget that.'

She *had* seen his fear. Ashamed, Quintus nodded jerkily.

'There you are! I've been looking for you.' Fabricius came into the room from the hall. Short and compact, his close-cut hair was more grey now than brown. Clean-shaven, he had a ruddier complexion than Quintus, but possessed the same straight nose and strong jawline. He was already wearing his hunting clothes – an old tunic, a belt with an ivory-handled dagger, and heavy-duty leather sandals. Even in civilian dress, he managed to look soldier-like. 'Made your devotions?'

Quintus nodded.

'We had best get ready.'

'Yes, Father.' Quintus glanced at his mother.

'Go on,' Atia urged. 'I will see you later.'

Quintus took heart. She must think I'll succeed, he thought.

'It's time to choose your spear.' Fabricius led the way to one of the storerooms, where his weapons and armour were stored. Quintus had only entered the chamber a handful of times, but it was his favourite place in the house. A ripple of excitement flowed through him as his father produced a small key and slipped it into the padlock. It opened with a quiet click. Undoing the latch, Fabricius pulled wide the door, allowing the daylight in.

A dim twilight still dominated the little room, but Quintus' eyes were immediately drawn to a wooden stand upon which was perched a distinctively shaped, broad-brimmed Boeotian helmet. What made it stand out was its flowing red horsehair crest. Now faded by time, its effect was dramatic nonetheless. Quintus grinned, remembering the day his father had left the door ajar, and he'd illicitly tried the helmet on, imagining himself as a grown man, a cavalryman in one of Rome's legions. He longed for the day when he'd possess one himself.

A pair of simple bronze greaves made from the same material lay on the floor beneath the helmet. A round cavalry shield, made from ox-hide, was propped up nearby. Leaning against it was a long, bone-handled sword in a leather scabbard bound with bronze fastenings: a *gladius hispaniensis*. According to his father, the weapon had been adopted by Rome after they had encountered it in the hands of Iberian mercenaries fighting for Carthage. Although it was unusual still for a cavalryman to bear one, virtually every legionary was now armed with a similar sword. Possessing a straight, double-edged blade nearly as long as a man's arm, the gladius was lethal in the right hands.

Quintus watched in awe as Fabricius traced his fingers affectionately over the helmet, and touched the hilt of the sword. This evidence of his father's former life fascinated him; he also yearned to learn the same martial skills. While Quintus was proficient at hunting, he had undergone little in the way of weapons training. Romans received this when they joined the army, and that couldn't happen until he was seventeen. His lessons, which included military history and tactics, and hunting boar, would have to do. For now.

Finally, Fabricius moved to a weapons rack. 'Take your pick.'

Quintus admired the various types of javelin and hoplite thrusting spears before him, but his needs that day were quite specific. Bringing down a charging bear was very different to taking on an enemy soldier. He needed far more stopping power. Instinctively, his fingers closed on the broad ash shaft of a spear that he had used before. It had a large, double-edged, leaf-shaped blade attached to the rest of the weapon by a long hollow shank. A thick iron spike projected from each side of the base of this. They were designed to prevent the quarry from reaching the person holding the spear. Him, in other words. 'This one,' he said, trying to keep his mind clear of such thoughts.

'A wise choice,' his father said, sounding relieved. He clapped Quintus on the shoulder. 'What next?'

He was being given complete control of the hunt, Quintus realised with a thrill. The days and weeks he'd spent learning to track over the previous two years were over. He thought for a moment. 'Six dogs should be enough. A slave to control each pair. Agesandros can come too: he's a good hunter, and he can keep an eye on the slaves.'

'Anything else?'

Quintus laughed. 'Some food and water would be a good idea, I suppose.'

'Very good,' agreed his father. 'I'll go to the kitchen and organise those supplies. Why don't you select the slaves and dogs you want?'

Still astonished by their role reversal, Quintus headed outside. For the first time he felt the full weight of responsibility on his shoulders. It was critical that he make the correct decisions. Bear hunting was extremely dangerous, and men's lives would depend on him.

*　*　*

Not long after, the little party set off. In the lead was Quintus, with his father walking alongside. Both were unencumbered except for their spears and a water bag each. Next came Agesandros, a Sicilian Greek who had belonged to Fabricius for many years. Trusted by his master, he also carried a hunting spear. A pack hung from his back, containing bread, cheese, onions and a hunk of dried meat.

Through sheer hard work, Agesandros had worked his way up to become the *vilicus*, the most important slave on the farm. He had not been born into captivity, though. Like many of his people, Agesandros had fought alongside the Romans in the war against Carthage. Captured after a skirmish, he had been sold into slavery by the Carthaginians. It was ironic, thought Quintus, that the Sicilian had become the slave of a Roman. Yet Fabricius and Agesandros got on well. In fact, the overseer had a good relationship with the entire family. His genial manner and willingness to answer questions meant that he had been a favourite with Quintus and Aurelia since they were tiny children. Although he was now aged forty or more, the bandy-legged vilicus was in excellent physical shape, and ruled over the slaves with an iron grip.

Last came three sturdy Gauls, chosen by Quintus because of their affinity with the hunting dogs. One in particular, a squat, tattooed man with a broken nose, spent all his free time with the pack, teaching them new commands. Like the other slaves, the trio had been toiling in the fields under Agesandros' supervision that morning. It was sowing time, when they had to work from dawn till dusk under the hot sun. The diversion of a bear hunt was therefore most welcome, and they chatted animatedly to each other in their own tongue as they walked. In front of each man ran a pair of large brindle dogs, straining at the leather leashes tied around their throats. With broad heads and heavily muscled bodies, they were the opposite of Fabricius' smaller dogs, which had tufted ears and feathered flanks. The former were scent hounds, while the latter relied on sight.

The sun beat down from a cloudless sky as they left behind the fields of wheat that surrounded the villa. The sundial in the courtyard had told Quintus it was only just gone *hora secunda*. The characteristic whirring sound of cicadas was starting up, but the heat haze that hung in the air daily had not yet formed. He led the way along a narrow track that twisted and wound through the olive trees dotting the slopes above the farm.

Having traversed an area of cleared earth, they entered the mixed beech and oak woods that covered most of the surrounding countryside. Although the hills were much lower than the Apennines, which ran down Italy's spine, they were home to an occasional bear. It was unlikely that he would find traces this near the farm, however. Solitary by nature, the large creatures avoided humans if at all possible. Quintus scanned the ground anyway, but seeing nothing, he picked up speed.

Like every other large town, Capua held its own *ludi*, or games, affording Quintus the opportunity to see a bear fight once before. It had not been a pretty sight. Terrified by the alien environment and baying crowds, the beast had had little chance against two trained hunters armed with spears. He had vivid memories, though, of the tremendous power in its strong jaws and slashing claws. Facing a bear in its own territory, alone, would be an entirely different prospect to the one-sided spectacle he'd witnessed in Capua. Quintus' stomach clenched into a knot, but his pace did not slacken. Fabricius, like all Roman fathers, held the power of life and death over his son, and he had chosen the task. Quintus could not let down his mother either. It was his duty to succeed. By sunset, I'll be a man, he thought proudly. Quintus couldn't help imagining, however, that he might end his days bleeding to death on the forest floor.

They climbed steadily, leaving the deciduous woods behind. Now they were surrounded by pines, junipers and cypress trees. The air grew cooler and Quintus began to worry. He'd seen piles of dung, and treetrunks with distinctive claw marks scratched into the bark, in this area before. Today, he saw nothing that wasn't weeks, even months, old. He kept going, praying to Diana, the goddess of the hunt, for a sign, but his request was in vain. Not a single bird called; no deer broke from cover. Finally, not knowing what else to do, he stopped, forcing everyone else to do the same. Acutely aware of his father at his back, Agesandros staring, and the Gauls giving each other knowing looks, Quintus racked his brains. He knew this ground like the back of his hand. Where was the best place to find a bear on such a warm day?

Quintus glanced at his father, who simply stared back at him. He would get no help.

Attempting to conceal his laughter, one of the Gauls coughed loudly. Quintus flushed with anger, but Fabricius did nothing. Nor did Agesandros. He looked at his father again, but Fabricius' gaze was set. He would get no sympathy, and the Gaul no reprimand. Today of all days he had to earn the vilicus' and the slaves' respect. Again Quintus pondered. At last an idea popped into his mind.

'Blackberries,' he blurted. 'They love blackberries.' Higher up, in the clearings on the south-facing slopes, were sprawling bramble bushes, which fruited far earlier than those growing on slopes with a different orientation. Bears spent much of their life in search of food. It was as good a place to look as any.

Right on cue, the staccato sound of a woodpecker broke the silence. A moment later, the noise was repeated from a different location. His pulse racing, Quintus searched the trees, finally seeing not one, but two black woodpeckers. The elusive birds were sacred to Mars, the warrior god. Good omens. Turning on his heel, Quintus headed in an entirely different direction.

His smiling father was close behind, followed by Agesandros and the Gauls.

None was laughing now.

Not long after, Quintus' prayers were answered in royal style. He'd checked several glades, with no luck. Finally, though, in the shade of a tall pine tree, he found a lump of fresh dung. Its shape, size and distinctive scent was unmistakable, and Quintus could have cheered at the sight. He stuck a finger into the dark brown mass. The centre had not grown completely cold, which meant that a bear had passed by in the recent past. There were also plenty of brambles nearby. Jerking his head at the tattooed man, Quintus pointed at the ground. The Gaul trotted up, and his two dogs instantly converged on the pile of evidence. Both began whining frantically, alternately sniffing the dung and the air. Quintus' pulse quickened, and the Gaul gave him an enquiring look.

'Let them loose,' ordered Quintus. He glanced at the other slaves. 'Those too.'

Aurelia's foul mood crept up on her after Quintus and their father had left. The reason for her ill humour was simple. While her brother went hunting for a bear, she had to help her mother, who was supervising the slaves in the garden outside the villa. This was one of the busiest times of the year, when the plants were shooting up out of the ground. Lovage sat alongside mustard greens, coriander, sorrel, rue and parsley. The vegetables were even more numerous, and provided the family with food for most of the year. There were cucumbers, leeks, cabbages, root vegetables, as well as fennel and brassicas. Onions, a staple of any good recipe, were grown in huge numbers. Garlic, favoured for both its strong flavour and its medicinal properties, was also heavily cultivated.

Aurelia knew that she was being childish. A few weeks earlier, she had enjoyed setting the lines where the herbs and vegetables would grow, showing the slaves where to dig the holes and ensuring that they watered each with just the right amount of water. As usual, she had reserved the job of dropping the tiny seeds into place for herself. It was something she'd done since she was little. Today, with the plants growing well, the main tasks

35

consisted of watering them and pulling any weeds that had sprouted up nearby. Aurelia couldn't have cared less. As far as she was concerned, the whole garden could fall into rack and ruin. She stood sulkily off to one side, watching her mother direct operations. Even Elira, with whom she got on well, could not persuade her to join in.

Atia ignored her for a while, but eventually she had had enough. 'Aurelia!' she called. 'Come over here.'

With dragging feet, she made her way to her mother's side.

'I thought you liked gardening,' Atia said brightly.

'I do,' muttered Aurelia.

'Why aren't you helping?'

'I don't feel like it.' She was acutely aware that every slave present was craning their neck to hear, and hated it.

Atia didn't care who heard her. 'Are you ill?' she demanded.

'No.'

'What is it then?'

'You wouldn't understand,' Aurelia mumbled.

Atia's eyebrows rose. 'Really? Try me.'

'It's . . .' Aurelia caught the nearest slave staring at her. Her furious glare succeeded in making him look away, but she got little satisfaction from this. Her mother was still waiting expectantly. 'It's Quintus,' she admitted.

'Have you had an argument?'

'No.' Aurelia shook her head. 'Nothing like that.'

Tapping a foot, Atia waited for further clarification. A moment later, it was clear that it would not be forthcoming. Her nostrils flared. 'Well?'

Aurelia could see that her mother's patience would not last much longer. In that moment, however, she caught sight of a buzzard hanging overhead on the thermals. It was hunting. Like Quintus. Aurelia's anger resurged and she forgot about their captive audience. 'It's not fair,' she cried. 'I'm stuck here, in the *garden*, while he gets to track down a bear.'

Atia did not look surprised. 'I wondered if that was what this is about. So you would also hunt?'

Glowering, Aurelia nodded. 'Like Diana, the huntress.'

Her mother frowned. 'You're not a goddess.'

'I know, but . . .' Aurelia half turned, so the slaves could not see the tears in her eyes.

Atia's face softened. 'Come now. You're a young woman, or will be soon. A beautiful one too. Consequently, your path will be very different to that of your brother.' She held up a finger to quell Aurelia's protest. 'That doesn't mean your destiny is without value. Do you think I am worthless?'

Aurelia was aghast. 'Of course not, Mother.'

Atia's smile was broad, and reassuring. 'Precisely. I may not fight or go to war, but my position is powerful nonetheless. Your father relies on me for a multitude of things – as your husband will one day. Maintaining the household is but one small part of it.'

'But you and Father chose to marry each other,' Aurelia protested. 'For love!'

'We were lucky in that respect,' her mother acknowledged. 'Yet we did so without the approval of either of our families. Because we refused to follow their wishes not to wed, they cut us off.' Atia's face grew sad. 'It made life quite difficult for many years. I never saw my parents again, for example. They never met you or Quintus.'

Aurelia was flattered. She'd never heard any of this before. 'Surely it was worth it?' she pleaded.

There was a slow nod. 'It may have been, but I would not want the same hard path for you.'

Aurelia bridled. 'Better that, surely, than being married to some fat old man?'

'That won't happen to you. Your father and I are not monsters.' Atia lowered her voice. 'But realise this, young lady: we *will* arrange your betrothal to someone of our choice. Is that clear?'

Seeing the steel in her mother's eyes, Aurelia gave in. 'Yes.'

37

Atia sighed, glad that her misgivings had gone unnoticed. 'We understand each other then.' Seeing Aurelia's apprehension, she paused. 'Do not fear. You will have love in your marriage. It can develop over time. Ask Martialis, Father's old friend. He and his wife were betrothed to each other by their families, and ended up devoted to one another.' She held out her hand. 'Now, it's time to get stuck in. Life goes on regardless of how we feel, and our family relies on this garden.'

With a faint smile, Aurelia reached out to grasp her mother's fingers. Maybe things weren't as bad as she'd thought.

All the same, she couldn't help glancing up at the buzzard, and thinking of Quintus.

Quintus had followed the pack for perhaps a quarter of an hour before there was any hint that the quarry had been found. Then a loud yelping bark rang out from the trees ahead. It quickly died away to a shrill, repetitive whine. With a racing heart, Quintus came to a halt. The dogs' role was merely to bring the bear to bay, but there was always one more eager than its fellows. Its fate was unfortunate, but unavoidable. What mattered was that the bear had been found. In confirmation, a renewed succession of growls was met by a deep, threatening rumble.

The terrifying sound made a hot tide of acid surge up Quintus' throat. Another piercing yelp told him that a second dog had been hurt, or killed. Ashamed of his fear, Quintus willed away his nausea. This was no time for holding back. The dogs were doing their job, and he must do his. Muttering more prayers to Diana, he pounded towards the din.

As he burst into a large clearing, Quintus frowned in recognition. He had often picked berries here with Aurelia. A sprawl of thorny brambles, taller than a man, ran across the floor of the glade, which was bathed in dappled sunlight. A stream pattered down the slope towards the valley below. Fallen boughs lay here and there amidst a profusion of wildflowers, but what drew

Quintus' eyes was the struggle going on in the shadow cast by a nearby lofty cypress. Four dogs had a bear cornered against the tree's trunk. Growling with fury, the creature made frequent lunges at its tormentors, but the hounds dodged warily to and fro, just beyond reach. Each time the bear moved away from the tree, the dogs ran in to bite at its haunches or back legs. It was a stalemate – if the bear left the tree's protection, the dogs swarmed in from all sides, but if the beast remained where it was, they could not overcome it.

Two motionless shapes lay outside the semicircle, the casualties Quintus had heard. A cursory glance told him that one dog might survive. It was bleeding badly from deep claw wounds on its ribcage, but he could see no other injuries. The second, on the other hand, would definitely not make it. Shallow movements of its chest told him it still lived, but half its face had been torn off, and shiny, jagged ends of freshly broken bone protruded from a terrible injury to its left foreleg, the result of a bite from the bear's powerful jaws.

Quintus approached with care. Rushing in would carry a real risk of being knocked over, and the Gauls would soon be here. Once they called off the hounds, his task would begin in earnest. He studied the bear, eager for any clue that might help him kill it. Preoccupied with the snapping dogs, it paid him little notice. Its sheer size meant that it had to be a male. The creature's dense fur was yellowish-brown, and it had a typical large, rounded head and small ears. Massive shoulders and a squat body at least three times bigger than his own reinforced Quintus' awareness of just how dangerous his prey was. He could feel his pulse hammering in the hollow at the base of his throat, its speed reminding him that he was not in total control. Calm down, he thought. Breathe deeply. Concentrate.

'Thinking of the berries was a good idea,' said Fabricius from behind him. 'You've found a big bear too. A worthy foe.'

Startled, Quintus turned his head. The others had arrived. All eyes were on him. 'Yes,' he replied, hoping that the growling and snarling a dozen steps away would hide the fear in his voice.

Fabricius moved closer. 'Are you ready?'

Quintus quailed mentally. His father had seen his anxiety, and was prepared to step in. A fleeting look at Agesandros and the slaves was enough to see that they also understood the question's double meaning. A trace of disappointment flashed across the Sicilian's visage, and the Gauls slyly eyed each other. Damn them all, Quintus thought, his guts churning. Have they never been scared? 'Of course,' he replied loudly.

Fabricius gave him a measured stare. 'Very well,' he said, coming to a halt.

Quintus wasn't sure that his worried father would obey. There was more at stake than his life now, though. Killing the bear would prove nothing if the Sicilian and the slaves thought he was a coward, who relied on Fabricius for back-up. 'Do not interfere,' he shouted. 'This is my fight. I must do this on my own, whatever the outcome.' He glanced at his father, who did not immediately respond.

'Swear it!'

'I swear,' Fabricius said reluctantly, stepping back.

Quintus was satisfied to see the first signs of respect return to the others' faces.

A dog howled as the bear caught it with a sweeping arm. It was thrown through the air by the powerful blow, landing with an ominous thud by Quintus' feet. He squared his shoulders and prepared himself. Three hounds weren't enough to contain the quarry. If he didn't act at once, it had a chance of escaping. 'Call them back,' he shouted.

With shrill whistles, the Gauls obeyed. When the enraged dogs did not comply, the tattooed man ran in. Ignoring the bear, and using a leash as a whip, he beat them backwards, out of the way. His actions worked for two of the hounds, but the largest, its lips and teeth reddened with the bear's blood, did not want to withdraw. Cursing, the Gaul half turned, trying to kick it out of the way. He missed, and it darted past him, intent on rejoining the fray.

Aghast, Quintus watched as the dog jumped, sinking its teeth into the side of the bear's face. Rearing up in pain, the bear lifted it right into the air. At once this allowed it to use its front legs, raking the dog's body repeatedly with its claws. Far from releasing its grip, the hound clamped its jaws tighter than ever. It had been bred to endure pain, to hold on no matter what. Quintus had heard of such dogs having to be knocked unconscious before their mouths could be prised open. Yet this stubborn courage would not be enough: it needed help from its companions, which were now restrained. Or from him. The Gaul was in the way, though, screaming his anger and distress. He swung the useless leash across the bear's head, once, twice, three times. It harmed the beast not at all, but would hopefully distract it from killing his favourite dog. That was the theory, anyway.

The Gaul's plan failed. With the skin and hair on both sides of the hound's abdomen ripped away, the bear eviscerated it with several powerful rakes of its claws. Slippery loops of pink bowel tumbled out into the air, only to be sheared off like so many fat sausages. Sensing the dog's grip on its face weaken, the bear redoubled its efforts. Quintus felt his gorge rise as purple lumps of liver tissue cascaded to the ground. Finally a claw connected with a major blood vessel, tearing it asunder. Gouts of dark red blood sprayed from the ruin of the dog's belly, and its jaws loosened.

A moment later, it dropped lifelessly away from the bear.

'Get back!' Quintus screamed, but the Gaul ignored him.

Instead, the wild-eyed slave launched another attack. The loss of his canine friend had driven him into battle rage, which Quintus had often heard of, but never seen. The Romans and Gauls were enemies of old and had fought numerous times. More than a hundred and seventy years before, Rome itself had been sacked by the fierce tribesmen. Just six years previously, more than seventy thousand of them had invaded northern Italy again. They had been defeated, but stories still abounded of berserker warriors who, fighting naked, threw themselves at oncoming legionaries with complete disregard for their own safety.

This man was no such enemy, however. He might be a slave, but his life was still worth saving. Quintus jumped forward, shoving his spear at the bear. To his horror, the animal moved at the last moment, and his blade ran deep into its side rather than its chest, as he had intended. His blow was not mortal, nor was it enough to stop the beast reaching up to seize the Gaul by the neck. A short choking cry left the man's lips, and the bear shook him as a dog would a rat.

Not knowing what else to do, Quintus thrust his spear even deeper. The only reaction was an annoyed growl. In his haste, he'd stabbed into the creature's abdomen. It was potentially a mortal wound, but not one that would stop it quickly. Satisfied that the Gaul was dead, the bear flung him to one side. Naturally, its gaze next fell upon Quintus, who panicked. Although his spear was buried in its flesh, the creature's deep-set eyes showed no fear, just a searing anger. Bears normally avoided conflict with humans, but when aroused they became extremely aggressive. This individual was irate. It snapped at his spear shaft and splinters flew into the air.

There was nothing for it. Quintus took a deep breath and pulled his spear free. Roaring with pain, the bear revealed a genuinely fearsome set of teeth, the largest of which were as long as Quintus' middle fingers. Its red, gaping mouth was big enough to fit his entire head inside, and was well capable of crushing his skull. Quintus wanted to move away, but his muscles were paralysed by terror.

The bear took a step towards him. Gripping his spear in both hands, Quintus aimed the point at its chest. Advance, he told himself. Go on the attack. Before he could move, the animal

lunged at him. Catching the end of the spear, it swept the shaft
to one side as though it were a twig. With nothing between them,
they stared at each other for a breathless moment. In slow motion,
Quintus saw its muscles tense in preparation to jump. He nearly
lost control of his bladder. Hades was a whisker away, and he
could do nothing about it.

For whatever reason, however, the bear did not leap at once,
and Quintus was able to bring down his spear again.

His relief was momentary.

As Quintus moved to the attack, he slipped on a piece of
intestine. Both of his feet went from under him, and he landed
flat on his back. With a rush, all the air left his lungs, winding
him. Quintus was vaguely aware of the butt of his spear catching
in the dirt and wrenching itself free of his grasp. Frantically, he
lifted his head. To his utter horror, he could see the bear not five
paces away, just beyond his sandals. It roared again, and this time
Quintus received the full force of its fetid breath. He blinked,
knowing that death was at hand.

He had failed.

Chapter III: Capture

The Mediterranean Sea

Hours passed in a blur of driving rain and pounding waves. Darkness fell, which increased the magnitude of the friends' terror manyfold. The small boat was tossed up and down, back and forth, helpless before the sea's immense power. It took all of Hanno's energy just to stay on board. Both of them were sick multiple times, vomiting a mixture of food and wine over themselves and the vessel's floor. Eventually there was nothing left but bile to come up. Flashes of lightning regularly illuminated the pathetic scene. Hanno wasn't sure which was worse: not being able to see his hand in front of his face, or looking at Suniaton's wan, terrified features and puke-spattered clothes.

Slumped on the bench opposite, his friend alternated between hysterical bouts of weeping, and praying to every god he could think of. Somehow Suniaton's distress helped Hanno to remain in control of his own terror. He was even able to take some solace from their situation. If Melqart had wanted to drown them, they would already be dead. The storm had not reached the heights it would have done in winter, nor had their boat capsized. Besides these minor miracles, there had been no further leaks. Sturdily built from cypress planks, its seams were sealed with lengths of tightly packed linen fibre as well as a layer of beeswax. They had not lost the oars, which meant that they could row to land, should the opportunity arise. Moreover, every stretch of coastline had its Carthaginian trading post. There they could make themselves known, promising rich reward for a passage home.

Hanno pinched himself out of the fantasy. Don't get your hopes up, he thought bitterly. The bad weather showed no signs of letting up. Any one of the waves rolling in their direction was capable of flipping the boat. Melqart hadn't drowned them yet, but deities were capricious by nature, and the sea god was no different. All it would take was a tiny extra surge in the water for their craft to overturn. Hanno struggled to hold back his own tears. What real chance had they? Even if they survived until sunrise and their families worked out where they had gone, the likelihood of being found on the open sea was slim to none. Adrift with no food or water, they would both die, painfully, within a few days. At this stark realisation Hanno closed his eyes and asked for a quick death instead.

Despite the heavy rain which had soaked him to the skin, Malchus had returned from the meeting with the Council of Elders in excellent humour. He stood now, a cup of wine in hand, under the sloping portico that ran around the house's main courtyard, watching the raindrops splashing off the white marble mosaic half a dozen steps away. His impassioned speech had gone down as he'd wished, which relieved him greatly. Since Hannibal's messenger had given him the weighty task a week before of announcing to the elders and suffetes that the general planned to attack Saguntum, Malchus had been consumed by worry. What if the council did not back the Barca? The stakes were higher than he'd ever known.

Saguntine reprisals against the tribes allied to Carthage were purportedly the reason for Hannibal's assault, but, as everyone knew, its intent was to provoke Rome into a response. Yet, thanks to the general's perfect timing, that response would not be militaristic. Severe unrest in Illyricum meant that the Republic had already committed both consuls and their armies to conflict in the East. For the upcoming campaign season, Rome would only be able to issue empty threats. After that, however, retribution would undoubtedly follow. Hannibal was not worried. He was convinced that the time for war with their old enemy was ripe, and Malchus agreed with him. Nonetheless, bringing those who led Carthage round to the same opinion had been a daunting prospect.

It was a pity, thought Malchus, that Hanno had not been there to witness his finest oratory yet. By the end, he'd had the entire council on their feet, cheering at the idea of renewed conflict with Rome. Meanwhile Hanno had most likely been *fishing*. News of the huge shoals of tunny offshore that day had swept the city. Now Hanno was probably spending the proceeds of his catch on wine and whores. Malchus sighed. A moment later, hearing Sapho and Bostar's voices in the corridor that led to the street, his mood lifted. At least two of his sons had been there. They soon emerged into view, wringing out their sodden cloaks.

'A wonderful speech, Father,' said Sapho in a hearty tone.

'It was excellent,' agreed Bostar. 'You had them in the palm of your hand. They could only respond in one way.'

Malchus made a modest gesture, but inside he was delighted. 'Finally, Carthage is ready for the war that we have been preparing for these years past.' He moved to the table behind him, upon which sat a glazed red jug and several beakers. 'Let us raise a toast to Hannibal Barca.'

'Shame Hanno didn't hear your speech too,' said Sapho, throwing a meaningful glance at Bostar. Busily pouring wine, their father didn't see it.

'Indeed,' Malchus replied, handing each a full cup. 'Such occasions do not come often. For the rest of his life, the boy will regret that he was playing truant while history was made.' He swallowed a mouthful of wine. 'Have you seen him?'

There was a short, awkward silence.

He looked from one to the other. 'Well?'

'We ran into him this morning,' Sapho admitted. 'On our way to the Agora. He was with Suniaton.'

Malchus swore. 'That must have been just after he'd scarpered out of the house. The little ruffian ignored my shouts! Did the pair of them give you the slip?'

'Not exactly,' Sapho replied awkwardly, giving Bostar another pointed stare.

Malchus caught the tension between his sons. 'What's going on?'

Bostar cleared his throat. 'We talked, and then let them go.' He rephrased his words. '*I* let them go.'

'Why?' Malchus cried angrily. 'You knew how important my speech was.'

Bostar flushed. 'I'm sorry, Father. Perhaps I acted wrongly, but I couldn't help thinking that, like us, Hanno will soon be at war. For the moment, though, he's still a boy. Let him enjoy himself while he can.'

Tapping a finger against his teeth, Malchus turned to Sapho. 'What did you say?'

'Initially, I thought that we should force Hanno to come with us, Father, but Bostar had a point. As he was the senior officer present, I gave way to his judgement.' Bostar tried to interrupt, but Sapho continued talking. 'In hindsight, it was possibly the wrong decision. I should have argued with him.'

'How dare you!' Bostar cried. 'I made no mention of rank! We made the decision together.'

Sapho's lip curled. 'Did we?'

Malchus held up his hands. 'Enough!'

Throwing each other angry looks, the brothers fell silent.

Malchus thought for a moment. 'I am sorely disappointed in

you, Sapho, for not protesting more at your brother's desire to let Hanno do as he wished.' He regarded Bostar next. 'Shame on you, as a senior officer, for forgetting that our primary purpose is to gain revenge on Rome. In comparison, frivolities such as fishing are irrelevant!' Ignoring their muttered apologies, Malchus raised his cup. 'Let us forget Hanno and his wastrel friend, and drink a toast to Hannibal Barca, and to our victory in the coming war with Rome!'

They followed his lead, but neither brother clinked his beaker off the other's.

Hanno's wish for an easy death was not granted. Eventually the storm passed, and the ferocious waves died down. Dawn arrived, bringing with it calm seas and a clear sky. The wind changed direction; it was now coming from the northeast. Hanno's hopes rose briefly, before falling again. The breeze was not strong enough to carry them back home, and the current continued to carry their small vessel eastwards. Silence reigned; all the seabirds had been driven off by the inclement weather. Suniaton's exhaustion had finally got the better of him, and he lay slumped on the boat's sole, snoring.

Hanno grimaced at the irony of it. The peaceful scene could not have been more at odds with what they had endured overnight. His sodden clothes were drying fast in the warm sunshine. The boat rocked gently from side to side, wavelets slapping off the hull. A pod of dolphins broke the surface nearby, but the sight did not bring the usual smile to Hanno's face. Now, their graceful shapes and gliding motion were an acute reminder that he belonged on the land, which was nowhere to be seen. Apart from the dolphins, they were utterly alone.

Regret, and an unfamiliar feeling, that of humility, filled Hanno. I should have done my duty, he thought. Gone to that meeting with Father. The idea of listening to dirtbags like Hostus and his cronies was now most appealing. Hanno stared bleakly at the western horizon, knowing that he would never see his home, or his family, again. Suddenly, his sorrow became overwhelming. Hanno's eyes filled with tears, and he was grateful that Suniaton was asleep. Their friendship ran deep, but he had no wish to be seen crying like a child. He did not despise Suni for his extreme reaction during the storm, though. Thinking that a calm mien might help his friend was all that had prevented him from acting similarly.

A short time later, Suniaton awoke. Hanno, who was still feeling fragile, was surprised and irritated to see that his spirits had risen somewhat.

'I'm hungry,' Suniaton declared, glancing around with greedy eyes.

'Well, there's nothing to eat. Or drink,' Hanno replied sourly. 'Get used to it.'

Hanno's foul mood was obvious and Suniaton had the wisdom not to reply. Instead he busied himself by bailing out the hands-breadth of water in the bottom of the boat. His housekeeping complete, he lifted the oars and placed them in their rowlocks. Squinting at the horizon and then the sun, he began rowing due south. After a moment, he started whistling a ditty that was currently popular in Carthage.

Hanno scowled. The tune reminded him of the good times they had spent carousing in the rough taverns near the city's twin ports. The pleasurable hours he had spent with plump Egyptian whores in the room above the bar. 'Isis', as she called herself, had been his favourite. He pictured her kohl-rimmed eyes, her carmine lips framing encouraging words, and his groin throbbed. It was too much to bear. 'Shut up,' he snapped.

Hurt, Suniaton obeyed.

Hanno was spoiling for a fight now. 'What are you doing?' he demanded, pointing at the oars.

'Rowing,' Suniaton replied sharply. 'What does it look like?'

'What's the point?' Hanno cried. 'We could be fifty miles out to sea.'

'Or five.'

Hanno blinked, and then chose to ignore his friend's sensible answer. He was so angry he could hardly think. 'Why choose south? Why not north, or east?'

Suniaton gave him a withering glance. 'Numidia is the nearest coastline, in case you hadn't realised.'

Hanno flushed and fell silent. Of course he knew that the southern shore of the Mediterranean was closer than Sicily or Italy. In the circumstances, Suniaton's plan was a good one. Nonetheless, Hanno felt unwilling to back down, so he sat and stared sulkily at the distant horizon.

Stubbornly, Suniaton continued to paddle southwards.

Time passed, and the sun climbed high in the sky.

After a while, Hanno found his voice. 'Let me take a turn,' he muttered.

'Eh?' Suniaton barked.

'You've been rowing for ages,' said Hanno. 'It's only fair that you have a break.'

'"What's the point?"' Suniaton angrily repeated his friend's words.

Hanno swallowed his pride. 'Look,' he said. 'I'm sorry, all right? Heading south is as good a plan as any.'

Suniaton's nod was grudging. 'Fair enough.'

They changed position, and Hanno took control of the oars. A more comfortable atmosphere fell, and Suniaton's good humour returned. 'At least we're still alive, and still together,' he said. 'How much worse would it have been if one of us had been washed overboard? There'd be no one to throw insults at!'

Hanno grimaced in agreement. He lifted his gaze to the burning disc that was the sun. It had to be nearly midday. It was baking hot now, and his tongue was stuck to the roof of his dry mouth. What I'd give for a cup of water, he thought longingly. His spirits reached a new low, and a moment later, he shipped the oars, unable to work up the enthusiasm to continue rowing.

'My turn,' said Suniaton dutifully.

Hanno saw the resignation he was feeling reflected in his friend's eyes. 'Let's just rest for a while,' he murmured. 'It looks set to remain calm. What does it matter where we make landfall?'

'True enough.' Despite the lie, Suniaton managed to smile. He didn't vocalise what they were both thinking: if, by some miracle, they did manage to reach the Numidian coastline, would they find water before succumbing to their thirst?

Some time later, they both took another turn at the oars, applying themselves to the task with a vigour born of desperation. Their exertions produced no discernible result: all around, the horizon was empty. They were totally alone. Lost. Abandoned by the gods. At length, exhausted by thirst and the extreme heat, the friends gave up and lay down in the bottom of the boat to rest. Sleep soon followed.

Hanno dreamed that he was on one side of a door while his father was on the other, hammering on the timbers with a balled fist and demanding he open it at once. Hanno was desperate to obey, but could find no handle or keyhole on the door's featureless surface. Malchus' blows grew heavier and heavier, until finally Hanno became aware that he was dreaming. Waking to a pounding headache and a feeling of distinct disorientation, he opened his eyes. Above, the limitless expanse of the blue sky. Beside him, Suniaton's slumbering form. To Hanno's amazement, the thumping in his head was replaced by a regular, and familiar, cadence: that of men singing. There was another voice too, shouting indistinct commands. It was a sailor, calling the tune for the oarsmen, thought Hanno disbelievingly. A ship!

All weariness fell away, and he sat bolt upright. Turning his head, Hanno searched for the source of the noise. Then he spotted it: a low, predatory shape not three hundred paces distant, its decks lined with men. It had a single mast with a square sail supported by a complex set of rigging, and two banks of oars. The red-coloured stern was curved like a scorpion's tail, and there was a small forecastle at the prow. Amidst his exultation, Hanno felt the first tickle of unease. This didn't look like a merchant vessel; it was clearly no fishing smack either. However, it was not large enough to be a Carthaginian, or even a Roman, warship. These days, Carthage had very few biremes or triremes, relying instead on the bigger, more powerful quinqueremes and, to a lesser extent, quadriremes. Rome possessed some smaller ships, but he could see none of their standards. Yet the craft had a distinctly military air.

He nudged Suniaton. 'Wake up!'

His friend groaned. 'What is it?'

'A ship.'

Suniaton shot into a sitting position. 'Where?' he demanded.

Hanno pointed. The bireme was beating a northward course, which would bring it to within a hundred paces of their little boat. It was in a hurry to be using both its sail and the power of its oars, and it seemed no one had seen them. Hanno's stomach lurched. If he didn't act, it might pass them by.

He stood up. 'Here! Over here,' he began shouting in Carthaginian. Suniaton joined in, waving his arms like a man possessed. Hanno repeated his cry in Greek. For a few heart-stopping moments, nothing happened. Finally, a man's head turned. With the sea almost flat calm, it was impossible not to see them. Guttural shouts rang out, and the chanting voices halted abruptly. The oars on the port side, which was facing them, slowed and stopped, reducing the bireme's speed at once. Another set of bellowed commands, and the sail was reefed, allowing the ship to bear away from the wind. The nearest banks of oars began to back water, turning the bireme towards them. Soon they could see the base of the bronze ram that was attached to the bow. Carved in the shape of a creature's head, it was only possible to make out the top of the skull and the eyes. Now pointing straight at them, the vessel gave off a most threatening air.

The two friends looked at each other, suddenly unsure.

'Who are they?' whispered Suniaton.

Hanno shook his head. 'I don't know.'

'Maybe we should have kept quiet,' said Suniaton. He began muttering a prayer.

Hanno's certainty weakened, but it was far too late now.

The sailor who led the oarsmen's chant began a slower rhythm than before. In unison, the oars on both sides lifted and swept gracefully through the air before arcing down to split the sea's surface with a loud, splashing sound. Encouraged by the shouts of their overseer, the oarsmen sang and heaved together, dragging their oars, carved lengths of polished spruce, through the water.

Before long, the bireme had drawn alongside. Its superstructure was decorated red like the stern, but around each oar hole a swirling blue design had been painted. It was still bright and fresh, showing the work had been done recently. Hanno's heart sank as he studied the grinning men – a mixture of nationalities from Greek and Libyan to Iberian – lining the rails and forecastle. Most were clad in little more than a loincloth, but all were armed to the teeth. He could see catapults on the deck as well. He and Suniaton had only their daggers.

'They're fucking pirates,' Suniaton muttered. 'We're dead meat. Slaves, if we're lucky.'

'Would you rather die of thirst? Or exposure?' Hanno retorted, furious at himself for not seeing the bireme for what it was. For not keeping silent.

'Maybe,' Suniaton snapped back. 'We'll never know now, though.'

They were hailed by a thin figure near the prow. With black hair and a paler complexion than most of his dark-skinned comrades, he could have been Egyptian. Nonetheless, he spoke in Greek, the dominant language of the sea. 'Well met. Where are you bound?'

His companions snorted with laughter.

Hanno decided to be bold. 'Carthage,' he declared loudly. 'But, as you can see, we have no sail. Can we take passage with you?'

'What are you doing so far out to sea in just a rowing boat?' the Egyptian asked.

There were more hoots of amusement from the crew.

'We were carried away by a storm,' Hanno replied. 'The gods were smiling, however, and we survived.'

'You were lucky indeed,' agreed the other. 'Yet I wouldn't give much for your chances if you stay out here. By my reckoning, it is at least sixty miles to the nearest landfall.'

Suniaton gestured towards the south. 'Numidia?'

The Egyptian threw back his head and laughed. It was an unpleasant, mocking sound. 'Have you no sense of direction, fool? I talk of Sicily!'

Hanno and Suniaton gaped at one another. The storm had carried them much further than they could have imagined. They had been mistakenly rowing out into the Mediterranean. 'We have even more reason to thank you,' said Hanno boldly. 'As our fathers will, when you return us safely to Carthage.'

The Egyptian's lips pulled up, revealing a sharp set of teeth. 'Come aboard. We can talk more comfortably in the shade,' he said, indicating the awning in the forecastle.

The friends exchanged a loaded glance. This hospitality was at odds with what their eyes were telling them. Every man in sight looked capable of slitting their throats without even blinking. 'Thank you,' said Hanno with a broad smile. He rowed around to the back of the bireme. There they found a jolly boat about the same size as theirs tied to an iron ring. A knotted rope had already been lowered to their level from above. A pair of grinning sailors waited to haul them up.

'Trust in Melqart,' Hanno said quietly, tying their boat fast.

'We didn't drown, which means he has a purpose for us,' Suniaton replied, desperate for something to believe in. Yet his fear was palpable.

Struggling not to lose his own self-control, Hanno studied the planks before him. This close, he could see the black tar that covered the hull below the waterline. Telling himself that Suniaton was right, Hanno took hold of the rope. How else could they have survived that storm? It *must* have been Melqart. Helped by the sailors, he ascended, using his feet to grip on the warm wood.

'Welcome,' said the Egyptian as Hanno reached the deck. He raised a hand, palm outwards, in the Carthaginian manner.

Pleased by this, Hanno did the same.

Suniaton arrived a moment later, and the Egyptian greeted him similarly. Leather water bags were then proffered, and the two drank greedily, slaking their fierce thirst. Hanno began to wonder if his gut instinct had been wrong.

'You're from Carthage?' The question was innocent enough.

'Yes,' replied Hanno.

'Do you sail there?' asked Suniaton.

'Not often,' the Egyptian replied.

His men sniggered, and Hanno noticed many were lustfully eyeing the gold charms that hung from their necks. 'Can you take us there?' he asked boldly. 'Our families are wealthy, and will reward you well for our safe return.'

The Egyptian rubbed his chin. 'Will they indeed?'

'Of course,' Suniaton asserted.

A prolonged silence fell, and Hanno grew more uneasy.

At last the Egyptian spoke. 'What do you think, boys?' he asked, scanning the assembled men. 'Shall we sail to Carthage and collect a handsome prize for our efforts?'

'No bloody way,' snarled a voice. 'Just kill them and have done.'

'Reward? We'd all be crucified, more like,' shouted another.

Suniaton gasped, and Hanno felt sick to the pit of his stomach.

Crucifixion was one of the punishments reserved for lawbreakers of the worst kind. Pirates, in other words.

Raising his eyebrows mockingly, the Egyptian lifted a hand, and his companions relaxed. 'Unfortunately, people like us aren't welcome in Carthage,' he explained.

'It doesn't have to be Carthage itself,' Hanno said nonchalantly. Beside him, Suniaton nodded in nervous agreement. 'Any town on the Numidian coast will do.'

Raucous laughter met his request, and now Hanno struggled not to despair. He glanced at Suniaton, but he had no inspiration to offer.

'Supposing we agreed to that,' said the grinning Egyptian, 'how would we get paid?'

'I would meet you afterwards with the money, at a place of your choosing,' Hanno replied, flushing. The pirate captain was playing with him.

'And you'd swear that on your mother's life, I suppose?' the Egyptian sneered. 'If you had one.'

Hanno swallowed his anger. 'I did, and I would.'

Catching him off guard, the Egyptian swung forward and delivered a solid punch to his solar plexus. The air shot from Hanno's lungs, and he folded over in complete agony. 'Enough of this shit,' the Egyptian announced abruptly. 'Take their weapons. Tie them up.'

'No!' Hanno mumbled. He tried to stand upright, but strong hands grabbed his arms from behind, pinioning them to his sides. He felt his dagger being removed, and a moment later the gold charm around his neck was torn away. Weaponless and without the talisman he had worn since infancy, Hanno felt utterly naked. Alongside, the same was happening to Suniaton, who screamed as his earrings were ripped out. Greedy hands pulled and tugged at their valuables as the pirates fought for a share of the spoils. Hanno glared at the Egyptian. 'What are you going to do with us?'

'You're both young and strong. Should fetch a good price on the slave block.'

'Please,' begged Suniaton, but the pirate captain had already turned away.

Hanno hawked and spat after him, and received a heavy blow across the head for his pains. They then had their arms tied tightly behind their backs and were bundled unceremoniously below decks, into the cramped space where the slaves sat on two tiers of benches. Slumped over their oars, and with barely enough room to sit erect, they sat twenty-five to each row, fifty on each side of the bireme. At the base of the steps, on a central walkway, stood a lone slave, the man whose chant had woken Hanno. Near the stern, a narrow iron cage contained a dozen or so prisoners. Hanno and Suniaton glanced at each other. They weren't alone.

It was hot outside, but here the presence of more than a hundred sweating men increased the temperature to that of an oven. Countless pairs of deadened eyes stared at the newcomers, but not a single slave spoke. The reason soon became apparent. Bare feet slapped off the timbers as a short barrel of a man approached. The friends stood head and shoulders over him, but the crop-haired newcomer's muscles were enormous, reminding Hanno of Greek wrestlers he'd seen. His only garment was a leather skirt, but he exuded authority, not least because of the knotted whip dangling from his right fist. His scarred features were roughly hewn, as if from granite, his lips a mere slit in the stone.

Still winded, Hanno couldn't stop himself from meeting the overseer's cold, calculating eyes.

'Fresh meat, eh?' His voice was nasal and irritating.

'Two more for the slave market, Varsaco,' answered one of the men holding Hanno.

'Consider yourself lucky. Most prisoners end up on the benches, but we have a full complement at the moment.' Varsaco gestured at the long-haired wretches all around them. 'So you get to stay in our select accommodation.' He jerked a thumb at the cage and laughed.

Hanno felt a thrill of dread. Their fate would be no better than that of the oarsmen. They would be totally at the mercy of whoever bought them.

Suniaton's eyes were pools of terror. 'We could end up anywhere,' he whispered.

His friend was right, thought Hanno. The Carthaginians' weakened navy no longer had the power to keep the western Mediterranean free of pirates, and thus far the Romans had not bothered to police the high seas. The bireme could roam wherever it wanted. There were few ports indeed where the security inspection was more than cursory. Sicily, Numidia or Iberia were possibilities. As was Italy. Every decent-sized town had a slave market. Hanno felt as if he was drowning in an ocean of despair.

The Egyptian's voice carried from the deck above. 'Varsaco!'

The overseer answered straightaway. 'Captain?'

'Resume former course and speed.'

'Yes, sir.'

Hanno and Suniaton were ignored as Varsaco bellowed orders at the oarsmen on the starboard side. Leaning into the task, the slaves used their oars to back water until the overseer gestured at them to stop. At once the figure on the walkway began singing a chant that set the oarsmen into a steady rhythm.

His duties in hand, Varsaco returned. There was a predatory look in his eyes that had not been there before. 'You're a handsome boy,' he said, running his stubby fingers down Hanno's arm. He slipped a hand under Hanno's tunic and tweaked a nipple. Hanno shuddered and tried to pull away, but with a man either side of him, he could not go far. 'I prefer those with a bit more meat on their bones, though,' Varsaco confided. He moved to Suniaton's side and roughly squeezed his buttocks. Suniaton twisted away, but the pirates holding him tightened their grip. 'But look, you're hurt.' Varsaco touched one of Suniaton's still oozing earlobes, then, to Hanno's horror, licked the blood off his fingertip.

Suniaton wailed with fear.

'Leave him alone, you whoreson,' Hanno roared, struggling uselessly to free himself.

'Or what?' teased Varsaco. Abruptly, his voice hardened. 'I am the master below decks. I do as I please. Take him over there!'

Tears of rage streamed down Hanno's face as he watched his friend being dragged to a large block of wood nailed down near the bow. Its surface, approximately the length of a man's torso, was covered in irregular, dark patches, and heavy iron fetters were in place at each corner at floor level. Releasing Suniaton from his bonds, the pirates slammed him face down on to the wood. He kicked and struggled, but his captors were too many. An instant later, the manacles clicked shut around his wrists and ankles.

Varsaco moved to stand behind him and, realising what was about to happen, Suniaton began to scream. His protests intensified as the overseer was handed a knife and used it to slit his breeches from waistband to crotch. Varsaco did the same to Suniaton's undergarment, laughing as the tip of the blade snagged in his flesh, causing him to moan with pain. Finally, the overseer pulled apart the cut fabric, and his face twisted with lust. 'Very nice,' he muttered.

'No!' cried Suniaton.

It was too much for Hanno to bear. Summoning every reserve of his strength, he twisted and bucked like a wild horse. Engrossed by the spectacle, the two men holding him were caught unawares, and he slipped their grasp. Sprinting forward, he reached Varsaco in a dozen steps. The overseer's broad back was towards him, and he was busily unbuckling the belt that held up his leather skirt. It dropped to the floor and he sighed with satisfaction, shuffling forward to complete the outrage.

Panting with fury, Hanno steadied himself and did the only thing he could think of. Drawing back his right leg, he swung it through the air and between Varsaco's thighs. With a meaty thump, the front of his sandal connected with the soft mass of the overseer's dangling scrotum. Letting out a high-pitched scream, Varsaco collapsed to the deck in a heap. Hanno snarled with delight. 'How do you like that?' he screamed, stamping his iron-studded sole on the side of Varsaco's head for good measure. He managed to deliver several more kicks before the men who had been holding him came barrelling in. Hanno saw one raising the butt of his sword. He half turned, awkward because of the ropes binding his arms, but was unable to avoid the blow. Stars exploded across Hanno's vision as the hilt connected with the back of his head. His knees buckled and he toppled forward to land on the semi-conscious Varsaco. A rain of blows followed and he slipped into the darkness.

'Wake up!'

Hanno felt someone nudge him in the back. Slowly, he came to. He was lying on his side, still trussed up like a hen for the pot. Every part of his body hurt. His head, belly and groin had obviously received special attention, however. It was agony to breathe in, and Hanno suspected that two or three of his ribs were cracked. He could taste blood, and warily he used his tongue to check that all his teeth were still in place. They were, thankfully, although two felt loose, and his top lip was bruised and swollen.

He was prodded again.

'Hanno! It's me, Suniaton.'

Finally, Hanno focused on his friend, who was lying only a few steps away. To his surprise, they were on the forecastle deck, under the cloth awning he had spied earlier. As far as he could tell, they were alone.

'You've been unconscious for hours.' Suniaton's voice was concerned.

The temperature had dropped significantly, Hanno realised. In the gap between the gunwale and the awning, he could see an orange tinge to the sky. It was nearly sunset. 'I'll live,' he croaked. His last memories came flooding back. 'What about you? Did Varsaco . . . ?' He couldn't finish the question.

Suniaton screwed up his face. 'I'm fine,' he muttered. Amazingly, he grinned. 'Varsaco couldn't stand for a long time, you know.'

'Good! The fucking bastard.' Hanno frowned. 'Why didn't his men kill me?'

'They were going to,' whispered Suniaton. 'But—'

Hearing the stairs that led to the main deck creak, he fell silent. Someone was approaching. A moment later, the Egyptian stooped over Hanno. 'You've come back to us,' he said. 'Good. A man who sleeps too long after a beating like that often doesn't wake.'

Hanno glared.

'Don't give me that look,' said the Egyptian reproachfully. 'If it wasn't for me, you'd be dead by now. Raped before you died, like as not.'

Suniaton flinched, but Hanno's fury knew no bounds. 'Am I supposed to be grateful?'

The Egyptian squatted down alongside him. 'Spirited, aren't you? A different prospect to your friend.' He nodded in approval. 'I hope to sell you as a gladiator. You'd be wasted as an agricultural or household slave. Are you able to get up?'

Hanno let the other help him to a sitting position. A stabbing pain from his chest made him grimace in pain.

'What is it?'

Hanno was disconcerted by the Egyptian's concern. 'It's nothing. Just a couple of broken ribs.'

'That's all?'

'I think so.'

The Egyptian smiled. 'Good. I thought I'd come too late. It wouldn't be the first time that one of Varsaco's little games got out of hand.'

'"Little games"?' Suniaton asked faintly.

The Egyptian made an offhand gesture. 'Usually, he's content to screw whichever poor bastard takes his fancy. Several times a day, normally. As long as that's it, I don't mind. It doesn't affect their sale value. After what you did, though, he would have killed you both. I don't mind him having his fun, but there's no point destroying valuable merchandise. That's why you're up here, where I sleep. Varsaco has a key to the cage, and I wouldn't trust him not to slip a knife between your ribs one night.'

Hanno longed to wrap his fingers around the captain's throat, choking the life out of him, ridding his face of its perpetual smug expression. It stung that their lives had been saved for purely financial reasons. Deep down, though, Hanno was unsurprised by the Egyptian's action. He'd once seen his father stop a slave from beating a mule for much the same reason.

'This is the best place on the ship. You're out of the sun here, and it catches the evening breeze as well.' The Egyptian got to his feet. 'Make the most of it. We're on course for Sicily, and then Italy,' he said, disappearing from view.

'At least in Iberia or Numidia, we might have had a chance of getting word to Carthage,' muttered Suniaton despairingly.

Hanno's nod was bitter. Instead, they were to be sold to their people's worst enemies, as gladiators. 'Melqart can't be solely responsible for this ill fortune. There's more to it.' He cast his mind about, wondering why they should suffer such a terrible fate. All at once, the memory of how he had left home came crashing back. Hanno cursed. 'I'm a fool.'

Suniaton threw him a confused look. 'What is it?'

'I didn't ask for Tanit's blessing as I walked out of the front door.'

Suniaton's face paled. Although she was a virginal mother figure, Tanit was the most important Carthaginian deity. She was also the goddess of war. Angering her carried the risk of severe punishment. 'It's not a crime to forget,' he said, before quickly adding, 'but you could ask pardon of her anyway.'

In a cold sweat, Hanno did as his friend advised.

Great Mother, he pleaded. Forgive me. Do not forget us, please.

The next morning, Hanno had not returned home. In itself, that was not particularly unusual. But the hours passed, and still there was no sign of him. At midday, Bostar began to look worried. He paced up and down the corridor from the courtyard, checking the street for his youngest brother. By the early afternoon, he could take it no more. 'Where is Hanno?'

'Nursing a hangover somewhere, probably,' Sapho growled.

Bostar pursed his lips. 'He's never been this late before.'

'Maybe he heard about Father's speech, and got even drunker than normal.' Sapho looked at their father for approval. Surprisingly, he got none.

Malchus' face now also registered concern. 'You're right, Bostar. Hanno always comes back in time for his lessons. I'd forgotten, but this afternoon, at his request, we were to discuss the battle of Ecnomus again.'

Sapho frowned. 'He wouldn't miss it then.'

'Precisely.'

Suddenly, the situation felt very different.

A familiar voice cut through their dismay. 'Malchus? Are you at home?'

All three turned to see a stout, bearded man appearing in the courtyard's entrance. A long cream linen robe reached almost to his feet, and a headcloth concealed his hair.

Bowing, Malchus hurried forward. 'Bodesmun. I am honoured by your presence.'

Behind him, Sapho and Bostar were also making obeisance. Eshmoun was not their family's favoured god, but he was an important deity. His temple at the top of Byrsa Hill was the largest in Carthage, and Bodesmun was one of the senior priests there.

'Can I offer you refreshment?' asked Malchus. 'Some wine or pomegranate juice? Bread and honey?'

Bodesmun waved a podgy hand in dismissal. His round, gentle face was worried. 'Thank you, but no.'

Malchus was nonplussed. He had little in common with a peace-loving priest. 'How can I help you?' he enquired awkwardly.

'It's about Suniaton.'

Malchus' response was instant. 'What's Hanno made him do?'

Bodesmun managed a weak grin. 'It's nothing like that. Have you seen Suni today?'

Malchus' heart gave an involuntary leap. 'No. I could ask you the same about Hanno.'

The smile left Bodesmun's face. 'He hasn't returned yet either?'

'No. Apparently, the tunny were running in their thousands yesterday. Any fool with a net could catch a boatload, and I'm sure they did the same. When Hanno didn't return, I presumed they had gone out to celebrate,' Malchus replied heavily, his imagination already running riot. 'It's odd that you should arrive when you did. I was just starting to get worried. Hanno has never skipped a lesson on tactics before.'

'Suni has never missed the devotions in the temple at midday either.'

Bostar's face fell. Even Sapho frowned.

The two older men stared at each other in disbelief. All at once, they had a great deal in common. Bodesmun was close to tears. 'What should we do?' he asked in a quavering voice.

Malchus refused to let the panic that had flared in his breast grow. He was a soldier. 'There'll be some easy explanation to this,' he declared. 'We might have to check every inn and whore-house in Carthage, but we'll find them.'

Bodesmun's normal commanding demeanour had disappeared. He nodded meekly.

'Sapho! Bostar!'

'Yes, Father,' they replied in unison, eager to be given some-thing to do. By now, Bostar was distraught. Sapho didn't look happy either.

'Rouse as many soldiers as you can from the barracks,' Malchus ordered. 'I want the city combed from top to bottom. Concentrate on their favourite haunts around the ports. You know the ones.'

They nodded.

Despite his best efforts, Malchus' temper frayed. 'Go on, then! When you're done, find me here, or in the Agora.'

Bostar turned at the entrance to the corridor. 'What are you going to do?'

'Talk to the fishermen at the Choma,' Malchus answered grimly. His mind was full of the storm that had battered the city the previous night. 'I want to know if anyone saw them yesterday.' He glanced at Bodesmun. 'Coming?'

The priest pulled himself together. 'Of course.'

With a sinking feeling in their bellies, they left the house.

On the Choma, Malchus and Bodesmun found scores of the fishermen who plied the waters off the city. Their day's work was long done. With their boats tied up nearby, they lounged about, gossiping and repairing holes in their nets. Unsurprisingly, the appearance of a noble and a high-ranking priest filled them with awe. Most went their entire lives without ever being in the presence of someone so far up the social scale. Their guttural argot was also quite hard to understand. Consequently, it was hard to get a word of sense out of them.

'We're wasting our time. They're all idiots,' Malchus muttered in frustration. He forced himself not to scream and lash out with rage. Losing his temper would be completely counterproductive. The best chance of discovering anything about their sons' disappearance was surely to be found here.

'Not all, perhaps.' Bodesmun indicated a wiry figure sitting on an upturned boat, whose silver hair marked him out as older than his companions. 'Let's ask him.'

They strolled over. 'Well met,' Bodesmun said politely. 'The blessings of the gods be upon you.'

'The same to you and your friend,' replied the old man respectfully.

'We come in search of answers to some questions,' Malchus announced.

The other nodded, unsurprised. 'I was thinking that you were after more than fresh fish.'

'Were you out on the water yesterday?'

There was a faint smile. 'With the tunny running like they were? Of course I was. It's just a shame that the weather changed so early, or it would have been the best day's catch in the last five years.'

'Did you see a small skiff, perhaps?' Malchus asked. 'With two crew. Young men, well dressed.'

His urgent tone and Bodesmun's anxious stance would have been obvious to all but an imbecile. Nonetheless, the old man did not answer immediately. Instead, he closed his eyes.

Each instant that went by felt like an eternity to Malchus. He clenched his fists to stop himself from grabbing the other by the throat.

It was Bodesmun who cracked first. 'Well?'

The old man's eyes opened. 'I did spot them, yes. A tall lad and a shorter, stockier one. Well dressed, as you say. They're out here regularly. A friendly pair.'

Malchus and Bodesmun gave each other a look full of hope, and fear.

'When did you last see them?'

The old man's expression became wary. 'I'm not sure.'

Malchus knew when he was being lied to. A tidal wave of dread swamped him. There was only one reason for the other to withhold the truth. 'Tell us,' he commanded. 'You will come to no harm. I swear it.'

The old man studied Malchus' face for a moment. 'I believe you.' Taking a deep breath, he began. 'When the wind rose sharply, I saw that a storm was coming. I quickly pulled my net on board and headed for the Choma. Everyone else was doing the same. Or so I thought. When I was safe on dry land, I saw one skiff still over the tunny. I knew it for the young men's craft by its shape. At first I imagined that they had been consumed by greed and were trying to catch even more fish, but as it was carried out of sight, I realised I was mistaken.'

'Why?' Bodesmun's voice was strangled.

'The boat appeared to be empty. I wondered if they'd fallen overboard and drowned. That seemed improbable, for the sea was still not that rough yet.' The old man frowned. 'I came to the assumption that they were asleep. Oblivious to the weather.'

'What do you take us for?' cried Malchus. 'One dozing, maybe, but both of them?'

The old man quailed before Malchus' wrath, but Bodesmun laid a restraining hand on his arm. 'That is a possibility.'

Wild-eyed, Malchus turned on Bodesmun. 'Eh?'

'A flask of good wine is missing from my cellar.'

Malchus gave him a blank look. 'I don't understand.'

'Suniaton is the likely culprit,' Bodesmun revealed sadly. 'They must have drunk the wine and then fallen asleep.'

'When the wind began to rise, they didn't even notice,' Malchus whispered in horror.

Tears formed in Bodesmun's eyes.

'So they were just washed out to sea?' Malchus muttered in disbelief. 'You are old. I can understand why you might have held back, but those?' Furiously, he indicated the younger fishermen. 'Why did none of them help?'

The old man found his voice once more. 'They were your sons, I take it?'

Anguish overtook Malchus' fury, and he nodded.

The other's eyes filled with an unhealed sorrow. 'I lost my only child to the sea ten years hence. A son. It is the gods' way.' There was a short pause. 'The rules of survival are simple. When a storm strikes, it is every craft for itself. Even then, death is quite likely. Why would those men risk their own lives for two youths they barely knew? Otherwise Melqart would likely have had more corpses entering his kingdom.' He fell silent.

Part of Malchus wanted to have every person in sight crucified, but he knew that it would be a pointless gesture. Glancing back at the old man, he was struck by his calm manner. All his deference had vanished. Looking once more into the other's eyes, Malchus understood why. What difference would threats make here? The man's only son was dead. He felt strangely humbled. At least he still had Sapho and Bostar.

Beside him, silent sobs racked Bodesmun's shoulders.

'Two deaths is enough,' Malchus acknowledged with a heavy sigh. 'I'm grateful for your time.' He began fumbling in his purse.

'I need no payment,' the old man intoned. 'Such terrible news is beyond a price.'

Mumbling his thanks, Malchus walked away. He was barely aware of a weeping Bodesmun following him. While he retained his composure, Malchus too was riven by grief. He had expected to lose one son – perhaps more – in the impending war with Rome, but not beforehand, and so easily. Had Arishat's death not been enough unexpected tragedy for one lifetime? At least he'd been able to say goodbye to her. With Hanno, there hadn't even been that chance.

It all seemed so cruel, and so utterly pointless.

Several days went by. The friends were kept on the forecastle and given just enough food to keep them alive: crusts of stale bread, a few mouthfuls of cold millet porridge and the last, brackish drops from a clay water gourd. Their bonds were untied twice a day for a short period, allowing them to stretch the cramped muscles in their arms and upper backs. They soon learned to answer calls of nature at these times, because at others their guards would laugh at any request for help. On one occasion, desperate, Hanno had been forced to soil himself.

Fortunately, Varsaco was not allowed near them, although he sent frequent murderous glances in their direction. Hanno was pleased to note that the overseer walked with a decided limp for days. Other than making sure Hanno was recovering from his injuries, the Egyptian ignored them, even moving his blankets to the base of the mast. Strangely, Hanno felt some pride at this clear indication of their value. Their solitude also meant that the pair had plenty of occasions to confer with each other. They spent all their time plotting ways to escape. Of course both knew that their fantasies were merely an attempt to keep their spirits up.

The bireme reached the rugged coastline of Sicily, travelling past the walled towns of Heraclea, Acragas and Camarina. Keeping a reasonable distance out to sea meant that any Roman or Sicilian triremes could be avoided. The Egyptian made sure that the friends saw Mount Ecnomus, the peak off which the Carthaginians had suffered one of their greatest defeats to the Romans. Naturally, Hanno had heard the story many times. Sailing over the very water where so many of his countrymen had lost their lives nearly forty years before filled him with a burning rage: partly against the Egyptian for his lascivious telling of the tale, but mainly against the Romans, for what they had done to Carthage. The *corvus*, a spiked boarding bridge suspended from a pole on every enemy trireme, had been an ingenious invention. Once dropped on to the Carthaginian ships' decks, it had allowed the legionaries to storm across, fighting just as they would on land. In one savage day, Carthage had lost nearly a hundred ships, and her navy had never recovered from the blow.

A day or so after rounding Cape Pachynus, the southernmost point of Sicily, the bireme neared the magnificent stronghold of Syracuse. Originally built by the Corinthians more than five hundred years before, its immense fortifications sprawled from the triangular-shaped plateau of Epipolae on the rocky outcrop above the sea, right down to the island of Ortygia at the waterline. Syracuse was the capital of a powerful city-state, which controlled the eastern half of Sicily and was ruled by the aged tyrant Hiero, a long-term ally of the Republic, and enemy of Carthage. The Egyptian took his ship to within half a mile of the port before deciding not to enter it. Large numbers of Roman triremes were visible, the captains of which would relish crucifying any pirates who fell into their hands.

It mattered little to Hanno and Suniaton where they landed. In fact, the longer their journey continued, the better. It delayed the reality of their fate.

Rather than make for the towns located on the toe or heel of Italy, the Egyptian guided the bireme into the narrow strait between Sicily and the mainland. Only a mile wide, it afforded a good view of both coasts.

'It's easy to see why the Romans began the war with Carthage, isn't it?' Hanno muttered to Suniaton. Sicily dominated the centre of the Mediterranean, and, historically, whoever controlled it, ruled the waves. 'It's so close to Italy. Our troops' presence must have been perceived as a threat.'

'Imagine if our people hadn't lost the war,' Suniaton replied sadly. 'We would have stood a chance of being rescued by one of our ships now.'

It was another reason for Hanno to hate Rome.

In the port of Rhegium, on the Italian mainland, the pirate captain prepared to sell his captives. The street gossip soon changed his mind. The forthcoming games at Capua, further up the coast, had produced an unprecedented demand for slaves. It was enough to make the Egyptian set sail for Neapolis, the nearest shore town to the Campanian capital.

As the end of their voyage drew near, Hanno found that his increasing familiarity with the pirates was, oddly, more comforting than the unknown fate that awaited him. But then he remembered Varsaco: remaining on the bireme was an impossibility for it would only be a matter of time before the brutal overseer took his revenge. It was with a sense of relief, therefore, that two days later Hanno clambered on to the dock at Neapolis. The walled city, formerly a Greek settlement, had been one of the *socii*, allies of the Republic, for over a hundred years. It possessed one of the largest ports south of Rome, a deep-water harbour filled with warships, fishing boats and merchant vessels from all over the Mediterranean. The place was jammed, and it had taken the Egyptian an age to find a suitable mooring spot.

With Hanno were Suniaton and the other captives, a mixture of young Numidians and Libyans. The Egyptian and six of his burliest men accompanied the party. To prevent any attempt at escape, the iron ring around each captive's neck was connected to the next by a length of chain. Enjoying the solidity of the quayside's broad stone slabs beneath his feet, Hanno found himself beside a heap of roughly cut cedar planks from Tyre. Alongside those lay golden mounds of Sicilian grain and bulging bags of almonds from Africa. Beyond, stacked higher than a man, were wax-sealed amphorae full of wine and olive oil. Fishermen bantered with each other as they hauled their catch of tunny, mullet and bream ashore. Off-duty sailors in their striking blue tunics swaggered along the dock in search of the town's fleshpots. Laden down by their equipment, a squad of marines prepared to embark on a nearby trireme. Spotting them, the sailors filled the air with jibes. Bristling, the marines began shouting back. The groups were only stopped from coming to blows by the intervention of a pug-nosed *optio*.

Hanno couldn't help himself from drinking the hectic scene in. It was so reminiscent of home, and his heart ached with the pain of it. Then, amidst the shouts in Latin, Greek and Numidian, Hanno heard someone speaking Carthaginian, and being answered in turn. Complete shock, then joy, filled him. At least two of his countrymen were here! If he could speak with them, word might be carried to his father. He glanced at Suniaton. 'Did you hear that?'

Stricken, his friend nodded.

Hanno frantically stood on tiptoe, but the press on the quay was too great.

With a brutal yank, the Egyptian pulled on the chain, forcing his captives to follow. 'It's only a short walk to the slave market,' he announced with a cruel smile.

Hanno dragged his feet, but the pull around his neck was inexorable. To his immense distress, within a dozen paces he could no longer discern his mother tongue from the plethora of other languages being spoken. It was as if the last window of opportunity had been shut in their faces. It felt a crueller blow than anything that had befallen them thus far.

A tear rolled down Suniaton's cheek.

'Courage,' Hanno whispered. 'Somehow we will survive.'

How? his mind screamed. *How?*

Chapter IV: Manhood

The bear lunged at his feet, and Quintus lashed out, delivering a flurry of kicks in its direction. He had to bite his tongue not to scream in terror. At this rate, the animal would seize him by the thigh, or groin. The pain would be unbelievable, and his death lingering, rather than the swift end suffered by the Gaul. Quintus could think of no way out. Desperately, he continued flailing out with his *caligae*. Confused, the animal growled, and it batted at him with a giant paw. It half ripped off one of Quintus' sandals.

A moan of fear ripped free of his lips at last.

Footsteps pounded towards Quintus, and relief poured through his veins. His life might not be over. He was simultaneously consumed by shame. He did not want to live the rest of his days known as the coward who had had to be rescued from a bear.

'HOLD!' shouted his father.

'But Quintus—' Agesandros protested.

'He must do this on his own. He said so himself,' Fabricius muttered. 'Stand back!'

Waves of terror washed over Quintus. In obeying his wishes, his father was consigning him to certain death. He closed his eyes. Let it be quick, please. A moment later, he realised that the bear had not pressed home its attack. Quintus peered at the animal, which was still only a few steps away. Was it Agesandros' charge, or his father's voice that had caused it to hesitate? He wasn't sure, but it gave him an idea. Taking a deep breath, Quintus let out a piercing cry. The animal's small ears flattened, which encouraged him to repeat the shrill sound. This time, he waved his arms as well.

To Quintus' immense relief, the bear backed off a pace. He was able to climb to his feet, still shrieking his head off. Unfortunately, his spear was beyond his reach. It lay right beneath the animal's front paws. Quintus knew that without it, he had no chance of success. Nor would there be any pride to be had in driving off the bear with noise. He had to regain his weapon and kill it. Swinging his arms like a madman, he took a step towards it. The animal's head swung suspiciously from side to side, but it gave way. Remembering Agesandros' advice about what to do if confronted by a bear in the forest, Quintus redoubled his efforts. His damaged sandal was still attached to his calf by its straps, and he had to take great care how he placed his feet. Despite this hindrance, it wasn't long before he regained his spear.

Quintus could have cheered. The animal was now looking all around it, searching for a way to escape, but there was no easy way. Fabricius had directed the others to spread out. They formed a loose circle around the pair. The remaining dogs filled the air with an eager clamour. His courage renewed, Quintus went on the offensive. After all, the bear was wounded. It had to be within his ability to kill it now.

He was mistaken.

Every time he stabbed his spear at the animal, it either snapped at the blade, or swept it out of the way with its massive arms. Quintus' heart thumped off his ribs. He would have to go a lot closer. How, though, could he deliver a death stroke without coming within range of its deadly claws? The bear's reach was prodigious. He could think of only one way. He'd seen pigs slaughtered many times in the farmyard, had even wielded the knife himself on occasion. With their tough skin and thick layer of subcutaneous fat, they were difficult animals to kill, quite unlike sheep or oxen. The best way was to run the blade into their flesh directly under the chin, cutting the major vessels that exited the heart. Quintus prayed that bears' anatomy was similar, and that the gods granted him a chance to finish the matter like this.

Before he could carry out his plan, the animal lunged forward on all fours, catching Quintus off guard. He backed away hastily, forgetting his damaged sandal. Within a few steps, the studded sole snagged on a protruding root. They pulled the straps attached to his calf taut, in the process unbalancing him. Quintus fell heavily, landing this time on his backside. Somehow, he hung on to his spear, which landed flat on the glade floor beside him. That didn't stop his heart from shrivelling with fear. The bear's attention focused in on him and, moving incredibly fast, it swarmed in his direction.

Quintus' eyes flickered to one side. The shocked expression on his father's face said it all. He was about to die.

Despite his horror, Fabricius kept his oath. He did not budge from his position.

Quintus' gaze returned to the bear. Its gaping mouth was no more than a handsbreadth from his feet. He had but the briefest instant to react before it ripped one of his legs off. Fortunately, the end of his spear protruded beyond his sandals. Gripping the shaft, he raised it off the ground. Sunlight flashed off the polished iron tip, and bounced into the bear's eyes, distracting it, and causing it to snap irritably at the blade. Swiftly, Quintus pulled his legs to one side. At the same time, he jammed the weapon's butt into the earth by his elbow and gripped it fiercely with both hands.

When the bear closed in, he aimed the sharp point at the flesh below its wide-open jaws. Intent on seizing him, it paid no attention. Lowering its head, it lunged at his legs. Desperately, Quintus slid them away as fast as he could. The movement brought the animal right on to his spear, and its momentum was great enough for the razor-sharp iron to slice through the skin. There was a grating feeling as it pushed over the larynx before running onwards into the deeper, softer tissues. Fully capable of tearing him apart yet, the bear bucked and reared, its immense strength threatening to rip Quintus' weapon from his hands. He hung on for dear life as, half suspended above him, the animal clawed furiously at the thick wooden shaft. It was so close that his nostrils were filled with its pungent odour. He could almost touch the fangs that had torn apart the Gaul and three of the dogs.

It was utterly terrifying.

The animal's immense weight eventually worked against it, forcing the deadly blade further into its flesh. Quintus was far from happy, however. The bear was very much alive, and it was drawing ever nearer. It filled his entire range of vision – a great angry mass of teeth and claws. Any closer and it would rip him to shreds. Could the protruding spikes at the base of the iron shank take the strain? Quintus' mouth was bone dry with fear. *Die, you whoreson. Just die.*

It lurched a further handsbreadth down the spear shaft.

He thought his heart would stop.

Abruptly, the bear gagged, and a bright red tide of blood sprayed from its mouth, covering the ground beyond Quintus. He had sliced through a large artery! Jupiter, let its heart be next, he prayed. *Before it reaches me.* The shaft juddered as the iron spikes slammed against the creature's neck, and it came to an abrupt stop. It snarled in Quintus' face, and he closed his eyes. There was no more he could do.

To his immense relief, the bear stopped struggling. Another torrent of blood poured from its gaping jaws, covering Quintus' face and shoulders. Disbelieving, he looked up, stunned to see the light in its amber eyes weaken, and then go out. All at once, the bear was a dead weight on the end of his spear. Quintus' exhausted muscles could take the pressure no longer, and he let go.

The animal landed on top of him.

To Quintus' immense relief, it did not move. And although he could barely breathe, he was alive.

An instant later, he felt the bear's body being hauled off.

'You're unhurt,' his father cried. 'Praise be!'

Agesandros growled his agreement.

Quintus sat up gingerly. 'Someone was watching over me,' he muttered, wiping some of the bear's blood away from his eyes.

'They were indeed, but that doesn't take away from what you've done,' said Fabricius. There was tangible relief in his voice. 'I was sure you were going to be killed. But you held your nerve! Few men can do that when faced with certain death. You should be proud. Not only have you proved your courage, but you've honoured our ancestors in the finest way possible.'

Quintus glanced at Agesandros and the two slaves, who were regarding him with new respect. His chin lifted. He had succeeded! Thank you, Diana and Mars, he thought. I will make a generous offering to you both. Inevitably, though, Quintus' eyes were drawn to the tattooed slave's body. Guilt seized him. 'I should have saved him too,' he muttered.

'Come now!' Fabricius replied. 'You are not Hercules. The fool should have known better than to risk his life for a dog. Your achievement is worthy of any Roman.' He drew Quintus to his feet and embraced him warmly.

Quintus' emotions suddenly became overwhelming: sadness at the Gaul's death mixed with relief that he had triumphed over his fear. He struggled not to cry. During the fight, he'd forgotten about becoming a man. Somehow, he had achieved the task set out by his father.

At last they drew apart.

'How does it feel?' Fabricius asked.

'No different,' Quintus replied with a grin.

'Are you sure?'

Quintus stared at the bear and realised that things *had* changed.

Before, he'd been unsure of his ability to kill such a magnificent creature. Indeed, he'd nearly failed because of his terror. Staring death in the face was a lot worse than he'd imagined. Yet wanting to survive had been a gut instinct. He looked back to find Fabricius studying him intently.

'I saw that you were afraid,' his father said. 'I would have intervened, but you had made me promise not to.'

Quintus flushed, and opened his mouth to speak.

Fabricius raised a hand. 'Your reaction was normal, despite what some might say. But your determination to succeed, even if you died in the attempt, was stronger than your fear. You were right to make me swear not to step in.' He clapped Quintus on the arm. 'The gods have favoured you.'

Quintus remembered the two woodpeckers he'd seen, and smiled.

'As you are to be a soldier, we shall have to visit the temple of Mars as well as that of Diana.' Fabricius winked. 'There's also the small matter of buying a toga.'

Quintus beamed. Visits to Capua were always to be looked forward to. Living in the countryside afforded few opportunities for socialising or pleasure. They could visit the public baths and his father's old comrade, Flavius Martialis. Flavius' son, Gaius, was the same age as he was, and the two got along famously. Gaius would love to hear the story of the bear hunt.

First, though, he had to tell Aurelia and his mother. They would be waiting eagerly for news.

While Agesandros and the slaves stayed to bury the tattooed Gaul and to fashion carrying poles for the bear, Quintus and his father headed for home.

It didn't take the Egyptian long to sell the friends. Thanks to the impending games at Capua, sales at the Neapolis slave market were brisk. There were few specimens on sale to compare with the two Carthaginians' muscular build, or the Numidians' wiry frames, and buyers crowded round the naked men, squeezing their arms and staring into their eyes for signs of fear. Although Hanno's miserable demeanour was not that of a combatant, he impressed nonetheless. Cleverly, the Egyptian refused to sell them except as a pair. Several dealers bid against each other to purchase the two friends, and the eventual victor was a dour Latin by the name of Solinus. He also bought four of the Egyptian's other captives.

Hanno took little notice of what was going on in the noisy market place. Suniaton's efforts to revive his spirits with whispers of encouragement were futile. Hanno felt more hopeless than he ever had in his life. Since surviving the storm, every possible chance of redemption had turned to dust. Unknowingly, they had rowed out to sea rather than towards the land. Instead of a merchant vessel, fate had brought them the bireme. In a heaven-sent opportunity, Carthaginians had been present at Neapolis, but he hadn't been able to speak to them. Lastly, they were to be sold as gladiators rather than the more common classes of slaves, which guaranteed their death. What more proof did he need that the gods had forgotten them completely? Hanno's misery coated him like a heavy, wet blanket.

Along with an assortment of Gauls, Greeks and Iberians, the six captives were marched out of the town and on to the dusty road to Capua. It was twenty miles from Neapolis to the Campanian capital, a long day's walk at most, but Solinus broke the journey with an overnight stop at a roadside inn. As the prisoners watched miserably, the Latin and his guards sat down to enjoy a meal of wine, roast pork and freshly baked bread. All the captives got was a bucket of water from the well, which afforded each man no more than half a dozen mouthfuls. At length, however, a servant delivered several stale loaves and a platter of cheese rinds. However paltry the portions, the waste food tasted divine, and revived the captives greatly. As Suniaton bitterly told Hanno, they would be worth far less if they arrived in Capua at death's door. It was therefore worth spending a few coppers on provisions, however poor.

Hanno didn't respond. Suniaton soon gave up trying to raise his spirits, and they sat in silence. Deep in their own misery, and strangers to each other, none of the other slaves spoke either. As it grew dark, they lay down side by side, staring at the glittering vista of stars illuminating the night sky. It was a beautiful sight, reminding Hanno again of Carthage, the home he would never see again. His emotions quickly got the better of him, and, grateful for the darkness, he sobbed silently into the crook of an elbow.

Their current suffering was nothing. What was to come would be far worse.

In the morning, Quintus had his first hangover. During the celebratory dinner the previous night, Fabricius had plied him with wine. Although he had often taken surreptitious tastes from amphorae in the kitchen, it had been the first time Quintus was officially permitted to drink. He had not held back. His approving mother had not protested. With Aurelia hanging on his every word, Elira casting smouldering glances each time she delivered food and his father throwing him frequent compliments, he'd felt like a conquering hero. Agesandros too had been full of praise when, after dinner, he had brought the freshly skinned bear pelt to the table. Flushed with success, Quintus rapidly lost count of how many glasses he'd downed. While the wine was watered down in the traditional manner, he was not used to handling its effects. By the time the plates were cleared away, Quintus had been vaguely aware that he was slurring his words. Atia had swiftly moved the jug out of his reach and, soon after, Fabricius had helped him to bed. When a naked Elira had slipped under the covers a short time later, Quintus had barely stirred; he hadn't noticed her leave either.

Now, with the early morning sun beating down on his throbbing head, he felt like a piece of metal being hammered on a smith's anvil. It was little more than an hour since his father had woken him, and even less since they had set off from the farm. Nauseous, Quintus had refused the breakfast proffered him by a sympathetic Aurelia. Encouraged by a grinning Agesandros, he'd drunk several cups of water, and mutely accepted a full clay gourd for the journey. There was still a foul taste in Quintus' mouth, though, and every movement of the horse between his knees threatened to make him vomit yet again. So far, he'd done so four times. The only things keeping him on the saddle blanket were his vice-like hold on the reins, and his knees, which were tightly gripping the horse's sides. Fortunately, his mount had a placid nature. Eyeing the uneven track that stretched off into the distance, Quintus muttered a curse. Capua was a long distance away yet.

They travelled in single file, with his father at the front. Dressed in his finest tunic, Fabricius sat astride his grey stallion. His gladius hung from a gilded baldric, necessary protection against bandits. Also armed, Quintus came next. The tightly rolled bear pelt was tied up behind his saddle blanket. It needed to dry out, but he was determined to show it to Gaius. His mother and his sister were next, sitting in a litter carried by six slaves. Aurelia would have ridden, but Atia's presence precluded that. Despite the tradition that women did not ride, Quintus had given in to his sister's demands years before. She had turned out to be a natural horse-woman. Their father had happened to see them practising one day, and had been amazed. Because of her ability, Fabricius had chosen to indulge her in this, but Atia had been kept in the dark. There was no way that she would have agreed to it. Knowing this, Aurelia had not protested as they'd left.

Taking up the rear was Agesandros, his feet dangling either side of a sturdy mule. He was to visit the slave market and find a replacement for the dead Gaul. A metal-tipped staff was slung over his back, and his whip, the badge of his office, was jammed into his belt. The Sicilian had left his deputy, a grinning Iberian with little brain but plenty of brawn, to supervise the taking in of the harvest. Last of all came a pair of prize lambs, bleating indignantly as Agesandros dragged them along by their head ropes.

Time passed and gradually Quintus felt more human. He drained the water gourd twice, refilling it from a noisy stream that ran parallel to the road. The pain in his head was lessening, allowing him to take more of an interest in his surroundings. The hills where they had hunted the bear were now just a hazy line on the horizon behind them. On either side sprawled fields of ripe wheat, ground which belonged to their neighbours. Campania possessed some of the most fertile land in Italy, and the proof lay all around. Groups of slaves were at work everywhere, wielding their scythes, gathering armfuls of the cut stalks, stacking sheaves. Their activities were of scant interest to Quintus, who was beginning to feel excited about wearing his first adult toga.

Aurelia drew the curtain as the litter came alongside. 'You look better,' she said brightly.

'A little, I suppose,' he admitted.

'You shouldn't have drunk so much,' Atia scolded.

'It's not every day a man kills a bear,' Quintus mumbled.

Fabricius turned his head. 'That's right.'

Aurelia's lips thinned, but she didn't pursue the issue.

'A day like yesterday comes along only a few times in a lifetime. It is right to celebrate it,' Fabricius declared. 'A sore head is a small price to pay afterwards.'

'True enough,' Atia admitted from the depths of the litter. 'You have honoured your Oscan, as well as your Roman, heritage. I'm proud to have you as my son.'

Shortly after midday, they reached Capua's impressive walls. Surrounded by a deep ditch, the stone fortifications ran around the city's entire circumference. Watchtowers had been built at regular intervals, and six gates, manned by sentries, controlled the access. Quintus, who had never seen Rome, loved it dearly.

Originally built by the Etruscans more than four hundred years before, Capua had been the head of a league of twelve cities. Two centuries previously, however, marauding Oscans had swept in, seizing the area for their people. My mother's race, thought Quintus proudly. Under Oscan rule, Capua had grown into one of the most powerful cities in Italy, but was eventually forced to seek aid from Rome when successive waves of Samnite invaders threatened its independence.

Quintus' father was descended from a member of the Roman relief force, which meant that his children were citizens. Campania's association with the Republic meant that its people were also citizens, but only the nobility were allowed to vote. This distinction was still the cause of resentment among many Campanian plebeians, who had to present themselves for military service alongside the legions, despite their lack of suffrage. The loudest among them claimed that they were remaining true to their Oscan ancestors. There was even some talk of Capua regaining its independence, which Fabricius decried as treason. Quintus felt torn if he thought about their protests, not least because his mother conspicuously remained silent at such times. It seemed hypocritical that local men who might fight and die for Rome were not permitted to have a say in who ran the Republic. It also brought Quintus to the thorny question of whether he was denying his mother's heritage in favour of his father's? It was a point that Gaius, Flavius Martialis' son, loved to tease him about. Although they had Roman citizenship and could vote, Martialis and Gaius were Oscan nobility through and through.

Their first stop was the temple of Mars, which was located in a side street a short distance from the forum. While the family watched, one lamb was offered up for sacrifice. Quintus was relieved when the priest pronounced good omens. The same assertion was made at Diana's shrine, delighting him further.

'No surprise there,' Fabricius murmured as they left.

'What do you mean?' asked Quintus.

'After hearing what happened on the hunt, the priest was hardly going to give us an unfavourable reading.' Fabricius smiled at Quintus' shock. 'Come now! I believe in the gods too, but we didn't need to be told that they were pleased with us yesterday. It was obvious. What was important today was to pay our respects, and that we have done.' He clapped his hands. 'It's time to clean up at the baths, and then buy you a new toga.'

An hour later, they were all standing in a tailor's shop. Thanks to its proximity to the fullers' workshops, the premises reeked of stale urine, increasing Quintus' desire to get on with the matter in hand. Workers were busy in the background, raising the nap on rolls of cloth with small spiked boards, trimming it with cropping shears to give a soft finish, and folding the finished fabric before pressing it. The proprietor, an obsequious figure with greasy hair, laid out different qualities of wool for them to choose from, but Atia quickly motioned at the best. Soon Quintus had been fitted in his toga *virilis*. He shifted awkwardly from foot to foot while a delighted Atia fussed and bothered, adjusting the voluminous folds until they met with her approval. Fabricius stood in the background, a proud smile on his lips while Aurelia bobbed up and down excitedly alongside.

'The young master looks very distinguished,' gushed the shopkeeper.

Atia gave an approving nod. 'He does.'

Feeling proud but self-conscious, Quintus gave her a tight smile.

'A fine sight,' Fabricius added. Counting out the relevant coinage, he handed it over. 'Time to visit Flavius Martialis. Gaius will want to see you in all your glory.'

Leaving the proprietor bowing and scraping in their wake, they walked outside. There Agesandros, who had taken their mounts to a stables, was waiting. He bowed deeply to Quintus. 'You are truly a man now, sir.'

Pleased by the gesture, Quintus grinned. 'Thank you.'

Fabricius looked at his overseer. 'Why don't you go to the market now? You know where Martialis' house is. Just come along when you've bought the new slave.' He handed over a purse. 'There's a hundred *didrachms*.'

'Of course,' Agesandros replied. He turned to go.

'Wait,' Quintus cried on impulse. 'I'll tag along. I need to start learning about things like this.'

Agesandros' dark eyes regarded him steadily. '"Things like this"?' he repeated.

'Buying slaves, I mean.' Quintus had never really given much thought to the process before, which, for obvious reasons, still impacted on Agesandros. 'You can teach me.'

The Sicilian glanced at Fabricius, who gave an approving nod.

'Why not?' Atia declared. 'It would be good experience for you.'

Agesandros' lips curved upwards. 'Very well.'

Aurelia rushed to Quintus' side. 'I'm coming too,' she declared.

Agesandros arched an eyebrow. 'I'm not sure . . .' he began.

'It's out of the question,' said Fabricius.

'There are things in the slave market which are not fitting for a girl to see,' Atia added.

'I'm almost a woman, as you keep telling me,' Aurelia retorted. 'When I've been married off, and I'm mistress of my own house, I will be able to visit such places whenever I choose. Why not now?'

'Aurelia!' Atia snapped.

'You do what I say!' interrupted Fabricius. 'I am your father. Remember that. Your husband, whoever he may be, will also expect you to be obedient.'

Aurelia dropped her eyes. 'I'm sorry,' she whispered. 'I just wanted to accompany Quintus as he walked through the town, looking so fine in his new toga.'

Disarmed, Fabricius cleared his throat. 'Come now,' he said. He glanced at Atia, who frowned.

'Please?' Aurelia pleaded.

There was a long pause, before Atia gave an almost imperceptible nod.

Fabricius smiled. 'Very well. You may go with your brother.'

'Thank you, Father. Thank you, Mother.' Aurelia avoided Atia's hard stare, which promised all kinds of dressing-down later.

'Go on, then.' Fabricius made a benevolent gesture of dismissal.

As Agesandros silently led them down the busy street, Quintus gave Aurelia a reproving look. 'It's not only my exercises that you've been spying on, eh? You're quite the conspirator.'

'You're surprised? I have every right to listen in to your little conversations with Father.' Her blue eyes flashed. 'Why should I just play with my toys while you two discuss possible husbands? I may be able to do nothing about it, but it's my right to know.'

'You're right. I should have told you before,' Quintus admitted. 'I'm sorry.'

Suddenly, her eyes were full of tears. 'I don't want an arranged marriage,' she whispered. 'Mother says that it won't be that bad, but how would she know?'

Quintus felt stricken. Such a bargain might help them climb to the upper level of society. If so, their family's fate would be changed for ever. The price required made him feel very uncomfortable, however. It didn't help that Aurelia was right beside him, waiting for his response. Quintus didn't want to tell an outright lie, so, ducking his head, he increased his pace. 'Hurry,' he urged. 'Agesandros is leaving us behind.'

She saw through his pretence at once. 'See? You think the same.'

Stung, he stopped.

'Father and Mother married for love. Why shouldn't I?'

'It is our duty to obey their orders. You know that,' said Quintus, feeling awful. 'They know best, and we must accept that.'

Agesandros turned to address them, abruptly ending their

conversation. Quintus was relieved to see that they had reached the slave market, which was situated in an open area by the town's south gate. Already it was becoming hard to make oneself heard above the din. Aurelia could do little but fall into an angry silence.

'Here we are,' the Sicilian directed. 'Take it all in.'

Mutely, the siblings obeyed. Although they had seen the market countless times, neither had paid it much heed before. It was part of everyday life, just like the stalls hawking fruit and vegetables, and the butchers selling freshly slaughtered lambs, goats and pigs. Yet, Quintus realised, it *was* different here. These were people on sale. Prisoners of war or criminals for the most part, but people nonetheless.

Hundreds of naked men, women and children were on display, chained or bound together with rope. Chalk coated everyone's feet. Black-, brown- and white-skinned, they were every nationality under the sun. Tall, muscular Gauls with blond hair stood beside short, slender Greeks. Broad-nosed, powerfully built Nubians towered over the wiry figures of Numidians and Egyptians. Full-breasted Gaulish women clustered together beside rangy, narrow-hipped Judaeans and Illyrians. Many were sobbing; some were even wailing with distress. Babies and young children added their cries to that of their mothers. Others, catatonic from their trauma, stared into space. Dealers stalked up and down, loudly extolling the qualities of their merchandise to the plentiful buyers who were wandering between the lines of slaves. On the fringes of the throng, groups of hard-faced, armed men lounged about, a mixture of guards and *fugitivarii*, or slave-catchers.

'The choice is enormous, so you have to know what you want in advance. Otherwise, it would take all day,' said Agesandros. He looked enquiringly at Quintus.

Quintus thought of the tattooed Gaul, whose primary duty had been working in the fields. His skill with the hunting dogs had merely been an added bonus. 'He needs to be young and physically fit. Good teeth are important too.' He paused, thinking.

'Anything else?' Agesandros barked.

Quintus was surprised by the change in the Sicilian, whose usual genial manner had disappeared. 'There should be no obvious infirmities or signs of disease. Hernias, poorly healed fractures, dirty wounds and so on.'

Aurelia screwed up her face in distaste.

'Is that it?'

Irritated, Quintus shook his head. 'Yes, I think so.'

Agesandros pulled out his dagger, and Aurelia gasped. 'You're forgetting the most important thing,' the Sicilian said, raising the blade. 'Look in his eyes, and decide how much spirit he has. Ask yourself: will this whoreson ever try to cut my throat? If you think he might, walk away and choose another. Otherwise you might regret it one dark night.'

'Wise words,' Quintus said, levelly. Now, put him on the back foot, he thought. 'What did my father think when he looked in your eyes?'

It was Agesandros' turn to be surprised. His eyes flickered, and he lowered the dagger. 'I believe he saw another soldier,' he answered curtly. Turning on his heel, he plunged into the crowd. 'Follow me.'

'He's just playing games, that's all. Trying to impress me,' Quintus lied to Aurelia. He actually reckoned that Agesandros had been trying to scare him. It had partially worked too. The only reply he got, though, was a scowl. His sister was still angry with him for not telling her what he thought of her chances of happiness in an arranged marriage. Quintus walked off. *I'll sort it out later.*

The Sicilian ignored the first slaves on offer, and then stopped by a line of Nubians, poking and prodding several, and even opening the mouth of one. Their owner, a scrawny Phoenician with gold earrings, instantly scuttled to Agesandros' side, and began waxing lyrical about their quality. Quintus joined them, leaving Aurelia to simmer in the background. After a moment, Agesandros moved on, ignoring the Phoenician's offers. 'Every tooth in that Nubian's head was rotten,' he muttered to Quintus. 'He wouldn't last more than a few years.'

They wandered up and down for some time. The Sicilian said less and less, allowing Quintus to decide which individuals fitted the bill. He found several, but with each Agesandros found a reason not to buy. Quintus decided to stand his ground when he found the next suitable slave. A moment later, two dark-skinned young men with tightly curled black hair caught his eye. He hadn't noticed them before. Neither was especially tall, but both were well muscled. One kept his gaze firmly directed at the ground, while the other, who had a snub nose and green eyes, glanced at Quintus, before looking away. He paused to assess the pair. There was enough spare chain for the slaves to step out of line. Beckoning the first forward, Quintus began his examination, watched closely by the Sicilian.

The youth was about his age, in excellent physical condition, with a good set of teeth. Nothing he did made the slave look at him, which increased his interest. Agesandros' warning was still fresh in his mind, so Quintus grabbed the other's chin and lifted it. Startlingly, the slave's eyes were a vivid green colour, like those of his companion. Quintus saw no defiance there, just an inconsolable sadness. He's perfect, he thought. 'I'll take this one,' he said to Agesandros. 'He meets your requirements.'

The Sicilian glanced the youth up and down. 'Where are you from?' he demanded in Latin.

The slave blinked, but did not answer.

He understood that question, thought Quintus with surprise.

Agesandros appeared not to have noticed, though. He repeated his question in Greek.

Again no reply.

Sensing their interest, the dealer, a dour Latin, moved in. 'He's Carthaginian. His friend too. Strong as oxen.'

'Guggas, eh?' Agesandros spat on the ground. 'They'll be no damn use.'

Quintus and Aurelia were both shocked at the change in his demeanour. The abusive term meant 'little rat'. Immediately, Agesandros' past came to Quintus' mind. It was Carthaginians who had sold the Sicilian into slavery. That wasn't a reason not to buy the slave, however.

'There's been a lot of interest in them this morning,' said the dealer persuasively. 'Good gladiator material, they are.'

'You haven't managed to sell them, though,' replied Quintus sarcastically; beside him, Agesandros snorted in agreement. 'How much are you asking?'

'Solinus is an honest man. 150 didrachms each, or 300 for the pair.'

Quintus laughed. 'Nearly twice the price of a farm slave.' He made to leave. His face a cold mask, Agesandros did too. Then Quintus paused. He was growing tired of the Sicilian's negative attitude. The Carthaginian *was* as good as any of the others he'd seen. If he could barter the Solinus down, why not buy him? He turned. 'We only need one,' he barked. The slaves glanced fearfully at each other, confirming Quintus' hunch that they spoke Latin.

Solinus grinned, revealing an array of rotten teeth. 'Which?'

Ignoring Agesandros' frown, Quintus pointed at the slave he'd examined.

The Latin leered. 'How does 140 didrachms sound?'

Quintus made a dismissive gesture. 'One hundred.'

Solinus' face turned hard. 'I have to make a living,' he growled. '130. That's my best price.'

'I could go ten didrachms more, but that's it,' said Quintus.

Solinus shook his head vehemently.

Quintus was incensed by Agesandros' delighted look. 'I'll give you 125,' he snapped.

Agesandros leaned in close. 'I haven't got that much,' he muttered sourly.

'I'll sell the bear pelt, then. That's worth at least twenty-five didrachms,' Quintus retorted. He'd planned on using it as a bed cover, but winning this situation came first.

Suddenly keen, Solinus stepped forward. 'It's a fair price,' he said.

Agesandros' fists closed over the purse.

'Give it to him,' ordered Quintus. When the Sicilian did not react, his anger boiled over. 'I am the master here. Do as I say!'

Reluctantly, Agesandros obeyed.

The small victory pleased Quintus no end. 'That's a hundred. My man here will bring the rest later,' he said.

Even as he pocketed the money, Solinus' mouth opened in protest.

'My father is Gaius Fabricius, an equestrian,' Quintus growled. 'The balance will be paid before nightfall.'

Solinus backed off at once. 'Of course, of course.' Pulling a bunch of keys from his belt, he selected one. He reached up to the iron ring around the Carthaginian's neck. There was a soft click, and the slave stumbled forward, freed.

For the first time, Aurelia looked at him. I have never seen anyone so handsome, she thought, her heart pounding at the sight of his naked flesh.

The Carthaginian's dazed expression told Quintus that he hadn't quite taken in what was happening. It was only when his companion muttered something urgent in Carthaginian that the realisation sank in. Tears welled in his eyes, and he turned to Quintus.

'Buy my friend as well, please,' he said in fluent Latin.

I was right, thought Quintus triumphantly. 'You speak my language.'

'Yes.'

Agesandros glowered, but the siblings ignored him.

'How come?' Aurelia asked.

'My father insisted I learn it. Greek too.'

Aurelia was fascinated, while Quintus was delighted. He had made a good choice. 'What's your name?'

BEN KANE

'Hanno,' the Carthaginian answered. He indicated his comrade. 'That's Suniaton. He's my best friend.'

'Why didn't you answer the overseer's question?'

For the first time, Hanno met his gaze. 'Would you?'

Quintus was thrown by his directness. 'No . . . I suppose not.'

Encouraged, Hanno turned to Aurelia. 'Buy us both – I beg you. Otherwise my friend could be sold as a gladiator.'

Quintus and Aurelia glanced at each other in surprise. This was no peasant from a faraway land. Hanno was well educated, and from a good family. So was his friend. It was a bizarre, and uncomfortable, feeling.

'We require one slave. Not two.' Agesandros' clarion voice was a harsh call back to reality.

'We could come to some arrangement, I'm sure,' said Solinus ingratiatingly.

'No, we couldn't,' the Sicilian snarled, cowing him into submission. He addressed Quintus. 'The last thing the farm needs is an extra mouth to feed. Your father will already want to know why we spent so much. Best not blow any more of his money, eh?'

Quintus wanted to argue, but Agesandros was right. They only needed one slave. He gave Aurelia a helpless look. Her tiny, anguished shrug told him she felt the same way. 'There's nothing I can do,' he said to Hanno.

The smirk of satisfaction that flickered across Agesandros' lips went unnoticed by all except Hanno.

The two slaves exchanged a long glance, laden with feeling. 'May the gods guide your path,' Hanno said in Carthaginian. 'Stay strong. I will pray for you every day.'

Suniaton's chin trembled. 'If you ever get home, tell my father that I am sorry,' he said in an undertone. 'Ask him for his forgiveness.'

'I swear it,' vowed Hanno, his voice choking. 'And he will grant it, you may be sure of that.'

Quintus and Aurelia could not speak Carthaginian but it was

impossible to misunderstand the overwhelming emotion passing between the two slaves. Quintus took his sister's arm. 'Come on,' he said. 'We can't buy every slave in the market.' He led her away, without looking at Suniaton again.

Agesandros waited until they were out of earshot, then he whispered venomously in Hanno's ear, in Carthaginian. 'It wasn't my choice to buy a gugga. But now you and I are going to have a pleasant time on the farm. Don't think you can run away either. See those types over there?'

Hanno studied the gang of unshaven, roughly dressed men some distance away. Every one was heavily armed, and they were watching the proceedings like hawks.

'They are fugitivarii,' Agesandros explained. 'For the right price, they'll track down any man. Bring him back alive, or dead. With his balls, or without. Even in little pieces. Is that clear?'

'Yes.' A leaden feeling of dread filled Hanno's belly.

'Good. We understand each other.' The Sicilian grinned. 'Follow me.' He strode off after Quintus and Aurelia.

Hanno turned to look at Suniaton one last time. His heart felt as if it was going to rip apart. It hurt even to breathe. Whatever his fate, Suni's would undoubtedly be worse.

'You can't help me,' Suniaton mouthed. Remarkably, his face was calm. 'Go.'

Hot tears blinded Hanno at last. He turned and stumbled away.

Chapter V: Malchus

Carthage

I n what had become his daily routine, Malchus finished his breakfast and left the house. Although Bostar had already shipped for Iberia, Sapho was still at home. However, he mostly stayed at his rooms in the garrison's quarters. When Sapho did call by, it was rare for him even to mention Hanno, which Malchus found slightly odd. It was his eldest son's way of dealing with bereavement, he supposed. His was to shun all human contact. It meant that apart from the rare occasions when he had visitors, Malchus' only companions were the domestic slaves. It had been thus since Hanno's disappearance a few weeks before. Scared of Malchus' fierce temper and obvious sorrow, the slaves tiptoed around, trying not to attract his attention. In consequence, Malchus was even more aware of – and annoyed by them. While he longed to lash out, the slaves were not to blame, so he bit down on his anger, bottling it up. Yet he could not bear to stay indoors, staring at the four walls, obsessed with thoughts of Hanno, his beloved youngest son – his favourite son – whom he would never see again.

Malchus headed towards the city's twin harbours. Alone. The adage that one's grief eased with time was utter nonsense, he thought bitterly. In fact, it grew by the day. Sometimes he wondered if his sorrow would overcome him. Render him unable to carry on. A moment later, Malchus caught sight of Bodesmun. He cursed under his breath. He found it increasingly hard even to look at Suniaton's father. The opposite seemed true of the priest, who sought him out at every opportunity.

Bodesmun raised a solemn hand in greeting. 'Malchus. How are you today?'

Malchus scowled. 'The same. And you?'

Bodesmun's face crumpled with anguish. 'Not good.'

Malchus sighed. The same thing happened every time they met. Priests were supposed to lead by example, not crack under pressure. He had enough problems of his own without having to deal with Bodesmun's too. Was he not carrying the weight of two losses on his shoulders? Malchus' rational side knew that he was not responsible for the death of either Arishat, his wife, or Hanno, but the rest of him did not. During the frequent nights when he lay awake, Malchus had become painfully aware that his self-righteousness was partly to blame for Hanno's bad behaviour. After Arishat's death, he had become somewhat of a fanatic, interested in nothing except Hannibal Barca's plans for the future. There had been no brightness or light in the house, no laughter or fun. Sapho and Bostar, already adult men, had not been so affected by his melancholy, but it had hit Hanno hard. Since that realisation, guilt had clawed at Malchus constantly. I should have spent more time with him, he thought. Even gone fishing, instead of droning on about ancient battles. 'It's hard,' he said, doing his best to be sympathetic. He ushered the priest out of the way of a passing cart. 'Very hard.'

'The pain,' Bodesmun whispered miserably. 'It just gets worse.'

'I know,' Malchus agreed. 'There are only two things I know of that make it ease somewhat.'

A spark of interest lit in Bodesmun's sorrowful brown eyes. 'Tell me, please.'

'The first is my loathing of Rome and everything it stands for,' Malchus spat. 'For years, it seemed that the opportunity for revenge would never come. Hannibal has changed all this. At last, Carthage has a chance at settling the score!'

'It's more than two decades since the war in Sicily ended,' Bodesmun protested. 'More than a generation.'

'That's right.' Malchus could remember how weakened the flames of his hatred had been before Hannibal's emergence on to the scene. Now, they had been fanned white-hot by his grief for Hanno. 'Even greater reason not to forget.'

'That can be of no help to me. Begetting violence is not Eshmoun's way,' Bodesmun murmured. 'What's your other means of coping?'

'I scour the streets near the merchant port, listening to conversations and studying faces,' Malchus answered. Seeing the confusion on the other's face, he explained. 'Looking for a clue, the smallest snippet of information, anything that might help to ascertain what happened to Hanno and Suni.'

Bodesmun looked baffled. 'But we know what took place. The old man told us.'

'I know,' Malchus muttered, embarrassed at having to reveal his innermost secret. He had spent a fortune on sacrifices to Melqart, the 'King of the City', his sole request being that the god had somehow seen a way to prevent the boys' boat from sinking. Of course, he'd had no answer, but he wouldn't give up. 'It's just possible that they might be alive. That someone found them.'

Bodesmun's eyes widened. 'That's a dangerous thing to go on believing,' he said. 'Be careful.'

Malchus' nod was brittle. 'How do you go on?'

Bodesmun looked up at the sky. 'I pray to my god. I ask him to look after them both in paradise.'

That was too much for Malchus. Too final. 'I have to go,' he muttered. He strode off, leaving a forlorn Bodesmun in his wake.

A short while later, Malchus reached the Agora. Seeing large numbers of senators and politicians, he cursed. He'd forgotten that there was an important debate on this morning. He considered changing his plans and attending, but decided against it. The majority in the Senate now backed Hannibal solidly, and this was unlikely to change in the foreseeable future. As well as restoring Carthaginian pride with his conquests of Iberian tribes and intimidation of Saguntum, a Roman ally, Hannibal had helped to restore the city's wealth. Although his long-term plans weren't common knowledge, there could be few elders who didn't suspect the truth.

Catching sight of Hostus, Malchus' lip curled. He for one thought war against Rome was coming, and was forever speaking out against it. The fool, thought Malchus. As Carthage's prosperity and pride returned, so conflict with Rome was inevitable. The annexation of Sardinia was a primary reason, and just one example of the wrongs visited upon his people by the Republic. In recent years it had continued to treat them in a disrespectful manner. Constantly sending snooping embassies to Iberia, where it had no jurisdiction, Rome had forged an alliance with Saguntum, a Greek city many hundreds of miles from Italy. It had then had the effrontery to impose a unilateral treaty on Carthage, forcing it not to expand its territories northwards towards Gaul.

Deep in thought, Malchus did not see Hostus recognise him. By the time the fat man had waddled self-importantly to his side, it was too late to get away. Cursing his decision to take the shorter route to the harbours, Malchus gave Hostus a curt nod.

Hostus flashed a greasy smile. 'Not coming to the debate this morning?'

'No.' Malchus tried to brush past.

Moving adroitly for his size, Hostus blocked the way. 'We have noted your absence in the chamber of late. Missed your valuable insights.'

Malchus stopped in his tracks. Hostus wouldn't care if he died, let alone wasn't present at council meetings. He fixed the other with a flinty stare. 'What do you want?'

'I know that of late you have had more important things than Carthage on your mind.' Hostus leered. 'Family matters.'

Malchus wanted to choke Hostus until his eyeballs popped out, but he knew that would be rising to the bait. 'Of course you always act for the good of Carthage,' he snapped. 'Never for the silver from the Iberian mines.'

A tinge of colour reddened Hostus' round cheeks. 'The city has no more loyal servant than I,' he blustered.

Malchus had had enough. He elbowed past without another word.

Hostus wasn't finished. 'If you tire of visiting Melqart's temple, there is always the Tophet of Baal Hammon.'

Malchus spun around. 'What did you say?'

'You heard me.' Hostus' smile was more of a grimace. 'You may have only livestock to offer, but there are plenty in the slums who will sell a newborn or young child for a handful of coins.' Seeing Malchus' temper rising, Hostus gave him a reproving look. 'Such sacrifices have saved Carthage before. Who is to say a suitable offering would not please Baal Hammon and bring your son back?'

Hostus' barbed taunt sank deep, but Malchus knew that the best form of defence was attack. Give the dog no satisfaction. 'Hanno is dead,' he hissed. 'Any fool knows that.'

Hostus flinched.

Malchus poked a finger in his chest. 'Unlike you, I would not murder another's child to make a request of a god. Nor would I have ever offered my own, unlike some around here. To do so is the mark of a savage. Not of someone who truly loves Carthage and would lay down his own life for it.' Leaving Hostus gaping in his wake, Malchus stalked off.

His patrol of the port area that morning yielded nothing. It was little more than Malchus had come to expect. He had overheard talk of the weather conditions between Carthage and Sicily, the most auspicious place to make an offering to the Scylla, and an argument over which of the city's whorehouses was best. He'd seen merchant captains holding guarded conversations, trying to glean information from each other without giving away any of their own, and drunken sailors singing as they weaved back to their ships. Housewives sat in the open doorways of their houses, working their spinning wheels, but the whores had gone to bed. Trickles of smoke rose from the chimneys of the pottery kilns a short distance away. The open-fronted taverns that dotted the streets weren't busy at this time of day, but the stalls selling fresh bread were a different story. Stopping to buy a loaf, Malchus ran into an acquaintance, a crippled veteran of the war in Sicily whom he paid to listen out for any interesting news. So far, the man had provided him with nothing.

Nonetheless, Malchus paid for the other's bread. It didn't cost much to retain the goodwill of the poor, something Hostus would never understand. Together they walked down the street, ignoring the urchins who pestered them for a crust. Malchus watched as the cripple devoured his food before silently handing over his own. This too disappeared rapidly. Studying the man's lined, weary face, Malchus wondered if he had ever had a wife and family. Been faced with an offer from a creature like Hostus for one of his children. It didn't bear thinking about, and Malchus was grateful that the dark practices that went on in the Tophet were no longer practised by many.

'Thank you, sir,' mumbled the veteran, wiping crumbs from his lips.

Malchus inclined his head. He waited, out of habit rather than any expectation, for any information.

The veteran coughed uneasily, and scratched at the shiny red stump that was the only remnant of his lower right leg. 'I saw something last night,' he said. 'It was probably nothing.'

Malchus stiffened. 'Tell me.'

'Down on the docks, I noticed a bireme I've never seen before.' The veteran paused. 'That in itself is nothing unusual, but I thought the crew were a bit sharp-looking for ordinary traders. Seemed like they were trying too hard, if you know what I mean, sir? Talking loudly about their goods, and the prices they hoped to get for them.'

Malchus felt his heart begin to beat faster. 'Could you point the ship out?'

'Better than that, sir. I happened to spot the captain and some of his crew this morning. They were in a tavern, maybe four streets away. Much the worse for wear too.' The veteran hesitated, looking awkward.

Even the poorest can have pride, thought Malchus. 'You will be well rewarded.'

Clutching his homemade crutch with renewed vigour, the smiling veteran hobbled off.

Malchus was one step behind him.

A short time later, they had arrived at the hostelry, a miserable low-roofed brick structure with crudely hewn benches and tables arrayed outside. Although it was early, this tavern was packed. Sailors, merchants and lowlifes of every nationality under the sun sat cheek by jowl with each other, swigging from clay cups or singing out of tune. Prostitutes with painted faces were sitting on men's laps, whispering in their ears in an attempt to win some business. Amidst the pieces of broken pottery littering the sawdust-covered ground, scrawny mongrels fought over half-gnawed bones. Malchus' stomach turned at the stench of cheap wine and urine, but he followed the veteran to an empty table. They both took a seat. Neither looked at the other customers. Instead they occupied themselves by trying to attract the attention of the tavern keeper or his assistant, a rough-looking woman in a low-cut dress.

Finally, they succeeded. A glazed red jug and two beakers arrived at the table soon after, borne by the owner. He cast an idle glance at the mismatched pair, but was called away before he could decide what to make of them. The veteran poured the wine, and handed a cup to Malchus.

He took a sip, and wrinkled his face with disgust. 'This is worse than horse piss.'

The veteran took a deep swallow. He gave an apologetic shrug. 'Tastes fine to me, sir.'

There was silence then, and the customers' din washed over them.

'They're right behind me,' whispered the veteran at length. 'Four men. One looks like an Egyptian. Another is the ugliest man you've ever seen, with scars all over his mug. The others could be Greek. Do you see them?'

Casually, Malchus glanced over the other's shoulder. At the next table, he saw a thin, pale-skinned figure with black hair sitting beside a barrel of a man whose scarred features could have been carved from granite. Their two companions had their backs towards Malchus, but he could see from their dark skin and raven hair that the veteran's guess at their nationality was probably correct. Dressed in ochre and grey woollen tunics, with daggers at their belts, the quartet were similar to many of the other customers. And yet they weren't. Malchus studied them carefully from the corner of his eye. Their faces were cruel, almost hatchet-like. Not the faces of merchants.

Gradually, Malchus began to discern their voices from the others around them. They were speaking in Greek, which was not unusual when individuals of more than one nationality crewed together. It was, after all, the predominant language used at sea. 'It's good to visit a big city at last,' mumbled one of the men with his back to Malchus. 'Not like where we usually berth. At least here there's more than one tavern to visit.'

'Plenty of whorehouses too, with decent-looking women,' growled the figure beside him.

'And boys,' added the scarred man with a leer.

The Egyptian laughed unpleasantly. 'Never change, do you, Varsaco?'

Varsaco smirked. He lowered his voice slightly. 'I just want a piece of Carthaginian arse.'

The Egyptian wagged a reproachful finger.

One of their companions sniggered, and Varsaco scowled.

'You've got a long memory,' said the last man. 'Is this revenge for the one that got away?'

'Watch your mouth,' the Egyptian snarled, confirming Malchus' suspicion that he was the leader of the group. A subdued silence fell for a moment before Varsaco and the Egyptian began whispering to each other. They cast frequent glances at the other tables.

At once, Malchus looked down. Carefully, he considered what he'd heard and seen. The men did not visit cities often. They looked a lot tougher than merchants should do. The veteran thought the same of their shipmates. Tellingly, they had had a Carthaginian crewmember in the recent past. Or had he been a prisoner? Alarm bells were now ringing in Malchus' mind. Not once since Hanno's disappearance had he had anything to go on like this. It wasn't much, but Malchus didn't care. Sliding a coin across the table with a fingertip, he watched the veteran's eyes widen. 'Stay here,' he whispered. 'If I haven't returned by the time they leave, follow them. Use a street urchin to bring me news of their location.'

'Where are you going?'

Malchus' smile was mirthless. 'To get some help.'

Malchus went straight to Sapho's commanding officer. His status was such that the captain fell over himself to be of assistance. At once, a dozen Libyan spearmen were put at Malchus' disposal. Although they had little idea of their mission, the men liked the sound of escaping weapons drill.

Sapho had been asleep when Malchus arrived, but the mention of possible news about Hanno sent him leaping from his bed.

While Bostar had the guilt of knowing he should have made Hanno and Suniaton stay in the city, Sapho was saddled with the fact that he should not have given way. His darkest secret was that part of him was glad that Hanno was gone. Hanno had never done what Malchus wanted, while he, Sapho, did everything according to the book. Yet it was Hanno who had made their father's eyes light up. Of course Bostar knew nothing of Sapho's feelings. Unsurprisingly, the two brothers had fallen out over the matter anyway, and it hadn't been long before they were barely speaking. The issue had only subsided with Bostar's recent departure for Iberia. Hearing Malchus' news scraped raw Sapho's guilt. As he threw on his long tunic and bronze muscled cuirass, and donned his Thracian helmet and greaves, he bombarded his father with questions. Malchus had the answers to almost none of them.

'The sooner we get down there, the sooner we'll find out something,' he growled.

Half an hour after he'd left the tavern, Malchus returned with Sapho and the spearmen in tow. The Libyans wore simple conical bronze helmets, and each was clad in a beltless, knee-length red tunic. They were armed with short thrusting spears.

Malchus was mightily relieved to see that the veteran and the four men he'd been watching over were still at their respective tables. The Greeks were dozing; Varsaco was talking to the Egyptian. As Malchus and his companions came to a halt outside the tavern, the two sailors looked around. Their faces twisted briefly with concern, but they did not move a muscle.

'Where are they?' demanded Sapho.

There was no need for concealment any longer. Malchus pointed. He was delighted when the Egyptian and Varsaco jumped to their feet and tried to escape. 'Seize them,' he shouted.

The soldiers swarmed forward and surrounded the pair with a circle of threatening spear points. The two sleeping men were kicked awake and heaved into the ring with their companions. All four were forced to throw down their daggers. Ignoring the bleary stares of the other customers, Malchus stalked forward and into view.

'What's this about?' asked the Egyptian in fluent Carthaginian. 'We've done nothing wrong.'

'I'll be the one to decide on that,' replied Malchus. He jerked his head.

'Back to the barracks,' Sapho ordered. 'Quickly!'

The veteran looked on in amazement as the captives were escorted away. A metallic clunk drew his attention back to the table surface. On it lay four gold coins, their faces decorated with the image of Hannibal Barca.

'One for each of the whoresons,' said Malchus. 'If they turn out to be the right men, I'll give you the same again.' Leaving the veteran stuttering his thanks, he followed Sapho and the soldiers.

There was urgent business to attend to.

It didn't take long to reach the Libyans' quarters, which were located east of the Agora, in the wall that faced on to the sea. Whole series of rooms, on two tiers, stretched for hundreds of paces in either direction. Dormitories led to eating and bathing areas. Officers' quarters were situated beside armouries, administrative and quartermasters' offices. Like any military base, there were also cells. It was to these last that Sapho guided the spearmen. Nodding in a friendly manner at the gaolers, he directed the party into a large room with a plain concrete floor. It was empty apart from the sets of manacles that hung from rings on the wall, a glowing brazier and a table covered in a variety of lethal-looking metal instruments and tools.

As the last man entered, Sapho slammed the door shut and locked it.

'Chain them up,' ordered Malchus.

As one, the soldiers placed their spears aside, and turned on the prisoners. Struggling uselessly, the four were restrained side by side. Terror filled the two Greeks' eyes, and they began to wail. Varsaco and the Egyptian tried to maintain their composure, filling the air with questions and pleas. Studying the implements on the table, Malchus ignored them until silence fell.

'What are you doing in Carthage?'

'We're traders,' muttered the Egyptian. 'Honest men.'

'Really?' Malchus' tone was light and friendly.

The Egyptian looked confused. 'Yes.'

Malchus stared at the faces of the Egyptian's companions. He turned to Sapho. 'Well?'

'I think he's lying.'

'So do I.' Malchus' intuition was screaming at him now. These were definitely no merchants. The idea that they might know something about Hanno became all-consuming. Malchus wanted information. Fast. How they obtained it was immaterial. He indicated one of the Greeks. 'Break his arms and legs.'

Clenching his jaw, Sapho picked up a lump hammer. He moved to stand in front of the man Malchus had indicated, who was now moaning in fear. Silently, Sapho delivered a flurry of blows, smashing first the Greek's arms, and then his lower legs, against the wall. His victim's screams made a thin, cracked sound that reverberated throughout the room.

It took a long time, but Malchus waited until the man's cries had died to a low moaning. 'A different question this time,' he said coldly. 'Who was the Carthaginian you were talking about earlier?'

The Egyptian shot a venomous glance at Varsaco.

A surge of adrenaline surged through Malchus. He waited, but there was no response. 'Well?'

'He was nobody, just one of the crew,' muttered Varsaco fearfully. 'He didn't like my attentions, so he deserted at some shithole settlement on the Numidian coast.'

Again Malchus looked at his son.

'Still lying,' growled Sapho.

'It's the truth,' Varsaco protested. He glanced at the Egyptian. 'Tell him.'

'It is as he says,' the Egyptian agreed with a nervous laugh. 'The boy ran away.'

'What kind of fool do you take me for? There's far more to it than that,' snapped Malchus. He pointed at Varsaco. 'Cut his balls off.'

Sapho laid down his hammer and picked up a long, curved dagger.

'No,' pleaded Varsaco. 'Please.'

Stone-faced, Sapho unbuckled Varsaco's belt and threw it to the floor. Next, he cut away the bottom of his tunic, exposing his linen undergarment. Sliding the blade underneath the fabric on each side of Varsaco's groin, Sapho slit it from top to bottom. The garment dropped to the floor, leaving Varsaco naked from the waist down, and gibbering with fear. 'There were two of them,' he babbled, squirming this way and that. 'They were adrift off the coast of Sicily.'

The Egyptian's visage twisted with fury. 'Shut up, you fool! You'll only make things worse.'

Varsaco ignored him. Tears were running down his scarred cheeks. 'I'll tell you everything,' he whispered.

Sapho began to feel very guilty indeed. Taking in a shuddering breath, he looked over his shoulder.

Malchus motioned his son to stand back. Volcanic emotions swept through him. The walls came pressing in, and he could feel the blood rushing in his ears. 'Speak,' he commanded.

Varsaco nodded eagerly. 'There was a bad storm a few weeks back. We were caught in it, and our bireme nearly sank. We didn't, thank the gods. The next day, we came across an open boat, with two young men in it.'

Sapho leaped up and placed his dagger across Varsaco's throat. 'Where were they from?' he screamed. 'What were their names?'

'They came from Carthage.' Varsaco's eyes flickered like those of a cornered rat. 'I don't remember what they were called.'

Malchus grew very calm. 'What did they look like?' he asked quietly.

'One was tall, and had an athletic build. The other was shorter. Both had black hair.' Varsaco thought for a moment. 'And green eyes.'

'Hanno and Suniaton!' Sapho's face twisted with anguish. Despite his relief at Hanno's disappearance, he couldn't bear that this might be the dreadful truth.

Malchus felt physically sick. 'What did you do with them?'

Varsaco turned a pasty shade of grey. 'Naturally, we were going to return them to Carthage,' he stammered. 'But the ship had sprung a leak during the storm. We had to make for the nearest land, which was Sicily. They disembarked there, in Heraclea, I think it was.' He looked to the Egyptian and received a nod of confirmation. 'Yes, Heraclea.'

'I see.' An icy calm blanketed Malchus. 'If that's the case, why have they not returned? Finding a ship to Carthage from the south coast of Sicily should pose a problem to no man.'

'Who knows? Young lads who have just left home are all the same. Only interested in wine and women.' Varsaco shrugged as nonchalantly as he could.

'"Just left home"?' Malchus shouted. 'You make it sound as if they had chosen to be washed out to sea. That it was a matter of no consequence. If you let them off in Heraclea, then my name is Alexander of Macedon.' He glanced at Sapho. 'Castrate him.'

Sapho lowered his knife.

'Not that, please, not that,' Varsaco shrieked. 'I'll tell the truth!'

Malchus raised his hand, and Sapho paused. 'You've probably guessed by now that you and these other sewer rats are dead men. You have condemned yourself with your own words.' Malchus paused to let his sentence sink in. 'Tell me honestly what you did with my son and his friend, and you'll keep your manhood. Receive a quick death too.'

Varsaco nodded dully in acceptance of his fate. 'We sold them as slaves,' he whispered. 'In Neapolis. We got an excellent price for both, according to the captain. That's why we came to Carthage. To abduct more.'

Malchus took a deep breath. It was much as he had suspected. 'Whom did you sell them to?'

'I don't know,' Varsaco stuttered. 'I wasn't there. The captain did it.' His gaze turned to the Egyptian, who spat contemptuously on the floor.

'So you are the one who is responsible for this outrage?' Cold fury bathed Malchus once more. 'Cut *his* balls off instead,' he roared.

At once Sapho stripped the Egyptian of his clothing. Grabbing hold of the moaning pirate captain's scrotum, he tugged down to draw it taut. Sapho threw a quick glance at Malchus, and received a nod. 'This is for my brother,' he muttered, lining his blade up, praying that the act would assuage his guilt.

'Varsaco was the one who would have raped them,' shouted the Egyptian. 'I stopped him.'

'How good of you,' Malchus snarled. 'You had no problem selling them, though, did you? Who bought them?'

'A Latin. I didn't get his name. He was going to take both to Capua. Sell them as gladiators. I don't know any more.' The Egyptian looked down at Sapho, and then towards Malchus. All he saw from both was an implacable hatred. 'Give me a quick death, like Varsaco,' he pleaded.

'You expect me to keep my word after what you have done to two innocent boys? Those who engage in piracy merit the most terrible fate possible.' Malchus' voice dripped with contempt. He turned to the soldiers. 'You've heard what these scum have done to my boy and his friend.'

An angry growl left the Libyans' throats, and one stood forth. 'What shall we do with them, sir?'

Malchus let his gaze linger on the four pirates, one by one. 'Castrate them all, but cauterise the wounds so they do not bleed to death. Break their arms and legs, and then crucify them. When you're done, find the rest of their crew and do the same to every last one.'

To a background of terrified protests, the spearman snapped off a salute. 'Yes, sir.'

Malchus and Sapho watched impassively as the soldiers set about their task. Dividing into teams of three, they stripped the prisoners with grim purpose. Light flashed off knife blades as they rose and fell. The screaming soon grew so loud that it was impossible to talk, but the soldiers did not pause for breath. Blood ran down the pirates' legs in great streams to congeal in sticky pools on the floor. Next, the stench of burning flesh filled the air as red-hot pokers were used to stem the flow from the prisoners' gaping wounds. The pain of the castration and cautery was so severe that all the pirates passed out. Their respite was brief. A moment later, they were woken by the agony of their bones breaking beneath the blows of hammers. Low repetitive thuds mingled with their shrieks in a new, dreadful cacophony.

Malchus pressed his lips to Sapho's ear. 'I've seen enough. Let's go.'

Even in the corridor outside, with the door closed, the din was incredible. Although it was now possible to talk, father and son looked at each other in silence for long moments.

Malchus spoke first. 'He could still be alive. They both could.' Rare tears glinted in his eyes.

Sapho felt bad for Hanno. Drowning was one thing, but fighting as a gladiator? He hardened his heart. 'They won't be for long. It's a mercy in a way.'

Unaware of Sapho's motivations, Malchus clenched his jaw. 'You're right. We can do no more than to hope that they died well. Let us join Hannibal Barca's army in Iberia, and wage war on Rome. One day, we will bring ruination, fire and death to Capua. Then, vengeance will be ours.'

Sapho looked stunned. 'Hannibal would invade Italy?'

'Yes,' replied Malchus. 'That is his long-term plan. To defeat the enemy on their own soil. I am one of only a handful of men who know this. Now you are another.'

'The secret is safe with me,' whispered Sapho. Obviously, he and Bostar had not been party to all of the information carried by Hannibal's messenger. Finally, he understood his father's threat to raze Capua. 'Our revenge will come one day,' he muttered, thinking of the golden opportunities to prove his worth that would arise.

'Speak after me,' ordered Malchus. 'Before Melqart, Baal Saphon and Baal Hammon, I make this vow. With all my might, I will support Hannibal Barca on his quest. I will find Hanno, or die avenging him.'

Slowly, Sapho repeated the words.

Satisfied, Malchus led the way outside.

The screaming continued unabated behind them.

Chapter VI: Servitude

Near Capua, Campania

Hanno trudged despondently behind Agesandros' mule, swallowing the clouds of dust sent up by those in front. Ahead of the Sicilian was the litter containing Atia and Aurelia, and beyond that, in the lead, were Fabricius and Quintus. It was the morning following his purchase by Quintus, and, after spending the night at Martialis' house, the family was returning to their farm. During their short stay, Hanno had been left in the kitchen with the resident household slaves. Dazed, still unable to believe that he had been separated from Suniaton, he had simply slumped in a corner and wept. Other than placing a loincloth, a beaker of water and a plate of food beside him, no one had offered him any comfort. Hanno would remember their curious stares afterwards, however. No doubt it was something they had all seen countless times before: the new slave, who realises that his life will never be the same again. It had probably happened to most of them. Mercifully, sleep had finally found Hanno. His rest had been fitful, but it had provided him with an escape of sorts: the possibility of denying reality.

Now, in the cold light of day, he had to face up to it.

He belonged to Quintus' father, Fabricius. Like his family, Suni was gone for ever.

Hanno still didn't know what to make of his master. Since a cursory examination when they had first returned to Martialis' house, Fabricius had paid him little heed. He had accepted his son's explanation that, because of his literacy and skill with languages, the Carthaginian was worth his high purchase price, the balance of which Quintus was paying anyway. 'It's your business the way you spend your money,' he'd said. He seemed decent enough, thought Hanno, as did Quintus. Aurelia was but a child. Atia, Fabricius' wife, was an unknown quantity. So far, she'd barely even looked at him, but Hanno hoped that she would prove a fair mistress.

It was strange to be considering people whom he'd always considered evil as normal, yet it was Agesandros whom Hanno was most concerned about. The Sicilian had taken a set against him from the beginning. For all his concerns, at least his own situation had a positive side to it, for which he felt immensely guilty. Suniaton's fate still hung by a thread, and Hanno could only ask every god he knew to intercede on his friend's behalf. At the worst, to let him die bravely.

Hearing the word 'Saguntum' mentioned, he pricked his ears. A Greek city in Iberia, allied to the Republic, it had been the focus of Hannibal's attention for months. Indeed, it was where the war on Rome would start.

'I thought that the Senate had decided there was no real threat to Saguntum?' asked Quintus. 'After the Saguntines had demanded recompense for the attacks on their lands, all Hannibal did was to send them a rudely worded reply.'

Hanno hid his smirk. He'd heard that insult several weeks before, at home. 'Scabby, flea-bitten savages,' Hannibal had called the city's residents. As everyone in Carthage knew, the rebuttal presaged his real plan: an attack on Saguntum.

'Politicians sometimes underestimate generals,' said Fabricius heavily. 'Hannibal has done far more than issue threats now. According to the latest news, Saguntum is surrounded by his army. They've started building fortifications. It's going to be a siege. Carthage has finally regained its bite.'

Quintus threw an angry glance at Hanno, who looked down at once. 'Can nothing be done?'

'Not this campaigning season,' Fabricius replied crossly. 'Hannibal couldn't have picked a better moment. Both the consular armies are committed to the East, and the threat there.'

'You mean Demetrius of Pharos?' asked Quintus.

'Yes.'

'Wasn't he an ally of ours until recently?'

'He was. Then the miserable dog decided that piracy is more profitable. Our entire eastern seaboard has been affected. He's been threatening Illyrian cities under the Republic's protection too. But the trouble should be over by the autumn. Demetrius' forces have no chance against four legions and double that number of socii.'

Quintus couldn't hide his disappointment. 'I'll miss it all.'

'Never fear. There'll always be another war,' said his father with an amused smile. 'You'll get your turn soon enough.'

Quintus was partly mollified. 'Meanwhile, Saguntum just gets left to hang in the wind?'

'It's not right, I know,' his father replied. 'But the main faction in the Senate has decided that this is the course we shall follow. The rest of us have to obey.'

So much for Roman *fides*, thought Hanno contemptuously.

Father and son rode in silence for a few moments.

'What will the Senate do if Saguntum falls?' probed Quintus.

'Demand that the Carthaginians withdraw, I imagine. As well as hand over Hannibal.'

Quintus' eyebrows rose. 'Would they do that?'

Never, thought Hanno furiously.

'I don't think so,' Fabricius replied. 'Even the Carthaginians have their pride. Besides, their Council of Elders will have known about Hannibal's plan to besiege Saguntum. They're hardly going to offer their support on that only to withdraw it immediately afterwards.'

Unseen, Hanno spat on to the road. 'Damn right they're not,' he whispered.

'Then war is unavoidable,' Quintus cried. 'The Senate won't take an insult like that lying down.'

Fabricius sighed. 'No, it won't, even though it's partly to blame for the whole situation. The indemnities forced on Carthage at the end of the last war were ruinous, but the seizure of Sardinia soon after was even worse. There was no excuse for it.'

Hanno could scarcely believe what he was hearing: a Roman express regret for what had been done to his people. Perhaps they weren't all monsters? he wondered for the second time. His gut reaction weighed in at once. *They are still the enemy*.

'That conflict was a generation ago,' said Quintus, bridling. 'This is now. Even if it comes late, Rome has to defend one of her allies who has been attacked without due cause.'

Fabricius inclined his head. 'She does.'

'So war with Carthage is coming, one way or another,' said Quintus. He threw a further look at Hanno, who affected not to notice.

'Probably,' Fabricius replied. 'Not this year perhaps, but next.'

'I could be part of that!' Quintus cried eagerly. 'But I want to know how to use a sword properly first.'

'You're proficient with both bow and spear,' admitted Fabricius. He paused, aware that Quintus was hanging on his every word. 'Strictly speaking, of course, it's not necessary for the cavalry, but I suppose a little instruction in the use of the gladius wouldn't go amiss.'

Quintus' grin stretched from ear to ear. 'Thank you, Father.' He raised a hand to his mouth. 'Mother! Aurelia! Did you hear that? I am to become a swordsman.'

'That's good news indeed.' Coming from the depths of the litter, Atia's voice was muffled, but Quintus thought he detected a tinge of sadness in it.

Aurelia lifted the cloth and stuck her head outside. 'How wonderful,' she said, forcing a smile. Inside, she was consumed by jealousy.

'We'll start tomorrow,' said Fabricius.

'Excellent!' Instantly, Quintus forgot both his mother and Aurelia's reactions. His head was full of images of him and Gaius serving in the cavalry, winning glory for themselves and Rome.

Despite his guilt over Suniaton, Hanno's spirits had also risen. While he had Agesandros to contend with, he was not destined to die as a gladiator. And, although he might not be able to take part, his people were about to take on Rome again, with Hannibal Barca to lead them. A man whom his father reckoned to be the finest leader Carthage had ever seen.

For the first time in days, a spark of hope lit in Hanno's heart.

One summer morning, word came from the port that Malchus and Sapho had landed. Bostar shouted with delight at the news. As he hurried through the streets of New Carthage, the city founded by Hasdrubal nine years before, he couldn't stop grinning. Catching a glimpse of the temple of Aesculapius, which stood on the large hill to the east of the walls, Bostar offered up a prayer of thanks to the god of medicine and his followers. If it hadn't been for the injury to his sword arm, sustained in overexcited training with naked blades, he would have already set out for Saguntum with the rest of the army. Instead, on the orders of Alete, his commanding officer, Bostar had had to stay behind. 'I've seen too many wounds like that turn bad,' Alete had muttered. 'Remain here, in the care of the priests, and join us when you've recovered. Saguntum isn't going to fall in a day, or a month.' At the time, Bostar had not been happy. Now, he was overjoyed.

It wasn't long until he'd reached the port, which looked out over the calm gulf beyond New Carthage. The city's location was second to none. Situated at the point of a natural, enclosed bay which was furthest from the Mediterranean, it was surrounded on all sides by water. To the east and south lay the sea, while to the north and west was a large, saltwater lagoon. The only connection with the mainland was a narrow, heavily fortified causeway, which made the city almost impregnable. It was no surprise that New Carthage had replaced Gades as the capital of Carthaginian Iberia.

Bostar sped past the ships nearest the quay. New arrivals would have to moor further away. As always, the place was extremely busy. The vast majority of the army might have left with Hannibal, but troops and supplies were still coming in daily. Javelins clattered off each other as they were laid in piles, and stacks of freshly made helmets glinted in the sun. There were wax-sealed amphorae of olive oil and wine, rolls of cloth and bags of nails. Wooden crates of glazed crockery stood beside bulging bags of nuts. Gossiping sailors coiled ropes and swept the decks of their unloaded vessels. Fishermen who had been out since before dawn sweated as they hauled their catch on to the dock.

'Bostar!'

He craned his head, searching for his family among the dense forest of masts and rigging. Finally, Bostar spotted his father and Sapho on the deck of a trireme that was tied up two vessels from the quay. He vaulted on to the first craft's deck and made his way to meet them. 'Welcome!'

A moment later, they had been reunited. Bostar was shocked by the change in both. They were different men since he'd last seen them. Cold. Hard-faced. Ruthless. He bowed to Malchus, trying not to let his surprise show. 'Father. It is wonderful to see you at last.'

Malchus' severe expression softened briefly. 'Bostar. What happened to your arm?'

'It's a scratch, nothing more. A stupid mistake during training,' he replied. 'Lucky it happened, though, because it's the only reason I'm still here. I receive treatment daily at Aesculapius' temple.' He turned to Sapho, and was surprised to see that his brother looked downright angry. Bostar's hopes for a reconciliation vanished. The rift caused by their argument over releasing Hanno and Suniaton was clearly still present. As if he didn't feel guilty enough, thought Bostar sadly. Instead of an embrace, he saluted. 'Brother.'

Stiffly, Sapho returned the gesture.

'How was your journey?'

'Pleasant enough,' Malchus answered. 'We saw no Roman triremes, which is a blessing.' His face twisted with an unreadable emotion. 'Enough of that. We have discovered what happened to Hanno.'

Bostar blinked with shock. 'What?'

'You heard,' snapped Sapho. 'He and Suni didn't drown.'

Bostar's mouth opened. 'How do you know?'

Malchus took over. 'Because I never lost faith in Melqart, and because I had eyes and ears in the port, who looked and listened out day and night for any clues.' He smiled sourly at Bostar's bafflement. 'A couple of months ago, one of my spies struck gold. He overheard a conversation he thought might interest me. We took the men in for questioning.'

Bostar was riveted by his father's story. Hearing that Hanno and Suniaton had been captured by pirates, he began to weep. Neither of the others did, which only increased his grief. His anguish grew deeper with the revelation of the pair's sale into slavery. *I thought it was a kind gesture to let them go fishing. How wrong I was!* 'That's a worse fate than drowning. They could have been taken anywhere. Bought by anyone.'

'I know,' Sapho snarled. 'They were sold in Italy. Probably as gladiators.'

Bostar's eyes filled with horror. 'No!'

'Yes,' Sapho shot back venomously, 'and it's all your fault. If

117

you had stopped them, Hanno would be standing here beside us today.'

Bostar swelled with indignation. 'That's rich coming from you!'

'Stop it!' Malchus' voice cut in like a whiplash. 'Sapho, you and Bostar came to the decision together, did you not?'

Sapho glowered. 'Yes, Father.'

'So you are both responsible, just as I am for not being easier on him.' Malchus ignored his sons' surprise at his admission of complicity. 'Hanno is gone now, and fighting over his memory will serve none of us. I want no more of this. Our task now is to follow Hannibal, and take Saguntum. If we are lucky, the gods will grant us vengeance for Hanno afterwards, in the fight against Rome. We must put everything else from our minds. Clear?'

'Yes, Father,' the brothers mumbled, but neither looked at the other.

Bostar had to ask. 'What did you do to the pirates?'

'They were castrated, and then their limbs were broken. Lastly, the scum were crucified,' Malchus replied in a flat tone. Without another word, he climbed up on to the dock and headed for the city's centre.

Sapho held back until they were alone. 'It was too good for them. We should have gouged out their eyes too,' he added viciously. Despite his apparent enthusiasm, the horror of what he'd seen still lingered in his eyes. Sapho had thought that the punishments would stop him feeling relief at Hanno's disappearance, but he'd been wrong. Seeing his younger brother again rammed that home. I will be the favourite! he thought savagely. 'Just as well that you weren't there. You wouldn't have been up to any of it.'

Despite the implication about his courage, Bostar retained his composure. He wasn't about to pull rank here, now. He was also uncertain what his own reaction might have been if he'd been placed in the same situation, handed the opportunity for revenge on those who had consigned Hanno to a certain death. Deep down, Bostar was glad that he had not been there. He doubted that either his father or Sapho would understand. Melqart, he prayed, I ask that my brother had a good death, and that you allow our family to put aside its differences. Bostar gained small consolation from the prayer, but it was all he had at that moment.

That, and a war to look forward to.

Checking that Agesandros was nowhere in sight, Hanno pulled the mules to a halt. The sweating beasts did not protest. It was nearly midday, and the temperature in the farmyard was scorching. Hanno jerked his head at one of the others who was threshing the wheat with him. 'Water.'

The Gaul made a reflex check for the Sicilian before putting down his pitchfork, and fetching the leather skin which lay by the storage shed. After drinking deeply, he replaced the stopper and tossed it through the air.

Hanno nodded his thanks. He swallowed a dozen mouthfuls, but was careful to leave plenty of the warm liquid for the others. He threw the bag to Cingetorix, another Gaul.

When he was done, Cingetorix wiped his lips with the back of his hand. 'Gods, but it's hot.' He spoke in Latin, which was the only language he and his countrymen had to communicate with Hanno. 'Does it never rain in this cursed place? At home . . .' He wasn't allowed to finish.

'We know,' growled Galba, a short man whose sunburnt torso was covered with swirling tattoos. 'It rains much more. Don't remind us.'

'Not in Carthage,' said Hanno. 'It's as dry there as it is here.'

Cingetorix scowled. 'You must feel right at home then.'

Despite himself, Hanno grinned. For perhaps two months after his arrival, the Gauls, with whom he shared sleeping quarters, had ignored him completely, speaking their own rapid-fire, guttural tongue at all times. He'd done his best to win them over, but it had made no difference. When it came, the change had been gradual. Hanno wasn't sure whether the extra, unwanted attention he received from Agesandros was what had prompted the tribesmen to extend the hand of friendship to him, but he no longer cared. The camaraderie they now shared was what made his existence bearable. That, and the news that Hannibal's iron grip on Saguntum had tightened. Apparently, the city would fall before the end of the year. Hanno prayed for the Carthaginian army's success every night. He also asked that one day he be granted an opportunity to kill Agesandros.

There were five of them in the yard altogether, continuing the work which had begun weeks previously with the harvest. It was late summer, and Hanno had grown used to life on the farm, and the immense labour expected of him every day. Things were made much harder by the heavy iron fetters that had been attached to his ankles, preventing him moving at any speed faster than a shuffle. Hanno had thought he was fit beforehand, but soon realised otherwise. Working twelve or more hours a day in summer heat, wearing manacles and fed barely enough, he was a taut, wiry shadow of his former self. His hair fell in long, shaggy tresses either side of his bearded face. The muscles on his torso and limbs now stood out like whipcord, and every part of exposed skin had darkened to a deep brown colour. The Gauls looked no different. We're like wild beasts, Hanno thought. It was no wonder that they rarely saw Fabricius or his family.

Catching sight of Agesandros in the distance, he whistled the agreed signal to alert his companions. Swiftly, the skin was hurled back to its original position. Hanno dragged his mules into action again, pulling a heavy sledge over the harvested wheat, which had been laid right across the hard-packed dirt of the large farmyard. The Gauls began winnowing the threshed crop, tossing it into the air with their pitchforks so that the breeze could carry away the unwanted chaff. Their tasks were time-consuming and mind-numbing, but they had to be done before the wheat could be shovelled into the back of a wagon and deposited in the nearby storage sheds, which were built on brick stilts to prevent rodent access.

When Agesandros arrived a few moments later, he stood in the shade cast by the buildings and watched them silently. Uneasy, the five slaves worked hard, trying not to look in the Sicilian's direction. Soon a fresh coat of sweat coated their bodies.

Every time he turned the sledge, Hanno caught a glimpse of Agesandros, who was staring relentlessly at him. He was unsurprised when the overseer stalked in his direction.

'You're walking the mules too fast! Slow down, or half the wheat won't come off the stalks.'

Hanno tugged on the nearest animal's lead rope. 'Yes, sir,' he mumbled.

'What's that? I didn't hear you,' Agesandros snarled.

'At once, sir,' Hanno repeated loudly.

'Stinking gugga. You're all the damn same. Useless!' Agesandros drew his whip.

Hanno steeled himself. It didn't seem to matter what he did. The mules' speed was just the latest example. His technique with the scythe and pitchfork, and how long he took to fetch water from the well had also recently been called into question. Everything he did was wrong, and the Sicilian's response was the same every time.

'You're all idle bastards.' Lazily, Agesandros drew the long rawhide lash along the ground. 'Motherless curs. Cowards. Vermin.'

Hanno clicked his tongue at the mules, trying to block out the insults.

'Maybe you did have a mother,' Agesandros admitted. He paused. 'She must have been the most diseased whore in Carthage, though, to spawn something that looks like you.'

Hanno's knuckles tightened with fury on the lead rope, and his shoulders bunched. From the corner of his eye, he saw Galba, who was behind the Sicilian, shaking his head in a gesture that said 'No'. Hanno forced himself to relax, but Agesandros had already seen his barb's effect.

'Didn't like that?' The Sicilian laughed, and raised his right arm. A heartbeat later, the whip came singing in to wrap itself across Hanno's back and under his right armpit. *Crack* went the tip as it opened the skin under his right nipple. The pain was intense. Hanno stiffened, and his pace decreased a fraction. It was all Agesandros needed. 'Did I tell you to slow down?' he screamed. The whip was withdrawn, only to return. Hanno counted three, six, a dozen lashes. Although he did his utmost not to make a sound, eventually he couldn't help but moan.

The overseer smiled at this proof of Hanno's weakness, and ceased. His skill with the lash was such that Hanno was always left in extreme pain, but still able to work. 'That should keep you moving at the right speed,' he said.

'Yes, sir,' Hanno muttered.

Satisfied, Agesandros gave the Gauls a hard stare and made as if to go.

Hanno did not relax. There was always more.

Sure enough, Agesandros turned. 'You'll find your bed softer tonight,' he confided.

Slowly, Hanno raised his gaze to meet that of the Sicilian.

'I've pissed in it for you.'

Hanno did not speak. This was even worse than Agesandros spitting in his food, or halving his water ration. His anger, which had been reduced to a tiny glow in the centre of his soul, was suddenly fanned to a white-hot blaze of outrage and indignation. With supreme effort, he kept his face blank. Now is not the time, he told himself. Wait.

Agesandros sneered. 'Nothing to say?'

I won't give the bastard what he wants, thought Hanno furiously. 'Thank you, sir.'

Cheated, Agesandros snorted and walked away.

'Dirty fucker,' whispered Galba when he was out of earshot.

There was a rumble of agreement from the others. 'You can have some of our bedding. We'll replace the wet stuff in the morning in case he checks up on you.'

'Thanks,' muttered Hanno absently. He was imagining running after the overseer and killing him. Thanks to Agesandros' expert needling, his warrior spirit had just reawakened. If he was to meet Suniaton in the next world, he wanted to be able to hold his head up high. Things would come to a head soon, Hanno realised. But it didn't matter. Death would be better than this daily indignity.

Unusually, Quintus found himself at a loose end one fine morning. It had rained overnight, and the temperature was cooler than it had been for many months. Invigorated by the crisp, fresh air, he decided to make amends with Aurelia. Over the previous few months, much to her displeasure, Aurelia had been put in the care of a strict tutor, a sour-faced Greek slave loaned to Atia by Martialis. Rather than roaming the farm as she pleased, nowadays Aurelia had to sit demurely and learn Greek and mathematics. Atia continued to teach her how to weave and sew, and how to comport herself in polite company. Aurelia's protests fell on deaf ears. 'It's time you learned to be a lady, and that's an end to it,' Atia had snapped a number of times. 'If you keep protesting, I'll give you a good whipping.' Aurelia dutifully obeyed, but her stony silences at the dinner table since revealed her true opinion.

Fabricius knew better than to intervene in his wife's business, which left Quintus as Aurelia's only possible ally. However, he felt caught in the middle. While he felt guilty at his sister's plight, he also knew that an arranged marriage was the best thing for the family. All his attempts to lighten her mood failed, and so Quintus began to avoid her company when his day's work was done. Hurt, Aurelia spent more and more time in her room. It was a vicious circle from which there seemed no way out.

Meanwhile Quintus had been fully occupied with the work his father set him: paperwork, errands to Capua and regular lessons in the use of the gladius. Despite the time that had passed, Quintus still missed his sister keenly. He made a snap decision. It was time to make her an apology and move on. They did not have for ever. Although Fabricius had found no suitable husband for Aurelia yet, he had begun the search during his visits to Rome.

Throwing some food into a pack, Quintus headed for the chamber off the courtyard where Aurelia took her lessons. Barely pausing to knock, he entered. The tutor glanced up, a small frown of disapproval creasing his brow. 'Master Quintus. To what do we owe the pleasure?'

Quintus drew himself up to his full height. He was now three fingers width taller than his father, which meant that he towered over most people. 'I am taking Aurelia on a tour of the farm,' he announced grandly.

The tutor looked taken aback. 'Who sanctioned this?'

'I did,' Quintus replied.

The tutor blew out his cheeks with displeasure. 'Your parents—'

'Would approve wholeheartedly. I will explain everything to them later.' Quintus made an airy gesture. 'Come on,' he said to Aurelia.

Her attempt to look angry faded away, and she jumped to her feet. Her writing tablet and stylus clattered unnoticed to the floor, drawing reproving clucks from the tutor. Yet the elderly Greek did not challenge Quintus further, and the siblings made their way outside unhindered.

Since killing the bear, Quintus' confidence had grown leaps and bounds. It felt good. He grinned at Aurelia.

Abruptly, she remembered their feud. 'What's going on?' she cried. 'I haven't seen you for weeks, and then suddenly you barge into my lessons unannounced.'

He took Aurelia's hand. 'I'm sorry for deserting you.' To his horror, tears formed in her eyes, and Quintus realised how hurt she had been. 'Nothing I said seemed to make any difference,' he muttered. 'I couldn't think of a way to help you. Forgive me.'

She smiled through her grief. 'I was at fault too, staying in a mood for days. But come, you're here now.' A mischievous look stole across her face. 'A tour of the farm? What have I not seen a thousand times before?'

'It was all I could think of,' he replied, embarrassed. 'Something to get you out of there.'

Grinning, she nudged him. 'It was enough to shut up the old fool. Thank you. I don't care where we go.'

Arm in arm, they strolled along the path that led to the olive groves.

Hanno could see that Agesandros was in a bad mood. Any slave who so much as missed a step was getting a tongue-lashing. Ten of them were walking ahead of the Sicilian, carrying wicker baskets. Fortunately, Hanno was near the front, which meant that Agesandros was paying him little attention. Their destination was the terraces containing plum trees, the fruit of which had lately, and urgently, become ripe. Picking the juicy crop would be an easy task compared to the work of the previous weeks, and Hanno was looking forward to it. Agesandros could only be so vigilant. Before the day was over, plenty of plums would have ended up in his grumbling belly.

A moment later, he cursed his optimism.

Galba, the man behind him, missed his footing and fell heavily to the ground. There was a grunt of pain, and Hanno turned to see a nasty gash on his comrade's right shin. It had been caused by a sharp piece of rock protruding from the earth. Blood welled in the wound, running down Galba's muscular calf and on to the dry soil, where it was soaked up at once.

'That's your day over,' Hanno said in a low voice.

'I doubt Agesandros would agree,' Galba replied, grimacing. 'Help me up.'

Hanno bent to obey, but it was too late.

Shoving past the other slaves, the Sicilian had reached them in a dozen strides. 'What in the name of Hades is going on?'

'He fell and hurt his leg,' Hanno began to explain.

Agesandros spun around, his eyes like chips of flint. 'Let the piece of shit explain for himself,' he hissed before turning back to Galba. 'Well?'

'It's as he said, sir,' said the Gaul carefully. 'I tripped and landed on this rock.'

'You did it deliberately, to get out of work for a few days,' Agesandros snarled.

'No, sir.'

'Liar!' The Sicilian tugged free his whip and began belabouring Galba.

Hanno's fury overflowed at last. 'Leave him alone,' he shouted. 'He didn't do anything.'

Agesandros delivered several more strokes and a hefty kick before he paused. Nostrils flaring, he glared at Hanno. 'What did you say?'

'Picking plums is an easy job. Why would he try and get out of it?' he growled. 'The man tripped. That's it.'

The Sicilian's eyes opened wide with disbelief and rage. 'You dare to tell me what to do? You piece of maggot-blown filth!'

Hanno would have given anything for a sword in that instant. He had nothing, though, but his anger. In the rush of adrenaline, it felt enough. 'Is that what I am?' he spat back. 'Well, you're nothing but low-born Sicilian scum! Even if my feet were covered in shit, I wouldn't wipe them on you.'

Something inside Agesandros snapped. Raising his whip, he smashed the metal-tipped butt into Hanno's face.

There was a loud crunch and Hanno felt the cartilage in his nose break. Half blinded by the intense pain, he reeled backwards, raising his hands protectively against the blow he knew would follow. He had no opportunity to pick up a rock, anything to defend himself. Agesandros was on him like a lion on its prey. Down came the whip across Hanno's shoulders, its tip licking around to snap into the flesh of his back. It whirled away but came singing back a heartbeat later, lacing cut after cut across his bare torso. He backed away, but the laughing Sicilian followed. When Hanno stumbled on a tree root, Agesandros shoved him in the chest, sending him sprawling. Winded, he could do nothing as the other loomed over him, his face twisted in triumph. A mighty kick in the chest followed, and the ribs broken by Varsaco cracked for the second time. The pain was unbearable and, hating himself, Hanno screamed. Worse was to follow. The beating went on until he was barely conscious. Finally, Agesandros rolled him on to his back. 'Look at me,' he ordered. Prompted by more kicks, Hanno managed to open his eyes. The moment he did, the Sicilian lifted his right leg high, revealing the hobnailed sole of his sandal. 'This is for all my comrades,' he muttered. 'And my family.'

Hanno had no idea what Agesandros was talking about. The bastard is going to kill me, he thought dazedly. Strangely, he didn't really care. At least his suffering would be over. He felt a numbing sense of sorrow that he would never see his family again. There would be no opportunity to apologise to his father either. Let it be so. Resigned, Hanno closed his eyes and waited for Agesandros to end it.

The blow never fell.

Instead, a commanding voice shouted, 'Agesandros! Stop!'

Initially, Hanno didn't grasp what was going on, but when the order was repeated, and he sensed the Sicilian back away, the realisation sank in. Someone had intervened. Who? He lay back on the hard ground, unable to do anything more than draw shallow breaths. Each movement of his ribcage stabbed knives of pain through every part of his being. It was the only thing that kept him from lapsing into unconsciousness. He was aware of Agesandros throwing hate-filled glances in his direction, but the Sicilian did nothing further to him.

A heartbeat later, Quintus and Aurelia, Fabricius' children, appeared at the edge of Hanno's vision. Outrage filled both their faces.

'What have you done?' Aurelia cried, dropping to her knees by Hanno's side. Although the bloodied Carthaginian was almost unrecognisable, her stomach still fluttered at the sight of him.

Hanno tried to smile at her. After Agesandros' cruel features, she resembled a nymph or other suchlike creature.

'Well?' Quintus' voice was stony. 'Explain yourself.'

'Your father leaves the running of the farm, and the care of the slaves, to me,' Agesandros blustered. 'That's the way it has been since before you were born.'

'And if you killed a slave? What would he say then?' Aurelia challenged.

Agesandros was taken aback. 'Come now,' he said in a placating manner. 'I was administering a beating, nothing more.'

Quintus' laugh was derisory. 'You were about to stamp on his head. On this rocky ground, a blow like that could stave a man's skull in.'

Agesandros did not reply.

'Couldn't it?' Quintus demanded. His fury at the Sicilian, who had looked intent on murder, had doubled when he realised the victim's identity. Any residual awe he felt towards Agesandros had evaporated. 'Answer me, by all the gods.'

'I suppose so,' Agesandros admitted sullenly.

'Was that your intention?' Aurelia demanded.

The Sicilian glanced at Hanno. 'No,' he said, folding his arms across his chest. 'My temper got the better of me, that's all.'

Liar, thought Hanno. Above him, Aurelia's face twisted with disbelief, reinforcing his conviction.

Quintus could also see that Agesandros was lying, but to accuse him further would bring the situation into completely uncharted waters. He didn't feel quite that confident. 'How did it happen?'

Agesandros indicated Galba. 'That slave fell deliberately and injured his leg. He was trying to get off work. It's an old trick, and I saw through it at once. I laid a few blows into the dog to teach him a lesson, and the gugga told me to stop, that it had been

a genuine accident.' He snorted. 'Such defiance cannot be toler-
ated. He needed to be taught the error of his ways on the spot.'

Quintus looked down at Hanno. 'I think you succeeded,' he
said sarcastically. 'He's halfway to Hades.'

One corner of Agesandros' mouth tugged upwards.

The only one to see it was Hanno. *Agesandros wants me dead.
Why?*

It was the last coherent thought he had.

Quintus' confidence was bolstered by his success over Agesandros.
Rather than let the injured Hanno be carried back to the villa like
a sack of grain as the Sicilian wanted, he insisted that a litter be
fetched. Galba could limp alongside. Scowling, Agesandros could
do little but obey his command, sending a slave off at the run.
The overseer watched with a surly expression as, using a strip of
cloth, Aurelia cleaned the worst of the blood from Hanno's face.
Tears poured down her cheeks, but she did not make a sound.
She would not give Agesandros the satisfaction.

A short time later, when Hanno had been carefully transferred
into the litter, she finally stood. A mixture of blood and dust
covered the lower half of her dress, from where she had knelt in
the dirt. Though reddened, her eyes were full of anger, and her
face was set. 'If he dies, I will see that Father makes you pay,'
she said. 'I swear it.'

Agesandros tried to laugh it off. 'It takes more than that to kill
a gugga,' he declared.

Aurelia glared at him, afraid and yet unafraid.

'Come,' said Quintus, gently leading her away. Agesandros
made to follow, but Quintus had had enough. 'Go about your
business,' he barked. 'We will care for the two slaves.'

They installed Hanno on blankets and a straw mattress in an
empty stable off the farmyard, where he lay as still as a corpse.
Quintus was concerned by his pale face. If the Carthaginian died,
his father would be severely out of pocket, so he ordered hot

water to be fetched from the kitchen, along with strips of linen and a flask of *acetum*, or vinegar. When they arrived, he was surprised by Aurelia's reaction. She would suffer no other to clean the Carthaginian's wounds. Meanwhile Elira treated Galba, with Quintus watching appreciatively. The Illyrian's medical knowledge was good, courtesy of her upbringing. As she'd told Quintus, her mother had been the woman to whom everyone in the tribe came with their ailments. First she washed the wound with plenty of hot water. Then, ignoring Galba's hisses of discomfort, she sluiced the area with *acetum* before patting it dry and applying a dressing. 'Two days' rest, and light duties for a week,' Quintus said when she was done. 'I'll make sure Agesandros knows.'

Muttering his gratitude, the Gaul shuffled off.

There was a moan from behind him, and Quintus turned. Hanno's face twisted briefly at whatever Aurelia was doing, before relaxing again. 'He's alive,' he said with relief.

'No thanks to Agesandros,' Aurelia shot back vehemently. 'Imagine if we hadn't come along! He might still die.' Her voice tailed off as she bit back a sob.

Quintus patted her shoulder, wondering why she was so upset. Hanno was only a slave, after all.

Elira moved to the bed. 'Let me take a look at him,' she said.

To Quintus' surprise, Aurelia moved aside. They watched in silence as the Illyrian ran expert hands over Hanno's battered body, gently probing here and there. 'I can find no head injury apart from his broken nose,' she said eventually. 'He has three cracked ribs, and all these flesh wounds from the whip.' She pointed to his prominent ribcage and concave belly. 'Someone hasn't been feeding him enough either. He's strong, though. Some good nursing and decent food, and he could be up and about inside a week.'

'Jupiter be thanked,' Aurelia cried.

Quintus smiled his own relief and went in search of Fabricius. Agesandros' cruelty must be reported at once. He suspected that his father would not seriously punish the Sicilian, who, no doubt, would deny everything if challenged. He could hear Fabricius' voice already. Discipline was part of the overseer's remit, and no slave had the right to question his authority as Hanno had. This was the first time that Agesandros had gone overboard. In Fabricius' eyes, it would be a one-off occurrence. Quintus knew what he had seen, however. His jaw hardened.

Agesandros would have to be watched from now on.

Hanno was woken by the pain radiating from his ribs each time he took a breath. The dull throbbing from his face reminded him of his broken nose. He lifted his hands, feeling the heavy strapping that circled his chest. The manacles around his ankles had been removed. This could hardly be Agesandros' work. Quintus must have insisted I be treated, Hanno thought. His surprise grew when he opened his eyes. Instead of the damp straw in his miserable cell, he was lying on blankets in an empty stable. Occasional whinnies told him that there were horses nearby. He eyed the stool alongside him. Someone had been keeping vigil.

A shadow fell across the threshold and Hanno looked up to see Elira carrying a clay jug and two beakers.

Her face lit up. 'You're awake!'

He nodded slowly, drinking her beauty in.

She rushed to his side. 'How do you feel?'

'Sore all over.'

She reached down and lifted a gourd from the floor. 'Drink some of this.'

'What is it?' he asked suspiciously.

Elira smiled. 'A dilute solution of *papaverum*.' Seeing his confusion, she explained. 'It will dull the pain.'

He was too weak to argue. Taking the gourd, Hanno took a deep swallow of the painkilling draught, screwing up his face at the bitter taste of the liquid within.

'It won't take long to work,' Elira murmured reassuringly. 'Then you can sleep some more.'

Abruptly, the Sicilian came to mind, and he tried to sit up. The small effort felt exhausting. 'What about Agesandros?'

'Don't worry. Fabricius has seen your injuries, and warned him to leave you alone. The gods must have been in good humour, because he also agreed to let me care for you. It took a bit of persuasion, but Aurelia won him over,' Elira said. She raised a hand to his sweating face. 'Look, you are as weak as a kitten,' she scolded. 'Lie down.'

Hanno obeyed. Why would Aurelia care what happened to him? he wondered. Feeling the papaverum begin to take effect, he closed his eyes. It was a huge relief to know that one of his owner's children was on his side, but Hanno doubted that Aurelia could shield him from Agesandros' ill will. She was only a girl. Still, he thought wearily, his situation was better now than it had been. Perhaps the gods were showing him favour once more? Keeping that idea uppermost, Hanno relaxed and let sleep take him.

Chapter VII: A Gradual Shift

Hanno did little more than sleep and eat for the next three days. Under Elira's approving eyes, he devoured plate after plate of food from the kitchen. His strength returned, and the pain of his injuries subsided. Soon he insisted that the strapping around his chest be removed, complaining that it was restricting his breathing. By the fourth day, he felt alert enough to venture outside. Fear stopped him, however. 'Where's Agesandros?'

Elira's full lips flattened. 'The whoreson is in Capua, thankfully.'

Relieved, Hanno shuffled outside. The yard was empty. All the slaves were at work in the fields. They sat down together in the sunshine and rested their backs against the cool stone of the stable walls. Hanno didn't mind that there was no one around. It meant he could be alone with Elira, whose physical attractions were daily becoming more obvious. As the ache in his groin constantly told him, he hadn't had a woman for many months. Yet merely to entertain such thoughts was dangerous. Even if Elira was willing, slaves were forbidden from having sexual relations with each other. What's more, Hanno had seen the way she and Quintus looked at one another. Stay well away, he told himself sternly. Screwing the master's son's favourite slave would not be clever. There was a simpler way of satisfying himself. Less enjoyable, but far safer.

He needed something to take his mind off sex. 'How did you come to be a slave?'

Elira's surprise was instantly replaced by sadness. 'That's the first time anyone has asked me such a question.'

'I guess it's because we all have the same miserable story,' said Hanno gently. He raised his eyebrows in an indication that she should continue.

Elira's eyes took on a distant look. 'I grew up in a little village by the sea in Illyricum. Most people were fishermen or farmers. It was a peaceful place. Until the day that the pirates came. I was nine years old.' Her face darkened with anger, and sorrow. 'The men fought hard, but they weren't warriors. My father and my older brother, they . . .' Her voice wobbled for a moment. 'They were killed. But what happened to Mother was just as bad.' Tears formed in her eyes.

Horrified, Hanno reached out to squeeze Elira's hand. 'I'm sorry,' he whispered.

She nodded, and the movement made the tears spill down her cheeks. 'We were taken to their ships. They sailed to Italy and sold us there. I haven't seen Mother or my sisters since.'

As Elira wept, Hanno cursed himself for opening his mouth. Yet the Illyrian's sorrow made her even more attractive. It was hard not to imagine wrapping her in his arms to comfort her. He was therefore relieved to see Aurelia approaching from the direction of the villa. Nudging Elira, he scrambled to his feet. The Illyrian had barely enough time to pull her hair down around her face and wipe away her tears.

Aurelia felt a tinge of jealousy at seeing Elira so close to Hanno. 'You're up and about!' she said tartly.

He bobbed his head. 'Yes.'

'How do you feel?'

Hanno touched his ribs. 'Much better than I did a few days ago, thank you.'

Aurelia's sympathy surged back at the sight of Hanno

wincing. 'It's Elira you should be grateful to. She's a marvel.'

'She is,' agreed Hanno, giving Elira a slanted grin.

The Illyrian blushed. 'Julius will be wondering where I am,' she muttered, before hurrying off.

Aurelia's annoyance returned, but, irritated with herself for even feeling it, she dismissed it at once. 'You're Carthaginian, aren't you?'

'Yes,' Hanno replied warily. He'd never yet had a proper conversation with Fabricius or any of his family. In his mind, they were still very much the enemy.

'What's Carthage like?'

He couldn't help himself. 'It's huge. Perhaps a quarter of a million people live there.'

Despite herself, Aurelia's eyes widened. 'But that's far bigger than Rome!'

Hanno had the sense not to utter the sarcastic response that rose to his lips. 'Indeed.' Aurelia seemed interested, so he launched into a description of his city, picturing it in his mind's eye as he did. Realising eventually that he had lost the run of himself, Hanno fell silent.

'It sounds beautiful,' Aurelia admitted. 'And you looked so happy while you were talking.'

Feeling utterly homesick, Hanno stared at the ground.

'It's not surprising, I suppose,' said Aurelia kindly. Looking curious, she tipped her head to one side. 'I remember that you speak Greek as well as Latin. In Italy, only nobles learn that tongue. It must be much the same in Carthage. How did someone so well educated end up as a slave?'

Balefully, Hanno lifted his gaze to hers. 'I forgot to ask a blessing of our most powerful goddess before I went on a fishing trip with my friend.' He saw her enquiring expression. 'Suni, the one you saw in Capua. After catching plenty of tunny, we drank some wine and fell asleep. A sudden storm took us far out to sea. Somehow, we survived the night, but the next day a pirate ship found us. We were sold in Neapolis, and taken to Capua to be sold as gladiators. Instead I was bought by your brother.' Hanno hardened his voice. 'Who knows what happened to my friend, though?' He was pleased to see her flinch.

Annoyed, Aurelia recovered quickly. Handsome or not, he's still a slave, she thought. 'Everyone at the slave market has a sad story. That doesn't mean that we can buy them all. Consider yourself lucky,' she snapped.

Hanno bowed his head. *She might be young, but she's got spirit.* An awkward silence fell.

It was broken by Atia's voice. 'Aurelia!'

Aurelia's face took on a hunted look. 'I'm in the yard, Mother.'

Atia appeared a moment later. She was wearing a simple linen stola and elegant leather sandals. 'What are you doing here? We were supposed to be practising the lyre.' Her gaze passed over Hanno. 'Isn't this the slave whom Agesandros beat? The Carthaginian?'

'Yes, Mother.' A touch of colour appeared in Aurelia's cheeks. 'I was checking with Elira that his recovery was satisfactory.'

'I see. It's good that you are taking an interest in things like that. It's all part of running the household.' Atia eyed Hanno with more interest. 'That broken nose isn't healed, but otherwise he looks fine.'

Hanno shifted from foot to foot, uncomfortable with being talked about as if he weren't present.

Aurelia became a little flustered. 'I suppose . . . Elira didn't say when he'd be ready to return to work.'

'Well?' Atia demanded. 'Are you sufficiently recovered?'

Hanno couldn't exactly refuse. 'Yes, mistress,' he murmured.

'He's got three cracked ribs,' Aurelia protested.

'That's no reason to stop him working in the kitchen,' Atia replied. She stared at Hanno. 'Is it?'

It would be far less effort than toiling in the fields, thought Hanno. He bowed his head. 'No, mistress.'

Atia nodded. 'Good. Follow us back to the house. Julius will have plenty for you to do.'

Secretly delighted, Aurelia followed her mother. She would no longer need an excuse to come and see Hanno.

'Quintus wants us to watch him sparring with your father,' said Atia in a proud yet wistful tone.

'Oh.' Aurelia managed to convey all of her disapproval and jealousy in one word.

Atia turned. 'Enough of that attitude! Would you rather spend the time playing the lyre or talking Greek with your tutor?'

'No, Mother,' Aurelia muttered furiously.

'Fine.' Atia's frown eased. 'Come on then.'

Hanno was fascinated. All the girls he'd ever met were perfectly happy to stick with womanly pursuits. Aurelia was made from a different mould.

They entered the house via a small postern gate. It was incorporated into one of the two large timber doors that formed the entrance. Hanno looked around keenly. It was the first time he had been in the villa proper. The simple elegance of its design did not fail to impress him. Carthaginian homes were typically built for functionality, rather than beauty. Elegant mosaics and colourful wall paintings were the exception, not the rule.

In the courtyard, they found Fabricius and Quintus moving carefully around each other. Both were clad in simple belted tunics, and carrying wooden swords and round cavalry shields.

Seeing Atia and Aurelia, they paused.

Fabricius raised his weapon in salute to Atia, who smiled.

'Finally,' said Quintus drolly to his sister.

Aurelia did her best to look enthusiastic. This *is* better than music lessons, she told herself. 'I'm here now.'

Quintus looked to his father. 'Ready?'

'When you are.'

The two stepped closer, raising their swords. The points met with a dull clunk. Both remained still for a moment, trying to gauge when the other would move.

Atia clapped her hands. 'Fetch some fruit juice,' she ordered Hanno. She pointed. 'The kitchen is over there.'

He tore his eyes away from the contest. 'Yes, mistress.' Adopting the preferred slave walk, slow and measured, Hanno did as he was told. Happily, he was able to continue observing.

Quintus was first to act. He swept his gladius down, carrying his father's blade towards the ground. In the same movement, he drew back his right arm and thrust forward, straight at the other's chest. Fabricius quickly met the attack with his shield. With a great heave, he lifted it in the air. Quintus' sword was also carried up by the move, which exposed his right armpit. Knowing that his father would strike at his weak point, Quintus desperately twisted to the left and retreated several steps. Fabricius was on him like a striking snake. Despite his father's ferocity, Quintus managed to hold off the assault. 'Not bad,' Fabricius said at length, pulling back. They paused to catch their breath before renewing the engagement.

To Quintus' delight, he drew first blood. His success came thanks to an unexpected shoulder charge at his father that enabled him to thrust his gladius around their shields. The point snagged in the left side of Fabricius' tunic. Despite the fact that the blade was wooden, it tore a great hole in the fabric, raked along his ribs and broke the skin. He bellowed in pain, and staggered backwards. Knowing that his father would now find it agonising to lift his sword, Quintus prepared to follow through and win the bout.

'Are you all right?' Aurelia cried.

Fabricius did not answer. 'Come on,' he growled at Quintus. 'Think you can finish me?'

Stung, Quintus lifted his gladius and ran forward. When he was only a step away, he feinted to the right and then to the left. A backward slash at Fabricius' head followed, and his father's response was barely enough to prevent the blow from landing. Quintus crowed with triumph and pushed on, keen to press home his advantage. Surprising him utterly, Fabricius backed away so fast that Quintus overbalanced and fell. As he landed, Fabricius spun round and placed his sword tip at the base of Quintus' neck. 'Dead meat,' he said calmly.

Furious and embarrassed, Quintus got to his feet. Catching sight of Hanno, he scowled. 'What are you looking at?' he yelled. 'Get about your business!'

Ducking his head to conceal his own anger, Hanno headed for the kitchen.

'Don't take it out on a slave,' cried Aurelia. 'It's not his fault.'

Quintus glared at his sister.

'Calm down,' said Fabricius. 'You were undone because you were overconfident.'

Now Quintus' face went beetroot.

'You did well until then,' reassured his father. In the background, Atia was nodding in agreement. 'If you'd just taken your time, I would have had no chance.' He lifted his left arm and showed Quintus the long bloody graze along the side of his chest. 'Even a scratch like this slows a man right down. Remember that.'

Pleased, Quintus smiled. 'I will, Father.'

At that moment, Hanno emerged with a polished bronze tray. Perched upon it were a fine glass jug and four cups of the same style. Seeing him, Quintus beckoned peremptorily. 'Get over here! I'm thirsty.'

Arrogant little shit, thought Hanno as he hurried to obey.

Fabricius waited until the whole family had a drink before raising his cup. 'A toast! To Mars, the god of war. That his shield always remains over us both.'

Hanno blocked out the words as best he could and prayed silently to his own martial god. Baal Saphon, guide Hannibal's army to victory over Saguntum. And Rome.

Gulping down his juice, Fabricius indicated that Hanno should pour him a refill. He frowned in recognition. 'Fully recovered?'

'Very nearly, master,' Hanno replied.

'Good.'

'I was impressed to find Aurelia checking up on his progress,' Atia added. 'He's not up to field work yet, but I didn't see any reason why Julius couldn't put him to use in the kitchen.'

'Fair enough. He's ready to go back to his cell then.' Aurelia's mouth opened in protest, and Fabricius raised a hand. 'He's not a horse,' he said sternly. 'That stable is needed. His manacles should be replaced too.' Seeing the apprehension in Hanno's face, Fabricius' face softened. 'Obey orders, and Agesandros will not lay a hand on you. You have my word on that.'

Hanno muttered his thanks, but his mind was racing. Despite Fabricius' reassurance, his troubles were far from over. Agesandros would undoubtedly be holding a grudge against him. He would constantly have to be on his guard. Without thinking, Hanno remained where he was, close to the family.

An instant later, Quintus turned and their eyes met. I'd love to take you on in a swordfight, thought Hanno. Teach you a lesson. Almost as if he understood, Quintus' top lip curled. 'What are you still doing here? Get back to the kitchen.'

Hanno quickly retreated. He was grateful for the smile Aurelia threw in his direction.

The conversation resumed behind him.

'Can we practise again tomorrow, Father?' Quintus' voice was eager.

'The enthusiasm of youth!' Touching his side, Fabricius grimaced. 'I doubt that my ribs would permit it. But I can't anyway.'

'Why not?' Quintus cried.

'I must travel to Rome. The Senate is meeting to consider how it will respond when Saguntum falls. I want to hear for myself what they plan.'

War, thought Hanno fervently. I hope they decide on war. Because that's what they're going to get in any case.

Quintus was crestfallen, but he didn't argue further. 'How long will you be gone?'

'At least ten days. Maybe more. It depends on the success of my other mission,' Fabricius replied. He fixed Aurelia with his grey eyes. 'To find a suitable husband for you.'

Aurelia paled, but she did not look away. 'I see. I'm not to be allowed to fall in love as you and Mother did, then?'

'You'll do as you're damn well told!' Fabricius snapped.

Atia flushed and looked down.

'Never mind, children,' intervened Atia in a brisk tone. 'It will be an opportunity for both of you to catch up on your studies. Quintus, the tutor reports that your grasp of geometry is not what it should be.'

Quintus groaned.

Atia turned to Aurelia. 'Don't think that you're going to escape either.'

Even as she scowled, Aurelia was struck by an idea. Her heart leaped at its brilliance. If she could pull it off, neither of them would care about extra lessons. And it would help her not to think about her father's quest.

Like all the best plans, Aurelia's was simple. She wasn't sure if Quintus would go along with it, however, so she said nothing until their father had been gone for several days. By then, her brother's frustration at not being able to do any weapons training was reaching new highs. Aurelia picked her moment carefully, waiting until her mother was occupied with the household accounts. Quintus' morning lessons had ended a short time before, and she found him pacing around the fountain in the centre of the courtyard, angrily scuffing his sandals along the mosaic.

'What's wrong?'

He glanced at her, scowling. 'Nothing, apart from the fact that

I've had to spend two hours trying to calculate the volume of a cylinder. It's impossible! And it's not as if I'll ever use the method again. Typical bloody Greeks for discovering how to work out something so stupid in the first place.'

Aurelia made a sympathetic noise. She wasn't fond of the subject either. 'I was wondering . . .' she began. Deliberately, she did not continue.

'What?' Quintus demanded.

'Oh, it's nothing,' she replied. 'Just a silly idea.'

The first trace of interest crossed Quintus' face. 'Tell me.'

'You've been complaining a lot about Father being away.'

He gave an irritable nod. 'Yes, because I can't practise my sword play.'

Aurelia smiled impishly. 'There might be a way around that.'

Quintus' look was pitying. 'Riding to Capua and back to train with Gaius each day isn't an option. It would take far too long.'

'That's not what I've got in mind.' Aurelia found herself hesitating. Say it! she thought. You've got nothing to lose. 'I could be your sparring partner.'

'Eh?' His eyebrows rose in shock. 'But you've never used a sword before.'

'I learn fast,' Aurelia shot back. 'You said so yourself when you taught me to use a sling.' She held her breath, praying that he would agree.

A slow grin spread across Quintus' face. 'We could go "for a walk" up to the woods, to the place where I train.'

'That's exactly what I was thinking,' cried Aurelia delightedly. 'Mother doesn't mind what we do as long as all of our homework is done, and our duties are completed.'

A frown creased his brow. 'What's in it for you? You'll never be able to do it again once you're . . .' He gave her a guilty look.

'That's precisely why,' Aurelia said fervently. 'I'll be married off within the year, most likely. Then I'll have to resign myself to childminding and running a household for the rest of my life. What an opportunity to forget that fate!'

'Mother will kill you if she finds out,' Quintus warned.

Aurelia's eyes flashed. 'I'll face that day if, or when, it comes.'

Quintus saw his sister's resolve, and nodded. In truth, he felt glad to be able to help her, even if it would only be a temporary affair. He wouldn't want the future she'd painted. 'Very well.'

Aurelia stepped in to kiss his cheek. 'Thank you. It means a lot to me.'

The moment that their tasks were done the following day, they met up in the atrium. Quintus slung an old sack over his shoulder; within were two of the wooden gladii, as well as a few snares. The latter could be pulled out in the event of any awkward questions from their mother. 'Ready?' Aurelia whispered excitedly.

He nodded.

They had gone a dozen steps when Atia appeared from the tablinum, a roll of parchment in one hand. She threw them a curious glance. 'Where are you two going?'

'For a walk,' Aurelia replied lightly. She lifted the wicker basket in her right hand. 'I thought you might like some mushrooms.'

'I need to set some traps as well,' Quintus added. He tapped his bow. 'This is in case I see a deer.'

'Make sure you're back well before dark.' Atia had taken a few steps when she turned. 'Actually, why don't you take the new slave with you? Hanno, I think he's called. While he's working in the kitchen, he might as well learn about foraging and catching game.'

'That's a good idea,' said Aurelia, her face lighting up. Despite the fact that Hanno now worked in the house, she had found there was still hardly ever a chance to speak to him.

'Is it?' asked Quintus, looking irritated. 'He might run away.'

Atia laughed. 'With the manacles he's wearing? I don't think so. Besides, you can both practise your Greek with him. You'll all be learning something.'

'Yes, Mother,' Quintus muttered unenthusiastically.

With an absent smile, Atia left them to it.

Aurelia poked Quintus. 'She didn't suspect a thing!'

Quintus grimaced. 'No, but we've got to take the Carthaginian with us.'

'So what? He can carry the sack.'

'I suppose,' Quintus admitted. 'Go and get him then. Let's not hang around.'

A short time later, they were following one of the narrow tracks that led through the fields to the edge of the farm. Shuffling because of his manacles, a bemused Hanno took up the rear. Aurelia's offer of a trip into the woods had come as a welcome surprise. Although his job in the kitchen kept him safe from Agesandros, Hanno had begun to miss being in the open air. He longed for the companionship of Galba, Cingetorix and the other Gauls too. Julius and the rest of the domestic slaves were pleasant, but they were soft, and did little but gossip with each other. He wouldn't see the Gauls today, but Hanno liked the sound of picking mushrooms, an activity that was unknown in Carthage, and of hunting, something he enjoyed greatly. Today he would have no time to brood.

It was when the two young Romans stopped in a large clearing that Hanno started to feel suspicious. The mushrooms that Aurelia had shown him on the way up had grown in shady areas under fallen trees, and only a fool would lay a snare or try waiting for a deer in the middle of an open space.

Quintus stalked over. 'Give me the sack,' he ordered.

Hanno obeyed. A moment later, he was most surprised to see two wooden swords clattering on to the soft earth. Gods, but how long it had been since he'd held a weapon! He still hadn't fully realised what was going on when Quintus tossed one of the gladii to Aurelia.

'These hurt like Hades if you land a blow, but they're not likely to spill your guts on the ground.'

Aurelia moved the blade to and fro once or twice. 'It feels very unwieldy.'

'It's double the weight of a real sword, to build up your fitness.' Quintus saw her frown. 'We don't have to do this.'

'Yes, we do,' she retorted. 'Show me how to hold the damn thing properly.'

Smiling, Quintus obeyed, gripping her wrist to move it slowly through the air. 'As you know, it was made to cut and thrust. But it can slash too, which is how we use it in the cavalry.'

'Shouldn't we have shields too?'

He laughed. 'Of course. But I think Mother might have realised what we were up to. Give me a few days. I'll take them up here on my own one evening, when she's taking her bath.'

Quintus began to teach Aurelia how to thrust the gladius forward. 'Keep your feet close together as you move. It's important not to over-extend yourself.'

After a while, Hanno began to grow bored. He would have loved to take Aurelia's place, but that wasn't going to happen. He glanced at his nearly empty basket, and coughed to get the young Romans' attention.

Quintus turned, a frown creasing his brow. 'What?'

'We didn't find many mushrooms on the way here. Should I go and pick some more?'

Quintus nodded in surprise. 'Very well. You're not to go far. And don't get any ideas about running away.'

Aurelia looked more grateful. 'Thank you.'

Hanno left them to it. He cast about the edge of the clearing, but found no mushrooms. Unnoticed by Quintus and Aurelia, he moved off into the undergrowth. The sounds of their voices became muffled and then were lost. Sunlight pierced the dense canopy above, lighting up irregular patches of the forest floor. Nonetheless, the air felt heavy. Hanno's presence made birds flit from branch to branch, sounding their alarm calls. Soon he felt as if he was the only person in the world. He felt free. Right on cue, the manacles around his ankles clanked, and reality struck. Hanno cursed. Even if he tried to run, he wouldn't get far. The moment Agesandros was alerted, he'd get out the hunting dogs. They'd track him down in no time. And of course there was the debt he owed Quintus. Sighing, Hanno got back to his task.

His luck was in. A quarter of an hour later, he returned to the clearing with a full basket.

Aurelia saw him first. 'Well done!' she cried, rushing over. 'Those slender mushrooms with the flat caps are delicious when fried. You'll have to try some later.'

Hanno's lips turned up. 'Thank you.'

Quintus glanced at the basket, but didn't comment. 'Race you to the stream,' he said to Aurelia. 'We can cool off before going back.'

With a giggle, she took off towards the far side of the clearing, from where the babble of running water could be heard.

'Hey!' Quintus shouted. 'That's cheating!' Aurelia didn't reply, and he sprinted after her.

Hanno looked after them wistfully, remembering similar good times with Suniaton. An instant later, though, his gaze fell on the two wooden swords, which had been left on the ground nearby. Quintus' bow and quiver lay alongside. Without thinking, Hanno walked over and picked up a gladius. As Aurelia had said, it was awkward to hold, but Hanno didn't care. Gripping the hilt tightly, he thrust it to and fro. It was the most natural thing to imagine sticking it in Agesandros' belly.

'What are you doing?'

Hanno almost jumped out of his skin. He turned to find a

dripping wet Quintus regarding him with extreme suspicion. 'Nothing,' he muttered.

'Slaves aren't allowed to use bladed weapons. Drop it!'

With great reluctance, Hanno let the gladius fall.

Quintus picked it up. 'No doubt you were thinking about murdering us all in our beds,' he said in a hard voice.

'I'd never do that,' Hanno protested. Agesandros is a different matter of course, he thought. 'I owe you my life twice over. That's something I will never forget.'

Quintus was nonplussed. 'I only bought you in the first place because Agesandros didn't want me to. As for when he was beating you, well, injuring a slave badly is a waste of money.'

'That's as may be,' Hanno muttered. 'But if it weren't for you, I'd surely be dead by now.'

Quintus shrugged. 'Don't pin your hopes on paying me back. There aren't too many dangers around here!' He pointed at his sack. 'Pick that up. I've spotted a good place on the bank to set a snare.'

Stooping so that Quintus didn't see his scowl, Hanno obeyed. Curse him and his arrogance, he thought. I should just run away. But his pride wouldn't let him. A debt was a debt.

Quintus and Aurelia managed to fit in three more trips to the clearing before Fabricius' return a week later. Atia had been so pleased by the basket of mushrooms that Quintus insisted Hanno accompany him and his sister each time. Hanno was glad to obey. Aurelia was friendly, and Quintus' manner towards him had changed fractionally. He wasn't exactly warm, but his high-handed manner, which Hanno despised, was no longer so evident. Whether it was because he had revealed the debt that he owed to Quintus, Hanno could not tell.

Although Fabricius' homecoming meant that the secret trips stopped, Hanno was pleased to learn that his master was soon to return to Rome. Eavesdropping as he served food to the family, Hanno heard how the debates in the Senate about Hannibal were constant now, with some factions favouring negotiations with Carthage and others demanding an immediate declaration of war. 'There's far more interest in that than the eligible daughter of a country noble,' Fabricius revealed to Atia.

Aurelia was barely able to conceal her delight, but her mother pursed her lips. 'Have you found no one suitable?'

'I've found plenty,' Fabricius replied reassuringly. 'I just need more time, that's all.'

'I want to know the best candidates,' said Atia. 'I can write to those of their mothers who are living. Arrange a meeting.'

Fabricius nodded. 'Good idea.'

Let it take for ever, Aurelia prayed. In the meantime, I can practise with Quintus. It had been a joy to discover that handling a sword came naturally to her. She burned to train further, while she still could.

Her brother's reaction, however, was the opposite to hers. 'How long will you be gone?' he asked glumly.

'I'm not sure. It could be weeks. I'll definitely be back for Saturnalia.'

Quintus looked horrified. 'That's months away!'

'It's not the end of the world,' said Fabricius, clapping him on the shoulder. 'You'll be starting your military training next spring anyway.'

Quintus was about to protest further but Atia intervened. 'Your father's business is far more important than your desire to train with a gladius. Be content that he is here now.'

Reluctantly, Quintus held his silence.

Bending their heads together, their parents fell into a private conversation.

It was probably about her prospective husbands, thought Aurelia furiously. She kicked Quintus under the table and framed the words 'We can go to the clearing more often' at him. When he raised his eyebrows, she repeated them and thrust an imaginary sword at him.

At last Quintus understood, and a happier expression replaced the sullen one.

Hanno hoped that Quintus and Aurelia would take him along too. Agesandros could not do a thing to him while he was with them. Moreover, he had come to enjoy the outings.

'Do you still think this is a good idea?' asked Atia when the children were gone.

Fabricius grimaced. 'What do you mean?'

'You said yourself that no one suitable is interested in finding a bride at the moment.'

'So?'

'Maybe we should leave it for six months or a year?'

His frown deepened. 'Where's the benefit in that? Don't tell me that you're having second thoughts?'

'I—'

'You are!'

'Do you remember our reason for getting married, Fabricius?' she asked gently.

A guilty look stole on to his face. 'Of course I do.'

'Is it so surprising, then, that it's hard for me to think of forcing Aurelia into an arrangement against her will?'

'It's difficult for me too,' he objected. 'But you know why I'm doing it.'

Atia sighed.

'I'm trying to better our family. I can't do that with a huge debt hanging over my head.'

'You could always ask Martialis for help.'

'I might owe thousands of didrachms to a moneylender in Capua, but I've still got my pride!' he retorted.

'Martialis wouldn't think any less of you.'

'I don't care! I wouldn't ever be able to look him in the eye again.'

'It's not as if you gambled the money away on chariot racing!

You needed the money because of the terrible drought two years ago. There's no shame in telling him that we had no crops to sell.'

'Martialis isn't a farmer,' said Fabricius heavily. 'He might understand if my problems were about property, but this . . .'

'You could try,' Atia murmured. 'He's your oldest comrade, after all.'

'A friend is the worst possible person to borrow from. I'm not doing it.' He fixed her with his stare. 'If we don't want the farm to be repossessed in the next few years, the only way forward is to marry Aurelia into a wealthy family. That knowledge alone will keep the moneylender off our backs indefinitely.'

'Maybe so, but it won't make the money appear from thin air.'

'No, but with the gods' favour, I will win more recognition in this war than I did in the last. After it's over, I'll secure a local magistrate's job.'

'And if you don't?'

Fabricius blinked. 'It'll be down to Quintus. With the right patronage, he could easily reach the rank of tribune. The yearly pay that position brings in will make our debts seem like a drop in the ocean.' He leaned in and kissed her confidently. 'You see? I have it all worked out.'

Atia didn't have the heart to protest any further. She couldn't make Fabricius go to Martialis, nor could she think of another strategy. She smiled bravely, trying not to think of an alternative, but entirely possible scenario.

What if Fabricius didn't come home from the war? What if Quintus never achieved the tribuneship?

Over the following weeks, it became the siblings' daily norm to go to the clearing. Pleased by the constant stream of mushrooms, hazelnuts, and the occasional deer brought down by Quintus' arrows, Atia did not protest. Because Aurelia had given Hanno the credit for their haul, he was allowed to accompany them. To Hanno's surprise, Aurelia's skill with the gladius was slowly improving, and Quintus had begun teaching her to use a shield. Not long after that, he brought two genuine swords with him. 'These are just to give you an idea of what using the real thing feels like,' he said, as he handed one to Aurelia. 'I want no funny stuff.'

Hanno eyed the long, waisted blade in Aurelia's hand with unabashed pleasure. It wasn't that different to the weapon he'd owned in Carthage.

Quintus saw his interest and frowned. 'You know how to use one of these?'

Hanno jerked back to the present. 'Yes,' he muttered unwillingly.

'How?'

'My father used to train me.' Hanno deliberately made no mention of his brothers.

'Is he a soldier?'

'He was,' lied Hanno. The less Quintus knew, the better.

'Did he fight in Sicily?'

Hanno nodded reluctantly.

Quintus looked surprised. 'So did mine. He spent years in the cavalry there. Father says that your people were worthy enemies, who only lacked a decent leader.'

No longer, thought Hanno triumphantly. Hannibal Barca will change all that. With an effort, he shrugged at Quintus. 'Maybe.'

Quintus' mouth opened to ask another question.

'Let's practise!' interjected Aurelia.

To Hanno's relief, the moment passed. Quintus responded to his sister's demand, and the two began sparring gently with the gladii.

Hanno headed off to check their snares. Shortly afterwards, and some distance from the clearing, he found the trail of a wild boar. He hurried back with the news as fast as his manacles would let him. Because of its rich flavour, boar meat was highly prized. The creatures were secretive too, and hard to find. An opportunity to kill one should not be passed up. Hanno's news immediately stopped Quintus practising with Aurelia. Sheathing the gladii, he rolled them up in a blanket and stuffed them into his pack. 'Come on!' he cried, sweeping up his bow.

Aurelia rushed after him. She was as keen as any to bring a boar back to the house.

Within a hundred paces, Hanno had fallen well behind. 'I can't go any faster,' he explained when the young Romans turned impatiently.

'We might as well give up now, then,' said Quintus with a scowl. 'Or you can just stay here.' He had the grace to flush.

Despite this, Hanno clenched his fists. I found the damn trail, he thought. Not you.

There was a short, uncomfortable pause.

'I can help,' Aurelia announced suddenly. From inside her dress she produced a small bunch of keys. Kneeling by Hanno's side, she tried several on one of his anklets before it fell apart.

'What do you think you're doing?' demanded Quintus.

Aurelia ignored him. Smiling broadly at Hanno, she opened the other. She couldn't help thinking how like the statue of a Greek athlete he looked.

Incredulous, Hanno lifted his feet one after another. 'Baal Hammon's beard, that feels good.'

Quintus stepped forward. 'How in Hades did you get those keys?'

Aurelia swelled with pride. 'You know how Agesandros likes to drink in the evenings. He's often snoring before *Vespera*. All I had to do was creep in and take an impression of each in wax, and get the smith to make them for me. I told him that they were for Father's chests, and gave him a few coins to make sure he told no one.'

Quintus' eyes widened at his sister's daring, but he still wasn't happy. 'Why did you do it?'

Aurelia wasn't going to admit the real reason, which was that she had come to abhor Hanno's fetters. Most slaves didn't have theirs removed until they'd been around for years and were no longer deemed a flight risk, but a small number were never trusted. Naturally, Agesandros had persuaded Fabricius that Hanno fell into this category. 'For a day like this,' she challenged, lifting her chin. 'So we could hunt properly.'

'He'll run away!' Quintus cried.

'No, he won't,' Aurelia retorted hotly. She turned to Hanno. 'Will you?'

Caught off guard by the bizarre situation, and stunned by Aurelia's action, Hanno stuttered to find an answer. 'N-no, of course not.'

'There!' Aurelia gestured in triumph at her brother.

'You believe that? He's a slave!'

Aurelia's eyes blazed. 'Hanno is trustworthy, Quintus, and you know it!'

Quintus matched her gaze for a moment. 'Very well.' He looked at Hanno. 'Do you give your word not to run away?'

'I swear it. May Tanit and Baal Hammon, Melqart and Baal Saphon be my witnesses,' said Hanno in a steady voice.

'If you're lying,' muttered Quintus, 'I'll hunt you down myself.'

Hanno stared stolidly back at him. 'Fine.'

Quintus gave him a curt nod. 'Lead on, then.'

Relishing the freedom of being able to run for the first time in months, Hanno bounded off towards the spot where he'd seen the boar's spoor. Of course he thought of escape, but there was no way Hanno would break the vow he'd just made.

Frustratingly, the boar proved elusive to the point of exasperation.

An hour later, they had still not laid eyes on it. The animal's trail had led them to a point where the forest thinned as it climbed the mountain slope above, and there it had disappeared. A large area of bare rock meant that their chances of finding it again were very slim.

Quintus looked at the darkening sky and cursed. 'We'll have

to give up soon. I don't fancy spending the night here. Let's spread right out. That's probably our best option.'

While Aurelia walked off to Quintus' left, Hanno moved slowly to the right. He kept his eyes fixed on the ground, but saw nothing at all for a good two hundred paces. His gaze wandered to the slopes above them. Much of the ground was covered in short scrubby grass, and fit only for sheep or goats.

Hanno frowned. Some distance above them, and partially obscured by a scattering of juniper and pine trees, he could see a small wooden structure. Smoke rose lazily from a hole in the apex of its roof. Latticed fencing around it revealed the presence of sheep pens. It didn't surprise him. Like most landowners, Fabricius' flocks wandered the hills during the spring and summer, accompanied by solitary shepherds and their dogs. Makeshift huts, and enclosures for the animals, were situated regularly across the landscape, shelter in case of bad weather and protection against predators such as wolves. To his astonishment, however, Hanno heard the sound of bleating. He looked up at the sky. It was early for the animals to be back from pasture. He glanced at Quintus, who was still casting about for signs of the boar. Aurelia was visible beyond. She too appeared oblivious.

Hanno was about to give a low whistle, when something stopped him. Instead, he trotted back towards the two Romans.

Quintus grew excited as he saw Hanno approach. 'Seen something?'

'The sheep up there are penned in,' said Hanno. 'A bit soon, isn't it?'

Quintus raised a hand to his eyes. 'By Jupiter, you're right,' he admitted, annoyed that he hadn't noticed first. 'Libo is the shepherd around here. He's a good man, not one to avoid work.'

Hanno's stomach clenched.

'I'm not happy.' Quintus took off his pack and emptied it on the ground. He unrolled the cloak. Carefully shoving one gladius into his belt, he handed the other to Aurelia, who had caught up with them. 'You probably won't need it,' he said with a falsely confident smile. Bending the stave with his knee, Quintus slipped his bowstring into place. There were ten arrows in his quiver. Plenty, he thought.

'What's wrong?' Aurelia demanded.

'Probably nothing,' replied Quintus reassuringly. 'I'm just going to take Hanno and check out that hut.'

Fear flared in Aurelia's eyes, but when she spoke, her voice was steady. 'What shall I do?'

'Remain here,' Quintus ordered. 'Stay hidden. Under no circumstances are you to follow us. Is that clear?'

She nodded. 'How long should I wait?'

'A quarter of an hour, no more. If we haven't reappeared by then, return to the farm as fast as you can. Find Agesandros, and tell him to bring plenty of men. Well armed.'

At this, Aurelia's composure cracked. 'Don't go up there,' she whispered. 'Let's just fetch Agesandros together.'

Quintus thought for a moment. 'Libo could be in danger. I have to check,' he declared. He patted Aurelia's arm. 'Everything will be fine, you'll see.'

Aurelia saw that her brother was not to be swayed. She took a step towards Hanno, but stopped herself. 'Mars protect you both,' she whispered, hating the way her voice trembled.

And Baal Saphon, thought Hanno, invoking the Carthaginian god of war.

Leaving Aurelia peering from behind a large pine, the two young men began to ascend. Quintus was surprised by the imperceptible change that had already taken place in their relationship. Although they could see no human activity above, both were instinctively using the few bushes present for cover. As soldiers would. *Don't be stupid. He's a slave.* 'It's bandits,' Quintus muttered to himself. 'What else can it be?'

'That's what it would be in the countryside around Carthage,' replied Hanno.

Quintus cursed. 'I wonder how many there are?'

Hanno shrugged uneasily, wishing he had a weapon. It wasn't surprising that Quintus had given the other gladius to Aurelia, but it grated on him nonetheless. 'Your guess is as good as mine.'

Quintus' lips had gone very dry. 'What if there are too many for me to take on?'

'We try not to shit ourselves, and then crawl out of there on our bellies,' Hanno answered dryly. 'Before going to get help.'

'That sounds like a good plan.' Despite himself, Quintus grinned.

The rest of the climb was made in silence. The last point of cover before the shepherd's hut was a stunted cypress tree, and they reached it without difficulty. Recovering their breath, each took turns to peer at the pens and the miserable structure alongside, which was little more than a leanto. His lips moving silently, Quintus counted the sheep. 'I make it more than fifty,' he whispered. 'That's Libo's entire flock.'

Be logical, thought Hanno. 'Maybe he's ill?'

'I doubt it,' Quintus replied. 'Libo is as hard as nails. He's lived in the mountains all his life.'

'Let's wait a moment then,' Hanno advised. 'No point rushing into a situation without assessing it first.'

Hanno's observation made Quintus bridle. Slaves do not advise their masters, he told himself angrily. Yet the Carthaginian's words were wise. Biting his lip, he drew a goose-feathered arrow from his quiver. It was his favourite, and he'd killed with it many times. Never a man, he thought with a rush of fear. Taking a deep breath, Quintus exhaled slowly. It might not come to that. Nonetheless, he picked out three more shafts and stabbed them into the earth by his feet. Suddenly, an awful thought struck him. If there were bandits about, and he was outnumbered, his bow was the only advantage he had. That might not be enough. Quintus was prepared for the potential danger he'd placed himself in, but he hadn't really considered his sister. He turned to Hanno. 'If anything happens to me, you're to run down and get Aurelia the hell out of here. Do you understand?'

It was too late to say that Quintus should have given him a sword, thought Hanno angrily. It would have been two of them against however many bandits might be in the hut. He nodded. 'Of course.'

It wasn't long before there was movement inside the building, which was perhaps twenty paces away. A man coughed, and cleared his throat in the manner of someone who has just woken. Quintus stiffened, listening hard. Hanno did likewise. Then they heard the rickety door on the far side of the hut being thrown open. A short figure wearing a sheepskin waistcoat over a home-spun tunic stepped into view. Stretching and yawning, he pulled down his breeches and began to relieve himself. Glancing sunlight lit up the yellow arc of his urine.

Quintus cursed under his breath.

Despite the other's reaction, Hanno had to ask. 'Is that the shepherd?' he whispered.

Quintus' lips framed the word 'No.' Carefully, he fitted his favourite arrow to his bowstring and drew a bead on the stranger.

'Could it be another shepherd?'

'I don't recognise him.' Quintus drew back until the goose feathers at the base of the arrow nearly touched his ear.

'Wait!' Hanno hissed. 'You have to be sure.'

Quintus was again angered by Hanno's tone. Nonetheless, he did not release: he too had no desire to kill an innocent man.

'Caecilius? Where are you?' demanded a voice from inside the hut.

The pair froze.

With a final shake, the man pulled up his trousers. 'Out here,' he replied lazily. 'Taking a piss on the shepherd. Making sure he's still dead.'

There was a loud guffaw. 'Not much chance of the whoreson being anything else after what you did to him.'

'You can't talk, Balbus,' added a third voice. 'He screamed the most when you were using the red hot poker.'

Quintus threw Hanno a horrified glance.

Balbus laughed, a deep, unpleasant sound. 'What do you think, Pollio?' There was no immediate answer, and they heard Balbus kicking someone. 'Wake up, you drunken sot.'

'The point of my boot up his arse should do the trick,' Caecilius bellowed, heading for the door.

Desperately, Hanno turned his head to tell Quintus to loose before it was too late. He barely had time to register the arrow as it flashed past his eyes and shot through the air to plant itself in the middle of Caecilius' chest. With a stunned look, the bandit dropped to his knees before toppling sideways to the dirt. He made a few soft choking sounds and lay still.

'Well done,' whispered Hanno. 'Three left.'

'At least.' Quintus did not think about what he had done. He notched another shaft and waited. The layout of the hut was such that if the remaining bandits merely looked out of the doorway, they would see Caecilius' body without exposing themselves to his arrows. Jupiter, Greatest and Best, he begged silently, let the next scumbag come right outside.

Hanno clenched his teeth. He too could see the danger.

'Caecilius? Fallen over your own prick?' demanded Balbus.

There was no answer. A moment later, a bulky-framed man with long greasy hair emerged partially into view. It took the blink of an eye for him to notice his companion's body, to take in the arrow protruding from his chest. A strangled cry left Balbus' throat. Frantic to regain the safety of the hut, he spun on his heel.

Quintus released. His shaft flew straight and true, driving deep into Balbus' right side with a meaty thump. The bandit cursed in pain, but managed to get through the doorway. 'Help me,' he cried. 'I'm hit.'

Shouts of confusion and anger rang out from within. Hanno heard Balbus growl, 'Caecilius is dead. An arrow to the chest.

No, Sejanus, I don't fucking know who did it.' Then, apart from low muttering, everything went silent.

'They know that I'm just outside,' Quintus whispered, suddenly wondering if he'd bitten off more than he could chew. 'But they have no idea that I'm on my own. How will they react?'

Hanno scowled. *You're not on your own, you arrogant fool.* 'What would you do?'

'Try to get away,' Quintus said, fumbling for an arrow.

In the same instant, loud cracking sounds filled the air and the back wall of the hut disintegrated in a cloud of dust. Three bandits burst into the open air, hurtling straight towards them. In the lead was a skinny man in a wine-stained tunic. He grasped a hunting spear in both hands. This had to be Pollio, thought Hanno. Beside him ran a massive figure carrying a club. Hanno blinked in surprise. It was not Balbus, because he was two steps behind, clutching the arrow in his side with one hand and a rusty sword with the other. Despite being twice Balbus' size, the big man was his spitting image. The pair had to be brothers.

The two sides goggled at each other for a heartbeat.

Pollio was the first to react. 'They're only children. And one isn't even armed,' he screamed. 'Kill them!' His companions needed no encouragement. Bellowing with rage, the trio charged forward.

Perhaps fifteen paces now divided them. 'Quick,' Hanno shouted. 'Take one of the bastards down.'

Quintus' heart hammered in his chest, and he struggled to notch his arrow correctly. Finally it slipped on to the string, but, desperate to even the odds, he loosed too soon. His shaft flashed over Pollio's shoulder and into the wreckage of the hut. He had no time to reach for another. The bandits were virtually upon them. Dropping his bow, he pulled the gladius from his belt. 'Get out of here!' he shouted. 'You know what to do!'

Facing certain death if he stayed without a weapon, Hanno turned and fled.

'Let him go!' shouted Pollio. 'The shitbag looks as if he can run like the wind.'

Quintus had just enough time to throw up a prayer of thanks to Jupiter before Pollio, leaping over a fallen log, reached him.

'So you're the one who would murder a man while he takes a piss,' the bandit snarled, lunging forward with his spear.

Quintus dodged sideways. 'He got what was coming to him.'

Leering, Pollio stabbed at him again. 'It was a quicker death than the shepherd had.'

Quintus tried not to think of Libo, or of the fact that he was outnumbered three to one. Holding his gladius with both hands, he swept the spear shaft away. Sejanus, the big man, was still a few steps away, but already there was no sign of Balbus. Where is the son of a whore? Quintus wondered frantically. He might be wounded, but he's still armed. The realisation made him want to vomit. *The bastard's coming to stab me in the back*. All Quintus could think of doing was to place himself against a tree. Driving Pollio off with a flurry of blows, he sprinted towards the nearest one he could see, a cypress with a thick trunk. He could make a stand there.

To Quintus' exhilaration, he made it.

The only trouble was that, a heartbeat later, he had the grinning bandits ringed around him in a semicircle.

'Surrender now, and we'll give you an easy death,' said Pollio. 'Not like the poor shepherd had.'

Even the wounded Balbus laughed.

What have I done? Somehow, Quintus swallowed down his fear. 'You're fucking scum! I'll kill you all,' he shouted.

'You think?' sneered Pollio. 'It's your choice.' Without warning, he thrust his spear at Quintus' midriff.

Quintus threw himself sideways. Too late, he realised that Sejanus had aimed his club at the very spot he was heading for. In utter desperation, he deliberately fell to the ground. With an almighty *crack*, the club smacked into the treetrunk. The

160

knowledge that the blow would have brained him if it had landed drove Quintus to his feet. Seizing his opportunity, he slashed out at Sejanus' arm and was delighted when his blade connected with the big man's right arm. The flesh wound it cut was enough for Sejanus to bellow in pain and stagger backwards, out of the way. Quintus' relief lasted no more than an instant. The injury wouldn't be enough to stop the brute from rejoining the fight. To survive, he immediately had to disable or kill one of the other two.

With that, a sword hilt smashed into the side of his head. Stars burst across Quintus' vision, and his knees buckled. Half-conscious, he dropped to the ground.

Hanno had probably run fifty paces before he glanced over his shoulder. Delighted that no one was pursuing him, he sprinted on for another fifty before looking back again. He was on his own. In the clear. Safe. So too, therefore, was Aurelia.

What of Quintus? he wondered with a thrill of dread.

You ran. Coward! Hanno's conscience screamed.

Quintus told me to, he thought defensively. The idiot couldn't bring himself to trust me with a gladius.

Does that mean you should leave him to die? his conscience shot back. What chance has he against three grown men?

Hanno screeched to a halt. Turning, he ran uphill as fast as his legs could take him. He took care to count his steps. At eighty, he slowed to a trot. Peering through the trees, he saw the three bandits standing over a motionless figure. Claws of fear savaged Hanno's guts as he took refuge behind a bush. *No! He can't be dead!* When Pollio's kick made Quintus moan, Hanno was nearly sick with relief. Quintus was alive still. Clearly, he wouldn't be for long. Hanno clenched his empty fists. *What in the name of Baal Saphon can I do?*

'Let's take him back to the hut,' Pollio declared.

'Why?' complained Balbus. 'We can just kill the fucker here.'

'That's where the fire is, stupid! It won't have gone out yet,' replied Pollio with a laugh. 'I know you're injured, but Sejanus and I can carry him between us.'

A cruel smile spread across Balbus' face. 'Fair enough. There'll be more sport with some heat, I suppose.' He watched each of his comrades take one of Quintus' arms and begin dragging him towards the hut. There was little resistance, but they retained their weapons nonetheless.

This is my chance. All three men had their backs to him, and half a dozen steps separated Balbus from the others. Hanno's mouth felt very dry. His prospects of success were tiny. Like as not, he'd end up dead, or being tortured alongside Quintus. He could still run. A wave of self-loathing swept over him. *He saved you from Agesandros, remember?*

Clenching his teeth, Hanno emerged from his hiding place. Grateful for the damp vegetation, which muffled the sound of his feet, he stole forward as fast as he could. Balbus was limping after his comrades, who were alternately grumbling about how much Quintus weighed and waxing lyrical about what they'd do to him. Hanno fixed his gaze on the rusty sword that dangled from Balbus' right hand. First, he *had* to arm himself. After that, he had to kill one of the bandits. After that . . . Hanno didn't know. He'd have to trust in the gods.

To Hanno's relief, his first target didn't hear him coming. Taking careful aim, he thumped Balbus near the point where Quintus' arrow had entered his flesh, before neatly catching the sword as it dropped from the screaming bandit's fingers. Switching it to his right hand, Hanno sprinted for the other two. 'Hey!' he shouted.

Their faces twisted with alarm, but Hanno's delight turned to fear as they dropped Quintus like a sack of grain. Do not let him be hurt, Hanno prayed. Please.

'You must be a slave,' Pollio growled. 'You were unarmed before. Why don't you join us?'

'We'll let you kill your master,' offered Sejanus. 'Any way you want.'

Hanno did not dignify the proposal with a reply. Sejanus was nearest, so he went for him first. The big man might have been injured, but he was still deadly with his club. Hanno ducked under one almighty swing, and dodged out of the way of another before seeing Pollio's spear come thrusting in at him. Desperate, Hanno retreated a few paces. Sejanus lumbered in immediate pursuit, blocking his comrade's view of Hanno. There was a loud curse from Pollio, and Sejanus' attention lapsed a fraction.

Hanno darted forward. As the other's eyes widened in disbelief, Hanno slid his sword deep into his belly. The blade made a horrible, sucking sound as it came out. Blood spurted on to the ground. Sejanus roared with agony; his club fell from his nerveless fingers and both his hands came up to clutch at his abdomen.

Hanno was already spinning to meet Pollio's attack. The little bandit's spear stabbed in, narrowly missing his right arm. His heart pounding, Hanno shuffled backwards. His eyes flickered to the side. Despite being in obvious pain, Balbus was about to join the fray. He'd picked up a thick branch. It wouldn't kill, thought Hanno, but if Balbus landed a blow, he'd easily knock him from his feet. Panic bubbled in his throat, and his sword arm began to tremble.

Get a grip of yourself! Quintus needs you.

Hanno's breathing steadied. He fixed Balbus with a hard stare. 'Want a blade in the guts as well as that arrow?'

Balbus flinched, and Hanno went for the kill. 'Creating fear in an enemy's heart wins half the battle,' his father had been fond of saying. 'Carthage!' he bellowed, and charged forward. Even if Pollio took him down from behind, Hanno was determined that Balbus would die.

Balbus saw the suicidal look in Hanno's eyes. He dropped his length of wood and raised both his hands in the air. 'Don't kill me,' he begged.

Hanno didn't trust the bandit as far as he could throw him; he didn't know what Pollio was doing either. Dropping his right shoulder, he crashed into Balbus' chest, sending him flying.

When he turned to face Pollio, the skinny bandit was gone. Pumping his arms and legs as if Cerberus himself were after him, he tore up the slope and was soon lost to view among the trees. Let the bastard go, Hanno thought wearily. He won't come back. A few steps away, Balbus was in the foetal position, moaning. Further off, Sejanus was already semi-conscious from the blood he'd lost.

The fight was over.

Elation filled Hanno for a moment – before he remembered Quintus.

He rushed to the Roman's side. To his immense relief, Quintus smiled up at him. 'Are you all right?' Hanno asked.

Wincing, Quintus lifted a hand to the side of his head. 'There's an apple-sized lump here, and it feels as if Jupiter is letting off thunderbolts inside my skull. Apart from that, I'll be fine, I think.'

'Thank the gods,' said Hanno fervently.

'No,' replied Quintus. 'Thank you – for coming back. For disobeying my orders.'

Hanno coloured. 'I'd never have been able to live with myself if I hadn't.'

'But you didn't have to do it. Even when you did, you could have taken up the bandits' offer. Turned on me.' A trace of wonder entered Quintus' voice. 'Instead, you took on the three of them, and won.'

'I—' Hanno faltered.

'I'm only alive because of you,' interrupted Quintus. 'You have my thanks.'

Seeing Quintus' sincerity, Hanno inclined his head. 'You're welcome.'

As the realisation sank in that they had survived the most desperate of situations, the two grinned at each other like maniacs.

These were strange circumstances for both. Master saved by his slave. Roman allied with Carthaginian. Yet both were very aware of a new bond: that of comradeship forged in combat.

It was a good feeling.

Chapter VIII: The Siege

Outside the walls of Saguntum, Iberia

Malchus regarded the immense fortifications with a baleful eye and spat on the ground. 'They're determined, you have to give them that,' he growled. 'They must know now that there's no help coming from Rome. But the pig-headed Greek bastards still won't give up.'

'Neither will we,' Sapho responded fiercely. His breath plumed in the cool, autumn air. 'And when we get inside, the defenders will regret the day they slammed the gates in our faces. The whoresons won't know what hit them. Eh, Bostar?' He elbowed his brother in the ribs.

'The sooner the city falls, the better. Hannibal will find a way,' Bostar replied confidently, sidestepping Sapho's needling. In the months since their argument in New Carthage, their relationship had improved somewhat, but Sapho never missed an opportunity to undermine him, or to call into question his loyalty to their cause. *Just because I don't enjoy torturing enemy prisoners,* thought Bostar sadly. *What has he become?*

In a way, though, it was unsurprising that Sapho resorted to violence in his attempts to garner intelligence that might gain them entry. Nearly six months had elapsed since Hannibal's immense army had begun the siege, and they were not much nearer to taking Saguntum. A mile from the sea, it sat on a long, naked piece of rock that towered three to four hundred paces above the plain below. The position was one of confident dominance, and made it a fearsome prospect to besiege. The only way of approaching the city, which was encircled by strongly built fortifications, was from the west, where the slope was least steep. Naturally, it was here that the defences were strongest. Surrounded by thick walls, a mighty tower sat astride the tallest part of the rock. Hannibal had encamped the majority of his forces below this point. He had also ordered the erection of a wall that ran all the way around the base of the rock. The circumvallation was dotted with towers whose function was merely to ensure that no enemy messengers escaped.

'The gods willing, *we* are that way,' Malchus added.

Both his sons nodded. Hannibal had shown their family considerable honour by picking their units to lead the impending attack. The rest of those who would take part, thousands of Libyans and Iberians, waited on the slopes below.

Sapho's face twitched, and he gestured at the massed ranks of their spearmen, who were arrayed around the massive shapes of four *vineae*, or 'covered ways', attacking towers with a massive battering ram at their base. These would form the basis for their assault. 'The men are nervous. It's no surprise either. We've been waiting for an hour. Where is he?'

Bostar could see that Sapho was right. Some soldiers were chatting loudly with each other, their voices a tone higher than normal. Others remained silent, but their lips moved in constant prayer. A nervous air hung over every phalanx. Hannibal will come soon, he told himself.

'Patience,' advised Malchus.

Reluctantly, Sapho obeyed, but he burned to prove himself once and for all. Show his father that he was the bravest of his sons.

Moments later, their attention was drawn by murmurs of anticipation, which began spreading forward from the rear of the throng.

'Listen!' said Malchus in triumph. 'Hannibal is talking to them as he passes by. There are many things that make a good general, and this is one of them. It's not just about leading from the front. You have to engage with your soldiers as well.' He gave Bostar an approving nod, which made Sapho mutter something under his breath.

Bostar's temper frayed. This was an area he paid a lot of attention to. 'What?' he demanded. 'If you tried that instead of punishing every tiny infraction of the rules, your troops might respect you more.'

Sapho's face darkened, but before he could reply, loud cheering broke out. Men began stamping their feet on the ground in a repetitive, infectious rhythm. The other officers did nothing to intervene. This was what they had all been waiting for. The noise grew and grew, until gradually a single word became audible. 'HANN-I-BAL! HANN-I-BAL! HANN-I-BAL!'

Bostar grinned. One could not help but be infected by the soldiers' enthusiasm. Even Sapho was craning his neck to see.

Eventually, a small party emerged from the midst of the spearmen. It was a hollow square, formed by perhaps two dozen *scutarii*. These Iberian infantry were some of Hannibal's best troops. As always, the scutarii were wearing their characteristic black cloaks over simple tunics and small breastplates. Their fearsome array of weapons included various types of heavy throwing spear, most notably the all-iron *saunion*, as well as long, straight swords, and daggers. Within their formation walked a lone figure, partially obscured from view. This was who everyone wanted to see. Finally, nearing Malchus and his sons, the scutarii fanned out in two lines. The man within was revealed.

Hannibal Barca.

Bostar gazed at his general with frank admiration. Like most senior Carthaginian officers, Hannibal wore a simple Hellenistic gilded bronze helmet. Sunlight flashed off its surface, reflecting into the soldiers' eyes. The blinding light concealed Hannibal's face apart from his beard. A dark purple cloak hung from his broad shoulders. Under it, he wore a tunic of the same colour, and an ornate muscled bronze cuirass, its details picked out in silver. Layered strips of linen guarded the general's groin, and polished bronze greaves covered his lower legs. His feet were encased in sturdy leather sandals. A hide baldric swept down from his right shoulder to his left hip, suspending a falcata sword in a well-worn scabbard. He moved forward, limping slightly.

The commander of the scutarii barked an order, and in unison his soldiers slammed their brightly painted shields on to the rock. The crashing sound instantly silenced the assembled troops. 'Your general, the lion of Carthage, Hannibal Barca!' screamed the officer.

Everyone stiffened to attention and saluted.

'General!' cried Malchus. 'You honour us with your presence.'

The corners of Hannibal's mouth tugged up. 'At ease, gentlemen.' He made his way to Malchus' side. 'Are you ready?'

'Yes, sir. We have checked over the siege engines twice. Every man knows his task.'

Malchus' sons muttered in agreement.

Hannibal glanced at each of them in turn before giving a satisfied nod. 'You will do well.'

'May Baal Saphon strike us down if we do not,' said Sapho fervently.

Hannibal looked a little surprised. 'I hope not. The city will fall eventually, but we haven't succeeded so far. Who's to say that today will be any different? And valuable officers are hard to come by.' Ignoring Sapho's obvious discomfort, he smiled at Malchus. 'Understand that you're only being granted this chance because I can't run.' He touched the heavy strapping on his right thigh.

'Your injury was most unfortunate, sir,' said Malchus, 'but we are grateful for the opportunity that it has granted us today.'

Hannibal smiled. 'Your eagerness is commendable.'

Bostar could still picture the heart-stopping moment several weeks previously, during an assault similar to the one they were about to lead. As was his nature, Hannibal had been at the front. Bostar wished it had been he who had taken the arrow through the thigh. 'How's it healing, sir?'

'Slowly enough.' Hannibal grimaced. 'I should be thankful, I suppose, that the defenders aren't better archers.'

Father and sons laughed nervously. That eventuality was something no one wanted to entertain.

'Well, don't let me stand in your way. The Saguntines await you.' Hannibal indicated the walls, which were thickly manned. He pointed back down the steep slope at the other companies of troops: reinforcements should the attack break through. 'So do they.'

'Yes, sir.' Malchus lifted his sword.

His men, who had been watching closely, stiffened.

'Gods, but I wish Hanno were here,' muttered Bostar.

Sapho's face hardened. 'Eh? Why?'

'He spent his time dreaming about things like this.'

'Well, he's dead,' Sapho whispered back savagely. 'So you're wasting your time.'

Bostar gave him a furious stare. 'Don't you miss him?'

Sapho had no chance to reply.

'What are you waiting for?' Malchus demanded, who had missed the exchange. 'Get into position!'

With a quick salute to Hannibal, Bostar and Sapho sprinted off to join their respective phalanxes. Each was in charge of one of the vineae, and their increasingly bitter rivalry meant that both burned to command the siege engine which smashed the decisive hole in the walls, and allowed their comrades a way into Saguntum. Of course it might not be they who succeeded, thought Bostar.

Their father commanded the third vinea, and Alete, a doughty veteran whom both brothers admired, had the last.

Malchus waited until they were in place before he chopped his arm downward. 'Forward!' he shouted.

Using whistles, the officers encouraged the Libyans towards the walls. Dozens of men who had been selected earlier handed their spears to comrades and ran to place their shoulders against the backs of the vineae, or to stand alongside the wheels. Scores of others used their large shields to form protective screens around those who were now unprotected. More commands rang out, and the soldiers around the siege engines began to push. With loud creaks, the vineae rumbled forward, past Hannibal. When the machines were perhaps fifty paces up the slope, the remaining Libyans began to follow in tight phalanxes.

As they drew nearer, Bostar's stomach clenched. He could clearly see the faces of those above, the defenders who were waiting to rain death down upon him and his men. Upon his father and brother. Baal Saphon, let us smash the enemy's walls asunder, he prayed. Keep your shield over all of us. As the first missiles came pattering down, Bostar couldn't help wondering if Sapho was asking for similar protection for him.

He doubted it.

Taking great care, Bostar peered out at the ramparts above him. Perhaps an hour had passed, and the assault was going well. The battering rams suspended in the bottoms of the vineae were smashing great holes in the base of the wall. Thanks to the siege engines' wooden and leather roofs, which had been pre-soaked in water, the defenders' clouds of fire arrows, stones and spears were having limited effect. Bostar had lost fifteen men, which was perfectly acceptable. The phalanxes on either side, those of Sapho and Alete, looked to have suffered much the same.

Soon after, a large section of the wall collapsed. A wry grin split Bostar's face at the sight. The area lay directly between his and Sapho's positions, so neither could claim the credit. That wasn't the point now, of course. Hannibal was watching them. Bostar roared at his men to redouble their efforts. He fancied he heard Sapho's voice above the din, enjoining his soldiers to do the same. Their efforts were not in vain. Before long, two, and then three, towers had fallen outwards, crushing dozens of the garrison, and spearmen, to death. But a sizeable breach had now been forced, large enough to gain entry. Bostar did not wait until the dust had settled. This opportunity had to be seized by the throat, before the bewildered defenders had a chance to react. Screaming at his men to pick up their weapons and follow him, he climbed on to the mounds of broken masonry that stood before the siege engines. He was pleased to note that Sapho's soldiers were also spilling into view. Catching sight of his brother twenty paces away, Bostar raised his spear in salute. 'I'll see you inside!'

'Not if I get there before you,' Sapho snarled back. He turned to his soldiers, who were straining like hunting dogs on the leash. 'Five gold pieces to the first man to get within the walls. Forward!'

Bostar sighed. Even this had to be a contest. So be it, he thought angrily.

The race was on.

Pursued by their men, the two brothers scrambled up towards the breach. They risked their lives with every step, not just from the continuing rain of missiles from the ramparts to either side, but from the treacherous footing beneath. Carrying a spear in one hand and a shield in the other made it even more difficult to balance. Bostar kept his gaze fixed firmly on the ground. The enemy missiles were beyond his control, but he could make sure that he didn't break an ankle in the ascent. He'd seen it happen before, consigning the unfortunates affected to being trampled by their comrades, or killed by the torrent of death being thrown by the Saguntines.

Bostar was first to reach the highest point of the smashed wall. The clouds of dust sent up by the towers' collapse formed a choking cloud that hid any defenders from sight. Perhaps there were none? wondered Bostar. His heart leaped, but then he glanced around and cursed. In his haste, he'd outstripped his soldiers. The nearest were twenty paces down the slope. 'Get a move on,' he roared. 'This isn't a walking party!'

An instant later, Sapho arrived from the gloom. He had a dozen or more Libyans in tow; more were hauling themselves up nearby. A happy smile spread across his face when he saw that Bostar was alone. 'On your own still? It's not surprising, really. Nothing like the promise of gold to speed things along.'

Bostar bit back his instinctive response. 'This is not the time for such bullshit,' he snarled. 'Let's seize the damn breach. We can argue later.'

Sapho gave a nonchalant shrug. 'As you wish.' He levelled his spear. 'Third Phalanx! On me! Form a line!'

Only four of Bostar's men had arrived. He watched in frustration as his brother led his spearmen forward. Of course he would be following in the blink of an eye, but it still rankled. A moment later, Bostar was glad that he hadn't been first into the gap. Like avenging ghosts, scores of screaming Saguntines emerged from the dust cloud. Every one of them carried a *falarica*, a long javelin with a burning ball of pitch-soaked tow wrapped around the middle of the shaft.

'Look out!' Bostar screamed, knowing that his warning was already too late.

Responding to an officer's command, the Saguntines drew back and released. They aimed short. Clouds of flaming missiles scudded through the air. Horror-struck, Sapho and his soldiers slowed down. And then the falaricae landed. Driving through shields. Maiming, killing and setting men alight.

Cursing, Bostar counted his spearmen. There were about twenty of them now. It wasn't enough, but he couldn't just stand by. If he did, Sapho would be killed, and his soldiers would run away. Their chance would be lost. 'Forward!' Raising his shield,

Bostar ran at the enemy. He did not look back. To his immense relief, he felt his men's presence at each shoulder. Death might take them all, thought Bostar, but at least they followed him through loyalty, not lust for gold.

He aimed for the spot where it looked as if Sapho's soldiers might be overwhelmed. Seeing him, the nearest Saguntines took aim and released their falaricae. Hunching his shoulders, Bostar ran on. Streaming flames, the javelins hummed right past him. There was a strangled scream, and he looked around. He wished he hadn't. A falarica had struck the man to his rear in the shoulder, driving deep into his flesh. In turn, the burning section had set alight the soldier's tunic. Gobbets of white-hot tow were dropping on to his face and neck. His screams were ear-splitting. Bostar's nostrils filled with the stench of cooking flesh. 'Leave him!' he roared at the men who instinctively went to help. 'Keep moving!' Grateful it wasn't him, and hoping the soldier died quickly, he spun back to the front.

If there was one small advantage to be gained from the enemy's secret weapon, it was that after launching them, the defenders were momentarily defenceless. In addition, many weren't even wearing armour. Snarling with fury, Bostar charged at a skinny Saguntine who was frantically trying to tug free his sword. He didn't succeed. Bostar's spear took him through the chest, punching through his ribcage with ease. The man's eyes nearly popped out of their sockets with the force of the impact. He was dead before Bostar pulled free his weapon, showering the ground in gouts of blood.

Panting, Bostar rounded on the next soldier within reach, a youth who couldn't have been more than sixteen. Despite his rusty sword and blood-curdling cries, he looked petrified.

Bostar parried his clumsy blows with little difficulty before sliding his spear into the youngster's belly. He killed two more defenders before an opportunity presented itself to assess the situation.

Perhaps a hundred of his own men were present; more were still arriving. A similar number of Sapho's soldiers were battling steadily around them. No doubt their father and Alete's phalanxes were trying to reach them too. Remarkably, however, they were being held back by the Saguntines, who were performing acts of heroism and suicidal bravery. No ground had been gained at all. Bostar realised why as he took in hundreds of civilians, who, just a few steps from the periphery of the fighting, were frantically repairing the breach with their bare hands. He could see old men, women and even children heaving rocks into place. Grudging respect filled him. Knowing that their loved ones were so close would make any man, soldier or not, fight like a demon. Bostar was not dismayed. Even now, thousands more troops would be climbing the slope to join them. Against such overwhelming numbers, even the gallant Saguntines could not hold for much longer. All they needed to do was to press home the attack.

Abruptly, his attention was drawn back to the present. Through the dust, he could make out a line of flickering flame approaching from the enemy citadel. Bostar's stomach clenched as the vision came into full focus. It was two further waves of warriors, carrying scores more burning falaricae. 'Shields up!' he yelled. 'Incoming javelins!'

His men hurried to obey.

Responding to a shouted order, the enemy lines came to a halt perhaps fifty paces away. Drawing back, the Saguntines threw their falaricae up in a steep arc, far over their own men. Over Bostar and Sapho's soldiers.

'Clever bastards,' Bostar muttered. 'They don't want to hit us.' He watched in total dread as the flaming javelins turned to point downwards. Like deadly shooting stars, they returned to earth to land amidst the still ascending Carthaginian troops. Thanks to the clouds of dust, these densely packed men had no idea what was about to hit them until the very last moment. Understandably, the falaricae caused utter chaos. Practically every one found a home in human flesh, running through shields and mail shirts with impunity. Yet their effect was far more profound. It was why the Saguntines had aimed at the unsuspecting soldiers to the rear, thought Bostar as the screams and wails of the injured filled his ears. The falaricae struck fear into the heart of every man who stood in their path. He knew exactly why. Who could bear to watch his comrades being turned into pillars of flame, or having the flesh blistered from their bones? No amount of training could prepare soldiers for that.

The entire advance below him had already come to a halt. As Bostar watched, the second wave of enemy javelins came rocketing down. An instant later, the Carthaginian attack became a rout. Despite the shouts of their officers, hundreds of men turned and fled. They hurled themselves down the slope with such abandon that many fell and were trampled by those following. The soldiers to either side, who had not been struck by the enemy volley, took one look at their retreating comrades and stopped dead. Then, as one, they turned on the spot and began running too.

Bostar cursed. The moment was lost. No one, even Hannibal, could turn this situation around. He caught the arm of the nearest spearman. 'Pull back! Our reinforcements are withdrawing. We have to save ourselves. Spread the word.' Repeating his command to every soldier he passed, Bostar fought his way through the press to Sapho's side. Oblivious to the volley's effect, his brother was urging a quartet of spearmen forward at a bunch of poorly armed defenders.

'Sapho!' Bostar yelled. 'Sapho!'

Eventually his brother heard him. 'What?' he snarled over his shoulder.

'We must pull back!'

Sapho's face contorted with anger. 'You're crazy! Any moment, the whoresons will break, and then we'll have them. Victory is at hand!'

'No, it isn't!' Bostar bellowed. 'We have to retreat. NOW.'

Some of Sapho's soldiers began to look uneasy.

Sapho glared furiously at Bostar, but realised that he was serious. Shouting encouragement to his men, Sapho elbowed his way out of the front rank. With his arms and face covered in blood, he was like some creature from the underworld. 'Have you entirely lost your wits?' he hissed. 'The enemy is giving ground at last. Another big push, and they'll break.'

'It's too late,' Bostar replied in a flat tone. 'Have you not seen what those fucking falaricae have done to the troops behind us?'

Sapho's rejoinder was instantaneous. 'No. I keep my eyes to the front, not the back.'

Bostar's fists clenched at the imputation. 'Well,' he muttered, 'let me tell you, our entire attack has come to a halt.'

Sapho bared his teeth. 'So? Those motherless curs will turn and run any moment. Then we'll get a foothold inside the walls.'

'Where we will be cut off and annihilated.' Bostar jabbed a finger into Sapho's chest for emphasis. 'Don't you understand? We're on our own up here!'

'Coward!' Sapho screamed. 'You're scared of dying, that's all.'

Bostar's anger surged out of control. 'When the time comes, I will fight and die for Hannibal,' he shouted. 'What's more, I will do it proudly. But there's a difference between dying well, and like a fool. There's nothing to be gained from sacrificing your life, or those of your men, here.'

Spitting on the ground, Sapho made to return to the fight.

'Stop!' Bostar's order was like the crack of a whip.

Stiff-backed, Sapho came to a halt, but he did not turn to face Bostar.

'As your superior officer, I command you to withdraw your men at once,' Bostar cried, making sure that every soldier within earshot heard him.

Defeated, Sapho spun around. 'Yes, *sir*,' he snarled. He raised his voice. 'You heard the order! Fall back!'

It didn't take long for Sapho's men to get the idea. Re-energised by the effect that their volleys had had on the ascending Carthaginian troops, the defenders were beginning to advance again. Behind them, freshly lit falaricae were being carried forward. Encouraged by this, even the civilians who were repairing the breach joined in, hurling stones and fist-sized pieces of masonry at the spearmen.

This increased the ignominy and fuelled Sapho's anger to new levels, all the more because he could now see that Bostar had been right to sound the recall. 'Fool,' he told himself nonetheless. 'It was there for the taking.'

Hannibal was waiting with Malchus and Alete at the bottom of the slope. The general greeted the brothers warmly. 'We were getting worried about you,' he declared.

Malchus rumbled in agreement.

'Sapho here didn't want to leave the fight,' said Bostar generously.

'Last on the field?' Hannibal clapped Sapho on the shoulder. 'But still with the sense to withdraw. Good man! Once the whoresons had panicked your reinforcements, there was no point staying there, eh?'

Sapho flushed and hung his head. 'No, sir.'

'It was a good effort from both of you,' said Malchus encouragingly. 'But it wasn't to be.'

Hannibal took Sapho's reaction to be disappointment. 'Never mind, man. My spies tell me that their food is fast running out. We'll take the place soon! Now, see to your injured.' He waved a hand in dismissal.

'Come on,' said Bostar, leading Sapho away.

'Let go!' Sapho whispered after a few steps. 'I'm not a child!'

'Stop acting like one then!' said Bostar, releasing his grip. 'The least you could do is thank me. I didn't have to cover up for you there.'

Sapho's lip curled. 'I'm damned if I'll do that.'

Bostar threw his eyes to heaven. 'Of course not! Why would

you recognise that I just saved your arse from a severe reprimand?'

'Fuck you, Bostar,' Sapho snapped. He felt completely backed into a corner. 'You're always right, aren't you? Everyone loves you, the perfect fucking officer!' Turning on his heel, he stalked off.

Bostar watched him go. Why couldn't he have gone fishing instead of Hanno? he thought. His remorse for even thinking such a thing was instant, but the feeling lingered as he began organising rescue parties for the injured.

For the next two months, the siege went on in much the same fashion. Every full frontal assault made by the Carthaginians was met with dogged, undying determination by the defenders. The vineae regularly smashed more holes in the outer wall, but the attackers could not press home their advantage fully, despite their overwhelming superiority of numbers. Relations between Bostar and Sapho did not improve, and the constant activity meant that it was easy to avoid each other. When they weren't fighting, they were sleeping or looking after their wounded. Malchus, who had not only his own phalanx to deal with, but the extra duties given him by Hannibal, remained unaware of the feud.

Incensed by the manner in which the siege was dragging on, Hannibal eventually ordered the construction of more siege engines: vineae, which protected the men within, and an immense multi-storey tower on wheels. This last, holding catapults and hundreds of soldiers on its various levels, could be moved to whichever point was weakest on a particular day. Its firepower was so great that the battlements could be cleared of defenders within a short time, allowing the wooden terraces which would protect the attacking infantry to be carried forward without hindrance. Fortunately for the Carthaginians, the ramparts had been built on a base of clay, not cement. Using pickaxes, the troops in the terraces set to work, undermining the base of the walls. In this way, a further breach was made, and the attackers' spirits were briefly lifted. Yet all was not as it seemed. Beyond the gaping hole, the Carthaginians found that a crescent-shaped fortification of earth had been thrown up in preparation for this exact eventuality. From behind its protection came repeated volleys of the terrifying falaricae.

At this point, despite the showers of burning javelins, the Carthaginians' relentless determination and superior numbers began to tell. The Saguntines did not have time to rebuild the new damage to their defences properly, and repeated waves of attack finally smashed a passage behind the walls. Despite the defenders' heroism, the position was held. Further successes followed in the subsequent days, but then, with winter approaching, Hannibal was called away by a major rebellion of the fierce tribes that lived near the River Tagus. Maharbal, the officer he left in command, proceeded vigorously with the assault. He gained further ground, driving the weakened defenders into the citadel. The attackers' situation was strengthened by the fact that cholera and other illnesses were now causing heavy casualties among the Saguntines; their food and supplies were also running dangerously low.

By the time Hannibal had put down the uprising and returned, the end was near. The Carthaginian general offered terms to the Saguntine leaders. Incredibly, they were rejected out of hand. With the end of the year nigh, preparations were made for a final, decisive assault. Thanks to their repeated valour, Malchus, his sons and their spearmen had been chosen to be part of the last attack. Typically, Hannibal and his corps of scutarii were also present.

Long before the winter sun had tinted the eastern horizon, they assembled some fifty paces from the walls. Behind them, reaching all the way to the bottom of the slope, were units from every section of the army except the cavalry. Apart from the occasional jingle of mail or muted cough, the soldiers made little noise. The

breath of thousands plumed the chill, damp air, the only mani-
festation of the excitement every man felt. As reward for their
long struggle and because of the Saguntines' refusal to parley,
Hannibal had told his troops that they had free rein when the city
fell. Carthage would take some of the spoils, but the rest was
theirs, including the inhabitants: men, women and children.

In serried ranks, they waited as the wooden terraces were
pushed forward by torchlight. There was no longer any need for
the huge tower with its slingers, spearmen and catapults. Either
from lack of men, or missiles, the defenders had recently given
up trying to destroy the Carthaginian siege engines. This good
fortune meant that the work to undermine the fortifications had
been able to proceed much faster than before. According to the
engineer in charge, the citadel itself would fall by mid-morning
at the latest.

His prediction was accurate. As the first orange fingers of
sunlight crept into the sky, ominous rumbles began to fill the air.
Within moments, great clouds of smoke began to rise from the
centre of the citadel. The crackle of burning wood could also be
heard. The Carthaginians paid it no heed. They no longer cared
what the Saguntines were doing. With all possible speed, the
majority of the soldiers at work in the terraces were pulled back.
The danger of being crushed had grown too great. Yet, despite
the extreme danger, some remained to finish the task.

They did not have to wait long. With frightening speed, a large
piece of the citadel wall suddenly tumbled to the ground. In a
chain reaction, it precipitated the thunderous collapse of other,
bigger sections. With loud cracks, brickwork and carved stones,
which had been in place for decades, even centuries, crumbled
and gave way. The noise as they fell more than five storeys was
deafening. Inevitably, some of those in the wooden terraces failed
to escape in time. A short chorus of strangled screams announced
their horrifying demise. Bostar clenched his jaw at the sound. It
was what he had expected. As his father had said, ordinary soldiers

were expendable. The loss of a certain number meant nothing. And yet to Bostar it did, like the widespread rape, torture and killing of civilians that would shortly take place. Malchus' grim nature and Sapho's even darker personality appeared not to be affected by such things, but Bostar felt it damage his soul. He did not let his determination weaken, however. There were too many things at stake. The defeat of Rome. Revenge for his beloved younger brother, Hanno. The building of a new relationship with Sapho. Whether he would ever achieve any of them, Bostar had no idea. Somehow the last seemed the most unlikely.

Immense clouds of dust clogged the air, but as they finally began to clear, the waiting Carthaginians could see an indefensible breach had been created. A swelling cheer rippled down the slope. At last, victory was at hand.

Bostar felt his spirits rise. He threw Sapho a tight smile, but all he got in return was a scowl.

Drawing his falcata sword, Hannibal led the advance.

It was at this precise moment, because of a warning from the surviving defenders on the battlements perhaps, that the screams began. Ululating, despairing, yet still with shreds of dignity, they filled the air. The Carthaginians' heads shot up. No one could ignore such terrible sounds.

'It's the nobility burning themselves to death.' Malchus' voice revealed an unusual respect. 'They're too proud to become slaves. May it never fall to that in Carthage.'

'Ha! That day will never come,' Sapho replied.

Bostar's instinctive reaction, however, was to utter a prayer to Baal Hammon. Watch over our city for ever, he prayed. Keep it safe from savages such as the Romans.

Hannibal wasn't listening to the noise. He was keen to end the matter. 'Charge!' he screamed in Iberian, and then, for the benefit of the Libyans, he repeated it in his own tongue. Followed by his faithful scutarii, he trotted towards the gaping hole in the citadel. Bellowing the same command, Malchus, Sapho and Bostar sprang forward with their men. Behind them, the order rang out in half a dozen languages, and, like so many thousand ants, the host of soldiers followed.

Sapho and Bostar's rivalry resurfaced with a vengeance. Whoever reached the top of the breach first would win praise from Hannibal and the respect of the entire army. Outstripping their men, they clambered neck and neck across the uneven and treacherous piles of rubble and broken masonry. With their spears in one hand, and their shields in the other, they had no way of breaking a fall. It was lunacy, but there was no going back now. Hannibal was leading, and they must follow. Soon, the brothers had drawn alongside their leader, who was two steps in front of his scutarii. Hannibal gave them an encouraging grin, which they reciprocated, before glaring at each other.

Glancing over his shoulder an instant later, Bostar's eyes widened. The downward angle of the gradient afforded him a perfect view of the Carthaginian attack. It was a magnificent and terrible sight, guaranteed to drive terror into the hearts of the defenders who remained on the walls. Bostar doubted that any would dare. With the leaders immolating themselves rather than surrender, the ordinary soldiers would be cowering in their homes with their families, or also committing suicide.

He was wrong. Not all the Saguntines had given up the struggle.

As his gaze returned to the slope before him, his attention was drawn by movement up and to the right, on a section of the battlements that was still complete. There Bostar saw six men crouched around an enormous block of stone. Working together, they were pushing it towards the broken end of the walkway that ran along the top of the wall. Bostar followed the trajectory the block would take when it fell, and his heart leaped into his mouth. While the Saguntines' purpose was to cause as many casualties as possible, the potential cost to the Carthaginians was far greater. Bostar could see that within a few heartbeats, Hannibal would be standing full square in the stone's path. A glance at Sapho, and at Hannibal himself, told Bostar that he was the only one to have seen the danger.

When he looked up again, the irregularly shaped block was already teetering on the edge. As Bostar opened his mouth in a warning shout, it tipped forward and fell. Gathering speed unbelievably fast, the stone tumbled and bounced down the slope. Its passage sent showers of brick and masonry into the air, each piece of which was capable of smashing a man's skull. Screaming with delight, the defenders turned and fled, secure in the knowledge that their final effort would kill dozens of Carthaginians.

Bostar did not think. He simply reacted. Dropping his spear, he charged sideways at Hannibal. The air filled with a sudden thunder. Bostar did not look up, for fear of soiling himself. Several scutarii, whose advance his action was checking, mouthed confused curses. Bostar paid no heed. He just prayed that none of the Iberians would think he was trying to harm Hannibal and get in his way. Now he had covered six steps. A dozen. Sensing Bostar's approach, Hannibal turned his head. Confused, he frowned. 'What in the name of Baal Hammon are you doing?' he demanded.

Bostar didn't answer. Leaping forward, he swept his right arm around Hannibal's body and drove them both to the ground, with the general trapped beneath. With his left arm, Bostar raised his shield to cover both their heads. There was a heartbeat's delay, and then the earth shook. Their ears were filled with a reverberation of sound that threatened to deafen them. Thankfully it did not last, but diminished as the block crashed down the slope.

Bostar's first concern was not for himself. 'Are you hurt, sir?'

Hannibal's voice was muffled. 'I don't think so.'

Thank the gods, thought Bostar. Gingerly, he moved his arms and legs. To his delight, they all seemed to work. Discarding his shield, he sat up, helping Hannibal to do the same.

The general swore softly. Perhaps three steps from their position, lay a scutarius. Or at least, what had once been a scutarius.

The man had not so much been broken apart as smeared across the uneven ground. His bronze helmet had provided little protection. Chunks of brain matter were spread like white paste on the rocks, providing a sharp contrast to the bright red blood that oozed from the tangled mess of tissue that had been his body. Jagged pieces of brick protruded from the scutarius' back, poking holes in his tunic. His limbs were bent at unnatural, terrible angles, exposing in multiple places the gleaming white ends of broken bones.

He was just the first casualty. Below the corpse stretched a swathe of destruction as far as the eye could see. Bostar had never witnessed anything like it. Dozens of soldiers, perhaps more, had been killed. No. Pulverised, Bostar thought. A wave of nausea washed over him, and he struggled not to be sick.

Hannibal's voice startled him. 'It appears that I owe you my life.'

Numbly, Bostar nodded.

'My thanks. You are a fine soldier,' said Hannibal, clambering to his feet. He helped Bostar to do the same.

In the same instant, those of Hannibal's scutarii who had not been harmed came swarming in, their faces twisted with alarm. Naturally, the attack had been stalled by the Saguntines' daring action. Anxious questions filled the air as the Iberians established that their beloved commander had not been hurt. Hannibal quickly brushed them off. Picking up his falcata sword, which had fallen to the ground, he looked at Bostar. 'Are you ready to finish what we started?' he asked.

Bostar was stunned by the speed at which Hannibal's composure had returned. He himself was still in shock. He managed to nod his head. 'Of course, sir.'

'Excellent,' replied Hannibal with a brief smile. He indicated that Bostar should advance beside him.

Retrieving his spear, Bostar obeyed. He barely took in the pleased grin that Malchus gave him, and the equally poisonous expression on Sapho's face. Elation had replaced his terror, and he could try to patch things up with his brother later.

For now, it was all about following Hannibal.

A true leader of men.

Chapter IX: Minucius Flaccus

Near Capua, Campania

Hanno leaned against the wall of the kitchen, admiring the view as Elira bent over a table laden down with food. Her dress rode up, exposing her shapely calves and tightening over the swell of her buttocks. Hanno's groin throbbed, and he shifted position to avoid his excitement being obvious. Elira and Quintus were still lovers, but that didn't mean Hanno couldn't admire her from a distance. Alarmingly, Elira had noticed his glances, and returned them with smouldering ones of her own, but Hanno had not risked taking things any further. His newly born – and potentially valuable – friendship with Quintus was too fragile to survive a revelation like that.

Since the fight at the hut, his circumstances had become much easier. Fabricius had been impressed by Quintus' account of the fight and the physical evidence of two live, if wounded, prisoners. Hanno's reward was to be made a household slave. His manacles were removed and he was allowed to sleep in the house. Initially, Hanno was delighted. At one stroke, he had been removed from Agesandros' grasp. Weeks later, he was not so sure. The harsh reality of his situation seemed starker than ever before.

Three times a day, Hanno had to attend the family at their

meals. Naturally, he was not allowed to eat with them. He saw Aurelia and Quintus daily from morning to night, but could not talk to them unless no one else was about. Even then, conversations were hurried. It was all so different from the time they had spent together in the woods. Despite the enforced distance between them, Hanno was relieved that the palpable air of comradeship – which had so recently sprung up – had not vanished. Quintus' occasional winks and Aurelia's shy smiles now lit up his days. Lastly, there was Elira, whose bedroll was not twenty paces from his, on the floor of the atrium, and whom he dared not approach. Hanno knew that he should be grateful for his lot. On the occasions that he and Agesandros came face to face, it was patently clear that the Sicilian still wished him harm.

'Father!' Aurelia's delighted voice echoed from the courtyard. 'You're back!'

As curious as any, Hanno followed the other kitchen slaves to the door. Fabricius hadn't been expected home for at least two weeks.

Dressed in a belted tunic and sandals, Fabricius stood by the main fountain. A broad smile creased his face as Aurelia raced up to him. 'I'm filthy,' he warned. 'Covered in dust from the journey.'

'I don't care!' She wrapped her arms around him. 'It's so good to see you.'

He gave her an affectionate hug. 'I have missed you too.'

A pang of sadness at his own plight plucked at Hanno's heart, but he did not allow himself to dwell on it.

'Husband. Thank the gods for your safe return.' With a sedate smile, Atia joined her husband and daughter. Aurelia pulled away, allowing Fabricius to kiss his wife on the cheek. They gave each other a pleased look, which spoke volumes. 'You must be thirsty.'

'My throat's as dry as a desert riverbed,' Fabricius replied.

Atia's eyes swivelled to the kitchen doorway, and the gaggle of watching slaves. She caught Hanno's gaze first. 'Bring wine! The rest of you, back to work.'

The doorway emptied in a flash. Every slave knew not to cross Atia, who ruled the household with a silken yet iron-hard grip. Quickly, Hanno reached down four of the best glasses from the shelf and placed them on a tray. Julius, the friendly slave who ran the kitchen, was already reaching for an amphora. Hanno watched as he diluted the wine in the Roman fashion with four times the amount of water. 'There you go,' Julius muttered, placing a full jug on the tray. 'Get out there before she calls again.'

Hanno hurried to obey. He was keen to know what had brought about Fabricius' early return. With pricked ears, he carried the tray towards the family, who had just been joined by Quintus.

Quintus grinned broadly, before he remembered that he was now a man. 'Father,' he said solemnly. 'It is good to see you.'

Fabricius pinched his son's cheek. 'You've grown even more.'

Quintus blushed. To cover his embarrassment, he turned expectantly to Hanno. 'Come on, then. Fill them up.'

Hanno stiffened at the order, but did as he was told. His hand paused over the fourth glass, and he looked to Atia.

'Yes, yes, pour one for Aurelia too. She's practically a woman.'

Aurelia's happy expression slipped away. 'Have you found me a husband?' she asked accusingly. 'Is that why you've come back?'

Atia frowned. 'Do not be so presumptuous!'

Aurelia's cheeks flamed red and she hung her head.

'I wish it were that simple, daughter,' Fabricius answered. 'While I have made some progress in that regard, there are far greater events occurring on the world stage.' He clicked his fingers at Hanno, whose heart raced as he moved from person to person, distributing the wine.

'What has happened?' asked Atia.

Instead of answering, Fabricius raised his glass. 'A toast,' he said. 'That the gods, and our ancestors, continue to smile on our family.'

Atia's face tightened a fraction, but she joined in the salutation.

Quintus was less ruled by decorum than his mother, and jumped in the moment his father had swallowed. 'Tell us why you've returned!'

'Saguntum has fallen,' Fabricius replied flatly.

Blood rushed through Hanno's ears, and he was acutely aware of Quintus spinning to regard him. Carefully, he wiped a drop of wine from the jug's lip with a cloth. Inside, every fibre of his being was rejoicing. Hannibal! his mind shouted. Hannibal!

Quintus' gaze shot back to his father. 'When?'

'A week ago. Apparently, they spared virtually no one. Men, women, children. The few who survived were taken as slaves.'

Atia's lips tightened. 'Absolute savages.'

Hanno found Aurelia staring at him with wide, horrified eyes. It's not as if your people don't do exactly the same thing when they sack a city, he thought furiously. Of course he could say nothing, so he turned his face away.

In contrast to his sister, Quintus looked angry. 'It was bad enough that the Senate did nothing to help one of our allies for the last eight months. Surely they'll act now?'

'They will,' Fabricius replied. 'In fact, they already have.'

The following silence echoed louder than a trumpet call.

'An embassy has been sent to Carthage, its mission to demand that Hannibal and his senior officers be handed over immediately to face justice for their heinous actions.'

Hanno squeezed the cloth so hard that it dripped wine on to the mosaic between his feet.

No one noticed. Not that Hanno would have cared. How dare they? his mind screamed. Bastard Romans!

'They will hardly do that,' said Atia.

'Of course not,' Fabricius answered, unaware of Hanno's silent but fervent agreement. 'No doubt Hannibal has his enemies, but the Carthaginians are a proud race. They will want redress for the humiliations we subjected them to after the war in Sicily. This grants them that opportunity.'

Quintus hesitated for a moment. 'You're talking about war?'

Fabricius nodded. 'I think that's what it will come to, yes. There are those in the Senate who disagree with me, but I think they underestimate Hannibal. A man who has achieved what he has in a few short years would not have embarked on the siege of Saguntum without it being part of a larger plan. Hannibal wanted a war with Rome all along.'

How right you are, thought Hanno exultantly.

Quintus was also jubilant. 'Gaius and I can join the cavalry!'

Fabricius' obvious pride was tempered by Atia's reticence. Even she could not hide the sadness that flashed across her eyes. Her composure returned quickly. 'You will make a fine soldier.'

Quintus blew out his chest with satisfaction. 'I must tell Gaius. Can I go to Capua?'

Fabricius gave an approving nod. 'Go on. You'll need to hurry. It's not long until dark.'

'I'll come back tomorrow.' With a grateful smile, Quintus was gone.

Looking after him, Atia sighed. 'And the other matter?'

'There is some good news.' Seeing Aurelia's instant interest, Fabricius clammed up. 'I'll tell you later.'

Aurelia's face fell. 'Everything is so unfair,' she cried, and hurried off to her room.

Atia touched Fabricius' arm to still his rebuke. 'Let her go. It must be hard for her.'

Hanno was oblivious to the family drama. Suddenly, his desire to escape, to reach Iberia and join his countrymen in their conflict, was overwhelming. It was what he had dreamed of for so long! Yet his debt to Quintus loomed large in his mind too. Had it been repaid by what he'd done at the shepherd's hut or not? Hanno wasn't sure. Then there was Suniaton. How could he even entertain leaving without trying to find his best friend? Hanno was grateful when he heard Julius' voice calling him. The conflicting emotions in his head were threatening to tear him apart.

* * *

Time went by, and Hanno was still working in the kitchen. Although an answer regarding his obligation to Quintus evaded him yet, he could not bring himself to abandon the farm without some attempt to find Suniaton. How the quest would be achieved, Hanno had no idea. Apart from him, who knew, or even cared, where Suniaton was now? The unanswerable dilemma kept him awake at night, and even distracted him from his usual lustful thoughts about Elira. Tired and irritable, he paid little attention one day when Julius announced an exhaustive menu that Atia had ordered for the following evening. 'Apparently, she and the master are expecting an important visitor,' said Julius pompously. 'Caius Minucius Flaccus.'

'Who in the name of Hades is that?' asked one of the cooks.

Julius gave him a disapproving look. 'He's a senior figure in the Minucii clan, and the brother of a former consul.'

'He'll be an arrogant prick then,' muttered the cook.

Julius ignored the titters this produced. 'He's also a member of the embassy that has just returned from Carthage,' he declared as if the matter were of some importance to him.

Hanno's stomach turned over. 'Really? Are you sure?'

Julius' lips pursed. 'That's what I heard the mistress saying,' he snapped. 'Now get on with your work.'

Hanno's heart was thudding off his ribs like that of a caged bird as he went out to the storage sheds. Would Fabricius' visitor speak of what he'd seen? Hanno begged the gods that he would. Passing the entrance to the heated bathroom, he saw Quintus stripping off. Well for him, thought Hanno sourly. He hadn't had a hot bath since leaving Carthage.

Blithely unaware of Hanno's feelings, Quintus' excitement was rising by the moment. Wanting to look his best that evening, he bathed, before enjoying a massage by a slave. Sleepily imagining how Flaccus might recount everything that had gone on in Carthage, he was barely aware of Fabricius entering the room.

'This visit is very important, you know.'

Quintus opened his eyes. 'Yes, Father. And we will play our part in the war, if it comes.'

Fabricius half smiled. 'That goes without saying. When Rome calls, we answer.' Clasping his hands behind his back, he walked up and down in silence.

The feel of the strigil on his skin began to irritate Quintus, and he gestured at the slave to stop. 'What is it?'

'It's about Aurelia,' Fabricius answered.

'You've arranged to marry her off, then,' he said, shooting his father a bitter glance.

'It's not definite yet,' said Fabricius. 'But Flaccus liked what he heard of Aurelia when I visited him in the capital some time ago. Now he wants to see her beauty for himself.'

Quintus scowled at his naïveté. Why else would a high-ranking politician pay a social visit to equestrians as lowly as they?

'Come now,' said Fabricius sternly. 'You knew this would happen one day. It's for the good of the family. Flaccus is not that old, and his clan is powerful and well connected. With the support of the Minucii, the Fabricii could go far.' He stared at Quintus. 'In Rome, I mean. You understand what I'm saying?'

Quintus sighed. 'Does Aurelia know yet?'

'No.' It was Fabricius' turn to look troubled. 'I thought I would speak to you first.'

'Make me part of it?'

'Don't take that line with me. You would also benefit,' snapped his father.

Excitement flared in Quintus' breast, and he hated himself for it. He'd seen Aurelia mooning over Hanno. An impossible infatuation for her, but one he'd done nothing to end. And now this. 'What made you decide on Flaccus?'

'I've been trying to organise something for the last two years,' Fabricius replied. 'Searching for the right man for our family, and for Aurelia. It's a tricky business, but I think Flaccus could be the one. He was going to be passing close to here anyway upon his return from Carthage. All I did was to make sure that an invitation was waiting for him when he landed.'

Quintus was surprised by his father's cunning. No doubt his mother had had a hand in it, he thought. 'How old is he?'

'Thirty-five or so,' said Fabricius. 'That's a lot better than some of the old goats who wanted to meet her. I hope she appreciates that.' He paused. 'One last thing.'

Quintus looked up.

'Don't ask any questions about what happened in Carthage,' his father warned. 'It is still a matter of state secrecy. If Flaccus chooses to fill us in on some of the details, so be it. If he does not, it's none of our business to ask.' With that, he was gone.

Quintus lay back on the warm stone slab, but all his enjoyment was gone. He would go to Aurelia the moment his father had finished speaking with her. What he would say, Quintus had no idea. His mood dark, he got dressed. The best place to watch Aurelia's doorway unobtrusively was from a corner of the tablinum. Quintus made his way to the large reception room. He hadn't been there long when Hanno entered, carrying a tray of crockery.

Seeing Quintus, Hanno smiled. 'Looking forward to this evening?' I am, he thought with glee.

'Not really,' Quintus replied dourly.

Hanno raised his eyebrows. 'Why not? You don't receive many visitors.'

Quintus was surprised to find that his excitement about what Flaccus might say was muted by his friendship with Hanno. 'It's hard to explain,' he replied awkwardly.

At that moment, Fabricius strode from Aurelia's room, banging the door behind him. His jaw was set with anger.

Their conversation instantly came to an end. Hanno could only watch as Quintus entered his sister's chamber in turn. Hanno was genuinely fond of Aurelia. Part of him wondered what was going on, but part of him didn't care. Finally, Carthage was at war with Rome once more.

Somehow, he would be involved in it.

Quintus found Aurelia lying on her bed, huge sobs racking her body. He rushed to kneel by her side. 'It will be all right,' he whispered, reaching out to stroke her hair. 'Flaccus sounds like a good man.'

Her crying redoubled, and Quintus muttered a curse. Mentioning the man's name was the worst possible thing he could have done. Not knowing what to do, he rubbed Aurelia's shoulders comfortingly. They stayed in that position without talking for a long time. Finally, Aurelia rolled over. Her cheeks were red and blotchy, and her eyes swollen from weeping. 'I must look terrible,' she said.

Quintus gave her a crooked smile. 'You're still beautiful,' he replied.

She stuck out her tongue. 'Liar.'

'A bath will help,' advised Quintus. He put on a jovial face. 'Won't it?'

Aurelia could not keep up the pretence. 'What am I going to do?' she whispered miserably.

'It was going to happen sometime,' said Quintus. 'Why don't you give him the benefit of the doubt? If you really hate him, Father would not make you go ahead with the marriage.'

'I suppose not,' Aurelia replied dubiously. She thought for a moment. 'I know I have to do what Father says. It's so hard, though, especially when . . .' Her voice died away, and new tears filled her eyes.

Quintus raised a finger to her lips. 'Don't say it,' he whispered. 'You can't.' He didn't want to hear it spoken out loud.

With great effort, Aurelia regained control of her emotions. She nodded resolutely. 'Better get ready, then. I have to look my best tonight.'

Quintus drew her into a warm embrace. 'That's the spirit,' he whispered. Possessing courage was not an exclusively male quality, he realised. Nor was it confined to the battlefield or the hunt. Aurelia had just shown that she had plenty of it too.

Flaccus arrived mid-afternoon, accompanied by a large party of slaves and soldiers, and was immediately ushered to the best guest room to freshen up. Apart from his personal slaves, most of Flaccus' retinue stayed outside, where they were quartered in the farmyard. Hanno was busy in the kitchen and saw little of the proceedings for some time. An hour later, loud voices announced the appearance of Martialis and Gaius. They were greeted jovially by Fabricius, and guided to the banqueting hall off the courtyard where, following tradition, they were first served *mulsum*, a mixture of wine and honey. Elira performed this task, leaving Hanno to wait impatiently in the kitchen. As darkness fell, he walked around the courtyard, lighting the bronze oil lamps that hung from every pillar. At the corner furthest from the tablinum, Hanno sensed movement behind him. He turned, gaining an impression of a handsome man in a toga with thick black hair and a big nose before Flaccus disappeared into the banqueting hall. Quintus and his sister arrived soon after, wearing their best clothes. Hanno had never seen Aurelia wearing make-up before. To his surprise, he liked what he saw.

Finally, the meal was ready, and Hanno could enter the room with the other slaves. He was to remain there for the duration of the meal, serving food, clearing away plates and, most importantly of all, listening to the conversation. He waited attentively behind the left-hand couch, where Fabricius reclined with Martialis and Gaius. As an important guest, Flaccus had been given the central couch, while Atia, Quintus and an impassive Aurelia occupied the right-hand one. In customary fashion, the fourth side of the table had been left open.

Flaccus spent much of his time complimenting Aurelia on her

looks and trying to engage her in conversation. His attempts met with little initial success. Finally, when Atia began to glare at her openly, she started to respond. To Hanno, it was obvious that she was being insincere, merely doing what her mother wished. Flaccus did not seem to notice this, or that apart from Fabricius, the others present did not dare to address him. Quintus and Gaius alone cast frequent glances at Flaccus, hoping in vain for news of Carthage. Quaffing large amounts of mulsum and wine, the black-haired politician seemed more and more taken by Aurelia as the night went on.

Over the sweet platters, Flaccus turned to Fabricius. 'My compliments on your daughter. She is as beautiful as you said. More so, perhaps.'

Fabricius inclined his head gravely. 'Thank you.'

'I think we should talk further on this matter in the morning,' boomed Flaccus. 'Come to a mutually satisfactory arrangement.'

Fabricius allowed himself a small smile. 'That would be a great honour.'

Atia murmured her agreement.

'Excellent.' Flaccus looked at Hanno. 'More wine.'

Hanno hurried forward, his face a neutral mask. He wasn't sure how he felt about what had just been said. Not that it mattered, he reflected bitterly. Here I am a slave. His resentment over his status surged back, stronger than ever, and he dismissed his concern about Aurelia's possible betrothal. The bonds that tied him to the farm were weakening. If Aurelia married Flaccus, she would go to live in Rome. Quintus was always talking about joining the army. When he left, Hanno would be left friendless and alone. On the spot, he resolved to begin planning his escape.

Quintus had decided that Flaccus seemed quite personable and glanced sidelong at Aurelia. He was delighted to see no sign of distress in her face, and marvelled at her equanimity. Then he noted the slight flush to her cheeks, and her empty glass. Was she drunk? It wouldn't take much. Aurelia rarely consumed wine.

In spite of this, Quintus found his head full of the possibilities that an alliance between the Fabricii and Minucii would create. Aurelia and Flaccus would get used to each other, he told himself. That's the way most marriages worked. He reached out to touch Aurelia's hand. She smiled, and he was reassured.

The conversation flitted about for some time, with talk of the weather, the crops and the quality of the games in Capua compared to Rome. No one mentioned the one topic that everyone wanted to know about: what had happened in Carthage?

It was Martialis who eventually broached the subject. As was his wont, he had been drinking large amounts. Draining his cup yet again, he saluted Flaccus. 'They say that the Carthaginian wines are very drinkable.'

'They are agreeable enough,' accepted Flaccus. He pursed his lips. 'Unlike the people who produce them.'

Martialis was oblivious to Fabricius' frowns. 'Will we be seeing such vintages in Italy more often?' he asked with a wink.

Flaccus dragged his eyes away from Aurelia. 'Eh?'

'Tell us what happened in Carthage,' begged Martialis. 'We are all dying to know.'

Hanno held his breath, and he could see Quintus doing the same.

Slowly, Flaccus took in the rapt faces around him. His features took on a self-important expression, and he smiled, pompously. 'Nothing I say is to travel beyond these walls.'

'Of course not,' Martialis murmured. 'You can be assured of our discretion.'

Even Fabricius joined in with the buzz of agreement.

Satisfied, Flaccus began. 'I was but a minor member of the party, although I like to think my contribution was noted. We were led by the two consuls, Lucius Aemilius Paullus and Marcus Livius Salinator. Our spokesman was the former censor Marcus Fabius Buteo.' He let the important names sink in. 'From the start, it seemed that our mission would be successful. The omens were good, and the crossing from Lilybaeum uneventful. We reached Carthage three weeks ago to the day.'

Hanno closed his eyes and imagined the scene. The massive fortifications gleaming in the winter sun. The magnificent temple of Eshmoun dominating the top of Byrsa Hill. The twin harbours full of ships. Home, he thought with a jolt of longing. Will I ever see it again?

Flaccus' next words brought him back to earth with a jolt. 'Arrogant sons of whores,' he growled. He glanced at Atia. 'My apologies. But the most significant men in Rome had arrived, and who had they sent to meet us? A junior officer of the city guard.'

Martialis' face went purple with rage, and he nearly choked on a mouthful of wine.

Fabricius was of a calmer disposition. 'It must have been a mistake, surely,' he said.

Flaccus scowled. 'On the contrary. The gesture was quite deliberate. They had made up their minds before we even disembarked from our ships. Instead of being allowed time to wash and recover from the journey, we were escorted straight to the Senate.'

Martialis snorted. 'Typical bloody guggas. No sense of decorum.'

Aurelia cast Hanno a quick, sympathetic glance.

The Carthaginian was so angry that he dared not look back at her. He longed to smash the clay jug in his hands over Martialis' head, but of course he did nothing. Punishment aside, what Flaccus had to say next was of far more importance.

'And when you got there?' asked Quintus eagerly.

'Fabius announced who we were. No one responded. They just stood there looking at us. Waiting, like so many jackals around a corpse. And so Fabius demanded to know if Hannibal's attack on Saguntum had been carried out with their approval.' Flaccus paused, breathing heavily. 'Do you know what they did then?' A vein pulsed in his forehead. 'They laughed at us.'

Martialis slammed his beaker on the table. Fabricius spat a

curse, while Quintus and Gaius gaped at each other, stunned that anyone would treat the Republic's most prominent statesmen in such a manner. Atia took the opportunity to mutter something in Aurelia's ear. Hanno, meanwhile, had to bite the inside of his cheek to stop himself from laughing out loud. Carthage had not lost all of its pride when it lost Sicily and Sardinia to Rome, he reflected proudly.

'There were some who spoke out against Hannibal,' Flaccus conceded. 'The loudest among them was a fat man called Hostus.'

Treacherous bastard! thought Hanno. What I'd give to stick a knife in his belly.

'But they were shouted down by the vast majority, who disputed the treaty signed by Hasdrubal six years ago and rejected any need to acknowledge Saguntum's links with Rome. They were shouting and hurling abuse at us,' growled Flaccus. 'We took counsel with each other, and decided we had only one option.'

Quintus glanced at Hanno. He had had no idea that the Carthaginians would react with such force. Stunned by what he saw, he looked again. Quintus knew Hanno's body language well enough to realise that he *had* known. Flaccus' voice stopped him from dwelling on the matter further.

'Fabius walked into the middle of the chamber. That shut the guggas up,' said Flaccus fiercely. 'Gripping the folds of his toga, he told them that within he held both peace and war. They could have whichever they pleased. At his words, the place descended into chaos. It was impossible even to hear yourself speak.'

'Did they opt for war?' demanded Fabricius.

'No,' revealed Flaccus. 'Instead, the presiding suffete told Fabius that he should choose.'

By now everyone in the room, even Elira, was hanging on his every word.

'Fabius looked at us to confirm that we were of one mind, and then he told the guggas that he let fall war.' Flaccus barked a short, angry laugh. 'They've got balls, I'll grant them that. Fabius had hardly finished speaking when practically every single man in the chamber stood up and yelled, "We accept it!"'

Hanno found he could no longer conceal his delight. Picking up two handfuls of dirty plates, he headed for the kitchen. No one except Aurelia noticed him leave. But once outside the door, Hanno's desire to hear more was so great that he lingered on, eavesdropping.

'I always hoped that another war with Carthage could be avoided,' said Fabricius heavily. His jaw hardened. 'But they leave us no choice. Insulting you and your colleagues, and especially the consuls, in that manner is unforgivable.'

'Absolutely right,' thundered Martialis. 'The curs must be taught an even better lesson than last time.'

Flaccus was pleased by their reactions. 'Good,' he muttered. 'Why don't you both come with me to Rome? Much needs to be arranged, and we will need men who have fought Carthage before.'

'It would be my honour,' replied Fabricius.

'And mine,' added Martialis. An embarrassed look crossed his florid face, and he tapped his right leg. 'Except for this. It's an old injury, from Sicily. Nowadays, I can barely walk more than a quarter of a mile without stopping for a rest.'

'You have more than done your duty for Rome,' said Flaccus reassuringly. 'I shall just take Fabricius.'

Quintus was on his feet before he knew it. 'I want to fight too.'

Gaius echoed his cry a heartbeat later.

Flaccus' smile was patronising. 'Both quite the dogs of war, aren't you? But I'm afraid that you're still too young. This struggle needs to be won fast, and the best men to do that are veterans.'

'I'm seventeen,' protested Quintus. 'So is Gaius.'

Flaccus' face darkened. 'Remember whom you are speaking to,' he snapped.

'Quintus! Sit down,' Fabricius ordered. 'You too, Gaius.' As the two reluctantly obeyed, he turned to Flaccus. 'My apologies. They're eager, that's all.'

'It's of no matter. Their time will come,' Flaccus replied smoothly, shooting Quintus a look of venom. It was gone so fast that no one else noticed. Quintus wondered if he'd been mistaken, but a moment later he saw something else. Aurelia made her excuses and retired for the night. Flaccus watched her retreating back as a serpent might look at a mouse. Quintus blinked, trying to clear his head, which was fuzzy from wine. When he looked again, Flaccus' expression was benevolent. I must have been imagining it, he concluded. Quintus was then disappointed to see the three older men gather in a huddle and begin muttering in low voices. Atia jerked her head at him in a clear sign of dismissal. Frustrated, Quintus beckoned Gaius outside to the courtyard.

Their appearance startled Hanno. Having hidden from Aurelia, he was only just emerging from behind an ornamental statue. Looking guilty, he scuttled off to the kitchen.

Gaius frowned. 'What in Hades is he up to?'

Later, Quintus was not sure whether it was because of the wine he'd drunk or his anger at the treatment of the Roman embassy. Either way, he wanted to lash out at someone. 'Who cares?' he snapped. 'He's a gugga. Let him go.' Quintus regretted the words the instant they left his mouth. He made to walk after Hanno, but Gaius, who was laughing, dragged him over to a stone bench by the fountain. 'Let's talk,' his friend muttered drunkenly.

Quintus dared not pull away. The darkness concealed his stricken face.

His shoulders stiff with repressed fury, Hanno did not look back. It was ten more steps to the kitchen, where he clattered the dishes angrily into the sink. So much for friendship with a Roman, he thought, bitterness coursing through his veins. He knew that Aurelia was sympathetic towards him, but he could not be sure of anyone else. Especially Quintus. The anger he'd heard in all the nobles' voices at Flaccus' revelation was natural, yet it changed Hanno's situation completely. In principle, he was now an enemy. His own delight at the matter would have to be buried so deeply that no one could see it. In the close confines of the house, Hanno knew how difficult this would prove. He exhaled slowly. An important decision had just been made for him. He should run away. Soon. But to Carthage or Iberia? And was there any chance of finding Suniaton before he left?

Chapter X: Betrayal

The next morning Quintus had another hangover, and his memories of Flaccus' facial expressions were hazy. Enough disquiet remained in his mind, however, for him to seek out his father. He found Fabricius closeted in his office with Flaccus. The pair were busily drawing up Aurelia's betrothal papers, and looked irritated by the distraction. Fabricius brushed off Quintus' muttered request for a word. Seeing his son's disappointment, he relented slightly. 'Tell me later,' he said.

Glumly, Quintus shut the door. He had other things on his mind too. He had insulted Hanno cruelly and he was ashamed. The Carthaginian's status meant that Quintus could treat him in any way he chose, but of course that was not the point. He saved my life. We are friends now, thought Quintus. I owe him an apology. Yet his quest to resolve this problem proved as frustrating as his attempt to speak with his father. He found Hanno easily enough, but the Carthaginian pretended not to hear Quintus' voice when he called, and avoided all attempts to make eye contact. Quintus didn't want to make a scene, and there was so much going on that he could not even find a quiet corner to explain. Fabricius' decision to accompany Flaccus to Rome and thence to war meant that the place was a flurry of activity. Every household slave was occupied in one way or another. Clothes, furniture and blankets had to be packed, armour polished and weapons sharpened.

Quintus went miserably in search of Aurelia. He wasn't sure whether he should mention anything about Flaccus. All he had to go on were two fleeting glimpses, observed while under the influence of too much wine. He decided to see what frame of mind Aurelia was in before saying a word. If she was still feeling positive about the marriage, he would say nothing. The last thing Quintus wanted to do was upset his sister's fragile acceptance of her lot.

To his surprise, Aurelia was in excellent humour. 'He is so handsome,' she gushed. 'And not that old either. I think we will be very happy.'

Burying his doubts, Quintus nodded and smiled.

'He strikes me as being quite arrogant, but what man of his position isn't? His loyalty to Rome is beyond doubt, and that is all that matters.' Aurelia's face grew troubled. 'I felt so sorry for Hanno last night. The horrible names they were calling his people were so unnecessary. Have you spoken with him?'

Quintus looked away. 'No.'

Aurelia reacted with typical female intuition. 'What's wrong?' she demanded.

'Nothing,' Quintus replied. 'I have a hangover, that's all.'

She bent to catch his eye. 'Did you argue with Hanno?'

'No,' he answered. 'Yes. I don't know.'

Aurelia raised her eyebrows, and Quintus knew that she would not leave it alone until he told her. 'When I left with Gaius, it looked like Hanno had been eavesdropping outside the door,' he said.

'Is that surprising? We were talking about a war between his people and ours,' Aurelia observed tartly. 'What does it matter anyway? He was there in the room when Flaccus told us the most important part of his story.'

'I know,' Quintus muttered. 'It seemed suspicious, though.

Gaius wanted to challenge him, but I told him not to bother. That Hanno was just a gugga.'

Aurelia's hand rose to her mouth. 'Quintus! How could you?'

Quintus hung his head. 'I wanted to say sorry straightaway . . . but Gaius wanted to talk,' he finished lamely. 'I couldn't walk off and leave him.'

'I hope you've apologised this morning,' Aurelia said sternly.

Quintus could not get over Aurelia's level of self-assurance. It was as if her betrothal had added five years to her age. 'I've tried,' he answered. 'But there's too much going on to get a quiet moment alone with him.'

Aurelia pursed her lips. 'Father is leaving in a few hours. There will be plenty of time after that.'

Finally, Quintus met her gaze. 'Don't worry,' he said. 'I'll do it.'

He had cause to rethink his opinion of Flaccus later that morning. With the betrothal agreement signed, the black-haired politician suddenly started to make much of his new brother-in-law-to-be. 'No doubt this war with Carthage will be over quickly – maybe even before you've completed your military training,' he declared, throwing an arm around Quintus' shoulders. 'Never fear. There will be other conflicts for you to win glory in. The Gauls on our northern borders are forever causing trouble. So too are the Illyrians. Philip of Macedon cannot be trusted either. A brave young officer like you could go far indeed. Perhaps even make tribune.'

Quintus grinned from ear to ear. While the Fabricii were of equestrian rank, their status was not so high that it was likely he'd reach the tribuneship. Under the patronage of someone really powerful, however, the process would be much more straightforward. Flaccus' words did much to soothe Quintus' disappointment at not accompanying his father. 'I look forward to serving Rome,' he said proudly. 'Wherever it may send me.'

Flaccus clapped him on the back. 'That's the attitude.' Seeing

Aurelia, he pushed Quintus away. 'Let me talk with my betrothed before I go. It's a long time until June.'

Delighted by the prospect of a glittering military career, Quintus put down Flaccus' powerful shove as nothing more than the excitement of a prospective bridegroom. Aurelia was turning into a beautiful young woman. Who wouldn't want to marry her? Leaving Flaccus alone, Quintus went in search of his father.

'Aurelia!' called Flaccus, entering the courtyard.

Aurelia, who had been wondering what married life would be like, jumped. She made a stiff little bow. 'Flaccus.'

'Walk with me.' He made an inviting gesture.

Twin points of colour rose in Aurelia's cheeks. 'I'm not sure Mother would approve . . .'

'What do you take me for?' Flaccus' tone was mildly shocked. 'I would never presume to take you outside the villa without a chaperone. I meant a stroll here in the courtyard, where everyone can see us.'

'Naturally,' Aurelia replied, flustered. 'I'm sorry.'

'The fault is all mine for not explaining,' he said with a re-assuring smile. 'I merely thought that, with us to be wed, it would be good for us to spend a little time together. War is coming, and soon occasions such as this will be impossible.'

'Yes, of course.' She hurried to his side.

Flaccus drank her in. 'Bacchus can make the most crab-faced crone look appealing, and the gods know I drank enough of his juice to think that last night. But your beauty is even more evident in the light of the sun,' he said. 'That *is* a rare quality.'

Unused to such compliments, Aurelia blushed to the roots of her hair. 'Thank you,' she whispered.

They strolled around the perimeter of the courtyard. Awkward with the silence, Aurelia began pointing out the plants and trees that occupied much of the space. There were lemon, almond and fig trees, and vines snaking across a wooden latticework that formed an artificial shaded corridor. 'This is such a bad time of year to see it,' she said. 'During the summer, the place is so beautiful. By the Vinalia Rustica, you can barely move for the fruit.'

'I'm sure it's spectacular, but I didn't come here to talk about grapes.' Seeing her embarrassment increase, Flaccus continued, 'Tell me about yourself. What do you like to do?'

Anxious, Aurelia wondered what he'd want to hear. 'I enjoy speaking Greek. And I'm better at algebra and geometry than Quintus.'

The corners of his mouth twitched. 'Are you indeed? That's wonderful. An educated girl, then.'

She flushed again. 'I suppose.'

'You'd probably give me a run for my money. Mathematics was never my favourite subject.'

Aurelia's confidence grew a little. 'What about philosophy?'

He looked down his long nose at her. 'The concepts of *pietas* and *officium* were being taught to me before I'd even been weaned. My father made sure that serving Rome means everything to me and my brother. We had to be schooled too, of course. Before we had any military experience, he sent us to study at the Stoic school in Athens. I didn't enjoy my time there much, however. All they did was sit around and talk in stuffy debating chambers. It reminds me a little of the Senate.' Flaccus' face brightened. 'Soon, though, I might be granted a senior position in one of the legions. I'm sure that will be more to my style.'

Aurelia found his enthusiasm endearing. It reminded her of Quintus, which made her think of what he might achieve once she had married into such an important family. 'Your brother has already served as consul, hasn't he?'

'Yes,' Flaccus replied proudly. 'He crushed the Boii four years ago.'

Aurelia had never heard of the Boii, but she wasn't going to admit it. 'I've heard Father mention that campaign,' she said knowledgeably. 'It was a fine victory.'

'May the gods grant that I achieve the same level of success one day,' Flaccus said fervently. His gaze went distant for a moment before returning to Aurelia. 'Not to say I don't like ordinary pleasures like watching chariot races, or going riding, and hunting.'

'So do I,' Aurelia said without thinking.

He smiled indulgently. 'The racing in Rome is the best in Italy. I'll take you to see it as often as you wish.'

Aurelia felt slightly annoyed. 'That's not what I meant.'

There was a small frown. 'I don't understand.'

Her courage wavered for a moment. Then she thought naïvely, If he's to be my husband, we should tell each other everything. 'I love riding too.'

Flaccus' frown grew. 'You mean watching your father or Quintus as they train their horses?'

'No. I can ride.' She was delighted by his astonishment.

It was Flaccus' turn to be irritated. 'How? Who taught you?' he demanded.

'Quintus. He says I'm a natural.'

'Your brother taught you how to ride?'

Pinned by his direct stare, Aurelia's confidence began to seep away. 'Yes,' she muttered. 'I made him.'

Flaccus barked a short laugh. 'You *made* him? Fabricius mentioned none of this when he was singing your praises.'

Aurelia looked down. I should have kept my mouth shut, she thought. Lifting her head, she found Flaccus scrutinising her. She shifted uneasily beneath his gaze.

'Do you fight also?'

Aurelia's mouth opened at his unexpected tack.

He thrust his right arm forward, mimicking a sword thrust. 'Can you wield a gladius?'

Worried by what she'd already revealed, Aurelia kept her lips sealed.

'I asked you a question.' Flaccus' voice was soft, but his eyes were granite hard.

What I've done isn't a crime, thought Aurelia angrily. 'Yes, I can,' she retorted. 'I'm far better with a sling, though.'

Flaccus threw his hands in the air. 'I'm to be married to an Amazon!' he cried. 'Do your parents know of this?'

'Of course not.'

'No, I don't suppose Fabricius would be too pleased. I can only imagine what Atia's reaction might be.'

'Please don't tell them,' Aurelia begged. 'Quintus would be in so much trouble.'

He watched her for a moment, before a wolfish smile crossed his lips. 'Why would I say a word?'

Aurelia couldn't believe her ears. 'You don't mind?'

'No! It shows your Roman spirit, and it means that our sons will be warriors.' Flaccus held up a warning finger. 'Don't expect that you can carry on using weapons when we're married, however. Such behaviour is not acceptable in Rome.'

'And riding?' Aurelia whispered.

'We'll see,' he said. He saw her face fall, and a strange look entered his eyes. 'My estate outside the capital is very large. Unless I tell them, no one knows what goes on there.'

Overwhelmed by Flaccus' reaction, Aurelia missed the silky emphasis he laid on the last seven words. Perhaps marriage would not be as bad as she'd thought. She took his arm. 'It's your turn to tell me about yourself now,' she murmured.

He gave her a pleased look, and began.

Quintus found his father outside, supervising the loading of his baggage on to a train of mules.

Fabricius smiled as he emerged. 'What was it that you wanted to tell me earlier?'

'It was nothing important,' Quintus demurred. He had decided to give Flaccus the benefit of the doubt. He cast a dubious eye over the pack animals, which were laden down with every piece of his father's military equipment. 'How long do you think this war will last? Flaccus seems certain that it will be over in a few months.'

Fabricius checked that no one was in earshot. 'I think he's a little overconfident. You know what politicians can be like.'

'But Flaccus is talking about getting married in June.'

Fabricius winked. 'He wanted to settle on a date. I obliged. What could be better than the most popular month of the year? And if it can't take place because we're still on campaign, the betrothal agreement ensures that it will happen at some stage.'

Quintus grinned at Fabricius' guile. He thought for a moment, deciding that his father was more likely to be correct than Flaccus about the war's duration. 'I'm already old enough to enlist.'

Fabricius' face turned serious. 'I know,' he said. 'As well as keeping an eye on you, I have asked Martialis to enrol you in the local cavalry unit, alongside Gaius. In my absence, your mother is obviously responsible for Aurelia and the care of the farm, but you will have to help her in every way possible. Yet I see no reason why you should not also begin your training.'

Quintus' eyes glittered with delight.

'Don't get any madcap ideas,' his father warned. 'There is no question of being called up in the immediate future. The horsemen supplied by Rome and its surrounding area will be more than enough for the moment.'

Quintus did his best not to look disappointed.

Fabricius took him by the shoulders. 'Listen to me. War is not all valour and glory: far from it. It's about blood, filth and fighting until you can barely grip a sword. You'll see terrible things. Men bleeding to death for lack of a tourniquet. Comrades and friends dying in front of you, crying for their mothers.'

It was becoming more difficult to hold his father's gaze.

'You are a fine young man,' said Fabricius proudly. 'Your time to fight in the front line will come. Until then, gain every bit of experience you can. If that means you miss the war with Carthage, so be it. Those initial weeks of training are vital if you want to survive more than the first few moments of a battle.'

'Yes, Father.'

'Good,' said Fabricius, looking satisfied. 'May the gods keep you safe and well.'

'And you also.' Despite his best effort, Quintus' voice wobbled.

Atia waited until Quintus had gone inside before emerging. 'He's almost a man,' she said wistfully. 'It only seems the blink of an eye since he was playing with his wooden toys.'

'I know.' Fabricius smiled. 'The years fly by, don't they? I can remember saying goodbye to you before leaving for Sicily as if it were yesterday. And here we are again, in much the same situation.'

Atia reached up to touch his face. 'You have to come back to me, do you hear?'

'I will do my best. Make sure that the altar is well stocked with offerings,' he warned. 'The lares have to be kept happy.'

She pretended to look shocked. 'You know I'll do that every day.'

Fabricius chuckled. 'I do. Just as you know that I'll pray daily to Mars and Jupiter for their protection.'

Atia's face became solemn. 'Are you still sure that Flaccus is a good choice for Aurelia?'

His brows lowered. 'Eh?'

'Is he the right man?'

'I thought he came across well last night,' said Fabricius with a surprised look. 'Arrogant, of course, but one expects that from someone of his rank. He was plainly taken with Aurelia too, which was good. He's ambitious, presentable and wealthy.' He eyed Atia. 'Isn't that enough?'

She pursed her lips.

'Atia?'

'I can't put my finger on it,' she said eventually. 'I don't trust him.'

'You need more than a vague idea, surely, for me to break off a betrothal with this potential?' asked Fabricius, looking irritated. 'Remember how much money we owe!'

'I'm not saying that you should call off the arrangement,' she said in a conciliatory tone.

'What then?'

'Just keep an eye on Flaccus when you're in Rome. You'll be spending plenty of time with him. That will give you a far better measure of the man than we could ever gain in one night.' She caressed his arm. 'That's not too much to ask, is it?'

'No,' he murmured. A relenting smile twitched across his lips, and he bent to kiss her. 'You do have a knack of sniffing out the rotten apple in the barrel. I'll trust you one more time.'

'Stop teasing me,' she cried. 'I'm serious.'

'I know you are, my love. And I'll do what you say.' He tapped the side of his nose. 'Flaccus won't have a clue, but I'll be watching his every move.'

Atia's expression lightened. 'Thank you.'

Fabricius gave her backside an affectionate squeeze. 'Now, why don't we say goodbye properly?'

Atia's look grew kittenish. 'That sounds like an excellent idea.' Taking his hand, she led him into the house.

An hour later, and a deathly quiet hung over the house. Promising a quick victory over the Carthaginians, Fabricius and Flaccus had departed for Rome. Feeling thoroughly depressed, Quintus sought out Hanno. There was little left to do in the way of household chores, and the Carthaginian could not refuse when Quintus asked him out into the courtyard.

An awkward silence fell the instant they were alone.

I'm not going to speak first, thought Hanno. He was still furious.

Quintus scuffed the toe of one sandal along the mosaic. 'About last night,' he began.

'Yes?' snapped Hanno. His voice, his manner was not that of a slave. At that moment, he didn't care.

Quintus bit back his reflex, angry response. 'I'm sorry,' he said sharply. 'I was drunk, and I didn't mean what I said.'

Hanno looked in Quintus' eyes and saw that, despite his tone, the apology was genuine. Immediately, he was on the defensive. This wasn't what he had expected, and he wasn't yet willing to back down himself. 'I am a slave,' he growled. 'You can address me in whatever way you please.'

Quintus' face grew pained. 'First and foremost, you are my friend,' he said. 'And I shouldn't have spoken to you the way I did last night.'

Hanno considered Quintus' words in silence. Before being enslaved, any foreigner with the presumption to call him 'gugga' would have received a bloody nose, or worse. Here, he had to smile and accept it. Not for much longer, Hanno told himself furiously. Just keep up the pretence for now. He nodded in apparent acceptance. 'Very well. I acknowledge your apology.'

Quintus grinned. 'Thank you.'

Neither knew quite what to say next. Despite Quintus' attempt to make amends, a distance now yawned between them. As a patriotic Roman citizen, Quintus would back his government's decision to enter into conflict with Carthage to the hilt. Hanno, while unable to join Hannibal's army, would do the same for his people. It drove a wedge deep into their friendship, and neither knew how to remove it.

Long moments dragged by, and still neither spoke. Quintus didn't want to mention the impending war because both had such strong feelings about it. He wanted to suggest some weapons practice, but that also seemed like a bad idea: for all that he now trusted Hanno, it seemed too much like the impending combat between Roman and Carthaginian. Irritated, he waited for Hanno to speak first. Angry yet, and fearful of giving away something of his escape plan, Hanno kept his lips firmly shut.

Both wished that Aurelia were present. She would have laughed and dissipated the tension in a heartbeat. There was no sign of her, however.

This is pointless, thought Hanno at last. He took a step towards the kitchen. 'I'd best get back to work.'

Irritated, Quintus moved out of his way. 'Yes,' he said stiffly.

As he walked away, Hanno was surprised to feel sadness rising in his chest. For all of his current resentment, he and Quintus shared a strong bond, forged by the incredible, random manner of his purchase, followed by the fight at the shepherd's hut. Another thought struck Hanno. It must have taken a lot for Quintus to come and apologise, particularly because of their difference in status. Yet here *he* was, haughtily walking off as if he were the master, and not the slave. Hanno turned, an apology rising to his lips, but it was too late.

Quintus was gone.

Several weeks passed, and the weather grew warm and sunny. Encouraged by the officers, widespread rumours of Hannibal's intentions had spread throughout the huge tented encampment outside the walls of New Carthage. It was all part of the general's plan. Because of the vastness of his host, it was impossible to inform every soldier directly about what was going to happen. This way, the message could be put across rapidly. By the time Hannibal called for a meeting of his commanders, everyone knew that they would be heading for Italy.

The entire army assembled in formations before a wooden platform not far from the gates. The soldiers covered an enormous area of ground. There were thousands of Libyans and Numidians, and even greater numbers of Iberians from dozens of tribes. Roughly dressed men from the Balearic Islands waited alongside rows of proud, imperious Celtiberians. Hundreds of Ligurians and Gauls were also present, men who had left their lands and homes weeks before so that they could join the general who would wage war on Rome. A small proportion of the soldiers would be able to see and hear whoever stood before them, but interpreters had been positioned at regular intervals to relay the news to the rest. There would only be a short delay before everyone present heard Hannibal's words.

Malchus, Sapho and Bostar stood proudly at the front of their Libyan spearmen, whose bronze helmets and shield bosses glittered in the morning sun. The trio knew exactly what was going to happen, but the same nervous excitement controlled them all. Since returning from their mission weeks before, Bostar and Sapho had put their differences aside to prepare for this moment. Now history was about to be made, in much the same fashion as when Alexander of Macedon had set forth on his extraordinary journey more than a hundred years previously. The greatest adventure of their lives was just beginning. With it, as their father said, came the chance of further revenge for Hanno. Although he didn't voice it, Malchus treasured a tiny, deeply buried hope that he might actually be alive. So too did Bostar, but Sapho had given up trying to feel anything similar. He was still glad that Hanno was gone. Malchus gave Sapho more attention and praise now than he could ever remember receiving before. And Hannibal knew his name!

The army did not have to wait long. Followed by his brothers Hasdrubal and Mago, the cavalry commander Maharbal, and the senior infantry officer Hanno, Hannibal approached the platform and climbed into view. A group of trumpeters came last, and filed around in front of the general's position, where they waited for their orders. Their leaders' appearance caused spontaneous cheering to break out among the assembled troops. Even the officers joined in. The men whistled and shouted, stamped their feet on the ground and clashed their weapons off their shields. As those who could not see joined in, the clamour swelled immeasurably. On and on it went, louder and louder, in a dozen tongues. And, as he had done on similar occasions, Hannibal did nothing to stop it. Raising both his arms, he let his soldiers' acclaim wash over him. This was his hour, which he had spent years preparing for, and moments like this boosted morale infinitely more than a host of minor victories.

Finally, Hannibal signalled to the musicians. Raising their instruments to their lips, the men blew a short set of notes. It was the call to arms, the same sound that alerted soldiers to the nearby presence of enemy forces. Immediately, the crescendo of sound died away, leaving in its place an expectant hush. Bostar excitedly nudged Sapho in the ribs, and received a similar dig in return. An admonitory look from Malchus had them both standing to attention as if on parade. This was no time for childish behaviour.

'Soldiers of Carthage,' Hannibal began. 'We stand on the brink of a great adventure. But there are those in Rome who would stop us from the outset.' He held up a hand to quell his men's angry response. 'Would you hear the words of the latest Roman embassy to visit Carthage?'

A few moments went by as the interpreters did their work, and then an enormous cry of affirmation went up.

'"The heinous and unwarranted attack on Saguntum cannot go unanswered. Deliver to us, in chains, the man they call Hannibal Barca, and all of his senior officers, and Rome will consider the matter closed. If Carthage does not comply with this request, it should consider itself at war with the Republic."' Hannibal paused, letting the translations sink in, and his soldiers' fury build. He gestured dramatically at those behind him on the platform. 'Should these men and I hand ourselves in to the nearest Roman ally so that justice can be done?'

Again, a short delay. But the roar of 'NO!' that followed exceeded the combined volume of all the cries that had gone before.

Hannibal smiled briefly. 'I thank you for your loyalty,' he said, sweeping his right arm from left to right, encompassing the entire host.

Another immense cheer shredded the air.

'Instead of accepting Rome's offer then, I would lead most of you to Italy. To carry the war to our enemies,' Hannibal announced to more deafening acclaim. 'Some must remain here, under the command of my brother Hasdrubal; your mission is to protect our Iberian territory. The rest will march with me. Because the Romans control the sea, we will travel overland and take them by surprise. You might imagine that we would be alone in Italy, and surrounded by hostile forces. But do not fear! Theirs is a fertile region, and ripe for the plunder. We will also have many allies. Rome controls less of the peninsula than you might think. The tribes in Cisalpine Gaul have promised to join us, and I have no doubt that the situation will be the same in the central and southern parts. It will not be an easy struggle, and I ask only those men who would freely accompany me to engage in this enterprise.' Hannibal let his gaze wander from formation to formation, catching the eye of individual soldiers. 'With all of your help,' he continued, 'the Republic will be torn asunder. Destroyed, so that it can no longer threaten Carthage!' Calmly, he waited for his message to spread.

It did not take long.

The noise of over a hundred thousand men expressing their agreement resembled a rumbling, threatening thunder. Malchus, Sapho and Bostar trembled to hear it.

Hannibal raised a clenched fist in the air. 'Will you follow me to Italy?'

There was but one answer to his question. And, as every man in his army gave voice to the loudest cry of all, Hannibal Barca stood back and smiled.

In the weeks following their argument, Hanno and Quintus both made half-hearted attempts at reconciliation. None succeeded.

Hurt by the other's attitude, and full of youthful self-importance, neither would give way. Soon they had virtually stopped talking to one another. It was a vicious circle from which there was no escape. Aurelia did her best to mediate, but her efforts were in vain. Yet for all of his resentment, Hanno had realised that he could not now run away. Despite his feud with Quintus, he owed him and Aurelia too much. And so, growing increasingly morose, he remained, wary always of Agesandros' menacing presence in the background. Quintus, meanwhile, threw himself into his cavalry training with the socii. He was often absent from the house for days at a time, which suited him fine. It meant that he didn't even have to see Hanno, let alone speak to him.

Spring was well underway when a note from Fabricius arrived. Followed by an eager Aurelia, Atia took it to the courtyard, which was filled with watery sunshine. Quintus, who was outside with Agesandros, would have to hear the news later.

Aurelia watched excitedly as her mother opened the missive and began to read. 'What does it say?' she demanded after a moment.

Atia looked up. The disappointment on her face was clear. 'It's a typical man's letter. Full of information about politics and what's going on in Rome. There's even a bit about some chariot race he went to the other day, but almost nothing about how he's feeling.' She traced a finger down the page. 'He asks after me, obviously, and you and Quintus. He hopes that there are no problems on the farm.' At last Atia smiled. 'Flaccus has asked him to send you his warmest regards, and says that although your marriage will have to be postponed because of the war, he cannot wait until the day it comes to pass. Your father has given him permission to write to you directly, so you may receive a letter from him soon.'

Aurelia was pleased by news of the postponement, but the thought of her wedding day – and night – still made her turn scarlet. Catching sight of Hanno in the kitchen doorway, she went an even brighter shade of red. His being a slave did not stop her from thinking – yet again – that, despite his newly crooked nose, he was extremely good-looking. For an instant, Flaccus was replaced by Hanno in her mind's eye. Aurelia stifled a gasp and shoved the shocking image away. 'That's nice. What else has Father to say?'

Hanno was oblivious to Aurelia's emotions. He was pleased because Julius had just told him to sweep the courtyard, which in turn allowed him to listen in on the conversation. With his ears pricked, he poked the broom into the crevices gaping between some of the tesserae on the mosaic floor, carefully hooking out as much dirt as possible.

Atia read on, sounding more interested. 'The majority of what he writes about is the Republic's response to Hannibal. The Minucii and their allies are working tirelessly to help the preparations for war. Flaccus hopes to be made tribune of one of the new legions. Most importantly of all, Tiberius Sempronius Longus and Publius Cornelius Scipio, the two new consuls, have been granted the provinces of Sicily and Africa, and Iberia, respectively. The mission of the former is to attack Carthage while that of the latter is to confront, and defeat, Hannibal. Father is pleased that he and Flaccus will serve with Scipio.'

'That's because all the glory will fall on the army that defeats Hannibal,' mused Aurelia. Sometimes she wished she were a man, so that she too could go to war.

'Men are all the same. We women have to stay behind and worry,' said her mother with a sigh. 'Let's just ask the gods to bring both of them back safely.'

Hanno didn't like what he had heard. Hated it, in fact. Stinking bloody Romans, he thought bitterly. There were no generals of any ability in Carthage, which meant that the Senate would recall Hannibal to defend the city, thus ending his plans to attack Italy. His departure would leave Iberia, Carthage's richest colony, at the mercy of an invading Roman army. Hanno's fingers clenched furiously on his broom handle. The war seemed over before it had begun.

Aurelia frowned. 'Didn't an assault on Carthage come close to succeeding in the previous war?'

'Yes. And Father says that whatever Hannibal's qualities, Rome will be victorious. We have no reason to believe that the Carthaginians' resolve is any stronger than it was twenty years ago.'

Hanno's black mood grew even worse. Fabricius was right. His city's record in the face of direct attacks was not exactly glorious. Of course Hannibal's return would make a huge difference, but would it be enough? His army wouldn't be with him: even without the Romans' control of the seas, the general simply didn't possess enough ships to transport tens of thousands of troops back to Africa.

It was then that Quintus arrived. Instantly, he took in Aurelia standing over his mother with the letter in her hand. 'Is that from Father?'

'Yes,' Atia replied.

'What news does he send?' he asked eagerly. 'Has the Senate decided on a course of action?'

'To attack Carthage and Iberia at the same time,' answered Aurelia.

'What a fantastic idea! They won't know what hit them,' Quintus cried. 'Where is Father to be sent?'

'Iberia. So too is Flaccus,' said Atia.

'What else?'

Atia handed the parchment to Quintus. 'Read it for yourself. Life goes on here, and I have to talk to Julius about the provisions that need buying in Capua.' She brushed past Hanno without as much as a second glance.

Hanno's anger crystallised. Whatever debt he might owe, it was time to run away. Carthage would now need every sword she could get. Nothing and no one else mattered. What about Suni?

221

asked his conscience. I have no idea where he is, thought Hanno desperately. What chance is there of finding him?

Quintus scanned the letter at top speed. 'Father and Flaccus are going to Iberia,' he muttered excitedly. 'And I am nearly finished my training.'

'What are you talking about?' Aurelia demanded.

He gave her a startled look. 'Nothing, nothing.'

Aurelia knew her brother well. 'Don't go getting any crazy ideas,' she warned. 'Father said you were to remain here until called for.'

'I know.' Quintus scowled. 'From the sound of it, though, the war *will* actually be over in a few months. I don't want to miss it.' His gaze flickered across the courtyard and made contact with Hanno. Instantly, Quintus glanced away, but it was too late.

Hanno's fury overflowed at last. 'Are you happy now?' he hissed.

'What do you mean?' Quintus replied defensively.

'The guggas will be defeated, again. Put in their rightful place. I expect you're delighted.'

Quintus' face grew red. 'No, that's not how it is.'

'Isn't it?' Hanno shot back. Clearing his throat, he spat on the mosaic floor.

'How dare you?' Quintus roared, taking a step towards Hanno. 'You're nothing but a—'

'Quintus!' cried Aurelia, aghast.

With great effort, her brother stopped himself from saying any more.

Contempt twisted Hanno's face. 'A slave. Or a gugga! Is that what you were going to say?'

Quintus' visage turned a deeper shade of crimson. Bunching his fists with anger, he turned away.

'I've had enough of this.' Hanno grabbed his broom.

Aurelia could take no more. 'Stop it, both of you! You're acting like children.'

Her words made no difference. Quintus stormed out of the house, and Aurelia followed him. Hanno retreated to the kitchen, where misery settled over him as it never had before. The news he'd heard a few months before, of Hannibal's successful siege of Saguntum, and the challenge it had issued, had bolstered his flagging spirits. Given him a reason to go on. Fabricius' letter had destroyed this utterly. Rome's plan seemed unbeatable. Even if he reached Hannibal's army, what difference could he make?

Aurelia came looking for Hanno upon her return. She found him slumped on a stool in the kitchen. Ignoring the other slaves' curious stares, she dragged Hanno outside. 'I've spoken to Quintus,' she muttered the moment they were alone. 'He didn't mean to offend you. It was just a spontaneous reaction to you spitting.' She gave Hanno a reproachful look. 'That was so rude.'

Hanno flushed, but he didn't apologise. 'He was gloating at me.'

'I know it seemed like that,' said Aurelia. 'But I don't think that's what he was doing.'

'Wasn't it?' Hanno shot back.

'No,' she replied softly. 'Quintus isn't like that.'

'Why did he call me a gugga originally, then?'

'People say things that they don't mean when they're drunk. I suppose that you haven't called him any names in your head since?' Aurelia asked archly.

Stung, Hanno did not answer.

Aurelia glanced around carefully, before reaching out to touch his face.

Startled by the intimacy this created, Hanno felt his anger dissipate. He looked into her eyes.

Alarmed by her suddenly pounding heart, Aurelia lowered her hand. 'On the surface, this argument looks quite simple,' she began. 'If it weren't for your misfortune, you would be a free man and, in all probability, enlisting in the Carthaginian army.

Like Quintus will do in the legions. There would be nothing wrong with either of those actions. Yet Quintus is free to do as he chooses, while you are a slave.'

That's it in a nutshell, thought Hanno angrily.

Aurelia wasn't finished. 'The real reason, however, is that first you, and then Quintus, were hurt by what the other said. Both of you are too damn proud to make a sincere apology and put it behind you.' She glared at him. 'I'm sick of it.'

Amazed by Aurelia's insight and sincerity, Hanno gave in. The quarrel had been going on long enough. 'You're right,' he said. 'I'm sorry.'

'It's not me you should be saying that to.'

'I know.' Hanno considered his next words with care. 'I will apologise to him. But Quintus has to know that, whatever the law of this land, I am no slave. I never will be.'

'Deep down, I'm sure he knows that. That's why he stopped himself from calling you one earlier,' Aurelia replied. Her face grew sad. 'Obviously, I don't think of you like that. But to everyone else, you *are* a slave.'

Hanno was about to tell Aurelia of his plans, when, out of the corner of his eye, he sensed movement. Through the open doors of the tablinum, he could see into part of the atrium. Outside the square of floor illuminated by the hole in its roof, everything lay in shadow. There Hanno could discern a tall figure, watching them. Instinctively, he pulled away from Aurelia. When Agesandros walked into the light, Hanno's stomach constricted with fear. What had he seen or heard? What would he do?

Aurelia saw the Sicilian in the same moment. She drew herself up proudly, ready for any confrontation.

To their surprise, Agesandros came no nearer. A tiny smile flickered across his face, and then he disappeared whence he had come.

Hanno and Aurelia turned back to each other, but Elira and another domestic slave emerged from the kitchen. The brief moment of magic they had shared was gone. 'I will talk to Quintus,' said Aurelia reassuringly. 'Whatever happens, you must hold on to your friendship. As we two will.'

Keen to make things as they were before he left the farm for ever, Hanno nodded. 'Thank you.'

Unfortunately, Aurelia was unable to remonstrate with her brother that day. As she told Hanno later, Quintus had taken off for Capua without a word to anyone but the bowlegged slave who worked in the stable. The afternoon passed and night fell, and it became apparent that he would not be returning. Hanno didn't know whether to feel angry or worried by this development. 'Don't be concerned,' Aurelia said before retiring. 'Quintus does this sometimes, when he needs time to think. He stays at Gaius' house, and returns in a few days.'

There was nothing Hanno could do. He lay back on his bedroll and dreamed of escape.

Sleep was a long time coming.

Chapter XI: The Quest for Safe Passage

After the fall of Saguntum, Bostar took to visiting his wounded men every morning, talking to those who were conscious and passing his hand over those who were still asleep, or who would never wake. There were more than thirty soldiers in the large tent, of whom half would probably never fight again. Despite the horror of his soldiers' injuries, Bostar had begun to feel grateful for his losses. All things considered, they had been slight. Far more Saguntines had died when Hannibal's troops had entered the city, howling like packs of rabid wolves. For an entire day, the predominant sound throughout Saguntum had been that of screams. Men's. Women's. Children's. Bostar squeezed his eyes shut and tried to forget, but he couldn't. Butchering unarmed civilians and engaging in widespread rape was not how he made war. While he hadn't tried to stop his men – had Hannibal not promised them a free rein? – Bostar had not taken part in the slaughter. Commanded by their general to guard the chests of gold and silver that had been found in the citadel, Malchus had not either. Bostar sighed. Inevitably, Sapho had.

A moment later, Malchus' touch on his shoulder made him jump. 'It's good that you're up so early checking on them.' Malchus indicated the injured men in their blankets.

'It's my job,' Bostar replied modestly, knowing that his father would have already visited his own casualties.

'It is.' Malchus fixed him with a solemn stare. 'And I think Hannibal has another one for you. Us.'

Bostar's heart thudded off his ribs. 'Why?'

'We've all been summoned to the general's tent. I wasn't told why.'

Excitement filled Bostar. 'Does Sapho know?'

'No. I thought you could tell him.'

'Really?' Bostar tried to keep his tone light. 'If you wish.'

Malchus gave him a knowing look. 'Do you think I haven't noticed how you two have been with each other recently?'

'It's nothing serious,' lied Bostar.

'Then why are you avoiding my gaze?' demanded Malchus. 'It's about Hanno, isn't it?'

'That's how it started,' Bostar replied. He began to explain, but his father forestalled him.

'There are only two of you now,' said Malchus sadly. 'Life is short. Resolve your differences, or one of you might find that it's too late.'

'You're right,' replied Bostar firmly. 'I'll do my best.'

'As you always do.' Malchus' voice was proud.

A pang of sadness tore at Bostar's heart. Did I do my best by letting Hanno go? he wondered.

'I'll see you both outside the headquarters in half an hour.' Malchus left him to it.

After telling his orderly to polish his armour, Bostar headed straight for Sapho's tent. There wasn't much time for getting ready, never mind a reconciliation. But their father had asked, so he would try.

Recognising the tent lines of Sapho's phalanx by their standard, Bostar quickly located the largest tent, which, like his, was pitched on the unit's right. The main flap was closed, which meant that his brother was either still in bed, or busy with his duties. Given his brother's recent habits, Bostar suspected the former. 'Sapho?' he called.

There was no answer.

Bostar tried again, louder.

Nothing.

Bostar took a step away. 'He must be with his men,' he said to himself in surprise.

'Who is it?' demanded an annoyed voice.

'Of course he's not,' Bostar muttered, turning back. He untied the thong that kept the tent flap closed. 'Sapho! It's me.' A moment later, he threw wide the leather. Sunlight flooded inside, and Bostar lifted a hand to his nose. The reek of stale sweat and spilt wine was overpowering. Stepping over the threshold, he picked his way over discarded pieces of clothing and equipment. Bostar was shocked to see that every item was filthy. Sapho's shield, spear and sword were the only things that had been cleaned. They leaned against a wooden stand to the side. He came to a halt before Sapho's bed, a jumble of blankets and animal skins. His brother's bleary eyes regarded him from its depths. 'Good morning,' said Bostar, trying to ignore the smell. He hasn't even washed, he thought with disgust.

'To what do I owe the pleasure?' Sapho's voice was acid.

'We've been summoned to a meeting with Hannibal.'

Sapho's lips thinned. 'The general told you that over breakfast, did he?'

Bostar sighed. 'Despite what you may think, I didn't save Hannibal's life to curry favour, or to make you jealous. You know I'm not like that.' He was pleased when Sapho's eyes dropped away. He waited, but there was no further response. Bostar pressed on. 'Father sent me. We need to be there in less than half an hour.'

Finally, Sapho sat up. He winced. 'Gods, my head hurts. And it tastes like something died in my mouth.'

Bostar kicked the amphora at his feet. 'Drank too much of this?'

Sapho gave him a rueful grin. 'Not half! Some of my men broke into a wine merchant's when the city fell. We've kept it under guard since. You should see the place. There's vintage stuff from all over the Mediterranean!' His expression grew hawkish. 'Shame his three daughters aren't still alive. We had some fun with them, I can tell you.'

Bostar wanted to punch Sapho in the face, but instead he proffered a hand. 'Get up. We don't want to be late. Father thinks Hannibal has a task for us.'

Sapho looked at Bostar's outstretched arm for a moment before he accepted it. Swaying gently, he looked around at the chaos of his tent floor. 'I suppose I'd better start cleaning my breastplate and helmet. Can't appear in front of Hannibal with filthy gear, can I?'

'Can't your orderly do it?'

Sapho made a face. 'No. He's down with the flux.'

Bostar frowned. Sapho was in no state to wash himself, prepare his uniform and present himself to their general in the time remaining. Part of him wanted to leave his brother to it. That's what he deserves, Bostar thought. The rest of him felt that their feud had been going on too long. He made a snap judgement. His own servant would have everything ready by now. It would only take him a few moments to get ready. 'Go and stick your head in a barrel of water. I'll clean your armour and helmet.'

Sapho's eyebrows rose. 'That's kind of you,' he muttered.

'Don't think I'm going to do it for you every day,' Bostar warned. He gave Sapho a shove. 'Get a move on. We don't want to be late. Hannibal must have something special lined up for us.'

At this, Sapho's pace picked up. 'True,' he replied. He stopped by the tent's entrance.

Bostar, who was already following with Sapho's filthy breastplate, paused. 'What?'

'Thank you,' said Sapho.

Bostar nodded. 'That's all right.'

The air between them grew a shade lighter, and for the first time in months, they smiled at each other.

Bostar and Sapho found their father waiting for them near Hannibal's tent. Malchus eyed their gleaming armour and helmets and gave an approving nod.

'What's this about, Father?' asked Sapho.

'Let's go and find out,' Malchus answered. He led the way to the entrance, where two dozen smartly turned-out scutarii stood. 'The general is expecting us.'

Recognising Malchus, the lead scutarius saluted. 'If you'll follow me, sir.'

As they were led inside, Bostar winked at Sapho, who returned the gesture. Excitement gripped them both. Although they had met Hannibal before, this was the first time they'd been invited into his headquarters.

In the tent's main section, they found Hannibal, his brothers Hasdrubal and Mago, and two other senior officers grouped around a table upon which a large map was unrolled. The scutarius came to a halt and announced them.

Hannibal turned. 'Malchus. Bostar and Sapho. Welcome!'

Father and sons saluted crisply.

'You will know my brother Hasdrubal,' said Hannibal, nodding at the corpulent, brooding man with a florid complexion and full lips beside him. 'And Mago.' He indicated the tall, thin figure whose eager, hawk-like face and eyes threatened to fix one to the spot. 'This is Maharbal, my cavalry commander, and Hanno, one of my top infantry officers.' The first man had a mop of unruly black hair and a ready smile, and the other a stolid but dependable look.

The trio saluted again.

'For many years, Malchus acted as my eyes and ears in

Carthage,' Hannibal explained. 'Yet when the time came for first his sons, and then he himself, to join me here in Iberia, no one was better pleased than I. They are good men all, and they proved their worth more than once during the siege, most recently when Bostar saved my life.'

The officers murmured in loud appreciation.

Malchus inclined his head, while Bostar flushed at the attention. Beside him, he was aware of Sapho glowering. Bostar cursed inwardly, praying that the fragile peace between him and his brother had not just been broken.

Hannibal clapped his hands together. 'To business! Come and join us.'

They eagerly crossed to the table, where the others made room.

At once Bostar's eyes drank in the undulating coast of Africa, and Carthage, their city. The island of Sicily, almost joining their homeland to its arch-enemy, Italy.

'Obviously, we are here, at Saguntum.' Hannibal tapped his right forefinger halfway up the east coast of the Iberian peninsula. 'And our destination is here.' He thumped the boot-like shape of Italy. 'How best to strike at it?'

Silence reigned. It was an affront to every Carthaginian's pride that Rome enjoyed supremacy over the western Mediterranean, an historical preserve of Carthage. Transporting the army by ship would be foolish in the extreme. Yet no one dared to suggest the only alternative.

Hannibal took the initiative. 'There will be no assault by sea. Even if we took the short route to Genua, our entire enterprise could be undone in a single battle.' He moved his finger northeast, across the River Iberus, to the narrow 'waist' that joined Iberia to Gaul. 'This is the route we shall take.' Hannibal continued to the Alps, where he paused for a moment before moving into Cisalpine Gaul, and thence into northern Italy.

Bostar's heart quickened. Although Malchus had told him of Hannibal's plan, the general's daring still took his breath away.

A glance at Sapho told him that his brother shared his feeling. Their father's face, however, remained expressionless. How much does he know? Bostar wondered. He himself had no idea how the immense task Hannibal had just mentioned would be achieved.

Hannibal saw Sapho straining forward eagerly. He raised an eyebrow.

'When do we march, sir?'

'In the spring. Until then, our Iberian allies have permission to return to their families, and the rest of the army can rest at New Carthage.' He saw Sapho's disappointed look and chuckled. 'Come now! Winter is no time to wage war, and things will be hard enough for us as it is.'

'Of course, sir,' Sapho muttered awkwardly.

'There are some things in our favour, however. Earlier in the year, my messengers journeyed to Cisalpine Gaul. They were received favourably by nearly all the tribes that they encountered,' Hannibal said. 'In fact, the Boii and the Insubres promised immediate aid when we arrive.'

Malchus and his two sons exchanged pleased glances. This was new information for all of them. Hannibal's companions did not react, however, instead studying the trio intently.

Hannibal held up a warning finger. 'There are many hurdles to cross before we reach these possible allies. Traversing the Alps will be the greatest by far, but another will be the fierce natives north of the Iberus, who will undoubtedly give violent resistance. We already have plans in train for our journey through these regions. However, there is an area about which we know very little.' Hannibal's forefinger returned to the mountains between Iberia and Gaul. He tapped the map meaningfully.

Bostar's mouth went dry.

Hannibal stared at Malchus. 'I need someone to sound out the tribes' possible reactions to a massive army entering their land. To discover how many might fight us. I must have this information by the onset of spring. Can you do it?'

Malchus' eyes glittered. 'Of course, sir.'

'Good.' Hannibal regarded Bostar and Sapho next. 'The old lion might lead the pack, but he still needs young males to hunt successfully. Will you accompany your father?'

'Yes, sir!' the brothers cried in unison. 'You show our family great honour by entrusting this mission to us, sir,' Sapho added.

The general smiled. 'I am sure that you will repay my trust amply.'

Delighted by this recognition of Sapho, Bostar gave his brother a small, pleased look. He was rewarded with a fierce nod.

'What are your thoughts, Malchus?'

'We'll need to set out at once, sir. It's a long way to the Iberus.'

'Nearly three thousand stades,' agreed Hannibal. 'As you know, it is generally peaceful as far as the river. After that, up to the border with Gaul, may be a different matter. The place is a jumble of mountains, valleys and passes, and the tribes there are rumoured to be fiercely independent.' He paused. 'How many men will you require?'

'Winning our passage by force of arms is simply not an option. Nor is it our purpose. We are to be an embassy, not an army,' said Malchus. 'What's important are the abilities to move fast and to see off possible attacks by bandits.' He looked at his sons, who nodded in agreement. 'Two dozen of my spearmen and the same number of scutarii should be sufficient, sir.'

'You shall have the pick of any unit you wish. And now, a toast to your success!' Hannibal clicked his fingers and a slave appeared from the rear of the tent. 'Wine!' As the man scurried off, the general looked solemnly at each of those around the table. 'Let us ask Melqart and Baal Saphon, Tanit and Baal Hammon to guide and protect these valiant officers on their mission.'

As the room filled with muttered agreement, Bostar added a request of his own. *Let Sapho and I put aside our differences once and for all.*

*   *   *

233

Braving frost, mud and bitter winter wind, the embassy slogged its way to the Iberus. Thereafter, the inhabitants inland could not be trusted, and so Malchus led them along the more secure coastal route, a densely inhabited area full of towns used to traders from overseas. The party passed by Adeba and Tarraco, before safely reaching the city of Barcino, which was located at the mouth of the River Ubricatus.

There were several routes through the mountains that led to Gaul, and Hannibal had advised that he would probably divide his army between them. This necessitated visiting the tribe that controlled each of the passes. A period of unseasonably calm, dry weather prompted Malchus to head north into the mountainous terrain first, rather than starting with the easiest way into Gaul, that which hugged the coastline via the towns of Gerunda and Emporiae. That could be left until last. Hiring locals as guides, the embassy spent many days on narrow paths that wound and twisted into the hills and valleys. Inevitably, the weather worsened, and a journey that might have taken several weeks stretched into two months. Pleasingly, their ordeals were not all in vain. The chieftains who received the Carthaginians seemed impressed with the tales of Hannibal's military victories throughout Iberia, and the descriptions of his enormous army. Most importantly, though, they welcomed the gifts Malchus offered: the bags of silver coinage, the finely made *kopides* and Celtiberian short swords.

Eventually, the only people left to contact were the Ausetani, who controlled the coastal route into Gaul. Having returned to the town of Emporiae to reshoe their horses and stock up on supplies, Malchus retired to the one inn which was large enough to quarter all of his men. He immediately demanded a meeting with their guides, three swarthy hunters. Soon after sunset, they convened around a table in his room. Small oval oil lamps cast a warm amber glow on to the grubby plaster on the wall. Malchus' sons sat opposite each other. Their relationship remained civil, even fairly cordial, but Bostar had stopped trying to be Sapho's friend. Each time he'd tried, his brother had remained indifferent to his advances. So be it, Bostar decided. It's better than fighting all the time. Such thoughts always brought Hanno, and his guilty wish that it had been Sapho who had been lost at sea, to mind. Disquieted, Bostar shoved away the idea.

Malchus himself served the guides with wine. 'Tell me about this tribe,' he commanded in rough Iberian.

The three glanced at one another. The oldest, a wiry man with a nut-brown, weather-beaten face, leaned forward on his chair. 'Their main village is in the foothills above the town, sir. It's a straightforward journey.'

'Not like the paths that we had to take before, then?'

'No, sir, nothing like that.'

Bostar and Sapho were both relieved. Neither had enjoyed the days spent on winding, treacherous tracks, where a single slip meant a precipitous fall.

'How far?'

'It's not quite a day's ride, sir.'

'Excellent! We'll set out at dawn,' Malchus declared. He eyed his sons. 'A night's rest upon our return, and we'll head south. Spring is around the corner, and we mustn't keep Hannibal waiting any longer.'

The lead guide cleared his throat. 'The thing is, sir, we were wondering if . . .' His nerve failed him and he stopped.

Keen to get in before Bostar, Sapho jumped in. 'What?'

The man rallied his courage. 'We wondered if you could pay us and make your own way there,' he said falteringly. 'We've spent so long away from our wives and families, you see?'

Malchus' brows lowered.

'The directions are simple. There's no way that you could get lost.' He looked at his two companions, who shook their heads in vigorous agreement.

Malchus did not answer. Instead, he glanced at Bostar and Sapho. 'What do you think?' he asked in Carthaginian.

Sapho bared his teeth. 'He's lying,' he snarled in Iberian. 'I say we tie the double-crossing dog down on the table and see what he says after I've cut a few strips of skin off him.' He calmly placed a dagger before him. 'This will make the shitbag sing like a caged bird.'

'Bostar?' asked Malchus.

Bostar studied the three guides, who seemed absolutely terrified. Then he looked at his brother, who was tapping his blade off the table's surface. He didn't want to upset Sapho, but nor was he prepared to see innocent individuals suffer for no reason. 'I don't think there's any need for torture,' Bostar said in Iberian, ignoring Sapho's scowl. 'These men have been with us day and night for weeks. They've had no chance to commit treachery. I think they're probably scared of the Ausetani. But I see no reason why they shouldn't fulfil their oath, which was to guide us until we discharged them.'

Malchus considered their answers in silence. At length, he turned to the lead guide. 'Has my son the right of it? Are you frightened of the Ausetani?'

'Yes, sir. They're prone to banditry.' There was a brief pause. 'Or worse.'

Alarm filled Bostar. Before he could react, Sapho butted in again. 'When, precisely, were you going to tell us this?' he demanded.

He got no answer.

Sapho threw a triumphant look at Bostar. 'Why don't we just get the directions, and then kill them?'

Perhaps his brother was correct, thought Bostar resentfully. He didn't want to admit that he'd made a bad judgement by trusting the guides.

His father's challenge surprised him. 'And if they had warned us? What would we have done?'

A flush spread slowly up Sapho's face and neck. 'Gone to the village anyway,' he muttered.

'Precisely,' replied Malchus evenly. He glared at the guides. 'It's not that I wouldn't end your miserable lives for withholding vital information, but I see no point in killing you when we would have followed the same course of action anyway.'

The three stammered their thanks. 'We will be honoured to guide you to the Ausetani settlement tomorrow, sir,' said the lead guide.

'That's right. You will.' Malchus' tone was silky soft, but there was no mistaking the threat in it. 'Myrcan! Get in here.'

A broad-chested spearman entered from the corridor. 'Sir?'

'Take these men's weapons and escort them to their quarters. Set guards at the windows and door.'

'Yes, sir.' Myrcan held out a meaty hand and the guides meekly handed over their knives before following him from the room.

'It appears you both still have something to learn about judging men's characters,' Malchus admonished. 'Not everyone is as honourable as you, Bostar. Nor do they all require torturing, Sapho.'

Both of his sons took a sudden interest in the tabletop before them.

'Get some rest,' Malchus said in a more kindly voice. 'Tomorrow will be a long day.'

'Yes, Father.' As one, the brothers shoved back their chairs and headed for the door.

Neither spoke on the way to their bedchambers.

The guide's estimate of the distance to the Ausetani village was accurate. After nearly a day's ride, the fortified settlement finally came into view at the end of a long, narrow valley. Perhaps half a mile away, it occupied a high, easily defensible point. Like many such in Iberia, it was ringed by a wooden palisade. The tiny figures of sentries could be seen patrolling the ramparts. Flocks of sheep and goats grazed the slopes to either side. It was a peaceful scene, but the guides looked most unhappy.

Malchus gave them a long, contemptuous stare. 'Go!'

The three men goggled at him.

'You heard me,' Malchus growled. 'Unless you'd like to spend some time with Sapho here.'

They needed no further encouragement and had the sense not to mention payment. Turning their mules' heads, the trio fled.

'It appears that we are about to enter a den of hungry wolves.' Malchus regarded each of his sons in turn. 'What's our best option?'

'Go straight in there and demand to see the headman,' Sapho declared boldly. 'As we did in every other village.'

'We can't go back to Hannibal without some information,' Bostar admitted. 'But nor should we foolishly place our heads on the executioner's block.'

Sapho's top lip curled. 'Are you afraid even to enter that excuse for a settlement?'

'No,' retorted Bostar hotly. 'I'm just saying that we know nothing about these whoresons. If they're as untrustworthy as the guide said, charging in there like raging bulls will get their backs up from the very outset.'

Sapho shot him a disbelieving look. 'So what? We're emissaries of Hannibal Barca, not some pisspot Iberian chieftain.'

They glared at each other.

'Peace,' said Malchus after a moment. 'As usual, both your opinions have some merit. If we had the time, I would perhaps advise waylaying one of their hunting parties. A few hostages would make a powerful bargaining tool before we made an entry. That might take days, however, and we must act now.' He glanced at Sapho. 'Not in quite the way you advised. We will take a more peaceable approach. Remember, the stroked cat is less likely to scratch or bite. Yet we must be confident or, like a cat, they will turn on us anyway.'

Turning to their escorts, Malchus laid out the situation in Carthaginian and basic Iberian. There was little reaction. The

Libyans and scutarii had been chosen for their loyalty and bravery. They would fight and, if necessary, die, for Hannibal. Wherever, and whenever, they were ordered to.

'Which of you two speaks the best Iberian?' Malchus asked his sons. While rusty, his command of the language sufficed most of the time. In a dangerous situation, however, it was best to minimise the chance of miscommunication.

'I do,' replied Bostar at once. Although he and Sapho had spent roughly the same amount of time in Iberia, it was he who had shown more aptitude for the rapid-fire, musical tribal tongues.

Sapho concurred with a reluctant nod.

'You act as interpreter, then,' Malchus directed.

Bostar didn't try to hide his smirk.

Without further ado, they set off. Malchus took the lead, with Bostar and a glowering Sapho following. Their escorts marched to their rear, first the spearmen, and last the scutarii. The party had not gone far when a horn blared out from the nearest hillside. It was quickly echoed by another nearer the village. Shouts rang out on the ramparts. When they were about four hundred paces from the settlement, the front gates creaked open, and a tide of warriors poured out. Forming up in an unruly mass that blocked the entrance, they waited for the Carthaginians to approach.

Bostar felt his stomach clench. He glanced sidelong at Sapho, who was half pulling his sword from its sheath before slamming it home again. He's worried too, thought Bostar. In front, the only sign of tension in their father was his rigid back. Bostar took heart from Malchus' self-assurance. Show no fear, he told himself. They will smell it the way a wolf scents its prey. Taking a deep breath, he fixed his features into a stony expression. Coming to the same realisation, Sapho let go of his sword hilt. Their escorts marched solidly behind them, reassurance that if there was trouble, plenty of men would die before they did.

Malchus rode his horse straight up to the mob of Ausetani. Taken aback by his confidence and the size of his mount, some of the warriors retreated a little. The advantage did not last long. Prompted by their companions' angry mutters, the men stepped forward once more, raising their weapons threateningly. Shouted challenges rang out, but Malchus did not move a muscle.

Like most Iberian tribesmen, few of the Ausetani were dressed identically. Most were bareheaded. Those who wore headgear sported sinew, bronze bowl or triple-crested helmets. The majority carried a shield, although these also varied in size and shape: tall and straight-sided with rounded ends, oval, or round with a conical iron boss. All were brightly painted with swirling serpents, diamonds, or alternating thick bands of colour. The Ausetani were also heavily armed. Every man carried at least one saunion, but many had two. In addition, each warrior had a dagger and either a *kopis* or a typical Celtiberian straight-edged sword.

Malchus turned his head. 'Tell them who we are, and why we're here.'

'We are Carthaginians,' said Bostar loudly. 'We come in peace.' He ignored the sniggers that met this remark. 'With a message for your chieftain, from our leader, Hannibal Barca.'

'Never heard of the prick,' bellowed a hulking figure with a black beard. Hoots of amusement from his comrades followed. Encouraged by this, the warrior shoved his way out of the throng. Long raven tresses spilled out from under his bronze helmet. His black quilted linen tunic could not conceal the massive muscles of his chest and upper arms, and his sinew greaves barely fitted around his trunk-like calves. He was so big that the shield and saunion clutched in his ham fists looked like child's toys. The warrior gave the Libyans and scutarii a contemptuous glance, before returning his cold gaze to Bostar. 'Give me one good reason why we shouldn't just kill you all,' he snarled.

Snarls of agreement followed his challenge, and the Ausetani moved forward a step.

Bostar tensed, but managed to keep his hands in his lap, on his reins. He watched Sapho sidelong and was relieved when his brother didn't reach for his sword either.

'The guide was telling the truth,' Malchus remarked dryly under his breath. He raised his voice. 'Tell him that we bring a message, and gifts, for his leader from our general. His chieftain will not be pleased if he does not hear these words for himself.'

Carefully, Bostar repeated his father's words in Iberian. It was exactly the right thing to say. Confusion and anger mixed on the big man's face for a moment, but a moment later, he stood back. When one of his companions queried his action, the warrior simply shoved him aside with an irritated grunt. Relief flooded through Bostar. The first hurdle had been crossed. It was like watching a landslide beginning. First one man moved out of the way, then a second and a third, followed by several more, until the process took on a life of its own. Soon the group of Ausetani had split apart, leaving the track that led to the village's front gate clear apart from the warrior with the black beard. He trotted ahead to carry the news of their arrival.

Without looking to left or right, Malchus urged his horse up the slope.

The rest of the party followed, shadowed closely by the mass of warriors.

Inside, the settlement was like a hundred others Bostar had seen before. A central open area was ringed by dozens of single-storey wooden and brick huts, the outermost of which had been built right up against the palisade. Plumes of smoke rose from the roofs of many. Small children and dogs played in the dirt, oblivious to the drama about to unfold. Hens and pigs scuffled about, searching for food. Women and old people stood in the doorways of their houses, watching impassively. The acrid smell of urine and faeces, both animal and human, laced the air. At the far side of the open space stood a high-backed wooden chair, which was occupied by a man in late middle age, and flanked by ten warriors in mail shirts and crimson-crested helmets. The bearded hulk was there too, busily muttering to the chieftain.

Without hesitation, Malchus headed for this group. Reaching it, he dismounted, indicating that his sons should do the same. At once three Libyan spearmen darted forward to take the horses' reins. Malchus made a deep bow towards the chief. Bostar quickly copied him. It was prudent to treat the Ausetani leader with respect, he thought. The man was head of a tribe, after all. Yet he looked an untrustworthy ruffian. The chieftain's red linen tunic might be woven from quality fabric, and the sword and dagger on his belt well made, but the tresses of lank, greasy hair that dangled on to his pockmarked cheeks told a different story. So did his flat, dead eyes, which reminded Bostar of a lizard. Sapho was last of all to bend from the waist. His gesture was shallower than the others had been. His insolence did not go unnoticed; several of the nearby warriors snarled with anger. Bostar glared at his brother, but the harm had been done.

The trio of Carthaginians and the Ausetani leader stared at each other in silence for a moment, each trying to gauge the other. The chieftain spoke first. He aimed his words at Malchus, the embassy's obvious leader.

'He says that our message must indeed be important to keep his men from their sport,' muttered Bostar.

'He's playing with us. Trying to put fear in our hearts,' Malchus murmured contemptuously. 'He's not about to kill us out of hand, or his warriors would have done so already. The news of our presence in the area must have reached him before now, and he wants to hear what we have to say for himself. Tell him what we told the other leaders. Lay it on thick about the size of our army.'

Bostar did as he was told, politely explaining how Hannibal and his host would arrive in the next few months, seeking only safe passage to Gaul. There would be well-paid jobs for Ausetani warriors who wished to serve as guides. Any supplies required by the Carthaginians would be purchased. Looting and theft of the locals' property or livestock would be forbidden, on pain of death. As he spoke, Bostar studied the chief intently but was frustrated in his attempt to gauge what the man was thinking. All he could do was to continue in a confident, self-assured vein. Hope for the best.

Bostar began to wax lyrical about the different groups that made up Hannibal's immense force, describing the thousands of spearmen and scutarii like those who stood behind him; the slingers and skirmishers who softened up an enemy before the real fighting began; the peerless Numidian cavalry, whose stinging attacks no soldiers in the world could withstand; and the elephants, which were capable of smashing apart troop formations like so much firewood. Bostar was still in mid-flow when the chieftain peremptorily held up his hand, stopping him. 'And you say this army is how big?' he demanded.

'A hundred thousand men. At the very least.' The instant the words had left his lips, Bostar could see that the Ausetani leader did not believe him. His spirits fell. It was an enormous figure to take in, yet the other tribes visited by the embassy had done so. Perhaps, thought Bostar, it was because they were a lot smaller than the Ausetani. In those villages, the fifty Carthaginian soldiers had seemed altogether more intimidating than they did here. This tribe was a different proposition; reportedly, there were numerous other villages like this one. Combined, the Ausetani might be able to field a force of two or even three thousand warriors, which for Iberia was a considerable achievement. Imagining a host thirty to fifty times larger than that number called for a good imagination.

Sure enough, the chief and his bodyguards exchanged a series of disbelieving looks.

'Scum,' Sapho whispered furiously in Carthaginian. 'They'll shit themselves when they actually see the army.'

Not knowing what else to do, Bostar ploughed on. 'Some evidence of our good faith.' He clicked his fingers and a quartet of scutarii trotted forward, carrying heavy, clinking bags and armfuls of tightly rolled leather. Placing the items in front of the chieftain, they returned to their positions.

The gifts were opened and examined with unseemly speed. Avarice glittered in the faces of every Ausetani watching as mounds of silver coins showered on to the ground. There were loud mutters of appreciation too for the shining weaponry that emerged into view as the leather bundles were unrolled.

Malchus' attitude was still confident, or appeared to be so. 'Ask the chief what answer he would have us take back to Hannibal,' he directed Bostar.

Bostar obeyed.

The Ausetani leader's face grew thoughtful. For the space of twenty heartbeats, he sat regarding the riches laid out before him. Finally, he asked a short question.

'He wants to know how much more they can expect when Hannibal arrives,' Bostar relayed unhappily.

'Greedy bastard,' Sapho hissed.

Malchus' eyebrows drew together in disapproval, yet he did not look surprised. 'I can promise him the same again, and the dog will probably let us go,' he said. 'But I have no idea if Hannibal will agree with my decision. We've already handed over a fortune.' He glanced at his sons. 'What do you think?'

'Hannibal will think we are fools, pure and simple,' muttered Sapho, his nostrils flaring. 'All the other tribes have accepted our gifts, yet this one got twice as much?'

'We can't offer him more or the son of a whore will think we're a walkover,' Bostar conceded. He scowled. 'Hannibal's goodwill should be more than enough for him!'

'But I don't think it will be,' said Malchus grimly. 'If that amount of silver and weaponry hasn't done it, then a vague promise certainly won't.'

Bostar could see no way out that didn't involve major loss of face. Although he and his companions were few in number, *they*

244

were the representatives of a major power, not these cut-throats around them. To accede to the chieftain's demand would show fear on their part, and by implication, weakness on the part of their general. His eyes narrowed as an idea struck. 'You could promise him a private meeting with Hannibal,' he suggested. 'Suggest that an alliance between his people and Carthage would be beneficial to both parties.'

'We don't have the authority to grant that,' growled Sapho.

'Of course we don't,' Bostar replied witheringly. 'But it's not a climbdown either.'

'I like it,' breathed Malchus. He glanced at Sapho, who gave a sulky shrug. 'I think it's our best shot. Tell him.'

Calmly, Bostar delivered their answer.

A ferocious scowl spread across the chieftain's face straightaway, and he spat out an irate, lengthy response. It was delivered so fast that Malchus and Sapho struggled to understand much of it. Bostar did not bother translating before he replied. At once the leader's bodyguards and the huge warrior moved forward in unison. Simultaneously, the men who had followed the Carthaginians inside fanned out on either side of the party, surrounding it.

'What in the name of all the gods did he say?' Malchus demanded.

Bostar's lips thinned. 'That the Ausetani have no need of an alliance with the louse-ridden son of a Phoenician whore.'

Sapho clenched his fists. 'How did you answer?'

'I told him that an immediate sincere apology *might* mean Hannibal's clemency when the army arrives. Otherwise, he and his entire tribe could expect to be annihilated.'

Malchus clapped him on the arm. 'Well said!'

Even Sapho gave Bostar a look of grudging admiration.

Malchus eyed the circle of warriors around them. 'It appears that our road ends here then,' he said in a hard voice. 'We will never have the opportunity to avenge Hanno. Yet we can die well.

Like men!' He turned towards their escorts, and repeated his words. He was pleased when, as one, they laid hands to their weapons.

'On your command, sir,' muttered the officers in charge.

'Wait,' interrupted Sapho. 'I have an idea.' Without asking for Malchus' approval, he drew his sword and moved to stand in front of the hulk who had laughed at them when they arrived. The warrior leered unpleasantly. 'Can this freak actually fight?' Sapho demanded in reasonable Iberian.

The Ausetani leader couldn't believe his ears. Sapho barely reached up to the warrior's shoulder. 'That's my eldest son. He's never been beaten in single combat.'

'What's he doing?' Bostar whispered to Malchus.

For once, Malchus looked worried. 'I don't know, but I hope the gods are smiling on him.'

Sapho raised his voice. 'If I defeat him, then you will apologise, accept Hannibal's gifts and allow us to leave unharmed. When our army arrives, you will offer it safe passage.'

The chieftain laughed. So did everyone within earshot. 'Of course. If you fail, though, he will take your head, and those of all your companions, as trophies.'

'I would expect no less,' Sapho replied disdainfully.

The chieftain gave a callous shrug. At his command, the mass of warriors formed a large, hollow circle. Malchus seized the initiative and used his soldiers to force a passage through so that they could form part of what was to be the combat area. He and Bostar stood at the very front. Many of the Ausetani did not like this move, and began pushing and shoving at the Carthaginian troops, until an angry shout from their leader stopped them. Surrounded by his bodyguards, the chief took up a position directly opposite Malchus.

Gripping his drawn sword, Sapho stalked through a narrow corridor of leering, unfriendly faces. A few paces behind him, the huge warrior received a rapturous welcome. When they were both in the centre of the circle, the crowd of Ausetani closed ranks. From a distance of perhaps a dozen paces, the two faced each other. Sapho was armed with a sword and a dagger. In contemptuous concession, his opponent had laid aside his shield and saunion, leaving him with a long, straight, double-edged blade. It still looked like a totally uneven match.

Bostar's gorge rose. Sapho was a skilled swordsman, but he'd never faced a prospect like this. Judging by his father's clenched jaw and fixed expression, he was thinking similar thoughts. Whatever he had been thinking about Sapho recently, Bostar didn't want him to die losing to this giant. Closing his eyes, he prayed to Baal Saphon, the god of war, to help his brother. To help them all.

Sapho rolled his shoulders, loosening his muscles and wondering what was his best course of action. Why had he thrown down such a stupid challenge? The explanation was simple. Since Bostar had saved Hannibal's life, Sapho's jealousy had soared to new heights. There had always been a keen rivalry between them, but this was a step too far. In the months since they'd left Saguntum, Sapho had appeared to go along with Bostar's wish to lay the matter to rest, but the feeling gnawed constantly at his guts like a malignant growth. Perhaps now some of his wounded pride could be reclaimed. Sapho studied his opponent's bulging muscles and tried not to despair. What chance had he of succeeding? He had only one, Sapho realised with a thrill. His speed.

The chieftain raised his right arm, and a hushed silence fell. Glancing at both men to ensure they were ready, he made a downward chopping gesture.

With an almighty roar, the warrior launched himself forward, his sword raised high. For him, the contest was to be ended quickly. Brutally. Closing in on Sapho, he hammered down an immense blow. Instead of cleaving flesh, the blade whistled through the air to clash off the pebble-strewn ground, sending up a shower of sparks. Sapho was gone, dancing nimbly around to his opponent's rear. The warrior bellowed with rage and spun to face him. Again he swung at Sapho, to no avail. He didn't seem to care. With greater strength and reach, and a longer weapon, he had all the advantage.

Speed isn't enough, thought Sapho. Desperately, he twisted away from a thrust that would have driven through both his bronze breastplate and his ribcage had it connected. So far, the warrior's quilted linen tunic had turned away the glancing blows he had managed to land. Without getting dangerously close, it was impossible to do any more. Backing away from his sneering opponent, Sapho did not see one of the Ausetani stretch out his foot. An instant later, he tripped over it and fell backwards on to the hard packed dirt. Fortunately, he retained hold of his sword.

The warrior stepped closer and Sapho saw death looking him in the eyes. He waited until his enemy had begun to swing downwards, and then, with all his might, he rolled away into the centre of the circle. Behind him, Sapho heard his opponent's sword slam into the ground with a bone-jarring thump. Knowing that speed was of the essence, he turned over and over before trying to get up. Mocking laughs from the watching Ausetani filled the air, and the huge warrior raised his arms in anticipation of victory. Rage filled Sapho at their treachery. He knew too that this fight couldn't be won by ordinary means. It was time to cast the dice. Take his chance. He drew his dagger with his left hand, ignoring the jeers this provoked.

Breathing deeply, Sapho waited. What he needed the warrior to do was take a great sideways slash at him. The only way he could think of drawing the hulk in was to stay put – without defending himself. It was a complete gamble. If the other didn't take the bait and respond exactly as he wished, he'd be dead, but Sapho couldn't think of anything else to do. Weariness threatened to overcome him, and his shoulders slumped.

The huge warrior shuffled in, grinning.

With a thrill, Sapho realised that his opponent thought he'd given up. He didn't move a muscle.

'Prepare to die,' the warrior growled. Lifting his right arm, he swung his sword around in a curving arc, aiming for the junction between Sapho's neck and shoulders. The blow was delivered with unstoppable force, at a target that was standing stock still. To those watching, it looked as if the duel was over.

At the last moment, Sapho dropped to his knees, letting the other's blade split the air over his head. Throwing himself forward, he stretched out his arm and plunged his dagger into the warrior's left thigh. It wasn't a fatal wound, but nor was it meant to be. As he landed helplessly on his chest, Sapho heard a loud scream of pain. A grimace of satisfaction twisted his lips as he scrambled to his feet, still clutching his sword. A few steps away, the bleeding warrior was listing to one side like a ship in a storm. All his attention was focused on pulling the knife from his leg. Stabbing him in the back would be simple.

A quick glance at the snarling faces surrounding them helped Sapho to make a snap decision. Mercy would be far more useful here than ruthlessness. Swiftly, he swept in and completed the task. Drawing his blade across the back of his enemy's left leg, he hamstrung him. As the bellowing warrior collapsed, Sapho stamped on his right hand, forcing him to drop his weapon. Touching the point of his blade to the other's chest, he growled, 'Yield.'

Moaning with pain, the warrior extended both his hands upwards, palms extended.

Sapho lifted his gaze to the chieftain, whose face registered stunned disbelief. 'Well?' he asked simply.

Eventually, the chief managed to compose himself. 'I apologise for insulting Hannibal, your leader. The Ausetani accept these generous gifts, with thanks,' he muttered with bad grace. 'You and your companions are free to go.'

'Excellent,' replied Sapho with a broad smile. 'Your son will be coming with us.'

The chief jumped to his feet. 'He needs medical attention.'

'Which he will receive in plenty. We will leave him in the care of the best surgeon in Emporiae. You have my word on that.' Sapho leaned on his sword slightly, eliciting a loud moan from the huge warrior. 'Or I can end it right here. It's your choice.'

The chieftain's lips peeled back with fury, but he was powerless in the face of Sapho's resolve. 'Very well,' he replied.

Only then did Sapho glance at his father and Bostar. Both gave him fierce nods of encouragement. Sapho found himself grinning like an idiot. Against all the odds, he had redeemed the situation, won his father's approval and his brother's admiration. Inside, though, he knew that the Ausetani would have to be defeated before this particular passage to Gaul was safe.

Chapter XII: Plans

Aboot in the ribs woke Hanno the next morning. Grunting in pain, he opened his eyes. Agesandros was standing over him, flanked by two of the largest slaves on the farm. Hanno knew them for dumb brutes who did whatever they were told. Sets of manacles hung from their ham-like fists. Confusion and dread filled Hanno. Quintus' and Fabricius' absence hit home like hammer blows. This had to be more than coincidence. 'What was that for?' he croaked.

Instead of answering, the Sicilian kicked him again. Several times.

Protecting his head with his hands, Hanno rolled into the foetal position and prayed that Aurelia would hear.

At length, Agesandros ceased. He'd made no effort to remain quiet. 'Gugga son of a whore,' he snarled.

Through squinted eyes, Hanno looked up. He was alarmed to see the Sicilian clutching a dagger in one hand and a small purse in the other.

'I found these under your pathetic pile of possessions. So you would steal money and weapons from your owner?' Agesandros thundered. 'Probably cut all our throats in the middle of the night too, before running away to join your scumbag countrymen in their war against Rome.'

'I've never seen those things before in my life,' Hanno cried. Immediately, an image of Agesandros lurking in the atrium came to mind. That's what the Sicilian had been doing! 'You bastard,' Hanno muttered, trying to sit up. He received a kick in the face for his troubles. Sprawling back on his bedroll, waves of agony washed over him. Blood filled his mouth, and a moment later he spat out two teeth.

Agesandros laughed cruelly. 'Fit him with manacles,' he ordered. 'Neck as well as ankles.'

Dazed, Hanno watched as the slaves stepped forward and fastened the heavy iron rings around his flesh. Three loud clicks, and he was back to where he'd been in the slave market. As before, a long chain extended from the metal band around his neck. With a brutal tug, Hanno was jerked to his feet and towards the door.

'Stop!'

All eyes turned.

Still in her nightdress, Aurelia stood framed in the doorway to her room. 'Just what do you think you are doing?' she screeched. 'Hanno is a household slave, not one of the farm workers, to do with as you please.'

The Sicilian bowed extravagantly. Mockingly. 'Forgive me, my lady, for waking you so early. After hearing of the news in your father's letter, I became concerned about how this slave would react. I worried that he was planning to do you and your family harm, before escaping. Unfortunately, I was correct.' He held up the evidence. 'These clearly aren't his.'

Horrified, Aurelia's gaze shot to Hanno. She flinched at the sight of his bloodied face.

'*Someone* planted them among my things,' Hanno muttered, throwing Agesandros a poisonous look.

Understanding at once, Aurelia started forward. 'You see?'

The Sicilian chuckled. 'He would say that, wouldn't he? Every gugga's a liar, though.' He jerked his head at the two hulks. 'Come on. We have a long journey ahead of us.'

'I forbid you,' Aurelia shouted. 'Do not move another step.'

The slaves holding Hanno froze, and Agesandros turned. 'Forgive me, my lady, but in this instance I am going to override your authority.'

Atia's voice cut in like a whiplash. 'What about mine?' she demanded. 'In Fabricius' absence, I am in charge, not you.'

Agesandros blinked. 'Of course you are, mistress,' he replied smoothly.

'Explain yourself.'

Agesandros held up the knife and purse once more and repeated his allegations.

Atia looked suitably horrified.

'What would Fabricius say if he found out that I had left such a dangerous slave on the premises, mistress?' the Sicilian asked. 'He would have me crucified, and rightly so.'

You clever bastard, thought Hanno. Make your move when you only have two women to intimidate. Fabricius was far away, and who knew when Quintus would return?

Atia nodded in acceptance. 'Where are you taking him?'

'To Capua, mistress. Clearly, the dog is too dangerous to sell as an ordinary slave, but I've heard of a local government official who died there recently. The funeral is in two days, and the man's son wants to honour his father's passing with a gladiator fight. A pair of prisoners are to fight each other to the death, and then the survivor is to be executed.'

Atia's lips thinned. 'I see. Will my husband be out of pocket?'

'No, mistress. For an event like this, I'll get far more than we paid for him.'

Tears of impotent rage ran down Aurelia's cheeks. Frantically, she racked her brains. What could she do?

Atia crossed to give Aurelia a hug. 'Don't fret. He's a slave, dear,' she said. 'A murderous one too.'

'No,' Aurelia whispered. 'Hanno wouldn't do something like that.'

Atia frowned. 'You've seen the evidence for yourself. The only way we can confirm the Carthaginian's guilt is have him tortured and see what he says. Is that what you want?'

Defeated, Aurelia shook her head. 'No.'

'Fine. The matter's closed,' her mother said firmly. 'Now, I'm going for a bath. Why don't you join me?'

'I couldn't,' whispered Aurelia.

'Suit yourself,' said Atia. She turned to Agesandros. 'Better get going, hadn't you? It's a long way to Capua.'

The Sicilian flashed an oily smile. 'Yes, mistress.'

With a satisfied nod, Atia disappeared from sight.

Hanno, meanwhile, was in a daze. Agesandros must have been planning this ever since Quintus and Aurelia rescued me, he realised. Waiting for the right time.

His horror was only to grow.

'I forgot to say.' Revelling in the moment, the Sicilian looked from Hanno to Aurelia and back. 'The other fighter is also a gugga. A friend of this shitbag, I believe.'

Hanno's stomach lurched. It seemed too much of a coincidence to be true. 'Suniaton?'

Agesandros revealed his teeth. 'That's his name, yes.'

'No,' cried Aurelia. 'That is so cruel.'

'Quite apt, I thought,' said Agesandros.

Hanno's relief that Suni was alive vanished. Blinding fury consumed him, and he lunged forward, desperate to close with Agesandros. Within three steps, he was pulled up short. The slave holding the chain attached to his neck had simply tightened his grip. Hanno ground his teeth in rage. 'You will pay for this,' he growled. 'I curse you for ever. May the gods of the underworld act as my witness.'

There were few who were not afraid of such powerful oaths, and Agesandros flinched. But he regained control quickly. 'It's you who will be visiting Hades, along with your friend. Not me.' Clicking his fingers at the slaves, he stalked to the front door.

Hanno could not bear to look at Aurelia as he was dragged away. It hurt too much. The last thing he heard was the patter of her feet on the mosaic, and her voice calling for Elira. Then he was outside, in bright spring sunshine. Walking to Capua, where he would fight Suniaton to the death. Hanno stared at Agesandros' broad back, begging all the gods for a lightning bolt to strike him down on the spot. Of course, nothing happened.

The last remnants of Hanno's hope disappeared.

It returned within a matter of moments. They had not even reached the end of the lane before shouts and cries rang out behind them. Agesandros spun around, and his eyes widened. Without even looking at Hanno, he sprinted back towards the farm buildings. In slow motion, Hanno turned to see what was happening. To his amazement, tendrils of smoke were rising from one of the granaries. Aurelia, he thought, exultantly. She must have started a fire.

There was no way under the sun that Agesandros could have done anything but return. Aurelia had bought him some time. How would that be enough? Hanno wondered, desperation tearing at his soul.

It was several hours before the blaze was brought under control. Roaring like a demon, Agesandros supervised as every slave on the farm ferried water to the grain stores. Even Hanno had his manacles unfastened for the task. Hurling the contents of their buckets on to the flames, the slaves ran to the well and back, over and over again. Aurelia and Atia watched from a distance. Horrified expressions adorned both their faces. There was no sign of Elira.

The Sicilian let no one rest until he was happy that the fire was dying down. Despite himself, Hanno felt a grudging admiration for Agesandros. Covered in soot from head to toe like everyone else, he looked exhausted. The granary's stone construction had helped, but the supreme effort the overseer had exacted from everyone was the main reason that the blaze had not spread to more of the farm buildings.

By the time the last of the flames had been extinguished, the afternoon was over. There was no question of walking to Capua that day. To Hanno's relief, the Sicilian didn't bother beating him further. His manacles were replaced, and he was locked into a small cell that adjoined Agesandros' quarters. In pitch darkness, Hanno slumped to the floor and closed his eyes. He was absolutely parched with thirst, and his belly was growling like a wild beast, but Hanno doubted that any food or drink would be forthcoming. He could only try to rest, and hope that Aurelia had another trick up her sleeve.

Hours passed. Hanno dozed fitfully, but the cold and his manacles prevented him from sleeping properly. Nonetheless, he dreamed of many things. The streets of Carthage. His two brothers, Sapho and Bostar, training with swords. Hannibal's messenger visiting by night. Fishing with Suniaton. The storm. Slavery and his unlikely friendship with Quintus and Aurelia. Bloody war between Carthage and Rome. Two gladiators fighting before a baying crowd. The last images were horrifyingly violent. Covered in sweat, Hanno jerked upright.

Desolation swamped him. After all his requests to be reunited with Suniaton, this is what it would come to. They would die together to commemorate the death of a crusty Roman official. Frustration and rage filled Hanno by turns. Alone in the darkness, he prayed that Agesandros stayed to watch the fight. When he and Suniaton were handed their weapons, they could make a suicidal attack on the Sicilian. Gain some retribution before they died. His plan was implausible, but Hanno hung on to it for dear life.

Some time later, he was startled by the sound of a key entering the lock. Surely dawn had not come yet? Hanno backed fearfully away from the door, raising his hands against the arc of light that spread into the room. To his utter surprise, the person who entered was none other than Quintus, clad in a heavy cloak. He was clutching a bunch of keys in one hand and a small bronze lamp in the other. A sheathed gladius hung from a baldric over his right shoulder.

Hanno was stunned. 'What are you doing here?'

'Helping a friend,' replied Quintus simply. Placing the lamp on the floor, he tried a key on Hanno's fetters. It didn't work, but the second one did. A moment later, he had also unlocked the iron ring around his neck. Quintus grinned. 'Let's go.'

Hanno could scarcely contain his joy. 'How did you know to come back?'

A wry smile tugged Quintus' lips upwards. 'You can thank Aurelia. The instant you had left, she sent Elira to find me. Next she set a fire in the granary.'

Hanno was still confused. 'But the keys,' he said. 'There was no time to make an impression of them.'

'These are the originals,' replied Quintus. He saw Hanno's bewilderment, and explained. 'I commended Agesandros on his excellent work by giving him a jug of Father's best wine. The fool was delighted. What he didn't know was that I had laced it with enough papaverum to knock out an elephant. I simply waited until he had drunk it and fallen asleep. Then I took his keys.'

'You're a genius. So is Aurelia.' He grabbed Quintus' arm. 'Thank you. I owe you both my life for the second time.'

Quintus nodded. 'I knew that Agesandros was lying about you planning to kill us. If you wanted me dead, you wouldn't have come back to save me at the hut. Besides, I know you would help me in a similar situation.' He moved towards the door. 'Now, come on. Dawn is not far off. Aurelia is at the pens, feeding the dogs scraps to keep them from barking, but she can't stay there for ever. She said to say that you would be in her prayers.' He didn't mention his sister's tears. What was the point? Hers was an impossible fantasy.

Sad that he would not see Aurelia, and unaware of Quintus'

emotions, Hanno followed him outside. The farmyard was deserted, and the only audible sounds were Agesandros' loud snores. Within a hundred paces, they had left the buildings behind. Along the lane, the cypress trees stood tall and threatening, their branches creaking in the slight breeze. A crescent moon hung low in the sky, reminding Hanno of Tanit and home. And Suniaton. Suddenly, the immense relief he had felt at Quintus' appearance began to ebb away. He might be free, but his friend was not.

Quintus stopped when they reached the shadow of the trees. He lifted the baldric over his shoulder and handed the gladius to Hanno. 'You'll need this.' Next, he proffered his thick woollen cloak and a leather satchel.

Hanno muttered his thanks.

'The bag contains food for several days, and twenty-five didrachms. Make your way to the coast and take passage to Syracuse. You should be able to find a merchant ship there which can take you to Carthage.'

'I'm going nowhere without Suniaton,' said Hanno.

Quintus' face changed. 'Have you gone mad?' he hissed. 'You don't even know where he is being held.'

'I'll find him,' Hanno answered stolidly.

'And get yourself killed into the bargain.'

'Would you leave Gaius behind if you were in my shoes?' Hanno demanded.

'Of course not,' Quintus retorted.

'Well, then.'

'Stubborn bloody Carthaginian. There's no telling you.' Quintus scowled. 'Going to Capua on your own is tantamount to committing suicide. I can't let you do that. Not after all the trouble I've gone to. Can you find the shepherd's hut where we fought the bandits?'

Hanno stared at Quintus, not understanding. 'I think so, yes.'

'Head up there and wait for me. I'll see about finding Suniaton later.'

The immensity of Quintus' offer sank in. 'You don't have to do this.'

'I know.' Quintus regarded him solemnly. 'But you are my friend.'

A lump rose in Hanno's throat. 'Thank you. If I can ever repay this debt, I will. You have my word.'

'Let us pray that I never have need to call on you.' Quintus pushed him towards the hills. 'Go.'

With a lightness in his heart that he had not felt since leaving Carthage, Hanno ran off into the darkness.

Hanno made his way to the hut without difficulty, reaching it less than two hours after sunrise. He spent the climb marvelling at how he'd escaped Agesandros' clutches for the second time. Of course it was solely thanks to Quintus and Aurelia. Yet again, Hanno was forced to admit that Romans were capable of great kindness. They were not all the deceitful monsters described by his father. His charitable feelings did not last long. Hanno only had to think of Flaccus and his tale to remember the incredibly harsh conditions imposed on Carthage at the end of the last war, and the arrogant manner with which Rome had treated her over Saguntum. Even the genial Martialis didn't like the Carthaginians. 'Typical guggas,' he'd said.

He calmed himself with thoughts of how a Roman – Quintus – was at this very moment trying to free Suniaton, a Carthaginian condemned to die. His ploy didn't last long. As the hours dragged by, Hanno found it ever harder not to head for Capua. His promise to Quintus was what made him stay. He busied himself by repairing the hut, which had been left damaged after the fight. First Hanno collected every piece of fallen wood he could find. Then, using some old but serviceable tools he found lying inside, he sawed and chopped the timber into suitable lengths. He was no carpenter, but the construction was straightforward. All he had to do was study the undamaged sides, and copy them. It was undemanding yet rewarding labour and, as the sun set, Hanno stood back and admired his handiwork.

Worry was niggling away at him, however. He could no longer ignore the fact that Quintus would not return that day. Did this mean that his attempt had failed? Hanno had no idea. He pondered his options for some time, concluding that it was too dangerous to return to the farm. Agesandros would be on the lookout for trouble. Nor was there any point in making for Capua. Hanno knew no one there, and if he didn't manage to find Quintus, he would have no idea what had transpired since the morning. His only choice was to stay put. Slightly more at ease, Hanno lit a fire in the hut's stone-ring fireplace, and wolfed down some of the olives, cheese and bread he found in the satchel.

Wrapped in Quintus' cloak, Hanno sat watching the yellow-orange flames and thinking of the people he held most dear in the world. His father. Sapho and Bostar. Suniaton. Hanno paused before adding two more individuals to the list. Quintus. Aurelia. How many of them would he ever see again? Sadness, his constant companion since the storm, washed over Hanno in great waves. In all likelihood, he would never be reunited with his family. They were probably with Hannibal's army in Iberia by now, with every chance of being killed. Although it was his greatest desire to find them, doing so in the midst of a war would be virtually impossible. Finding Suniaton was perhaps his best hope, Hanno realised. If, by some stroke of luck, this came to pass, he would leave, never to see Quintus or Aurelia again. That conclusion brought even more pain. All he could wish for was a reunion with his loved ones in the next world. This bleak insight was the last thing Hanno remembered as sleep drew him into its embrace.

Dawn found Hanno in a better frame of mind. There was much to be grateful for. Despite what he had been through, he was no longer a captive. Moreover, Quintus had a greater chance of freeing Suniaton than he did. If the attempt was successful, he and his friend had a reasonable chance of making it to the coast, and finding a ship bound for Carthage. Never give up hope, Hanno thought. Without it, life is pointless.

He spent the morning practising with his gladius and scanning the slopes below for movement. It was nearly midday when Hanno spotted a lone figure on horseback. His heart leaped in his chest at the sight. There was no way of knowing who it was, so he withdrew into the cover granted by a clump of juniper trees some fifty paces from the hut. With bated breath, Hanno waited as the rider drew nearer. From its broad shoulders, he judged it to be male. There was no sign of any dogs, which pleased him. It increased the likelihood that this was not someone sent to track him down.

Finally, he recognised Quintus' features. Disappointment flooded Hanno that Suniaton was not with him. As the other drew close enough to speak, Hanno emerged from his hiding place.

Quintus raised a hand in apologetic salute.

'What happened? Did you discover anything about Suniaton?'

Quintus' lips twisted in a grimace. 'He's still alive, but he was injured during training two days ago. The good news is that he won't be able to take part in the *munus*.' He saw Hanno's alarm. 'It's just a flesh wound. Apparently, he'll be fine in a month or so.'

Hanno closed his eyes to relish the wave of relief. Suni wasn't dead! 'The official's son wouldn't sell him, then?'

Quintus shook his head. 'He didn't seem to care that you and Suniaton wouldn't be fighting each other,' he said. 'But he didn't want to sell Suni either. Stupidly, I let the mangy dog see how much I wanted to buy him. The prick told me to come back when Suniaton is fully recovered and I can see a demonstration of his full abilities. "That will show you his true worth," he said. I wouldn't hold your breath, though. The man fancies himself as a gladiator trainer. There must have been a dozen slaves with weapons training in his yard. I'm sorry.'

Hanno felt the last of his reborn hope slipping away.

Quintus glanced uneasily down the slope. 'You'd be wise to get moving.'

Hanno gave him a questioning look.

'Agesandros was furious when he discovered that you were gone,' Quintus said. 'The arrogant bastard wouldn't take it from me that I had freed you. He said only my father had the power to do that. Naturally, my mother agreed with him. She's furious with me,' he added glumly.

'But your father won't be back for months.'

Quintus gave him a grim nod. 'Precisely. Which makes you a runaway, and hunting *them* down is something Agesandros is rather good at. I told him that you headed towards Capua, and I think he believed me. He started looking in that direction.' He winked. 'Fortunately, Aurelia made Elira drag an old tunic of yours all the way to the river, and then swim downstream to a ford where her tracks would be mixed up with plenty of others. She left the garment in the water, which should trick the hounds.'

'Your sister is incredible,' said Hanno in amazement.

Quintus grinned briefly. 'It would still be best to get a head start now. Skirt around the farm to arrive at Capua tomorrow morning. Agesandros should have returned home by that stage, and you can catch a boat downriver to the coast.'

A knot formed in Hanno's stomach. 'I can't desert Suniaton,' he muttered. 'He's so near.'

'And so far,' Quintus replied harshly. 'He might as well be in Hades for all you can do.'

'That's as may be,' Hanno retorted. 'But you said the official's son would talk again in a few weeks.'

Unsurprised, Quintus sighed. 'Stay, then,' he said. 'I'll bring you food every two or three days. I will try to keep an eye on Suniaton. We'll work out some way of getting him out.'

Hanno could have cried with relief. 'Thank you.'

Quintus pulled around his horse's head. 'Be vigilant. You never know when Agesandros might appear.'

* * *

Bostar's phalanx was marching behind those of Sapho and his father, so the messenger reached him first. 'Is there a Captain Bostar here?' he cried.

'Yes. What do you want?'

'Hannibal wants to talk to you, sir. Now,' he said, matching the Libyans' pace easily.

Bostar stared at the strapping scutarius, who was one of the general's bodyguard. 'Do you know what it's about?'

'No, sir.'

'Did he want to see my father or brother?'

'Just you, sir,' replied the Iberian stolidly. 'What shall I say to the general? He's pulled out of the column about a mile back.'

'Tell him I will be there at once.' Bostar thought for a moment. 'Wait! I'll come with you.'

The scutarius looked pleased. 'Very good, sir.'

Bostar muttered instructions to his second-in-command, who was riding beside him, before turning his horse's head and directing it out of his soldiers' way. Few of the men looked up as he trotted by, but those who did grinned. Bostar nodded in acknowledgement, glad that his efforts in winning their trust had paid off. The Libyans' large round shields knocked off their backs as they walked, and their short spears looked skywards in a forest of points. A junior officer was situated every fifty paces, and beside each marched a standard-bearer. Their wooden poles were decorated with sun discs, lunar crescents and red decorative ribbons.

Bostar eyed the long, winding column approaching from the southwest. 'Feast your eyes on that,' he said to the scutarius, who was trotting alongside. 'It's some spectacle.'

'I suppose so, sir.' The man cleared his throat and spat. 'It would look a damn sight better with forty thousand more of my countrymen, though.'

'Not all are as loyal as you and your comrades,' replied Bostar. In his heart, he too was sorry that the host had shrunk by more than a third in little over three months. Much of the decrease could be accounted for by the casualties suffered thus far, and those who made up the garrisons along the route back to Iberia. In addition, plenty of men, perhaps ten thousand more, had been discharged by Hannibal before they could desert. To discuss the matter with an ordinary soldier was bad for morale, so Bostar kept his lips sealed. His spirits soon lifted, however. It was impossible not to be exhilarated by the sight of such a massive Carthaginian army, the first such to go on the offensive against Rome in more than a generation.

After the last of the spearmen had passed, there was a short delay until the next units reached them. These were massed ranks of fierce-looking, tattooed Libyan skirmishers in bare feet and red goatskin tunics. They were armed with small round shields and handfuls of javelins. Hundreds of Balearic slingers followed, wild half-dressed men from the Mediterranean islands, whose skill with their slings was legendary. Bostar wouldn't have trusted a single man among them, but they were a supreme asset to Hannibal's army.

After came the light Iberian infantry, the *caetrati*, with their round leather bucklers, javelins and falcata swords. Further down the track, Bostar made out Hannibal and his officers, surrounded by the mounted part of his bodyguard, local cavalry in crested bronze helmets and red cloaks. Behind the general marched the heavy Celtiberian foot, the scutarii.

Bostar could not see the final units of the army, which trailed behind the baggage train, thousands of laden-down mules led by Iberian peasants. Protecting the rear were thirty-seven elephants, and more Celtiberians. Bostar thought that their uniform was probably the most striking in the entire force: black cloaks, bronze helmets with crimson crests and greaves made of sinew. Their shields were either round like those of the caetrati, or flat, elongated ovals, and they carried short straight swords and all-iron spears. Last of all, mobile and fast moving, were the many protective squadrons of Iberian and Numidian cavalry. These – the finest horsemen in the world – were Hannibal's secret weapon.

They reached the general's position not long after. The scutarius gave the password to the cavalryman who challenged them, which saw the protective cordon open up. Bostar dismounted quickly and threw his reins to the Iberian. As he approached, he felt Hannibal's eyes upon him. Bostar moved even faster. He snapped off a salute. 'You wished to see me, sir?'

Hannibal smiled. 'Yes. I wasn't expecting you so soon.'

Bostar couldn't help but grin. 'I wanted to find out what you had in mind for me, sir.'

Hannibal glanced at the officers to either side. 'Eager, this lion cub, isn't he?'

There was a ripple of laughter, and Bostar flushed, not least because the general and his brothers – the sons of Hamilcar Barca – were known as the 'lion's brood'.

Hannibal noticed at once. 'Do not take offence, for I meant none. It's soldiers like you who are the backbone of this army. Not like the thousands of men I had to let go after our recent campaign. Faint hearts.'

Bostar nodded gratefully. 'Thank you, sir.'

Hannibal turned his eyes to the southwest, whence they had come. 'It's hard to believe that we only crossed into Gaul a few weeks ago, isn't it? Seems like we haven't fought a battle in an age.'

'I won't forget the journey in a hurry, sir.' After the hostile, sun-scorched lands north of the Iberus, Bostar appreciated the fertile land of southern Gaul, with its tilled fields, large villages and friendly natives.

Hannibal's nod was rueful. 'Nor will I. Losing ten thousand men in under three months was most unfortunate. But it couldn't be helped. Speed was of the essence, and our tactics worked.'

Mago shot his brother a disgruntled look. 'Don't forget the

same number of troops, plus cavalry, that you had to leave to keep the bastards pacified.'

'Soldiers who will also protect the area against Roman invasion,' retorted Hannibal. 'After defeating the troublesome natives, they should be able to take on a legion or two.' He scratched his beard and eyed Bostar. 'The worst of the lot were that tribe you had trouble with. The whoresons who would have slaughtered you but for the duel your mad brother fought.'

Bostar hid his amusement at Hannibal's description of Sapho. 'The Ausetani, sir.'

'The same ones who wouldn't allow the army to march through their lands unhindered. They were fools. But brave all the same,' Hannibal acknowledged. 'At the end, hardly any of them had wounds in their backs.'

'They fought well, sir,' agreed Bostar. 'Especially the champion whom Sapho defeated. I counted ten of our soldiers lying around his corpse. His wound from the duel hadn't even healed either.'

'Malchus pointed him out to me afterwards,' said Hannibal. 'It's incredible that your brother managed to beat him in single combat. The man was as big as Herakles.'

'He was, sir,' agreed Bostar fervently. His memories of the fight were still vivid. 'Sapho had the gods on his side that day.'

'He did. For all his bravery, though, your brother has a tendency to be rash. To act first, and think later.'

'If you say so, sir.' While Bostar agreed with his general's assessment, it felt wrong to openly say so.

Hannibal gave him a shrewd look. 'Your loyalty is commendable, but don't think I didn't hear about his refusal to pull back during that attack on Saguntum. If it hadn't been for you, hundreds of men would have lost their lives unnecessarily. Eh?'

Bostar met his general's gaze with reluctance. 'Maybe so, sir.'

'That's why you're here. Because you think before you take action.' Hannibal waved at the rolling countryside, much of which was full of ripe wheat and barley. 'Things are easy now. We can buy as much grain as we need from the locals, and live off the land the rest of the time. But the journey won't all be like this. The weather will get worse and, sooner or later, we'll come across someone who wants to fight us.'

'Indeed, sir,' said Bostar soberly.

'We can only pray that it's not the Romans at any stage before we reach Cisalpine Gaul. Hopefully, those bastards still have no idea of our plans. The good news is that my scouts, who have just returned from the River Rhodanus, saw no sign of them.'

Mago's smile was like that of a wolf. 'And the trail a legion leaves can't be missed, so we have one less thing to worry about. For now.'

'Have you heard of the Rhodanus?' asked Hannibal.

'Vaguely, sir,' said Bostar. 'It's a big river quite near the Alps.'

'That's right. By all accounts, most of the tribes in the area are well disposed towards us. Naturally, there's one that is not. The Volcae, they're called, and they live on both sides of the water.'

'Will they try to deny us the passage, sir?'

'It would appear so,' Hannibal answered grimly.

'That could be very costly, sir, especially when it comes to taking the horses and elephants across.'

Hannibal scowled. 'That's right. Which is why, while the army prepares to cross, you're going to lead a force upriver of the Volcae camp. You'll swim over at night, and find a hidden position nearby. Your dawn signal will tell me to order the boats launched.' He smacked a fist into his palm. 'We'll squash them like a man stamps on a beetle. How does that sound?'

Bostar's heart thumped in his chest. 'It sounds good, sir.'

'That's what I like to hear.' Hannibal gripped his shoulder. 'You'll get further instructions nearer the time. Now, you'll be wanting to get back to your men.'

Bostar knew when he was being dismissed. 'Yes, sir. Thank you, sir.'

Hannibal called out when Bostar was ten steps away. 'Not a word about this to anyone.'

'Of course, sir,' Bostar replied. The order was a relief, for it meant that Sapho would have no chance to be jealous because he had not been selected for the duty. Yet Bostar was already worrying how his brother would react when he did find out.

Chapter XIII: Departure

Hanno soon grew used to living in the hut, which had lain vacant since the shepherd's murder. According to Quintus, Fabricius' sheep were being grazed elsewhere and there was little likelihood of anyone passing by. Nonetheless, Hanno stayed alert. While Agesandros was his main concern, he had no wish to be seen at all. Hanno's luck held out; the only visitors he had were Quintus, and occasionally Aurelia.

There was little news of Suniaton. Quintus did not want to appear too eager by visiting the official's son earlier than had been arranged. Finally, though, Quintus reported that Suniaton had made an uneventful recovery. Hanno's spirits soared upon hearing this, but his hopes were immediately dashed. 'The whoreson still won't sell. He says Suniaton is too promising a fighter. He wanted 250 didrachms for him.' Quintus gave Hanno an apologetic look. 'I haven't got that type of money. Father does, of course, but I'm not sure he'd give it to me, even if I managed to find him.'

'We can't give up now. There must be another way,' said Hanno fiercely.

'Unless we can bribe someone to let Suniaton escape . . . I just don't know who to approach.' Quintus' frown disappeared. 'I could ask Gaius.' He held up a reassuring hand as Hanno jerked forward in alarm. 'Gaius and I have been friends since we could walk. He doesn't necessarily approve of my helping you escape, but he won't tell a soul. Who knows? He might be prepared to help.'

Hanno forced himself to sit down. Gaius' trustworthiness had already been proved by the fact that nobody had come looking for him at the shepherd's hut. It also seemed as if he was Suniaton's only hope. 'Let us pray to the gods that he agrees, then.'

'Leave it to me,' said Quintus, hoping that his confidence in Gaius was not misplaced. In an effort to protect Hanno, he had concealed the fact that Suniaton was already fighting as a gladiator once more.

Time was not on their side.

When Quintus finally brought word that Gaius' efforts had come to fruition, Hanno's relief was overwhelming. Autumn had arrived, and the woods were a riot of colour. The temperature had dropped noticeably too. Hanno was growing used to being woken by the cold at night. Quintus' direction to pack all his gear was most welcome. Hopefully, he'd be leaving the hut for ever. 'What are we going to do?' he asked as they headed towards Capua.

'Gaius didn't want me to say,' Quintus replied, avoiding Hanno's gaze.

Worry clawed at Hanno's insides. 'Why?'

Quintus shrugged. 'I'm not sure. I think he wants to tell you himself.' He saw Hanno's disappointment. 'It's only a few hours longer.'

'I know,' Hanno replied, forcing a smile. 'And I owe you both so much for what you've done.'

'It's not about debts,' said Quintus generously. 'A man tries to help his friends if he can. Let's just hope that Gaius' idea works.'

Hanno nodded grimly. If it didn't, there was a hard choice to be made. He couldn't hang around for ever.

It was nearly dark by the time they reached Capua. Their journey had been uneventful, but Hanno still faltered as the massive walls loomed into view. Even though he was coming to help free Suniaton, entering the city now meant real danger. There would be guards at the gate, who could ask awkward questions. Descriptions of him pinned to the walls of houses. Hanno knew how fugitive slaves were hunted in Carthage. It wouldn't be much different here. His feet dragged to a halt.

Quintus turned. 'What is it?'

'I'm not just an escaped slave. What if someone recognises me as a Carthaginian?'

Quintus' chuckle died away as he saw Hanno's real distress. 'You don't have to worry,' he said reassuringly. 'There are plenty of dark-skinned slaves in Capua. Greeks, Libyans, Judaeans. No one knows the difference. And apart from Gaius, no one knows what you've done. Nor do they care. You're a slave, remember? Most people won't even notice you, let alone challenge you.' He dismounted. 'Follow me. Look miserable and don't catch anyone's eye.'

'Very well,' said Hanno, wishing that he had the comfort of a weapon to defend himself.

To his relief, things went smoothly. The sentries didn't even look up as he shuffled after Quintus. It was the same on the streets, which, thanks to the fast-approaching sunset, were emptying fast. People were more interested in getting home safely than studying a young noble and his slave. Housewives with baskets full of food muttered a few words with each other rather than having a full-blown gossip. Stallholders were boxing up their unsold produce and loading it on to mules. Many of the shops were already boarded up for the night.

Before long, they had reached Martialis' house. Quintus' loud knock was answered at once by Gaius himself, who grinned at his friend as he pulled open the gate. 'I've been waiting for you.' He gave Hanno a hard glance, but did not speak.

All of Hanno's doubts returned. He ducked his head awkwardly, telling himself that Gaius must be prepared to help. Why else were they here?

With several domestic slaves looking on, however, there was no chance of asking. One of them scurried past to take the horse's reins, and Gaius threw an arm around Quintus' shoulders. 'Let's go inside. Father can't wait to see you. He ordered a piglet roasted in your honour.' Gaius eyed the stable boy. 'Make sure my friend's slave gets fed. Find him a bed too.'

'Yes, sir.'

Hanno's unease abated a little when Quintus turned and gave him a wink. Hanno forced himself to relax as the gate shut, leaving him on the street. He followed the boy around the corner of the house to the stables, which were in a separate walled courtyard. The young slave proved to be as taciturn as he was ugly. They rubbed down, fed and watered Quintus' mount in complete silence, which suited Hanno down to the ground. Next they entered Martialis' kitchen through a door in the adjoining wall. Similar to Julius' jurisdiction, it was a hot, busy place, filled with the clatter of pans and shouted orders. The rich smell of cooking pork filled Hanno's nostrils and set his stomach rumbling. Keen to avoid attention, he found a quiet spot in the corridor that led to the pantry, where he sat down.

A few moments later, the stable boy appeared bearing two plates heaped high with bread, roast meat and vegetables. He shoved one at Hanno. 'You're in luck tonight. The piglet could feed twenty people, so the master won't notice if his slaves also have a share.'

'Thank you.' Hanno seized the platter. This was a better feed than he'd had in months.

When they'd finished, the stable boy squinted at Hanno. 'Do you play dice?'

Hanno did, but he felt as tense as the arm on a cocked catapult. So much was at stake tonight. 'No.'

Looking vaguely disappointed, the slave shuffled off. 'Come on. I'll show you a place to sleep.'

Hanno was taken back to the stables, and shown a quiet corner near the door. 'No lights can be left in here. Too great a risk of fire.' The stable boy indicated his small oil light. 'I'll be taking this with me.'

'Fine,' replied Hanno.

With a shrug, the slave left him to it. As the flickering glow of the other's lamp receded, Hanno was left in complete darkness. He didn't mind about that. It was more the fact that, with Suniaton's escape so close, he was about to spend several hours alone. After a while, he began to look forward to the occasional stamp of a hoof or a gentle whinny. The frequent noise of rats scurrying to and fro was less welcome, but it was a minor inconvenience compared to his reason for being there.

To Hanno's annoyance, the evening dragged by more slowly than an entire week. He spent an age praying to the gods, asking for their aid in ensuring that Gaius helped to free Suniaton. Growing frustrated with the overwhelming silence that met each of his requests, Hanno tried to sleep. He had no luck at all. His spirits rose when the stable boy and two other slaves entered the building. Despite his frustration, time *was* passing. Pretending to be asleep, Hanno heard them clamber up the rickety ladder to the hay store over the horses' stalls. Their incoherent mumbling led him to assume that they'd been drinking. Their oil light was extinguished almost immediately, and it wasn't long before a cadence of snores from above filled Hanno's ears. After what seemed an age, he felt his way over to the kitchen door, where Quintus had told him to wait.

When the door opened smoothly inwards, it caught Hanno unawares. 'Who is it?' he whispered nervously.

'Pluto himself, come to carry you away,' Quintus muttered. 'Who do you think?'

Hanno shivered. Even mentioning the Roman god of the

underworld felt like bad luck. He offered up another prayer to Eshmoun, asking for his protection.

Quintus was followed by Gaius, who was carrying a small, shuttered lantern. Both were wearing dark cloaks.

Hanno could take it no more. 'What are we going to do?'

'Outside.' Gaius led them to the stable door, where he lifted the locking bar and gently laid it on the floor. A waft of cool air hit their faces as he tugged the door open. Gaius padded out and checked the street. 'All clear!' he hissed an instant later.

Quintus shoved Hanno out first, and pulled the portal to behind them.

'Come on, Gaius. Are you finally going to tell us what you've planned?' asked Quintus.

Hanno's stomach clenched into a knot.

'I will,' muttered Gaius, 'but your slave should know something first.'

'He's not a slave any more,' Quintus hissed. 'I freed him.'

'You and I know that that holds about as much water as a leaky bucket.'

Quintus did not reply.

Hanno's breath caught in his chest. Gaius was clearly cut from different cloth to Quintus. He wanted to leave, but that would mean extinguishing whatever hope there was of freeing his friend. Gritting his teeth, he waited.

'I was stunned when you first told me what you'd done, Quintus,' Gaius whispered. 'I said nothing of course. You're my oldest friend. But you took a step too far when you asked me to help free another slave. That I could not do.'

'Gaius, I—' Quintus began. The poor light could not conceal the embarrassment in his voice.

'I changed my mind, however, when I found out who owned the slave you were interested in.' Gaius paused. 'The official who died was none other than the biggest persecutor of Oscan nobility that this city has ever seen. His shitbag of a son is little better.

Stealing . . . freeing . . . one of his slaves is the least I would do to the bastard.'

Hanno let out a long sigh.

'Thank you, Gaius,' whispered Quintus. He wasn't going to question his friend's motives at a moment such as this.

At once Gaius brought them into a little huddle. 'I started off by spending days hanging around in the street where the official's son lives. I found out little, but I did get to know the faces of everyone who lived in his house. Then my luck changed. About a week ago, I saw the major-domo coming out of a brothel in a different part of town.'

'So what?' demanded Quintus. 'That's hardly unusual.'

Gaius' teeth flashed white in the darkness. 'Except when I went inside and asked who he'd been fucking, the madam went all coy. I slipped her a few coins, and she soon changed her tune. It seems that the major-domo has a taste for young boys.'

'Filthy bastard,' muttered Quintus.

An image of Hostus popped into Hanno's mind. His father's enemy was known for a similar taste in flesh. 'It's disgusting, but is it a crime?' he asked. 'It's not in Carthage, unfortunately.'

'The practice is frowned upon by many, but it isn't against the law for citizens, like us,' Gaius replied. 'Slaves are a different matter, however. I doubt that the official's son would be too pleased to find out about his major-domo's habits. The madam said that he tends to get overexcited. Violent. She's had to intervene a number of times to stop her boys from being badly injured.'

'Fucking animal,' said Quintus, looking revolted.

Hanno was just grateful that he and Suniaton hadn't been sold to a similar fate. 'So you're blackmailing him?'

'Basically, yes,' Gaius answered. 'He's agreed to drug the slave who guards the door, which will give him a chance to let Suniaton out. Of course the poor bastard doorman will probably end up on a cross for letting another slave escape, but the major-domo doesn't care about that. He's only thinking of his own skin.'

'And if he doesn't play along?' enquired Quintus. His words made Hanno's stomach clench.

'His owner will receive an anonymous letter detailing his sordid activities to the letter, and giving the brothel's address should he wish to corroborate the details.'

'Excellent,' murmured Quintus.

For a moment, Hanno's delight at Gaius' plan was soured by the knowledge that an innocent slave would suffer, or even die, so that Suni might be free. He quelled the thought without remorse. He would kill to save his friend. How was this any different? 'It sounds foolproof,' he said. 'Thank you.'

'I'm not doing it for you,' Gaius replied curtly. 'I'm doing it because it gives me an opportunity to get back at the official's son.' He chuckled at the others' confusion. 'By sunset tomorrow, everyone in the town will have heard the rumour that he likes to screw young boys. Not the best way to start a political career, is it?' He looked at Gaius, who gave a resigned shrug. 'Best get moving now, though. Stay close.'

Telling himself that it didn't matter what Gaius' reasons for helping were, Hanno followed the two Romans through the darkened streets. The only living thing that they encountered was a scrawny dog, which raised its hackles and growled at the interlopers to its territory. It darted, yelping, out of the way when Gaius aimed a hefty kick at it, and it wasn't long before they were crouched by the front door of a nondescript house, three shadows that could barely be seen. Apart from the chinks of light that escaped the wooden shutters of a flat on the opposite side of the lane, it was pitch black.

Checking the street yet again, Gaius rapped lightly on the door with his knuckles. There was no response from within, and Hanno began to panic. He glanced at the myriad of stars that lit the night sky. Eshmoun, he begged, do not forget Suniaton, your devoted follower, and son of your priest in Carthage. Great Tanit, have mercy.

276

His prayers were answered a moment later when, with a faint creak, the door opened inwards. 'Who is it?'

'Gaius.'

A short man emerged cautiously on to the street. Seeing Quintus and Hanno, he stiffened. Gaius was quick to jump in with the reassurance that they were friends, and the figure relaxed a fraction. His receding hair, long nose, and darting eyes made him resemble a rat, thought Hanno distastefully. It was no surprise that he fucked little boys. Yet this was the major-domo of the house, who was also about to set Suniaton free.

'Well, where's the Carthaginian?' demanded Gaius.

'Just inside. I'll get him,' the major-domo replied, bobbing his head. 'And you'll say nothing to my master?'

'I give you my word,' Gaius answered dryly.

The other nodded uneasily, knowing that this was all he'd get. 'Very well.'

He scuttled from view, and Hanno felt a tinge of suspicion at his speed. There was a short delay before he heard the sound of shuffling feet. Then Hanno saw a stooped figure framed in the doorway, and he leaped forward. 'Suniaton?'

'Hanno?' croaked the other.

Throwing his arms around Suniaton, Hanno clung to his friend like a drowning man. He was dimly aware of the door shutting and a bolt sliding across to lock it. Hanno didn't care. Hot tears of joy scalded his cheeks; he felt moisture soak into his tunic as Suniaton wept too. For a moment, they just stood there, each revelling in the fact that the other was still alive. Abruptly, Suniaton's knees gave way beneath him. Hanno had to stop him from falling. He studied Suniaton's face. Gone was the round-faced young man he was familiar with. In his place stood a gaunt-cheeked, unshaven wretch with long hair. 'You're half starved,' Hanno cried.

'It's not that,' replied Suniaton. His eyes were deep pools of pain. 'I'm hurt.'

Suddenly, Hanno understood the reason for Suniaton's hunched posture. 'How badly?'

'I'll live.' Despite his brave words, Suniaton grimaced. 'I got beaten in a fight two days ago. I've got several wounds, but the worst is a slash across the top of my right thigh.'

Gaius thumped on the door. 'Treacherous bastard! You said nothing about this.'

To his surprise, the major-domo replied. 'I was told only to bring him out at the appointed hour. No one said anything about whether he was well or not.'

'You whoreson!' hissed Hanno. 'I should cut your balls off.' He leaned his shoulder against the timbers and heaved.

Quintus intervened. 'It's not safe here.' He moved to stand by Suniaton. 'You take one arm, and I'll take the other,' he said to Hanno.

Hanno nodded. There was no point wasting time. The major-domo could take his own chances now. Only the gods knew whether the drugging of the doorman would fool his master. It mattered not at all. They had to get Suniaton back to Gaius' house, where they could examine his wounds.

Fortunately, Suniaton was proved to be right about his injuries. Although he was in considerable pain, the clean sword cuts were not life-threatening. As far as Hanno could tell, they had been stitched reasonably well. Yet the worst wound concerned him greatly. The biggest muscle in Suniaton's right thigh had nearly been severed. There was nothing they could do about it, and so they prepared to leave. They had to get to safety before dawn. Bidding farewell to Gaius, the pair heaved Suniaton up on to Quintus' mount. Having bribed a sentry, they passed out of the town with relative ease. The horse's movement caused Suniaton so much pain, however, that he soon passed out. Hanno could do nothing but support his friend as he walked alongside. He would ask Quintus to get some papaverum from Elira later. For now, he thanked Tanit and Eshmoun, and asked for their continued blessing. Hopefully, Suniaton just needed time. Hanno was desperate to head for Iberia, but he would not leave his friend behind now.

The war would have to wait.

Bostar eyed the figures on the other side of the Rhodanus. Although the deep, fast-flowing water was more than five hundred paces across at this point, the Volcae camp was easy to make out between the trees that dotted the far bank. There were scores of tents and lines of tethered horses, denoting the presence of hundreds of warriors. Sentries patrolled the waterline day and night. Given that the tribesmen normally lived on both sides of the river, their intent could not be more plain. They would pay dearly for their combative stance, thought Bostar. Hannibal had given him his orders not an hour since. Once he'd made an offering to the gods, it was time to go. His phalanx and the three hundred scutarii the general had insisted he also take were already assembled beyond the Libyans' tent lines. Their destination, an island at a narrow point in the river, was a day's march to the north.

Sapho's voice made him jump. 'Why couldn't the stupid bastards be like the other tribes around here?'

'Sell us boats and supplies, you mean?' Bostar asked, trying to look pleased to see his brother. What was Sapho, who still had no idea of his mission, doing here at this early hour? Why did I mention it to Father? thought Bostar, panicking. He took a deep breath. Calm down. I asked him not to mention it to a soul. He won't have.

'Yes. Instead, they'll kill a tiny fraction of our troops before being annihilated themselves. Even simple savages such as they must know that our army can't be stopped from crossing the Rhodanus.'

Bostar shrugged. 'I suppose they're like the Ausetani. Defending their territory is a matter of pride. It doesn't matter how badly they're outnumbered. Death in battle is not something to be ashamed of.'

'Sheep-shagging inbreds,' said Sapho with a derisive snort. 'Why can't they understand that all we want to do is cross this poxy river and be on our way?'

Bostar refrained from asking the obvious question: wasn't the response of the Volcae how Sapho, or he, might act in a similar situation? 'Never mind. Hannibal gave them their chance. Now, what was it that you wanted? I was about to take my phalanx out on a march,' he lied bluffly, unable to think of what else to say.

'Gods, your men must *love* you. Haven't we done enough of that recently? That explains why you're in full uniform at this hour.' Sapho made a dismissive gesture. 'It was nothing that can't wait. Just that I noticed plenty of game trails leading down to the water's edge. I thought I'd follow them beyond the camp. Would you like to come along?'

Bostar was completely taken aback by this. 'What, and go looking for boar?' he faltered.

'Or deer.' Sapho threw him a crooked, awkward grin. 'Anything to vary our current diet.'

'A bit of fresh meat wouldn't go amiss,' Bostar admitted ruefully. He felt torn. The proposal was clearly a bridge-building effort on Sapho's part, but he couldn't disobey Hannibal's orders; nor could he reveal them. They were still top secret. What to say? 'I'd love to, but not today,' he managed eventually. 'Who knows what time I'll get back?'

Sapho wasn't to be put off. 'How about tomorrow?' he asked cheerfully.

Bostar's anguish grew. Great Melqart, he thought, what have I done to deserve this? He and his men would only be getting into position by the following evening. On the far bank. 'I'm not sure . . .' he began.

Sapho's good humour fell away. 'So you'd rather spend time with your men than your own brother?'

'It's not that,' Bostar protested. 'Going hunting with you sounds wonderful.'

'What is it then?' Sapho snarled.

Bostar's mind was empty of ideas. 'I can't say,' he muttered.

Sapho's lip curled even further. 'Admit it. I'm not good enough for you, am I? Never have been!'

'That's not true. How can you say such a thing?' Bostar cried, horrified.

'Bostar!' Their father's cheerful voice cut across the argument like a knife. Startled, both brothers glanced around. Malchus was approaching from the direction of his tent lines. 'I thought you'd be gone by now,' he said as he drew nearer.

'I was just leaving,' replied Bostar uneasily. Let me get away without any more problems, Baal Saphon, he prayed. 'I'll see you later.'

Bostar's plea was not answered; Malchus gave him a broad wink. 'Good luck.'

'Eh?' said Sapho with a puzzled frown. 'Why would he need that on a training march?'

Malchus looked uncomfortable. 'You never know, he might break an ankle. The trails around here are very uneven.'

'That's a lie if I ever heard one. Besides, when have you ever wished us luck for so trivial a matter?' Sapho scoffed. He turned on Bostar. 'Something else is going on, isn't it? That's why you won't come hunting!'

Bostar felt his face grow red. 'I've got to go,' he muttered, picking up his shield.

Furious, Sapho blocked his path. 'Where are you going?'

'Get out of my way,' said Bostar.

'Is that an order, *sir*?' Contempt dripped from the last word.

'Move, Sapho!' snapped Malchus. 'Your brother's orders come from Hannibal himself.'

'It's like that, is it?' Sapho stepped aside, his eyes filled with jealousy. 'You could have said. Just a hint.'

Bostar looked at him, and knew he'd made a mistake. 'I'm sorry.'

'No, you're not,' Sapho hissed. He lowered his voice even further. 'Lick-arse. Perfect fucking officer.'

A towering fury took hold of Bostar. Somehow, he managed to keep it in check. 'Actually, I said nothing because I didn't want you to feel that you'd been overlooked.'

'You're so fucking kind,' Sapho shouted, the veins in his neck bulging. 'I hope you get killed wherever you're going.'

Malchus' mouth opened in rebuke, but Bostar held his hand up. Oddly, his anger had been replaced by sorrow. 'I trust that you wish the mission to be successful at least?'

Shame filled Sapho's face, but he had no chance to reply.

Bostar turned to Malchus. 'Farewell, Father.'

Malchus' eyes were dark pools of sorrow. 'May the gods watch over you and your men.'

Bostar nodded and walked away.

'Bostar!'

He ignored Sapho's cry.

It felt as if he'd just lost another brother.

Two days later, Bostar and his men were in position. Theirs had been a hard journey. After a long march on the first day, their guides had brought them to a fork in the Rhodanus. The island in the centre of the river had made their crossing much easier. Not knowing if there were any Volcae on the opposite bank, they had waited until nightfall. Then, using rafts constructed from a combination of chopped-down trees and inflated animal skins, Bostar and ten handpicked men had swum to the other side. To their immense relief, the woods had been empty of all but owls and foxes. Soon after, the remaining soldiers had safely joined him. Bostar had not forgotten to give thanks to the gods for this good fortune. Hannibal and the entire army were relying on them. If they failed, hundreds, or even thousands, of men would die at the hands of the Volcae when the Carthaginian forces began to cross.

At sunrise, they had marched south, halting only when the enemy encampment had been identified. Leaving his party to rest in the dense thickets that occupied the high ground overlooking the river, Bostar and a few sentries had spent the night on their bellies, watching the Volcae sitting around their fires. The tribesmen seemed oblivious to any danger, which pleased him. Somehow that made his anguish over the argument with Sapho easier to bear. Bostar had no wish to be enemies with his brother. Let us both survive the struggle to come, he prayed, and make our peace afterwards.

As dawn arrived, it became possible to make out the enormous Carthaginian camp on the far bank. With growing tension, Bostar waited until he could see troops near the water's edge, cavalrymen climbing into the larger craft, and infantry scrambling into the canoes. He even spied Hannibal in his burnished cuirass, directing operations. Still Bostar held on. Picking the right moment to charge was vital. Too soon, and he and his men risked being slaughtered; too late, and innumerable soldiers in the boats would die.

It wasn't long before the Volcae sentinels noticed the activity opposite their position and raised the alarm. Clutching their weapons, hundreds of warriors emerged from their tents and ran down to the bank. There they paced threateningly up and down, screaming abuse at the Carthaginians and bragging of their exploits. Bostar was thrilled. The enemy's camp had been abandoned, and every man's gaze was fixed on the flotilla of vessels opposite. It was time to move. 'Light the fires!' he hissed. 'Quickly!'

A trio of kneeling spearmen, who had been regarding him nervously, struck their flints together. *Clack, clack, clack,* went the stones. Sparks dropped on to the little mounds of dry tinder before each man. Bostar sighed with relief as a tiny flame licked first up the side of one pile, and then another. The third heap took flame a moment later. The soldiers encouraged the fires by blowing on them vigorously.

Fretfully chewing a fingernail, Bostar waited until each blaze was strong enough. 'Add the green leaves,' he ordered. He watched intently as thick eddies of smoke from the damp foliage curled up into the air and climbed above the tops of the trees. The instant it had, Bostar's gaze shot to the opposite bank. 'Come on,' he muttered. 'You have to be able to see it now.'

His prayers were answered as Hannibal and his soldiers sprang into action. Boat after boat was pushed out into the water. The larger craft, carrying the cavalrymen, who were each leading six or seven horses, stayed upstream. Their size and number helped to reduce the impact of the powerful current on the smaller vessels containing the infantry. The Volcae responded at once. Every man with a bow or spear pushed forward to the water's edge and waited for his chance.

'Come on,' muttered Bostar to his three spearmen. 'It's time to give those shitbags a surprise they'll never forget.'

Moments later, he and most of his force were trotting down the slope towards the riverbank. The remainder, a hundred scutarii, were heading for the Volcae camp. They ran in silence, hard and fast. Rivulets of sweat ran from under Bostar's bronze helmet to coat his face. He did his best to ignore it, counting his steps instead. During the long wait, he had made repeated estimates of the distance from where they had lain hidden to the water's edge. Five hundred paces, Bostar told himself. To the enemy tents, it was only 350. It seemed an eternity, but the Volcae were so busy shouting at the approaching boats that they had soon covered a hundred paces without being challenged. Then it was 150; 175. Hannibal's boats had reached the midpoint of the river. As Bostar counted two hundred, he saw a figure turn to address one of his companions. An expression of stunned disbelief crossed the man's face as he took in the mass of soldiers running towards him. Bostar had covered another ten steps before the warrior's warning cry ripped through the air. It came far too late, he thought triumphantly.

Bostar threw back his head and roared, 'Charge! For Hannibal and Carthage!'

There was an inarticulate roar of agreement from his men as they closed in on the bewildered Volcae, who were already wailing in fright at the prospect of being attacked from the front and rear. Suddenly, their enemies' distress grew even greater and Bostar glanced over his shoulder. To his delight, the Volcae tents were going up in flames. The scutarii were following their orders perfectly.

The warriors' disarray helped greatly to reduce the Carthaginian casualties. The tribesmen were far more concerned with protecting their own backs than aiming missiles at the helpless troops in their boats. However, their poor discipline and general panic meant that the Volcae had little success with Bostar's soldiers either. They loosed their spears and arrows in ragged, early volleys that had barely enough power to reach the spearmen's front ranks. Fewer than two dozen men had been downed before they had come within what Bostar considered proper range.

Calmly, he ordered his soldiers to throw their spears. This massed effort stood in stark comparison to the tribesmen's pathetic efforts. Hundreds of shafts curved up into the air, to fall in dense shoals among the unprepared Volcae, most of whom were not wearing armour. The volley caused heavy casualties. The screams of the injured and dying served to increase the warriors' fear and confusion. Bostar laughed at the magnificence of Hannibal's plan. One moment, the Volcae had been waiting for an easy slaughter, and the next, they were being attacked from behind while their tents went up in flames.

It was then that the lead Carthaginian boats pulled into the riverbank. Led by their general, scores of scutarii and caetrati threw themselves into the shallows. Their fierce battle cries were the final straw for the terrified Volcae, who could take no more. Faces twisted in fear, they broke and ran. 'Draw swords!' Bostar shouted delightedly, leading his men to complete the rout. The crossing of the river was theirs, which proved that the gods were still smiling on Hannibal and his army.

Within a quarter of an hour, it was all over. Hundreds of Volcae lay dead or dying on the grass, while the broken survivors ran for their lives into the nearby woods. Squadrons of whooping Numidians were already in pursuit. Few of the fugitives would live to tell the tale of the ambush, thought Bostar. But some would, and the legend of Hannibal's passing would spread. Bloody lessons such as this were like the siege of Saguntum. They sent a clear message to the surrounding tribes that to resist the Carthaginian army resulted in just one thing. Total defeat. Bostar wished vainly that it proved to be this simple with the Romans.

His task completed, he stood his men down and went in search of Hannibal. By now, the bank was thronged with infantry, slingers and cavalrymen leading their horses away from the river. Officers shouted in frustration, trying to assemble their scattered units. The river was dotted with dozens of boats travelling in each direction. The mammoth task of ferrying tens of thousands of men and vast quantities of supplies over the Rhodanus was under way.

Bostar threaded his way through the soldiers, scanning the faces for his family. When he saw Malchus, his heart leaped with joy. Sapho was by his side. Bostar hesitated, before recognising that he felt relief at the sight of his brother. He was grateful for this gut instinct. Whatever the circumstances of their parting, blood was thicker than water.

Telling himself that all would be well, Bostar raised a hand. 'Father! Sapho!' he shouted.

It rapidly became clear that Suniaton would take months to recover; that was, if his wounds ever healed fully. Hanno was not at all sure they would. Certainly, his friend would never be fit to fight again. There was little doubt now that Suniaton's heavy limp would be lifelong. But, as he repeatedly told Hanno, at least he was alive.

Hanno nodded and smiled, trying to ignore the resentment that clawed at his happiness over Suniaton's rescue. He failed, because his friend was not fit to journey on his own, and might never be. Hanno grew irritable and withdrawn, and took to spending his time outside the hut, away from Suniaton. This made him feel even worse, but when he returned, determined to make amends, and saw his friend hobbling about on his home-made crutch, Hanno's anger always returned.

On the fourth day, the pair had an unexpected visit from Quintus and Aurelia. 'It's all right, there's been no news from Capua,' Quintus said as he dismounted.

Hanno relaxed a fraction. 'What brings you here then?'

'I thought you'd want to know. Father and Flaccus are about to leave. Finally, Publius Cornelius Scipio and his legions are ready.'

Hanno's heart stopped for a moment. 'Are they headed for Iberia?'

'Yes. The northeast coast. That's where they think that Hannibal is,' replied Quintus in a neutral tone.

'I see,' said Hanno, fighting to remain calm. Inside, his desire to leave had resurfaced. 'And the army that's bound for Carthage?'

'It will be leaving soon too.' Quintus looked awkward. 'I'm sorry.'

'There's nothing to be sorry for,' Hanno muttered gruffly. 'It's not your doing.'

Quintus was still uncomfortable, because he moved off to check Suniaton's injured thigh without answering. Hanno thought guiltily, I should be doing that. For all the good it would do, his mind retorted. He'll never walk properly again.

Aurelia's voice cut into his reverie. 'We won't see Father for months,' she said sadly. 'And Quintus never stops talking about going to join him. Before long, Mother and I may be left alone.'

Hanno made a sympathetic gesture, but he wasn't concentrating; all he could think of was following Scipio'ss army to Iberia.

Aurelia mistook his silence for sorrow. 'How could I be so thoughtless? Who knows when you will see your family?'

Hanno scowled, but not because of what she'd said. Hannibal and his host would shortly face a Roman consular army. Meanwhile, he was stuck here with Suniaton.

'Hanno? What is it?'

'Eh?' he answered. 'Nothing.'

Aurelia followed his gaze to Suniaton, who was gingerly following Quintus' instructions. The realisation hit her at once. Like a cat, she pounced. 'You want to go to war too,' she whispered. 'But you can't, because of your loyalty to Suni.'

Stricken, Hanno stared at the ground.

Aurelia touched his arm. 'There is no greater love you could show a friend than standing by him in his time of need. It requires true courage.'

Hanno swallowed hard. 'I should be happy to stay with him, though, not angry.'

'You can't help it.' Aurelia sighed. 'You're a soldier, like my father and brother.'

Almost on cue, Quintus came striding over. 'What's that?'

Neither Aurelia nor Hanno answered.

Quintus grinned. 'What's the big secret? Have you guessed that I'm going to go and find Father?'

Aurelia's mouth opened in horror. Hanno was similarly shocked, but before either could respond, Suniaton joined them, obviously intent on speaking. Surprised by the Carthaginian's interruption, Quintus deferred to him. Suni's words struck everyone dumb. 'I know how hard it is for you, Hanno. Waiting for me to recover, when all you want to do is join Hannibal's army.'

Hanno's guilt swelled immeasurably. 'I will stay with you as long as necessary. That's all there is to it,' he declared. Quickly, he turned to Quintus. 'What made you decide to leave now?'

'I have to tell Father about the way Agesandros has been carrying on. Power has gone to his head.'

Aurelia butted in angrily. 'That's not your reason. It would be crazy to get rid of an experienced overseer at a time like this, and you know it. Besides, Agesandros hasn't done enough to warrant being replaced. We'll have to live with him.'

Quintus set his jaw. 'Well, I'm going anyway. My training is finished. The war could be over in a few months. I'll miss it if I just wait to be called up.'

You underestimate Hannibal, thought Hanno darkly.

'You're crazy,' accused Aurelia. 'How will you find Father in the middle of a war?'

A flicker of fear flashed across Quintus' face. 'I'll reach him before that,' he declared, full of apparent bravado. 'All I need to do is take passage to the Iberian port that Scipio made for. I'll buy a horse there, and follow the legions. By the time I find Father, it will be far too late to send me back.' He glared, daring Hanno and his sister to challenge him.

'It's madness to talk about travelling so far on your own,' Aurelia cried. 'You've never been further than Capua before.'

'I'll manage,' Quintus muttered, glowering.

'Really?' demanded Aurelia sarcastically. She was surprised by how angry she felt when she'd known this was going to happen sooner or later.

'Why wouldn't I?' Quintus shot back.

An awkward silence fell.

Suniaton cleared his throat. 'Why don't you go with Quintus?' he asked, astonishing Hanno. 'Two swords on the road will be better than one.'

Suddenly, Aurelia's heart started pounding. Shocked by her emotions, she had to bite her lip not to protest aloud.

Hanno saw the flash of hope in Quintus' eyes. To his surprise and shame, he felt the same emotion in his heart. 'I'm not leaving you, Suni,' he protested.

'You've done more than enough for me, especially when it's my fault that we're here in the first place,' insisted Suniaton. 'You have been waiting your whole life for this war. I have not. You know that I'd rather be a priest than a soldier. So, with Quintus' and Aurelia's permission, I will remain here.' Quintus nodded his acquiescence, and Suniaton continued, 'When I'm fully recovered, I will travel to Carthage, alone.'

'I don't know what to say,' Hanno stuttered, his feelings fluctuating between sadness and excitement.

Suniaton held up a hand, stalling his protest. 'I will have it no other way.'

Hanno's protest died in his throat. 'I'm still in your debt, Quintus,' he said. 'Accompanying you might repay part of that obligation. What do you say?'

'I'd be honoured to have you as a companion,' said Quintus, bowing his head to conceal his relief.

Now, Aurelia's grief knew no bounds. She was going to lose not only her brother, but also Hanno, and there was nothing she could do about it. A tiny sob escaped her lips. Quintus put an arm around her, and Aurelia managed to rally herself. 'Come back safely.'

'Of course I will,' he murmured. 'Father will also.'

Nervously, Aurelia fixed her eyes on Hanno. 'You too,' she whispered.

Quintus' mouth opened as the two words hung in the air.

Hanno was stunned. Aurelia was promised to another, and a high-ranking Roman at that. Did she really mean what he thought? He studied her face for a moment.

'I will,' he said finally. 'One day.'

Chapter XIV: Confrontation

Massilia, on the southern coast of Gaul

Fabricius stared at the Greek columns on the temples opposite the quay and smiled. 'Very different to those at home,' he said. 'It feels good to be in a foreign land at last.'

Five days before, the Roman fleet and its commander, the consul Publius Cornelius Scipio, had finally set sail. Fabricius and Flaccus had been on board one of the sixty quinqueremes that had left from Pisae, on the west coast of Italy. Hugging the Ligurian shoreline all the way to the Greek city of Massilia, a long-term Roman ally on the south coast of Gaul, the flotilla had arrived not two hours previously.

'Too many months were spent talking,' Flaccus agreed. 'It's time now to carry war to the Carthaginians, and settle the matter swiftly.' He eyed Fabricius, who was nodding in vigorous agreement. 'You don't like sitting on your hands, eh?'

'No.' His recent spell in Rome had brought home to Fabricius the fact that he was no politician. He'd stayed in the capital because he was eager to fight. His desire for action, however, had vanished beneath a wave of debates in the Senate, just one of which could take more than a week. 'I know that the politicians' original reasons for delaying were simple,' he admitted. 'With most of the army disbanded, it was logical to wait for the new consuls to be appointed before making any far-reaching decisions. But to take so long after that?'

'Don't forget the other matters of foreign policy which had to be discussed.' Flaccus' tone was reproving. 'Rome has many concerns other than what goes on in Iberia.'

'Of course.' Fabricius sighed. That had been one of the hardest lessons for him to learn.

'Philip V of Macedon has never been the greatest friend of Rome,' said Flaccus. 'But giving refuge to Demetrius of Pharos showed that he really wishes us ill.'

'True.' Demetrius, the deposed King of Illyricum, had himself been the cause of much recent trouble to the Republic. 'Is a month of debates about the two of them really necessary, though?'

Flaccus' face took on a pompous expression. 'Such is the Senate's way, as it has been for nearly three hundred years. Who are we to question such a hallowed process?'

Fabricius bit back his pithy response. In his mind, the Senate would work far more efficiently if only the debates were better controlled. He smiled diplomatically. 'To be fair, it reacted fast when word came of the unrest among the Gaulish tribes.'

Flaccus looked pleased. 'And as soon as it became clear that the proposed new Latin colonies at Placentia and Cremona would not be enough, it requisitioned one of the legions from our expeditionary force. While I was stuck in Rome, raising and training the new units that were required, at least you got a taste of action!' He wagged a finger at Fabricius. 'Three months of it.'

Fabricius had grown used to the other's patronising manner, but still found it irritating. 'You weren't there. The Boii and Insubres are no pushover,' he growled. 'Don't you remember Telamon? We did well to end it so swiftly. Hundreds of our soldiers were slain, and many more were injured.'

Flaccus flushed. 'I apologise. I did not mean to belittle your efforts, or those of the men who died.'

'Good,' Fabricius replied, placated. 'It doesn't take away from the fact that we should have been in Iberia three months ago!'

Flaccus made a conciliatory gesture. 'At least we're in Massilia now. Soon the Saguntines will be avenged.'

'A bit late, isn't it?' demanded Fabricius sourly. The Senate's refusal to act had meant leaving the Saguntines to their fate, which had not sat well with his conscience. It still didn't.

'Come now,' entreated Flaccus. 'We've just been through all that.'

'I know,' Fabricius replied heatedly. 'But an ally of Rome should never be treated as Saguntum was.'

Flaccus' voice grew soft. 'You know that I agree with you. Did I not speak repeatedly in the Senate about the dishonour of abandoning the city?'

'You did.' Yet you probably knew that your words would make little difference, thought Fabricius. It had sounded good, however, and showed a pleasingly combative side to his prospective son-in-law's character.

'Thank all the gods that we're serving under Scipio rather than Tiberius Sempronius Longus,' said Flaccus. 'We shall see action far sooner than they will. Last I heard, Longus' fleet wasn't going to be ready for another month.'

'How frustrating.'

'Whereas we can set sail the moment that the fleet's supplies of food and water have been renewed.' Flaccus rattled the hilt of his ornamental sword.

'Let's not forget to hear what information the local intelligence has gathered,' warned Fabricius. 'Nothing has been heard of Hannibal for several months.'

'That's because he's sitting on his hairy gugga arse in Iberia, drinking local wine and waiting for us to arrive!' Flaccus sneered.

'Maybe he is,' said Fabricius with a smile, 'but being forewarned is to be forearmed.'

He had no idea that, within the next few hours, his words would be proven true.

Hannibal was no longer in Iberia.

According to the exhausted Massiliote messengers who rode in on lathered mounts, he was probably no more than a day's march away.

Flaccus and the other senior officers received an immediate summons to attend Scipio in his headquarters, a sprawling tent at the centre of one of the legions' temporary forts. Fabricius was pleased and surprised to receive a similar order less than an hour later. As he arrived, Fabricius saw Flaccus standing outside with the other high-ranking officers, including Gnaeus, Scipio'ss elder brother, a former consul who was also his *legatus*, or second-in-command. Fabricius saluted, and nodded at Flaccus. To his surprise, his future son-in-law barely acknowledged the gesture. Indeed, his face wore such a thunderous expression that Fabricius wondered what had gone on in the moments prior. He had no time to find out. Recognising Fabricius, the officer in charge of the sentries ushered him inside at once.

They found Scipio talking animatedly with a young Massiliote soldier over a table on which a crudely drawn map had been laid out. Both men were wearing Hellenistic bronze cuirasses, layered pteryges, which protected the groin and the tops of the thighs, and bronze greaves. Yet there was no question, even to the untrained eye, who was in charge. The Massiliote's armour was well made, but, with its magnificent depiction of Hercules' face, Scipio'ss positively exuded quality and wealth. The same could be said of his ornate plumed Attic helmet, which sat on a nearby stool. Although the Massiliote towered over the grey-haired consul, Scipio's confidence more than made up for the difference in height. Fabricius had come to know his commander a little, and liked him. Scipio's calm presence and direct manner were popular with everyone, from the rank and file to the military tribunes. Gnaeus, his brother, was no different.

Scipio looked up. 'Ah, Fabricius! Thank you for coming.'

Fabricius saluted. 'How can I be of service, sir?'

'First meet the commander of the unit that brought us the dramatic news. Fabricius, this is Clearchus. Clearchus, meet Fabricius, of whom I have spoken.'

The two exchanged courteous nods.

'Obviously, you have heard about Hannibal's whereabouts,' Scipio enquired archly. 'You'd have to be deaf not to.'

Fabricius grinned. The news *had* been shouted from the rooftops. 'They say that he and his army have crossed the Rhodanus, sir, and are camped on the eastern shore.'

'Indeed.' Scipio regarded the Massiliote. 'Clearchus?'

'Since word came that Hannibal had crossed into Gaul, we have been patrolling deep inland, using small, highly mobile cavalry units. One such sighted the Carthaginians about two weeks ago, and shadowed them to the river's western bank. It's a long day's ride from here.'

Fabricius' heart thumped in his chest. The rumour *was* true. 'And their number?'

'Perhaps fifty thousand men all told. Not quite a quarter of that is made up of cavalry.'

Fabricius' eyebrows rose. This was a larger army than he'd ever faced in Sicily.

Scipio saw his reaction. 'I was surprised too. Hannibal means to attack Italy. Fortuna had been generous indeed to alert us to his purpose before he arrived. Go on, Clearchus.'

'They camped by the river for several days, constructing rafts and boats, and no doubt planning their tactics against the Volcae, the hostile natives on the eastern side. The result was extraordinary, sir. Hannibal sent a strong force upriver, which crossed undetected and fell on the tribesmen's rear.' Clearchus made a circle of his thumb and forefinger. 'They crushed them with ease. Nearly the whole army has traversed safely since then. Only the elephants remain on the far bank.'

'Imagine if we had landed a week earlier, and been there to

contest the passage of the river. The war might already be over!' Scipio cried in frustration. His face turned cunning. 'We still might have a chance, though, Clearchus?'

'That's right, sir. Getting the elephants across will take at least two to three days. Perhaps more. Several attempts have already failed.'

'Excellent. Now, I need someone to take a look at the Carthaginian army. A Roman officer.' Scipio glanced at Clearchus. 'Not to belittle our Massiliote allies in any way.'

'No insult taken, sir,' said Clearchus, raising his hands.

'Naturally, others wanted this job, but I felt that the task was suited to a veteran. A man who knows how to keep his cool. I thought of you.' Scipio fixed his eyes on Fabricius. 'Well?'

Fabricius felt his breath quicken. Had Flaccus asked for the duty, and been turned down? That might explain his sour expression. 'Of course I'll do it, sir.'

Scipio gave a small smile of approval. 'Speed is of the essence. If you leave at once, you could be back by tomorrow night. The next day, at the latest. I will want good estimates of their numbers, and a breakdown of the troop types.'

Fabricius wasn't going to back down from a challenge like this. 'I will do my best, sir.'

'How many men have you?'

'About two hundred and fifty, sir.'

'Take all of them. Clearchus will guide you.' Scipio looked at the Massiliote. 'How strong is your force?'

'Two hundred riders, sir, all experienced.'

'It should be enough.' Scipio turned back to Fabricius. 'You're in charge. Avoid contact with the enemy unless it cannot be helped. Return quickly. I'll have the army ready to march the moment you return.'

'Yes, sir.' Fabricius saluted crisply; Clearchus did the same. They left the consul poring over his map.

* * *

Fabricius wasted no time. Less than an hour later, he led the ten *turmae* – cavalry units – under his command out of the camp and towards Massilia's north gate. It was a pity that he hadn't had time to replace his losses from the recent campaign, thought Fabricius. Still, he was reasonably happy with the rest of his cavalrymen, who had fought well during the summer. As citizen cavalry, his men were equestrians, and most dressed in a Hellenistic style similar to his own. They wore Boeotian helmets and bleached white tunics, which had a purple stripe running from each shoulder to the hem. Sturdy leather boots that completely enclosed the feet were ubiquitous. All carried thrusting spears, and round cavalry shields, made of ox hide. Few carried swords. The heavy cavalry cloak, or *sagum*, owned by each man and used in bad weather, was tied up in a roll behind the saddlecloth.

They met Clearchus and his riders just outside the city walls. The Massiliote cavalry were irregulars, and no two were dressed alike. With their helmets, spears and small shields, however, they were similar in appearance to the Roman cavalrymen. Fabricius was re-assured by Clearchus' calm manner, and the way his men responded to his orders. If it came to a fight, they'd probably do all right.

With the Massiliotes in the lead, they rode north, stopping only when it grew too dark to continue. Clearchus knew the country-side well, but, as he confided to Fabricius, it was possible that Carthaginian patrols could be operating in the area too. There was no point exposing themselves to unnecessary danger, and riding at night fell into that category. Fabricius did not argue. Clearchus' judiciousness made perfect sense. Ordering no fires to be lit, he had the men set up camp. Double the normal number of sentries were stationed around the perimeter. Long after the soldiers had retired, Fabricius walked from picket to picket, his ears pricked. This was a mission of the utmost importance. If that meant hardly any sleep, then so be it. Nothing could go wrong. Thankfully, he heard nothing other than the occasional screech of an owl.

He and Clearchus had their men up long before dawn. Tension among both sets of riders was immediately palpable. Contact with the enemy was likely before the day was out. After a brief chat with Clearchus, Fabricius sent ten Massiliote riders to scout the trail a mile in advance of the main party. One turma, under the command of his best decurion, accompanied them. Their orders were to return at the slightest hint of anything untoward.

Fabricius' hunch turned out to be the best decision he had ever made.

They had ridden for an hour or so when an outrider returned at the gallop. He dragged his horse to a stop beside Fabricius and Clearchus, who were riding together, and saluted.

Fabricius took a deep breath. 'What news?'

'We've spotted a group of Numidians, sir. Perhaps two miles away.'

Fabricius went very still. His memories of fighting against the lightly armed African horsemen were exclusively bad. 'Did they see you?'

The cavalryman grinned. 'No, sir. We were able to get behind a stand of trees.'

Fabricius hissed in relief. Their mission had escaped discovery – for the moment. 'How many of them were there?'

'Perhaps three hundred in total, sir.'

'Anything else?'

'Yes, sir. The decurion said to tell you that there's a copse about a mile from here that would make a perfect place for an ambush. If you move fast, you could get in place before the Numidians reach it.'

Fabricius' mouth went dry. Scipio had ordered him to avoid confrontation at all costs. How was that possible in this situation, however? To let the enemy cavalry pass while continuing with their own mission would leave his patrol at risk of attack from behind. Aware that everyone's eyes were on him, Fabricius closed his eyes. 'Three hundred men, you say?' he demanded.

'Yes, sir.'

Fabricius made up his mind. They were 450 strong. Easily enough. Opening his eyes, he laid a hand to his sword and was pleased by Clearchus' fierce nod of agreement. 'Swiftly, then,' he said. 'Take us to the copse.'

A short time later, Fabricius found himself in an excellent position overlooking the narrow track they had been following. Thanks to Clearchus' quick-witted suggestion, the entire patrol had ridden up and out of view well before the far entrance to the stand of trees. The trap would be sprung long before the Numidians saw their incriminating tracks – he hoped. Fabricius also wished that they could have concealed themselves better, and effected some method of preventing the Numidians from retreating. With time running out, that had not been possible. Instead, they had to place their trust in the gods. He glanced to either side, seeing the same tense expression on his riders' faces that he felt twisting his own.

The reasons were simple.

Soon, they would set eyes upon the first Carthaginian troops to act in aggression against Rome for more than twenty years. The enemy were not on Sicily either, their historical hunting grounds. The unthinkable had happened, and Fabricius still couldn't quite take it in. Hannibal was in Gaul, and heading for Italy! Calm down, he thought. Of more relevance right now was the fact that if he and his men weren't very lucky, the approaching Numidians would spot them and flee before the ambush began.

The following quarter of an hour felt like eternity to Fabricius. Focusing his gaze on the point where the track entered the copse, he ignored the faint jingle of harness around him, and bird song from the branches above. He couldn't block out all sound, however. A horse stamped a hoof as it grew restless. Someone coughed, drawing a muttered rebuke from the nearest officer. Fabricius glared at the rider responsible before returning his attention to the path. Spotting movement, he blinked. Then his arm shot out, pointing. 'Pssst!' he hissed to the man on either side. A judder of anticipation rippled through the line of waiting cavalrymen.

Amazingly, the pair of enemy scouts who emerged into view were only a short distance in front of the main body of their countrymen. The Numidians appeared no different to the men Fabricius had fought in Sicily. Dark-skinned, lithe, athletic, they rode small horses without saddles, bridles or bits. Their loose tunics had large armholes and were pinned at the shoulder and belted at the waist. The Numidians carried javelins and light, round shields without bosses. Instead of looking around for danger, they were busy talking to each other. Given the empty countryside, thought Fabricius delightedly, it wasn't that surprising. He'd made similar mistakes himself before, and been lucky enough to get away with it.

In they rode, without so much as a glance up the gentle slopes where the Romans and Massiliotes lay hidden. Fabricius held his breath, counting the distance. Eighty, then fifty paces. The front ranks of Numidians entered the copse, and Fabricius' mind flashed back to the war in Sicily. They did not look like much, but these were some of the finest cavalry in the world. Sublime horsemen, they were best at skirmishing, and frustrating the enemy with their stinging attacks. He knew from personal experience that the Numidians' pursuit of a vanquished foe was even more deadly.

It was too soon to sound the charge. As many riders as possible had to come into the copse where the trees would ensnare them. With every passing moment, though, the risk of being discovered grew. Fabricius' stomach clenched painfully, but he did not stir. By the time two-thirds of the horsemen had ridden in, he saw that his men were on the verge of breaking ranks. He could no longer take the pressure either. 'Charge!' he shouted, urging his horse down the slope. 'For Rome!' Bellowing with excitement, 250 cavalry followed. An instant later, Clearchus and his Massiliotes emerged from the other side of the track, screaming at the top of their lungs.

Fabricius revelled in the look of stunned disbelief on the Numidians' faces. It was their job to ambush and fall on an unsuspecting enemy, not the other way around. Surprised, outnumbered and with the advantage of height against them, they instantly wheeled their mounts' heads and tried to flee. Within the space of a dozen heartbeats, total confusion reigned. Although some of those at the rear were already riding away, the vast majority were trapped by the trees. Horses reared in panic; men shouted contradictory orders at each other. Only an occasional rider prepared to fight. All the rest wanted to do was escape. Fabricius bared his teeth exultantly. They had ridden within thirty paces of the enemy without suffering a single casualty, and things were about to get even better. For all their horsemanship and skirmishing skill, the tribesmen were poor at close combat. 'Ready spears,' Fabricius yelled. 'Kill as many as you can!'

With an inarticulate roar, his men obeyed.

Casting fearful looks over their shoulders, the surviving Numidians fled for their lives. Eyeing the bodies littering the ground, Fabricius estimated that more than a hundred of their number had been slain or injured in the initial ambush. The Roman and Massiliote casualties were perhaps half that number. Given the circumstances, this was more than satisfactory. Catching sight of Clearchus, Fabricius beckoned him urgently. 'We've got to follow them,' he said. 'Stick tight to their tails, or there'll be no chance to assess Hannibal's forces.'

Clearchus nodded. 'The wounded, sir?'

'They can fend for themselves. We'll pick them up on the way back.'

'Very good, sir.' The Massiliote turned to relay the order.

'Clearchus?'

'Sir?'

'I want no further engagement with the enemy. A running battle could easily lead to disaster, especially if we encounter more Carthaginian forces. Our mission is more important now than killing a few more Numidians. Understood?'

Clearchus' teeth flashed in the sunshine. 'Of course, sir. Scipio is waiting for us.'

Soon all the able-bodied men had formed up and were ready to ride. Without a backward glance, Fabricius and Clearchus led them after the Numidians. This time, there was no advance party. They rode at top speed, four abreast, knowing that the chance of an attack from the panicked enemy riders was slim to none. It wasn't long before they glimpsed the last of the tribesmen, who screamed in dismay. At once Fabricius ordered his men to slow down. He was relieved when his command was obeyed without question. Poor discipline was too often the reason for battles being lost.

They followed the Numidians along the winding track for perhaps five miles. The flat terrain and the well-beaten track made the pursuit easy. Fabricius had no idea how far the Rhodanus was, but Clearchus reached him as they neared a low, stone-topped hill that stood alone, dominating the surrounding wooded area.

'The river is on the other side of that, sir.'

Immediately, Fabricius held up his hand. 'Halt!' As his order was obeyed, he fixed the Massiliote with his stare. 'Let's go up. Just you and me.'

Clearchus looked startled. 'Are you sure, sir? There could be enemy pickets at its crest.'

'They'll be running after the Numidians!' Fabricius replied confidently. 'And when we come leathering back down here, I want everyone ready to ride, not bunched up on a narrow path.'

Clearchus blinked; then a mischievous smile twitched across his lips. 'I suppose two men against an entire host are as good as a few hundred.'

With a fierce grin, Fabricius slapped his thigh. 'That's the attitude.' He turned to the nearest of his decurions. 'Rest the men. We're going to take a look at what's on the other side of the hill. I want you ready to leave at a moment's notice.'

'Yes, sir!'

Fabricius led the way up the path. He was surprised to find himself feeling more nervous than he had in years. He would never have expected to be the first Roman to set eyes on Hannibal's army. Yet here he was.

Nearing the crest, they found evidence of a sentry post: a stone fireplace full of smoking ash, and bedding rolls, which still bore the imprint of those who'd been sitting on them. They dismounted and tethered their horses before clambering to the peak. Instinctively, Fabricius went down on his belly. The first thing that caught his attention as he peered over the edge was the mob of yelling Numidians driving their horses down the slope. Behind them were a dozen or more running figures: the sentries from the abandoned picket. Fabricius' lips peeled up in a snarl of satisfaction, but as he took in the scene beyond, his mouth fell open in wonder.

In the middle distance glittered the wide band that was the River Rhodanus. Perhaps a hundred paces from the water's edge, the enemy tent lines began. They stretched as far as the eye could see. Fabricius was used to legionary camps that could hold 5,000 men, or even 10,000. What lay before him was much less organised, but far larger. It was more than twice as large as a consular army, which was made up of approximately 20,000 men. 'You weren't exaggerating. This host is immense!' he muttered to Clearchus. 'Scipio should have moved on your intelligence. We'd have caught the bastards napping.'

The Massiliote looked pleased.

Fabricius scanned the encampment, mentally noting everything he saw. Hannibal had superior numbers of horsemen compared to an equivalent Roman force, which worried him. Few things were more important than the quantity of horse at one's disposal.

There were the usual Carthaginian stalwarts: Libyan spearmen and skirmishers, Balearic slingers and Numidian and Iberian cavalry. Most plentiful of all were the infantry, the majority of which were scutarii and caetrati. And last but not least, there were the elephants: the battering rams that had so terrified Roman armies in the past. Perhaps twenty of the massive beasts were already on the near bank. 'Gods,' Fabricius whispered in amazement. 'How in the name of Jupiter did they get them over the river?'

Clearchus touched his arm and pointed. 'On those.'

Fabricius peered at the two massive wooden rafts being pulled back to the far side by rowing boats. There, he could see a dozen or more elephants waiting to be ferried across. Before them, an enormous jetty formed by a double line of square platforms projected some sixty paces out into the fast-flowing water. Dozens of ropes and cables secured the makeshift affair to trees upriver from the pier. He shook his head at the scale of the engineering that had gone into the pier's construction. 'I've heard that elephants are intelligent creatures. Surely they wouldn't just walk on to a floating square of wood?'

Clearchus squinted into the bright light. 'I can see a layer of earth all along the walkway. Maybe it's meant to look like dry land?'

'Clever bastards. So they lead their charges to the end of the jetty, and on to the rafts. Then they cut them free and row across the river.' Rapt, Fabricius watched as, encouraged by its mahout, an elephant was slowly led down the walkway. Even from a distance, it was clear that the creature was not happy. Bugles of distress blared out again and again. It had only walked a third of the jetty's length before it stopped dead in its tracks. In an effort to make the elephant continue, a group of men behind it began shouting and playing drums and cymbals. However, instead of continuing to the raft, which was now tethered to the end of the pier, the creature jumped into the water. There was a wail from its unfortunate mahout as he disappeared from sight, and Fabricius closed his eyes. What a way to die, he thought. When he looked up, the elephant was swimming strongly across the river. Fabricius was engrossed. He had never seen such an incredible sight before.

Suddenly, Clearchus tugged at his arm. 'The Numidians have raised the alarm, sir.'

At the edge of the camp, Fabricius could see the tribesmen milling around. Many were pointing at the hill and beyond. Faint shouts of anger carried through the air, and he smiled mirthlessly. 'Time to go. Scipio will want to hear the news. Good, and bad.'

Fabricius was delighted by Scipio's instantaneous response to his dramatic news. The consul was not afraid of confrontation. Ordering the heavy baggage to be loaded on to the quinqueremes for safety, Scipio led the army north as soon as was humanly possible. Nonetheless, it was three full days before the legions and their allies arrived at the point where the Carthaginians had crossed the river. It was a huge disappointment to find the vast encampment abandoned. As the Roman officers picked their way across the remnants of thousands of campfires, the only life to be seen were the skulking forms of jackals looking for scraps, and the countless birds of prey that hovered overhead for similar reasons.

Hannibal had gone. North, to avoid a battle.

Scipio had difficulty concealing his amazement. 'Who would have thought it?' he muttered. 'He is heading for the Alps, and thence to Cisalpine Gaul.'

Fabricius was still astonished too. He knew no one who had even contemplated that Hannibal would pursue such a plan. Stunning in its simplicity, it had taken them all completely unawares. It was lucky chance that had them standing here today. Now Scipio faced a hard choice. What was the best thing to do?

The consul immediately convened a meeting of his senior

officers on the riverbank. As well as Gnaeus, his legatus, there were twelve tribunes present, six for each regular legion. Following tradition, alternate legions had three senior tribunes, men who had served for more than ten years, while the others had two. The junior tribunes needed only to have seen five years' service. It was a mark of the times, and of the influence of the Minucii, that Flaccus, who had no military experience, should be accorded even the lower rank of junior tribune. As the patrol leader, Fabricius was also present. He felt distinctly nervous in the presence of so many senior officers.

'We are faced with four choices, all of them difficult,' Scipio began. 'To pursue Hannibal and force him to fight, or to withdraw to the coast and return with the whole army to Cisalpine Gaul. The third option would be merely to send word to the Senate of Hannibal's intentions, before continuing as charged to Iberia. Or . . . I could bring the news to Rome myself while Gnaeus takes the legions west.' He scanned his officers' faces, waiting for a response.

Fabricius thought that either the second or fourth options were the best, but he certainly wasn't going to say anything before any of his superiors did. As the silence lengthened, it appeared that none of them were prepared to speak up either. Fabricius fumed. This was one of the most pivotal moments in Roman history, and no one wanted to say the wrong thing. That is, he realised, apart from one. Flaccus was shifting from foot to foot like a man possessed. Fabricius struggled to master his exasperation. Probably all that kept Flaccus' mouth shut was the desire not to breach military protocol by speaking out of turn, before the five senior tribunes.

Eventually, Scipio grew impatient. 'Come now,' he said. 'Let us be frank. You may speak without fear of retribution. I want your honest opinions.'

Gnaeus cleared his throat. 'In theory, Hannibal should be confronted immediately. However, I wonder if it would be the right thing to do?'

'We know that his forces outnumber ours by at least two to one, sir,' added a senior tribune quickly. 'And if we suffered a setback, or even a defeat, what then? Massilia's defences aren't up to withstanding a siege. All of the other legions are occupied on other duties, either in Cisalpine Gaul, or in Sicily with Consul Longus. We have no support to call on.'

Sensible words, thought Fabricius. He was surprised to see Flaccus' face grow red with indignation.

Another senior tribune, an older man than the rest, stepped into view. 'Is the enemy's strength so important, sir?' he demanded angrily. 'Our legionaries are the finest soldiers in the world! They are used to winning victories against vastly superior numbers, and have done so against Carthaginian armies in the past. Why should they not do the same against this . . . *Hannibal*?' He filled the last word with contempt. 'I say we follow him, and stamp on the gugga serpent before it slides into Cisalpine Gaul and prepares to bite us in the heel.'

It was difficult to respond to the tribune's fierce words without seeming unpatriotic, and the first speakers sealed their lips. Even Gnaeus looked unsure. Naturally, Flaccus beamed and nodded in agreement, turning to his fellow junior tribunes for support. Cupping his chin with one hand, Scipio gazed at the nearby fast-flowing water. Everyone waited for his response.

Roman soldiers are indeed without equal, thought Fabricius, but the Carthaginian forces who had left this camp were led by a man who, in less than a year, had conquered large areas of Iberia, passed through the mountains into Gaul and, despite fierce opposition, successfully crossed an enormous river, elephants included. Chasing after Hannibal could prove disastrous.

Scipio held his counsel for an age. At length, he looked up. 'It seems to me that pursuing a larger enemy force into unknown territory would be most unwise. As some have already said, we are alone here apart from our Massiliote allies, who do not number more than a few thousand. We must reconcile ourselves to the fact that the Carthaginians will enter Cisalpine Gaul within the next two months.' Ignoring the shocked gasps this comment produced, Scipio continued, 'Let us also not forget where Hannibal's main base is. If his access to that is cut off, his chance of supplies and reinforcements will be greatly reduced. With this in mind, I propose to hand the command of the consular army to my brother, and for him to lead it to Iberia.' Scipio acknowledged Gnaeus' accepting bow. 'I myself will return to Italy with all speed. I intend to be waiting for Hannibal when he makes his descent from the Alps. In this way both our problems will have been addressed, the gods willing.'

Scipio's decisive manner was good enough for most of the tribunes, who muttered in agreement. Only the older man and Flaccus seemed unhappy. The former was experienced enough to know when to keep quiet, but the latter was not. Ignoring Fabricius' warning look, Flaccus started forward. 'Think again, sir! Hannibal may win many allies among the discontented tribes in Cisalpine Gaul. The next time you meet his army, it could be far bigger.'

Scipio's eyebrows rose at Flaccus' temerity. 'Is that so?' he said icily.

Fabricius was impressed by his future son-in-law's insight, but it was time to shut up. Angering a consul was not an intelligent thing to do. Again, however, Flaccus ignored his pointed stare.

'It is, sir! For the honour of Rome, you must follow Hannibal and defeat him. Think of the shame of a foreign enemy, especially a Carthaginian one, setting his foot on Italian soil.' Seeing his fellow officers' horrified expressions, Flaccus faltered. Then he looked for support. Finding none among his compatriots, his gaze finally fell on Fabricius. 'You agree with me, don't you?'

Suddenly, Fabricius was the centre of attention. He did not know what to say. Agreeing would make him party to Flaccus' insult to the consul. Refusing to agree would, in effect, renege on the newly founded alliance between his family and the Minucii. Both choices seemed as bad as the other.

To his intense relief, Scipio leaped in. 'At first I thought you courageous for speaking your mind. Now I see that it was your arrogance. How dare you speak of Rome's honour when you have never drawn a sword in her defence? The only one here who has not, I might add.' As Flaccus' cheeks flushed crimson, Scipio continued. 'Just so you know, I too hate the idea of an enemy on Roman soil. Yet there is no shame in waiting to face an opponent on the best terms possible, and in Cisalpine Gaul we shall have the entire Republic's resources behind us.'

'I'm sorry, sir,' Flaccus muttered. 'I spoke out of turn.'

Scipio did not acknowledge the apology. 'Next time you place your foot in your mouth, do not try to redeem yourself by asking a junior officer such as Fabricius to disagree with a consul. *That* is a shameful act.' He stalked off with Gnaeus. The other tribunes fell to talking among themselves. They pointedly ignored Flaccus.

Fortunately, Flaccus' outrage was so great that he assumed Fabricius was of the same opinion as he. Complaining bitterly about the public humiliation he had just suffered, he accompanied Fabricius back to the legions. For his part, Fabricius was content to remain silent. He had dismissed Atia's concerns out of hand before, but Flaccus' rash action revealed monstrous arrogance, but also a worrying lack of awareness. What else was he capable of?

Chapter XV: The Alps

Hunching his shoulders against the early-morning chill, Bostar emerged from his tent. He gazed in awe at the towering mountains that reared up before him. The range stretched from north to south above the fertile plain, and occupied the entire eastern horizon. A dense network of pine trees covered the lower slopes, concealing any potential routes of ascent. The sky was clear, but the jagged peaks above were hidden yet by shrouds of grey cloud. Despite this, they were a magnificent sight.

'Lovely to look at, eh?'

Bostar jumped. Not many of the soldiers were stirring, but it was no surprise that his father was already up. 'They are incredible, yes.'

'And we've got to cross them.' Malchus grimaced. 'Our passage of the River Rhodanus seems trivial now, doesn't it?'

Bostar's laugh was a trifle hollow. If anyone had made such a statement a few weeks before, he wouldn't have believed it. Looking at the harsh slopes above, he knew that his father might well be correct. Expecting more than fifty thousand men, thousands of pack animals and thirty-seven elephants to climb into the realm of gods and demons bordered on genius – or madness. Feeling disloyal for even thinking the latter, Bostar glanced around. He was surprised to see Sapho approaching. After the Rhodanus, the brothers had ostensibly patched up their relationship, but the reconciliation had been little more than a façade for their father's benefit. The two avoided each other if at all possible. Bostar forced a smile. 'Sapho.' Try as he might, he could not help but feel hurt when his brother silently responded with a salute.

'That's not necessary, is it?' Malchus' tone was sharp.

'Sorry,' said Sapho offhandedly. 'I'm still half asleep.'

'Yes, it's not exactly your time of day, is it?' retorted Bostar acidly. 'That would be more like midday.'

'Enough!' barked Malchus before Sapho could respond. 'Why can't you at least be civil to each other? There's far more at stake here than your stupid feud.'

As always, their father's outburst silenced the brothers. Unusually, it was Sapho who made the first effort. 'What were you talking about?' he asked.

His attempt made Bostar feel obliged to reply. 'Those.' He pointed at the mountains.

Sapho's face soured. 'Ill fortune awaits us up there. Countless men will be lost, I know it.' He made the sign against evil.

'We've had such good fortune since the Rhodanus, though,' protested Bostar. 'The Romans didn't pursue us. Then the Cavares gave us gifts of food, shoes and warm clothing. Since we entered their territory, their warriors have kept the Allobroges at bay. Who's to say that the gods won't continue to smile on us?'

'The year's practically over. Winter will be here soon. It will be a superhuman task.' An impossible task, thought Sapho dourly. Hell awaits us. He had never liked heights, and the prospect of ascending the Alps – especially in late autumn – filled him with a murmuring dread. Of course he could not admit to that, nor to his resentment of Hannibal for choosing such a difficult route, or for favouring Bostar above him. He jerked his head towards the south. 'We should have travelled along the coast of Gaul.'

311

'That would have meant a pitched battle with the forces our cavalry encountered near the Rhodanus, which was something Hannibal wanted to avoid.' Despite his robust words, Bostar felt his spirits being dragged down. With the friendly Cavares returning to their homes, and nowhere to go other than up, there was no denying what they had let themselves in for. He was grateful when his father intervened.

'I want to hear no more talk like that. It's bad for morale,' growled Malchus. He had similar concerns, but he wouldn't admit them to anyone. 'We must keep faith with Hannibal, as he does with us. His spirits were high last night, weren't they?' He glared at his sons.

'Yes, Father,' Sapho conceded.

'He doesn't *have* to wander around his men's campfires for half the night, sharing their poxy rations and listening to their miserable life stories,' Malchus continued sternly. 'He doesn't sleep alongside them, wrapped only in his cloak, for the good of his health! Hannibal does it because he loves his soldiers as if they were his children. The least we can do is to return that love with utmost fealty.'

'Of course,' Sapho muttered. 'You know that my loyalty is beyond question.'

'And mine,' added Bostar fervently.

Malchus' scowl eased. 'I'm glad to hear it. I know that the next few weeks will be our toughest test yet, but it's officers such as we who will have to give an example. To lead the men when they falter. We must show no weakness, just a steely resolve to reach the top of whichever pass Hannibal chooses. Don't forget that from there, we will fall upon Cisalpine Gaul, and after it, Italy, like ravening wolves.'

Finally, the two brothers gave each other a pleased look. It lasted only an instant before they broke eye contact.

Malchus was already ten strides away. 'Get a move on. Hannibal wants us all to see the sacrifice.'

The brothers followed.

The flat, well-watered land where the Carthaginians were camped had provided respite to man and beast before the rigours that were to come. It also offered, Bostar realised, a place where Hannibal could address his troops, as he had at New Carthage before they'd left. Even though his forces were now considerably smaller, there were still far too many soldiers to be able to witness personally their general make an offering to the gods. That was why the commanders of every unit in the army had been ordered to bring a score or more of their men to the ceremony.

They made their way past rank-smelling Balearic slingers clad in animal skins and slender, dark-skinned Numidians with oiled ringlets in their hair. Burly scutarii and caetrati in sinew helmets and crimson-edged tunics stood with their arms folded. Alongside was Alete with twenty of his Libyan spearmen. Groups of bare-chested Gauls, their necks and arms decorated with torcs of gold, eyed the others present with supercilious stares.

Before the gathered soldiers stood a strongly built low wooden platform, and upon it a makeshift altar of stone slabs had been erected. In front stood fifty of Hannibal's bodyguards. A ramp led from the foot of the dais to the top, and beside it, a large black bull had been tethered. Six robed priests waited with the beast, which was snorting with unease. As Malchus led them to a position within a dozen steps of the soothsayers, Bostar shivered. In their gnarled hands – through the divination to come – lay the power to raise the army's morale, or to send it into the depths. Gazing at the nearby soldiers, Bostar saw the same concern twisting their faces that he was experiencing. There was little conversation; indeed an air of apprehension hung over the entire gathering. Bostar glanced at Sapho, whom he could read like a book. His brother was feeling the same way, or worse. Bostar sighed. Despite the ease of the last few days, the mountains' physical immensity had cast a shadow over men's hearts. There

313

was only one person who could cast out that gloom, he thought. Hannibal.

The man himself bounded into view a moment later, ascending the ramp as if he were on the last lap of a foot race. A loud cheer met his arrival. Hannibal's bronze helmet and breastplate had been polished until they shone as if lit from within. In his right hand his falcata sword glinted dangerously; in his left, he carried a magnificent shield emblazoned with the image of a prowling male lion. Without a word, Hannibal strode to the edge of the platform and lifted his arm so everyone could see his blade. He let the troops focus on it before he pointed it to his rear.

'After so long, there they are! The Alps,' Hannibal cried. 'We have halted at our enemies' very gates to prepare for our ascent. I can see by your faces that you are worried. Scared. Even exhausted.' The general's eyes moved from soldier to soldier, daring them to hold his gaze. None could. 'Yet after the brutal campaign in Iberia, and the crossing of the Rhône, what are the Alps?' he challenged. 'Can they be anything worse than high mountains?' He paused, glancing around questioningly as his words were translated. 'Well?'

Bostar felt worried. Despite the truth in Hannibal's words, few men looked convinced.

'No, sir,' Malchus answered loudly. 'Great heaps of rock and ice is all they are.'

Hannibal's lips tightened in satisfaction. 'That's right! They can be climbed, by those with the strength and heart to do so. It's not as if we will be the first to cross them either. The Gauls who conquered Rome passed by this same way, did they not?'

Again the delay as the interpreters did their work. Finally, there was a mutter of accord.

'Yet you despair of even being able to get near that city? I tell you, the Gauls brought their women and children through these mountains! As soldiers carrying nothing but our weapons, can we not do the same?' Hannibal raised his sword again, threateningly this time. 'Either confess that you have less courage than the Romans, who we have defeated on many occasions in the past, or steel your hearts and march forward with me, to the plain which stands between the River Tiber and Rome! There we will find greater riches than any of you can imagine. There will be slaves and booty and glory for all!'

Malchus waited as the general's words were translated into Gaulish, Iberian and Numidian, but as a rumble of agreement began to sweep through the assembled troops, he raised a fist into the air. 'Hannibal!' he roared. 'Hannibal!'

Quickly, Bostar joined in. He noted that Sapho was slow to do the same.

Shamed by their general's words, the soldiers bellowed a rippling wave of approval. The Gauls chanted in deep voices, the Libyans sang and the Numidians made shrill ululating sounds. The cacophony rose into the crisp air, bouncing off the imposing walls of rock before the gathering and thence up into the empty sky. The startled bull jerked futilely at the rope tethering its head. No one paid it any heed. Everyone's gaze was locked on Hannibal.

'Last night, I had a dream,' he cried.

The cheering quickly died away, and was replaced by an expectant hush.

'I was in a foreign landscape, which was full of farms and large villages. I wandered for many hours, lost and without friends, until a ghost appeared.' Hannibal nodded as his words spread and the superstitious soldiers glanced nervously at each other. 'He was a young man, handsome, and clad in a simple Greek tunic, but there was an ethereal glow about him. When I asked who he was, he laughed and offered to guide me, as long as I did not look back. Although I was unsure, I accepted his proposal.'

Hannibal had everyone's attention now, even that of the priests. Men were making the sign against evil, and rubbing their lucky amulets. Bostar's heart was thudding off his ribs.

315

'We walked for maybe a mile before I became aware of a loud crashing noise behind us,' Hannibal went on. 'I tried not to turn and see what was going on, but the sound grew so great that I could not help myself. I glanced around. What I saw made my throat close with fear. There was a snake of wondrous size following us, crushing every tree and bush in its path. Black thunderclouds sat in the sky above it, and lightning bolts flashed repeatedly through the air. I froze in terror.' Hannibal paused.

'What happened next, sir?' cried one of Alete's Libyans. 'Tell us!'

An inchoate roar of agreement followed. Bostar found himself shouting too. Visions like this – for surely that was what Hannibal had had – could portend a man's future, for good or ill. Dread filled Bostar that it was the latter.

Sapho could not dispel his unease about what lay before them. 'He's making it up. So we'll follow him up into those damn mountains,' he muttered.

Bostar gave him a disbelieving glance. 'He wouldn't do that.'

Sapho's jealousy of his brother grew. 'Really? With so much at stake?' he retorted.

'Stop it! You'll anger the gods!' said Bostar.

Belatedly scared by what he'd said, Sapho looked away.

'Wait,' hissed Malchus. 'There's more.'

'The young man took my arm, and ordered me not to be afraid,' shouted Hannibal suddenly. 'I asked him what the snake signified, and he told me. Do you want to hear what he said?'

There was a short pause.

'YES!' The bellow exceeded anything that had gone before.

'The devastation represents what will happen to Rome at the hands of my army!' the general said triumphantly. 'The gods favour us!'

'Hurrah!' Bostar was so thrilled that he threw an arm around Sapho's shoulders and hugged him. His brother tensed, before stiffly returning the gesture. The exhilaration in the air was infectious. Even Malchus' normal solemnity had been replaced by a broad smile.

'HANN-I-BAL! HANN-I-BAL! HANN-I-BAL!' yelled the delighted soldiers.

While his troops cheered themselves hoarse, Hannibal made a gesture to the priests. With the aid of a dozen scutarii, the bellowing bull was hauled up the ramp until it stood in front of the altar. Hannibal stood to one side. At once the applause died away, and the worried looks returned to men's faces. Success was by no means guaranteed yet. The omens from the sacrifice also had to be good. Bostar found himself clenching his fists.

'O Great Melqart, accept this prize beast as a sacred offering, and as a gesture of our good faith,' intoned the high priest, an old man with a grey beard and fleshy cheeks. His companions repeated his words. Raising the hood on his robe, the priest then accepted a long dagger. The bull's head was pulled forward, stretching its neck. Without further ado, the old man extended his arm and yanked it back, drawing the blade across the underside of the bull's throat with savage force. Blood gouted from the large wound, covering the priest's feet. The kicking beast collapsed to the platform, and the unneeded scutarii were waved back. Swiftly, the old man moved to kneel between the bull's front and back legs. With sure strokes, he slit open the skin and abdominal muscles. Steaming loops of bowel slithered into view. The priest barely glanced at them as, still gripping the dagger, he shoved both his arms deep into the abdominal cavity.

'He's seen nothing bad so far. That's good,' whispered Bostar.

It's probably all been arranged in advance, thought Sapho sourly, but he no longer dared speak his mind.

A moment later, the old man stood up to face Hannibal. His arms were bloodied to the shoulder, and the front of his saturated robe had turned crimson. In his hands, he held a purple, glistening lump of tissue. 'The beast's liver, sir,' he said gravely.

'What does it tell you?' There was the slightest trace of a quaver in Hannibal's voice.

'We shall see,' replied the priest, studying the organ.

'Told you!' Bostar gave Sapho a hefty nudge. 'Even Hannibal is unsure.'

Sapho looked at Hannibal, whose face was now etched with worry. If their general was an actor, he was a damn good one. Fear suddenly clogged Sapho's throat. What was I thinking to call Hannibal's dream into question? Sapho couldn't think of a better way to call down the gods' wrath than to say what he just had. And there was Bostar, beside him, who was unable to put a foot wrong. Bitterness coursed through his veins.

'It is very clear,' the priest announced loudly.

Every man present craned his neck forward, eager to hear.

'The passage of the mountains will be difficult, but not impossible. The army will descend upon Cisalpine Gaul, and there allies will flock to our cause. The legions that come to meet us will be swept away, as the mightiest of trees are by a winter storm. Victory awaits!'

'Victory! Victory! Victory!' chanted the soldiers.

Raising his hands for silence, Hannibal stepped forward. 'I told you of my dream. You have heard the soothsayer make his pronouncement. Now, who will follow me across the Alps?'

The watching troops surged forward, shouting their acceptance.

Looking elated, Malchus and Bostar were among them. Sapho followed, telling himself that everything would be all right. The knot of fear and unease in his belly told another story, however.

Four days later, Sapho was beginning to wonder if his misgivings had been overblown. While the Carthaginians had encountered some resistance from the Allobroges, it had been swept aside by Hannibal's fierce response. Life in the mountains had settled into a reassuring routine, the same as they'd followed for months. Rise at dawn. Strike camp. Eat a cold breakfast. Assemble the men. Assume position at the head of the enormous column. Join the path eastwards. March. Sapho was immensely proud that Hannibal had picked his unit to lead the army. Let Bostar suck on that, he thought. His brother's phalanx marched behind his. Malchus and his soldiers were with the rearguard, more than ten miles back down the stony track.

His duty carried with it huge responsibility. Sapho was on the lookout for danger at all times. For the thousandth time that morning, he eyed the heights around the flat-bottomed valley in which they currently found themselves. Nothing. Intimidated by Hannibal's seizure of their main settlement and, with it, all their supplies, the Allobroges had vanished into the bare rocks. 'Good enough for the cowardly scumbags,' muttered Sapho. He spat contemptuously.

'Sir!' cried one of the guides, a warrior of the Insubres tribe. 'Look!'

To Sapho's surprise, the figures of men could be seen appearing on the track ahead. Where in the name of hell had they come from? He lifted his right arm. 'Halt!' At once the order began passing back down the line. Sapho's jaw clenched nervously as he listened to it. He was stopping the progress of the entire army. It had to be done, however. Until proven otherwise, every person they encountered was an enemy.

'Should we advance to meet them, sir?' asked an officer.

'Not bloody likely. It could be a trap,' Sapho replied. 'The fuckers can come to us.'

'What if they don't, sir?'

'Of course they will. Why else do you think they've slunk out of their rat holes?'

Sapho was right. Gradually, the newcomers approached: a group of perhaps twenty warriors. They were typical-looking Gauls, well built with long hair and moustaches. Although some wore tunics, many were bare-chested under their woollen cloaks.

Baggy woven trousers were ubiquitous. Some wore helmets, but only a handful had mail shirts. All were armed with tall, oval shields and swords or spears. Interestingly, the men at the front were carrying willow branches.

'Are the dogs coming in peace?' asked Sapho.

'Yes, sir,' answered the guide. 'They're Vocontii, I think.' He saw Sapho's blank look. 'Neighbours – and enemies – of the Allobroges.'

'Why doesn't that surprise me?' sneered Sapho. 'Do any of you Gauls get on with each other?'

The guide grinned. 'Not too often, sir. There's always something to fight over.'

'I'm sure,' Sapho said dryly. He glanced to either side. 'Front rank, shields up! First and second ranks, ready spears!'

Wood clattered off wood as the spearmen obeyed his command. An instant later, the phalanx presented a solid wall of overlapping shields to its front. Over the shield rims, scores of spear tips poked forward like the spines on a forest of sea urchins.

Looking alarmed, the warriors stopped.

Sapho's lips peeled upwards. 'Tell them that if they come in peace, they have nothing to fear.'

'Yes, sir.' The guide bellowed a few words in Gaulish.

There was a brief pause, and then the Vocontii continued walking towards them. When they were twenty paces away, Sapho held up his hand. 'That's close enough.'

The guide translated his words, and the tribesmen dutifully halted.

'Ask them what they want,' Sapho ordered. He fixed his attention on the one man who had answered all the guide's questions. A fine mail shirt covered the middle-aged warrior's barrel chest, and three gold torcs announced his wealth and status. What Sapho didn't like, or trust, was the man's wall-eye and permanent leer.

'They have heard of the size of our army and of our victories over the Allobroges, sir, and wish to assure us of their friendship,' said the guide. 'They want to guide us through their territory, to the easiest pass over the Alps.'

'How charming,' Sapho replied caustically. 'And why in Melqart's name should we believe them?'

There was a shifty smile from the wall-eyed warrior as the guide interpreted. A wave of his hand saw several fat heifers herded into view.

'Apparently, they have a hundred of these to offer us, sir.'

Sapho didn't let his pleasure show. That quantity of fresh meat would be very welcome. 'The beasts don't count for much if the Vocontii steal them straight back. Hannibal needs far more assurance than that. What kind of guarantee of safe passage can the dirtbags offer?'

A moment later, fully half of the tribesmen took a step forward. Most obvious was the wide-faced young warrior with blond pigtails and finely made weapons. He looked decidedly disgruntled. An explanation from the deputation's leader followed.

'Apparently, the youngster is the chieftain's youngest son, sir. The rest are high-ranking warriors,' said the guide. 'They are to be our hostages.'

'That's more like it,' said Sapho. He turned to the nearest of his officers. 'Go and find the general. Tell him what's happened. I think he'll want to hear their offer for himself.' As the officer hurried off to do his bidding, Sapho resumed his study of the heights above. The fact that they were bare did not reassure him in any way. Gut feeling told him that the Vocontii were as trustworthy as a nest of snakes.

It wasn't long before Hannibal appeared. When he wasn't marching near the army's head, the general was to be found at its tail, and today it was the former. Sapho was flattered that Hannibal was not accompanied by any of his senior officers. He saluted crisply. 'Sir!'

'Sapho.' Hannibal reached his side. 'So this is the deputation from the Vocontii, eh?'

'Yes, sir,' Sapho replied. 'The shifty-looking bastard over there is the leader.'

'Tell me again what they've said,' Hannibal ordered, scanning the warriors.

Sapho obeyed.

Hannibal rubbed his chin. 'A hundred cattle and ten hostages. Plus the guides who will stay with us. It's not a bad offer, is it?'

'No, sir.'

'You're not happy,' said Hannibal with a shrewd look. 'Why?'

'What's to stop them from simply rustling the beasts back from us, sir?' Sapho answered. 'Who's to say that the hostages aren't peasants, whom the Vocontii chieftain wouldn't ever miss if they were executed?'

'Should I reject their offer?'

Sapho's stomach did a somersault. Give the wrong answer now, and Hannibal probably wouldn't ask him to lead the army again. Give the correct one, and he would rise in the general's estimation. Sapho was desperate for the latter. 'There's no point, sir.'

'Why not?' Hannibal demanded.

Sapho met his general's fierce gaze. 'Because if you did, we'd have to fight our way through their territory, sir. If we play along instead, there's a reasonable chance of anticipating possible attacks while continuing the march without hindrance. If they prove to be trustworthy, so much the better. If not, then we at least gave it a try.'

Hannibal did not reply immediately, and Sapho began to worry that he'd said the wrong thing. He was thinking of retracting his words when the general spoke.

'I like your thinking, Sapho, son of Malchus. It is easier to avoid treading on a serpent that is watched than to find it under any one of a thousand stones. It would be foolish not to take steps to prevent disaster, though. The baggage train and the cavalry must be moved to a position just behind the vanguard. They're the most vulnerable to being cut off.'

At the front that could never happen, thought Sapho. 'Yes, sir.' He tried not to feel disappointed that Hannibal was taking charge. At least he'd led the army for a few days.

Hannibal surprised him. 'We still need infantry to lead us. You've been doing an excellent job, so I want you to continue in your position.'

Sapho grinned. 'Thank you, sir!'

'I also want you to guard the hostages. At the slightest sign of treachery, you know what to do.'

'I'll have them tortured and then crucified in full view of their compatriots, sir.'

'Excellent. Do whatever you see fit.' Hannibal clapped him on the arm. 'I'll have the cavalry move up to your position at once. Start marching again as soon as they're in place.'

'What about the mules, sir?'

'Getting them into position would be far too awkward now. We'll keep our fingers crossed for today and do it tomorrow.'

'Yes, sir. Thank you, sir.' Delighted, Sapho watched his general disappear back down the track. The passage of the mountains was proving to be far more rewarding than he could have anticipated.

For two days, the party of Vocontii led Sapho through their lands. The cavalry and baggage train followed slowly behind them, and after them came the rest of the army. Although there had been no attacks on the column, Sapho's distrust of the tribesmen who guided him remained. It grew stronger when, on the morning of the third day, the Vocontii chose a track that entered a valley much narrower than that in which they'd been marching. There was barely enough room for the ubiquitous pine trees to grow up its steep sides. Halting his soldiers, Sapho summoned the wall-eyed warrior. 'Why aren't we staying on this path?' Sapho indicated the larger way to the right, which continued off into the distance. 'It's wider, and the terrain looks to remain flatter.'

The guide repeated his words in the local tongue.

The warrior launched into a long, rambling explanation, which involved much pointing and gesticulating.

'Apparently it ends in a sheer cliff face about five miles away, sir. We'd just have to turn around and come back here. This narrow one, on the other hand, leads gradually upwards and will take us to the lowest pass in the area.'

Sapho glared at the warrior, who simply shrugged. One of his eyes was looking at him, while the other was staring off into the sky. Sapho found it infuriating. It also made judging whether the warrior was lying exceptionally hard. He made up his mind. Sending a runner to ask Hannibal, who was with the rearguard, would entail a delay of three hours or more. 'Fine,' he growled. 'We'll do as he says. Tell him, though, that if there's any trickery, he'll be the first to die.' Sapho was pleased to see the warrior's throat work nervously when his threat was translated. He led the way confidently enough, however, allaying Sapho's concern a fraction.

His unease soon returned. It wasn't the stony and uneven track. That was much the same as those they'd followed since entering the Alps. No, thought Sapho, it was the sheer rock faces that pressed in from both sides. They went on and on with no sign of widening out. It created a feeling of real claustrophobia. He didn't know exactly how high the cliffs were, but it was enough to reduce significantly the light on the valley floor. Sapho wasn't alone in disliking the situation. He could hear his men muttering uneasily to each other. Behind, there were indignant brays from the mules. Many of the cavalrymen were dismounting in order to lead their reluctant horses forward.

Sapho set his jaw. He had committed the army to this route. With a ten-mile column following, there was no turning back now. They just had to get on with it. Loosening his sword in his scabbard, Sapho ensured that he stayed close to the wall-eyed warrior. If anything happened, he *would* carry out his threat.

Pleasingly, they made slow but continuous progress for what remained of the morning. Men's spirits rose, and even the animals grew used to the confined space. Sapho remained on edge, constantly scanning the skyline above for any sign of movement. He tried to ignore the crick that was developing in his neck from always looking straight up in the air.

What attracted Sapho's attention first was not motion, but sound. One moment all that he could hear was the noises he'd heard daily since leaving New Carthage. Soldiers gossiping with each other. An occasional laugh, or curse. Officers barking orders. The creak of leather and jingle of harness. Hacking coughs from those with bad chests. The sound of men spitting. Brays from mules. Horses' whinnies. The next moment, Sapho's ears rang with a terrible, screeching resonance. He flinched instinctively. It was the noise of rock scraping off rock. With a terrible sense of dread, he looked up.

For a moment, Sapho saw nothing, but then the irregular edge of a block of stone appeared at the edge of the cliff far above. Frantically, Sapho raised a hand to his mouth. 'We're under attack! Raise shields! Raise shields!' In the same instant, his head was turning, searching for the wall-eyed warrior. As the air filled with panicked shouts, Sapho saw the man had already elbowed past his comrades and was shouting at them to follow him. 'You treacherous bastard!' Sapho shouted, drawing his sword. He was too late. Enraged, he watched as the Vocontii disappeared into a fissure in the rock not twenty paces away. Sapho cursed savagely. He had to stay where he was, and do what he could for his men. If he wasn't killed himself. One thing was certain: if any of the hostages, who were kept deep in the middle of his phalanx, survived, they would die the instant he could get to them.

The air filled with a rumbling thunder and Sapho glanced upwards again. It was a terrifying sound, amplified a thousand times by the confining valley walls. Awestruck, he watched as several boulders, each the size of a horse, were pushed over the edge high above them. They picked up speed fast, and tumbled with ever-increasing speed down the vertiginous cliff face. Relief battled with horror as Sapho realised that none would strike him. Loud screams rose from the soldiers directly underneath the rocks, who could do nothing but watch their death hurtle towards them. Their cries revealed their awful, helpless terror. Aghast, Sapho could not take his eyes off the plummeting pieces of stone. A hot tide of acid flooded the back of his mouth as they struck their targets with deafening thumps, silencing their victims for ever.

Their ordeal wasn't over, either. Further down the cliff tops, in a position over the cavalry and the baggage train, Sapho could see more boulders being pushed towards the edge. He groaned. There was nothing he could do for those men and beasts either. Sapho took a deep breath. Best see to the injured, he thought. At least those can be helped.

The scream of battle cries filled their ears before they could do a thing. To Sapho's fury, files of Vocontii warriors came spilling from the fissure into which their guides had just vanished. More issued from another one alongside it. A red mist of rage replaced Sapho's dismay. He recognised the wall-eyed man and others of their guides among their number. Raising his spear, he roared, 'Eyes front! Enemy attack!' His soldiers responded with alacrity. 'Shields up! Ready spears!'

From the shouts behind them, Sapho could tell that the column had been attacked in other places too. 'Rear five ranks, about turn!' he bellowed. 'Advance to meet the enemy. Engage at will.' That done, Sapho spun to face the Vocontii before them. The tribesmen were closing in fast, weapons held high. Sapho levelled his spear at the wall-eyed warrior. 'You're dead meat, you stinking whoreson!'

His answer was an inarticulate snarl.

To Sapho's frustration, he did not get to close with the other. The phalanx's rigid structure meant that he could not move from his position, and the warrior was heading for a different part of the front rank. Sapho had to forget about him, as a tribesman with a dense red beard thrust his sword at his face. Rather than ducking below his shield rim, thereby losing sight of his enemy, Sapho jerked his head to one side. The blade whistled past his left ear, and Sapho thrust forward with his spear. There was a grating feeling as it slipped between two ribs, and then it ran deep into the other's unprotected chest. Sapho had no chance to pull free his weapon from the dying man's flesh. Releasing his grip on the shaft, he dragged free his sword. The warrior slumped to the ground, a disbelieving expression still twisting his features, and was immediately replaced.

Sapho's second foe was a bellowing bull of a man with a thick neck and hugely muscled arms. To Sapho's shock, the triangular point of his enemy's spear punched clean through the bronze and leather facing of his shield and smacked into his cuirass. A ball of agony exploded from Sapho's lower belly, and he reeled several steps backwards, dropping his sword. Fortunately, the soldier behind was ready, and leaned forward, thereby preventing Sapho from falling over. Jammed in Sapho's shield, the tribesman's weapon was no longer usable. Quick as a flash, however, he ripped out a long dagger and reached over the top of Sapho's shield to lunge at his throat. Desperately, Sapho jerked his head backwards. Slash after slash followed, and he knew that it would only be a moment before his throat was ripped open by the wickedly wielded blade.

It was with the utmost relief that Sapho saw a spear come in from the side to pierce the warrior's throat. It stabbed right through, emerging scarlet-tipped from the right side of his neck. A dreadful, choking sound left the Gaul's gaping mouth. It was followed by a tide of bright red blood, which spattered the front of Sapho's shield and, below, his feet. The spear was withdrawn, letting the dead warrior collapse on top of Sapho's first opponent.

'Gods above,' Sapho muttered. He'd never been so close to death. He turned his head to regard his saviour. 'Thank you.'

The spearman, a gap-toothed youth, grinned. 'You're welcome, captain. Are you all right?'

Sapho reached a hand under the bottom edge of his cuirass, which had a great dent in it. He probed upwards, wincing at the pain this caused. When he pulled out his fingers, he was relieved to see that there was no blood on them. 'I seem to be,' he answered with relief. He stooped to pick up his sword. Returning his gaze to the fight, Sapho was gratified to see that the Vocontii charge had smashed apart against the phalanx's solid wall of shields. He wasn't surprised. While a few of his men might have been killed, it would take more than a charge by disorganised tribesmen to break them. It was time to lead a counter charge, thought Sapho. All reason left him, however, as he saw the wall-eyed warrior no more than twenty steps away, stooping to kill an injured Libyan even as he himself retreated. Dropping his useless shield, Sapho leaped forward. His desire to kill the deceitful tribesman gave him extra speed and he had covered maybe a third of the ground between them before the other even saw him. The warrior took one look and fled for his life. So did his comrades.

'Come back, you fucking coward!' Sapho screamed. He was oblivious to the fact that the phalanx's front-rankers had followed him. He increased his pace to a sprint, aware that if the other reached the gap in the rock, any chance of catching him would disappear. It was no good. The warrior seemed to have winged heels. But then fate intervened, and Sapho's enemy tripped on a protruding rock. He stumbled and fell to one knee. Sapho was on him like a dog cornering a rat. Instead of killing the tribesman, he smashed the hilt of his sword across the back of his head. Straightening, Sapho was able to slash another warrior's arm as he ran past. With a howl, the man blundered into the fissure and out of sight.

'Don't go in there!' Sapho shouted as the first of his spearmen arrived and made for the gap in the rock. 'It's a death trap.'

The soldiers reluctantly obeyed.

'I want twenty men stationed right here to make sure they don't try a counter attack.' Sapho kicked the wall-eyed warrior, who groaned. 'Someone, pick up this sack of shit. Find any of his compatriots who are alive, and tie them all up.'

'What are you going to do with them, sir?' asked an officer.

'You'll see,' Sapho replied with a wolfish smile. 'First, though, we need to see what's going on behind us.'

By the time they had reached the rear of the phalanx, the Vocontii who had been attacking there were gone. The corpses of fifteen or more warriors were sprawled on the ground, but that was of little satisfaction to Sapho. In this small section alone, at least fifty Carthaginian soldiers had been critically injured or crushed to death. Just beyond, so had the same number of mules and cavalry mounts. The ground was covered with blood, and the mangled bodies of men and beasts lay everywhere. The screaming of the injured, especially those who had been trapped when the boulders finally came to rest, was awful. Sapho closed his ears to their clamour, and concentrated on finding out what else had happened. Bostar was among the officers who reported to him.

Panicked by the falling rocks, an elephant had dashed three men to death with its trunk, before charging backwards into the column, there to cause untold damage. Fortunately, its companions had been kept calm by their mahouts. The most frustrating discovery was that the Vocontii had stolen dozens of mules, leading them up the same precipitous paths that had served to launch their daring attack. They had even seized some captives. Despite this, Sapho knew that there was no point in pursuing the raiders. Moving on was more important than trying to save a few unfortunate soldiers. Once the dead and the blocks of stone had been rolled out of the way, the column would have to resume its advance.

Before that, however, there was something that Sapho had to do.

He made his way back to where the Vocontii prisoners were. With the ten hostages, they had twenty-two in total, sitting together and surrounded by a ring of spearmen. The only one who did not look fearful was the wall-eyed warrior, who spat at Sapho as he approached.

'Shall we execute them, sir?' asked an officer eagerly.

An angry mutter of agreement went up from the Libyans.

'No,' Sapho replied. He ignored his men's shocked response. 'Tell them that despite their brethren's treachery, they are not to be killed,' he said to the interpreter. As his words were translated, Sapho was gratified to see traces of hope appear in some warriors' faces. He waited for a moment, enjoying his power.

'Please, sir, reconsider!' an officer enjoined. 'They can't go unpunished. Think of our casualties.'

Sapho's lips peeled into a snarl. 'Did I say that they would go unpunished?'

The officer looked confused. 'No, sir.'

'We shall do to them what they did to us,' Sapho pronounced. 'Do not translate that,' he snapped at the interpreter. 'I want them to watch, and wonder.'

'What do you want us to do, sir?'

'Tie the shitbags in a line. Next, get one of the elephants. Use it to shift a large rock. A rock so big that no men could ever move it.'

A slow smile spread across the officer's face. 'To dash out their brains, sir?'

'No,' reproached Sapho. 'We're not going to kill them, remember? I want the boulders dropped on their legs.'

'And then, sir?'

Sapho shrugged cruelly. 'We'll just leave them there.'

The officer grinned. 'It'll be dark before their scumbag companions can return. They'll be begging for death by that stage, sir.'

'Precisely. They might think before attacking us a second time.' Sapho clapped his hands. 'See to it!'

He watched as the Vocontii prisoners were forced to lie down by a rocky outcrop. Sapho intervened to make sure that the wall-eyed warrior was last in the line. There was a short delay as an elephant was brought up from its position with the baggage train. Sapho waited with the interpreter by the first of the warriors, whose eyes were now bulging with fear.

Sapho looked up at the mahout. 'Can you shift that boulder there?' He pointed.

'Yes, sir. Where?'

'On to these men's legs. But they mustn't be killed.'

The mahout's eyes widened. 'I think so, sir.'

'Get on with it, then.'

'Sir.' Leaning forward, the mahout whispered in his huge mount's ear before tapping it behind the ear with his hooked staff. The elephant lumbered up to the stone that Sapho had indicated, and gripped the top of it with its trunk. There was a moment's silence before the slab began to move out of its resting place. The mahout muttered another command, and the elephant stepped up to rest the front of its head against the boulder, preventing it from picking up speed. Slowly, the beast reversed towards the prisoners, controlling its load's progress down the slight slope. Realising at last what was about to happen, the Vocontii warriors began to wail in fear.

Sapho laughed. He scanned the heights above, and fancied he saw movement. 'Yes, you fuckers,' he screamed. 'Look! We're about to give your friends a dose of their own medicine.'

Several steps from the captives, the mahout made the elephant pause. He looked at Sapho questioningly.

'Do it.'

A murmured word in its ear, and the elephant moved aside, letting the stone roll on to the first three warrior's legs. Strangled screams shredded the air. The sound was met by an immense cheer from the hundreds of watching Carthaginian soldiers. This, in their eyes, was vengeance for their dead comrades. Meanwhile, the tribesmen's companions struggled uselessly against their bonds, which had been pegged to the ground.

'Tell them that this is Hannibal's retribution for double-crossing us,' Sapho thundered.

Pale-faced, the interpreter did as he was told. His words were met by a gabble of terrified voices. 'Some are saying that they didn't know that we would be attacked,' he muttered.

'Ha! They're liars, or fools, or both.'

'They're asking just to be killed.'

'Absolutely not.' Sapho waved a hand at the mahout. 'Do it again. Don't stop.'

Rock after rock was lowered into place, smashing the legs of all but the last Vocontii warrior. When the elephant had manoeuvred the final piece of stone into place, Sapho ordered the mahout to wait. Clicking his fingers to make sure that the interpreter followed him, he made his way to where the wall-eyed warrior lay. Purple-faced with rage, the tribesman spat a string of obscenities.

'Don't bother,' said Sapho with a sneer as the interpreter began to speak. 'I know what he's saying. Tell him that this is repayment for his deceit, and that a coward like him will never reach the warriors' paradise. Instead, his soul will rot for all eternity in hell.' He eyed the mahout. 'When he's finished, let the stone fall.'

The elephant driver nodded.

'What in the name of all the gods is going on?' Somehow Bostar's voice penetrated the cacophony of screams echoing throughout the narrow gorge.

The interpreter stopped speaking. The mahout sat motionless atop his beast. Stiff-backed with fury, Sapho turned to find his brother regarding him with an outraged expression. He inclined his head mockingly. 'I'm punishing these worthless whoresons. What does it look like?'

Bostar's face twisted. 'Could you think of a crueller way to kill them?'

'Several ways, actually,' Sapho replied amiably. 'They all took too long, though. This method might be crude, but it's effective. It will also send a strong message to the rest of their pox-ridden, louse-infested tribe that to fuck with us carries a heavy price.'

'You've already made your point!' Bostar indicated the line of screaming men. 'Why not just stab this man in the throat and have done?'

'Because this one' — and Sapho kicked the wall-eyed warrior in the head — 'is their leader. I've saved him until last, so he could watch his comrades suffer, and anticipate his own fate.'

Bostar recoiled. 'You're sick,' he spat. 'I command you to halt this outrage.'

'You might outrank me still, *brother*, but Hannibal entrusted the vanguard to me, not you,' Sapho said in a loud voice. 'I'm sure that our general would love to hear why you countermanded his orders.'

'Hannibal ordered you to kill any prisoners like this?' Bostar muttered in disbelief.

'He said I was to do as I saw fit,' snarled Sapho. 'Which I am doing. Now stand back!' He was delighted when, with slumped shoulders, Bostar obeyed. Sapho looked down for a final time at the wall-eyed warrior, who tried to spit at him again. Inspiration seized Sapho and he drew his dagger. Kneeling down, he shoved the tip into the man's right eye socket. With a savage wrench, he hooked out the eyeball. His victim's courage disappeared and a shriek of pure agony ripped free of his throat. Wiping his bloody hands on the warrior's tunic, Sapho stood. 'I'm leaving him one eye so that he can watch the mightiest army in the world pass by,' he said to the interpreter. 'Tell him that.' He glanced at Bostar. 'Watch and learn, little brother. This is how enemies of Carthage should be treated.' Without waiting for a response, Sapho jerked his head at the mahout. 'Finish it.'

Full of impotent anguish, Bostar walked away. He was unwilling to watch. Unfortunately, he couldn't block out the screams. What had his older brother become? he wondered. Why was Hanno the one who had been carried out to sea?

For the first time, Bostar allowed himself that thought without guilt.

Chapter XVI: Journeys

Naturally, the via Appia, the main road to Rome, led straight out of Capua. Not wishing to enter the town, Quintus first bypassed his father's farm and then took a smaller, cross-country track that meandered through a number of hamlets and past countless farms to join the larger way some miles to the north. Quintus rode his horse. As a supposed slave, Hanno sat on the back of an irritable mule, which was also laden down with equipment. They travelled in silence for the first hour. Both had much to think about.

Quintus now felt confident of finding his father. He was sad to have left Aurelia behind, but that was the way of the world. Their mother would look after her well. However, Quintus felt uneasy. Once their objective — that of finding his father — had been achieved, Hanno would depart to join the Carthaginian forces. Did that mean that they were *already* enemies? Thoroughly unsettled by this notion, Quintus tried not to think of it.

Hanno prayed that Suniaton would be all right and that they would find Fabricius swiftly. Then he would be free. He asked to be reunited with his father and brothers. If they were still alive, of course. Hanno tried to be upbeat, and concentrated on imagining marching to war against the Romans. At once, however, another disquieting image popped up. Quintus and Fabricius would be serving in the legions. Unknowingly, Hanno had the same disturbing thought as Quintus, and buried it deeply in the recesses of his mind.

Not long after they had joined the Via Appia, they came upon a party of infantry marching south.

'Oscans,' said Quintus, relieved to have something to talk about. 'They're heading for the port.'

Hanno knew that the River Volturnus ran in a southwesterly direction past Capua to terminate at the coast. 'To be transported to Iberia?'

Ill at ease again, Quintus nodded.

Hanno ignored him, focusing instead on the approaching group. Apart from Fabricius' escort, he hadn't seen many soldiers in Italy. These were socii, not regular legionaries, but such men would constitute up to half of any army that faced Hannibal's. They were the enemy.

Some of the Oscans were bareheaded, but most wore bronze Attic helmets decorated in striking fashion with horsehair or feathers, which were dyed red, black, white or yellow. Their short wool tunics were also eye-catching, ranging from red to ochre to grey. Few wore shoes or sandals, but all had a broad leather belt covered in bronze sheeting, which was fastened with elaborate hooks. The soldiers were armed with light javelins and thrusting spears of different lengths; the rare men with swords carried the slashing kopis, a curved weapon originally used by the Greeks. The majority of their shields were similar to *scuta*, concave and ribbed, but smaller.

'It wasn't many generations ago that they were fighting Rome,' Quintus revealed. 'Capua has only been under Roman rule for just over a century. Many locals think it should reclaim its independence.'

Hanno goggled. 'Really?'

'Yes. It's a favourite argument between Martialis and my father, especially when they've been drinking.' Quintus frowned, wondering if his mother felt similarly. She'd never said as much, but he knew that she was fiercely proud of her heritage.

Hanno was fascinated. His knowledge of the Republic's structure, and its relationship with the non-Roman cities and peoples of Italy, was patchy at best. It was interesting that natives of such a large and important city were unhappy being ruled by Rome. Could there be others who felt the same way? he wondered.

As one of the junior tribunes of a legion, Flaccus should have accompanied his unit to Iberia. After his foolish outburst in front of Scipio, it would also have been wise for him to lay low for a time. As Fabricius rapidly discovered, that was not his way. Discovering that, in addition to Fabricius' cavalry, the consul was taking a single cohort back to Italy, Flaccus begged to be included. One tribune was needed to command the legionaries, he reasoned. Why should it not be he? To Fabricius' utter amazement, Scipio did not explode at the request. While clearly annoyed, the consul acceded. 'By Jupiter, but you have a brass neck,' he muttered. 'Now get out of my tent.'

Fabricius took a mental note of the incident, which revealed how far the power of the Minucii stretched. Although it mattered little which tribune accompanied Scipio, Flaccus' gall in asking would have been punished had he been anyone else. Rather than punishment, though, he had got his wish. As he said smugly to Fabricius later, the Minucii had a finger in every pie. 'By the time we arrive in Italy, the clan will probably know about Hannibal's intentions.' The only way that could happen, thought Fabricius, was if you had sent a message ahead of us. He couldn't believe that was the case. Had Atia been right about Flaccus? Wishing that his prospective son-in-law were less of a braggart, Fabricius consoled himself by imagining how his family would benefit from the Minucii's influence once Aurelia was married.

For his part, Fabricius was delighted to be heading for Italy. Although there would be plenty of action there, he wanted to be part of the army that faced the main threat. Naturally, this was Hannibal, not the commander he had left in Iberia.

Sapho's brutal treatment of the prisoners did not stop the Vocontii from mounting further attacks. If anything, it increased their ferocity. More rocks were rolled down the slopes, causing heavy casualties among the soldiers and pack animals. During the late afternoon, the fighting grew so intense that the vanguard, including the cavalry and the baggage train, became separated from Hannibal and the bulk of the infantry. It remained so for the duration of the night. The following morning, to everyone's relief, the Vocontii had disappeared. Most supposed that their losses had eventually become heavy enough to make stealing supplies pointless. Yet the tribesmen had wreaked more than simple physical damage on the army. The terrifying ordeal helped morale to plummet among the less motivated units. Each night, hundreds of men vanished under cover of darkness. Hannibal had ordered that no one was to stop them. 'Soldiers who are coerced into fighting make poor comrades,' he said to Malchus.

The host marched on.

For eight days, the miserable, cold and footsore Carthaginians climbed. Their enemies were no longer the Vocontii or the Allobroges, but the elements and the terrain, which grew ever more treacherous. Wind chill, frostbite and exposure began to take their toll. From dawn until dusk, soldiers dropped to the ground like flies. At night they simply died in their sleep. They were weakened by hunger, exhaustion, insufficient clothing, or a combination of all three.

Hannibal's response to Sapho's robust defence of the vanguard had been to promote him. He had also left Sapho in charge of leading the column. Despite his joy at being equal to Bostar in rank, his responsibility was a double-edged sword. It was down to him and his men to act as trailbreakers, which was an utterly exhausting task. Boulders had to be moved. The track regularly needed repairing or strengthening. Casualties among Sapho's men soared. By the eighth night, he was on the point of physical and mental collapse. His dread of their passage of the mountains had been proved well founded. In his mind, they were all doomed. They would never find the promised pass that marked the high point of their journey. All that kept Sapho going was his pride. Asking Hannibal to relieve him of his command would be worse than jumping off a cliff. Yet Sapho didn't want to do that either. Incredibly, life was still better than death. Wrapped in five blankets, he huddled over a lukewarm brazier in his tent and tried to feel grateful. None of his men had the luxury of fuel to burn.

After a while, Sapho stirred. Although he didn't want to, it was time to check the sentries. It was also good for morale for him to be seen. He shed his blankets, pulled on a second cloak and wrapped a scarf around his head. As he unlaced the leather ties and opened the tent flap, a gust of bitingly cold wind entered. Sapho flinched, before forcing himself outside. Two sentries, Libyans, stood by the entrance. A pitch-soaked torch held upright by a small pile of stones cast a faint pool of light around them.

The pair stiffened to attention as they saw him. 'Sir,' they both mumbled through lips that were blue with cold.

'Anything to report?'

'No, sir.'

'It's as cold as ever.'

'Yes, sir,' the nearest man replied. He doubled over as a paroxysm of coughing took him.

'Sorry, sir,' said his companion nervously. 'He can't help it.'

'It's all right,' Sapho replied irritably. He eyed the first soldier, who was wiping bloody sputum from his lips. A dead man walking, he thought. Sudden pity filled him. 'Take the wretch inside to the brazier. Try and get him warm. You can stay there until I get back from my rounds.'

Stunned, the second Libyan stammered his thanks. Sapho grabbed the torch and stalked off into the darkness. He would only be gone for a quarter of an hour, but it might provide the sick man with some relief. A sour smile traced his chapped lips. I'm getting soft, like Bostar. Sapho hadn't seen his brother since their argument over the Vocontii prisoners. As far as he was concerned, that was fine.

Taking great care on the icy ground, Sapho traced his way past his soldiers' tents. He glanced at the pair of elephants Hannibal had ordered to stay with the vanguard. The miserable beasts stood side by side, trying to maximise their warmth. Sapho even pitied them. Soon after, he reached the first sentries, who were stationed some two hundred steps from his tent. They were in a line across the path where the advance had stopped for the night. Exposed on three sides, it was the worst place to stand watch in the whole army. No fire could survive in the vicious, snow-laden wind that whistled down from the peaks. In order that the soldiers here didn't all die from exposure, Sapho had ordered their periods on duty shortened to just an hour at a time. Even so, he lost men every night.

'Seen anything?' he shouted at the officer in charge.

'No, sir! Even the demons are in bed tonight!'

'Very good. As you were.' Pleased by the officer's attempt at humour, Sapho began to retrace his steps. He had only to check the sentries at the rear of the phalanx, and then he was done. Peering into the gloom, he was surprised to see a figure emerging around the corner of the outermost tent. Sapho frowned. The cliff might be twenty steps from the tent lines, but the wind was so powerful that a man could easily be carried over the edge. He had seen it happen several times already. Consequently, everyone walked between the tents, not around them. The man was carrying a torch, which meant that he was no enemy. Yet he'd just taken the most dangerous route past his phalanx. Why? What had he to hide?

'Hey!' Sapho shouted. 'Stop right there!'

The figure straightened, and the hood of his cloak whipped back. 'Sapho?'

'Bostar?' said Sapho incredulously.

'Yes,' his brother replied. 'Can we talk?'

Sapho staggered as a particularly savage gust of wind struck him. He watched, aghast, as it buffeted an unsuspecting Bostar sideways and on to one knee. As he struggled to stand up, another blast of air hit, carrying him backwards and out into the blackness.

Sapho couldn't believe his eyes. He ran to the edge of the precipice, where he was astonished to find his brother clinging desperately to the protruding branch of a stunted bush several steps below him.

'Help me!' Bostar shouted.

Silently, Sapho stared down at him. Why should I? he asked himself. Of what benefit is it to me?

'What are you waiting for?' Bostar's voice cracked. 'This damn branch will never hold!' Seeing the look in Sapho's eyes, he blanched. 'You want me to die, don't you? Just as you were happy when Hanno was lost.'

Sapho's tongue stuck to the roof of his mouth with guilt. How could Bostar know that? Still he didn't act.

The branch split.

'Fuck you to hell and gone!' screamed Bostar. Letting go with his left hand, he threw himself forward, searching for a fingerhold on the track. There would only be a moment before his body weight pulled him backwards and into the abyss. Knowing this, Bostar scrabbled frantically to gain any kind of purchase in the rock-hard, ice-covered earth. He found none. With a despairing cry, he started to slide backwards.

Sapho's gut instinct took over, and he leaned forward to grab his brother by the shoulders. With a great yank, he pulled him up and over the edge. A second effort saw them several paces away, on safer ground. They lay side by side for a few moments, their chests heaving. Bostar was the first to sit up. 'Why did you save me?'

Sapho met his gaze with difficulty. 'I'm not a murderer.'

'No,' Bostar snapped. 'But you were glad when Hanno vanished, weren't you? With him out of the way, you had a chance to become Father's favourite.'

Shame filled Sapho. 'I—'

'It's strange,' said Bostar, interrupting. 'If I had died just now, you'd have Father all to yourself. Why didn't you let me slip into oblivion?'

'You're my brother,' Sapho protested weakly.

'I might be, but you still stood there, looking at me when I first fell,' Bostar retorted furiously. He regained control of himself. 'Yet I have you to thank for saving my life. I am grateful, and I will repay my debt if I can.' He carefully spat on the ground between them. 'After that, you will be dead to me.'

Sapho's mouth gaped. He watched as Bostar got up and walked away. 'What will you tell Father?' he called out.

Bostar turned, a contemptuous expression twisting his face. 'Don't worry. I'll say nothing.' With that, he was gone.

Right on cue, a blast of icy wind hit Sapho, chilling him to the bone.

He had never felt more alone.

Quintus' and Hanno's departure left Aurelia feeling abandoned. Finding an excuse to head off to visit Suniaton was far from easy. She could not confide in her mother for obvious reasons, and she didn't like, or trust, her old Greek tutor. She was friendly with Elira, but the Illyrian had been in a bad mood recently, which made her poor company. Julius was the only other household slave Aurelia could be bothered with. After the excitement of her trips to the woods, however, discussion about what was on next week's menu was of little interest. Inevitably, she spent most of her time with her mother, who, since they'd been left alone, had thrown herself into household tasks with a vengeance. It was, Aurelia supposed, Atia's way of coping with Quintus' disappearance.

Foremost among their jobs was dealing with the vast amount of wool stockpiled in one of the sheds in the yard. It had been shorn from the sheep during the summer, and in the subsequent months, the women slaves had stripped the twigs and vegetation from the fleeces, before dyeing them a variety of colours: red, yellow, blue and black. Once dyed, the wool was ready for spinning, and then weaving. Although the majority of this work was done by slaves, Atia also contributed to the effort. She insisted Aurelia did so as well. Day after day, they sat in or walked around the courtyard, distaffs and spindles in hand, retreating to the atrium only if it rained.

'It's the job of a woman to keep the house and work in wool,' said Atia one crisp morning. Deftly pulling a few unspun fibres from the bundle on her distaff, she attached them to her spindle and set it spinning. Her eyes lifted to Aurelia. 'Are you listening, child?'

'Yes,' Aurelia replied, grateful that Atia hadn't noticed her rolling eyes. 'You've told me that a thousand times.'

'That's because it's true,' her mother replied primly. 'It's the mark of a good wife to be proficient at spinning and weaving. You'd do well to remember that.'

'Yes, Mother,' said Aurelia dutifully. Inside, she imagined that she was practising with a gladius.

'No doubt your father and Quintus will be grateful for any cloaks and tunics that we can send them too. I believe that the winters in Iberia can be harsh.'

Guiltily, Aurelia applied herself to her task with more vigour. This was the only tangible way of helping her brother. She was shocked to find herself wishing that she could do the same for Hanno. He's one of the enemy now, she told herself. 'Has there been any more news?'

'You know there hasn't.' There was an unmistakable trace of irritation in Atia's voice. 'Father will have no time to write to us. With the gods' blessing, however, he'll have reached Iberia by now.'

'With luck, Quintus will find him soon,' Aurelia responded.

Atia's composure cracked for an instant, revealing the sorrow beneath. 'What was he thinking to go on his own?'

Aurelia's heart bled to see her mother so upset. Until now, she hadn't mentioned that Hanno had left with her brother. Saying nothing made things far simpler. Now, though, her resolve wavered.

A discreet cough prevented her from saying a word. Aurelia was annoyed to see Agesandros standing by the atrium doors.

In the blink of an eye, Atia's self-possession returned. 'Agesandros.'

'My lady,' he said, bowing. 'Aurelia.'

Aurelia gave the Sicilian a withering look. Since his accusation of Hanno, she had avoided him like the plague. Now he had stopped her from consoling her mother.

'What is it?' asked Atia. 'A problem with the olive harvest?'

'No, mistress.' He hesitated. 'I have come to make an apology. To Aurelia.'

Atia's eyebrows rose. 'What have you done?'

'Nothing that I shouldn't have, mistress,' said Agesandros reassuringly. 'But the whole business with the Carthaginian slave was most . . . unfortunate.'

'Is that what you call it?' Aurelia interjected acidly.

Atia raised a hand, stalling her protest. 'Continue.'

Scipio was incensed, upon his arrival in Pisae nearly a week later, to be greeted by a messenger from the Senate. The consul's only thought was to travel north, to Cisalpine Gaul, and there take control of the legions presently commanded by a praetor, Lucius Manlius Vulso. Yet the note Scipio was handed suggested in no uncertain terms that it would be judicious to report to the Senate before taking further action against Hannibal. This was necessary because, as Scipio spat at Flaccus, he had '"exceeded his consular remit, by deciding not to proceed to Iberia with his army".'

Flaccus innocently studied his fingernails.

'Someone must have sent word before we left Massilia,' Scipio raged, staring pointedly at Flaccus. 'Yet nowhere do I see any mention of the word *provocatio*. In other words, I could ignore this disrespectful note. I probably should. With every day that goes by, Hannibal and his army march closer to our northern borders. Sempronius has no chance of travelling from Sicily quicker than I can reach the north. Journeying to Rome will delay me by two weeks, or more. If Hannibal turns up during that time, the result could be catastrophic.'

'That would scarcely be my fault,' Flaccus replied smoothly.

Scipio's nostrils flared white with fury. 'Is that so?'

Flaccus had the sense not to answer.

Reading the missive again, Scipio composed himself. 'I will return to Rome as asked, but any responsibility for what happens because of the delay will fall on the heads of the Minucii, and on you particularly. Should Hannibal already be in the area when I eventually reach Cisalpine Gaul, I will make sure to position you in the front line every time we encounter the Carthaginians.' Flaccus looked up in alarm, and Scipio snarled, 'There you can win all the glory you desire. Posthumously, I expect.' Ignoring Flaccus' shock, Scipio turned to Fabricius. 'We shall take but a single turma to Rome. I want two spare horses for every rider. Your other men can buy new mounts, and then head north to join Vulso with the cohort of infantry. See to it. We ride out in an hour.'

Flaccus followed Fabricius as he supervised the unloading of the mounts and equipment. The quayside at Pisae was a hive of activity. Freshly disembarked soldiers retrieved their equipment from piles on the dock and formed up in lines under their officers' eagle eyes. Fabricius' cavalrymen watched as specially constructed wooden frames lifted their horses out of the ships' bellies and on to dry land once more. Grooms stepped in, reassuring their unsettled charges, before leading them off to one side where they

345

could be readied for the impending journey. As soon as the opportunity presented itself, Fabricius rounded on Flaccus. 'What in the name of Hades is going on?'

Flaccus made a show of innocence. 'What do you mean?'

'Any fool knows that the best thing is not for Scipio to go to Rome, but to Cisalpine Gaul, and with all haste. Yet you have conspired to make sure that he does the former.'

Flaccus looked shocked. 'Who's to say that I had anything to do with the news reaching Rome? Anyhow, I cannot answer for the actions of more senior members of my clan. They are men greater than you or I, men whose only interest is that of Rome. They also know Scipio for an arrogant individual whose main aim is to gain glory for himself; his recent actions prove this. He must be brought to book by his fellows and reminded of his position before it's too late.

'It's not as if we are without forces in the north,' Flaccus went on persuasively. 'Lucius Manlius Vulso is already in the area with a full-sized consular army. Vulso is an experienced commander, and I have no doubt that he is skilled enough to face, and beat, the rabble Hannibal will lead out of the mountains. Would you not agree?'

Fabricius felt his position waver. Scipio's confident decision to send his army on to Iberia while he himself returned to Italy had certainly been out of the ordinary. Initially, Fabricius had thought Scipio was showing genuine foresight, but Flaccus' words sowed doubt in his mind. It was hard to credit that a faction in Rome would endanger the Republic just to score points over a political rival. The Minucii must have their reasons for demanding to see Scipio, he reasoned. In theory, the legions in Cisalpine Gaul were fully capable of defending their northern border. Fabricius glanced at Flaccus, and saw nothing but genuine concern. 'I suppose so,' he muttered.

'Good. Let us travel to the capital without worrying about Hannibal, and see what our betters in the Senate would say to

Scipio,' said Flaccus earnestly. 'The gugga can be dealt with immediately afterwards, if Vulso has not already wiped him from the
face of the earth. Are we agreed?' He stuck out his right arm in
the soldier's fashion.

Fabricius felt uneasy. One moment Flaccus was talking as if
those in Rome always acted unselfishly, and the next he was
implying that Scipio's recall was a political tactic made with scant
consideration of the danger posed by Hannibal. There was far
more going on here than met the eye. In Fabricius' mind, the sole
issue at hand was Hannibal, and how to deal with him. Those
who sat in the Senate obviously did not appreciate that. Yet did
it really matter, he wondered, if they went to Rome before
Cisalpine Gaul? If Hannibal did succeed in crossing the Alps, his
army would need a prolonged period of rest to recover from their
ordeal. Forewarned, Vulso would be ready, and Scipio would not
take long to travel from the capital. 'We are agreed,' he said,
accepting Flaccus' grip.

'Excellent.' Flaccus' eyes glittered with satisfaction. 'By the
way, don't take anything my brother says to heart. He is greatly
looking forward to meeting you in private.'

Feeling rather out of his depth, Fabricius nodded.

Hannibal's army reached the top of the pass the next day.
Thrillingly, the watery sunshine revealed flat plains far below.
The distant image could have been a mirage for all the use it was
to them, thought Bostar bitterly. The slopes that led down towards
Cisalpine Gaul were covered in frozen snow, which entirely
concealed the path. Achieving a secure footing from now on would
be more difficult than ever, and the price of failure was no less
lethal than it had been since they'd entered the mountains.

To relieve his troops' suffering, Hannibal let them rest for two
days at the summit. Of course there was more to his decision
than simple kindness. Hundreds of stragglers, soldiers who would
have died otherwise, managed to catch up with their comrades in

this time, where they were greeted with relief but little sympathy. Even if they'd wanted to speak of their ordeal, few would have found an audience. Despair clawed constantly at men's hearts, rendering them insensible to the suffering of others.

Remarkably, hundreds of mules that had gone missing during the ascent also made their way into the camp. Although the majority had lost their baggage, they were still a welcome sight. In an effort to raise morale, Hannibal allowed the weakest beasts, numbering two hundred or more, to be slaughtered on the last evening before the descent. The fires needed to cook this meal consumed most of the army's remaining wood, but for the first time in weeks, his soldiers went to sleep with fresh meat in their bellies.

Bostar's deeply held hope that Hanno was still alive, and the presence of his father, were what sustained him through the agonies of the following day and night. He tried not to think of Sapho at all, instead concentrating on helping his soldiers. If Bostar had thought that the journey through the mountains up to that point had been difficult, then the descent was twice as bad. After more than a week above the snow line, the troops were chilled to the bone. Despite the Cavares' gifts of clothing and footwear, many were still not suitably attired for the freezing, hazardous conditions. Slowed by the cold, the Carthaginians stumbled over the slightest obstacles, walked into snowdrifts and collided with each other. This, when a simple trip meant death, instantly from the fall, or by slipping away into a sleep from which there was no wakening.

The soldiers died in other ways as well. Sections of the path cracked away under the weight of snow and men, sending hundreds into oblivion, and forcing those behind to repair the track in order to continue. The unfortunate mules were now prone to panic at the slightest thing, and their struggles were the cause of more casualties. Bostar found that the only way not to go mad in the face of so much death and destruction was to act as if nothing had happened. To keep putting one foot in front of the other. Step by grim step, he plodded on.

Just when he thought that things could get no worse, they did. Late the next morning, the vanguard arrived at a point where a landslide had carried away the track for a distance of one and a half stades. Sapho sent word back that neither man nor beast could proceed without losing their life. Here the drop was at least five hundred paces. Undeterred, Hannibal ordered his Numidians to begin constructing a new path across the obstacle. The rest of the army was ordered to rest as best it could. The news made many soldiers break down and weep. 'Will our suffering never end?' wailed one of Bostar's men. Bostar was quick to issue a reprimand. Morale was painfully low, without being made worse by open despair.

All they had to go on were the garbled messages occasionally passed back from the vanguard. Bostar didn't know which to believe. The cavalry mounts were useful in pulling large boulders out of the way. Most of the work had to be done by bare hand. Hannibal had offered a hundred gold pieces to the first man over the obstacle. Ten men had fallen to their deaths when a section of the track had given way. It would take a week or more to clear the way for the elephants.

As darkness fell, Bostar's spirits were raised somewhat by a Numidian officer who was passing through Bostar's phalanx as he returned to his tent.

'Progress was good today. We've laid a new path over more than two-thirds of the landslide. If things proceed like this tomorrow, we should be able to continue.'

Bostar breathed a huge sigh of relief. After nearly a month in the mountains, Cisalpine Gaul would be within reach at last.

His optimism vanished within an hour of work resuming the following morning when the cavalrymen exposed a huge boulder. It completely blocked the way forward. With a diameter greater than the height of two men, the rock was positioned such that only a few soldiers could approach at a time. Horses weren't strong enough to move it, and there was no space to lead an elephant in to try.

As time passed, Bostar could see the last vestiges of hope disappearing from men's eyes. He felt the same way himself. Although they weren't speaking, Sapho looked similarly deflated. It wasn't long before Hannibal came to survey the problem. Bostar's usual excitement at seeing his general did not materialise. How could anyone, even Hannibal, find a way to overcome this obstacle? As if the gods were laughing, more snow began to fall. Bostar's shoulders slumped.

A moment later, he was surprised to see his father hurrying to speak with Hannibal. When Malchus returned, he had a new air of calmness about him. Bostar squinted at the soldiers who were hurrying back along the column. He grabbed his father's arm. 'What's going on?'

'All is not lost,' Malchus replied with a small smile. 'You will see.'

Soon after, the soldiers returned, each man bent double under a pile of firewood. Load after load was carried past and set carefully around the base of the rock. When the timber had been piled high, Malchus ordered it lit. Still Bostar did not understand, but his father would answer no questions. Leaving his sons to observe with increasing curiosity, he returned to Hannibal's side.

The soldiers who could see were also intrigued, but after the fire had been burning for more than an hour without any result, they grew bored. Grumbles about wasting the last of their wood began. For the first time since leaving New Carthage, Bostar did not immediately react. His own disillusionment was reaching critical levels. Whatever crackpot idea his father had had was not going to work. They might as well lie down and die now, because that was what would surely happen when night fell.

Bostar missed the construction of a wooden framework that

allowed a man to stand over the top of the rock. It was only when the first amphorae were carried past that he looked up. Finally, his curiosity got the better of his despair. The clay vessels contained sour wine, the troops' staple drink. Bostar saw his father gesturing excitedly as Hannibal watched. Quickly, two strapping scutarii climbed the frame. To combat the extreme heat now radiating from the rock, they had both soaked their clothes in water. The instant they had reached the top, the pair lowered ropes to the ground. Men below tied amphorae to the cables, which were hauled up. Without further ado, the scutarii cracked open the wax seals and poured the vessels' contents all over the boulder. The liquid sizzled and spat, sending a powerful smell of hot wine into the faces of those watching. Realisation of what they were trying to do struck Bostar like a hammer blow. He turned to tell Sapho before biting his lip and saying nothing.

The empty containers were discarded and replaced by full ones, and the process was repeated. There was more loud bubbling as the wine boiled on the superheated rock, but nothing else happened. The scutarii looked uncertainly at Malchus. 'Keep going! As fast as you can!' he shouted. Hastily, they obeyed, upending two more amphorae. Then it was four. Still the rock sat there, immovable, immutable. Malchus roared at the soldiers who stood close by to add more fuel to the blaze. The flames licked up, threatening to consume the platform upon which the scutarii stood, but they were not allowed to climb down. Malchus moved to stand at the frame's base, and exhorted the soldiers to even greater efforts. Another two amphorae were emptied over the boulder, to no avail. Bostar's hopes began to ebb away.

A succession of explosive cracks suddenly drowned out all sound. Chunks of stone were hurled high into the air, and one of the scutarii collapsed as if poleaxed. His skull had been neatly staved in by a piece of rock no bigger than a hen's egg. His panicked companion jumped to safety, and the soldiers who had been tending the fire all retreated at speed. More cracking sounds followed, and then the rock broke into several large parts. Parts that could be moved by men, or smashed into pieces by hammers. The cheering that followed rose to the very clouds. As word spread down the column, the noise increased in volume until it seemed that the mountains themselves were rejoicing.

Elated, Bostar and Sapho rushed separately to their father's side. Joyfully, they embraced him one by one. They were joined by Hannibal, who greeted Malchus like a brother. 'Our ordeal is nearly over,' the general cried. 'The path to Cisalpine Gaul lies open.'

The two friends' first sight of the capital was formed by the immense Servian wall, which ringed the city and dwarfed Capua's defences. 'The fortifications are nearly two hundred years old,' Quintus explained excitedly. 'They were built after Rome was sacked by the Gauls.'

May Hannibal be the next to do so, Hanno prayed.

'How does Carthage compare?'

'Eh?' said Hanno, coming back to reality. 'Many of her defences are much more recent.' They're still far more spectacular, he thought.

'And its size?'

Hanno wasn't going to lie about that one. 'Carthage is much bigger.'

Quintus did his best not to look disgruntled, and failed.

Hanno was surprised that within the walls, Carthage's similarities with Rome grew. The streets were unpaved, and most were no more than ten paces across. After months of hot weather, their surfaces were little more than an iron-hard series of wheel ruts. 'They'll be a muddy morass come the winter,' he said, pointing. 'That's what happens if it rains a lot at home.'

'As in Capua,' agreed Quintus. He wrinkled his nose as they passed an alleyway used as a dung heap. The acrid odour of human faeces and urine hung heavy in the air. 'Lucky it's autumn and not the height of summer. The smell then is apparently unbearable.'

'Do many buildings have sewerage systems?'

'No.'

'It's not much different to parts of Carthage,' Hanno replied. It was strange to feel homesick because of the smell of shit.

The fuggy atmosphere was aided by the fact that the closely built structures were two, three and even four storeys tall, creating a dimly lit, poorly ventilated environment on the street. Compared to the fresh air and open spaces of the Italian countryside, it was an alternative world. Most structures were open-fronted shops at ground level, with stairs at the side that snaked up to the flats above. Quintus was shocked by the filth of it all. 'They're where the majority of people live,' he explained.

'In Carthage, they're mostly constructed from mud bricks.'

'That sounds a lot safer. The *cenaculae* are built of wood. They're disease-ridden, hard to heat and easy to destroy.'

'Fire's a big problem, then,' said Hanno, imagining how easy it would be to burn down the city if it fell to Hannibal's army.

Quintus grimaced. 'Yes.'

Along with its sights and smells, the capital provided plenty of noise. The air was filled with the clamour of shopkeepers competing for business, the shrieks of playing children and the chatter of neighbours gossiping on the street corners. Beggars of every hue abounded, adding their cries for alms to the din. The clang of iron being pounded on anvils carried from smithies, and the sound of carpenters hammering echoed off the tall buildings. In the distance, cattle bellowed from the Forum Boarium.

Of course Rome was not their main destination: that was the port of Pisae, from which Scipio and his army had set sail. Yet the temptation of visiting Rome had been too much for either of the friends to resist. They wandered through the streets for hours, drinking in the sights. When they were hungry, they filled their bellies with hot sausages and fresh bread bought from little stalls. Juicy plums and apples finished off their satisfying meal.

Inevitably, Quintus was drawn to the massive temple of Jupiter, high on the Capitoline Hill. He gaped at its roof of beaten gold, rows of columns the height of ten men and façade of brightly painted terracotta. He came to a halt by the immense statue of a bearded Jupiter, which stood in front of the complex, giving it a view over much of Rome.

Feeling resentful, Hanno also stopped.

'This must be bigger than any of the shrines in Carthage,' said Quintus with a questioning look.

'There's one which is as big,' Hanno replied proudly. 'It's in honour of Eshmoun.'

'What god is that?' asked Quintus curiously.

'He represents fertility, good health and well-being.'

Quintus' eyebrows rose. 'And is he the leading deity in Carthage?'

'No.'

'Why has his temple the most prominent position then?'

Hanno gave an awkward shrug. 'I don't know.' He remembered his father saying that their people differed from the Romans by being traders first and foremost. This temple complex proved that Quintus' kind placed power and war before everything else. Thank all the gods that we have a real warrior in Hannibal Barca, he thought. If fools like Hostus were in charge, we would have no hope.

Quintus had come to his own conclusion. How could a race who gave pride of place to a fertility god's temple ever defeat Rome? And when the inevitable happens, what will happen to Hanno? his conscience suddenly screamed. Where will he be? Quintus didn't want to answer the question. 'We'd better find a bed for the night,' he suggested. 'Before it gets dark.'

'Good idea,' replied Hanno, grateful for the change of subject.

* * *

Agesandros gave a tiny nod of thanks and turned to Aurelia. 'I should have handled the matter far better. I wanted to apologise for it, and ask if we can make a new start.'

'A new start?' Aurelia snapped. 'But you're only a slave! What you think means nothing.' She was pleased to see pain flare in his eyes.

'Enough!' Atia exclaimed. 'Agesandros has served us loyally for more than twenty years. At the least, you should listen to what he has to say.'

Aurelia flushed, mortified at being reprimanded in front of a slave. She was damned if she'd just give in to her mother's wishes. 'Why would you bother apologising now?' she muttered.

'It's simple. The master and Quintus may be gone for a long time. Who knows? It could be years. Perhaps you'll have more of a hand with the running of the farm.' Encouraged by Atia's nod of acquiescence, he continued, 'I want nothing more than to do my best for you and the mistress here.' Agesandros made an almost plaintive gesture. 'A good working relationship is essential if we are to succeed.'

'He's right,' said Atia.

'You owe me an explanation before I agree to anything,' said Aurelia angrily.

The Sicilian sighed. 'True. I did treat the gugga slave harshly.'

'Harshly? Where do you get the gall?' Aurelia cried. 'You were going to sell a man to someone who would make him fight his best friend to the death!'

'I have my reasons,' Agesandros replied. A cloud passed across his face. 'If I were to tell you that the Carthaginians tortured and murdered my entire family in Sicily, would you think differently of me?'

Aurelia's mouth opened in horror.

'They did what?' demanded her mother.

'I was away, fighting at the other end of the island, mistress. A surprise Carthaginian attack swept through the town, destroying all in its path.' Agesandros swallowed. 'They slaughtered everyone in the place: men, women, children. The old, the sick, even the dogs.'

Aurelia could scarcely breathe. 'Why?'

'It was punishment,' the Sicilian replied. 'Historically, we had sided with Carthage, but had switched to give our allegiance to Rome. Many settlements had done the same. Ours was the first to be captured. A message had to be delivered to the rest.'

Aurelia knew that terrible things happened in war. Men died, or were injured terribly, often in their thousands. But the massacre of civilians?

'Go on,' said Atia gently.

'I had a wife and two children. A girl and a boy.' For the first time, Agesandros' voice cracked. 'They were just babies. Three and two.'

Aurelia was stunned to see tears in his eyes. She had not thought the vilicus capable of such emotion. Incredibly, she felt sorry for him.

'I found them some days later. They were dead. Butchered, in fact.' Agesandros' face twitched. 'Have you ever seen what a spear blade can do to a little child? Or what a woman looks like after a dozen soldiers have violated her?'

'Stop!' Atia cried in distaste. 'That's quite enough.'

He hung his head.

Aurelia was reeling with horror. Her mind was filled with a series of terrifying images. It was no wonder, she thought, that Agesandros had treated Hanno as he had.

'Finish your story,' Atia commanded. 'Quickly.'

'I didn't really want to live after that,' said Agesandros obediently, 'but the gods did not see fit to grant my wish of dying in battle. Instead, I was taken prisoner, and sold into slavery. I was taken to Italy, where the master bought me.' He shrugged. 'Here I have been ever since. That pair were some of the first guggas I had seen for two decades.'

'Hanno is innocent of any crime towards your family,' Aurelia hissed. 'The war in Sicily took place before he had even been born!'

'Let me deal with this,' said her mother sharply. 'Were you seeking revenge the first time that you attacked the Carthaginian?'

'Yes, mistress.'

'I understand. While it doesn't excuse your actions, it explains them.' Atia's expression hardened. 'Did you lie about finding the knife and purse among the slave's belongings?'

'No, mistress! As the gods are my witness, I told the truth,' said the Sicilian earnestly.

Liar, thought Aurelia furiously, but she dared say nothing. Her mother was nodding in approval. A moment later, her worries materialised.

'Agesandros is right,' Atia declared. 'Things will be hard enough in the months to come. Let us all make a new start.' She stared expectantly at Aurelia. Agesandros' expression was milder, but mirrored hers.

'Very well,' Aurelia whispered, feeling more isolated than ever.

Chapter XVII: Debate

Having found a cheap bed for the night, the two friends hit the nearest tavern. Drinking seemed the adult thing to do, but of course there was a darker reason behind it: their thoughts about the outcome of the war. Both felt more awkward than they had since falling out during Flaccus' visit. Aurelia was not there to mediate, so wine would have to do. Their tactic worked to some extent, and they chatted idly while eyeing the prostitutes who were working the room for customers.

It didn't take long before the wine began to affect them both. Neither were used to drinking much. Fortunately, they grew merry rather than morose, and the evening became quite enjoyable. Encouraged by a hooting Hanno, Quintus even relaxed enough to take one of the whores on to his lap and fondle her bare breasts. He might have gone further, but then something happened that took all their attention away from wine and women. Important news didn't take long to spread through cities and towns. People simply carried the word on foot, from shops to taverns, and market places to houses. Naturally, the accuracy of such gossip could not always be relied upon, but that did not mean there wasn't some truth to it.

'Hannibal is leading his army over the Alps!' cried a voice from outside the inn. 'When he falls upon Italy, we shall be murdered in our beds!'

As all conversation ceased, the two friends stared at each other, wide eyed. 'Did you know about this?' Quintus hissed.

'I had no idea,' Hanno replied truthfully. 'Why else would I have agreed to travel with you to Iberia?'

A moment later, a middle-aged man with a red face and double chin entered. His grubby tunic and calloused hands pointed towards him being a shopkeeper of some kind. He smiled self-importantly at the barrage of questions that greeted him. 'I have seen Scipio the consul with my own eyes, not an hour since,' he announced. 'He has returned from Massilia with this terrible news.'

'What else did you hear?' shouted a voice. 'Tell us!'

A roar of agreement went up from the other patrons.

The shopkeeper licked his lips. 'Running through the streets is thirsty work. A cup of wine would wet my throat nicely.'

Hurriedly, the landlord filled a beaker to the brim. Scurrying over, he pressed it into the newcomer's hand.

He took a deep swallow and smacked his lips with satisfaction. 'Tasty.'

'Tell us!' Quintus cried.

The shopkeeper smiled again at his temporary power. 'After landing at Massilia for supplies, Scipio heard word that Hannibal might be in the area. He sent out a patrol, which stumbled upon the entire Carthaginian army.' He paused, letting the shocked cries of his audience fill the air, and draining his cup. The innkeeper refilled it at once. The man raised a hand. Instantly, silence fell. 'When he heard, Scipio led his army north with all speed, his aim to force the enemy into battle. But when they arrived, Hannibal had gone. Vanished. His only intention can be to cross the mountains and enter Cisalpine Gaul. Before invading Italy.'

Wails of terror met his final remark. The room descended into chaos as everyone screamed to be heard. Some customers even ran away, back to their houses. Quintus' face bore an expression of total shock, while Hanno struggled to control his exhilaration.

Who else could be so daring, other than Hannibal? He wondered if his father had known about this tactically brilliant plan, and said nothing? At one stroke, his priorities had been changed utterly.

Quintus had realised the same thing. 'I suppose you'll be leaving now,' he said accusingly. 'Why travel to Iberia now? Just head to Cisalpine Gaul.'

Feeling guilty for even entertaining the idea, Hanno flushed. 'This changes nothing,' he replied. 'We are going to Iberia to find your father.'

Quintus looked Hanno in the eyes, and saw that he meant it. He hung his head. 'I'm sorry for doubting your honour,' he muttered. 'It's shocking to hear news like this.'

Their conversation was interrupted again. 'Do you not want to know why the consul has returned?' bellowed the messenger, who was already on his fourth cup of wine. He waited as the room grew quiet once more. 'Scipio has been recalled by the Senate because he sent his army on to Iberia rather than pursuing Hannibal. They say that the Minucii want him replaced with one of their own. Tomorrow, he will attend the Curia to explain his actions.'

All thoughts of leaving Rome at dawn vanished from the pair's heads. What did it matter if they delayed their departure for a few hours to witness this drama unfold?

Whatever Scipio's reception in the Senate might be, he was still one of the Republic's two consuls. At the walled gate that signalled the end of the Via Ostiensis, the road from Ostia, a fine litter borne by six strapping slaves awaited his arrival. He, Flaccus and Fabricius clambered aboard. A dozen lictores bearing fasces preceded the litter into the city. As soldiers under arms, Fabricius' thirty cavalrymen had to remain outside but this did not delay the party's progress. The lictores' mere presence, wearing their magnificent red campaign cloaks rather than just their usual togas, and with the addition of axes to their fasces, was enough to clear the streets. All citizens, apart from Vestal Virgins or married women, were obliged to stand aside, or face the consequences. Only the strongest and tallest men were picked to join the lictores, and they had been taught to use their fasces at the slightest opportunity. If ordered to do so, they could even act as executioners.

Fabricius had been to Rome several times, and always enjoyed the spectacle provided by the capital. The lictores' presence ensured that he gained the best possible impression of the city. People pushed inside the shops and into the alleyways to get out of the way. It was all a far cry from Capua, and even further from Fabricius' farm, and yet it felt very similar. He tried to ignore the feeling of homesickness that followed. Their rapid progress to the Forum Romanum ensured that he had no time to wallow in the emotion.

As they entered the Forum, Fabricius' eyes were drawn to the Curia, the home of the Senate. Unremarkable apart from its great bronze doors, it was nonetheless the focal point of the Republic. He picked out the Graecostasis, the area just outside, where foreign embassies had to wait until they were called in. Today, accompanying one of the two most important men in the land, there was no such delay. The lictores swept up to the entrance, scattering the crowd of senators' sons who were hovering outside, listening to the debates within. Scipio alighted right before the portals; so too did Flaccus and Fabricius. All three were clad in their finest togas. Naturally, Scipio wore the grandest, a shining white woollen garment with a purple border.

Before leaving, Fabricius had secreted a dagger in the folds of his toga. After months on campaign, he felt naked without a weapon, and had scooped it up without even thinking. Yet it was a risky move: the lictores alone were allowed to bear arms within the Curia. Now, Fabricius cursed his impulsive decision. There was no way of getting rid of the dagger, though. He would have to carry it inside and hope for the best. His heart began to pound. Scipio had asked him to be present because he was the only Roman officer to have seen Hannibal's army. His testimony was vital for

Scipio's defence. 'I'm relying on you,' the consul had said. 'I know you won't let me down. Just tell them what you saw at the Carthaginian camp.' Fabricius had promised to do so. He sneaked a glance at Flaccus, who looked rather pleased with himself. Confusion filled Fabricius. What role would he play in the drama to come?

The most senior lictor spoke with the guards before entering to announce Scipio's arrival. A hush fell inside. Upon the man's return, the twelve lictores re-formed in six columns of two. With a measured tread, they led the way into the Senate. Fabricius followed Scipio and Flaccus. He had to stop himself from staring like an excited boy. He'd never entered the seat of the Republic's democracy. Light flooded in through long, narrow windows set high in the walls. Running the length of the rectangular room, three low steps were lined by marble benches. Rank upon rank of standing toga-clad senators filled this space. To a man, their gaze was locked on Scipio and his companions. Struggling to control his awe, Fabricius kept his eyes averted from the senators. At the end of the chamber, he saw a dais upon which sat two finely carved rosewood chairs. These, the most important positions, were for the consuls.

The lictores reached the platform and fanned out to either side, leaving a space for Scipio to assume his seat. Flaccus and Fabricius remained at floor level. As Scipio sat down, the lictores smacked the butts of their fasces off the mosaic. The clashing sound echoed off the walls and died away.

There was a long pause.

Glancing sideways, Fabricius saw a tiny, satisfied smile flicker across the consul's lips. It was obviously up to Scipio to begin proceedings, and, in a pointed reminder of his rank, he was making the men who had recalled him to Rome wait. On and on the silence went. Soon Fabricius could see senators muttering angrily to one another. None dared to speak, however.

Finally, Scipio opened his mouth. 'As I speak, the greatest threat to Rome since the barbarian Brennus approaches us through the Alps.' He let his shocking words sink in. 'Yet instead of letting me fulfil my duty, that of defending the Republic, you would have me return to explain my actions. Well, I am here.' Scipio extended his arms, as if to welcome interrogation, and fell silent.

A deluge of questions followed. Practically half the senators present tried to speak at the same time. Many of their queries involved Brennus, the Gaulish chieftain who had led his fearsome warriors to the Capitoline Hill itself, and sacked Rome. In the process, he had left a weeping sore deep in the Roman psyche, a source of eternal shame. Fabricius did not know if Hannibal was truly that dangerous, but merely by mentioning Brennus, Scipio had scored the first points. Before the Minucii could make a single accusation, the Senate's attention had been neatly diverted to something far more primeval.

Scipio wasn't finished. Lifting a hand, he waited for quiet. 'I want to know why I was summoned here. Only then will I tell you anything of Hannibal and the enormous Carthaginian army which follows him.'

Cries and protests filled the air, but Scipio simply folded his arms and sat back on his chair.

Second round to Scipio, thought Fabricius. His respect for the consul was growing by the moment.

Both young men were up late the next morning. A brief visit to the public baths helped to ease their pounding heads. Fortunately, both also had the wits to drink copious amounts of water. Relieving themselves was not an issue: all they had to do was dart up one of the many alleyways that contained dung heaps. Breakfasting on bread and cheese, they made their way to the Forum Romanum. Naturally enough, conversation was limited until they reached their destination.

Quintus soaked up the sight of the long, rectangular space. 'It used to be a marsh, but now it's the largest open area within the city walls. This is the heart of the Republic,' he said proudly. 'The centre of religious, ceremonial and commercial life. People come here to socialise, to watch court cases or gladiator fights, and to hear important public announcements.'

'It has a lot in common with the Agora,' said Hanno politely. Although it's not half as big, he thought.

Hundreds of shops lined the Forum's perimeter. They ranged from ordinary butchers, fishmongers and bakers to the grander premises of lawyers, scribes and moneylenders. Crowds of people thronged the whole area.

Quintus had been taught the Forum's layout. 'There are the shrines of Castor and Pollux, and Saturn,' he cried as they walked along. 'And the circular temple of the Vestal Virgins.'

'What's that?' asked Hanno, pointing at a grubby building along the northern side of the Forum.

'I think it's the *comitium*,' Quintus replied. 'It's a temple which was built during the foundation of Rome more than five hundred years before.' His voice lowered. 'Inside it is the *lapis niger*, a stubby pillar of black stone which marks the spot where Romulus, the founder of Rome, ascended to heaven. Beside is the rostra, the speaker's platform, which is decorated with the prows of captured ships.' Quintus flushed and fell silent. The most recent additions were from Carthaginian triremes that had been captured in the last war.

Realising, Hanno glowered.

The friends soon discovered that they had arrived just after Scipio had entered the Curia, but consoled themselves with the fact that they would be close at hand when he emerged. Huge crowds were already present. The news about Hannibal had spread all over the city by now. Everyone in Rome wanted to know what would happen next. Wild rumours swept from one end of the gathering to the other.

'Hannibal has a host of more than a hundred and fifty thousand men,' cried a man with red-rimmed eyes.

'He has a hundred elephants, and twenty-five thousand Numidian cavalry,' wailed another.

'They say that Philip of Macedon has mobilised his army and is about to attack us from the northeast,' shot back the first man. 'He's going to join with the Carthaginians.'

'So is every tribe in Cisalpine Gaul,' added a third voice.

Hanno's anger over the rostra was replaced by delight. If only a fraction of the gossip was true, Rome faced a catastrophe of enormous proportions. He glanced at Quintus, who was staring rigidly at the Curia, pretending to ignore what was being said.

An awkward silence fell.

A hush fell in the Senate as a stocky figure with wavy black hair and a ruddy complexion made his way into view. Bushy eyebrows sat over a pair of calculating blue eyes and a prominent nose. The senators around him moved deferentially out of the way. Flaccus gave the man a tiny nod, and Fabricius knew at once who it was. He was Marcus Minucius Rufus, a former consul, and Flaccus' brother. This was the pre-eminent member of the Minucii clan, and one of the most powerful men in Rome. No doubt he was the person responsible for the letter to Scipio.

'Consul,' said Marcus, inclining his head in recognition. 'We thank you for returning to Rome. It is an honour to see you once more.' With the niceties over, his expression turned hawkish. 'We were alarmed to hear that your brother was leading your legions to Iberia. This, so that you could return to Italy. We have asked you back to explain your extraordinary about turn, which goes completely against the Senate's decision made here not six months ago. You and Longus, your co-consul, have supreme command of the Republic's military forces. That is beyond doubt. Yet neither of you are immune to challenge, should that be necessary.' Marcus half turned, smiling at the mutters of agreement that were becoming audible. 'Clearly, I am not the only one to hold such an opinion.'

One of Scipio's eyebrows arched. 'And what opinion might that be?' he asked in a silky smooth tone.

Marcus' reply was urbane. 'I speak of course, of the power of provocatio.'

Some of the senators hissed with disapproval at this, but others shouted in agreement. Fabricius felt a nerve twitch in his face. He'd never before heard of one of the Republic's supreme magistrates being threatened with a criminal charge. He shot a glance at Flaccus, but could glean nothing from his face. Why were the Minucii seeking to depose Scipio during his consulship? Fabricius wondered. What purpose would it serve?

'Have you nothing to say?' Marcus asked, taking a smug look around the room. Like a tide that had just turned, the noise of those who supported him began to grow.

Fabricius glanced at Flaccus again. This time, he saw the same self-satisfied expression as the one adorning Marcus' face. Then it hit him. Flaccus had believed Scipio's account of the threat posed by Hannibal and, in his letter, told his brother of his concerns. Now Marcus, a previously successful general in his own right, wanted to become consul so that he could claim the glory of defeating the Carthaginians instead of leaving it to Scipio. This possibility, no, probability, Fabricius thought angrily, defied belief. All that mattered was defeating an enemy who posed a serious threat to the Republic. Yet to some of these politicians, it was more about making a name for themselves.

Bizarrely, Scipio laughed. 'I find it remarkable,' he said, 'that I should be accused of exceeding my remit when in fact I have done more than my duty in fulfilling it. My army has been sent to Iberia as ordered; its commander, my brother Gnaeus, has a proven record in the field. Furthermore, upon realising the implications of Hannibal's march across the Alps, and knowing that my colleague Longus would not have time to react, I returned to Italy with the intention of facing the Carthaginians myself. Immediately. Does that not prove my loyalty to Rome? And what should we think about those who would prevent me from doing my duty?'

In the uproar that followed, Scipio and Marcus stared at each other with clear dislike. But Marcus' response was swift. 'I take it that you have seen Hannibal's "enormous" army with your own eyes? Made a realistic estimate of the number of enemy troops?'

'I have done neither,' replied Scipio in an icy tone.

'Are you a soothsayer, then?' Marcus asked, to gales of laughter from his supporters.

'Nothing like that.' Scipio coolly indicated Fabricius. 'I have with me the veteran cavalry officer who led the patrol that reconnoitred the Carthaginian camp's perimeter. He will be happy to answer any questions you may have.'

Marcus regarded Fabricius with thinly disguised contempt. 'Your name?'

Meeting Marcus' stare, Fabricius steeled his resolve. Whatever the other's rank, and however intimidating the scene, he would tell the truth. 'Gaius Fabricius, sir. Equestrian and landowner near Capua.'

Marcus made a dismissive gesture. 'Have you much military experience?'

'I spent nearly ten years in Sicily, fighting the Carthaginians, sir,' replied Fabricius proudly. He was delighted by the response of some of those watching. Many heads nodded in approval; other senators muttered in each other's ears.

Marcus pursed his lips. 'Tell us what you saw, then. Let the Senate decide if it truly poses the threat that Scipio would have us believe.'

Taking a deep breath, Fabricius began the tale of his patrol. He did not look at Marcus or anyone else. Instead he kept his gaze fixed on the bronze doors at the far end of the room. It was a good tactic, and he warmed to his topic as he continued. Fabricius spared no detail of the Carthaginian encampment, and was particularly careful to stress the number of enemy cavalry, the River

Rhodanus' immense width and the Herculean effort of ferrying the elephants across it. Finishing, he looked to Scipio. The consul gave an approving nod. Flaccus' expression had soured. Had his prospective son-in-law thought that having to appear before the entire Senate would be too much for him? From the alarmed looks many senators were now giving each other, the opposite was true. Suddenly, Marcus seemed to be on the back foot.

Seizing the initiative, Scipio moved to the front of the dais. 'Fabricius estimated the Carthaginian host to be greater in size than two consular armies. I'm talking about fifty thousand men, of whom at least a quarter are cavalry. Numidians, who bested our troops in Sicily on countless occasions. Do not forget the elephants either. Our combat record against *them* is less than valiant. We also have to consider the leader of this army. Hannibal Barca, a man who has recently conquered half of Iberia and taken an impregnable city, Saguntum, by storm. A general who is unafraid of leading his soldiers across the Alps in late autumn.' Scipio nodded as many senators recoiled. 'Many of you know the praetor Lucius Manlius Vulso, as I do. He is an honourable and able leader. But is he capable of beating a force twice the size of his, which also possesses superior numbers of horse, and elephants?' He looked around. 'Is he?'

A brief, disbelieving silence cloaked the room. Then, sheer pandemonium broke out. Hundreds of worried voices competed with each other, but no individual would listen to what another was saying. Marcus tried to calm those around him, but his efforts were in vain. Fabricius couldn't believe it. Here were the men who ruled the Republic, squabbling and shouting like frightened children. He glanced at Scipio, who was watching the spectacle, waiting for an opportunity to intervene. Impulsively, Fabricius pulled out his dagger and handed it over. 'It's yours, sir,' he said passionately. 'Like the sword of every citizen in Italy.' Scipio's initial surprise was replaced by a wolfish smile. He accepted the blade before muttering an order to his lictores. The hammering of fasces on the floor drew everyone's attention.

Scipio raised the dagger high. 'I have been handed this by Fabricius, who has broken the law by carrying it into the Curia. Yet he did it only because of his loyalty to the Republic. To show his willingness to shed his blood and, if necessary, to die in the struggle to overcome Hannibal. With determined soldiers like this, I promise you victory over the Carthaginian invaders! Victory!'

As a flock of birds seamlessly alters direction, the senators' mood changed. Their panic vanished, to be replaced by a frenzy of excitement. Spontaneous cheering broke out, and the atmosphere lightened at once. Scipio had won, thought Fabricius delightedly. Nobody but a fool would try and depose the consul now.

A moment later, Flaccus sidled over. 'Happy?' he hissed.

Fabricius had had enough. 'What was I supposed to do? Lie about what I saw?' he retorted. 'Hannibal's army is huge. It's well armed, and led by a very determined man. We underestimate it at our peril.'

Flaccus' expression grew softer. 'Of course, you are right. You spoke well. Convincingly,' he said. 'And the danger must be addressed fast. Clearly, Scipio is still the man to do it. The resolve he has shown here today is admirable.'

Looking at the displeasure twisting Marcus' face, Fabricius had difficulty in believing Flaccus' words. He shoved his disquiet away. Such things were no longer of importance.

All that mattered was defeating Hannibal.

Fabricius wasn't surprised when Scipio ordered him to proceed back to the city gate, there to ready his men. They would leave for Cisalpine Gaul within three hours. Flaccus would be with them too. Scipio rolled his eyes as he said it. 'Some things cannot be changed,' he muttered. Fabricius was relieved to be given his orders. He had seen enough of politics for a lifetime, and was uncertain what to think of Flaccus and his brother. Maybe Atia had been right? he wondered. Deciding to inform her of what had transpired by writing a quick letter before they set off, Fabricius exited the bronze doors and headed across the Forum.

Chapter XVIII: Cisalpine Gaul

There were only two occasions when the two friends heard something of what was going on inside. The first was when alarmed shouts rang out; the second, which followed directly after, was the sound of loud cheering. Almost at once, news spread through the assembled crowds that the Senate had given Scipio its resounding support. Now the consul was to head north with all speed, there to confront Hannibal. Before the pair had time to take the momentous information in, several figures hurried from the Curia. Suddenly, Quintus came to life. He gave Hanno a violent nudge. 'Look,' he hissed, taking a step forward. 'It's Father!'

'So it is,' Hanno muttered. He was even more shocked than Quintus. Why was Fabricius here? His next thought was far more worrying. How would Quintus explain his presence? A wave of terror struck him. What chance was there of Fabricius accepting Quintus' grant of freedom? Precious little. Hanno couldn't help thinking he should walk away into the crowd. He would be lost to sight in an instant. Free to make his own way north. Hanno wavered, but then his pride took over. I am no coward who runs away and hides.

Glancing around, Quintus sensed his unhappiness. Despite his excitement, he pulled himself up short. 'It's all right,' he said gently. 'I'm not going anywhere.'

'Eh? Why not?' Hanno cried. 'This is a perfect opportunity for you.'

'Maybe so, but it isn't for you.'

Hanno coloured. He didn't know what to say.

Quintus pre-empted him. 'What possibility is there that Father will honour your manumission?'

'I don't know,' Hanno muttered. 'Not much, I suppose.'

'Exactly,' Quintus replied. 'Which is the reason I'm staying right here. With you.'

'Why would you do that?' asked Hanno, caught off guard.

'Have you forgotten last night already?' Quintus cuffed him on the side of the head. 'You promised to accompany me to Iberia, even though you no longer had any need to go there. Plus you didn't make a run for it just now, which most people would have done. I have to repay your honour. Fair's fair.'

'It's not that simple.' Hanno indicated Fabricius, who was about to disappear from view. 'Maybe he's not going with the consul.'

'I'd say he is, but you're right. We should make sure.' Quintus strode off. 'Come on, let's follow him.'

Hanno hurried to catch up. 'What if he's going back to Iberia?'

'We'll talk about that afterwards,' Quintus answered. 'In that eventuality, I suppose it would make sense to split up. Otherwise, I'm travelling with you to Cisalpine Gaul.'

Hanno chuckled. 'You're crazy!'

'Perhaps.' Quintus gave him a lopsided smile. 'But I still have to do the right thing.'

'And once we get there?' Hanno asked uneasily.

'We'll part company. I'll find Father, and you' – there was an awkward pause – 'can seek out Hannibal's army.'

Hanno gripped Quintus' arm. 'Thank you.'

Quintus nodded. 'It's the least I can do.'

The army that straggled down into the green foothills of the Alps was a shadow of what it had been. All semblance of marching formation had long gone. Gaunt-faced, hollow-cheeked figures stumbled along, holding on to each other for support. The ribs on every surviving horse and mule stood out like the bare frame of a new-built ship. Although few had died, the elephants had suffered extraordinarily too. Bostar thought that they now looked like nothing more than giant skeletons covered by sagging folds of grey skin. The heaviest toll, however, was the number of men and beasts that had been lost during the passage of the mountains. The scale of it was hard to take in, but it was impossible to deny. Hannibal had insisted on a tally as his troops entered the flat plain where, exhausted beyond belief, they had first camped. Even when a margin of error was allowed for, the count revealed that perhaps 24,000 foot soldiers and more than 5,000 pack animals had deserted, run away or perished. Approximately 26,000 men remained, just a quarter of the number that had left New Carthage, and little more than one Roman consular army.

It was a sobering figure, thought Bostar worriedly, especially when there were peoples to fight other than the Romans. He was standing with other senior officers outside the fortified walls of Taurasia. It was the main stronghold of the Taurini, the hostile tribe into whose lands Hannibal's force had descended. To his left was Sapho's phalanx, and to his right, his father's. Alete was positioned beyond Malchus. Fully half of the Libyans were present: six thousand of Hannibal's best troops.

'Gentlemen.'

At the sound of Hannibal's voice, Bostar turned. He scarcely recognised the shambling figure before him, clad in a ragged military cloak. Dank tresses of brown hair fell from under a simple bronze helmet, framing a gaunt face streaked with filth. The man sported a padded linen cuirass, which had clearly seen better days, a thrusting spear and an old, battered shield. He was the worst dressed Libyan spearman Bostar had ever seen, and he stank to high heaven. Bostar glanced at the other officers, who appeared as stunned as he. 'Is that you, sir?'

The belly laugh was definitely Hannibal's. 'It is. Don't look at me as if I am mad.'

Bostar flushed. 'Sorry, sir. May I ask why are you dressed like that?'

'Two reasons. Firstly, as an ordinary soldier, I'm far less of a target to the enemy. Secondly, being anonymous allows me to mix with the troops and assess their mood. I've been doing that since we came down out of the mountains,' Hannibal revealed. He turned to include all those present. 'What do you think I've heard?'

Most of the officers, Bostar included, took a sudden interest in their fingernails, or a strap on their harness that needed tightening. Even Malchus cleared his throat awkwardly.

'Come now,' said Hannibal in a bluff tone. 'Did you really think that I wouldn't find out how low morale really is? Spirits are high amongst the cavalry, but that's because I looked after them so well in the mountains. Far fewer of them died. But they're unusual. Many of the men think we'll be annihilated the first time we encounter the Romans, don't they?'

'They'll fight anyway, sir!' Malchus cried. 'They love you as no other.'

Hannibal's smile was warm. 'Worthy Malchus, I can always rely on you and your sons. I know that your soldiers will stay true, and so will the bulk of the army. But we require an immediate victory to raise the men's spirits. More importantly, we need food to put in their bellies. Our intelligence tells me that the stores behind those walls' – he indicated the fortress – 'are full of grain. I would have bought it from the Taurini, but they rejected my overtures out of hand. Now they will learn the price of their foolishness.'

'What shall we do, sir?' Sapho asked eagerly.

'Take the place by storm.'

'Prisoners?'

'Leave none alive. Not a man, woman or child.'

Sapho's eyes lit up. 'Yes, sir!'

His words were echoed by a rumble of agreement from the others.

Hannibal stared at Bostar. 'What is it? Are you unhappy with my command?'

'Must everyone die, sir?' Terrible images from the fall of Saguntum filled Bostar's mind.

Hannibal scowled. 'Unfortunately, yes. Know that I order this for a particular reason. We are in a very fragile position. If a Roman army presented itself tomorrow, we would indeed struggle to defeat it. When they hear of our weakness, the Boii and Insubres will think twice before giving us the aid that they so eagerly promised last year. If that happens, we will have failed in our task before it has even begun. Is that what you want?'

'Of course not, sir,' Bostar replied indignantly.

'Good,' said Hannibal with a pleased look. 'Slaughtering the inhabitants of Taurasia will send a clear message to the area's tribes. We are still a lethal fighting force, and they either stand with us, or against us. There is no ground in between.'

Humbled, Bostar glanced down. 'I'm sorry, sir. I didn't understand.'

'Some of the others probably didn't either,' answered Hannibal, 'but they didn't have the courage to ask.'

'I understood, sir,' Sapho snarled.

'Which is the reason you're standing here today,' said Hannibal grimly. 'Monomachus too.' He nodded at a squat man with a bald head. 'The rest of you are present because I know that, as my finest officers, you will do exactly what I have ordered.' He pointed his spear at the fortress walls. 'I want the place reduced by nightfall. After that, your men can have the rest they so well deserve.'

Bostar joined in the cheering with more enthusiasm this time. He caught a sneering Sapho trying to catch his eye, and ignored him. He would follow Hannibal's orders, but for a very different reason to his brother. Loyalty, rather than sheer bloodthirstiness.

*   *   *

Despite Quintus' generosity in accompanying him north, Hanno found the journey grating. He still had to act like a slave. Quintus rode a horse, while he had to sit astride a cantankerous mule. He could not eat with Quintus, or share the same room. Instead, he had to take his meals with the domestic slaves and servants of the roadside inns they frequented, and to bed down in the stables with the animals. Oddly, Hanno's physical separation from Quintus began to restore the invisible differences between them.

In a bizarre way, both were relieved by this. What they'd seen and heard in Rome had hammered reality home as never before, shredding the camaraderie that had developed on the farm. They were travelling to a place where there could be no friendship between Carthaginian and Roman, only combat and death. Not speaking to each other obviated the need to think about what might happen in the future. Of course their silently adopted tactic did not work. Both felt great pain at their impending separation, which in all likelihood would be permanent.

The three hundred miles from Rome to Placentia dragged by, but the pair finally reached their destination having encountered few problems. All the empty ground outside the town was taken up with vast temporary encampments, full of legionaries, socii and cavalry. The tracks were jammed with units of marching men and ox carts laden with supplies. Stalls lined the margins of every way, hawking food, wine and equipment. Soothsayers offered their services alongside blacksmiths, butchers and whores. Musicians played drums and bone whistles, acrobats jumped and tumbled, tricksters promised a cure for every ailment under the sun. Snot-nosed children darted to and fro, playing with scrawny mongrels.

It was utter chaos, thought Hanno, but there was no denying that Hannibal had set himself a Herculean task. There were already tens of thousands of Roman troops in the area.

Quintus wasted no time. He hailed a passing centurion. 'Has the consul arrived from Rome?'

'You're behind the times! He got here four days ago.'

Quintus was unsurprised. Unlike them, Scipio and his party would have been changing their mounts every day. 'Where are his headquarters?'

The centurion gave him an odd look, but did not ask why. While young, Quintus was clearly an equestrian. He pointed down the road. 'That way. It's about a mile.'

Quintus nodded his thanks. 'What news of Hannibal?'

Hanno stiffened. This was the question he had been burning to ask.

The centurion's face darkened. 'Well, believe it or not, the whoreson succeeded in crossing the Alps. Who'd have thought it?'

'Amazing.' Quintus did not want to look at Hanno in case he was gloating. 'What has he been up to since?'

'He attacked the Taurini stronghold of Taurasia, and massacred its inhabitants. Apparently, he's now on his way here, to Placentia. We're blocking his route to the scumbag Boii and Insubres, see?' The centurion half drew his gladius from its scabbard and slammed it home again. 'There'll be one hell of a fight very soon.'

'May Mars and Jupiter keep us in the palm of their hands,' said Quintus.

'Aye. Now, I'd best be off, or my tribune will string me up by my balls.' With a cordial nod, the centurion marched away.

Quintus and Hanno looked at each other. Neither spoke.

'You're taking up half the fucking road. Get out of the damn way!' shouted a man leading a train of mules.

They led their mounts to one side and into a gap between two stalls.

'This is it, then,' said Quintus unhappily.

'Yes,' Hanno muttered. He felt awful.

'What will you do?'

Hanno shrugged. 'Travel west until I run into some of our forces.'

Your forces, thought Quintus, not mine. 'The gods grant you a safe passage.'

'Thank you. May you find your father quickly.'

'I don't think that will be a problem,' Quintus replied, smiling.

'Even you would find it hard to get lost now,' joked Hanno.

Quintus laughed.

'I wish that we could part under different circumstances,' said Hanno.

'So do I,' answered Quintus passionately.

'But we both have to do our duty by our people.'

'Yes.'

'Maybe we'll meet again one day. In peacetime.' Hanno cringed inwardly. His words sounded false even to his own ears.

Quintus did not rebuke him, however. 'I would like that too, but it will never happen,' he said gently. 'Go well. Stay safe. May your gods protect you.'

'The same to you.' At last, Hanno's eyes filled with tears. Clumsily, he reached out and embraced Quintus. 'Thank you for saving me and Suniaton. I will never forget that,' he whispered.

Quintus' emotions welled up. He awkwardly clapped Hanno on the back. 'You saved my life too, remember?'

Hanno's nod was jerky.

'Come on,' said Quintus, growing businesslike. 'You need to get as far from here by nightfall as you can. No point having to try and explain yourself to one of our patrols, is there?'

Hanno drew back. 'No.'

'Help me up.' Quintus lifted his left foot.

Grateful for the distraction, Hanno linked his hands together so that Quintus could step up and climb on to his horse's back. When it was done, he forced a smile. 'Farewell.'

'Farewell.' Quickly, Quintus pulled his horse's head around and urged it on to the roadway.

Hanno watched as his friend was swallowed up by the mass of men jostling along on the muddy track. It was only when he could no longer see Quintus that Hanno realised he had forgotten to send a last farewell to Aurelia. Sadly, he clambered aboard his mule and headed in the opposite direction. Despite the inevitability of their parting, Hanno felt a void inside. Let us never meet again, he prayed. Unless it happens in peacetime.

A hundred paces away, Quintus felt the same way. Only now could he allow himself to grieve the loss of a friend. They had been through a great deal together. If Hanno were a Roman, Quintus thought, I would be proud to stand beside him in battle. Sadly, it was only the opposite that could ever come to pass. Jupiter, Greatest and Best, never let this happen, he prayed.

Not long after, Quintus found the consul's headquarters, a large pavilion surrounded by the cavalry tent lines. The *vexillum*, a red flag on a pole, made sure that every soldier could see Scipio's position. A few questions guided Quintus in the direction of his father, whom he found outside his tent, talking to a pair of decurions. To his relief, Fabricius did not immediately explode. Instead he quietly dismissed the junior officers. The moment that they were gone, however, he rounded on Quintus. 'Look who it is!' Sarcasm dripped from his voice.

'Father.' Feeling distinctly nervous, Quintus dismounted. 'Are you well?'

'I'm fine,' Fabricius replied. His eyebrows arched. 'Surprised, though. Annoyed and disappointed too. You should be at home, looking after your mother and sister, not here.'

Quintus shuffled his feet.

'Not going to answer that charge?' his father snapped. 'Why are you not on a ship to Iberia? After all, that's where I should be.'

'I travelled to Rome first,' Quintus muttered. 'I was there when Scipio spoke in the Curia. I caught a glimpse of you outside.'

Fabricius frowned. 'Why in Jupiter's name didn't you come up to me there?'

'The press was too great to reach you, Father. I didn't know where you were staying, or even that you were heading north with the consul,' Quintus lied. 'I found out later. It was easy enough to follow you.'

'I see. Fortuna must have been guiding your path. The tribesmen around here aren't the friendliest,' said Fabricius dourly. 'It's a shame that you didn't make yourself known to me in Rome. You'd already be in Capua by now, or my name isn't Gaius Fabricius.' His dark eyes regarded Quintus carefully. 'And so you travelled up here alone?'

Quintus cursed inwardly. This was going even worse than he'd expected. He was such a poor liar when asked a direct question. 'No, Father.'

'Who was with you? Gaius, probably. He listens to Martialis as little as you do to me.'

'No,' Quintus mumbled.

'Who, then?'

Dreading his father's response, Quintus said nothing.

Fabricius' anger bubbled over. 'Answer me!'

'Hanno.'

'Who?'

'One of our . . . your . . . slaves.'

Fabricius' face purpled. 'That's not enough! Do you expect me to remember the name of every damn one?'

'No, Father,' Quintus said quickly. 'He's the Carthaginian that I bought after the bear hunt.'

'Oh, him. Where is the dirtbag? Putting up your tent?'

'He's not here,' replied Quintus, stalling for time.

Fabricius' eyes opened wide with disbelief. 'Say that again.'

'He's gone, Father,' Quintus whispered.

'Louder! I can't hear you!'

A passing officer glanced over, and Quintus' mortification soared. 'He's gone, Father,' he said loudly.

'What a surprise!' Fabricius cried. 'Of course he was going to run away. What else would the dog do with a host of his country-men so near? I bet that he waited until the very last moment before disappearing too. Congratulations! Hannibal has just gained himself another soldier.'

Quintus was stung by the truth in his father's words. 'It's not like that,' he said quietly.

'How so?' retorted Fabricius furiously.

'Hanno didn't run away.'

'He's dead then?' Fabricius demanded in a mocking tone.

'No, Father. I set him free,' Quintus blurted.

'*What?*'

With ebbing confidence, Quintus repeated himself.

Astonishment and disbelief mixed with the anger on Fabricius' face. 'This goes from bad to worse. How dare you?' Stepping closer, he slapped Quintus hard across the face.

He reeled backwards from the force of the blow. 'I'm sorry.'

'It's a little late for apologies, don't you think?'

'Yes, Father.'

'It is not within your power to act in this manner,' Fabricius ranted. 'My slaves belong to me, not you!'

'I know, Father,' Quintus muttered.

'So why did you do it? What in Hades were you thinking?'

'I owed him my life.'

Fabricius frowned. 'You're referring to what happened at Libo's hut?'

'Yes, Father. When he came back, Hanno could easily have turned on me. Joined the bandits. Instead, he saved my life.'

'That's still no reason to free him on a whim. Without my permission,' Fabricius growled.

'There's more to it than that.'

'I should damn well hope so!' Fabricius looked at him enquir-ingly. 'Well?'

Quintus snatched the brief respite from his father's tirade. 'Agesandros. He had it in for Hanno from the first moment I bought him. Don't you remember what happened when the Gaul hurt his leg?'

'An over-enthusiastic beating is no reason to free a slave,' Fabricius snapped. 'If it was, there would be no servile labour in the whole damn Republic.'

'I know it isn't, Father,' said Quintus humbly. 'But after your letter arrived in the spring, Agesandros planted a purse and a dagger among Hanno's belongings. Then he accused him of stealing them, and planning to kill us all before he fled. He was going to sell Hanno to the same owner who had bought his friend. They were to be forced to fight each other as gladiators at a munus, he said. And it was all a complete lie!'

Fabricius thought for a moment. 'What did your mother have to say?'

'She believed Agesandros,' Quintus answered reluctantly.

'Which should have been good enough for you,' Fabricius thundered.

'But he was lying, Father!'

Fabricius' brows lowered. 'Why would Agesandros lie?'

'I don't know, Father. But I'm certain that Hanno is no murderer!'

'You can't *know* something like that,' replied Fabricius dryly. Quintus took heart from the fact that some of the rage had gone from his voice. 'Never trust a slave totally.'

Quintus rallied his courage. 'In that case, how can you depend on Agesandros' word?'

'He's served me well for more than twenty years,' his father replied, a trifle defensively.

'So you'd trust him over me?'

'Watch your mouth!' Fabricius snapped. There was a short pause. 'Start at the beginning. Leave nothing out.'

Quintus realised that he had been granted a stay of execution. Taking a deep breath, he began. Remarkably, his father did not interrupt at all, even when Quintus related how Aurelia had set a fire in the granary, and how he and Gaius had freed Suniaton. When he fell silent, Fabricius stood, tapping his foot on the ground for several moments. 'Why did you decide to help the other Carthaginian?'

'Because Hanno would not leave without him,' Quintus answered. Then he added, passionately, 'He is my friend. I couldn't betray him.'

'Hold on!' interrupted Fabricius, ire creeping back into his voice. 'We're not talking about Gaius here. Freeing a slave without the permission of his owner is a crime, and you have done it twice over! This is a very serious matter.'

Quintus quailed before his father's fury. 'Of course, Father. I'm sorry.'

'Both of the slaves are long gone, if they have any sense,' mused Fabricius. 'Thanks to your impetuosity, I have been left more than a hundred didrachms out of pocket. So has the official's son in Capua.'

Quintus wanted to say that Gaius had tried to buy Suniaton, but his father's temper was at fraying point. Buttoning his lip, he nodded miserably.

'As your father, I am entitled to punish you how I choose,' Fabricius warned. 'Even to strike you dead.'

'I'm at your mercy, Father,' said Quintus, closing his eyes. Whatever might happen next, he was still glad that he'd let Hanno go.

'Although you and your sister have behaved outrageously, I heard the truth in your words – or at least the belief that you were speaking the truth. In other words, you did what you thought was right.'

Startled, Quintus opened his eyes. 'Yes, Father. So did Aurelia.'

'Which is why we'll say no more about it for the moment. The matter is far from settled, however.' Fabricius pursed his lips. 'And Agesandros will have some explaining to do when next I see him.'

I hope I'm there to see that, thought Quintus, his own anger at the Sicilian resurfacing.

'You still haven't explained why you abandoned your mother and sister to make your way here.' Fabricius pinned him with a hard stare.

'I thought the war might be over in a few months, like Flaccus said, Father. I didn't want to miss it,' Quintus said lamely.

'And that's a good enough reason to disobey my orders, is it?'

'No,' Quintus replied, flushing an ever deeper shade of red.

'Yet that's precisely what you did!' accused his father. He stared off into the distance. 'It's not as if I haven't got enough on my plate at the moment.'

'I'll get out of your way. Return home,' Quintus whispered.

'You'll do no such thing! The situation is far too dangerous.' Fabricius saw his surprise. 'Scipio has decided to lead his forces over the river Padus, into hostile territory. A temporary bridge has already been thrown over to the far bank. Tomorrow morning, we march westward, towards Hannibal's army. No Roman forces are to be left behind, and the local Gauls can't be trusted. You'd have your throat cut within five miles of here.'

'What shall I do, then?' asked Quintus despondently.

'You will have to come with us,' his father replied, equally unhappily. 'You'll be safe in our camp until an opportunity presents itself to send you back to Capua.'

Quintus' spirits fell even further. The shame of it! To have reached Scipio's army only to be prevented from fighting. It wasn't that surprising, though. His actions had stretched his father's goodwill to the limit. At least Hanno had got away, Quintus thought, counting himself lucky that Fabricius hadn't given him a good hiding.

'Fabricius? Where are you?' cried a booming voice.

'Mars above, that's all I need,' muttered Fabricius.

Astounded by his father's reaction, Quintus turned to see Flaccus emerge into view.

'There you are! Scipio wants another meeting about—' Flaccus stopped in astonishment. 'Quintus? What a pleasant surprise!'

Quintus grinned guiltily. At least someone was pleased to see him.

'You sent for Quintus, I presume?' Flaccus didn't wait for Fabricius to answer. 'What an excellent idea! His timing is impeccable too.' He raised a clenched fist at Quintus. 'Tomorrow, we're going to teach those bastard guggas a lesson they'll never forget.'

'I didn't send for him,' answered Fabricius stiffly. 'He saw fit to leave his mother and sister on their own and turn up here without so much as a by your leave.'

'The rashness of youth!' demurred Flaccus with a smile. 'Nonetheless, you'll let him ride out with us in the morning?'

'I hadn't planned on it, no,' said Fabricius curtly.

'What?' Flaccus threw him an incredulous look. 'And deny your son a chance to blood himself? To take part in what could be one of our greatest cavalry victories ever? Scipio's boy is to come along, and he's no older than Quintus here.'

'It's not that.'

'What is it, then?'

'It's none of your concern,' said Fabricius angrily.

Flaccus barely blinked at the rebuff. 'Come now,' he cajoled. 'Unless the lad has committed murder, surely he should be allowed to be part of this golden opportunity? This could be the glowing start to his career – a career that will only blossom once your family is allied to the Minucii.'

Furious, Fabricius considered his options. They were in this situation purely because of Flaccus' pushiness, yet it would look rude now for him to turn down Flaccus' proposal. It might also jeopardise Quintus' chances of advancement. Even when wedded to Aurelia, Flaccus would be under no legal obligation to help his brother-in-law. It was all down to goodwill. He made a show of looking pleased. 'Very well. I'll ask the consul for his permission to let Quintus join my unit.'

BEN KANE

'Excellent!' cried Flaccus. 'Scipio won't turn down a cavalry-man of your son's quality.'

Quintus couldn't believe the change in his fortunes. 'Thank you,' he said, grinning at both men. 'I won't let you down, Father.'

'Consider yourself lucky,' Fabricius growled. He stabbed a finger into Quintus' chest. 'You're not out of trouble yet either.'

'The glory he'll win tomorrow will make you forget anything he's done,' declared Flaccus, giving Quintus a broad wink. 'Now, we'd best not keep Scipio waiting any longer.'

'True,' replied Fabricius. He pointed at a nearby tent. 'There's an empty space in that one. Tell the men in it that I said you were to bunk in with them. We'll get you some equipment later.'

'Yes, Father. Thank you.'

Fabricius did not reply.

'Until tomorrow,' said Flaccus. 'We'll cover the field with gugga bodies!'

Instantly, an image of Hanno appeared in Quintus' mind's eye. Forcing a grin, he did his best to shove it away. Defeating the Carthaginians was all that mattered, he told himself.

386

Chapter XIX: Reunion

Hanno did not dare to try crossing the makeshift bridge over the Padus with his mount. He had tempted fate enough by riding out of the camp alone on his mule, a likely slave. There had to be at least two centuries of legionaries guarding the road that ran up to the crossing. No matter how dull their duty, Hanno doubted that they were stupid enough to let a dark-skinned man who spoke accented Latin pass by without question. He therefore rode west along the southern bank, searching for a suitable place to ford the river.

Winter gales had stripped the leaves from the trees, leaving the flat landscape stark and bare. It made it easy to spot movement of any kind. This suited Hanno down to the ground. Unarmed apart from a dagger, he had no desire to meet anyone until he crossed the river into the territory of the Insubres. They were mostly hostile towards the Romans. Even there, however, Hanno wanted to avoid human contact. In reality, he could trust no one but his own people, or the soldiers who fought for them. Although he was by no means safe yet, Hanno could not help feeling exhilarated. He could almost sense the presence of Hannibal's army nearby.

Hanno hardly dared to wonder if his own father and brothers were still alive, or with the Carthaginian forces. There was absolutely no way of telling. For all he knew, they could yet be in Iberia. Maybe they had been posted back to Carthage. What would he do if that were the case? Whom would he report to? At that moment, Hanno did not overly care. He had escaped, and, gods willing, would soon place himself under Hannibal's command: another soldier of Carthage.

For two days and nights, Hanno travelled west. He avoided settlements and farms, camping rough in dips and hollows where there was little chance of being discovered. Despite the severe cold, he forbore from lighting fires. His blankets were sufficient to prevent frostbite, but not to allow much sleep. It didn't matter. Staying alert now was critical. Despite Hanno's weariness, each new day of freedom felt better than the last.

His luck continued to hold. Early on the third day, Hanno reached a crossing point over the Padus. A collection of small huts huddled around the ford, but there was no one about. The days were short, and work on the land had ceased until spring. Like most peasants at this time of year, the inhabitants went to bed shortly after sunset and rose late. Nonetheless, Hanno felt very vulnerable as he stripped off by the water's edge. Placing his clothing in his pack, he rolled up the oiled leather tightly and tied it with thongs. Then, naked as the day he was born, he led the protesting mule into the river. The water was shockingly cold. Hanno knew that if they didn't cross it fast, his muscles would freeze up and he would drown. Winter rainfall ensured that its level was high, however, and for a time, his mount struggled against the current. Hanno, who was holding on to its reins and swimming as hard as he could, felt panic swelling in his chest. Thankfully, the mule possessed enough strength to carry them both into the shallows on the far side, and from there, on to the bank. The biting wind struck Hanno savagely, setting his teeth to chattering. Fortunately, only a small amount of water had entered his pack, meaning that his clothes were mostly dry. He dressed quickly. Then, wrapping his blanket around himself for extra warmth, he remounted and resumed his journey.

The day wore on and Hanno's excitement grew. He was deep in Insubres territory; Hannibal's army could not be far away. Since he'd been captured by the pirates, it had seemed impossible that he would ever be in such a position. Thanks to Quintus, it was now a reality. Hanno prayed that his friend would come through the impending war unharmed. Naturally enough, he quickly returned to thoughts of a reunion with his family. For the first time, Hanno's attention lapsed.

A short time later, he was brought back to reality with a jolt. Halfway down into a hollow, Hanno heard a blackbird sounding its alarm call, sharp and insistent. Scanning the trees on either side, he could see no reason for its distress. Yet birds did not react like that without cause. Acid-tipped claws of fear clutched at his belly. This was the perfect place for an ambush. For bandits to attack and murder a lone traveller.

Terror filled Hanno as, in the same instant, a pair of javelins scudded out of the bushes to his left and flew over his head. Praying that his attackers were on foot, he dug his heels into his mule's sides. It responded to his fear, and pounded gamely up out of the dip. Several more javelins hissed into the air behind them, but when Hanno glanced over his shoulder, his hopes vanished entirely. A group of mounted figures had emerged from the cover on each side. Six of them at least, and on horses. There was no chance of outriding his pursuers on a mule. Hanno cursed savagely. This was surely the cruellest turn of fate since he'd been washed out to sea. To have gone through all that he had, only to be murdered by a bunch of brigands a few miles from where Hannibal's forces lay.

He wasn't surprised when more horses and riders appeared on the road ahead, blocking it entirely. Gripping the dagger that was his solitary weapon, Hanno prepared to sell his life dearly. As the horsemen approached, however, his heart leaped. He had not seen any Numidian cavalry since leaving Carthage, but there could be no mistaking their identity. What other mounted troops scorned the use of saddles, bridles and bits? Or wore open-sided tunics even in winter?

Even as he opened his mouth to greet the Numidians, another flurry of javelins was hurled in his direction. This time, two barely missed him. Frantically, Hanno raised both his hands in the air, palms outwards. 'Stop! I am Carthaginian,' he shouted in his native tongue. 'I am Carthaginian!'

His cry made no difference. More spears were launched, and this time one struck his mule in the rump. Rearing in pain, it threw Hanno to the ground. The air shot from his lungs, winding him. He was vaguely aware of his mount trotting away, limping heavily. Within the blink of an eye, he had been surrounded by a ring of jeering Numidians. Three jumped down and approached, javelins at the ready. What a way to die, Hanno thought bitterly. Killed by my own side because they don't even speak my language.

From nowhere, inspiration hit him. He'd learned a few words of the sibilant Numidian tongue once. 'Stop,' Hanno mumbled. 'I . . . friend.'

Looking confused, the trio of Numidians paused. A barrage of questions in their tongue followed. Hanno barely understood one word in ten of what the warriors were saying. 'I not Roman, I friend,' he repeated, over and over.

His protests weren't enough. Drawing back his foot, one of the tribesmen kicked Hanno in the belly. Stars flashed across his vision, and he nearly passed out from the pain. More blows landed, and he tensed, expecting at any moment to feel a javelin slide into his flesh.

Instead, an angry voice intervened.

The beating stopped at once.

Warily, Hanno looked up to see a rider with tightly curled black hair standing before him. Unusually for a Numidian, he was wearing a sword. An officer, thought Hanno dully.

'Did I hear you speaking Carthaginian?' the man demanded.

'Yes.' Relieved and surprised that someone present spoke his tongue, Hanno sat up. He winced in pain. 'I'm from Carthage.'

The other's eyebrows rose. 'What in Melqart's name are you doing alone in the middle of this godforsaken, freezing land?'

'I was sold into slavery among the Romans some time ago,' explained Hanno. 'Hearing the news of Hannibal's invasion, I escaped to join him.'

The Numidian didn't look convinced. 'Who are you?'

'My name is Hanno,' he said proudly. 'I am a son of Malchus, who serves as a senior officer among our Libyan spearmen. If I reach Hannibal's army, I hope to be reunited with him, and my brothers.'

There was a long silence, and Hanno felt his fear return. Do not desert me now, great Tanit, he prayed.

'An unlikely story. Who's to say that you are not a spy?' the officer mused out loud. Several of his more eager men lifted their javelins, and Hanno's heart sank. If they killed him now, no one would ever know.

'Hold!' snapped the officer. 'If this man has really spent much time among the Romans, he may be useful to Hannibal.' He grinned at Hanno. 'And if you are telling the truth, I suspect that your father, whether he is with the army or no, would rather see you alive than dead.'

Hanno's joy knew no bounds. 'Thank you,' he said.

The officer barked an order and the Numidians swarmed in, hauling Hanno to his feet. His wrists were bound with rope, but he was offered no further violence. As the warriors mounted up, Hanno was picked up and thrown roughly across the neck of a horse, in front of its rider. He didn't protest. With his mule injured, there was no other way of returning to the Carthaginian camp at speed. At least they weren't dragging him behind one of the mounts.

As the Numidians began to ride west, Hanno gave thanks to

every god he could think of, but most importantly to Tanit, whom he'd forgotten to address before leaving his home in Carthage.

He wasn't out of the woods yet, but he felt that she was smiling on him once more.

Upon reaching Hannibal's camp, Hanno was lowered to the ground. He gazed around him in wonderment, absolutely exhilarated to see a Carthaginian host so near the Italian border. His heart throbbed with an unquenchable joy. He was back with his people! Yet Hanno was concerned by the army's size. It was far smaller than he'd expected. He was alarmed too by the soldiers' faces. Suffering was etched deep into every single one. Most had unkempt beards, and looked half starved. The pack animals, and particularly the elephants, looked even worse. Hanno shot a worried glance at the Numidian officer. 'The crossing of the Alps must have been terrible,' he said.

'You cannot even imagine it,' the Numidian replied with a scowl. 'Hostile natives. Landslides. Ice. Snow. Starvation. Between desertions and fatalities, we lost nearly twenty-five thousand men in a month. Practically half our army.'

Hanno's mouth fell open in horror. Immediately, he thought of his father and brothers, who could easily be among the dead. He caught the Numidian watching him. 'Why tell me this?' he stuttered.

'I can say what I like. The Romans will never find out,' replied the other amiably. 'It's not as if you could escape my men on foot.'

Hanno swallowed. 'No.'

'Just as well you were telling the truth about who you were, eh?'

Hanno met the Numidian's gimlet stare. A sudden pang of terror struck him. What if no one could be found to vouch for his identity? 'Yes, it is,' he snapped, praying that the gods would not dash the cup of success from his lips at this late stage. 'Take me to the Libyans' tent lines.'

With a mocking bow, the Numidian led the way. He hailed the first spearman they met. 'We are looking for an officer by the name of . . .' He looked questioningly at Hanno.

'Malchus.'

To Hanno's utter joy, the man jerked a thumb behind him. 'His tent is three ranks back. It's bigger than the rest.'

'So far, so good,' said the officer, dismounting gracefully. He indicated that Hanno should follow him. Three of his warriors took up the rear, their javelins at the ready. Carefully, they weaved their way between the closely packed tents.

'This looks like the one.' The officer came to a halt outside a large leather pavilion. It was held up by multiple guy ropes staked into the ground. A pair of spearmen stood on guard outside.

A volcanic wave of emotion battered Hanno. Terror that his father would not be within. Joy that he might. Relief that, after all his ordeals, he was perhaps about to be reunited with his family. He turned to the officer. 'Stay here.'

'Eh? You're not in charge,' the Numidian growled. 'Until I hear otherwise, you're a damn prisoner.'

'My hands are tied! Where am I going to go?' Hanno snapped back. 'Stick a fucking spear in my back if I even try. But I'm walking over there on my own.'

The Numidian saw the steel in Hanno's eyes. Suddenly, he realised that his captive might outrank him considerably. There was a gruff nod. 'We'll wait here,' he said.

Hanno made no acknowledgement. Stiff-backed, he walked towards the tent.

One of the spearmen started forward. 'What's your business?' he demanded in a brusque tone.

'Are these Malchus' quarters?' asked Hanno politely.

'Who wants to know?' came the surly reply.

The last of Hanno's patience ran out. 'Damn your insolence,' he snarled. 'Father? Are you there?'

The spearman, who had advanced a step, stopped in his tracks.

'Father?' called Hanno again.

Someone coughed inside the tent. 'Bostar? Is that you?'

Hanno began to grin uncontrollably. Bostar had also survived!

An instant later, Malchus emerged, fully dressed for battle. He looked at his guards first, and frowned. 'Who called my name?'

'It was I, Father,' answered Hanno joyfully, stepping forward. 'I have returned.'

Malchus went as white as a sheet. 'H-Hanno?' he stuttered.

With tears of happiness filling his eyes, Hanno nodded.

'Praise all the gods. This is a miracle!' cried Malchus. 'But what are you doing, tied up like this?'

Hanno jerked his head at the Numidians, who were looking decidedly awkward. 'They weren't sure whether to believe my story or not.'

Drawing his dagger, Malchus sawed at the ropes that bound Hanno's wrists. The instant they had dropped away, he drew his son into his arms. Great shudders of emotion racked his frame, and for long moments, he clung to Hanno with a grip of iron. Hanno delightedly returned the embrace. Finally, Malchus stepped back to study him. 'It is you,' he breathed. A rare smile split his face. 'How you've grown. You're a man!'

In contrast, Hanno could not get over how his father had aged. Deep lines now creased his forehead and cheeks. There were bags of exhaustion under his eyes, and his hair was more grey than black. But Malchus had a new lightness about him, an air Hanno had not seen since well before his mother's death. It was, he realised with a thrill, because of his return. 'I heard you call out Bostar's name. Is Sapho here too?'

'Yes, yes, they both are. The pair of them should be back any moment,' Malchus replied, filling Hanno with more joy. He glanced at the Numidians. 'To whom do I owe my thanks?'

Saluting, the officer hurried forward. 'Zamar, section leader, at your service, sir.'

'Where did you find him?'

'About ten miles east of here, sir.' Zamar shot an uneasy glance at Hanno. 'I'm sorry for the rough treatment, sir.'

'It's all right,' Hanno replied. 'Your men couldn't be expected to know that I was Carthaginian. At least you stopped them from killing me, and listened to my story.'

Zamar dipped his head in gratitude.

'Wait here,' ordered Malchus. Hurrying into the tent, he emerged with a large leather purse. 'A token of my appreciation,' he said, handing it over.

Zamar's eyes widened as he accepted the clinking gift, and his men exchanged excited looks. It didn't matter what was inside. The bag's obvious weight spoke volumes. 'Thank you, sir. I am delighted to have been of service.' Zamar made a deep bow, and withdrew.

'Come inside,' Malchus muttered. Ushering Hanno within, he fussed over him as he hadn't done in years. 'Are you hungry? Thirsty?'

Gratefully accepting a cup of wine, Hanno took a seat on a three-legged stool he remembered from their house in Carthage. Malchus sat opposite. Neither could take their eyes off the other, or stop smiling. 'It's wonderful to see you,' Hanno said.

'Likewise,' Malchus murmured. 'I had given you up for dead. To first of all survive a storm at sea . . . well, Melqart must have laid his hand upon you and Suniaton.' His brows lowered. 'Is Suni dead?'

Hanno grinned. 'No! He couldn't travel because he was injured, but he is being cared for by a friend. Soon he will be making his way to Carthage.'

Malchus' frown cleared. 'The gods be thanked. Now, you must tell me what happened.'

Hanno laughed. 'I could say the same thing, Father, seeing you here, on the wrong side of the Alps.'

'That is a story worth hearing,' Malchus agreed. 'But I want to listen to yours first.' He cocked his head. The sound of approaching voices carried inside, and he smiled. 'I guess it will have to wait a while. You won't want to be telling it twice.'

Hanno's face lit up. 'Is that Sapho and Bostar?'

'Yes.' His father winked. 'Just sit there. Don't say a word until they see you.'

Hanno watched excitedly as Malchus moved towards the front of the tent.

A moment later, two familiar figures entered. Hanno had to grip his stool to stop himself leaping up to greet them. 'Good news, Father. Apparently, more than ten thousand Gaulish warriors are on their way to join us,' Bostar announced.

'Excellent news,' Malchus replied offhandedly.

'Aren't you pleased?' asked Sapho.

'We have an unexpected visitor.'

Sapho snorted. 'Who could be more interesting than that information?'

Silently, Malchus turned and indicated Hanno.

Sapho blanched. 'Hanno?'

'No!' Bostar exclaimed. 'It cannot be true!'

Hanno could not contain himself any longer. He leaped up and ran to greet his brothers. Laughing and crying at the same time, Bostar wrapped him in a huge bear hug. 'We thought you were dead.'

Laughing too, Hanno managed to extricate himself from Bostar's grip. 'I should be, but the gods did not forget me.' He reached out to Sapho, who awkwardly drew him into an embrace. Surely he can't still be angry about what happened in Carthage? Hanno wondered.

Sapho stepped back after only a moment. 'How in hell did you get here?' he cried.

'Where is Suniaton?' Bostar demanded.

A stream of questions poured from their lips.

Malchus intervened. 'Let him tell the whole story.'

Hanno cleared his throat. All he could think of was the manner in which he'd left the family house on that fateful morning. He looked guiltily at Malchus. 'I'm sorry, Father,' he said. 'I ought never to have run off like that. I should have stayed to do my duty.'

'The meeting was of small consequence anyway. Like most of them,' Malchus admitted with a sigh. 'If I had been more under-standing, you might have been less bored by such things. Put it behind you, and tell us how you survived that storm.'

Taking a deep breath, Hanno began. His father and brothers hung off his every word. When he explained how he and Suniaton had been captured by the pirates, Sapho let out a grim chuckle. 'They got their just deserts eventually.'

'Eh?' Hanno gave his brother a confused look.

'I'll explain later,' said Malchus. 'Go on.'

Quelling his curiosity, Hanno obeyed. His family's fury over the pirates was as nothing compared with their reaction to his purchase by Quintus.

'Roman bastard!' Sapho spat. 'I'd love to have him here right now.'

Hanno was surprised by the defensive feelings that flared up at once. 'Not all Romans are bad. If it wasn't for him and his sister, I wouldn't be here.'

Sapho scoffed. Even Bostar looked unconvinced. Malchus alone did not react.

'It's true,' Hanno cried. 'You haven't heard all of my story yet.'

'True,' admitted Bostar.

Sapho raised an eyebrow. 'Surprise us,' he said.

Amazed by the speed at which his customary anger towards his eldest brother had returned, Hanno continued with his story. He emphasised how Quintus had engineered not only his escape, but that of Suniaton, and how the young equestrian had accom-panied him to Cisalpine Gaul rather than be reunited with his father in Rome.

'He sounds like a decent person. So does his sister, for all that she is a child. That in turn means that their father must be an honourable man,' Malchus agreed. His jaw hardened. 'It is a shame that the Roman Senate does not possess the same morals. You heard from the horse's mouth how the whoresons demanded Hannibal be handed over to receive Roman "justice", how they lied about us breaking the treaty which confined us to the area below the River Iberus. Their arrogance is without parallel! That's before dragging up Sicily, Sardinia and Corsica.'

Sapho and Bostar growled in agreement.

Hanno felt a momentary sadness. Yet it was time to forget the kindness he had received. His father's words had made old resentment bubble up from the depths. He took a deep breath and exhaled slowly. Finally, I am where I longed to be, he thought. With my family. With Hannibal's army. And I am a soldier of Carthage. The Romans are our enemies. So be it. 'You're right, Father. What is Hannibal's plan?'

Malchus gave him a wolfish smile. 'To attack! We continue our march east tomorrow, in search of their legions.'

'I know exactly where they are,' Hanno replied, trying, and failing, not to think of Quintus.

'We'd best take you to Hannibal then,' said Malchus, looking pleased.

'Really?'

'Of course. He'll want to hear everything you know.'

Hanno turned to his brothers. 'I'm to meet Hannibal!' he cried delightedly. Bostar grinned, but Hanno caught Sapho shooting him a sour glance. Old emotions flared up yet again. 'What?' he demanded. 'Are you not pleased?'

Sapho blinked. 'Yes,' he muttered.

'It doesn't look like it,' said Hanno hotly.

'That's because he isn't,' Bostar growled. 'Our older brother gets jealous of anyone who might win favour from our general.'

The veins in Sapho's neck bulged with fury. 'Fuck you,' he snapped.

'Sapho!' shouted Malchus. 'Curb your tongue! You too, Bostar. Can we not forget our differences for once, on this most joyful of days?'

Shame-faced, Sapho and Bostar nodded.

Taking Hanno by the hand, Malchus led him away. 'Come on,' he ordered over his shoulder. Pointedly ignoring each other, Sapho and Bostar followed.

Hanno couldn't get over the level of animosity between his brothers. What on earth had happened between them? He was amazed too at the ease with which Sapho still got his back up. Seeing Hannibal's tent in the distance, Hanno put his concerns from his mind. He was going to meet the finest Carthaginian general in history. The man who dared to attack Rome on its own territory.

With a ragtag, half-starved army, his cynical side added. Hanno could not let go of this worrying thought as his father led him and his brothers onward. How could they ever match the numbers of soldiers Rome could call upon?

Soon they had reached a large open area before their general's headquarters. The place was thronged. Hanno's eyes widened. Flanking the perimeter were hundreds of soldiers from all over the Mediterranean, men whom he'd heard much about, but never seen. Numidian and Iberian infantry mixed with Lusitanians. Spiky-haired, bare-chested Gauls stood shoulder to shoulder with Balearic slingers and Ligurian warriors. There were several nationalities of cavalrymen: Iberian, Gaulish and Numidian. Outside the main tent stood a large group of senior officers, resplendent in their polished muscled cuirasses, pteryges and crested helmets. Hannibal's purple cloak made him easy to pick out. A group of musicians was positioned nearby, their instruments at the ready: curved ceramic horns and *carnyxes*, vertical trumpets made of bronze, each topped by a depiction of a wild boar.

Hanno glanced at his father. 'What's going on?'

Even Sapho and Bostar looked confused.

Frustratingly, Malchus did not answer. He walked on, up to the party of officers. A quick word in the ear of one of Hannibal's bodyguards saw them led straight to their leader's side. Recognising Malchus, Hannibal smiled. Hanno felt as if he were in a dream come true.

Malchus saluted. 'A word, if I may, sir?'

'Of course. Make it quick, though,' Hannibal replied.

'Yes, sir. You know two of my sons, Sapho and Bostar,' said Malchus. 'But there is a third, Hanno.'

Hannibal gave Hanno a curious look. 'I seem to remember a tragedy at sea in which he'd been lost.'

'You have a fine memory, sir. I discovered afterwards, however, that by some miracle, Hanno had not been drowned. Instead, he and his friend were found adrift by some pirates. They sold both into slavery. In Italy.'

Hannibal's eyebrows rose. 'This couldn't be him?'

Malchus grinned. 'It is, sir.'

'Gods above!' Hannibal exclaimed. 'Come here!'

Self-conscious in his ragged, filthy clothes, Hanno did as he was told.

Hannibal appraised him for several, breath-holding moments. 'You have the look of Malchus all right.'

Hanno didn't dare reply. His heart was thumping off his ribs like that of a wild bird.

'How did you escape?'

'My owner's son let me go, sir.'

'Did he, by Melqart's beard? Why?'

'I saved his life once, sir.'

'Intriguing.' Hannibal stroked his chin. 'Have you travelled far?'

'No, sir. He released me near Placentia.'

'You are welcome. Your father and brothers are valuable officers. I hope that you will be too.'

Hanno made an awkward half-bow. 'I will do my best, sir.'

Hannibal made a gesture of dismissal.

'Wait, sir,' said Malchus eagerly. 'Hanno's awe at meeting you has curdled his brains. He didn't say that Placentia is where Scipio and his army were camped.'

Hannibal's face came alive with interest. 'Scipio, you say? One of the Scipiones?'

'Yes, sir,' Hanno replied, aware that every officer within earshot was now listening. 'After missing you at the Rhodanus, he returned to Italy with all speed.'

There was a general gasp of dismay.

'Has he brought his entire army with him?' asked Hannibal softly.

'No, sir. He sent it to Iberia, under the command of his brother.'

'A shrewd general, then.' Hannibal let out a slow breath. 'Hasdrubal and Hanno will also have a fight on their hands. It is to be expected, I suppose.' He fixed Hanno with his dark eyes again. 'What of Scipio now?'

'He has thrown a bridge over the Padus, and was intending to march west on the day I fled.'

Hannibal leaned forward. 'When was that?'

'Three days ago, sir.'

'So he cannot be far away. Excellent news!' Hannibal smacked a fist into his palm. 'What of his forces?'

Hanno did his best to recount all that he had seen and heard since leaving Rome.

'Well done, young man,' said Hannibal when he was done, making Hanno flush beetroot. 'We shall face the first of our great tests soon. What we are about to observe now seems even more apt. Stay here with me and watch, if you will.'

Stuttering his thanks, Hanno stood with Hannibal, Malchus and his brothers and watched as dozens of prisoners were led out into the open area before them.

'Who are they?' Hanno asked.

'Allobroges and Vocontii, prisoners taken during the passage of the Alps,' replied his father.

Hanno's stomach clenched. The men looked terrified.

A fanfare from the musicians' horns and carnyxes prevented any further conversation. Hannibal stood forth when it finished. At once an expectant hush fell over the gathered troops. Everyone watched as a line of slaves carried out bronze trays, some of which were laden with glittering mail shirts. On others, helmets were piled high. There were gold arm rings and torcs, fine cloaks decorated with wolf fur and gilt-handled swords.

Hannibal let the prisoners feast their eyes on the treasure before he spoke. 'You have been brought here to make a simple choice.' He paused to allow his message to be relayed to the captives. 'I will offer six men the chance to win their freedom. You will divide into pairs, and fight each other to the death. The three who survive will receive a good horse, their choice of everything on show and a guarantee that they will ride out of here unharmed. Those who do not volunteer will be sold as slaves.' Again Hannibal waited.

A moment later, the warriors began shouting and raising their clenched fists in the air.

The lead interpreter turned to Hannibal. 'They all want the honour, sir. Every last one.'

Hannibal smiled broadly. 'Announce that to my troops,' he ordered.

A loud sigh of appreciation rose from the watching soldiers as the Allobroges' reply was translated.

Malchus bent to whisper in Hanno's ear. 'Single combat to the death is much revered among the Gauls. This end is far superior to a life of slavery.'

Hanno still didn't understand.

'I will not allow every man to do this,' Hannibal proclaimed. 'Form up in two lines.' He waited as the prisoners were shoved into position. 'Pick out every fourth man until you have six,' he bellowed. His command was obeyed at once, and the remainder of the captives were shepherded to one side. The half-dozen warriors who had been chosen were each handed a sword and shield and, at a signal, were ordered to begin fighting. They went at each other like men possessed, and soon first blood had been spilled on the rock-hard ground.

'What's the point of this?' Sapho muttered after a few moments. 'We should just kill them all and have done.'

'Your damn response to everything,' Bostar retorted angrily.

'Shhh!' hissed Malchus. 'Hannibal does nothing by accident.'

Again Hanno was surprised by the degree of acrimony between his brothers, but he was granted no chance to dwell on this troubling development.

The duels were short, and savage. Before long, three bloodied warriors stood over the bodies of their opponents, waiting for Hannibal's promise to be fulfilled. And it was. Each man was allowed his choice of the rich goods on the trays, before selecting a horse from those tethered nearby. Then, with the cheers of everyone present ringing in their ears, they were allowed to leave.

'Even more than this can be yours,' shouted Hannibal to his men. 'For you the prize of victory is not to possess horses and cloaks, but to be the most envied of mankind, masters of all the wealth of Rome.'

The immense roar that followed his words rose high into the winter sky.

Impressed by Hannibal's tactic, Hanno glanced at Bostar.

'He will take us to the enemy's very gates,' said his brother.

'That's right,' declared Malchus.

'Where we'll slaughter every last one of the whoresons,' Sapho snarled.

Hanno's spirits soared. Rome *would* be defeated. He felt sure of it.

Chapter XX: Setbacks

Some days later, Quintus was huddled around a campfire with a group of his new comrades. It was a dank, cold afternoon. A gusty wind set lowering clouds scudding over the camp, threatening snow and increasing the general misery.

'I still can't believe it,' moaned Licinius, a garrulous Tarentine who was one of Quintus' tent mates. 'To have lost our first battle against the guggas. It's shameful.'

'It was only a skirmish,' said Quintus morosely.

'Maybe so,' agreed Calatinus, another of the men who shared their tent. Sturdily built, he was a year older than Quintus, but of similar outlook. 'It was a damn big one, though. I bet you're all glad to be sitting here now, eh?' He nodded as his companions shook their heads in agreement. 'Look at our casualties! Most of our cavalry and hundreds of *velites* killed. Six hundred legionaries taken prisoner, and Scipio gravely injured. Hardly a good start, was it?'

'Too true,' said Cincius, their last tent mate, a huge, ruddy-faced man with a shock of red hair. 'We've also retreated since. What must Hannibal think of us?'

'Why in Hades did we even pull back?' Licinius demanded. 'After the bridge had been destroyed, the Carthaginians had no way of crossing the Ticinus to get at us.'

Calatinus made sure no one else was in earshot. 'I reckon the consul panicked. It's not surprising, really, with him being out of action and all.'

'How would you know what Scipio thinks?' Quintus challenged irritably. 'He's far from a fool.'

'As if you'd know what the consul's like, new boy,' Cincius snapped.

Quintus scowled, but had the wisdom not to reply. Cincius looked ready for a fight, and he was twice Quintus' size.

'Why didn't Scipio take his chance when Hannibal offered battle before our camp?' Cincius went on. 'What an opportunity to miss, eh?'

There was a gloomy mutter of agreement.

'I say it's downright cowardly,' said Cincius, warming to his theme.

Quintus' anger flared. 'It's best to fight on the ground of one's choosing, at a time of one's choosing,' he declared, remembering what his father had said. 'You all know that! At the moment, we can do neither, and with Scipio injured, that position is unlikely to change in the near future. It made far more sense to remain in a position of security, here in the camp. Consider what might happen otherwise.'

Cincius glared at Quintus, but, seeing the others subside into a grumpy silence, chose to say no more for the moment.

Quintus felt no happier. While Scipio's courage was in little doubt, that of Flaccus was a different matter. It had taken a sea change in his view of his prospective brother-in-law as a hero even to countenance such a thought, but the reality of what had happened at the Ticinus could not be denied. Flaccus had ridden out with the cavalry on the ill-fated reconnaissance mission at his own request. Still ecstatic about being allowed to accompany the patrol, Quintus had been there too. He and his father had seen Flaccus as the clash began, but not after that. He hadn't reappeared until afterwards, when the battered remnants of the patrol retreated over the River Ticinus and reached the Roman camp. Apparently, he'd been swept out of harm's way by the tide of battle. Seeing that the Carthaginians had the upper hand, Flaccus had ridden for help. Naturally, the senior tribunes had declined to lead their legions, an infantry force, across a temporary bridge to face an enemy entirely made up of cavalry. What else could he have done? Flaccus had earnestly asked.

Of course there was no way of questioning Flaccus' account. Events were moving apace. They would just have to accept it. While Fabricius had not said as much to Quintus, he was clearly troubled by the possibility that Flaccus was a coward. Quintus felt the same way. Although he'd been terrified during the fight, at least he had stood his ground and fought the enemy. Aurelia must not marry a man, however well connected, who did not stick by his comrades in battle. Quintus poked a stick into the fire and tried not to think about it. He was annoyed to realise that the others had resumed their doleful conversation.

'My groom was drinking with some of the legionaries who guard Scipio's tent,' said Licinius. 'They said that a huge Carthaginian fleet has attacked Lilybaeum in Sicily.'

'No!' exclaimed Cincius.

Licinius nodded mournfully. 'There's no question of Sempronius Longus coming to our relief now.'

'How can you be so sure?' demanded Quintus.

'The soldiers swore on their mothers' graves it was true.'

Quintus gave him a dubious look. 'Why haven't we heard it from anyone else, then?'

'It's supposed to be top secret,' muttered Licinius.

'Well, *I* heard that the entire Boii tribe is marching north to join Hannibal,' interjected Cincius. 'If that's right, we'll be caught in a pincer attack between them and the guggas.'

Quintus remembered what his father had told him. A monstrous calf, which was somehow turned inside out to expose all of its internal organs, had been cut out of a cow that could not give birth on a farm nearby. The damn thing had been alive too. An officer whom Fabricius knew had seen it while on patrol. Stop it, thought Quintus, setting his jaw. 'Let's not get overexcited,' he advised. 'These stories are all too far-fetched.'

'Are they? What if the gods are angry with us?' retorted Licinius. 'I went to the temple of Placentia to make an offering yesterday, and the priests said that the sacred chickens would not eat. What better evidence do you need?'

Quintus' anger overflowed. 'Should we just surrender to Hannibal?'

Licinius flushed. 'Of course not!'

Quintus rounded on Cincius, who shook his head. 'Shut your damn mouths, then! Talk like that is terrible for morale. We're equestrians, remember? The ordinary soldiers look to us to set an example, not to put the fear of Hades in their hearts.'

Shame-faced, the others took a sudden interest in their sandals.

'I've had enough of your whingeing,' Quintus growled. He got up. 'See you later.' Without waiting for a response, he stalked off. His father would be able to shed a more positive light on what was going on. Quintus hoped so, because he was struggling with a real sense of despondency. He hid it well, but the savage clash with Hannibal's deadly Numidian horsemen had shaken him to the core. They were all lucky to have survived. No wonder his comrades were susceptible to the rumours sweeping the camp. Quintus had to work hard not to let his own fear become overwhelming.

His father was not in his tent. One of the sentries said that he'd gone to the consul's headquarters. The walk would do him good, Quintus decided. Blow out the cobwebs. His route took him past the tents of the Cenomani, local Gaulish tribesmen who fought for Rome. There were more than two thousand of the tribesmen, mostly infantry but with a scattering of cavalry. They were a clannish lot, and the language barrier compounded this difference. There was, however, a palpable air of comradeship between them and the Romans, which Quintus had come to enjoy. He hailed the first warrior he saw, a strapping brute who was sitting on a stool outside his tent. To his surprise, the man looked away, busying himself with the sword he was oiling. Quintus thought nothing of it, but a moment later, the same thing happened again. A bunch of warriors not ten steps from where he was walking gave him cold, stony stares, before turning their backs.

It's nothing, Quintus told himself. Scores of their men were killed the other day too. Half of them have probably lost a father or a brother.

'Aurelia! Aurelia!'

Atia's voice dragged Aurelia reluctantly from a pleasing dream, which had involved both Quintus and Hanno. Importantly, they'd still been friends. Despite the impossibility of this situation, and the urgency in her mother's tone, she was in a good mood. 'What is it, Mother?'

'Get out here!'

Aurelia shot out of bed. Pulling open her door, she was surprised to see Gaius standing in the atrium with her mother. Both looked decidedly serious. Suddenly self-conscious, Aurelia darted back and threw a light tunic over her woollen nightdress. Then she hurried out of her bedroom. 'Gaius,' she cried. 'How nice to see you.'

He bobbed his head awkwardly. 'And you, Aurelia.'

His grave manner made Aurelia's stomach lurch. She glanced at her mother and was horrified to see that her eyes were bright with tears. 'W-what is it?' Aurelia stammered.

'Word has come from Cisalpine Gaul,' said Gaius. 'It's not good.'

'Has our army been defeated?' Aurelia asked in surprise.

'Not exactly,' replied Gaius. 'But there was a big skirmish near the River Ticinus several days ago. Hannibal's Numidians caused heavy casualties among our cavalry and velites.'

Aurelia felt faint. 'Is Father all right?'

'We don't know.' Her mother's eyes were dark pools of sorrow.

'The situation is still very confused,' muttered Gaius. 'He's probably fine.'

'Heavy casualties,' repeated Aurelia slowly. 'How heavy, exactly?'

There was no answer.

She stared at him in disbelief. 'Gaius?'

'They say that out of three thousand riders, perhaps five hundred made it back to camp,' he answered, avoiding her gaze.

'How in the name of Hades can you say that Father is alive, then?' Aurelia shouted. 'It's far more likely that he's dead.'

'Aurelia!' barked Atia. 'Gaius is just trying to give us some hope.'

Gaius flushed. 'I'm sorry.'

Atia reached out to take his hand. 'There's nothing to apologise for. You have ridden out here at first light to bring us what information there is. We're very grateful.'

'I'm not! How could I be grateful for such news?' Aurelia yelled. Sobbing wildly, she ran towards the front door. Ignoring the startled doorman, she pulled it open and plunged outside. She ignored the cries that followed her.

Aurelia's feet led her to the stables. They had long been her refuge when feeling upset. She went straight to the solitary horse of her father's that had been left behind. A sturdy grey, it had been lame at the time of his departure. Seeing her, it whinnied in greeting. At once Aurelia's sorrow burst its banks and she dissolved in floods of tears. For a long time, she stood sobbing, her mind filled with images of her father, whom she would never see again. It was only when she felt the horse nibbling at her hair that Aurelia managed to regain some control. 'You want an apple, don't you?' she whispered, stroking its nose. 'And I've stupidly come empty-handed. Wait a moment. I'll get you one.'

Grateful for the interruption, Aurelia went to the food store at the end of the stables. Picking the largest apple she could find, she walked back. The horse's eagerly pricked ears and nickers of excitement made her sorrow surge back with a vengeance, however. Aurelia calmed herself with the only thing she could think of. 'At least Quintus is safe in Iberia,' she whispered. 'May the gods watch over him.'

Fabricius was closeted with Scipio, so Quintus didn't manage to meet with his father until later in the afternoon. When told about Quintus' comrades' scaremongering, Fabricius' reaction was typically robust. 'Despite the rumours, Scipio is doing fine. He'll be up and about in a couple of months. The rumour about a Carthaginian fleet attacking Sempronius Longus I also know to be untrue. Scipio would have mentioned it to me. It'd be the same if he'd had any intelligence about the Boii rising up. As for these bad omens – has a single one of your companions actually witnessed one?' Fabricius laughed as Quintus shook his head. 'Of course not. Apart from that calf, which was just a freak of nature, no one ever has. The chickens in Jupiter's temple might not be eating, but that's to be expected. Poultry are frail bloody creatures. They're forever falling sick, especially in weather like this.' He pointed to his head, and then his heart, and last of all at his sword. 'Trust in these before you worry about what other men say.'

Quintus was heartened by Fabricius' attitude. He was also grateful that his father no longer mentioned sending him home. Nothing had been said since the defeat at the Ticinus. Whether it was because of the number of riders who had fallen, or because Fabricius had become reconciled to the idea of him serving in the cavalry, Quintus did not know – or care. His good humour was added to by the bellyful of wine and hearty stew that his father had provided, and he left in much better spirits than he'd arrived.

His good mood did not last long, however. The currents of air that whipped around Quintus as he struggled back towards his tent were even more vicious than earlier in the day. They cut clean through his cloak, chilling his flesh to the bone. It was so easy to imagine the gods sending the storm down as punishment. There was an awful inevitability about the snow that began falling a moment later. His worries, only recently allayed, returned with a vengeance.

What few soldiers were about rapidly vanished from sight. Quintus couldn't wait to climb beneath his blankets himself, where he could try to forget it all. He was amazed, therefore, to see the Cenomani tribesmen outside. They stood around blazing fires, their arms around each other's shoulders, singing low, sorrowful chants. The warriors were probably mourning their dead, thought Quintus, shivering. He left them to it.

Licinius was first to catch Quintus' eye when he entered the tent. 'Sorry about earlier,' he muttered from the depths of his blankets. 'I should have kept my mouth shut.'

'Don't worry about it. We were all feeling down,' Quintus replied, shedding his damp cloak. He moved to his bedroll. It lay alongside that of Calatinus, who also gave him a sheepish look. 'You might be interested to know that Scipio knows nothing of a Carthaginian fleet attacking Sicily.'

An embarrassed grin creased Calatinus' face. 'Well, if he hasn't heard of it, we have nothing to worry about.'

'What about the Boii?' challenged Cincius aggressively.

Quintus grinned. 'No. Good news, eh?'

Cincius' glower slowly faded away.

'Excellent,' said Calatinus, sitting up. 'So we just have to wait until Longus gets here.'

'I think we should raise a toast to that day,' Cincius announced. He nodded at Quintus as if to say that their disagreement had been forgotten. 'Who's interested?'

There was a chorus of agreement, and Quintus groaned. 'I can feel the hangover already.'

'Who cares? There's no chance of any action!' Cincius leaped up and headed for the table where they kept their food and wine.

'True enough,' Quintus muttered. 'Why not, then?'

The four comrades were late getting to sleep. Despite his drunken state, Quintus was troubled by bad dreams. The most vivid involved squadrons of Numidian horsemen pursuing him across an open plain. Eventually, drenched in sweat, he sat up. It was pitch black in the tent, and freezing cold. Yet Quintus welcomed the chill air that moved across his face and arms, distracting him from the drumbeat pounding in his head. He squinted at the brazier, barely making out the last glowing embers. Yawning, he threw back the covers. If the fire was fed now, it might last until morning. As he stood, Quintus heard a faint noise outside. Surprised, he pricked his ears. It was the unmistakable crunching of snow beneath a man's feet, but rather than the measured tread of a sentry, this was being made by someone moving with great care. Someone who did not want to be heard.

Instinctively, Quintus picked up his sword. On either side and to the rear, the next tents were half a dozen paces away. In front, a narrow path increased that distance to perhaps ten. This was where the sound was coming from. Quintus padded forward in his bare feet. All his senses were on high alert. Next, he heard whispering. Adrenaline surged through him. This was not right. Groping his way back through the darkness, Quintus reached Calatinus and grabbed his shoulder. 'Wake up,' he hissed.

The only answer he got was an irritated groan.

At once the noise outside stopped.

Quintus' heart thumped with fear. He might have just attracted the attention of those on the other side of the tent leather. Letting go of Calatinus' tunic, he frantically pulled on his sandals. His fingers slipped on the awkward lacing, and he mouthed a savage curse. Finally, though, he was done.

As Quintus straightened, he heard a soft, choking sound. And another. There was more muttering, and a stifled cry, which was cut short. He rushed to Licinius' bedroll this time. Perhaps he wasn't so pissed. Placing a hand across the Tarentine's mouth, Quintus shook him violently. 'Wake up!' he hissed. 'We are under attack!' He made out the white of the other's shocked eyes as they opened. Licinius nodded in understanding, and Quintus took away his hand. 'Listen,' he whispered.

For a moment, they heard nothing. Then there was a strangled moan, which swiftly died away. It was followed by the familiar, meaty sound of a blade plunging in and out of flesh. Quintus and Licinius exchanged a horrified glance and they both leaped up. 'To arms! To arms!' they screamed in unison.

At last Calatinus woke up. 'What's going on?' he mumbled.

'Damn it, get up! Grab your sword,' Quintus shouted. 'You too, Cincius. Quickly!' He cursed himself for not raising the alarm sooner.

In response to their cries, someone pushed a blade through the front of the tent and sliced downwards. Ripping the leather apart, he stepped inside. Quintus didn't hesitate. Running forward, he stabbed the figure in the belly. As the man folded over, bellowing in pain, a second intruder entered. Quintus hacked him down with a savage blow to the neck. Blood spattered everywhere as the intruder collapsed, screaming. Unfortunately, a third man was close behind. So was a fourth. Loud, guttural voices from outside revealed that they had plenty of back-up.

'They're fucking Gauls!' yelled Licinius.

Confusion filled Quintus. What was happening? Had the Carthaginians scaled the ramparts? Ducking underneath a swinging sword, he thrust forward with his gladius, and was satisfied by the loud cry this elicited. Licinius joined him. Side by side, they put up a desperate resistance against the tide of warriors trying to gain entry. It was soon obvious that they would fail. Their new enemies were carrying shields, while they were in only their underclothes.

More ripping sounds came from Quintus' left and he struggled not to panic. 'The whoresons are cutting their way in. Calatinus! Cincius! Slash a hole in one of the back panels,' he shouted over his shoulder. 'We've got to get out.' There was no response, and Quintus' stomach clenched. Were their comrades already dead?

'Come on!' Calatinus screeched a moment later.

Relief flooded through Quintus. 'Ready?' he bellowed at Licinius.

'Yes!'

'Let's go, then!' Quintus delivered a desperate flurry of blows in the direction of his nearest opponent before turning and sprinting for the rear of the tent. He sensed Licinius one step behind. Quintus reached the gaping hole in the leather in a few strides. He hurled himself bodily through it, landing with a crash at the feet of the others. As they hauled him up, he peered inside, and was horrified to see Licinius – almost within arm's reach – trip and fall to his knees. Quintus had no time to react. The baying Gauls were on his comrade like hounds that have cornered a boar. Swords, daggers and even an axe chopped downwards. The poor light was not enough to prevent Quintus seeing the spurts of blood from each dreadful, mortal wound. Licinius collapsed on to the tent's floor without a word.

'You bastards,' Quintus screamed. Desperate to avenge his friend, he lunged forward.

Strong arms pulled him back. 'Don't be stupid. He's dead. We have to save ourselves,' Cincius snarled. Quickly, he and Calatinus dragged him off into the darkness.

There was no pursuit.

'Let me go!' Quintus shouted.

'You won't go back?' insisted Calatinus.

'I swear it,' Quintus muttered angrily.

They released him.

Quintus gazed around with horrified eyes. As far as he could see, pandemonium reigned. Some tents had been set on fire, vividly illuminating the scene. Groups of Gaulish warriors ran hither and thither, cutting down the confused Roman cavalrymen and legionaries who were emerging, half-clothed, into the cold night air. 'It doesn't look like an all-out attack,' he said after a moment. 'There aren't enough of them.'

'Some of the whoresons are already running away,' swore Calatinus, pointing.

Quintus squinted into the glow cast by the burning tents. 'What are they carrying?' His gorge rose as he realised. A great retch doubled Quintus over, and he puked up a bellyful of sour wine.

'The fucking dogs!' cried Cincius. 'They're heads! They've beheaded the men they've killed!'

With watering eyes, Quintus looked up. All he could see were the trails of blood the Gauls had left in the dazzling white snow.

Cincius and Calatinus began to moan with fear.

With great effort, Quintus pulled himself together. 'Quiet!' he hissed.

To his surprise, the pair obeyed. White-faced, they waited for him to speak.

Quintus ignored his instincts, which were screaming at him to search for his father. He had two men's lives in his hands. For the moment, they had to be the priority. 'Let's head for the *intervallum*,' he said. 'That's where everyone will be headed. We can fight the whoresons on a much better footing there.'

'But we're both barefoot,' said Cincius plaintively.

Quintus bridled, but if he didn't let the others equip themselves with caligae from nearby corpses, frostbite beckoned. 'Go on, then. Pick up a *scutum* each as well,' he ordered. A shield was vital.

'What about a mail shirt?' Calatinus tugged at a dead legionary. 'He's about my size.'

'No, you fool! We can't afford the time. Swords and shields will have to do.' Twitching with impatience, he waited until they

415

were ready. 'Follow me.' Keeping an eye out for Gaulish warriors, Quintus set off at a loping run.

He led them straight to the intervallum, the strip of open ground that ran around the inside of the camp walls. Normally, it served for the legion to assemble before marching out on patrol or to do battle. Now, it allowed the bloodied survivors of the covert attack to regroup. Many had had the same idea as Quintus. The area was packed with hundreds of milling, dis-organised legionaries and cavalrymen. Not many were fully dressed, but most had had the wits to pick up a weapon as they fled their tents.

Fortunately, this was where the discipline of officers such as centurions came into play. Recognisable even without their characteristic helmets, there were calm, measured figures everywhere, shouting orders and forming the soldiers into regular lines. Quintus and his companions joined the nearest group. At that point, it didn't matter that they were not infantry. Before long, the centurions had marshalled a large force together. Every sixth soldier was issued with one of the few torches available. It wasn't much, but would do until the attack had been contained.

At once, they began sweeping the avenues and tent lines for Gauls. To everyone's frustration, they had little success. Their desire for revenge could not be sated. It appeared that as soon as the alarm had been raised, the majority of the tribesmen had made their getaway. Nonetheless, the search continued until the entire area had been covered.

The worst discoveries were the numerous headless bodies. It was common knowledge that the Gauls liked to gather such battle trophies, but Quintus had never witnessed it before. He had never seen so much blood in his life. Enormous splashes of red circled every corpse, and wide trails of it ran alongside the Gauls' footprints.

'Jupiter above, this will look like a slaughterhouse in daylight,' said Calatinus in a hushed voice.

'Poor bastards,' replied Cincius. 'Most of them never had a chance.'

An image of his father sleeping in his tent made Quintus retch again. There was nothing left to come up except bile.

Calatinus looked concerned. 'Are you all right?'

'I'm fine,' Quintus barked. Forcing down his nausea, he carefully scanned each body they came across. He begged the gods that he would not find his father. To his immense relief, he saw none who resembled Fabricius. Yet this did not mean a thing. They had covered but a small part of the camp. Only when daybreak came could he be sure.

The centurions kept every soldier on high alert for what remained of the night. The sole compromise they would make was to allow each makeshift century in turn to go to their tents and retrieve their clothing and armour. Fully prepared for battle, the legionaries and cavalrymen then had to wait until dawn, when it became clear that there would be no further attack. The men were finally allowed to stand down, and were ordered to return to their respective units. The cleaning-up operation would take all day. Disregarding this, Quintus went in search of his father. Miraculously, he found him in his tent. Tears came to his eyes as he entered. 'You're alive!'

'There you are,' Fabricius declared, waving at the table before him, which was laid out for breakfast. 'Care for some bread?'

Quintus grinned. Despite his father's nonchalance, he had seen the flash of relief in his eyes. 'Thank you. I'm famished. It's been a long night,' he replied.

'Indeed it has,' Fabricius replied. 'And more than a hundred good men are gone thanks to those bastard Cenomani.'

'You're certain that's who it was?'

'Who else could it have been? There was no sign of the gate being forced, and the sentries on the walls saw no one.'

Realisation struck Quintus. 'That's why they were so surly yesterday!' Seeing his father's confusion, he explained.

'That clarifies a great deal. And now they've fled to the Carthaginian camp. No doubt their "trophies" will serve as an offering to Hannibal,' said Fabricius sourly. 'Proof that they hate us.'

Quintus tried not to think of Licinius' headless corpse, which he'd found in the wreckage of their tent. 'What will Scipio do?'

Fabricius scowled. 'Guess.'

'We're to withdraw again?'

His father nodded.

'Why?' cried Quintus.

'He thinks it's too dangerous on this side of the Trebia. After last night, that's hard to argue with.' Fabricius saw Quintus' anguish. 'It's not just that. The high ground on the far bank is extremely uneven, which will stop any chance of attacks by the Carthaginian cavalry. We'll also be blocking the roads that lead south through Liguria to the lands of the Boii.'

Quintus' protests subsided. Those reasons at least made sense. 'When?'

'This afternoon, as it's getting dark.'

Quintus sighed. The very manner of their retreat seemed cowardly, but it *was* prudent. 'And then we sit tight?' he guessed. 'Contain the Carthaginians?'

'Exactly. Sempronius Longus is travelling here with all speed. His forces will arrive inside a month.' Fabricius' expression grew fierce. 'Hannibal's forces will never stand up to two consular armies.'

For the second time since the Cenomani attack, Quintus had a reason to smile.

'There you are. Your mother's been worried. She thought you'd be here.'

At the sound of Elira's voice, Aurelia turned. The Illyrian was framed in the doorway to the stable. All at once, she felt very childish. 'Is Gaius still here?'

'No, he's gone. Apparently, his unit is to be mobilised soon. He said that you would be in his thoughts and prayers.'

Aurelia felt even worse.

Elira came closer. 'I heard the news,' she said softly. 'Everyone did. We all feel for you.'

'Thank you.' Aurelia threw her a grateful look.

'Who's to know? Your father may well be alive.'

'Don't,' Aurelia snapped.

'I'm sorry,' said Elira quickly.

Aurelia forced a smile. 'At least Quintus is still alive.'

'And Hanno.'

Aurelia shoved away the pang of jealousy that followed Elira's words. Mention of Hanno inevitably made her think of Suniaton. She hadn't taken him any food for four days. He'd be running out of provisions. Aurelia made her mind up on the spot. Seeing Suni now would cheer her up. She squinted at Elira. 'You liked Hanno, didn't you?'

Twin dimples formed in the Illyrian's cheeks. 'Yes,' she whispered.

'Would you help him again?'

'Of course,' Elira answered, looking puzzled. 'But he's gone, with Quintus.'

Aurelia smiled. 'Go to the kitchen and fill a bag with provisions. Bread, cheese, meat. If Julius asks, tell him that they're rations for our foraging trip. Fetch a basket too.'

'What if the mistress wants to know where you are?'

'Say that we're going to look for nuts and mushrooms.'

Elira's face grew even more confused. 'How will that help Hanno?'

'You'll see.' Aurelia clapped her hands. 'Well, get on with it then. I'll meet you on the path that leads up to the hills.'

With a curious glance, Elira hurried off.

Aurelia hadn't been waiting long before Elira came hurrying through the trees towards her. A small leather pack dangled from one hand, a cloak that matched her own from the other.

'Did anyone ask what you were doing?' Aurelia asked nervously.

'Julius did, but he just smiled when I told him what we were doing. He said to be careful.'

'He's such an old woman!' declared Aurelia. She looked down and realised that she'd come out without her dagger or sling. It doesn't matter, she told herself. We won't be gone for long. 'Come on,' she said briskly.

'Where are we going?' asked Elira.

'Up there,' replied Aurelia, waving vaguely at the slopes that loomed over the farm. Abruptly, she decided that there was no further need for subterfuge. 'Did you know that Hanno had a friend who was captured with him?'

Elira nodded.

'Suniaton was sold to become a gladiator in Capua.'

'Oh.' Elira didn't dare to say more, but her muted tone spoke volumes.

'Quintus and Gaius helped him to escape.'

The Illyrian was visibly shocked. 'Why?'

'Because Hanno was Quintus' friend.'

'I see.' Elira frowned. 'Has Suniaton got something to do with where we're going now?'

'Yes. He was injured when they rescued him, so the poor thing couldn't travel. He's much better now, thank the gods.'

Elira looked intrigued. 'Where is he?'

'At the shepherd's hut where Quintus and Hanno fought the bandits.'

'You're full of surprises, aren't you?' said Elira with a giggle.

Aurelia's misery lifted a fraction and she grinned.

Talking animatedly, they walked to the border of Fabricius' land. The fields on either side were empty and bare, lying fallow until the spring. Jackdaws were their only company; flocks regularly flew overhead, their characteristic squawks piercing the chill air. Soon they had entered the woods that covered the surrounding hills. The bird cries immediately died away, and the trees pressed in from all sides with a claustrophobic air that Aurelia did not like.

When Agesandros stepped out on to the path, she screamed in fright. So did Elira.

'I didn't mean to scare you,' he said apologetically.

Aurelia tried to calm her pounding heart. 'What are you doing here?' she demanded.

He raised the bow in his hands. An arrow was already notched to its string. 'Hunting deer. And you?'

Aurelia's mouth felt very dry. 'Looking for nuts. And mushrooms.'

'I see,' he said. 'I wouldn't stray too far from the farm on your search.'

'Why not?' asked Aurelia, trying desperately to sound confident.

'You never know who might be about. Bandits. A bear. An escaped slave.'

'There's little chance of that,' Aurelia declared boldly.

'Maybe so. You're unarmed, though. I could come with you,' the Sicilian offered.

'No!' Instantly, Aurelia regretted her vehemence. 'Thank you, but we'll be fine.'

'If you're certain,' he said, stepping back.

'I am.' Jerking her head at Elira, Aurelia walked past him.

'It's a bit late for mushrooms, isn't it?'

Aurelia's step faltered. 'There are still a few, if you know where to look,' she managed.

Agesandros nodded knowledgeably. 'I'm sure.'

Aurelia's skin was crawling as she walked away.

'Does he know?' whispered Elira.

'How could he?' Aurelia hissed back.

But it felt as if he did.

* * *

Many days passed by, and it became evident that there would be no battle. As Fabricius had said, no commander would choose to fight unless he could select the time and place. Scipio's refusal to move from the high ground and Hannibal's unwillingness to attack his enemy's position produced a stalemate. While the Carthaginians roamed at will across the plain west of the Trebia, the Romans stayed close to their camp. Hannibal's cavalry now severely outnumbered their horsemen. Patrols were so risky that they were rarely sent out. Despite this, Quintus found it hard to remain equable about their enforced inactivity. He was still suffering nightmares about what had happened to Licinius. He hoped that in battle he could purge himself of the disturbing images. 'I'm going crazy,' he told his father one night. 'How much longer do we have to wait?'

'We'll do nothing until Longus arrives,' Fabricius repeated patiently. 'If we marched down to the flat ground today and offered battle, the dogs would cut us to pieces. Even without the difference in cavalry, Hannibal's army outnumbers us man for man. You know that.'

'I suppose so,' Quintus admitted reluctantly.

Fabricius leaned back in his chair, satisfied that his point had been made.

Quintus stared gloomily into the depths of the brazier. What was Hanno doing at this very moment? he wondered. It didn't seem real that they were now enemies. Quintus also thought of Aurelia. When would his recently composed letter reach her? If Fortuna smiled on them both, he might get a reply within the next few months. It was a long time to wait. At least in the meantime he was serving alongside his father. His sister, on the other hand, was not so lucky. Quintus' heart ached for her.

'Here you both are!' A familiar booming voice broke the silence.

Fabricius made a show of looking pleased. 'Flaccus. Where else would we be?'

Quintus jumped up and saluted. What does he want? he wondered. Since the debacle at the Ticinus, they had hardly seen Aurelia's husband-to-be. The reason, all three knew, was Flaccus' conduct during that disaster. It was hard to dispel suspicion once it had taken root, thought Quintus. Yet he could not shake off his feeling. Nor, it appeared, could his father.

'Quite so, quite so. Who would be out tonight apart from the sentries and the deranged?' Chuckling at his own joke, Flaccus proffered a small amphora.

'How kind,' Fabricius murmured, accepting the gift. 'Will you try some?'

'Only if you will,' Flaccus demurred.

Fabricius opened the amphora with a practised movement of his wrist. 'Quintus?'

'Yes, please, Father.' Quickly, he fetched three glazed ceramic beakers.

With their cups filled, they eyed each other, wondering who would make the toast. At length, Fabricius spoke. 'To the swift arrival of Sempronius Longus and his army.'

'And to a rapid victory over the Carthaginians thereafter,' Flaccus added.

Quintus thought of Licinius. 'And vengeance for our dead comrades.'

Nodding, Fabricius lifted his cup even higher.

Flaccus beamed. 'That's fighting talk! Just what I wanted to hear.' He gave them a conspiratorial wink. 'I've had a word with Scipio.'

Fabricius looked dubious. 'About what?'

'Sending out a patrol.'

'Eh?' asked Fabricius suspiciously.

'No one has been across the river in more than a week.'

'That's because it's too damn dangerous,' Fabricius replied. 'The enemy controls the far bank in its entirety.'

'Hear me out,' said Flaccus in a placatory tone. 'When

Sempronius Longus arrives, he'll want fresh intelligence, and information on the terrain west of the Trebia. After all, that's where the battle will be.'

'What's wrong with waiting until he gets here?' demanded Fabricius. 'Some of his cavalry can do his donkey work.'

'It needs to be now,' urged Flaccus. 'Presenting the consul with all the information he needs would allow him to act fast. Just think of the boost it would provide to the men's morale when we come back safely!'

'We?' said Fabricius slowly. 'You would come too?'

'Of course.'

Not for the first time, Fabricius wondered if it had been a good idea to betroth Aurelia to Flaccus. Yet how could he be a coward and offer to take part in such a madcap venture? 'I don't know,' he muttered. 'It would be incredibly risky.'

'Not necessarily,' Flaccus protested. 'I've been watching the Carthaginians from our side of the river. By *hora decima* every afternoon, their last patrol has vanished from sight. It's at least *hora quarta* the following morning before they return. If we crossed at night, and rode out before dawn, we'd have perhaps two hours to reconnoitre the area. We would be back across before the Numidians had finished scratching their lice.'

Quintus laughed.

Fabricius scowled. 'I don't think it's a very good idea.'

'Scipio has already given his approval. I could think of no one better to lead the patrol, and he agreed,' said Flaccus. 'Come on, what do you say?'

Damn you, thought Fabricius. He felt completely out-manoeuvred. Refusing Flaccus' offer could be seen as a snub to Scipio himself, and that was not a wise course of action. Furious, Fabricius changed his mind. 'It could only be a small patrol. One turma at most,' he said. 'It would have to be under my sole command. You can come along – as an observer.'

Flaccus did not protest. He turned to Quintus. 'Your father is a shining example of a Roman officer. Brave, resourceful and eager to do his duty.'

'I'm coming too,' said Quintus.

'No, you're not,' snapped his father. 'It will be far too dangerous.'

'It's not fair! You did things like this when you were my age – you've told me!' retorted Quintus furiously.

Flaccus stepped in before Fabricius could reply. 'How can we deny Quintus such a chance to gain valuable experience? And think of the glory that will be heaped upon the men who brought Longus the information that helped him to defeat Hannibal!'

Fabricius looked at his son's eager face and sighed. 'Very well.'

'Thank you, Father,' said Quintus with a broad smile.

Fabricius kept showing a brave face, but inside he was filled with fear. It will be like walking past a pride of hungry lions, hoping that none of them sees us, he thought. Yet there was no going back now.

He had given his word to lead the mission.

Chapter XXI: Hannibal's Plan

One morning, not long after the Carthaginians had driven the Romans back over the Trebia, Malchus was ordered to Hannibal's tent. While this happened regularly, he always felt a tremor of excitement when the summons arrived. After so many years of waiting for revenge on Rome, Malchus still thrilled to be in the presence of the man who had finally begun the war.

He found Hannibal in pensive mood. The general barely glanced up as Malchus entered. As ever, he was leaning over his campaign table, studying a map of the area. Maharbal, his cavalry commander, stood beside him, talking in a low voice. A thin man with long, curly black hair and an easy grin, Maharbal was popular with officers and ordinary troops alike.

Malchus came to a halt several steps from the table. He stiffened to attention. 'Reporting for duty, sir.'

Hannibal straightened. 'Malchus, welcome.'

'You asked to see me, sir?'

'I did.' Still deep in thought, Hannibal rubbed a finger across his lips. 'I have a question to ask you.'

'Anything, sir.'

'Maharbal and I have come up with a plan. An ambush, to be precise.'

'Sounds interesting, sir,' said Malchus eagerly.

'We're hoping that the Romans might send a patrol across the river,' Hannibal went on. 'Maharbal here will organise the cavalry that will fall upon the enemy, but I want some infantry there too. They will lie in wait at the main ford, and prevent any stragglers from escaping.'

Malchus grinned fiercely. 'I'd be honoured to take part, sir.'

'I didn't have you in mind.' Seeing Malchus' face fall, Hannibal explained, 'I'm not losing one of my most experienced officers in a skirmish. I was thinking of your sons, Bostar and Sapho.'

Malchus swallowed his disappointment. 'They'd be well suited to a job like this, sir, and I'm sure delighted to be picked for it.'

'I thought so.' Hannibal paused for a moment. 'And so to my question. What about your other son?'

Malchus blinked in surprise. 'Hanno?'

'Is he battle-ready yet?'

'I put him into training straight after he returned, sir. Not being in Carthage, it was a little improvised, but he performed well.' Malchus hesitated. 'I'd say that he's ready to be commissioned as an officer.'

'Good, good. Could he lead a phalanx?'

Malchus gaped. 'Are you serious, sir?'

'I'm not in the habit of making jokes, Malchus. The crossing of the mountains left many units without officers to command them.'

'Of course, sir, of course.' Malchus gathered his thoughts. 'Before Hanno was lost at sea, I would have had grave reservations.'

'Why?' Hannibal's gaze was as fierce as a hawk's.

'He was a bit of a wastrel, sir. Only interested in fishing and girls.'

'That's hardly a crime, is it?' Hannibal chuckled. 'I thought he was too young to serve in the army back then?'

'He was, sir,' Malchus admitted. 'And, to be fair, he was

excellent when it came to lessons in military tactics. He was skilled at hunting too.'

'Good qualities. So, has your opinion changed since his return?'

'It has, sir,' Malchus replied confidently. 'He's changed. The things he experienced and had to live through would have broken many boys, but it didn't Hanno. He is a man now.'

'You're sure?'

Malchus met his general's gaze squarely. 'Yes, sir.'

'Fine. I want you and your three sons back here in an hour. That'll be all.' Hannibal turned back to Maharbal.

'Thank you, sir.' Grinning with excitement, Malchus saluted and withdrew.

Confusion filled Hanno when his father told him the news.

'What does he want with a junior officer like me?'

'I couldn't say,' Malchus replied neutrally.

Hanno's stomach twisted into a knot. 'Are Sapho and Bostar also to be present?'

'They are.'

That did little to reassure Hanno. Had he done something wrong?

'I'll leave you to it,' said Malchus. 'Make sure you're there in half an hour.'

'Yes, Father.' With a racing mind, Hanno set to polishing his new helmet and breastplate. He didn't stop until his arms burned. Then he rubbed his leather sandals with grease until they glistened. When he was done, Hanno hurried to his father's tent where there was a large bronze mirror. To his relief, Malchus wasn't there. He scowled at his reflection. 'It'll have to do,' he muttered.

As he walked to Hannibal's headquarters, Hanno was grateful that none of the soldiers hurrying to and fro gave him a second look. It wasn't until he reached the scutarii who stood guard outside the large pavilion that he became the focus of attention.

'State your name, rank and business!' barked the officer in charge of the sentries.

'Hanno, junior officer of a Libyan phalanx, sir. I'm here to see the general.' Hanno blinked, half expecting to be told to get lost.

Instead, the officer nodded. 'You're expected. Follow me.'

A moment later, Hanno found himself in a large, sparsely furnished chamber. Apart from a desk and a few hide-backed chairs, it held only a weapons rack. Hannibal was there, surrounded by a circle of his commanders. Among them were his father and brothers.

'Sir! Announcing Hanno, junior officer of the Libyan spearmen!' the officer bellowed.

Hanno flushed to the roots of his hair.

Turning, Hannibal smiled. 'Welcome.'

'Thank you, sir.'

'You all know about Malchus' prodigal son?' asked Hannibal. 'Well, here he is.'

Hanno's embarrassment grew even greater as the senior officers studied him. He could see Bostar grinning. Even his father had the trace of a smile on his lips. Sapho, on the other hand, looked as if he'd swallowed a wasp. Hanno felt a surge of annoyance. *Why is he like that?*

Hannibal looked at each of the brothers in turn. 'You're probably wondering why I summoned you this morning?'

'Yes, sir,' they answered.

'I'll come to my reason in a moment.' Hannibal looked at Hanno. 'You've heard no doubt of our severe casualties, suffered during the crossing of the Alps?'

'Of course, sir.'

'Since then, we've been short of not just men, but officers.'

'Yes, sir,' Hanno replied. What was Hannibal getting at? Hanno wondered.

The general smiled at his confusion. 'I'm appointing you to the command of a phalanx,' he said.

'Sir?' Hanno managed.

'You heard me,' replied Hannibal. 'It's a huge leap, I know, but your father assures me that you've returned a man.'

'I . . .' Hanno's gaze flickered to Malchus and back to Hannibal. 'Thank you, sir.'

'As you know, a phalanx should number four hundred men or so, but yours now barely musters two hundred. It's one of the weakest units, but the men are veterans, and they should serve you well. And, after your extraordinary ordeals, I have high expectations of you.'

'Thank you, sir,' said Hanno, acutely aware of the huge responsibility he'd just been handed. 'I am deeply honoured.' Bostar winked at him, but he was irritated to see that Sapho's lips were pursed.

'Good!' Hannibal declared. 'Now for the reason I called you all here today. As you probably know, there's been no action since we sent the Romans packing over the Trebia. Nor is there much chance of any in the near future. They know that our cavalry greatly outnumbers theirs, as does our infantry. From our point of view, it would be pointless to attack their camp. It's on such uneven ground that the advantage our horsemen grant us would be negated. The Romans know that too, so the mongrel bastards are happy just to block the road south and wait for reinforcements. We may have to wait until those forces arrive, but I'm not happy to sit about doing nothing.' Hannibal turned. 'Maharbal?'

'Thank you, sir,' said the cavalry commander. 'To try and encourage the enemy to send some men over the river, we've been giving the impression that our riders have become quite lax. Do you want to know how?' he asked.

'Yes, sir,' the three brothers replied eagerly.

'We never appear on our side of the Trebia until late in the morning, and we always leave well before dark. Understand?'

'You want them to try a dawn patrol, sir?' asked Bostar.

Maharbal smiled. 'Exactly.'

Hanno felt his excitement grow. He didn't feel confident enough to ask a question, however.

Sapho did it for him. 'What else, sir?'

Hannibal took over once more. 'Maharbal has five hundred Numidians permanently stationed in the woods about a mile from the main ford over the river. If the Romans take the bait, and send out a patrol, they'll have to ride past our men. Not many of the dogs will escape when the Numidians fall on them from behind, but some might. Which is where you and your Libyans will come in.'

Hanno shot a glance at Bostar and Sapho, who were grinning fiercely.

'I want a strong force of infantry to remain hidden near the crossing point. If any Romans do cross, they're not to be hindered, but when they return . . .' Hannibal clenched a fist. 'I want them annihilated. Is that clear?'

Hanno glanced at his brothers, who gave him emphatic nods. 'Yes, sir!' they cried in unison.

'Excellent,' declared Hannibal. His gaze hardened. 'Do *not* fail me.'

Shortly after darkness had fallen the following evening, Hanno and his brothers led their units out of the Carthaginian camp. As well as their tents and sleeping rolls, the men carried enough rations for three days and nights. To Hanno's delight, the Numidians who were to guide them into position were led by no less than Zamar, the officer who'd found him near the Padus. Following the horsemen, the phalanxes quietly marched to the east, following little-used hunting tracks. As the sound of rushing water filled everyone's ears, Zamar directed them to a hidden dell which lay a couple of hundred paces from the area's main crossing point over the River Trebia. It was a perfect hiding place. Spacious enough to contain their entire force, but sufficiently close to the ford. 'I'm leaving you six riders as messengers. Send them out the moment you see anything,' Zamar muttered before he left. 'And remember, when the Romans come, none are to be left alive.'

'Say no more,' Sapho snarled.

Although Bostar said nothing, Hanno saw a look of distaste flicker across his face. He waited until Zamar was out of sight before turning to his brothers. 'What's going on?' he demanded.

'What do you mean?' asked Sapho defensively.

'You two are permanently like a pair of cats in a bag with each other. Why?'

Bostar and Sapho scowled at each other.

Hanno waited. The silence dragged on for a few moments.

'It's really none of your business,' said Bostar at length.

Hanno flushed. He glanced at Sapho, whose face was a cold mask. Hanno gave up. 'I'm going to check on my men,' he muttered and stalked off.

They waited in vain through what remained of the night. By dawn, the Carthaginians were chilled through and miserable. To avoid any possibility of being spotted, no fires had been lit. While it hadn't rained, the winter damp was pervasive. Following strict orders, the soldiers remained in the clearing during daylight. The sole exceptions to this were a handful of sentries, who, with blackened faces, hid themselves among the trees lining the river-bank. Everyone else had to stay put, even when answering calls of nature. While some found the energy to play dice or knuckle-bones, most men stayed in their tents, chewing on cold rations or catching up on lost sleep. Still annoyed by his brothers' pettiness, Hanno spent his time talking to his spearmen, trying to get to know them. He knew by their muted reactions that his efforts would mean little until he'd led them into combat, but it felt better than doing nothing.

The day dragged past without event.

Night fell at last, and Hanno took charge of the sentries, who were stationed along the river's edge for several hundred paces either side of the ford. He spent his time wandering the bank, his eyes peeled for any enemy activity. There was little cloud cover. The myriad stars above provided enough light to see relatively well, yet hours went by without so much as a flicker of movement on the opposite side. By the time dawn was approaching, Hanno had grown bored and annoyed. 'Where are the fuckers?' he muttered to himself.

'Still in their beds, probably.'

Hanno jumped. Turning, he recognised Bostar's features in the dim light. 'Tanit above, you scared me! What are you doing here?'

'I couldn't sleep.'

'You should have stayed under your blankets anyway. It's a damn sight warmer than out here,' Hanno replied.

Bostar crouched down beside Hanno with a sigh. 'To be honest, I wanted to apologise about what happened yesterday with Sapho. Our argument shouldn't affect our dealings with you.'

'That's all right. I shouldn't have poked my nose where it didn't belong.'

A more comfortable air settled about them.

'We've actually been fighting for over a year,' Bostar admitted a moment later.

Hanno was grateful for the darkness, which concealed his surprise. 'What, the usual stuff with him being pompous and overbearing?'

Bostar's teeth glinted sadly in the starlight. 'I wish it was just that.'

'I don't understand.'

'It started when you'd been lost at sea.'

'Eh?'

'Sapho blamed me for letting you and Suniaton go.'

'But you both agreed to do so!'

'That's not how he saw it. We hadn't patched things up by the time I was posted to Iberia, and it flared up again the instant he and Father arrived from Carthage months later.'

'Why?'

'They'd had news of what had happened to you and Suni. Sapho was furious. He blamed me all over again.'

'You mean the pirates?' Suddenly, Hanno remembered Sapho's comment the day he'd returned, and his father's promise to tell him what had happened. 'I'd forgotten.'

'There was so much going on,' said Bostar. 'All that mattered was that you had returned.'

'We've got plenty of time now,' retorted Hanno. 'Tell me!'

'It was a few weeks after you'd disappeared. Thanks to one of his spies, Father got wind of some pirates in the port. Four of them were seized and taken in. Under torture, they admitted selling you and Suni into slavery in Italy.'

Vivid images flashed through Hanno's mind. 'Do you know any of their names?'

'No, sorry,' said Bostar. 'Apparently, the captain was an Egyptian.'

'That's right!' said Hanno, shivering. 'What happened to them?'

'They were castrated first. Then their limbs were smashed before they were crucified,' Bostar replied in a flat tone.

Hanno imagined the terrible scene for a moment. 'Not a good way to die,' he admitted.

'No.'

'But they deserved it,' declared Hanno harshly. 'Thanks to those whoresons, Suni and I should have died in the arena.'

'I know,' said Bostar with a heavy sigh. 'Yet seeing what happened to the pirates changed Sapho in some way. Ever since, he's been much harder. Crueller. You saw how he reacted to what Zamar said. I know that we have to kill any Romans who might cross the river. Orders are orders. But Sapho seems to take pleasure in it.'

'It's not nice, but it's not the end of the world, surely?' said Hanno, trying to make light of his brother's words.

'That's not all,' muttered Bostar. 'He thinks that I'll do anything to curry favour with Hannibal.' Quickly, he related how he'd saved Hannibal's life at Saguntum. 'You should have seen the expression on Sapho's face when Hannibal congratulated me. It was as if I'd done it to make him look bad.'

'That's crazy!' Hanno whispered. 'Are you sure that's what he thought?'

'Oh yes. "The perfect fucking officer" he's taken to calling me.'

Hanno was shocked into silence for a moment. 'Surely, it hasn't been all him? There are always two sides to every argument.'

'Yes, I've said some nasty things too.' Bostar sighed. 'But every time I try to sort it out, Sapho throws it back in my face. The last time I tried . . .' He hesitated for a heartbeat before shaking his head. 'I've given up on him.'

'Why? What happened?' asked Hanno.

'I'm not telling you,' said Bostar. 'I can't.' He looked away, out over the murmuring river.

Troubled by what Bostar had said, Hanno did not press him further. He tried to be optimistic. Maybe he could act as a mediator? Imagining a world in which Carthage was at peace once more, Hanno pictured himself hunting with his brothers in the mountains south of their city.

Bostar nudged him in the ribs, hard. 'Pssst! Do you hear that?'

Hanno came down to earth with a jolt. He leaned forward, listening with all his might. For a long time, he could make out nothing. Then, the jingle of harness. Hanno's senses went on to high alert. 'That came from across the water,' he muttered.

'It did,' replied Bostar excitedly. 'Hannibal was right: the Romans want information.'

They watched the far bank like wolves waiting for their prey to emerge. An instant later, their patience was rewarded. The sounds of horses, and men, moving with great care.

A surge of adrenaline pulsed through Hanno's veins. 'It has to be Romans!'

'Or some of their Gaulish allies,' said Bostar.

It wasn't long before they could make out a line of soldiers and mounts, winding their way down the track that led to the ford.

'How many?' hissed Bostar.

Hanno squinted into the darkness. An accurate head count was impossible. 'No more than fifty. Probably less. It's a reconnaissance patrol all right.'

Stopping, the Roman riders gathered together in a huddle.

'They're getting their last orders,' said Hanno.

A moment later, the first man quietly walked his horse into the ice-cold water. It gave a gentle, dissenting whinny, but some muttered reassurances in its ear worked wonders, and it continued without further protest. At once the others began to follow.

Bostar unwound his limbs and stood. 'Time to move. Go and tell Sapho what's happening. The Numidians must be alerted immediately. Clear?'

'Yes. What are you going to do?'

'I'll go along the bank to the next sentry, and keep an eye on them until they're out of sight. We need to be sure that no more of the bastards are going to cross.'

'Right. See you soon.' Hanno backed away slowly until he was behind the cover of the trees. Treading lightly on the hard ground, he sped back to their secret camp. He found Sapho pacing the ground before his tent. Quickly, he filled his brother in.

'Excellent,' said Sapho with a savage grin. 'Before long, you will get to blood your men's spears, and perhaps your own. A special moment for you.'

Hanno nodded nervously. Was he imagining Sapho's lasciviousness?

'Well, come on then! This is no time for standing around. Get your men up. I'll send out a few of the Numidians, and get my phalanx ready. Bostar will do the same no doubt, when he eventually gets here,' said Sapho.

Hanno frowned. 'No need for that,' he said. 'He'll be here any moment.'

'Of course he will!' Sapho laughed. 'Now get a move on. We'll need to move into position the instant the Romans have gone.'

Hanno put his head down and obeyed. He didn't understand the feud between his brothers, but one thing was certain: Sapho still liked telling him what to do. Irritated, Hanno began rousing his men. When he heard a man grumbling, Hanno lambasted him from a height. His tactic seemed to work; it didn't take long for the soldiers to assemble alongside Sapho's phalanx.

Soon after, Bostar's shape emerged from the gloom that hung over the trees that lined the riverbank. 'They've gone,' he declared. He whistled at the last three Numidians. 'Ride out at once. Trail the dogs from a distance. Return when the ambush has been sprung.'

With a quick salute, the cavalrymen sprang on to their horses' backs. They headed off at the trot.

Bostar approached his brothers. 'Our time here was not in vain,' he said with a smile.

'Finally,' drawled Sapho. 'We've been waiting for you.'

Why is he needling him like that? thought Hanno.

Bostar's jaw bunched, but he said nothing. Fortunately, his soldiers had heard their comrades getting up, and were doing the same. When he was done, the trio convened in front of their men.

'How are we going to work this?' asked Hanno.

'It's obvious,' said Sapho self-importantly. 'The phalanxes should form three sides of a square. The fourth side will be completed by the Numidians, who will drive the Romans into the trap. They'll have nowhere to go. All we have to decide is which phalanx holds each position.'

There was a momentary pause. Each of them had reconnoitred

the ground around the crossing point several times. The left flank was taken up by a dense patch of oak trees, while the right was a large swampy area. Neither constituted ground that horses would choose to ride over if given the choice. The best place to stand was on the track that led to the ford. That was where any action would take place.

As the youngest and most inexperienced, Hanno was content to take whichever of the flanks he was given.

'I'll take the central side,' said Bostar abruptly.

'Typical,' muttered Sapho. 'I want it as well. And you don't outrank me any more, remember?'

The two glowered at each other.

'This is ridiculous,' said Hanno angrily. 'It doesn't matter which one of you does it.'

Neither of his brothers answered.

'Why don't you toss a coin?'

Still neither Bostar nor Sapho spoke.

'Melqart above!' exclaimed Hanno. 'I'll do it, then.'

'That's out of the question,' snapped Sapho. 'You've got no combat experience.'

'Exactly,' added Bostar.

'I've got to start somewhere. Why not here?' Hanno retorted. 'Better this, surely, than in a massive battle?'

Bostar looked at Sapho. 'We can't stand around arguing all morning,' he said in a conciliatory tone.

Sapho gave a careless shrug. 'It would be hard for Hanno to get it wrong, I suppose.'

Feeling humiliated, Hanno looked down.

'That's unnecessary,' barked Bostar. 'Father has trained Hanno well. Hannibal himself picked him to lead a phalanx. His men are veterans. The chances of him fucking up are no greater than if I were in the centre.' He paused. 'Or you were.'

'What's that supposed to mean?' Sapho's eyes were mere slits.

'Stop it!' Hanno cried. 'You should both be ashamed of

438

yourselves. Hannibal gave us a job to do, remember? Let's just do it, please.'

Like sulky children, his brothers broke eye contact. In silence, they stalked off to stand before their phalanxes. Hanno waited for a moment before realising that it was up to him to lead the way. 'Form up, six men wide,' he ordered. 'Follow me.' He was pleased by his soldiers' rapid response. Many of them looked pleased by what had happened, which encouraged him further.

The three phalanxes deployed at the ford, in open order. Once they closed up, the spearmen would present a continuous front of overlapping shields. No horse would approach such an obstacle. The forest of spears protruding from it promised death by impalement to anyone foolish enough to try.

Hanno marched up and down, muttering encouraging words to his men. He was grateful that his father had advised him to recognise as many of his soldiers as possible. It was a simple ruse, yet not a man failed to grin when Hanno spoke to him by name. His efforts didn't take long, though, and soon time began to drag. Muscles that had been stirred into activity by their movement into position grew cold again. A damp breeze blew off the river, chilling the waiting soldiers to the bone. Allowing them to warm up was not an option, nor was singing, a common method of raising morale.

All they could do was wait.

Dawn came, but banks of lowering cloud concealed the sun. The sole sign of life was the occasional small bird fluttering among the trees' bare branches; the only sound the murmur of the river at their backs. Finally, Hanno's grumbling belly made him wonder if they should order an issue of rations. Before he could query this with his brothers, the sound of galloping hooves attracted everyone's attention. All eyes turned to the track leading west.

When two Numidians came thundering around the corner, there was a massed intake of breath.

'They're coming!' one shouted as he drew nearer.

'With five hundred of our comrades hot on their tails!' whooped the other.

Hanno scarcely heard. 'Close order!' he screamed. 'Ready spears!'

Chapter XXII: Face to Face

Quintus had hoped that his unease would dissipate as they left the Trebia behind them. Far from it. Each step that his horse took further into the empty landscape felt as final as if he had crossed the Styx to penetrate the depths of Hades itself. The eagerness he'd felt in his father's tent, with a belly full of wine, had totally vanished. Quintus said nothing, but a glance to either side confirmed that he was not alone in his feelings. The other riders' faces spoke volumes. Many were throwing filthy glances at Flaccus. Everyone knew that he was responsible for their misfortune.

At the front, Fabricius had no idea, or was choosing to ignore, what was going on. It was probably the latter, Quintus decided. These were some of the most experienced men in his command. Yet they were unhappy. Why had his father accepted the mission? Quintus cursed. The answer was startlingly simple. How would it look to Scipio if Fabricius had refused a duty like this? Terrible. Quintus eyed Flaccus sourly. If the fool hadn't put the idea in the consul's head, they'd all still be safe on the Roman side of the river. Guilt soon replaced Quintus' anger. By being so eager, he had probably helped push his father into accepting the suicide mission.

For, despite the fact that there was no sign of the enemy, that is what it felt like.

Quintus waited for only a short time before urging his horse forward to his father's position. Flaccus was riding alongside. He gave Quintus a broad wink. It wasn't entirely convincing.

He's frightened too, thought Quintus. That made up his mind.

Fabricius was intent on scanning the landscape. His rigid back told its own story. Quintus swallowed. 'Maybe this patrol was a bad idea, Father.' He ignored Flaccus' shocked reaction. 'We're visible for miles.'

Fabricius dragged his gaze around to Quintus. 'I know. Why do you think I'm keeping such a keen eye out?'

'But there's no sign of anyone,' protested Flaccus. 'Not even a bird!'

'For Jupiter's sake, that doesn't matter!' Fabricius snapped. 'All the Carthaginians need is one alert sentry. If there are any Numidians within five miles of here, they'll be after us within a dozen heartbeats of any alarm.'

Flaccus flinched. 'But we can't go back empty-handed.'

'Not without looking like fools, or cowards,' Fabricius agreed sourly.

They rode in silence for a few moments.

'There might be a way out,' Flaccus muttered.

Quintus was ashamed to feel a flutter of hope.

Fabricius laughed harshly. 'Not so keen now, are you?'

'Are you doubting my courage?' demanded Flaccus with an outraged look.

'Not your courage,' Fabricius growled. 'Your good judgement. Haven't you realised yet that Hannibal's cavalry are lethal? If we so much as see any, we're dead men.'

'Surely it's not that bad?' protested Flaccus.

'I should have refused this mission, regardless of how it looked to Scipio. Let you lead it on your own. If anyone would follow you, that is.'

Flaccus subsided into a sulky silence.

442

His father's outburst revealed the depths of his anger; Quintus was amazed.

Fabricius relented a fraction. 'So what's your bright idea? You might as well tell me.'

'We will report that the enemy cavalry was present in such numbers that we were unable to proceed far from the Trebia,' said Flaccus with bad grace. 'It's not cowardice to avoid annihilation. Who will gainsay us? Your men certainly won't talk about it, and no one else will be foolish enough to cross the river.'

'Your capacity for guile never ceases to amaze me,' snarled Fabricius.

'I . . .' Flaccus spluttered.

'But you're right. It's better to save the lives of thirty men in the way you suggest rather than throw them away through foolish pride. We will return at once.' Fabricius reined in his mount, and turned to issue the order to halt.

Quintus sagged down on to his horse's back. His relief lasted no more than a heartbeat. From some distance away came the unmistakable sound of galloping hooves.

The eyes of every man in the turma turned to the west.

A quarter of a mile distant, a tide of riders was emerging from behind a copse of trees.

'Numidians!' Fabricius screamed. 'About turn! Ride for your lives!'

His soldiers needed no urging.

Trying not to panic, Quintus did the same thing. The ambush might have been sprung early, but it remained to be seen if they could make it back to the Trebia before the enemy horsemen reached them.

It soon became clear that they would never reach the river in time. The Numidians were physically smaller than the Romans, and their mounts were faster. They were operating to a plan too. While some continued riding in direct pursuit from the south, others angled their path outwards and to the west, effectively hemming the patrol against the Trebia. The Romans had to flee northwards. Naturally, they made for the ford. There was no other option. It was the only one for miles in either direction.

'Get to the front,' Fabricius shouted at Quintus and Flaccus. 'Stay there. Stop for nothing.'

Flaccus obeyed without question, but Quintus held back. 'What about you?'

'I'm staying at the rear to prevent this becoming a complete rout,' snapped Fabricius. 'Now go!' His steely gaze brooked no argument.

Fighting back tears, Quintus urged his horse into a full gallop. It soon drew ahead of the other cavalrymen. Never had he been more glad of his father's insistence on taking the best mount available, or more ashamed that he could feel such relief. Quintus did not want to die like a rabbit chased down by a pack of dogs. With this dark thought fighting for supremacy, he leaned forward over his horse's neck and concentrated on one thing. Surviving. With luck, some of them would make it.

They had covered nearly a mile before the first Numidians had closed to within missile range. Riding bareback, half-clothed, the lithe, dark-skinned warriors did not look that threatening. Their javelins' accuracy proved otherwise. Every time Quintus looked around, another cavalryman had been struck, or fallen from his mount. Others had their horses injured, and were no longer able to keep up with their comrades. No one saw their swift and inevitable fate, yet their strangled cries followed in the survivors' wake, sending terror into their hearts. The Roman riders could not even respond. Their thrusting spears were not made to be thrown.

By the time Fabricius' men had covered another mile, the Numidians were attacking from three sides. Javelins were scudding in constantly, and Quintus could count only ten riders apart from himself, his father and Flaccus. At the bend in the track that led around and down to the ford, that number had been reduced to six. Desperately, Quintus urged his mount to even greater efforts. He didn't know why, but they seemed to have drawn slightly ahead of their pursuers. Perhaps they still had a chance? he wondered. With their horses' hooves throwing up showers of stones, they pounded around the corner and on to the straight stretch that led to the Trebia, a mere two hundred paces away.

All Quintus' hopes evaporated on the spot.

The tribesmen had held back in order to close the trap. Blocking the way ahead was a massed formation of spearmen. Their large, interlocking shields formed three sides of a square, leaving the open side towards him. Quintus' eyes flickered around in panic. A dense network of trees lined the right-hand side of the road. There was no escape there. On the left was a large area of boggy ground. Only a fool would try to ride across that, he thought.

Yet one of the cavalrymen took this second option. He swiftly learned his lesson. Within twenty paces, his horse was belly deep in glutinous sludge. When the rider tried to dismount, the same happened to him. Screaming with terror, he had soon sunk to his armpits. At last he stopped struggling, but it was too late. The best the man could hope for was an accurately thrown enemy javelin, thought Quintus bitterly. It was that, or drown in the mud.

Fabricius' voice snapped him back to the present. 'Slow down! Form a line,' he ordered in a stony voice. 'Let us meet our death like men.'

One of the five remaining cavalrymen began to make a low, keening noise in his throat.

Suddenly, Quintus' fear became overwhelming.

'Shut your fucking mouth!' Fabricius shouted. 'We are not cowards.'

To Quintus' amazement, the rider stopped wailing.

'Form a line,' Fabricius ordered again.

Moving together until their knees almost touched, the eight

men rode forward. Wondering why he hadn't had a javelin in the back by now, Quintus turned. The Numidians had slowed to a walk. We're being herded to the slaughter like so many sheep, he thought in disgust.

'Keep your eyes to the front,' Fabricius muttered. 'Show the whoresons that we are not afraid. We will look our fate in the eyes.'

About 150 paces separated the Romans from the phalanxes. To Quintus, the distance felt like an eternity. Part of him wished that the travesty would just end, but he was also desperate not to die. Inexorably, the gap narrowed. A hundred paces, then eighty. Terrified now, Quintus glanced at his father. All he received in the way of reassurance was a tight nod. Quintus took a deep breath, forcing himself to be calm.

I am a boy no longer. How I face my death is my decision alone. I will make it as brave an end as possible.

'Ready spears,' Fabricius ordered.

Quintus shot a look at Flaccus and was faintly pleased by his jutting chin. For all his arrogance, he was *not* a coward.

Sixty steps. They were nearing the distance of a long volley from the spearmen. As they crossed this invisible line, every one of the eight flinched. It was impossible not to. Yet nothing happened. Fabricius felt a new determination. They could ignore this torture if they wished. 'Let's take some of the bastards with us! At the trot. Choose your targets!' he yelled, pointing his spear at a bearded Libyan.

Relieved that the movements of his horse concealed his shaking arm, Quintus took aim at a man with a notched helmet. Let it be over soon, he prayed. May the gods look after Mother and Aurelia. He heard the shout of orders as the Carthaginian officers prepared their soldiers for a final volley, saw hundreds of men's torsos twist as their right arms went back. Quintus closed his eyes. The darkness this granted was somehow comforting. He was aware of his pounding heart, and his mount between his knees. Bounded on each side by its companions, it would not stray from its course. All he had to do was hold on.

'Quintus?' bellowed a voice.

With a jerk, Quintus opened his eyelids. That shout had come from within the Carthaginian ranks. He glanced at his father. 'Stop! You must stop!'

Something in Quintus' tone penetrated Fabricius' battle madness, and his fierce expression cleared. He raised his spear in the air. 'Halt!'

Pulling hard on their reins, the Romans screeched to a halt ten paces from the forest of bristling spear tips. Unsettled, their horses tried to shy away. More than one Libyan shoved his weapon forward in an attempt to reach them. Quintus heard a familiar voice cry out in Carthaginian. Goosebumps rose on his arms. Ignoring his companions' confusion, he scanned the enemy ranks. He couldn't believe it when Hanno, clad in a Carthaginian officer's uniform, elbowed his way out of the phalanx a moment later. Quintus lowered his spear. 'Hanno!'

'Quintus.' Hanno's tone was flat. He spoke in Latin. 'What are you doing here?'

'We were on a patrol,' he replied. 'A reconnaissance mission.'

Hanno made a sweeping gesture with his right arm. 'We control the whole plain. You must know that. What kind of fool would order an undertaking like that?'

'Our consul,' Quintus muttered. He wasn't going to reveal Flaccus' involvement.

Hanno gave a derisory snort. 'Enough said.'

Quintus had the sense not to reply. He glanced at his father and saw that he too had recognised Hanno. Sensibly, Fabricius also said nothing. Flaccus and the cavalrymen looked baffled, and fearful. Quintus turned back to Hanno. He tried to ignore the fierce stares of the enemy soldiers.

'Hanno!' cried an angry voice. A torrent of Carthaginian followed as two more officers emerged, one from the phalanx on either side. The first was short and burly, with thick eyebrows, while the other was tall and athletic, with long black hair. Their features were too similar to Hanno's to be coincidence. They had to be his brothers, thought Quintus. 'You found your family, then?'

'I did. And they want to know why you're still alive.' Turning to his siblings, Hanno launched into a long explanation. With his stomach knotted in tension, Quintus watched. Their very lives depended on what was said. There was plenty of shouting and gesticulating, but eventually Hanno seemed satisfied. The shorter of his brothers looked most unhappy, however. He continued muttering loudly as the taller brother approached the Romans. His face was hard, but not without kindness, thought Quintus warily. He had to be Bostar.

'Hanno says that he owes his life to you twice over,' Bostar said in accented Latin.

Quintus nodded. 'That's true.'

'For that reason, we have agreed not to slay you, or your father.' At this, Sapho launched into another tirade, but Bostar ignored him. 'Two lives for two debts.'

'And the others?' asked Quintus, feeling sick.

'They must die.'

'No,' Quintus muttered. 'Take them as prisoners. Please.'

Bostar shook his head and turned away.

Cries of fear rose from the cavalrymen. Flaccus, however, sat up straight on his horse, gazing with contempt at the Libyans.

Quintus' gaze shot to Hanno, and found no pity there. 'Show them some mercy.'

'We have our orders,' said Hanno in a harsh voice. 'But you and your father are free to go.' He snapped out a command, and the phalanx behind him split open, opening a passage to the ford.

An idea struck Quintus. 'There is one other family member here.'

Hanno turned. 'Who?' he demanded suspiciously.

448

Quintus indicated Flaccus. 'He is betrothed to Aurelia. Spare him also.'

Hanno's nostrils flared in belated recognition. 'If they are not married, he is not yet part of your family.'

'You would not deprive Aurelia of her prospective husband, surely?' Quintus pleaded.

Hanno was shocked to feel resentful. 'You ask for more than you know,' he said from between gritted teeth.

'I ask it nonetheless,' replied Quintus, meeting his gaze.

Hanno stalked closer to Flaccus. If the truth be known, he did not want to withdraw the hand of friendship so fast, but this *was* one of the enemy.

Incredibly, Flaccus spat a gob of phlegm at his feet.

Rage filled Hanno, and his hand fell to his sword. Before he could draw it, however, Sapho had stepped past. There was a spear gripped in his fists. Without saying a word, he shoved the blade deep into Flaccus' groin, below his armour, before ripping it out again. As his victim fell screaming to the ground, Sapho spun around. He aimed his bloody spear tip at Hanno. 'We're not here to be friendly with these fucking whoresons,' he snapped. 'You and Bostar might have overridden me over releasing two of them, but you're not setting another one free!'

Hanno pointed grimly at the ford. 'Go.'

Quintus stared helplessly at Flaccus, who was clutching his wound while blood spurted from between his fingers. There was already a large pool beneath him. We can't just leave the poor bastard to die, Quintus thought. But what other choice have we?

Fabricius took the initiative. 'May you meet each other in Elysium,' he muttered to the cavalrymen. 'Your family will be told that you died well,' he said to Flaccus. Then, without so much as a backward glance, he rode towards the river. 'Come on,' he hissed at Quintus.

Trying to think of what to say, Quintus took a last look at Hanno. Rather than meet his gaze, the Carthaginian stared right through him. There was to be no farewell. Gritting his teeth, Quintus followed his father. At once his ears were filled with the cries of the five unfortunate cavalrymen, who were promptly surrounded and dispatched by the clamouring Libyans.

Father and son made their way unhindered to the ford, and into the water.

On the other side, it finally sank in that they had escaped.

A long, shuddering breath escaped Quintus' lips. Never let me meet Hanno again, he prayed. His former friend *would* try to kill him: there was no doubt about that. And Quintus realised that he would do the same. As cold misery gripped his heart, he stared back across the river. The Libyans were already marching away. They had left the crumpled forms of the Roman dead on the riverbank. The sight caused Quintus' shame to soar. Everyone deserved to be buried, or burned on a pyre. 'Maybe we can retrieve the bodies tomorrow,' he muttered.

'We'll have to try, or I'll never be able to look Aurelia in the eyes again,' replied his father. *And the moment that the damn moneylenders hear that Flaccus is dead, they'll be all over me like a rash.* He glanced at Quintus. 'It's all my damn fault. Flaccus and thirty good men are dead, because I agreed to lead the damn patrol. I should have refused.'

'It's not up to you to make tactical decisions, Father,' Quintus protested. 'If you'd said no, Scipio could have demoted you to the ranks, or worse.'

Fabricius shot Quintus a grateful look. 'I'm only alive because of you. Helping the Carthaginian to escape and then manumitting him were good decisions. I'm grateful.'

Quintus nodded sadly. His friendship with Hanno might have saved their lives, but this was not the way he'd have wanted it to end. There was nothing he could do to change things, however. Quintus hardened his heart. Hanno was one of the enemy now.

* * *

Fabricius rode straight back to the camp, and from there to the consul's command tent. Leaping from his horse, he threw his reins at one of the sentries and started towards the entrance. Quintus watched miserably from the back of his mount. Scipio would not want to speak to a low-ranking cavalryman such as he.

His father stopped by the tent flap. 'Well?'

'You want me to come in?'

Fabricius laughed. 'Of course. You are the sole reason we're still breathing. Scipio will want to hear why.'

Re-energised, Quintus jumped down and joined his father. The sentries at the entrance, four sturdy *triarii* – veterans – wearing highly polished crested helmets and mail shirts, stood to attention as they passed. Quintus' chest swelled with pride. He was about to meet the consul! Until now, his only interactions with Scipio had been to salute and return a polite greeting.

They were ushered through various sections of the tent by a junior officer until they reached a comfortable area lined with carpets. The space was lit by large bronze lamps and contained a desk covered in parchments, ink pots and quills, various iron-bound chests and several luxurious couches. Bolstered by cushions, Scipio was reclining on the biggest. His face was still an unhealthy grey colour, and bulky dressings were visible on his injured leg. His son stood attentively behind him, reading from a half-unrolled manuscript. Scipio's eyes opened as they approached, and he acknowledged their salutes. 'Well met, Fabricius,' he murmured. 'Is that your son?'

'Yes, sir.'

'What's his name again?'

'Quintus, sir.'

'Ah, yes. So, you have returned from your patrol. Did you meet with any success?'

'No, sir,' Fabricius replied tersely. 'In fact, the complete opposite. Before getting anywhere near the Carthaginian camp, we were ambushed by a hugely superior enemy force. They pursued us right to the riverbank, where a strong force of spearmen was waiting.' He indicated Quintus. 'We are the only survivors.'

'I see.' Scipio's fingers drummed on the arm of his couch. 'How is it that you were not also killed?'

Fabricius met the consul's scrutiny with a solid gaze. 'Because of Quintus here.'

Scipio's brows lowered. 'Explain.'

Prompted by his father's nudge, Quintus told the story of how he had been recognised by a former slave of the family, whom he had befriended. He faltered when it came to explaining how Hanno had been freed, but encouraged by Scipio's nod, Quintus revealed everything.

'That is an incredible tale,' Scipio acknowledged. 'The gods were most merciful.'

'Yes, sir,' Quintus agreed fervently.

The consul looked up at his son. 'You're not the only one able to rescue his father,' he joked.

The younger Scipio blushed bright red.

Scipio's face turned serious. 'So, a whole turma has been wiped out, and we know no more about Hannibal's disposition than yesterday.'

'That's correct, sir,' Fabricius admitted.

'I see little point in sending further patrols across the Trebia. They would meet the same fate, and we have few enough cavalry as it is,' said Scipio. He pressed a finger against his lips, thinking. Then he shook his head. 'Our main priority is to block the passage south, which we are already doing. The Carthaginians will not attack us here, because of the uneven terrain. Nothing has changed. We wait for Longus.'

'Yes, sir,' Fabricius concurred.

'Very good. You may go.' Scipio waved a hand in dismissal.

Father and son made a discreet exit.

Quintus managed to contain his frustration until they were out of earshot. 'Why doesn't Scipio *do* something?' he hissed.

'You want revenge for what happened at the ford, eh?' asked Fabricius with a wry smile. 'I do too.' He bent close to Quintus' ear. 'I'm sure that Scipio would have moved against Hannibal again if he weren't . . . incapacitated. Of course he's not going to admit that to the likes of us. For the moment, we just have to live with it.'

'Will Longus want to fight Hannibal?'

'I'd say so,' replied his father with a grin. 'A victory before the turn of the year would show the tribes that Hannibal is vulnerable. It would also reduce the number of warriors who plan on joining him. Defeating him soon would be far better than leaving it until the spring.'

Quintus prayed that his father was correct. After all the setbacks they'd suffered, it was time for the tables to be turned. The quicker that was done, the better.

Chapter XXIII: Battle Commences

Bostar waited until they'd got back to the Carthaginian camp before he launched his attack. The moment that their men had been stood down, he rounded on Hanno. 'What the hell was that about?' he shouted. 'Don't you remember our orders? We were supposed to kill them all!'

'I know,' muttered Hanno. The sad image of Quintus and his father riding down to the Trebia was vivid in his mind's eye. 'How, though, could I kill the person who had saved my life, not once, but twice?'

'So your sense of honour is more important than a direct order given by Hannibal?' Sapho sneered.

'Yes. No. I don't know,' Hanno replied. 'Leave me alone!'

'Sapho!' Bostar snapped.

Sapho raised his hands and stepped back. 'Let's see what the general says when we report to him.' He made a face. 'I presume that you are going to tell him?'

Hanno felt a towering fury take hold. 'Of course I am!' he cried. 'I've got nothing to hide. What, were you going to tell Hannibal if I didn't?' His mouth opened as Sapho flushed. 'Sacred Tanit, you fucking were! Where did you get to be so poisonous? No wonder Bostar doesn't like you any more.' He saw Sapho's shock, and despite his anger, felt instant shame. 'I shouldn't have said that. I'm sorry.'

'It's a bit late,' retorted Sapho. 'Why should I be surprised that you've been talking about me behind my back? You little dirtbag!'

Hanno flushed and hung his head.

'I'll see you at the general's tent,' said Sapho sourly. 'We'll see what Hannibal thinks of what you've done then.' Pulling his cloak tighter around himself, he walked away.

'Sapho! Come back!' Hanno shouted.

'Let him go,' advised Bostar.

'Why is he being like that?'

'I don't know,' said Bostar, looking away.

Now you're the one who's lying, thought Hanno, but he didn't have the heart to interrogate his older brother. Soon he would have to explain his actions to Hannibal. 'Come on,' he said anxiously. 'We'd best get this over with.'

Hanno was relieved to find that Sapho had not entered Hannibal's tent, but was waiting outside for them. Zamar, the Numidian officer, was there too. Announcing themselves to the guards, they were ushered inside.

Hanno slipped to Sapho's side. 'Thank you.'

Sapho gave him a startled look. 'For what?'

'Not going in to tell your version of the story first.'

'I might disagree with what you did, but I'm not a telltale,' Sapho shot back in an angry whisper.

'I know,' said Hanno. 'Let's just see what Hannibal says, eh? After that, we can forget about it.'

'No more talking about me behind my back,' Sapho warned.

'It's not as if Bostar said much. He commented that after the pirates' capture, you had changed.'

'Changed?'

'Grown tougher. Harder.'

'Nothing else?' Sapho demanded.

'No.' What in Tanit's name happened between you two? Hanno wondered. He wasn't sure he wanted to know.

Sapho was silent for a moment. 'Very well. We'll put it behind us after we've reported to Hannibal. But understand this: if he asks me my opinion about the release of the two Romans, I'm not going to lie to him.'

'That's fine,' said Hanno heatedly. 'I wouldn't want you to.'

Their conversation came to an abrupt halt as they entered the main part of Hannibal's tent.

The general greeted them with a broad smile. 'Word of your success has already reached me,' he declared. He raised his glass. 'Come, taste this wine. For a Roman vintage, it's quite palatable.'

When they all had a glass in hand, Hannibal looked at them each in turn. 'Well?' he enquired. 'Who's going to tell me what happened?'

Hanno stepped forward. 'I will, sir,' he said, swallowing.

Hannibal's eyebrows rose, but he indicated that Hanno should continue.

Shoving away his nervousness, Hanno described their march to the Trebia, and the long wait in the hidden clearing. When he got to the point where the Roman patrol had crossed, he turned to Zamar. The Numidian related how his men had carried word to him of the enemy incursion, and of how the ambush had been sprung early by an overeager section leader. 'I've already stripped him to the ranks, sir,' he said. 'Thanks to him, the whole thing might have been a disaster.'

'But it wasn't, thankfully,' Hannibal replied. 'Did any make it to the river?'

'Yes, sir,' said Zamar. 'Eight.'

Hannibal winked. 'That didn't leave much work for nine hundred spearmen!'

They all laughed.

'Did you find any documents on the Roman commander?'

Hanno didn't know how to answer. 'No, sir,' he muttered. From the corner of his eye, he could see Sapho glaring at him.

Hannibal didn't notice Hanno's reticence. 'A shame. Still, never mind. It's unlikely that they would carry anything of importance on such a mission anyway.'

Hanno coughed awkwardly. 'I didn't manage to search him, sir.'

'Why not?' asked Hannibal, frowning.

'Because I let him go, sir. Along with one other.'

The general's eyes widened in disbelief. 'You had best explain yourself, son of Malchus. *Fast.*'

Hannibal's intense stare was unnerving. 'Yes, sir.' Hanno hastily began. When he had finished, there was a pregnant silence. Hanno thought he was going to be sick.

Hannibal eyed Sapho and Bostar askance. 'Presumably, he consulted with you two,' he snapped.

'Yes, sir,' they mumbled.

'What was your reaction, Bostar?'

'Although it was against your orders, sir, I respected his reason for wanting to let the two men go.'

Hannibal looked at Sapho.

'I violently disagreed, sir, but I was overruled.'

Hannibal regarded Zamar. 'And you?'

'I had nothing to do with it, sir,' the Numidian replied neutrally. 'I was a hundred paces away with my men.'

'Interesting,' said Hannibal to Hanno. 'One brother supported you, one did not.'

'Yes, sir.'

'Is this what I am to expect in future when I issue a command?' demanded Hannibal, his nostrils flaring.

'No, sir,' protested Bostar and Hanno. 'Of course not,' Hanno added.

Hannibal didn't comment further. 'Do I detect that there was quite an amount of disagreement?'

Hanno flushed. 'You do, sir.'

'Why was that?'

'Because we were given orders to let none survive, sir!' cried Sapho.

'Finally, we come back to the nub of the issue,' said Hannibal. In the background, Sapho smiled triumphantly. 'Under ordinary circumstances, this situation would be black and white. And if you'd disobeyed my orders as you have done, I would have had you crucified.'

His words hung in the air like a bad smell.

Fear twisted Sapho's face. 'Sir, I . . .' he began.

'Did I ask you to speak?' Hannibal snapped.

'No, sir.'

'Then keep your mouth shut!'

Humbled, Sapho obeyed.

Hanno wiped his brow, which was covered in sweat. I still did the right thing, he thought. I owed Quintus my life. Sure that, at the very least, a severe punishment was about to follow, he resigned himself to his fate. Beside him, Bostar was clenching and unclenching his jaw.

'Yet what transpired happens but once in a host of lifetimes,' said Hannibal.

Stunned, Hanno waited to hear what his general said next.

'A man can't go killing those who have helped him, even if they are Roman. I cannot think of a better way to anger the gods.' Hannibal gave Hanno a grim nod. 'You did the right thing.'

'Thank you, sir,' whispered Hanno. He'd never been so relieved in his life.

'I will let you off, Bostar, because of the unique nature of what happened.'

Bostar stood rigidly to attention and saluted. 'Thank you, sir!'

Hanno glanced at Sapho. His fear had been replaced by a poorly concealed expression of resentment. Did he want us to be punished? Hanno wondered uneasily.

'As well as satisfying your honour, your lenient gesture fulfilled another purpose,' Hannibal continued. 'Those two men will speak of little but the excellence of our troops. Some of their comrades will be demoralised by what they hear, which helps our cause. Despite your disobedience, you have achieved the result I wanted.'

'Yes, sir.'

'That's not all,' said Hannibal lightly.

Hanno's fear returned with a vengeance. 'Sir?'

'There can be no repeat of such behaviour.' Hannibal's voice had grown hard. 'You have paid off your obligation to this *Quintus*. Should you see either him or his father again, you can act in only one way.'

He's right, screamed Hanno's common sense. How can I remain friends with a Roman? Despite everything, his heart felt differently. 'Yes, sir.'

'Trust me, those men would bury a sword in your belly as soon as look at you. They are the enemy,' growled Hannibal. 'If you meet either again, you will kill them.'

'Yes, sir,' Hanno said, finally giving in. *But never let it happen.*

'Understand too that if any of you disobey my orders again, I will *not* be merciful. Instead, expect to end your miserable lives screaming on a cross. Understand?'

'Yes, sir,' replied Hanno, shaking.

'You're dismissed,' said Hannibal curtly. 'All of you.'

Muttering their thanks, Zamar and the three brothers withdrew.

Sapho sidled up to Hanno outside. 'Still think you did the right thing?' he hissed.

'Eh?' Hanno gave his brother an incredulous look.

'We could all be dead now, thanks to you.'

'But we're not! And it's not as if such a thing will ever happen again, is it?' demanded Hanno.

'I suppose not,' Sapho admitted, taken aback by Hanno's fury.

'I'm as loyal as you or any man in the damn army,' Hanno snarled. 'Line me up some Romans, and I'll chop off all their fucking heads!'

'All right, all right,' muttered Sapho. 'You've made your point.'

'So have you,' retorted Hanno angrily. 'Did you want us to be punished in there?'

Sapho made an apologetic gesture. 'Look, I had no idea he might crucify you.'

'Would you have said anything to Hannibal if you had?' challenged Bostar.

A guilty look stole across Sapho's face. 'No.'

'You're a fucking liar,' said Bostar. Without another word, he walked off.

Hanno glared at Sapho. 'Well?'

'Do you really think I'd want the two of you to die? Please!' Sapho protested. 'Have some faith in me!'

Hanno sighed. 'I do. I'm sorry.'

'So am I,' said Sapho, clapping him on the shoulder. 'Let's forget about it, eh? Concentrate on fighting the Romans.'

'Yes.' Hanno glanced after Bostar, and his heart sank. His other brother looked angered by the friendly gesture Sapho had just made. Gods above, he thought in frustration, can I not get on with the two of them?

It appeared not.

Saturnalia was fast approaching. Despite Atia and Aurelia's melancholy, preparations for the midwinter festival were well under way. It was a way, Aurelia realised, of coping with the void both of them felt inside at her father's probable death, and the lack of word from Quintus. Life had to go on in some fashion, and losing themselves in mundane tasks had proved to be an effective method of maintaining normality. There was so much to be done that the short winter days flashed by in a blur. Atia's list of things to do seemed never-ending. Each evening, Aurelia was worn out, and grateful that her exhaustion meant deep slumber without any bad dreams.

One night, however, Aurelia did not fall asleep as usual. Her mind was racing. She and her mother were going to Capua in two days on a final shopping expedition. Dozens of candles were still required as gifts for their family friends and the guests. Not all of the food for their impending feasts had been ordered yet – there had been a mix-up with the baker over what was needed, and the butcher wanted far too much money for his meat. Atia also wanted to purchase pottery figurines; these were exchanged on the last day of the celebrations.

Despite her best efforts, Aurelia found herself thinking about Suniaton. After meeting Agesandros, she and Elira had made their way to the hut without any difficulty. Pleasingly, Suni's leg had healed enough for him to leave. He's long gone, thought Aurelia sadly. Suniaton had been her last link with Hanno, and in a strange way, Quintus and her father. It was entirely possible that she would never see any of them again. On the spur of the moment, she decided to visit the isolated dwelling one more time. What for, Aurelia wasn't sure. Perhaps the gods would offer her some kind of sign there. Something that would make her grief more bearable. Keeping this idea to the forefront of her mind, she managed to fall asleep.

Waking early the next morning, Aurelia dressed in her warmest clothes. She was relieved to find only a finger's depth of snow covering the statues and mosaic floor in the courtyard. Pausing to tell a sleepy Elira where she was going, and to raise the alarm if she was not back by nightfall, Aurelia went to the stables and readied her father's grey horse.

She had never ridden so far from the farm in the depths of winter before, and was stunned by the beauty of the silent country-side. It was such a contrast to the spring and summer, when everything was bursting with life. Most of the trees had lost their leaves, scattering them in thick layers upon the ground, layers that were now frozen beneath a light covering of snow. The only movement was the occasional flash of wildlife: a pair of crows tumbling through the air in pursuit of a falcon, the suggestion of a deer in the distance. Once, Aurelia thought she saw a jackal skulking off into the undergrowth. Gratifyingly, she heard no wolves, and saw no sign of their spoor. Although it was rare for the large predators to attack humans, it was not unheard of. The chances of seeing them grew as she climbed, however, and Aurelia was grateful that she had taken a bow as well as her sling.

Her anticipation grew as she neared the hut. Its peaceful atmosphere would assuage her worries about her loved ones. With a growing sense of excitement, Aurelia tied up her horse outside. She scattered a handful of oats on the ground to keep it happy, and stepped towards the door. A faint sound from inside stopped her dead. Terror paralysed Aurelia's every muscle as she remembered the bandits whom Quintus and Hanno had fought. What had she been thinking to travel alone?

Turning on her heel, Aurelia tiptoed away from the hut. If she made it onto her saddle blanket, there was a good chance of escaping. Few men possessed the skill with a bow to bring down a rider on a galloping horse. She had almost reached her mount when it looked up from its oats, and gave her a pleased whinny. Frantically stroking its head to silence it, Aurelia listened. All she could hear was her heart pounding in her chest like that of a captured beast. Taking a good grip of the horse's mane, she prepared to scramble on to its back.

'Hello?'

Aurelia nearly jumped out of her skin with fright.

A moment passed. The door did not open.

Aurelia managed to calm herself. The voice had been weak and quavering, and certainly not that of a strong, healthy man. Gradually, her curiosity began to equal her fear. 'Who's there? I'm not alone.'

There was no response.

Aurelia began to wonder if it was a trap after all. She vacillated, torn between riding to safety and checking that whoever was inside did not need help. At length, she decided not to flee. If this was an ambush, it was the worst-laid one she could think of. Gripping her dagger to give her confidence, she padded towards the hut. There was no handle or latch, just a gap in the timbers to pull open the portal. With trembling fingers, Aurelia flipped the door towards her, placing her foot against the bottom edge to hold it ajar. She peered cautiously into the dim interior. Instead of the fire she might have expected, the round stone fireplace was full of ashes. Aurelia gagged as the acrid smell of human urine and faeces wafted outside.

Finally, she made out a figure lying sprawled on the floor. She had taken it first for a bundle of rags. When it moved, she screamed. 'S-Suni?'

His eyes opened wide. 'Is that you, Aurelia?'

'Yes, it is.' She darted inside and dropped to her knees by his side. 'Oh, Suniaton!' She struggled not to weep.

'Have you any water?'

'Better than that: I have wine!' Aurelia ran outside, returning with her supplies. Gently, she helped him to sit up and drink a few mouthfuls.

'That's better,' Suniaton declared. A tinge of colour began to appear in his cheeks, and he cast greedy eyes at Aurelia's bag.

Delighted by his revival, she laid out some bread and cheese. 'Eat a little at a time,' she warned. 'Your stomach won't be able to take any more.' She sat and watched him as he devoured the food. 'Why didn't you leave after my last visit?'

He paused between mouthfuls. 'I did, the next day. About half a mile down the track, I tripped over a jutting tree root and landed awkwardly. The fall tore the muscles that had just healed in my bad leg. I couldn't walk ten steps without screaming, never mind reach Capua or the coast. It was all I could do to crawl back to the hut. My food ran out more than a week ago, and my water two days after that.' He pointed at the hole in the roof. 'If it hadn't been for the snow that came through that, I would have died of thirst.' He smiled. 'They took their time, but the gods answered my prayers.'

Aurelia squeezed his hand. 'They did. Something told me to come up here. Obviously, you were the reason why.'

'But I can't stay here,' Suniaton said despairingly. 'One heavy fall of snow and the roof will give way.'

'Don't worry,' Aurelia cried. 'My horse can carry both of us.'

His expression was bleak. 'Where to, though? My leg will take months to heal, if it does at all.'

'To the farm,' she replied boldly. 'I will tell Mother and Agesandros that I found you wandering in the woods. I couldn't just leave you to die.'

'He might remember me,' Suniaton protested.

She squeezed his hand. 'He won't. You look terrible. Totally different from that day in Capua.'

Suniaton scowled. 'It's obvious that I am an escaped slave.'

'But there won't be any way of proving who you are,' Aurelia cried in triumph. 'You can act mute.'

'Will that work?' he asked with a dubious frown.

'Of course,' Aurelia declared robustly. 'And when you're better, you can leave.'

A spark of hope lit in Suniaton's weary eyes. 'If you're sure,' he whispered.

'I am,' Aurelia replied, patting his hand. Inside, however, she was terrified.

What other choice had they, though? her mind screamed.

More than two weeks later, Quintus was wandering through the camp with Calatinus and Cincius. The general mood had been improved dramatically seven days before by the arrival of Tiberius Sempronius Longus, the second consul. His army, which consisted of two legions and more than 10,000 socii, infantry and cavalry, had swelled the Roman forces to nearly 40,000 men.

Inevitably enough, the trio found their feet taking them in the direction of the camp headquarters. So far, there had been little news of what Longus, who had assumed control of all Republican forces, planned to do about Hannibal.

'He'll have been encouraged by what happened yesterday,' declared Calatinus. 'Our cavalry and velites gave the guggas a hiding that they won't forget in a hurry.'

'Stupid bastards got what was coming to them,' said Cincius. 'The Gauls are supposed to be their allies. If they go pillaging local settlements, it's natural that the tribesmen will come looking for help.'

'There were heavy enemy casualties,' Quintus admitted, 'but I'm not sure it was the total victory Longus is claiming.'

Both of his friends looked at him in astonishment.

'Think about it,' urged Quintus. It was what his father had said to him when he'd raved about the engagement. 'We had the upper hand from the start, but things changed immediately once Hannibal came on the scene. The Carthaginians held their ground then, didn't they?'

'So what?' Cincius responded. 'They lost three times more men than we did!'

'Aren't you pleased that we finally got the better of them?' demanded Calatinus.

'Of course I am,' said Quintus. 'We shouldn't underestimate Hannibal, that's all.'

Cincius snorted derisively. 'Longus is an experienced general. And in my book, any man who can march his army more than a thousand miles in less than six weeks shows considerable ability.'

'You've seen Longus a few times since his arrival. The man positively exudes energy,' added Calatinus. 'He's keen for a fight too.'

'You're right,' said Quintus at last. 'Our troops are better fed, and better armed than Hannibal's. We outnumber the Carthaginians too.'

'We just need the right opportunity,' declared Cincius.

'That will come,' said Calatinus. 'All the recent omens have been good.'

Quintus grinned. It was impossible not to feel enthused by his friends' words, and the recent change in their fortunes. As always when Quintus thought of the enemy, an image of Hanno popped into his mind. He shoved it away.

There was a war on.

Friendship with a Carthaginian had no place in his heart any longer.

Several days passed, and the weather grew dramatically worse. The biting wind came incessantly from the north, bringing with it heavy showers of sleet and snow. Combined with the shortened daylight, it made for a miserable existence. Hanno saw little of either his father or brothers. The Carthaginian soldiers huddled in their tents, shivering and trying to stay warm. Even venturing outside to answer a call of nature meant getting soaked to the skin or chilled to the bone.

Hanno was stunned, therefore, by the news that Sapho brought one afternoon. 'We've had word from Hannibal!' he hissed. 'We move out tonight.'

'In weather like this?' asked Hanno incredulously. 'Are you mad?'

'Maybe.' Sapho grinned. 'If I am, though, so too is Hannibal. He has ordered Mago himself to lead us.'

'You and Bostar?'

Sapho nodded grimly. 'Plus five hundred skirmishers, and a thousand Numidian cavalry.'

Hanno smiled to cover his disappointment at not also being picked. 'Where are you going?'

'While we've been hiding in our tents, Hannibal has been scouting the whole area. He discovered a narrow river that runs across the plain,' Sapho revealed. 'It's bounded on both sides by steep, heavily overgrown banks. We have to lie in wait there until the opportunity comes – if it comes – to fall upon the Roman rear.'

'What makes Hannibal think that they'll cross the river?'

Sapho's expression grew fierce. 'He plans to irritate them into doing so.'

'That means using the Numidians,' guessed Hanno.

'You've got it. They're going to attack the enemy camp at dawn. Sting and withdraw, sting and withdraw. You know the way they do it.'

'Will it drag the whole Roman army out of camp, though?'

'We'll see.'

'I wish I'd been chosen too,' said Hanno fervently.

Sapho chuckled. 'Save your regrets. The whole damn enter-prise might be a waste of time. While Bostar and I are freezing our balls off in a ditch, you and the rest of the army will be warmly wrapped up in your blankets. And if a battle does look likely, it's not as if you'll miss out, is it? We'll all have to fight!'

A grin slowly spread across Hanno's face. 'True enough.'

'We'll meet in the middle of the Roman line!' declared Sapho. 'Just think of that moment.'

Hanno nodded. It was an appealing image. 'The gods watch over you both,' he said. I must go and speak to Bostar, he thought. Say goodbye.

'And you, little brother.' Sapho reached out and ruffled Hanno's hair, something he hadn't done for years.

Quintus was in the middle of a fantasy about Elira when he became aware of someone shaking him. He did his best to stay asleep, but the insistent tugging on his arm proved too much. Opening his eyes irritably, Quintus found not Elira, but Calatinus crouched over him. Before he could utter a word of rebuke, he heard the trumpets sounding the alarm over and over. He sat bolt upright. 'What's going on?'

'Our outposts beyond the camp perimeter are under attack. Get up!'

The last of Quintus' drowsiness vanished. 'Eh? What time is it?'

'Not long after dawn. The sentries started shouting when I was in the latrines.' Calatinus scowled. 'Didn't help my diarrhoea, I can tell you.'

Smiling at the image, Quintus threw off the covers and began scrambling into his clothes. 'Have we had any orders yet?'

'Longus wants every man ready to leave a quarter of an hour ago,' replied Calatinus, who was already fully dressed. 'I've been shouting at you to no avail. The others are readying their mounts.'

'Well, I'm here now,' muttered Quintus, kneeling to strap on his sandals.

Before long, they had joined their comrades outside, by their tethered horses.

It was bitterly cold, and the north wind was whipping vicious little flurries of snow across the tent tops. The camp was in uproar as thousands of men scrambled to get ready. It wasn't just the cavalry who had been ordered to prepare themselves for battle. Large groups of velites were being addressed by their officers. Unhappy-looking *hastati* and *principes* – the men who stood in the legion's first two ranks – left their breakfasts to burn on their campfires as they ran to get their equipment. Messengers hurried to and fro, relaying information between different units. On the battlements, the trumpeters kept up their clarion call to arms. Quintus swallowed nervously. Was this the moment he had been waiting for? It certainly felt like it. Soon after, he was relieved to see his father's figure striding towards them from the direction of the camp's headquarters. Excited murmurs rippled through the surrounding cavalrymen. As one, they stiffened to attention.

'This is no parade. At ease,' said Fabricius, waving a hand. 'We ride out at once. Longus is deploying our entire cavalry force, as well as six thousand velites. He wants this attack thrown back across the Trebia without delay. We're taking no more nonsense from Hannibal.'

'And the rest of the army, sir?' cried a voice. 'What about them?'

Fabricius smiled tightly. 'They will be ready to follow us very soon.'

These words produced a rousing cheer. Quintus joined in. He wanted this victory as much as anyone else. The fact that his father hadn't mentioned Scipio must mean that the injured consul agreed with his colleague's decision, or had been overruled by him. Either way, they weren't going to sit by and do nothing.

Fabricius waited until the noise had died down. 'Remember to do everything I've taught you. Check your horse's harness is tightly fastened. Take a leak before you mount up. There's nothing worse than pissing yourself in the middle of a fight.' Hoots of nervous laughter met this comment, and Fabricius smiled. 'Ensure that your spear tip is sharp. Tie the chinstrap on your helmet. Watch each other's backs.' He scanned the faces around him with grave eyes. 'May the gods be with you all.'

'And with you, sir!' shouted Calatinus.

Fabricius inclined his head in recognition. Then, giving Quintus a reassuring look, he made towards his horse.

For the third time since dawn, Bostar scrambled up the muddy slope towards the sentry's position. More than anything, he wanted to warm up. Unfortunately, the climb wasn't long enough to shift the chill from his muscles. He glanced down at the steep-sided riverbank below him. It was filled with Mago's men: 1,000 Numidians and their horses, and 1,000 infantry, a mixture of Libyan skirmishers and spearmen. Despite the fact that the warmly dressed soldiers were packed as tightly as apples in a barrel, it seemed an eternity since they had arrived. In fact, it was barely five hours. Men are not supposed to spend a winter's night outdoors in this godforsaken land, thought Bostar bitterly.

His bones ached at the idea of the warm sunshine that bathed Carthage daily.

Reaching the top of the bank, Bostar crouched down, using the scrubby bushes that regularly dotted the ground as cover. He peered into the distance, but saw nothing. There had been no movement since the Numidian cavalry had quietly passed by, heading for the Roman side of the river. Bostar sighed. It would be hours before anything of importance happened. Nonetheless, he had to keep his guard up. Hannibal had given them the most important task of any soldiers in his army. For what felt like the thousandth time, Bostar slowly turned in a circle, scanning the landscape with eagle eyes.

The watercourse that formed their hiding place was a small tributary of the Trebia, and ran north–south across the plain that lay before the Carthaginian camp. Following Hannibal's instructions, they had secreted themselves half a mile to the south of the area upon which he wished to fight. The general's reasons were simple. Behind them, the ground began to climb towards the low hills that filled the horizon. If the Romans took the bait, they were unlikely to march in this direction. It was a good place to hide, thought Bostar. He just hoped that Hannibal's plan worked, and that they weren't too far away from the fighting if, or when, the time came to move.

He found Mago lying alongside the sentry in a shallow dip, seemingly oblivious to the cold. Bostar liked the youngest Barca brother. Like Hannibal, Mago was charismatic and brave. He was also indomitably cheerful, which provided a counterweight to Hannibal's sometimes serious disposition. Smaller than Hannibal, Mago reminded Bostar of a hunting dog: lean, muscular and always eager to be slipped from the leash. 'Seen anything, sir?' he whispered.

Mago turned his head. 'Restless, aren't you?'

Bostar shrugged. 'The same as everyone else, sir. It's difficult waiting down there without a clue what's going on.'

Mago smiled. 'Patience,' he said. 'The Romans will come.'

'How can you be sure, sir?'

'Because Hannibal believes that they will, and I trust in him.'

Bostar nodded. It was a good answer, he thought. 'We'll be ready, sir.'

'I know you will. That's why Hannibal picked you and your brother,' Mago replied.

'We're very grateful for the opportunity, sir,' said Bostar, thinking sour thoughts about Sapho. He and his older brother hadn't spoken since Hannibal's reprimand. Bostar felt regret that he'd only had the briefest of words with Hanno before they'd left the camp. He'd been angry that his younger brother seemed to be friendly with Sapho. Really, it was none of his business.

Mago got to his feet. 'Have the men eaten yet?'

'No, sir.'

'Well, if I'm famished, they must be too,' Mago declared. 'Let's break out the rations. It won't be a hot breakfast, like the lucky dogs back at camp will get, but anything's better than nothing. A man with a full belly sees the world with different eyes, eh?' He glanced at the sentry. 'You won't miss out. I'll send someone up to relieve you soon.'

The man grinned. 'Thank you, sir.'

'Lead on,' Mago said.

Bostar obeyed. Mention of the encampment brought his father and Hanno to mind. If it came to a battle, they would be in the front line. Not quite in the centre – that honour had been given to Hannibal's new recruits, the Gaulish tribesmen – but still in a dangerous position. The fighting everywhere would be intense. He sighed. The gods protect us all, he prayed. If it comes to it, let us die well.

Combining his riders with Scipio's depleted horsemen gave Sempronius Longus just over four thousand cavalry. The moment that the assembled turmae had heard their orders, they were sent out from behind the protection of the fortifications. Fabricius and his men were among the first to exit the camp.

Quintus blinked with surprise. Beyond the sentry posts lay open ground that rolled down to the river. It was normally empty of all but the figures of training soldiers or returning patrols. Now, it was occupied by thousands of Numidian tribesmen. Waves of yelling warriors were galloping into the Roman positions and loosing their javelins, before wheeling their horses in a tight circle and retreating. The unfortunate sentries, who only numbered four or five per outpost, received no respite. Scarcely had one set of Numidians disappeared before another arrived, whooping and screaming at the top of their lungs.

'Form a battle line!' Fabricius shouted. His call was already being echoed by other officers who were emerging from the camp.

With a pounding heart, Quintus obeyed. So did Calatinus, Cincius and his comrades, each turma fanning out six ranks wide and five riders deep. The instant they were ready, Fabricius shouted, 'Charge!'

His men went from the trot into a canter. This was followed immediately by a gallop. For maximum impact, they had to hit the Numidians at full speed. That was if the enemy riders stayed to fight, thought Quintus suspiciously. His experience with the fierce tribesmen had taught him otherwise. Yet Longus was doing the right thing. He could not just let his sentries be massacred within sight of his camp. Hannibal's men had to be driven off. With six thousand velites following hot on their heels, that would not be difficult.

The thunder of hundreds of hooves drowned out all sound except the occasional encouraging shout from Fabricius: 'Forward!' As they closed in, each man let go of his reins and transferred the spear from his left hand, which also held his shield, to his right. From here on in, they would guide their horses with their knees. Now the months of careful instruction they had received would pay off. For all his comrades' skill, Quintus was still wary of the Numidians, who learned to ride almost before they could walk. He was heartened by the thought of the velites. Their help would make all the difference.

'Look! They've seen us!' shouted Calatinus, pointing at the beleaguered sentries, whose terrified expressions were being replaced by elation. 'Hold on!'

'The poor bastards must have got the shock of their lives when the Numidians suddenly appeared,' replied Quintus.

'We're coming none too soon,' Calatinus added. 'Many of the outposts have no defenders left.'

They had closed to within fifty paces of the enemy.

'Time to even up the score,' cried Quintus, picking out a slight Numidian with braided hair as his target.

Cincius' lip curled. 'They'll turn and run any moment now, the way they always do.'

Instead, to their amazement, the enemy riders turned and began driving their horses straight at the Roman cavalry.

'They're going to fight, not run.' Quintus felt faintly nauseous, but he kept his eye on the Numidian, who was riding straight at him. Oddly, it seemed the warrior had also chosen him.

'Pick your targets,' Fabricius shouted, praying that the outcome of this clash proved different to the one at the Ticinus. 'Make every spear count.'

Seeing the Numidian loose a javelin in his direction, Quintus panicked. Fortunately, it missed, sailing between him and Calatinus. Quintus cursed savagely. The Numidian still had two javelins. Even as the thought went through his mind, the next one scudded his way. He bent low over his horse's neck, hearing it whistle overhead. Claws of desperation tore at him. How long would his luck hold out? He was fewer than twenty paces from his enemy. At that range and closing, the warrior could hardly miss.

The Numidian held on to his last javelin until he was practically on top of Quintus. His error meant that Quintus was able to catch the missile in his shield. He had to discard the useless thing, but he was also able to stab his spear deep into the Numidian's belly as he rode past. Side by side, Quintus and Calatinus struck the enemy formation. At once the world shrank to a small area in their immediate vicinity. Quintus' ears rang with the clash of arms and men's screams, a deafening cacophony that added hugely to the confusion. The press of opposing riders pushing against each other meant that he seldom fought the same opponent for more than a couple of strokes. Quintus' first opponent was a young Numidian who nearly took his eye out with a well-aimed javelin. He jabbed his spear unsuccessfully at the warrior before being swept twenty paces away, never to see him again.

In quick succession, Quintus fought two more Numidians, stabbing one in the arm and plunging his weapon into the other's chest. Next he went to the aid of a Roman cavalryman who was being attacked by three enemy riders. They fought desperately for what seemed an age, barely able to defend themselves against the Numidians' lightning-quick javelin thrusts. And then, like wraiths, the warriors were gone, galloping off into the distance. All across the battlefield, Quintus could see their companions doing the same. It was done with the ease of a shoal of fish changing direction. Unexpectedly, though, the Numidians reined in several hundred paces away. They began shouting insults at the Romans, who responded loudly and in kind.

'Mangy bastards!' shouted Cincius.

'Come back, you goat-fuckers!' roared Calatinus.

Quintus grinned. 'We've driven them a good distance from the camp already.'

'Yes,' agreed Calatinus, whose face was drenched in sweat. 'Time for a rest. I'm bloody exhausted.'

'And me,' added Cincius.

Fabricius and his fellow officers let the Roman cavalry catch their breath for a few moments. Clouds of condensation hung above the mass of horsemen, but were soon dispersed by the heavy sleet that began to fall.

'Time to move before you all freeze to death,' bellowed Fabricius.

Quintus glanced at Calatinus and Cincius. 'Ready for another bout?'

'Definitely,' they snarled in unison.

Right on cue, Fabricius' voice bellowed the command. 'Hold the line! Advance!' The call was repeated by all along the front rank. The Roman horsemen needed little encouragement, and urged their mounts forward. Once again, the ground shook as thousands of horses pounded across the soft ground. This time, the Numidians fought for only a short time before retreating. Yet the tribesmen did not go far. Instead, they turned to fight again. Without pause, the Roman cavalrymen charged at their enemies. Keeping up the momentum of an attack was vital.

Their confidence was boosted by the sight, to their rear, of six thousand velites pouring to their aid. The fact that they were on foot did not take away from the skirmishers' value. They would first consolidate and hold the area that had been taken back from the Numidians. If the enemy horsemen decided to stand their ground, the velites could support their comrades and tilt the balance in their favour. If, on the other hand, the Roman cavalrymen were driven back, then the velites would provide a protective screen for them to fall back through. It was a win-win situation, thought Quintus jubilantly.

At daybreak, the horns that normally signalled the Carthaginian troops to get up remained silent. Used to army routine, most men were already awake. Hanno smiled as he listened to the rumours filling the tents around him. The rank-and-file troops had no idea yet why they had not been ordered from their beds. The majority were happy not to enquire, but some of the more eager ones poked their heads outside. Their officers told them that nothing was wrong. Not wanting to pass up such a rare opportunity, the soldiers duly returned to the comfort of their blankets. For half an hour, an unusual calm fell over the encampment. To the Carthaginians, it was a small dose of heaven. Despite the inclement weather, they were dry, warm and safe.

Finally, the horns did sound. There was no alarm, just the normal notes that indicated it was time to rise. Hanno began moving from tent to tent, encouraging his men.

'What's going on, sir?' asked a short spearman with a bushy black beard.

Hanno grinned. 'You want to know?'

'Yes, sir,' came the eager reply.

Hanno was fully aware that every soldier within earshot was listening. 'The Numidians are attacking the Roman camp even as we speak.'

A rousing cheer went up, and Hanno raised his hands. 'Even if the whoresons take the bait and follow our cavalry, it will take them an age to cross the Trebia. You have plenty of time to get ready.'

Pleased mutters met this comment.

'I want you to prepare yourselves well. Stretch and oil your muscles. Check all your equipment. When you're ready, lay your arms aside and prepare a hot breakfast. Clear?'

'Yes, sir,' his men shouted.

Hanno retired to his own tent in search of food. When that was done, he lay down on his bed and instantly fell asleep. For the first time since leaving Carthage, Hanno dreamed of his mother, Arishat. She did not seem concerned that Malchus and her three sons were in Hannibal's army. Hanno found this immensely reassuring. His mother's spirit was watching over them all.

Soon after, he was roused by the horns sounding the call that meant 'Enemy in sight'.

Hanno sat bolt upright in bed, his heart racing. The Romans *had* followed the Numidians! He and every man in the army were about to be given their first chance to punish Rome for what it had done to his people.

They would grasp it with both hands.

Little more than an hour later, eight thousand of Hannibal's skirmishers and spearmen, with Hanno among them, had been deployed about a mile and a half east of their camp. Behind this protective screen, the rest of the army was slowly assuming battle formation. Hearing that the entire enemy host was crossing the Trebia, the Carthaginian general had finally responded. Hanno was delighted by Hannibal's ingenuity. Unlike the Romans, who had not eaten and were even now fording chest deep, freezing water, Hannibal's soldiers had full bellies and came fresh from their fires. Even at this distance, the chill air was filled with their ribald marching songs. He could hear the elephants bugling too, protesting as they were taken from their hay and sent out to the flanks.

Hanno was positioned at the easternmost point of the defensive semicircle, nearest the River Trebia. It was where contact with the Romans would first be made. To facilitate the Numidians' withdrawal, gaps had been left between each unit. These could easily be closed if necessary. Five score paces in front of the Libyans' bristling spears, hundreds of Balearic slingers waited patiently, the leather straps of their weapons dangling from their fists. The tribesmen didn't look that impressive, thought Hanno, but he knew that the egg-sized stones hurled by their slings could travel long distances to crack a man's skull. The ragged-looking skirmishers' volleys could strike terror into an advancing enemy.

The wind had died down, allowing the grey-yellow clouds to release heavy showers of snow on the waiting troops. They would have to bear with it, Hanno decided grimly. Nothing would happen for a while. The Numidians were still retreating across the Trebia. When the Roman cavalry arrived, they probably wouldn't attack the protective screen. He was correct. Over the following half an hour, squadron after squadron of Numidians escaped between the phalanxes. Soon after, Hanno was pleased to recognise Zamar approaching. He raised a hand in greeting. 'What news?'

Zamar slowed his horse to a walk. 'Things go well. I wasn't sure if the Romans were up for a fight to start off with, but they poured out of their camp like a tide of ants.'

'Just their cavalry?'

'No, thousands of skirmishers too.' Zamar grinned. 'Then the infantry followed.'

Thank you, great Melqart, thought Hanno delightedly.

'We fought and withdrew repeatedly, and gradually led them down to the river. That was where we took most of our casualties. Had to make it look as if we were panicking, see?' said Zamar with a scowl. His face lifted quickly. 'Anyway, it worked. The enemy foot soldiers followed their cavalry into the water and started wading across. To cap it all, that was when the snow really started falling. You could see the fuckers' faces turning blue!'

'Did they turn back?'

'No,' replied Zamar with a grim pleasure. 'They didn't. It might take the whoresons all day to get here, but they're coming. Their whole damn army.'

'This really is it then,' Hanno muttered. His stomach churned.

Zamar nodded solemnly. 'May Baal Saphon protect you and your men.'

'And the same to you,' Hanno replied. He watched sadly as the Numidian led his riders to the rear. Would they ever see each other again? Probably not. Hanno didn't wallow in the emotion. It was far too late for regret. They were all in this together. He and his father. Sapho and Bostar. Zamar and every other soldier in the army. Yes, bloodshed was inevitable. So too were the deaths of thousands of men.

Even as he saw the first files of Roman legionaries filing into view, Hanno believed that Hannibal would not let them down.

Chapter XXIV: At Close Quarters

With the Numidians gone, Fabricius regrouped his riders on the near riverbank. The mass of horsemen crossed together and went pounding up the track, past the spot where their patrol had been annihilated by Hanno and his men. Trying not to think about what had happened, Quintus squinted up at the low-lying cloud. For the moment, the snow had stopped. He tried to feel grateful. 'What time is it?' he wondered. 'It has to be *hora quinta* at least.'

'Who cares?' growled Calatinus. 'All I know is that I'm parched with thirst, and bloody famished.'

'Here.' Quintus handed over his water bag.

Grinning his thanks, Calatinus took a few deep swallows. 'Gods, that's cold,' he complained.

'Be grateful you're not a legionary,' advised Quintus. He pointed back towards the Trebia, where thousands of soldiers were already preparing to follow the cavalry across.

Calatinus scowled. 'Aye. Fording that was unpleasant enough on a horse. I pity the poor bastard infantry. The damn river must be chest deep.'

'It's the winter rain,' said Quintus. 'Even the parallel tributaries are waist high, so the poor bastards will have to immerse themselves repeatedly. It doesn't bear thinking about.'

'A fight will soon warm them up,' declared Cincius stoutly.

Quintus and his two comrades were among the first to emerge from the trees' protection. They reined in at once, cursing. Their chase was over.

A quarter of a mile away, stretching from left to right as far as the eye could see, stood the figures of thousands of waiting men. Carthaginian troops. 'Halt!' bellowed Fabricius. 'It's a protective screen. No point committing suicide.' Cheated of the chance for further revenge on the Numidians, his men shouted insults after the retreating enemy riders.

Fabricius found Quintus a moment later. He smiled to see his son unharmed. 'Quite a morning so far, eh?'

Quintus grinned. 'Yes, Father. We've got them on the run, eh?'

'Hmmm.' Fabricius was studying the brown-yellow clouds above. He frowned. 'There's more snow coming, and we're going to have a long wait before the real fight begins. The legions and the socii will take hours to get in position. By that time, the men will be half dead with cold.'

Quintus glanced around. 'Some of them don't even have cloaks on.'

'They were too keen to engage with the enemy,' replied Fabricius grimly. 'What's the betting that they didn't feed and water their horses?'

Quintus flushed. He hadn't remembered that most basic of duties either. 'What should we do?'

'Do you see those trees?'

Quintus eyed the dense stand of beech a short distance to their left. 'Yes.'

'Let's take shelter there. Longus might not like it, but he's not here. We'll still be able to respond fast if there's any threat to the legionaries. Not that that's likely. Hannibal threw out this protective screen deliberately. He wants a proper battle today,' Fabricius declared. 'Until the fighting starts, or orders come to the contrary, we should try to keep warm.'

Quintus nodded gratefully. There was more to war than simply defeating an enemy in combat, he realised. Initiative was also important.

And so, while the rest of the cavalry and the velites milled about uncertainly, watching the legionaries wading across the Trebia, Fabricius led his riders under cover.

By the time two hours had passed, Hanno was shivering constantly. His soldiers were in the same condition. It was absolute torture standing on an open plain in such bitter weather. Although the snow showers had died away, they had been succeeded by sleet, and the wind had recovered its viciousness. It whistled and whipped at Carthaginian and Roman alike with an unrelenting fury. The only opportunity Hanno's men had been given to warm up was when the instruction had come to withdraw towards their camp.

'Look at the whoresons!' cried Malchus, who had come over from his phalanx. 'Will they never stop coming?'

Hanno eyed the ground opposite their position, which was being filled with a plodding inevitability. 'It must be the entire Roman army.'

'I'd say so,' answered his father bleakly. Abruptly, he laughed. 'However cold you think your men are, those fuckers are in a far worse state. In all likelihood, they've had no food, and now they're all drenched to the skin too.'

Hanno shuddered. He could only imagine how cold the wind would feel on wet clothing and heavy mail, both of which carried heat away from the body anyway. Demoralising. Energy-sapping.

'Meanwhile,' his father went on, 'we're ready and waiting for them.'

Hanno glanced to either side. As soon as the Numidians had retreated safely, he and his men had pulled back to Hannibal's battle formation, which consisted of a single line of infantry in close order. The slingers and Numidian skirmishers were arrayed some three hundred paces in front of the main battle line. Their general had not placed his strongest infantry – the Libyans and Iberians – in the centre. Instead, that space was filled by about eight thousand Gauls. 'Surely we should be standing there?' he asked crossly. 'Instead, it's our newest recruits.'

Malchus gave him a calculating look. 'Think about it. Listen to them.'

Hanno cocked his head. The war cries and the carnyx blasts emanating from the Gauls' ranks were deafening. 'They're delighted with the honour that Hannibal has granted them. It will increase their loyalty.'

'That's right. To them, pride is everything,' answered Malchus. 'What could be better than being given the centre of the line? But there's another reason. The heaviest fighting, and the worst casualties will be there too. Hannibal is saving us and the Iberians from that fate.'

Hanno gave his father a shocked glance. 'Would he do such a thing?'

'Of course,' replied Malchus casually. 'The Gauls can easily be replaced. Our men, and the scutarii and caetrati, cannot. That's why we're on the wings.'

Hanno's respect for Hannibal grew further. He eyed the seventeen elephants standing just in front of their position. The rest were arrayed on the other wing, before the Iberian foot soldiers. Further protection for the heavy infantry, he realised. Outside, on each flank, sat five thousand Numidians and Hannibal's Iberian and Gaulish horse. The Carthaginian superiority in this area would hopefully afford Hannibal a good chance of winning the cavalry battle. Meanwhile, the Gauls would have to resist the hammer blow delivered by the Roman legions to the centre of the Carthaginian line. 'Will the Gauls hold?' he asked anxiously.

'There's a decided chance that they will not,' Malchus replied, clenching his jaw. 'They might be brave, but they're poorly disciplined.'

Hanno stared over at the tribesmen. Few of them wore armour. Even in this weather, most preferred to fight stripped to the waist. There was no denying that the legionaries' mail shirts and heavy scuta would provide them with a severe test. 'If they don't break, however, and our cavalry are successful . . .'

Malchus' grin was wolf-like. 'Our troops on each side will have a god-given opportunity to attack the sides of the Roman formation.'

'That's when Mago's force will appear.'

'We must hope so,' said his father. 'For all of our fates will lie with them.'

Hanno could hardly bear it. 'So many small things have to succeed for us to win the day.'

'That's right. And the Gauls will have the hardest task of any.'

Hanno closed his eyes and prayed that everything went according to plan. *Great Melqart, you have helped Hannibal thus far. Please do the same again today.*

In the event, Fabricius spotted one of the consul's messengers well before Quintus and his comrades had warmed up. He rode to confer with him, and returned at the double.

'Longus wants all citizen cavalry positioned on the right flank, and the allied horse on the left. We've got to ride north, to the far end of the battle line.'

'When?' asked Quintus irritably. His earlier excitement had been sapped by the mind-numbing cold.

'Now!' Fabricius called out to his decurions: 'Have the men form up. We ride out at once.'

As the cavalrymen emerged from the trees, Quintus could have sworn that the wind hit them with a new vigour, stripping away any of the warmth that they had briefly felt. That settled it, he thought grimly. The sooner the fighting began, the better. Anything rather than this torture.

Fabricius led them through the gaps in the three lines of soldiers to the front of the army. By the time they had reached open ground, Quintus had gained a good appreciation of the entire host. Longus had ordered the legions to deploy in traditional pattern, with a hundred paces between each line and the next. The veteran triarii were at the rear, in the middle were the principes, men in their late twenties and early thirties, and next came the ranks of the hastati, the youngest of the infantry. At the very front stood the exhausted velites, who, despite their recent travails, would be forced to engage the enemy first.

All three lines were composed of maniples. Those of hastati and principes comprised two centuries of between sixty and seventy soldiers. There were fewer triarii, however, and their maniples were made up of just two centuries of thirty men each. The units in each line did not yet form a continuous front. Instead, they were positioned one century in front of the other, leaving gaps equal to the maniple's frontage between each unit. The units of the second and third lines stood behind the spaces in front, forming a quincunx configuration like the '5' face on a gaming die. This positioning allowed a rapid transition to combat formation when the rear century in each maniple would simply run around to stand alongside the front one. It also permitted soldiers to retreat safely from the fighting, allowing their fresher comrades access to the enemy.

It was a long way to the edge of the right flank, so Quintus also had time to study the Carthaginian forces. These were arrayed about a quarter of a mile distant, sufficiently near to appreciate the enemy's superior numbers of cavalry, and the threatening outlines of at least two dozen elephants. The blare of horns and carnyxes carried through the air, an alien noise compared to the familiar Roman trumpets. It was clear that Hannibal retained fewer troops than Longus, but his host still made for a fearsome, if unusual, sight.

At length Quintus began to feel quite exposed. Fortunately, he didn't have to wait much longer. They passed the four regular legions, spotting Longus and his tribunes at the junction between these and the allied troops of the right wing. Finally, Fabricius' unit reached the Roman cavalry, which, with their arrival, numbered just under a thousand. There was more ribaldry as the assembled riders demanded to know where they had been.

'Screwing your mother!' shouted a wit among Fabricius' men. 'And your sisters!'

Angry roars rose from the joke's victims, and the air filled with insults. A smile twitched across Fabricius' lips. He glanced at Quintus and registered his surprise. 'Many of them are going to die soon,' he explained. 'This takes their minds off it.'

The mention of heavy casualties made Quintus feel nauseous. Would he survive to see the next dawn? Would his father, Calatinus or Cincius? Quintus looked around at the familiar faces, the men he had come to know over the previous weeks. He didn't like all of them, but they were still his comrades. Who would end the day lying bloodied and motionless in the cold mud? Who would be maimed, or blinded? Quintus felt the first fingers of panic clutch at his belly.

His father took his arm. 'Take a deep breath,' he said quietly.

Quintus shot him a worried glance. 'Why?'

'Do as I say.'

He obeyed, relieved that Calatinus and Cincius were deep in conversation with each other.

'Hold it,' Fabricius ordered. 'Listen to your heart.'

It wasn't hard to do that, thought Quintus. It was hammering off his ribs like that of a wild bird.

His father waited for a few moments. 'Now let the air out through your lips. Nice and slowly. When you've finished, do the same again.'

Quintus' eyes flickered around nervously, but nobody appeared to be watching. He did as he was told. By the third or fourth breath, the effect on his pulse was noticeable. It had slowed down, and he wasn't feeling as scared.

'Everyone is frightened before battle,' said his father. 'Even me. It's a terrifying thing to charge at another group of men whose job it is to kill you. The trick is to think of your comrades on your left and right. They are the only ones who matter from now on.'

'I understand,' Quintus muttered.

'You will be fine. I know it.' Fabricius clapped him on the shoulder.

Steadier now, Quintus nodded. 'Thank you, Father.'

With his army in place, Longus had the trumpeters sound the advance. Stamping their numb feet on the semi-frozen ground, the infantry obeyed. Loud prayers to the gods rose from the ranks, and the standard-bearers lifted their arms so that everyone could see the talismanic gilded animal that sat atop the wooden poles they bore. Each legion had five standards, depicting respectively an eagle, Minotaur, horse, wolf and boar. They were objects of great reverence, and Quintus wished that his unit possessed them too. Even the allied infantry bore similar standards. For reasons unclear to him, the cavalry didn't.

Victory will be ours regardless, he thought. Urging his horse on with his knees, he rode towards the enemy.

It was imperative that their enemies marched beyond Mago's hidden position. Consequently, the entire Carthaginian army had to stay put as the Romans approached. It was a nerve-racking time, with little to do other than pray or make last, quick checks of equipment. Imitating his father, Hanno had given his men a short address. They were here, he'd told them, to show Rome that it could not trifle with Carthage. To right the wrongs it had done to all of their peoples. The spearmen had liked Hanno's words, but they cheered loudest when he reminded them that they were here to follow Hannibal's lead and, most importantly, to avenge their heroic comrades who had fallen since their departure from Saguntum more than six months before.

Their racket was as nothing compared to that of the Gauls, however. The combination of drumming weapons, war chants and wind instruments made an incredible din. Hanno had never heard anything like it. Musicians stood before the assembled warriors, playing curved ceramic horns and carnyxes at full volume. The tribesmen's frenzied response was to clatter their swords and spears rhythmically off their shields, all the while chanting in unison. Some individuals were so affected that they broke ranks, stripped naked and stood whirling their swords over their heads, screaming like men possessed.

'They say that at Telamon, the ground shook with their noise,' his father shouted.

But they still lost, thought Hanno grimly.

The tension mounted steadily as the Roman battle line drew closer. It was immensely long, stretching off on both sides until it was lost to sight. The Carthaginian formation was considerably narrower, which threatened immediate flanking. Hanno's worries about this were forgotten as Hannibal ordered his skirmishers forward.

The Balearic slingers and Numidian javelin men bounded off, eager to start the battle proper. A vicious and prolonged missile encounter followed, from which the Carthaginians emerged clear victors. Unlike the wet, tired velites, who had been fighting for hours and had already thrown the majority of their javelins, Hannibal's men were fresh and keen. Stones and spears whistled and hummed through the air in their hundreds, scything down the velites like rows of wheat. Unable to respond in similar fashion, the Roman light troops were soon put to flight, retreating through the gaps in their front line. Hannibal immediately recalled his skirmishers, whose lack of armour made them vulnerable to the approaching hastati. As they trotted back through the spaces between the various Carthaginian units, they received a rousing cheer.

'A good start,' Hanno yelled to his men. 'First blood to us!'

A moment later, the Romans charged.

'Shields up!' Hanno yelled. From the corner of his eye, he was dimly aware of their Iberian and Gaulish cavalry, as well as the elephants, charging at the enemy's horsemen. He had literally an instant to pray that they succeeded.

Then the Roman *pila*, or javelins, began to arrive. Each hastatus carried two of the weapons, which gave their front line fearsome firepower. The missiles were thrown in such dense showers that the air between the two armies darkened as they flew. 'Protect yourselves!' Hanno screamed, but it was only those in the front rank who could do as he said. The phalanx's formation packed men together so tightly that it prevented the rest from raising their large shields. As the javelins came hammering down, they gritted their teeth and hoped not to be hit.

Topped by a pyramidal point, the pila were fully capable of punching through a shield and piercing its bearer's flesh. And they did exactly that: killing, wounding, cutting tissue apart with ease. Hanno's ears rang with the choking cries of soldiers who could no longer talk thanks to the iron transfixing their throats. Screams rang out from those who had been struck elsewhere. Wails of fear rose from the unhurt as they saw their comrades slain before their eyes. Hanno risked a look to the front and cursed. While their first volley flew, the hastati had continued to advance. They were now less than forty paces away, and preparing to release again. He couldn't help admiring the legionaries' discipline. They actually slowed down or even stopped to throw their pila. As he already knew, it was well worth the effort to make an accurate shot. Lesser foes would have already broken and run beneath the rain of iron-tipped terror. Hanno was grateful that he was commanding veterans. While his men had suffered terribly, their lines remained steady. His father's phalanx looked rock solid too.

To his left, the Gauls were also suffering heavy casualties. Hanno could see some of them wavering, a worrying sign so early. But their chieftains were made of sterner stuff, shouting and exhorting their followers to stand fast. To Hanno's relief, the tactic worked. As the second shower of javelins was launched, the Gauls swiftly lifted their shields. While their response reduced the number of wounded and killed, it stripped many of the warriors of their main protection. Few things were more useless than a shield with a bent pilum protruding from it. Weirdly, this looked more to the Gauls' liking. Shouting fiercely, they prepared to meet the hastati head on.

Many of the men at the front of Hanno's phalanx were also now without shields. He cursed savagely. The gaps would provide the legionaries with opportunities too good to pass up, but there was nothing Hanno could do to remedy the problem. 'Close order!' he shouted. As the command was repeated all along the line, he felt the shields of the men on either side slide against his to form a solid barrier. 'Front two ranks, raise spears!' Scores of wooden shafts clattered off each other as those in the second row shoved their weapons over the shoulders of the soldiers in front. Hanno gritted his teeth. 'This is it!' he roared. 'Hold fast!'

He could pick out individuals now: there a stocky figure with a pockmarked face; beside him a young man wearing a pectoral breastplate who couldn't have been more than eighteen. His own age. He looked a bit like Gaius, Martialis' son. Unsettled, Hanno blinked. Naturally, he was mistaken: Gaius was a noble, and would serve in the cavalry. Who cares? he thought harshly. They are all the enemy. Kill them. 'Steady,' he roared. 'Wait for my command!'

The hastati screamed as they closed in. Each man clutched a gladius in his right fist, and in the other he carried a heavy, elongated oval scutum with a metal boss. Like Hanno's men's shields, many Roman ones had designs painted on their hide covers.

Bizarrely, Hanno found himself admiring the charging boars, leaping wolves and arrangements of circles and spirals. They contrasted strongly with the more ornate patterns favoured by the Libyans.

Nervous, the man beside him shoved his spear forward too soon, and Hanno's attention snapped back to the present. 'Hold!' he ordered. 'Your first thrust has to kill a man!'

One heartbeat. Two heartbeats.

'Now!' Hanno roared at the top of his voice. In the same moment, he thrust forward with his weapon, aiming it at the face of the nearest hastatus. On either side, hundreds of Libyans did the same. Hanno's speed caught the legionary off guard, and his spear tip skidded over the top of the other's scutum to take him through the left eye. Aqueous fluid spattered everywhere and an agonising scream ripped free of the hastatus' throat. Hanno's instinct was to shove his spear even deeper, making the blow mortal, but he stopped himself. The man would probably die of his injury. More importantly, he would not take any further part in the battle. With a powerful twist, Hanno pulled the blade free. Iron grated off bone as he did so and the bellowing hastatus collapsed.

Hanno barely had time to breathe before another legionary came trampling over his first opponent and deliberately barged straight into him. If it hadn't been for the fact that his shield was locked with that of the man on either side, Hanno would have fallen over. As it was, he was knocked off balance and struggled to regain his footing. This was precisely what the hastatus had intended. Bending his right elbow, he stabbed his gladius over the top of Hanno's shield. Frantically, Hanno twisted his head to one side, and the blade gouged a deep line across the cheekpiece of his bronze helmet before skimming through the hair on the side of his head. The hastatus snarled with anger and pulled back his weapon to deliver another blow. Hanno struggled to use his spear, but his opponent was too close to reach him easily. Panic bubbled in the back of his throat. The battle had hardly started, and already he was a dead man.

Then, out of the blue, a spear took the hastatus through the throat, making his eyes bulge in shock. He made a choking gasp as the blade slid out of his flesh, and dropped like a stone, sending gouts of blood all over Hanno's shield and lower legs. 'My thanks!' Hanno shouted at the soldier behind him. He couldn't turn around to express his gratitude, because another hastatus was already trying to kill him. This time, Hanno managed to fend off his attacker with his spear. Cursing loudly, they traded blows back and forth, but neither could gain an advantage over the other. Things were taken out of both their hands a moment later when a man a few steps to Hanno's right, who had discarded his pilum-riddled shield, was killed. Two hastati forced their way into the space at once, shouting at their comrades to follow them. Hanno's opponent knew that this was too good a chance to pass up. In the blink of an eye, he had shoved his way after his fellows. To Hanno's relief, he was granted a brief respite.

Panting heavily, he glanced to either side. Claws of worry raked at his insides. The phalanxes were holding their own, but only just. To his left, the Gauls were struggling to contain the same intense assault. Worryingly, the hastati there had already been joined by the principes. The Gauls had even less prospect of holding back these legionaries, thought Hanno sourly. Most of the principes wore mail shirts, making them much harder to kill. Thus far, however, the tribesmen were not retreating. Despite their lack of armour, they persisted in fighting to the death. Already the ground beneath their feet was a churned-up morass of corpses, discarded weapons, mud and blood.

Desperately, Hanno cast his eyes to the Roman left flank. His heart lifted. Thanks to the Iberians and Gauls, it had been shorn of its cavalry protection. There was no sign of Hannibal's heavy cavalry, however, which meant it was still pursuing the Roman horse. Hanno's worry increased tenfold. If that battle hadn't been won, they might as well all give up now. Then his attention was drawn by hundreds of figures who were swarming towards the enemy's left flank. To his delight, he saw that they were hurling javelins and firing sling stones. It was the Carthaginian skirmishers!

A yelling hastatus jumped into the attack, preventing Hanno from any further thought. He fought back with renewed determination, using the greater length of his spear to stab at the Roman's face. The fight wasn't over by any means. There was hope yet.

As they rode towards the Carthaginians, Quintus forgot his father's reassuring words. He felt sick to the stomach. How could a thousand men prevail against what looked like more than five times that number? It simply wasn't possible.

Calatinus also looked unhappy. 'Longus should have split our horsemen equally,' he muttered. 'There are nearly three thousand allied riders on the other flank.'

'It's not fair,' moaned Cincius.

'The figures still don't equate,' Quintus replied wearily.

'I suppose. It's not even as if the bastards coming towards us will be scared. They've already tasted victory over us.' Calatinus cursed the consul heartily.

'Come on! We should be able to stall the enemy attack,' encouraged Quintus. 'Hold the line, and stop the enemy from having free rein over the battlefield.'

Calatinus' grunt conveyed all types of disbelief. Cincius didn't seem convinced either.

'Listen to our infantry,' cried Quintus. The noise of their tread was deafening. 'There are more than thirty-five thousand of them. How can Hannibal with his little army, made up of a hodgepodge of different nationalities, prevail against that type of might? He can't!'

His comrades looked a trifle more confident.

Wishing that he felt as certain as he sounded, Quintus again fixed his gaze to the front.

The first of the enemy riders were now very close. Quintus recognised them as Gauls by their mail shirts, round shields and long spears. He squinted at the small, bouncing objects tied to their horses' harnesses. To his horror, he realised they were severed human heads. These warriors could be some of their so-called allies, and the heads those of his former comrades. Of Licinius, perhaps.

Calatinus had seen the same thing. 'The fucking dogs!' he screamed.

'Yellow-livered sons of whores!' Cincius bellowed.

A towering rage also filled Quintus. He wasn't going to flee from cowards like these. Men who would kill others as they slept. I would rather die, he thought. Quintus raised his spear and chose a target, a warrior on a sturdy grey horse. The magnificent gold torc visible over the top of the Gaul's mail shirt revealed him to be an important individual. So did the three human heads bouncing off his mount's chest. He would be a good start, Quintus decided.

However, the tide of battle swept Quintus away from the Gaul he'd aimed for. In hindsight, it was a good thing. The tribesman was immensely skilled. Quintus watched in horror as a Roman rider fewer than twenty paces away was skewered through the chest by the Gaul's weapon. The force of the impact punched the man off his saddle blanket, dropping him dead to the dirt below. The horse behind stumbled over the corpse, unbalancing its rider, and rendering him easy prey for the Gaul, who was now swinging a long sword. He took off the cavalryman's head with a great sideways lop. Quintus had never seen blood spray so high in the air. Gouts of it went everywhere as the panicked horse galloped off. It was perhaps a dozen steps before its dead rider toppled off.

At once the Gaul sawed on his mount's reins and jumped down. Quintus' amazement turned to disgust. The warrior was after another head. He would have given anything just then to be able to reach the Gaul, but it was not to be. He nearly lost his own head to a swinging sword, managing to dodge it only because its bearer uttered a loud war cry as his killing stroke came down. As it was, Quintus nearly fell off his horse. With a speed born of utter desperation, he managed to regain his seat in time to parry his opponent's next powerful blow.

Fortuna was smiling on him in that instant, for the warrior was even younger than he, and, as Quintus realised, far less skilled. A more experienced man would have already despatched him. The Gaul was not lacking in bravery, however, and they hammered fiercely at each other for a few moments before Quintus found an opportunity to strike. The other's wild swings left his right armpit exposed. Taking a gamble that he could react faster than his enemy, Quintus did not defend against the next strike. Instead, bending low over his horse's neck, he listened to it whistle overhead. While the Gaul was still coming to the end of his swing, Quintus came up like a striking snake. He buried his spear in the other's side, sliding it neatly into the armhole of his mail shirt. With nothing but a tunic to stop its progress, the blade slid between the man's ribs, through one lung and into his heart. It was as clean a stroke as Quintus had ever made, killing instantaneously. He would always remember it not for that, however, but for the brief burst of shock and pain in the Gaul's eyes before they went dark for ever.

When Quintus looked up, he quailed. Most of the nearby Roman riders had been cut down. The others were fleeing. There was no sign of Calatinus, Cincius or his father. Quintus' vision was filled with Gauls. Behind them came hundreds of Iberians. He would be dead long before those riders arrived, however. Three Gaulish warriors were heading straight for him. Despairing, Quintus picked the man he thought would reach him first. It would make little difference, but he didn't care. His father was dead, and the cavalry battle half lost. What did it matter if he also fell?

Raising his spear, Quintus screamed a final cry of defiance. 'Come on, then, you bastards!'

The trio of warriors roared an inarticulate response.

A horrifying image of his own head as a trophy filled his mind. He banished the image. Just let the end be quick, Quintus prayed.

Chapter XXV: Unexpected Tactics

Bostar had barely been able to contain himself since the sentry's report that the enemy were crossing the river. He and Sapho had clambered up the bank to lie beside Mago, who was trembling with excitement. With every nerve stretched taut, they'd watched as the Roman cavalry and velites were gradually followed by the allied infantry and the regular legionaries. Only then did it sink in.

'The Roman commander has no interest in nibbling at the bait,' muttered Mago excitedly. 'He's swallowed it in one great bite. That's his whole fucking army!'

They exchanged nervous grins.

'The fighting will start soon,' said Sapho eagerly.

'It's not time to move yet,' interjected Bostar at once.

'That's right. We have to wait until the perfect moment to fall upon the Romans' rear,' warned Mago. 'Moving too early could cost us the battle.'

Knowing that Mago was correct, the brothers reluctantly stayed put. The wait that followed was the longest of Bostar's life. Mago's incessant twitching and the savagery with which Sapho bit his nails told him that they felt the same way. It was no more than three to four hours, but at the time it seemed like an eternity. Naturally, the news that the Romans were on the move had spread through their two thousand soldiers like wildfire. Soon it became difficult to keep them silent. It was understandable, thought Bostar. There was only so long that one could take pleasure in being out of harm's way rather than facing mortal danger – especially when one's comrades were about to fight for their lives.

Even when the clash of arms became audible, Mago did not move. Bostar forced himself to remain calm. The rival forces of skirmishers would meet first, and then pull back. Sure enough, the screams and cries soon abated. They were replaced by the unmistakable sound of thousands of feet tramping the ground in unison.

'The Roman infantry are advancing,' said Mago in an undertone. 'Melqart, watch over our men.'

A knot of tension formed in Bostar's belly. Facing so many of the enemy would be terrifying.

Beside him, Sapho shifted uneasily. 'The gods protect Father and Hanno,' he whispered. Their enmity momentarily forgotten, Bostar muttered the same prayer.

The crashing sound that reached their ears a moment later was as deafening as thunder. Yet there were no threatening storm clouds above, no flashes of lightning to sear their eyeballs. It was something altogether more lethal. More terrifying. Bostar trembled to hear it. He had witnessed terrible things since the war started: the immense block of stone that had nearly killed Hannibal; the scenes at the fall of Saguntum; avalanches sweeping away scores of screaming men in the Alps. But he had never heard the sound of tens of thousands of soldiers striking each other for the first time. It promised death in any number of appalling ways, and Hanno and his father were caught up in it. Somehow Bostar kept still, trying his best to block out the screams that were now discernible amid the crescendo of sound. His tactic didn't work for long. He looked at Mago, who gave him a tiny encouraging nod.

'Is it time yet, sir?' Bostar asked.

Mago's eyes glittered eagerly. 'Soon. Prepare your men to move out. Tell the same to the officer commanding the Numidians. At my signal, bring them up.'

'Yes, sir!' Bostar and Sapho grinned at each other as they hadn't done in an age, and hurried to obey.

From then on, time moved in a blur, a continuum that Bostar could only remember afterwards in a series of fractured images. The frisson of excitement that shivered through the waiting soldiers when they heard their orders. Mago's head silhouetted as he peered over the riverbank, and his beckoning arm. Reaching the top, and being awestruck by the colossal struggle going on over to their left. Who was winning? Was Hanno still alive? Mago shaking his arm and telling him to keep focused. Telling the men to unsling their shields from their backs and ready their weapons. Assembling their phalanxes in open order. Watching the thousand Numidians split, placing half their number on each side of the infantry. Mago's raised sword pointing at the enemy and his cry, 'For Hannibal and for Carthage!'

And the run. Bostar would never forget the run.

They did not sprint. It was more than half a mile to the battle-field. Exhausting themselves would give away all the advantage they had been granted. Instead they moved at a fast trot, leaving plumes of exhaled breath in their wake. The cold air was filled with the low, repetitive thuds of horses' hooves and men's boots and sandals on the hard ground. No one spoke. No one wanted to. Everyone's eyes were locked on what was unfolding before them. Amid the confusion, one thing was clear. There was no sign of the enemy's cavalry, which meant that the Iberian and Gaulish horsemen must have driven them off. On the Roman flanks, the allied infantry were struggling against the Carthaginian elephants, skirmishers and Numidian horsemen. In itself, these were major achievements, and Bostar wanted to cheer. But he did not utter a word. The battle's outcome still hung in the balance. As they drew closer, he saw that the fighting in the centre was incredibly fierce. The legionaries there had actually moved in front of their wings, which meant that they had pushed the Gauls who formed the central part of Hannibal's line backwards.

They had come not an instant too soon, thought Bostar.

Mago came to the realisation at the same time. 'Charge!' he screamed. 'Charge!'

With a wordless roar, Bostar, Sapho and their soldiers obeyed, increasing their speed to a dangerous, breakneck pace. Any man who tripped now risked breaking an ankle or a leg. But no one cared. All they wanted to do was to start shedding their opponents' blood. To bury their weapons in Roman flesh.

The last moments of their run were surreal. Exhilarating. Thanks to the deafening sounds of battle, there was no need to worry about how much noise they made. The triarii in the enemy's third rank – their targets – were not looking behind them. Unsurprisingly, the veterans were engrossed by the bitter struggle going on to their front, and were preparing to join in. They had no idea that two thousand Carthaginian soldiers were about to strike their rear at a full charge. Bostar would always remember the first faces that turned, casually, for whatever reason, to look around. The sheer disbelief and terror that twisted those faces to find a group of the enemy fewer than thirty paces away. The hoarse screams as the small number of triarii who were aware tried to warn their comrades of their deadly peril. And the satisfaction as they smashed into the Roman ranks, drawing their weapons down on the backs of men who did not even know they were about to die.

For the first time in his life, Bostar was overcome by battle rage. In the red mist surrounding him, it was easy to lose count of the number of men he killed. It was like stabbing fish in a rock pool off the coast of Carthage. Thrust forward. Run the blade in as deep as possible. Withdraw. Select another target. When eventually his blunted spear stuck in a triarius' backbone, Bostar simply discarded it and pulled out his sword. He was vaguely aware that his arm was bloody to the elbow, but he didn't care. *I'm coming, little brother. Stay alive, Father.*

Eventually, the veteran legionaries managed to turn and face their attackers. The fight became harder, but the advantage was still with Mago's men, who could now see that the enemy's flanks had broken. Bostar exulted. The combined wave of Carthaginian troops and cavalry on the allied infantry's undefended side had proved too much. Prevented from wheeling to face the threat, they had been mercilessly hacked to pieces.

Now, dropping their weapons, the survivors turned and ran for the Trebia. Bostar threw back his head and let free an animal howl of triumph. To the rear, he glimpsed thousands of their cavalrymen waiting for just such an eventuality. The allied troops would not go far. Suddenly, a veteran with a notched sword blade drove at him and Bostar was reminded that their own task was not over. Although the triarii were suffering heavy casualties, the rest of the legionaries were still moving forward into, and through, the lines of Gauls. Like a battering ram, they could only be resisted for so long. Bostar's elation died away as he realised that some of the Libyan phalanxes had also given way. They quickly crumbled before the legionaries' relentless assault. Catching Sapho's attention, Bostar pointed. His brother's face twisted in rage. With renewed energy, they both threw themselves at the triarii.

'Hanno! Father!' Bostar shouted. 'We're coming!'

Too late, his heart screamed back.

When Aurelia entered the bedroom, her mother barely stirred. Elira, who was sitting by the bed, turned.

'How is she?' Aurelia whispered.

'Better,' the Illyrian replied. 'Her fever has broken.'

Some of the tension went from Aurelia's shoulders. 'Thank the gods. Thank *you*.'

'Hush,' murmured Elira reassuringly. 'She was never that ill. It's a bad winter chill, that's all. She'll be up and about by Saturnalia.'

Aurelia nodded gratefully. 'I don't know what I'd do without you. It's not just caring for Mother these past few days. You made all the difference in Suni's—' She looked over her shoulder guiltily. To her relief, there was no one in the atrium. 'I mean Lysander's recovery.'

Elira waved a hand in dismissal. 'He's young, and strong. All he needed was some food and warmth.'

'Well, I'm thankful to you nonetheless,' said Aurelia. 'So is he.'

Elira bobbed her head, embarrassed.

Things had moved on since she had returned to the farm with a half-conscious Suniaton two weeks previously, thought Aurelia, looking down at her sleeping mother. Fortunately, Atia had not questioned her story of finding him in the woods. In a real stroke of luck, a heavy snowstorm later that night had concealed the evidence of her tracks up to the hut. Unsurprisingly, everyone had taken Suniaton for a runaway slave. As agreed, he had pretended to be mute. He also put on a good show of appearing simple. Agesandros had been suspicious, of course, but there had been no trace of recognition in his eyes at any stage.

Aurelia had given the Sicilian no chance to have anything to do with Suniaton. Any master who wanted his property back could come looking for the boy, she had said to her mother. Until then, she was going to keep him. 'Lysander, I'll call him, because he looks Greek.'

Atia had smiled in acceptance. 'Very well. If he even survives,' she'd joked.

Well, he had, thought Aurelia triumphantly. Suni's leg had recovered enough for him to limp about the kitchen under Julius' instruction. For the moment, he was safe.

What frustrated Aurelia most was the fact that she could rarely talk to him. The best they could manage was an occasional snatched conversation in the evenings, when the other kitchen slaves had gone to bed. Aurelia used these moments to ask Suni about Hanno. She now knew much about his childhood and family, his interests, and where he had lived. Aurelia's reason for wanting to know about Hanno was quite simple. It was a way of not thinking about her betrothal. Even if Flaccus had been killed with her father, her mother would soon find her another husband. If Flaccus had survived, they would be wed within the year. One way or another, she would have an arranged marriage.

'Aurelia.'

Her mother's voice jerked Aurelia back to the present. 'You're awake! How do you feel?'

'Weak as a newborn,' Atia murmured. 'But better than I did yesterday.'

'Praise all the gods.' Tears leaped unbidden to Aurelia's eyes. Finally, things were looking up.

Her mother's improvement lifted Aurelia's mood considerably. For the first time in days, she went for a walk. The chill weather meant that the snow that had fallen over the previous few days had not melted. Aurelia didn't want to go far from her mother or Suni. Just venturing a short distance along the track towards Capua felt wonderful, however. She relished the crunch of the frozen snow beneath her sandals. Even the way her cheeks rapidly went numb felt refreshing after all the time she'd spent indoors. Feeling more cheerful than she had in a while, Aurelia let herself picture a scenario in which her father had not been killed. She imagined the joy of seeing him walk through the front doors.

With this optimistic thought uppermost in her mind, she returned to the house.

As Aurelia crossed the courtyard, she saw Suniaton. He had his back to her, and was carrying a basket of vegetables into the kitchen. Her spirits lifted even higher. If he was able to do that, his leg must have improved further. She hurried after him. Reaching the door, Aurelia saw Suniaton lifting his load on to the work surface. All the other slaves were busy in other parts of the room. 'Suni!' she hissed.

He didn't react.

'Pssst! Suni!' Aurelia stepped inside the kitchen.

Still he did not respond. It was then that Aurelia noticed his stiff-backed stance. Claws of fear raked her belly. 'Sunny, it's so sunny outside,' she said loudly.

'I could have sworn you said S-u-n-i,' Agesandros purred, stepping from the shadows beside the kitchen door.

Aurelia blanched. 'No. I said it was sunny. Can't you see? The weather's changed.' She gestured outside at the blue sky above the courtyard.

She might as well have been speaking to a statue. 'Suni – Suniaton – is a gugga name,' said the Sicilian coldly.

'What's that got to do with anything?' Aurelia retorted desperately. Her gaze shot to Julius and the other slaves, but they were carefully pretending not to notice what was going on. Despair filled her. She wasn't the only one who was scared of the vilicus. And her mother was still sick in bed.

'Is this miserable wretch Carthaginian?'

'No. I told you, he's Greek. His name's Lysander.'

From nowhere, a dagger appeared in Agesandros' hand. He pricked it to Suniaton's throat. 'Are you a gugga?' There was no response, and the vilicus moved his blade to Suni's groin. 'Do you want your balls cut off?'

Petrified, Suniaton shook his head vehemently.

'Speak, then!' Agesandros shouted, returning the dagger to Suni's neck. 'Are you from Carthage?'

Suniaton's shoulders sagged. 'Yes.'

'You *can* talk!' crowed the Sicilian. He rounded on Aurelia. 'So you lied to me.'

'What if I have?' Aurelia cried, genuinely angry now. 'I know what you think of Carthaginians.'

Agesandros' eyes narrowed. 'It was odd when this scumbag arrived, half-dead. With a recently healed sword injury. I bet he's the runaway gladiator.' Like a hawk, he pounced on Suniaton's reactive flinch. 'I *knew* it!'

Think! Aurelia told herself. Quickly, she drew herself up to her full height. 'Surely not?' she snapped haughtily. 'That creature would have fled long ago.'

'He might have fooled you, but there's no drawing the wool over my eyes.' Agesandros leaned on his blade. 'You're no simpleton, are you?'

'No,' Suniaton mumbled wearily.

'Where's your friend?' the Sicilian demanded.

Don't say anything, thought Aurelia pleadingly. He's still not sure.

To her horror, Suniaton's courage flared one last time. 'Hanno? He's long gone. With any luck, he'll be in Hannibal's army by now.'

'Shame,' murmured Agesandros. 'You're of no further use, then.' Smoothly, he brought down his dagger and slipped it between Suniaton's ribs, guiding it into his heart.

Suniaton's eyes bulged in shock, and he let out a shuddering gasp of pain. His limbs went rigid before relaxing slowly. With an odd tenderness, Agesandros let him down. A rapid flow of blood soaked the front of Suni's tunic and spread on to the tile floor. He did not move again.

'No! You monster!' Aurelia shrieked.

Agesandros straightened. He studied his bloodied blade carefully.

Panicking, Aurelia took a step backwards, into the kitchen. 'No,' she cried. 'Julius! Help me!'

At last, the portly slave came hurrying to her side. 'What have you done, Agesandros?' he muttered in horror.

The Sicilian didn't move. 'I have done the master and mistress a service.'

Aurelia couldn't believe her ears. 'W-what?'

'How do you think he'd feel to discover that a dangerous fugitive – a gladiator – had contrived to join the household, placing his wife and his only daughter in danger of their lives?' asked

Agesandros righteously. He kicked Suniaton. 'Death is too good for scum like this.'

Aurelia felt herself grow faint. Suniaton was dead, and it was all her fault. She could do nothing about it either. She felt like a murderess. In her mother's eyes, the Sicilian's actions would be completely justifiable. A sob escaped her lips.

'Why don't you attend to the mistress?' There was iron below Agesandros' apparent solicitousness.

Aurelia rallied herself. 'He's to have a decent burial,' she ordered.

The Sicilian's lips quirked. 'Very well.'

Aurelia stalked from the kitchen. She needed privacy. To wail. To weep. She might as well be dead, like Suniaton – and her father. All she had to look forward to from now on was her marriage to Flaccus.

Suddenly, an outrageous image popped into Aurelia's mind. It was of her, standing on the deck of a ship as it sailed out from the Italian coast. Towards Carthage.

I could run away, she thought. Find Hanno. He—

Leave everything you've ever known behind to find one of the enemy? Aurelia's heart shouted. That's madness.

It was only the bones of an idea, but her spirits were lifted by its mere existence.

It would give her the strength to carry on.

Quintus didn't notice Fabricius appearing by his side. The first thing he knew was when his reins were grabbed from his hands and his horse's head was yanked around to face to the rear. Using his knees to control his own mount, Fabricius headed east. Quintus' steed was happy enough to follow. Although it had been trained for cavalry service, the middle of a battle was still a most unnatural place to be. Quintus' initial joy at seeing his father alive exceeded his desire to fight for a moment, but then the balance reversed. 'What are you doing?'

'Saving your life,' his father shot back. 'Are you not glad?'

Quintus glanced over his shoulder. There wasn't a living Roman cavalryman in sight, just a swarming mass of enemy horsemen and riderless mounts. Thankfully, the Gauls who'd been heading for him had already given up the chase. Like their compatriots, they had dismounted to hunt for trophies. A huge sense of relief filled Quintus. Despite his decision to stand his ground, he *was* glad to be alive. Unlike poor Calatinus, Cincius and his other comrades, who were probably dead. Shame followed swiftly on the heels of this emotion. He grabbed back his reins and concentrated on the ride. On either side, scores of other cavalrymen were also fleeing for their lives.

Their common destination seemed to be the Trebia.

Off to one side, both sets of opposing infantry were now locked together in a bitter struggle, the outcome of which was totally unclear. On the fringes of the conflict, Quintus could see the shapes of the enemy's elephants battering the allied foot soldiers. The massive beasts were supported by horsemen, and he guessed it had to be the Numidians. It could only be a matter of time before the Roman flanks folded. Then Hannibal's soldiers would be free to swing around and attack their rear. That was even before the rest of the Carthaginian cavalry returned to the conflict. Quintus blinked away tears of frustration and rage. How could this have happened? Just two hours before, they had been pursuing an enemy in disarray over the Trebia.

Hoarse shouting dragged Quintus' attention back to his own surroundings. To his horror, the Gauls to their rear had resumed the chase. With their gory trophies taken, the tribesmen were eager for more blood. His stomach churned. In their present state, the nearest cavalrymen were in no state to turn, stand and fight. Nor was he, he realised with shame. Quintus wondered if it was the same on the other flank, where the allied horse had been positioned. Had they too broken and fled?

Fabricius had also seen their new pursuers. 'Let's head that way.' Surprisingly, he pointed north. He saw Quintus' questioning look. 'There'll be too many trying to ford the river where we crossed before. It will be a slaughter.'

Quintus remembered the narrow approach to the main crossing point and shuddered. 'Where should we aim for?'

'Placentia,' his father replied ominously. 'No point returning to the camp. Hannibal could take that with little difficulty. We need the protection of stone walls.'

Quintus nodded in miserable acceptance.

Doing their best to bring along as many others as they could, they turned their horses' heads. Towards Placentia, where they might find refuge.

It was ironic, thought Hanno, that his life had been saved by Roman efficiency. It wasn't because he and his men had been victorious. Far from it. The Libyans' position adjoining the Gauls meant that many of them had shared the tribesmen's fate. When the Gauls had finally crumbled before the mass of heavily armed legionaries, some of the phalanxes had been dragged in. The spearmen in question were slaughtered to a man. Sheer luck had determined that Malchus and Hanno's units had not been affected. Battered and bloodied, they had fought on, even as they were pushed to one side by the massive block of Roman soldiers.

Somehow, Hanno utilised the natural breaks in the fighting to regain better control of his phalanx. He ordered the spearmen to the rear to pass their shields forward. The same was done with spears, allowing his unit to resume, at the front at least, a more normal appearance. Malchus emulated Hanno. With their defensive shield walls restored, the two phalanxes were a much harder proposition to overcome. Without their pila, the Romans had to rely on their gladii, which were shorter than the Libyans' spears. It did not take the legionaries facing Hanno's unit long to realise this. Seeing the hastati and principes to their right advancing without difficulty through the remnants of the Gauls, they broke away to follow their comrades.

Hanno's exhausted men watched with a sense of stunned relief.

Then, quite suddenly, the Romans were gone. Oddly, they didn't wheel around to attack the rear of the Carthaginian line. Hanno couldn't believe it. There were still isolated pockets of fighting, small groups of legionaries who had been cut off from their comrades, but the vast majority of the enemy infantry had broken through Hannibal's centre. They showed no interest, however, in doing anything except beating a path to the north. As far as Hanno was concerned, they could go. His men weren't capable of mounting a meaningful pursuit. Nor were his father's. No command issued from the musicians stationed by Hannibal's side, proving that their general was of the same mind. Having arrayed his foot soldiers in a single line, he had no reserve to send after the retreating legionaries.

Chest heaving, Hanno studied the scene. There was no sign of the allied infantry. The combination of elephants, Numidians and skirmishers must have routed them from the field. Off to his right, which had been the phalanx's front until the Romans had pushed them sideways, the battleground was now almost devoid of life. Suddenly, Hanno was overcome with a heady combination of exhilaration and fear. They had won, but at what price? He looked up at the leaden sky and offered up a heartfelt prayer: Thank you, great Melqart, all-seeing Tanit and mighty Baal Saphon, for your help in achieving this victory. You have been merciful in letting both me and my father survive. I humbly beseech that you have also seen fit to spare my brothers.

He took a deep breath. *If not, let all their wounds be at the front.*

Soon there was an emotional reunion with his father. Blood-spattered and steely-eyed, Malchus said nothing when they drew close. Instead he pulled Hanno into a tight hug that spoke volumes. When he finally let go, Hanno was touched to see the moisture in his own eyes mirrored in his father's. Malchus had shown more emotion in the last few weeks than at any time since his mother's death.

'That was a hard fight. You held your phalanx together well,' Malchus muttered. 'Hannibal will hear of it.'

Hanno thought he would burst with pride. His father's approval meant ten times that of their general.

Malchus' businesslike manner returned fast. 'There's still plenty of work to be done. Spread your men out. Advance. Tell them to kill any Romans that they find alive.'

'Yes, Father.'

'Do the same for those of our men who are badly injured,' Malchus added.

Hanno blinked.

Malchus' face softened for a moment. 'They'll die in far worse ways otherwise. Of cold, a wolf bite, or exposure. A swift end from a comrade is better than that, surely?'

Sighing, Hanno nodded. 'What about you?'

'Those who are lightly wounded might survive if we can carry them from the field. It will be dark within the hour, though. I must act fast.' He gave Hanno a shove. 'Go on. Look for Sapho and Bostar as well.'

Did his father mean alive or dead? Hanno wondered nervously as he walked away.

His men responded with enthusiasm to the idea of killing more Romans. Unsurprisingly, they reacted less well to doing the same to their comrades. Few objected, however, when Hanno explained the alternatives to them. Who wanted to die the lingering death that awaited when night fell?

In a long line, they began advancing across the battlefield. Beneath the struggle of so many men, the ground had been churned into a sludge of reddened mud that stuck to Hanno's sandals. Only the tiniest areas of snow remained untouched, startling patches of brilliant white amid the scarlet and brown coating everything else. Hanno was stunned by the scale of the horror. This was but a tiny part of the battlefield, yet it contained thousands of dead, injured and dying soldiers.

Pitifully small figures now, they lay alone, heaped over one another and in irregular piles, Gauls entwined with hastati, Libyans beneath principes, their enmity forgotten in the cold embrace of death. While some still clutched their weapons, others had discarded them to clutch at their wounds before they died. Spears dotted the bodies of many Romans, while countless pila were buried in the Carthaginian corpses. So many severed limbs were lying around that Hanno was soon sick. Wiping his mouth, he forced himself to continue searching. Again and again he saw Sapho and Bostar's faces among the slack-jawed dead, only to find that he was wrong. Inevitably, Hanno felt his hopes of finding his brothers alive wither and die.

It was especially hard to look at the soldiers who had lost their extremities. The lucky ones were already dead, but the rest were screaming for their mothers while what blood was left in them spurted and dribbled out on to the semi-frozen earth. It was a mercy to kill them. Yet for every gruesome sight that Hanno beheld, there was another one to exceed it. It was the suffering of those of his own side that tore at his heart the most. He had to force himself to examine these unfortunates. It was his job to judge the severity of their injuries and make a snap decision if they should live or die.

It was usually the latter.

Gritting his teeth, Hanno killed men who were shuddering their way into oblivion, holding their intestines, the rank smell of their own shit filling their nostrils. Those who lay moaning and coughing up the pink froth that signified a lung wound also had to be slain. More fortunate were the men who wailed and thrashed about, clutching at the arm that had been sliced open to the bone, or the leg that had been hamstrung. Their reaction to Hanno and his soldiers, the lone uninjured figures among them, was uniform. It did not matter whether they were Libyan, Gaulish or Roman. They reached out with bloodied hands, beseeching him for help. Muttering reassurances to the Carthaginian troops, Hanno offered the enemy wounded nothing but silence and a flashing blade. It was far worse than the savagery of close-quarters combat, and soon Hanno was utterly sick of it. All he wanted to do was find his brothers' bodies and return to the camp.

When first the familiar voice of Sapho, and then Bostar, called out his name, Hanno didn't react. As their shouts grew more urgent, he was thunderstruck. There they were, not fifty paces away, in the midst of Mago's men. It was a miracle, Hanno thought dazedly. It had to be, for all four of them to survive this industrial-scale butchery.

'Hanno? Is that you?' Sapho demanded, unable to keep the disbelief – and joy – from his voice.

Hanno blinked away his tears. 'It is.'

'Father?' Bostar's tone was strangled.

'He's unhurt,' Hanno yelled back, not knowing whether to laugh or cry. In the event, he did both. So did Bostar. An instant later, even Sapho had tears in his eyes as the three came together in a fierce embrace. Each stank of sweat, blood, mud and other smells too foul to imagine, but none of them cared.

Their arguments had been forgotten for the moment.

The only thing that mattered was that they were still alive.

At last, grinning like fools, the brothers pulled apart. Not quite believing their own eyes, they held on to one another's arms or shoulders for a long time afterwards. Inevitably, though, their gaze was drawn to the devastation all around. Instead of the din of battle, their ears rang with the sound of screams. The voices of the countless injured and maimed, men who were desperate to be found before darkness fell and a certain fate claimed them for ever.

'We won,' said Hanno in a wondering tone. 'The legionaries might have escaped, but the rest of them broke and ran.'

'Or died where they stood,' Sapho snarled, his customary

511

hardness already creeping back. 'After what they've done to us, the whoresons had it coming!'

Bostar winced as Sapho gestured at the piles of dead, but he nodded in agreement. 'Don't think that the war has been won,' he warned. 'This is just the start.'

Hanno thought of Quintus and his dogged determination. 'I know,' he replied heavily.

'Rome must pay even more for all the wrongs it has done to Carthage,' intoned Bostar, raising his reddened right fist.

'In blood,' Sapho added. He reached up to clasp Bostar's hand with his own.

Both looked expectantly at Hanno.

An image of Aurelia, smiling, popped into Hanno's head, filling him with confusion. It took but an instant, however, before he savagely buried the picture in the recesses of his mind. What was he thinking? Aurelia was one of the enemy. Like her brother and father. Hanno could not truly bring himself to wish any of the three ill, but nor could they be friends. How could that ever be possible after what had gone on here today? On the spot, Hanno decided never to think of them again. It was the only way he could deal with it.

'In blood,' he growled, lifting his hand to enclose those of his brothers.

They exchanged a fierce, wolfish smile.

That is what we are, thought Hanno proudly. Carthaginian wolves come to harry and tear at the fat Roman sheep in their fields. Let the farmers of Italy tremble in their beds, for we shall leave no corner of their land untouched.

Quintus' abiding memory of their ride to Placentia was the extreme cold. The wind continued to blow from the north, powerful gusts that threatened to dislodge an unwary rider from his seat. While it didn't succeed in doing that, the chill air penetrated every layer of Quintus' clothing. Initially, he had been kept warm by the effort and thrill of the chase, and latterly by the fear that kept his heart hammering off his ribs. Now, his sweat-soaked clothes felt as if they were about to freeze solid. Everyone was in the same position, of course, so he gritted his chattering teeth and rode on. After what they'd all been through, silence was best.

Lost in their own private worlds of misery, the twenty cavalry-men brought together by Fabricius simply followed where they were led. Hunched over their horses' backs, helmetless and with their sodden cloaks pulled tightly around them, they were a pathetic sight. It was as if each one knew that Hannibal's army had prevailed. Yet in reality, they didn't, thought Quintus. The battle had still been raging when they'd fled. It was hard to see how, though, with their flanks exposed, Longus' legions could have seized victory.

Quintus felt like a coward, but his fear had abated enough for him to consider fighting again. He'd ridden to the front of their little column a number of times, intent on remonstrating with his father.

Fabricius had been in no mood for conversation. 'Shut your mouth,' he snarled when Quintus had suggested turning back. 'What do you know of tactics?' A short while later, Quintus tried again. On this occasion, Fabricius let him have it. 'Once cavalry break, it's unheard of for them to rally and return to the fight. You were there! You saw the way they ran, the way I struggled to get this many men to follow me *away* from the battle. Do you think that in this weather, with night coming, they would turn and face the Gauls and Iberians again?' He glared at Quintus, who shook his head. 'In that case, what would you have us both do? Commit suicide by charging at the enemy alone? Where's the damn point in that? And don't give me the "death with honour" line. There's no honour in dying like a fool!'

Shaken by his father's anger, Quintus hung his head. Now he felt like a total failure as well as a coward.

They rode without speaking for a long time after that.

Fortuna finally lent the weary cavalrymen a hand, guiding them to a spot where the Trebia was fordable. By the time they'd reached the eastern bank, it was nearly dark. As miserable as he'd ever been in his life, Quintus looked back over the fast-flowing water into the gathering gloom. More snow was falling, millions of little white motes that clouded his vision even further. The scene was so peaceful and quiet. It was as if the battlefield had never existed. 'Quintus.' Fabricius' tone was gentler than before. 'Come. Placentia is still a long ride away.'

Quintus turned his back on the River Trebia. In a way, he realised, he was doing the same on Hanno and his friendship. Feeling hollow inside, he followed his father.

They reached Placentia about an hour later. Quintus had never been so glad to see the walls of a town, and to hear the challenge of a sentinel. The lines of frightened faces on the ramparts above soon distracted him from thoughts of sitting by a fire, however. Word of the battle had arrived before them. Despite the sentries' fear, Fabricius' status saw the gate opened quickly. A few barked questions at the officer of the guard revealed that a handful of cavalrymen had made it to the town ahead of them. Their garbled account appeared to have the entire army wiped out. There had been no sign of Longus or the infantry yet, which had only fuelled the fears of the soldiers who were manning the defences. Fabricius was incensed by the harm that the unsubstantiated reports would have already caused and demanded to see the most senior officer in the town.

Not long after, both men were wrapped in blankets and drinking warm soup in the company of no less than Praxus, the garrison commander. The rest of their party had been taken off to be quartered elsewhere. A stout individual with a florid complexion, Praxus barely fitted into his dirty linen cuirass, which had seen better days. He paced up and down nervously while father and son thawed out by a glowing cast-iron brazier. At length, he could hold in his concerns no longer. 'Should we expect Hannibal by morning?' he demanded.

Fabricius sighed. 'I doubt it very much. His soldiers will be in need of rest as much as we are. You shouldn't give up on Longus just yet either,' he advised. 'Last I saw, the legionaries were holding their own.'

Praxus winced. His Adam's apple bobbed up and down. 'Where are they then?'

'I don't know,' Fabricius replied curtly. 'But Longus is an able man. He will not give up easily.'

Praxus resumed his pacing and Fabricius left him to it. 'Worrying about it won't do any good. This fool won't be able to stop the rumours either. He probably started half of them,' he muttered to Quintus before closing his eyes. 'Wake me up if there's any news.'

Quintus did his best to stay alert, but it wasn't long before he too grew deliciously drowsy. If Praxus wanted his fireside chairs back, he could bloody well wake them up, Quintus thought as sleep claimed him.

Some time later, they were woken by a sentry clattering in, shouting that the consul had arrived at the gates. It seemed a miracle, but as many as ten thousand legionaries were with him. Quintus found himself grinning at his father, who winked back. 'Told you,' said Fabricius. Praxus' miserable demeanour also vanished, and he capered about like a child. His sense of self-importance returned with a vengeance. 'Longus will have need of my quarters,' he declared loftily. 'You'd best leave at once. One of my officers can find you rooms.' He didn't give a name.

Fabricius' top lip lifted at the sudden return of the other's courage, and his bad manners, but he got up from his chair without protest. Quintus did likewise. Praxus barely bothered to say goodbye. Fortunately, the officer who'd initially brought them from the gate was still outside, and upon hearing their story, agreed to let them share his quarters.

The three hadn't gone far before the heavy tramp of men marching in unison came echoing down the narrow street towards them. Torchlight flickered off the darkened buildings on either side. A surge of adrenaline shot through Quintus' tired veins. He glanced at his father, who looked similarly interested. Quintus' lips framed the word 'Longus'? His father nodded. 'Stop,' he requested. The officer complied, as eager as they to see who it was. Within a few moments, they could make out a large party of legionaries – *triarii* – approaching. The soldier at the outside edge of each rank carried a flaming torch, illuminating the rest quite well.

'Make way for the consul!' shouted an officer at the front.

Quintus sighed with relief. Sempronius Longus had survived. Rome had not lost all its pride.

The triarii scarcely broke step as they passed by. One of the two most important men in the Republic did not wait while a pair of filthy soldiers gaped at him. Especially on a night like this.

Quintus couldn't stop himself. 'What happened?' he cried.

His unanswered question was carried away by the wind.

They gave each other a grim look and resumed their journey. Soon after, they happened upon a group of principes. Desperate to know how the battle had ended, Quintus caught the eye of a squat man carrying a shield emblazoned with two snarling wolves. 'Did you win?' he asked.

The princeps scowled. 'Depends what you mean by that,' he muttered. 'Hannibal won't forget the legionaries who fought at the Trebia in a hurry.'

Quintus and Fabricius exchanged a shocked, pleased glance. 'Did you turn and fall on the Carthaginian rear?' asked Fabricius excitedly. 'Did the allied infantry throw back the elephants and the skirmishers?'

The soldier looked down. 'Not exactly, sir, no.'

They stared at him, not understanding. 'What then?' demanded Fabricius.

The princeps cleared his throat. 'After breaking through the enemy line, Longus ordered us to quit the field.' A shadow passed across his face. 'Our wings had already broken, sir. I suppose he wasn't certain that we could turn the situation around.'

'The allied troops?' Quintus whispered.

The silence that followed spoke a thousand words.

'Sweet Jupiter above,' swore Fabricius. 'They're dead?'

'Some may have escaped back to our camp, sir,' the princeps admitted. 'Only time will tell.'

Quintus' head spun. Their casualties could number in the tens of thousands.

His father was more focused. 'In that case, I think it's we who will be remembering Hannibal rather than the other way around,' he observed acidly. 'Don't you?'

'Yes, sir,' the princeps muttered. He threw a longing glance at his comrades, who were disappearing around the nearest corner.

Fabricius jerked his head. 'Go.'

In a daze, Quintus watched the soldier scuttle off. 'Maybe Praxus was right,' he muttered. 'Hannibal could be at the gates by dawn.'

'Enough talk like that,' his father snapped. His lips peeled back into a feral snarl. 'Rome does not give up after one defeat. Not with foreign invaders on her soil!'

Quintus' courage rallied a fraction. 'What of Hannibal?'

'He'll leave us to it now,' Fabricius declared. 'He will be content to gather support from the Gaulish tribes over the winter.'

Quintus was relieved by his father's certainty. 'And us?'

'We will use the time to regroup, and to form new legions and cavalry units. One thing Rome and her allies are not short of is manpower. By the spring, the soldiers lost today will all have been replaced.' *And I'll have won a promotion which will keep the money-lenders at bay.* Fabricius grinned fiercely. 'You'll see!'

At last Quintus took heart. He nodded eagerly. They would fight the Carthaginians again soon. On equal or better terms.

517

There would be a chance to regain the honour that, in his mind, they had left behind on the battlefield.

Rome would rise again, and wrench victory from Hannibal.

Author's Note

It is an immense privilege to be accorded the opportunity to write a set of novels about the Second Punic War (218–201 BC). I have been fascinated by the time period since I was a boy, and I, like many, regard this as one of history's most hallowed episodes. The word 'epic' is completely overused today, but I feel that it is justified to use it with reference to this seventeen-year struggle, the balance of which was uncertain on so many occasions. If it had tipped but a fraction in the opposite direction during a number of those situations, life in Europe would be a very different affair today. The Carthaginians were quite unlike the Romans, and not in all the bad ways history would have us believe. They were intrepid explorers and inveterate traders, shrewd businessmen and brave soldiers. Where Rome's interests so often lay in conquest by war, theirs lay more in assuming power through controlling commerce and natural resources. It may be a small point, but my use of the word 'Carthaginian' rather than the Latin-derived 'Punic' when referring to their language is quite deliberate. The Carthaginians would not have used the term.

Many readers will know the broad brush strokes of Hannibal's war with Rome; others will know less; a very few will be voracious readers of the ancient authors Livy and Polybius, the main sources for this period. For the record, I have done my best to stick to the historical details that have survived. In places, however, I have either changed events slightly to fit in with the story's development, or invented things. Such is the novelist's remit, as well as his/her bane. If I have made any errors, I apologise for them.

The novel starts with a description of Carthage in all its magnificence. In the late third century BC, it was an infinitely grander city than Rome. I have taken the liberty of describing the fortifications present at the time of the Third Punic War (149–146 BC). I did this because we do not know what defences were in place in Hannibal's time. Because the incredible and impressive structures that held off the Romans in the final conflict were built sometime in the fifty years after Hannibal's defeat, I did not feel that using them was a major digression from fact.

Describing Carthaginian soldiers, both native and non-native, is a whole minefield of its own. We have little historical information about the uniforms that Carthaginian citizens and the host of nationalities who fought for them wore, or the type of equipment and weapons that they carried. Without several textbooks and articles, which I'll name later, I would have been lost. Another difficult area was Carthaginian names. In short, there aren't very many, or at least not many that have come down to us, more than 2,200 years later. Most of the ones that have survived are unpronounceable, or sound awful. Some are both! Hillesbaal and Ithobaal don't exactly roll off the tongue. Hence the main Carthaginian protagonist is called Hanno. There were important historical characters with this name, but I desperately needed a good one for my hero, and they were in very short supply.

The siege of Saguntum happened much as I've described. Anyone who visits Spain's eastern coast could do worse than climb the huge rocky outcrop near modern-day Valencia. It's such an impressive place that it's not hard to imagine Hannibal's soldiers besieging it. The formidable size of his army is attested by the ancient sources, as are the ways it was reduced by deaths, desertions and release from service. Whether any troops were left as garrisons in Gaul, we do not know. There has been much argument over which route the Carthaginian army followed after the Pyrenees, and where it crossed the River Rhône. The Volcae were surprised from the rear by a party of Carthaginians who had crossed upriver; their commander was one Hanno, not Bostar, however. The elephants were ferried over the river in the manner I've described.

The dramatic confrontation between the Roman embassy and the Carthaginian Council of Elders apparently took place as I've portrayed it. So too did the chance encounter between a unit of Roman cavalry and one of Numidians in the countryside above Massilia. I altered events, however, to take Scipio back to Rome before he travelled to Cisalpine Gaul to face the invaders. Minucius Flaccus is a fictitious character, but Minucius Rufus, his brother, is not.

Most controversy over Hannibal's journey concerns which pass his host took through the Alps. Having no wish to enter into such debates, I merely used the descriptions which Polybius and Livy gave us to set the scene. I truly hope that I managed to convey some of the terror and elation that would have filled the hearts of those hardy souls who followed Hannibal up and over the Alps' lofty peaks. The speech he gave to his troops before they started climbing was very similar to the one I described. Although not every source mentions the scene with the boiling wine and the boulder, I felt that I had to include it.

The term 'Italy' was in use in the third century BC as a geographical expression; it encompassed the entire peninsula south of Liguria and Cisalpine Gaul. The term did not become a political one until Polybius' time (mid second century BC). I decided to use it anyway. It simplified matters, and avoided constant reference to the different parts of the Republic: Rome, Campania, Latium, Lucania, etc.

My description of the calf born with its internal organs on the outside is not a figment of my imagination – I have performed two caesarean sections on cows to deliver the so-called *schistosomus reflexus*. They were without doubt the most revolting things I've ever set eyes upon. On one occasion, the unfortunate calf was still alive. Although this happened only fifteen years ago, the farmer's superstition was obvious and he became extremely agitated until I had euthanased it. We can only imagine what kind of reaction such a creature might have provoked in ancient times.

The duels between the Carthaginian prisoners, and the rewards on offer to those who survived, are described in the ancient texts. So too is the fate of Taurasia. When it came to making a point, Hannibal was as ruthless as the next general. The Roman losses in the Ticinus skirmish were severe and the savage night attack by some of their so-called Gaulish allies only served as another knock to Scipio's confidence. I invented the Carthaginian ambush at the River Trebia, but the details of the remarkable battle that unfolded afterwards are as exact as I could make them. Hannibal's victory on that bitter winter's day proved beyond doubt that his crossing of the Alps was no fluke. As the Romans would repeatedly discover in the months that followed, he was a real force to be reckoned with.

A bibliography of the textbooks I used while writing *Hannibal: Enemy of Rome* would run to several pages, so I will mention only the most important, in alphabetical order by author: *The Punic Wars* by Nigel Bagnall, *The Punic Wars* by Brian Caven, *Greece and Rome at War* by Peter Connolly, *Hannibal* by Theodore A. Dodge, *The Fall of Carthage* by Adrian Goldsworthy, *Armies of the Macedonian and Punic Wars* by Duncan Head, *Hannibal's War* by J. F. Lazenby, *Carthage Must Be Destroyed* by Richard Miles, *The Life and Death of Carthage* by G. C. & C. Picard, *Daily Life in Carthage (at the Time of Hannibal)* by G. C. Picard, *Roman Politics 220–150 BC* by H. H. Scullard, *Carthage and the Carthaginians* by Reginald B. Smith and *Warfare in the Classical World* by John Warry. I'm grateful to Osprey

Publishing for numerous excellent volumes, to Oxford University Press for the outstanding *Oxford Classical Dictionary*, and to Alberto Perez and Paul McDonnell-Staff for their superb article in Volume III, Issue 4 of *Ancient Warfare* magazine. Thanks, as always, to the members of www.romanarmy.com, whose rapid answers to my odd questions are so often of great use. I also have to mention, and thank, the three Australian brothers Wood: Danny, Ben and Sam. Their excellent mini travel series, *On Hannibal's Trail*, couldn't have screened on BBC4 at a better time than it did, and was a great help to me when writing the chapter on crossing the Alps.

I owe gratitude too to a legion of people at my wonderful publishers, Random House. There's Rosie de Courcy, my indefatigable and endlessly encouraging editor; Nicola Taplin, my tremendous managing editor; Kate Elton, who was generous enough to welcome me into the big, brave world of Arrow Books; Rob Waddington, who ensures that my novels reach every possible outlet in the land; Adam Humphrey, who organises fiendishly clever and successful marketing; Richard Ogle, who, with the illustrator Steve Stone, designs my amazing new jackets; Ruth Waldram, who secures me all kinds of great publicity; Monique Corless, who persuades so many foreign editors to buy my books; David Parrish, who makes sure that bookshops abroad do so too. Thank you all so much. Your hard work on my behalf is very much appreciated.

So many other people must be named: Charlie Viney, my agent, deserves a big mention. Without him, I'd still be working as a vet, and plugging away at my first Roman novel. Thanks, Charlie! I'm very grateful to Richenda Todd, my copy editor, who provides highly incisive input on my manuscripts; Claire Wheller, my outstanding physio, who stops my body from falling to bits after spending too long at my PC; Arthur O'Connor, the most argumentative man in Offaly (if not Ireland), who also supplies excellent criticism and improvements to my stories.

Last, but most definitely not least, Sair, my wife, and Ferdia and Pippa, my children, ground me and provide me with so much love and joy. Thank you. My life is so much richer for having you three in it.

Glossary

acetum: vinegar, the most common disinfectant used by the Romans. Vinegar is excellent at killing bacteria, and its widespread use in Western medicine continued until late in the nineteenth century.

Aesculapius: son of Apollo, the god of health and the protector of doctors. Revered by the Carthaginians as well as the Romans.

Agora: we have no idea what Carthaginians called the central meeting area in their city. I have used the Greek term to differentiate it from the main Forum in Rome. Without doubt, the Agora would have been the most important meeting place in Carthage.

Alps: In Latin, these mountains are called *Alpes*. Not used in the novel (unlike the Latin names for other geographical features) as it looks 'strange' to modern eyes.

Assembly of the People: the public debating group to which all Carthaginian male citizens belonged. Its main power was that of electing the suffetes once a year.

Astarte: a Carthaginian goddess whose origins lie in the East. She may have represented marriage, and was perhaps seen as the protector of cities and different social groups.

atrium: the large chamber immediately beyond the entrance hall in a Roman house. Frequently built on a grand scale, this was the social and devotional centre of the home.

Baal Hammon: the pre-eminent god at the time of the founding of Carthage. He was the protector of the city, the fertilising sun, the provider of wealth and the guarantor of success and happiness. The Tophet, or the sacred area where Baal Hammon was worshipped, is the site where the bones of children and babies have been found, giving rise to the controversial topic of child sacrifice. For those who are interested, there is an excellent discussion on the issue in Richard Miles' book, *Carthage Must Be Destroyed*. The term 'Baal' means 'Master' or 'Lord', and was used before the name of various gods.

Baal Saphon: the Carthaginian god of war.

bireme: an ancient warship, which was perhaps invented by the Phoenicians. It had a square sail, two sets of oars on each side, and was used extensively by the Greeks and Romans.

caetrati (sing. *caetratus*): light Iberian infantry. They wore short-sleeved white tunics with a crimson border at the neck, hem and sleeves. Their only protection was a helmet of sinew or bronze, and a round buckler of leather and wicker, or wood, called a *caetra*. They were armed with *falcata* swords and daggers. Some may have carried javelins.

caligae: heavy leather sandals worn by the Roman soldier. Sturdily constructed in three layers – a sole, insole and upper – *caligae* resembled an open-toed boot. The straps could be tightened to make them fit more closely. Dozens of metal studs on the sole gave the sandals good grip; these could also be replaced when necessary.

carnyx (pl. *carnyxes*): a bronze trumpet, which was held vertically and topped by a bell shaped in the form of an animal, usually a boar. Used by many Celtic peoples, it was ubiquitous in Gaul, and provided a fearsome sound alone or in unison with other instruments. It was often depicted on Roman coins, to denote victories over various tribes.

Carthage: modern-day Tunis. It was reputedly founded in 814 BC, although the earliest archaeological finds date from about sixty years later.

cenaculae (sing. *cenacula*): the miserable multi-storey flats in which Roman plebeians lived. Cramped, poorly lit, heated only by braziers, and often dangerously constructed, the *cenaculae* had no running water or sanitation. Access to the flats was via staircases built on the outside of the building.

Choma: the manmade quadrilateral area which lay to the south/ southeast of the main harbours in Carthage. It was probably constructed to serve as a place to unload ships, to store goods, and to act as a pier head protecting passing vessels from the worst of the wind.

Cisalpine Gaul: the northern area of modern-day Italy, comprising the Po plain and its mountain borders from the Alps to the Apennines. In the third century BC, it was not part of the Republic.

consul: one of two annually elected chief magistrates, appointed by the people and ratified by the Senate. Effective rulers of Rome for twelve months, they were in charge of civil and military matters and led the Republic's armies into war. Each could countermand the other and both were supposed to heed the wishes of the Senate. No man was supposed to serve as consul more than once.

Council of Elders: Carthaginian politics, with its numerous ruling bodies, is very confusing. The Council of Elders was one of the most important, however. Its members were some of the most prominent men in Carthage, and its areas of remit included the treasury and foreign affairs. Another ruling body was the Tribunal of One Hundred and Four. Composed of members of the elite aristocracy, it supervised the conduct of government officials and military leaders; it also acted as a type of higher constitutional court.

crucifixion: contrary to popular belief, the Romans did not invent this awful form of execution; in fact, the Carthaginians may well have done so. The practice is first recorded during the Punic Wars.

decurion: the cavalry officer in charge of ten men. In later times, the decurion commanded a *turma*, a unit of about thirty men.

didrachm: a silver coin, worth two drachmas, which was one of the main coins in third century BC Italy. Strangely, the Romans did not make coins of their own design until later on. The *denarius*, which was to become the main coin of the Republic, was not introduced until around 211 BC.

Eshmoun: the Carthaginian god of health and well-being, whose temple was the largest in Carthage.

falaricae (sing. *falarica*): a spear with a pine shaft and a long iron head, at the base of which a ball of pitch and tow was often tied. This created a lethal incendiary weapon, used to great effect by the Saguntines.

falcata sword: a lethal, slightly curved weapon with a sharp point used by light Iberian infantry. It was single-edged for the first half to two-thirds of its blade, but the remainder was double-edged. The hilt curved protectively around the hand and back towards the blade; it was often made in the shape of a horse's head. Apparently, the *caetrati* who used *falcata* swords were well able to fight legionaries.

fasces: a bundle of rods bound together around an axe. The symbol of justice, it was carried by a lictor, a group of whom walked in front of all senior magistrates. The fasces symbolised the right of the authorities to punish and execute lawbreakers.

fides: essentially, good faith. It was regarded as a major quality in Rome.

fugitivarius (pl. *fugitivarii*): slave-catchers, men who made a living from tracking down and capturing runaways. The punishment branding the letter 'F' (for *fugitivus*) on the forehead is documented; so is the wearing of permanent neck chains, which had directions on how to return the slave to their owner.

Genua: modern-day Genoa.

gladius (pl. *gladii*): little information remains about the 'Spanish' sword of the Republican army, the *gladius hispaniensis*, with its waisted blade. It is not clear when it was adopted by the Romans, but it was probably after encountering the weapon during the First Punic War, when it was used by Celtiberian troops. The shaped hilt was made of bone and protected by a pommel and guard of wood. The *gladius* was worn on the right, except by centurions and other senior officers, who wore it on the left. It was actually quite easy to draw with the right hand, and was probably positioned like this to avoid entanglement with the *scutum* while being unsheathed.

gugga: in Plautus' comedy, *Poenulus*, one of the Roman characters refers to a Carthaginian trader as a 'gugga'. This insult can be translated as 'little rat'.

hastati (sing. *hastatus*): experienced young soldiers who formed the first ranks in the Roman battle line in the third century BC. They were armed with mail or bronze breast and back plates, crested helmets, and *scuta*. They carried two *pila*, one light and one heavy, and a *gladius hispaniensis*.

hora secunda, the second hour; *hora quarta*, the fourth hour; *hora undecima*, the eleventh hour: Roman time was divided into two periods, that of daylight (twelve hours) and of night-time (eight watches). The first hour of the day, *hora prima*, started at sunrise.

Iberia: the modern-day Iberian Peninsula, encompassing Spain and Portugal.

Iberus: the River Ebro.

Illyricum (or Illyria): the Roman name for the lands that lay across the Adriatic Sea from Italy: including parts of modern-day Slovenia, Serbia, Croatia, Bosnia and Montenegro.

intervallum: the wide, flat area inside the walls of a Roman camp or fort. As well as serving to protect the barrack buildings from enemy missiles, it could when necessary allow the massing of troops before battle.

kopis (pl. *kopides*): a Greek sword with a forward curving blade, not dissimilar to the *falcata* sword. It was normally carried in a leather-covered sheath and suspended from a baldric. Many ancient peoples used the *kopis*, from the Etruscans to the Oscans and Persians.

lictor (pl. *lictores*): a magistrates' enforcer. Only strongly built citizens could apply for this job. Essentially, *lictores* were the bodyguards for the consuls, praetors and other senior Roman magistrates. Such officials were accompanied at all times in public by set numbers of *lictores* (the number depended on their rank). Each *lictor* carried a fasces. Other duties included the arresting and punishment of wrongdoers.

Ligurians: natives of the coastal area that was bounded to the west by the River Rhône and to the east by the River Arno.

Lusitanians: tribesmen from the area of modern-day Portugal.

Massilia: the city of Marseille in modern-day France.

Melqart: a Carthaginian god associated with the sea, and with Hercules. He was also the god most favoured by the Barca family. Hannibal notably made a pilgrimage to Melqart's shrine in southern Iberia before beginning his war on Rome.

mulsum: a drink made by mixing four parts wine and one part honey. It was commonly drunk before meals and during the lighter courses.

munus (pl. *munera*): a gladiatorial combat, staged originally during celebrations honouring someone's death.

Padus: the River Po.

papaverum: the drug morphine. Made from the flowers of the opium poppy, its use has been documented from at least 1000 BC.

peristyle: a colonnaded garden which lay to the rear of a Roman house. Often of great size, it was bordered by open-fronted seating areas, reception rooms and banqueting halls.

pilum (pl. *pila*): the Roman javelin. It consisted of a wooden shaft approximately 1.2 m (4 ft) long, joined to a thin iron shank approximately 0.6 m (2 ft) long, and was topped by a small pyramidal point. The javelin was heavy and, when launched, all of its weight was concentrated behind the head, giving it tremendous penetrative force. It could strike through a shield to injure the man carrying it, or lodge in the shield, making it impossible for the man to continue using it. The range of the *pilum* was about 30 m (100 ft), although the effective range was probably about half this distance.

Pisae: modern-day Pisa.

Placentia: modern-day Piacenza.

praetor: one of four senior magistrates (in the years 228–198 BC approximately) who administered justice in Rome, or in its overseas possessions such as Sardinia and Sicily. He could also hold military commands and initiate legislation. The main understudies to the consuls, the praetors convened the Senate in their absence.

principes (sing. *princeps*): these soldiers – described as family men in their prime – formed the second rank of the Roman battle line in the third century BC. They were similar to the *hastati*, and as such were armed and dressed in much the same manner.

provocatio: an appeal on behalf of the Roman people, made against the order of a magistrate.

pteryges: also spelt *pteruges*. This was a twin layer of stiffened linen strips that protected the waist and groin of the wearer. It either came attached to a cuirass of the same material, or as a detachable piece of equipment to be used below a bronze breastplate. Although *pteryges* were designed by the Greeks, many nations used them, including the Romans and Carthaginians.

quinquereme: the principal Carthaginian fighting vessel in the third century BC. They were of similar size to triremes, but possessed many more rowers. Controversy over the exact number of oarsmen in these ships, and the positions they occupied, has gone on for decades. It is fairly well accepted nowadays, however, that the quinquereme had three sets of oars on each side. The vessel was rowed from three levels with two men on each oar of the upper banks, and one man per oar of the lower bank.

Rhodanus: the River Rhône.

Saguntum: modern-day Sagunto.

Saturnalia: a festival which began on 17 December. During the week long celebrations, ordinary rules were relaxed and slaves could dine before their masters; at this time, they could also treat them with less deference. The festival was an excuse for eating, drinking and playing games. Gifts of candles and pottery figures were also exchanged.

saunion: also called the *soliferreum*. This was a characteristic Iberian weapon, a slim, all-iron javelin with a small, leaf-shaped head.

scutarii (sing. *scutarius*): heavy Iberian infantry, Celtiberians who carried round shields, or ones very similar to those of the Roman legionaries. Richer individuals may have had mail shirts; others may have worn small breastplates. Many *scutarii* wore greaves. Their bronze helmets were very similar to the Gallic Montefortino style. They were armed with straight-edged swords that were slightly shorter than the Gaulish equivalent, and known for their excellent quality.

scutum (pl. *scuta*): an elongated oval Roman army shield, about 1.2 m (4 ft) tall and 0.75 m (2 ft 6 in) wide. It was made from two layers of wood, the pieces laid at right angles to each other; it was then covered with linen or canvas, and leather. The *scutum* was heavy, weighing between 6 and 10 kg (13–22 lbs). A large metal boss decorated its centre, with the horizontal grip placed behind this. Decorative designs were often painted on the front, and a leather cover was used to protect the shield when not in use, e.g. while marching. Some of the Iberian and Gaulish warriors used very similar shields.

Scylla: a mythical monster with twelve feet and six heads that dwelt in a cave opposite the whirlpool Charybdis, in the modern Straits of Messina.

socii: allies of Rome. By the time of the Punic Wars, all the non-Roman peoples of Italy had been forced into military alliances with Rome. In theory, these peoples were still independent, but in practice they were subjects, who were obliged to send quotas of troops to fight for the Republic whenever it was demanded.

stade: from the Greek word *stadion*. It was the distance of the original foot race in the ancient Olympic games of 776 BC, and was approximately 192 m (630 ft) in length. The word 'stadium' derives from it.

strigil: a small, curved iron tool used to clean the skin after bathing. First perfumed oil was rubbed in, and then the *strigil* was used to scrape off the combination of sweat, dirt and oil.

suffete: one of two men who headed the Carthaginian state. Elected yearly, they dealt with a range of affairs of state from the political and military to judicial and religious issues. It is extremely unclear whether they had as much power as Roman consuls, but it seems likely that by the third century BC they did not.

tablinum: the office or reception area beyond the *atrium*. The *tablinum* usually opened on to an enclosed colonnaded garden, the peristyle.

Tanit: along with Baal Hammon, the pre-eminent deity in Carthage. She was regarded as a mother goddess, and as the patroness and protector of the city.

Taurasia: modern-day Turin.

tesserae: pieces of stone or marble which were cut into roughly cubic shape and fitted closely on to a bed of mortar to form a mosaic. This practice was introduced in the third century BC.

Ticinus: the River Ticino.

Trebia: the River Trebbia.

tribune: senior staff officer within a legion; also one of ten political positions in Rome, where they served as 'tribunes of the people', defending the rights of the plebeians. The tribunes could also veto measures taken by the Senate or consuls, except in times of war. To assault a tribune was a crime of the highest order.

trireme: the classic ancient warship, which was powered by a single sail and three banks of oars. Each oar was rowed by one man, who on Roman ships was freeborn, not a slave. Exceptionally manoeuvrable, and capable of up to eight knots under sail or for short bursts when rowed, the trireme also had a bronze ram at the prow. This was used to damage or even sink enemy ships. Small catapults were also mounted on the deck. Each trireme was crewed by up to 30 men and had around 200 rowers; it could carry up to 60 infantry, giving it a very large crew in proportion to its size. This limited the triremes' range, so they were mainly used as troop transports and to protect coastlines.

triarii (sing. *triarius*): the oldest, most experienced soldiers in a legion of the third century BC. These men were often held back until the most desperate of situations in a battle. The fantastic Roman expression 'Matters have come down to the *triarii*' makes this clear. They wore bronze crested helmets, mail shirts and a greave on their leading (left) legs. They each carried a *scutum*, and were armed with a *gladius hispaniensis* and a long, thrusting spear.

tunny: tuna fish.

turmae (sing. *turma*): a cavalry unit of thirty men.

velites (sing. *veles*): light skirmishers of the third century BC who were recruited from the poorest social class. They were young men whose only protection was a small, round shield, and in some cases, a simple bronze helmet. They carried a sword, but their primary weapons were 1.2 m (4 ft.) javelins. They also wore bear- or wolf-skin headdresses.

Vespera: the first watch of the night.

vilicus: slave foreman or farm manager. Commonly a slave, the *vilicus* was sometimes a paid worker, whose job it was to make sure that the returns on a farm were as large as possible. This was most commonly done by treating the slaves brutally.

Vinalia Rustica: a Roman wine festival held on 19 August.

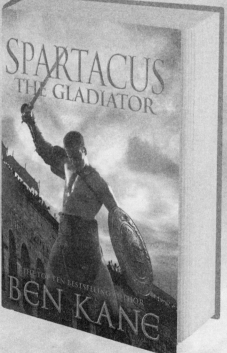

Chapter I

South-western Thrace, autumn 74 BC

When the village came into sight at the top of a distant hill, a surging joy filled him. The road from Bithynia had been long. His feet were blistered, the muscles of his legs hurt and the weight of his mail shirt was making his back ache. The chill wind snapped around his ears, and he cursed himself for not buying a fur cap in the settlement he'd passed through two days prior. He had always made do with a felt liner and, when necessary, a bronze helmet, rather than a typical Thracian fox-skin *alopekis*. But in this bitter weather, maybe warm clothing was more important than war gear. Gods, but he was looking forward to sleeping under the comfort of a roof, out of reach of the elements. The journey from the Roman camp where he'd been released from service had taken more than six weeks, and winter was fast approaching. It should have been less than half that, but his horse had gone lame only two days after he'd left. Since then, riding had been out of the question. Carrying his shield and equipment was as much as he could ask it to do without worsening its limp.

'Any other mount, and I'd have sacrificed you to the gods long ago,' he said, tugging the lead rope that guided the white stallion ambling along behind him. 'But you've served me well enough these last years, eh?' He grinned as it nickered back at him. 'No, I've no apples left. But you'll get a feed soon enough. We're nearly home, thank the Rider.'

Home. The mere idea seemed unreal. What did that mean after so long? Seeing his father would be the best thing about it, although he'd be an old man by now. The traveller had been away for the guts of a decade, fighting for Rome. A power hated by all Thracians, yet one that many served nonetheless. He had done so for good reasons. *To learn their ways so that one day I can fight them again. Father's idea was a good one.* It had been the hardest act of his life to take orders from some of the very soldiers he had fought against – men who had perhaps killed his brother and who had certainly conquered his land. But it had been worth it. He had learned a wealth of information from those whoresons. How to train men mercilessly, until they fought as one unit. How vital it was to obey orders, even in the red heat of battle. How trained soldiers could be made to stand their ground in the most extreme situations. Discipline, he thought. Discipline and organisation were two of the most vital keys.

It wasn't just the desire to learn their ways that had you leave your village, added his combative side. After its last defeat by the legions, your tribe had been thoroughly cowed. There was no chance of fighting anyone, least of all Rome. You are a warrior, who follows the rider god. You love war. Bloodshed. Killing. Joining the Romans gave you the opportunity to take part in never-ending campaigns. Despite everything that they've done to your people, you still took pleasure from waging war alongside theme.

I've had a bellyful of it for now. It's time to settle down. Find a woman. Start a family. He smiled. Once he would have scorned such ideas. Now they were appealing. During his service with the legions, he'd seen things that would turn a man's hair grey. He'd become used to them – in the red heat of battle, he had acted in much the same way, but sacking undefended camps and villages, and seeing women raped and children killed, were not things that sat especially well with him.

'Planning how to take the fight to Rome will do me for a while. The time for war will present itself again,' he said to the stallion. 'In the meantime I need a good Thracian woman to make lots of babies with.'

It nibbled his elbow, ever hopeful for a treat.

'If you want some barley, get a move on,' he said in an affectionate growl. 'I'm not stopping to give you a nosebag this near to the village.'

Above him and to his left, something scraped off rock, and he cursed silently for letting his attention lapse. Just because he'd encountered no one on the rough track that day didn't mean that it was safe. Yet the gods had smiled on him for the whole journey from Bithynia. This was a time when most Thracians avoided the bitter weather in favour of oiling and storing their weapons in preparation for the following campaigning season. For a lone traveller, this was the best time to travel.

I've done well not to have run into any bandits thus far. These ones are damn close to my village. Let there not be too many of them. Pretending to stretch his shoulders and roll his neck, he stole a quick glance to either side. Three men, maybe four, were watching him from their hiding places on the rocky slopes that bordered the rough track. Unsurprisingly for Thrace, they seemed to be armed with javelins. He eyed the tinned bronze helmet that hung from the pack on the stallion's rump, and decided against making a grab for it. Few peltasts could hit a man in the head. As for his shield, well, he could reach that while their first javelins were still in the air. If he was hit, his mail shirt would probably protect him. Trying to untie his thrusting spear would take too much time. He'd carry the fight to them with his *sica*, the curved Thracian blade that hung from his gilded belt. They were acceptable odds, he decided. As long as the brigands weren't expert shots. *Great Rider, watch over me with a ready sword.*

'I know you're there,' he called out. 'You might as well show yourselves.'

There was a burst of harsh laughter. About thirty paces away, one of the bandits stood up. Merciless eyes regarded the traveller from a narrow face pitted with scars. His embroidered woollen cloak swung open, revealing a threadbare, thigh-length tunic. A greasy fox-skin cap perched atop his head. He had scrawny legs, and his tall calfskin boots had seen better days. In his left hand, he carried a typical *pelte*, or crescent-shaped shield, and behind it a spare javelin; in his right, another light spear was cocked and ready to throw.

No armour, and apart from his javelins, only a dagger in his belt, noted the traveller. Good. His friends will be no better armed.

'That's a fine stallion you have there,' said the thug. 'A pity that it's lame.'

'It is. If it wasn't, you shitbags wouldn't have seen me for dust.'

'But it is, so you're on foot, and alone,' sneered a second voice.

The traveller looked up. The speaker was older than the first man, with a lined visage and greying hair. His hemp-woven clothing was equally ragged, but there was a fierce hunger in his brooding gaze. For all his poverty, his round shield was well made, and the javelin in his right fist looked to have seen good use. This was the most dangerous one. The leader. 'You want the stallion, I suppose,' the traveller said.

'Ha!' A third man stood up. He was larger than either of his companions; his arms and legs were heavily muscled, and instead of javelins, he carried a large pelte and a vicious-looking club. 'We want it all. Your horse, your equipment and weapons. Your money, if you have any.'

'We'll even take your food!' The fourth bandit was skeletally thin, with sunken cheeks and a sallow, unhealthy complexion. He had no shield, but three light spears.

'And if I give you all that, you'll let me go on my way?' His breath plumed in the chill air.

'Of course,' promised the first man. His flat, dead eyes, and his comrades' sniggers, gave the lie to his words.

The traveller didn't bother answering. He spun around, muttering 'Stay!' to the stallion. Even as he slid his hand under his large circular shield and snapped the thong that held it in place, he heard a javelin zipping over his head. Another followed behind on a lower arc. It struck the dust between the horse's hooves, making it skitter to and fro. 'Calmly,' he ordered. 'You've been through this plenty of times before.' Reassured by his voice, it settled.

'Oeagrus, stop, you fool!' shouted the leader. 'If you injure that beast, I'll gut you myself.'

Good. No more javelins. The stallion is too valuable. Keeping his back to his mount and raising the shield, he turned. The skinny bandit was to his rear now, but he wouldn't risk any more spears. Nor would the others. Drawing his sica, he smiled grimly. 'You'll have to come down and fight me.'

'Fair enough,' growled the first man. Using his heels as brakes, he skidded down the slope. His two comrades followed. Behind him, the traveller heard the thin brigand also descending. The stallion bared its teeth and screamed an angry challenge. *Let him even try to come close.*

When the trio reached the bottom, they conferred for a moment.

'Ready?' he asked mockingly.

'You whoreson,' snarled the leader. 'Will you be so arrogant when I cut your balls off and stuff them down your neck?'

'At least you'd be able to find mine. I doubt that any of you scumbags have any.'

The big man's face twisted with fury. Screaming at the top of his voice, he charged, pelte and club at the ready.

The traveller took a couple of steps forward. Placing his left leg behind the shield, he braced himself. He tightened his grip on his sica. *This has to be quick or the others will be on me as well.*

Fortunately, the thug was as unskilled as he was confident.

Driving his shield into his opponent's, he swung a wicked blow at his head. The traveller, rocking back slightly from the impact of the strike, ducked his head out of the way. Reaching around with his sica, he sliced the big man's left hamstring in two. A piercing scream rent the air, and the bandit collapsed in a heap. He had enough sense to raise his pelte, but the traveller smashed it out of the way with his shield and skewered him through the neck. The thug died choking on his own blood.

He tugged the blade free and kicked the corpse on to its back. 'Who's next?'

The leader hissed an order at the skinny man before he and the cap-wearing bandit split up. Like crabs, they scuttled out to either side of their victim.

The stallion trumpeted another challenge, and the traveller sensed it rear up on its hind legs. He stepped forward, out of its way. An instant later, there was a strangled cry, the dull *thump*, *thump* of hooves striking bone, and then the noise of a body hitting the ground. 'My horse might be lame, but he still has quite a temper,' he said mildly. 'Your friend's brains are probably decorating the road. Am I right?'

The two remaining brigands exchanged a shocked look. 'Don't even think of running away!' warned the leader. 'Oeagrus was my sister's son. I want vengeance for his death.'

Unobtrusively, the traveller lowered his shield a fraction, exposing his neck. *Let that tempt one of them.*

The man in the fox-skin cap clenched his jaw. 'Fuck whether the beast gets hit,' he said, hurling his javelin.

The traveller didn't move from the spear's path. He simply raised his shield, letting it smack directly into the layered wood and leather. Its sharp iron head punched two fingers' depth out through the inner surface, but did not injure him. Swinging back his left arm, he threw the now useless item at the thug, who scrambled away to avoid being hit. What he wasn't expecting was for the traveller to be only a few steps behind his flying shield.

When the bandit thrust his second javelin at his opponent, it was parried savagely out of the way.

Using his momentum to keep moving forward, the traveller punched his opponent in the face with his left fist. The man's head cracked back with the force of the blow, and he barely saw the sica as it came swinging back around to hack deep into the flesh where his neck met his torso. Spraying blood everywhere, and looking faintly surprised, he fell sideways into the road. Keeping time with the slowing beats of his heart, a crimson tide flooded the ground around him. *Three down, but the last is the most deadly.*

The traveller turned swiftly, expecting the leader's attempt to stab him in the back. The move saved him from serious injury, and the javelin skidded off the rings of his mail shirt and into thin air, causing the man to overreach and stumble. A massive backhand to the face sent him sprawling backwards on to his arse, losing his weapon in the process.

He stared up at the traveller, frank terror in his eyes. 'I have a wife. A f-family to f-feed,' he stammered.

'You should have thought of that before you ambushed me,' came the growled reply.

The bandit screamed as the sica slid into his belly, slicing his guts to ribbons. Sobbing with pain, he waited for the death blow. But it did not fall. He lay there, helpless, already passing in and out of consciousness.

A few moments later, he opened his eyes. His killer was watching him impassively. 'Don't leave me to die,' he begged. 'Even Kotys wouldn't do this to a man.'

'Kotys?' There was no response, so he kicked his victim. 'You were going to cut my balls off and feed them to me, remember?'

He swallowed down his agony. 'P-please.'

'Very well.' The sica rose high in the air.

'Who in all the gods' name are you?' he managed to whisper.

'Just a weary traveller with a lame horse.'

The blade scythed down, and the brigand's eyes went wide for the last time.

Ariadne scraped back her hair and carefully pushed a couple of bone pins into her long black tresses, fastening them into place. Sitting on a three-legged stool by a low wooden table, she angled the bronze mirror that sat there so that it caught the watery light entering through the hut's open doorway. The shaped piece of red-gold metal was her sole luxury, and using it occasionally served to remind her of who she was. This was one of those days. To the vast majority of the people in the settlement, she was not a woman, a relation or a friend. She was a priestess of Dionysus, and revered as such. Most of the time, Ariadne was content with this prestige. After her harsh upbringing, her elevated position was better than she'd have ever dreamed possible. But it didn't mean that she didn't have needs or desires. *What's wrong with wanting a man? A husband?* Her lips pursed. Currently, the only person showing interest in her was Kotys, the king of the Maedi tribe. Unsurprisingly, his interest had put paid to any other potential suitors. Those who crossed Kotys tended to end up dead – or so the rumour went. Not that there had been any before that, she reflected bitterly. Men with the courage to court a priestess were rare beasts indeed.

Ariadne did not want or appreciate Kotys' lecherous advances, but felt powerless to stop them. He hadn't yet tried to become physical, but she was sure that was because of her vaunted status – and the venomous snake that she kept in a basket by her bedding. Her situation was complicated by the fact that she had to remain in the village. She had been sent here by the high priests in Kabyle, Thrace's only city, which lay far to the north-east. Extraordinary circumstances notwithstanding, hers was an appointment for life. If she returned to Kabyle, Ariadne could expect to be performing menial duties in the main temple there for the rest of her days.

There was no question either of returning to her family. While she loved her mother, and prayed for her every day, Ariadne harboured two feelings for her father. Hate was the first, and loathing was the second. Her emotions stemmed from her brutal childhood. Ariadne's existence had consisted of beatings, humiliation and worse, all at the hands of her father. A warrior of the Odrysai tribe, he had despised her because she – his only child – was not male. During the long years of misery, her sole means of escape had been praying to Dionysus, the god of intoxication and ritual ecstasy. It was only when communing with him that she'd felt some inner peace, a state of affairs that still prevailed. To this day, Ariadne believed that Dionysus had helped her to survive the unending abuse.

Other than through marriage, the concept of escaping her father had never entered Ariadne's mind. There had been simply nowhere for her to go. Then, on her thirteenth birthday, things had changed utterly. In a remarkable intervention, Ariadne's downtrodden mother had persuaded her father to allow her attend the Dionysian temple in Kabyle as a prospective candidate for the priesthood. Once there, her burning determination had impressed the priests and allowed her to remain. More than a decade later, she still had no desire to return home. Unless, of course, it were to kill her father, which would be a pointless exercise. While Ariadne's position as a priestess elevated her above that of ordinary women, a patricide could expect but one fate.

No, her best option was to weather out Kotys' attentions – *Dionysus, let some doe-eyed beauty catch his eye soon* – and establish herself here. It had been a mere six months since she'd arrived at this, the main Maedi settlement. Not long at all. Ariadne's chin lifted. There was another option of course. If Kotys were deposed, a better man could take his place. She'd been here long enough to sense the seething discontent with his rule. Rhesus, the previous king, and Andriscus, his son, weren't especially missed, but Sitalkes, the noble who might have replaced them, had been a popular figure. They were careful not to do it within earshot of Kotys' bodyguards, but plenty of warriors spoke nostalgically of

Sitalkes and his two sons, of whom one had been killed in battle against the Romans and the other had gone to serve the conquerors as a mercenary, and never returned.

If only someone would step forward and harness the simmering rage against Kotys, thought Ariadne. A short, sharp fight and the bastard would be gone for ever. Not for the first time, she cursed the fact that she'd been born a woman. *No one would follow me.* She studied the familiar reflection in the bronze mirror before her. A heart-shaped face, with a straight nose and high cheekbones, framed by long black ringlets of hair. A determined chin. Creamy white skin, most unsuited to the blazing sun that bathed Thrace every summer. A swirling design of dots tattooed on both her forearms. Slim but muscular shoulders. Small breasts. What does Kotys see in me? she wondered. I'm no beauty. Striking perhaps, but not pretty. As ever, the same answer entered Ariadne's head. He sees my wild spirit and, being a king, wants it for his own. It was the same fieriness that had often got her in trouble during her training, and which had also helped her to become a priestess sooner than might have been expected. Ariadne valued her tempestuous nature greatly. Because of it, she could enter the maenad trances easily, and reach the zone where one might encounter Dionysus, and know his wishes. My spirit belongs to no man, Ariadne thought fiercely. Only to the god.

Standing, she moved to her simple bed, a blanket covering a thick layer of straw in one corner of the hut. It was the same as that used by everyone in the settlement. Thracians were known for their austerity, and she was no different. Ariadne donned her dark red woollen cloak. In addition to marking her position in life, it served as her cover at night. Picking up the wicker basket that lay at the bed's foot, she put it to her ear. Not a sound. She wasn't surprised. The snake within did not like the chilly autumn weather, and it was as much as she could do to rouse it occasionally from its torpor and wrap it around her neck before performing a rite at the temple. Thankfully, this simple tactic was enough to inspire awe in the villagers' minds. To Ariadne, however, the serpent was but a tool in maintaining her air of mystery. She respected the creature, indeed feared it a little, but she'd been exhaustively trained to handle it and its kind in Kabyle.

With the basket under one arm, she headed outside. Like most of the others in the settlement, her one-roomed, rectangular hut had been constructed using a lattice of woven branches, over which a thick layer of mud had been laid. Its saddle roof was covered with a mixture of straw and mud, with a gap at one end to let out smoke from the fire. To the hut's rear stood part of the rampart that ran around Kotys' living quarters. It was a defence within the circular settlement's outer wall, reinforcing the king's elevated position and serving against treachery from within. Other huts lay to either side, each surrounded by a palisade that kept in their owners' livestock. The dwellings followed the winding paths that divided the sprawling village. Like the regular dungheaps and mounds of refuse, they had evolved over centuries of inhabitation. Ariadne was eternally grateful that her hut was a reasonable distance from any of these necessary, but stinking, piles.

She followed the lane towards the centre of the settlement, acknowledging the respectful greetings of those she met with a grave smile, or a nod. Women with babes at the breast and the old asked for her blessing or advice, while all but the boldest of the warriors tended to avoid her gaze. Children tended to fall into two camps: those who were terrified of her and those who asked to see her snake. There were far more of the former than the latter. There was little to leaven the loneliness of Ariadne's existence. She forced her melancholy away. The god would send her a man, if he saw fit. And if he didn't, she would continue to serve him faithfully, as she had promised during her initiation.

The crowd in front of her parted, revealing a group of richly dressed warriors. Ariadne's heart sank. It wasn't just the men's swagger that told her who they were. Their red long-sleeved tunics with vertical white stripes, elaborate bronze helmets and silver-inlaid greaves shouted stature and importance. So too did their well-made javelins, *kopis* swords and long, curved daggers. Ariadne mouthed a silent curse. Wherever this many of his bodyguards were, Kotys wouldn't be far behind. Glancing to her left, she greeted an elderly woman whose sick husband she'd recently treated. A torrent of praise to Dionysus filled Ariadne's ears. Smiling, she moved nearer to the woman's hut, turning her back on the path. With a little luck, the warriors wouldn't have seen her. Perhaps they weren't even looking for her?

'Priestess!'

Ariadne cursed silently. She continued listening to the old woman's patter, but when the voice called again, it was right behind her.

'Priestess.'

The traveller didn't linger at the scene where he'd been ambushed. Of course, the brigands had nothing worth taking. All he'd had to do was clean his sica, snap off the javelin that had skewered his shield and retie the shield to the pack on his horse's back. Leaving the bodies where they'd fallen, he set out for the village. At this rate, they'd be lucky to reach it before dark. That eventuality did not bear thinking about. Banks of dull yellow clouds overhead promised an early fall of snow. His luck was in, however. Whether it was the adrenalin pumping through his mount's veins, or an intervention by the Great Rider, he did not know, but the stallion now seemed to move more easily on its bad leg. They made good progress, coming within sight of the settlement just as the first flakes began to fall.

Loud bleating carried through the air, and the traveller looked up. Aided by a pair of dogs, a small boy was herding a flock of sheep and goats on to the road just ahead. 'We're not the only ones seeking shelter,' he said to his mount. They halted, giving the lad space to usher his resentful charges on to the stony track. 'Some bitter weather coming. You're wise to head for home now,' he said in a friendly tone.

The boy made no move to come down off the slope. 'Who are you?' he demanded suspiciously.

'Peiros is my name,' he lied. Even this close to his home, he did not yet feel like revealing his true identity.

'Never heard of you,' came the dismissive reply.

'You were probably still crawling around on a bearskin rug at your mother's feet when I left the village.'

Some of the wariness left the boy's eyes. 'Maybe.' He began urging the last of the sheep and goats on to the road with sharp cries and waves of his arms. The dogs darted to and fro, ensuring that there were no stragglers. The traveller watched, and when the entire flock was safely down, he began to walk alongside the young shepherd. *I wonder what I can find out.* 'How's Rhesus?' he asked.

'Rhesus? The old king?'

'Yes.'

'He's been gone these four years. A plague took him.'

'His son Andriscus should be king then.'

The boy threw him a scornful look. 'You really have been away. Andriscus is dead too.' He glanced around warily before whispering, 'Murdered, like Sitalkes.' He saw the flash of horror in the traveller's eyes. 'I know, it was terrible. My father says that the Great Rider will punish Kotys eventually, but for now, we have to live with him.'

'Kotys killed Sitalkes?'

'Yes,' replied the lad, spitting.

'And now he's the king?'

A nod.

'I see.'

A silence fell, which the boy did not dare break. He wouldn't admit it, but the grim traveller scared him. A moment later, the man halted. 'You go on.' He gestured at his stallion. 'I mustn't make him walk too long on his bad leg. I'll see you in the village.'

With a relieved nod, the boy began chivvying the flock along the road again. The traveller waited until he was some distance away before closing his eyes. 'Guilt nipped at his conscience. *If only I had been here, things might have been different.* He didn't let the feeling linger. *Or they might not. I too might have been slain. Father's decision to send me away was a good one.* Somehow he knew that Sitalkes also would not have changed what had transpired. It was impossible to deny his sadness at the news of his father's murder, however. He thought of Sitalkes as he'd last seen him: strong, straight-backed, healthy. *Rest well.* All he'd wanted was to come home. For his service with his most hated enemies to end. To hear that his father was dead was bad enough, but if it was true that he had been murdered, there would be no warm homecoming. No rest. Yet to think of turning away from the settlement and retracing his steps was not an option. Vengeance had to be obtained. His honour demanded it. Besides, where would he go? Back into service with the legions? *Absolutely not.* It was time to return, no matter what reception awaited him. *I do not question your will, Great Rider. Instead I ask you to protect me, as you have always done, and to help me punish my father's killer.* The fact that this meant slaying a king did not weaken his resolve.

'Come on,' he said to the stallion. 'Let's find you a stable and some food.'

Ariadne turned slowly. 'Polles. What a surprise.' She made no attempt to keep the ice from her voice. Polles might be Kotys' champion, but he was also an arrogant bully who abused his position of authority.

'The king wishes to talk with you,' drawled Polles.

Despite the veneer of courtesy, this was an order. *How dare he?* Ariadne forced her face to remain calm. 'But we spoke only yesterday.'

Polles' thin lips twisted in a travesty of a smile. Everything about him from his striking good looks to his long black hair and oiled muscles smacked of self-importance. 'Nonetheless, he desires . . . the pleasure of your company once more.'

Ariadne did not miss the short but deliberate delay in his delivery. Judging by the other warriors' chuckles, neither had they. Filthy bastard, she thought. Just like your master. 'When?'

'Why, now,' he replied in a surprised tone.

'Where is the king?'

Polles waved languidly over his shoulder. 'In the central meeting area.'

Where all the people can see him. 'I'll be there in a moment.'

'Kotys sent us to accompany you to his side. At once,' said Polles, frowning.

'He may well have done, but I am busy.' Ariadne indicated the fawning old woman. 'Can't you see?'

Polles' face flushed with annoyance. 'I—'

'Are the king's wishes are more important than the work of the god Dionysus?' asked Ariadne, lifting the basket's lid.

'No, of course not,' Polles answered, retreating.

'Good.' Ariadne turned her back on him.

Angry muttering broke out behind her. 'I don't know what you should say to the king. Tell him that we can't find her. Tell him that she's in a trance. Make up something!' snapped Polles. Ariadne heard feet scurrying off and allowed herself a small smile. Soon, however, her conversation with the old woman petered out. It wasn't surprising. Having the king's champion a few steps away, no doubt staring daggers at both of them, would intimidate anyone. Murmuring a blessing on the crone, Ariadne glanced at Polles. 'I'm ready.'

With poor grace, he beckoned her into the midst of his warriors. They closed ranks smartly and Polles led the way forward, bawling at anyone foolish enough to get in his way. It didn't take long to reach the large open area which formed the settlement's centre. The space was roughly circular in shape, and fringed by dozens of huts. Crowds of women gossiped as they carried their washing back from the river. A ragtag assortment of children played or fought with each other in the dirt while skinny mongrels leaped excitedly around them, filling the air with shrill barks. Smoke trickled from the roof of a smithy off to one side; the clang of a hammer on an anvil could be heard from within. Several men waited outside, damaged weapons in hand. There were wooden stalls selling metalwork, hides and essential supplies such as grain, pottery and salt, a miserable inn, and three temples – one each to Dionysus, the rider god, and the mother goddess. That was it.

Like their fellow Thracians, the Maedi were not a race that depended on trade for a living. Their territory was poor in natural resources. Farming provided little more than a subsistence living, so they had evolved into fighters, whose sole purpose of existence was to make war, either in their own land or abroad. The people visible proved this point: they were mostly powerfully built warriors. The majority were red- or brown-haired, with dark complexions. Varying in age from stripling to greybeard, all had the same confident manner. Clad in pleated, short-sleeved tunics that ranged in colour from red and green to brown or cream, they wore sandals, or leather shoes with upturned toes. Many wore the ubiquitous *alopekis*, the pointed fox-skin cap with long flaps to cover the ears. Richer individuals sported bronze or gold torcs around their necks. A sword or a dagger – often both – hung from every man's belt or baldric. They stood around in groups, bragging of their exploits and planning hunting trips.

Polles and his men attracted the attention of everyone in the vicinity. Ariadne felt the weight of the onlookers' stares as they strode towards Dionysus' temple, a larger building than most, with a squat stone pillar on each side of the entrance. She heard their muttering too, and hated it. They were brave enough to fight in battle, but not to stand up to the king they resented. It made her feel very alone.

The king was waiting by the temple doors. He was flanked by bodyguards, while a throng of warriors stood before him. He cut a grand sight. Although he was nearly fifty, Kotys looked a decade younger. His wavy black hair showed not a trace of grey and there were few wrinkles on his shrewd, fox-like face. Over his purple knee-length tunic, Kotys wore a composite iron corselet with gold fittings and twin pectorals of the same precious metal. Layered linen pteryges protected his groin, and greaves inlaid with silver covered his lower legs. He was armed with an ivory-handled *machaira* sword, which hung in an amber-studded scabbard from his gold-plated belt. An ornate Attic helmet sat upon his head, marking his kingship.

As Polles and his men pushed through the throng, Kotys' eyes drank Ariadne in. 'Priestess! Finally, you grace us with your presence,' he called.

'I came as soon as I could, Your Majesty.' Ariadne did not explain further.

'Excellent.' Kotys made a peremptory gesture and her escorts moved aside. Reluctantly, she took a step forward, then a few more. Ariadne could sense Polles smirking. Turning her head, she glared at him. The gesture was not lost on Kotys, who waved his hands again. At this, the bodyguards withdrew some twenty paces to the smithy.

'You must forgive Polles' lack of manners,' said the king. 'He is ill suited to running errands.'

Why send him then? 'I understand,' she murmured, forcibly dampening her anger.

'Good.' One word was the limit of Kotys' own courtesy. 'It would be easy to make more suitable arrangements,' he said brusquely.

'And they would be?' Ariadne arched her eyebrows.

'Dine with me in my quarters some evening. There would be no need for Polles, no need for an escort.'

'I'm afraid that won't be possible,' Ariadne replied icily.

'Are you forgetting who I am?' asked Kotys with a scowl.

'Of course not, Majesty.' Ariadne lowered her eyes in a pretence of demureness. 'Evenings are the best time for communing with the god, however,' she lied.

'That couldn't happen every night,' he growled.

'No, the dreams are only occasional. Dionysus' ways are mysterious, as you would expect.'

He nodded sagely. 'The rider god is the same.'

'Naturally, the erratic nature of their arrival means that I must always be ready to receive them. Spending an evening away from the temple is out of the question. Now, if you would excuse me, I must pray to the god.' Although her heart was thumping in her chest, Ariadne bowed and gave Kotys a beatific smile, before making to move past him.

To Ariadne's shock, he seized her by the arm. She dropped the basket, but unfortunately the lid stayed on.

'You're hurting me!'

'You think that's painful?' Kotys laughed and thrust his face into hers. 'Know this, *bitch*. Toy with me at your peril. I won't tolerate it forever. Remember that I am also a priest. You *will* come to my bed, one way or another. And soon.' He suddenly released his grip, and Ariadne staggered away, white-faced.

What she would have given for a lightning bolt to flash down from the sky and strike him dead. Naturally, nothing of the sort happened. She might be the representative of a deity, but so was Kotys. In a situation such as this, Ariadne was powerless. Kabyle with its powerful council of priests was far, far away. Not that they'd intervene anyway. As ruler of the Maedi and high priest to the rider god, Kotys was the one with all the power. She managed a stiff little bow. Kotys' lips twitched in contemptuous amusement. 'We will speak again,' he said in a grating voice. 'Shortly.'

With trembling hands, Ariadne carried the basket to the temple doors, where she set it down. She lifted the heavy bar which held the portal closed, letting the light flood in to the dim interior. The moment that Kotys was gone, she let out a shuddering gasp. Her knees felt weak beneath her, and she fumbled her way to one of the benches that sat against the side walls. Closing her eyes, Ariadne inhaled deeply and held it as she counted her heartbeat. At the count of four, she let the air out gradually. Dionysus, help me, she begged. Please. She continued to take slow breaths. A vague sense of calm crept over her at last, and some of the tension left her shoulders. A lingering fear remained in Ariadne's belly, however. It would take far more than prayers to stop Kotys taking matters into his own hands. She felt utterly helpless.

A discreet cough interrupted her reverie.

Ariadne turned her head. The figure in the doorway was outlined by sunlight, preventing her from recognising who it might be. Needles of panic stabbed through her before she regained control. Kotys or Polles would not be so polite. 'Who is it?'

'My name is Berisades,' said a respectful voice. 'I'm a trader.'

Ariadne's professional mien took over. 'Come in,' she commanded, gliding towards him. Berisades was a short man in late middle age with a close-cut beard and deep-set, intelligent eyes. 'You've been on the road,' she said, eyeing his green tunic and loose trousers, which were covered in dust.

'I have come from the east. It was a long journey, but we made it without too many losses. I wanted to offer my thanks to the god immediately.' Berisades tapped the purse on his belt, which clinked.

Ariadne ushered the trader forward to the stone altar. Behind it, on a plinth, was a large painted statue of Dionysus. In one hand, the bearded god held a grapevine, and in the other a drinking cup. Waves lapped at his feet, showing his influence over water. A carved bull with the face of a man stood to one side of him while a group of satyrs cavorted on the other. At his feet lay bunches of withered dry flowers, miniature clay vessels containing wine and tiny statues in his likeness. Light winked off pieces of amber and glass. There were long razor clam shells, ribbed cockles and, most prized of all, a rare leopard cowrie shell.

Kneeling, Berisades placed his pouch amongst the other offerings.

Ariadne retreated, leaving him to his devotions. An image of a leering Kotys filled her mind's eye at once, and her spirits plunged. She could see no escape from him and despair overtook her. Thinking that meditation would make a difference, she closed her eyes and tried to enter the calm state that so often provided her with insight into the god's wishes and desires. She failed miserably, instead imagining Kotys manhandling her on to his bed.

'What do they call you, lady?' Berisades' voice was close by. With huge relief, she jerked back to the present. 'Ariadne.'

'You weren't here when last I visited.'

'No. I arrived here six months ago.'

He nodded. 'I remember at the time the old priest not being that well. Still, you're young and healthy. No doubt you'll be here for many years, to gladden the eyes of every grateful traveller wanting to pay his respects.'

'You're very kind,' murmured Ariadne, cringing inside. *If only you knew the truth.*

'It won't be long until the next pilgrim arrives, by the way.'

'No?' Ariadne was barely listening. She was already worrying about Kotys once more.

'I met a warrior yesterday who was returning here. He'd have come in with us, but his horse is lame. Spent years in the Roman auxiliaries, apparently. He wants to give thanks to the tribe's gods for his safe return. A quiet man, but he put himself across well.'

'Really?' replied Ariadne vacantly. She had little interest in the return of yet another tribesman who'd served as a mercenary for the Romans.

Berisades could see that her mind was elsewhere. 'My thanks, lady,' he muttered, withdrawing.

Ariadne gave him a bright smile. Inside, however, she was screaming.

As they climbed the slope to the palisaded settlement, old memories came flooding back. Hot summer days swimming with other boys in the fast-flowing river that ran past one side of the village. Herding the sturdy horses that served as mounts for the wealthier warriors. Hunting for deer, boar and wolves as a youth among the peaks that towered overhead. Being blooded as a warrior after killing his first man at sixteen. Kneeling in the sacred grove at the top of a nearby mountain, praying to the rider god for guidance. The hours of his life he'd spent wishing that his mother had not died birthing his sister, a babe that had lingered less than a month in this world. The day he'd heard the news that Rome had invaded Thrace. Riding to war against its legions with his father Sitalkes, brother Maron and the rest of the tribe. Their first glorious victory, and the bitter defeats that followed. The agonising death of Maron, a week after being thrust through the belly by a Roman sword, a *gladius*. The subsequent vain attempts to overcome the Roman war machine. Ambushes from the hills. Night attacks. Poisoning the rivers. Unions with other tribes that were undone by treachery or greed, or both.

'We Thracians never change, eh?' he asked the stallion. 'Never mind what might be best for Thrace. We fight everyone, even our own. Especially our own. Unite to fight a common enemy, such as Rome? Not a chance!' His barking laugh was short, and angry. The first part of the task his father had set him – serving with the Roman legions – had been completed. He had anticipated a period of relatively normal life before attempting the second part, that of trying to unify the tribes. It was not to be. The dark cloud of war with its bloody lining had found him yet again. Yet he did not try to ignore the adrenalin rush. Instead he welcomed it. *Kotys killed my father. The treacherous bastard. He must die, and soon.*

Used to both his soliloquies and his silences, the horse plodded on behind him.

Two sentries armed with shields and javelins stood by the walled settlement's large gates. They peered at him through jaundiced eyes, muttering to each other as he approached. Few travellers arrived at this late hour, in such bad weather. Even fewer possessed a mail shirt or tinned helmet. Although the newcomer's stallion was lame, it was of fine quality. It was also white – the colour prized by kings.

'Halt!'

He came to a stop, raising his left hand in a peaceful gesture. *Just let me in without too many questions.* 'It's an evil evening,' he said mildly. 'After paying respects to the rider god, it's one to spend by the fire with a cup of wine.'

'You speak our tongue?' asked the older guard in surprise.

'Of course.' He laughed. 'I'm Maedi, like you.'

'Is that so? I wouldn't recognise you from a dog turd,' snarled the second sentry.

'Me neither,' his comrade added in a slightly more civil tone.

'Maybe so, but I was born and raised in this village.' He frowned at their scowls. 'Is this the best welcome I can expect after nearly a decade away?' He was about to say that his name was Peiros, but the first guard spoke first.

'Who are you?' He peered at the newcomer's arms, noticing for the first time the spatters of blood, and then back at his face. 'Wait a moment. I know you! Spartacus?'

Shit! 'That's right,' he replied curtly, caressing the hilt of his sword.

An incredulous grin split the older man's face. 'By all the gods, why didn't you say? I'm Lycurgus. Sitalkes and I rode together.' He threw a warning look at the other guard.

'I remember you,' said Spartacus with an amiable nod. The stare he gave the second sentry was far less friendly. Mortified, the warrior took a sudden interest in the dirt between his feet.

'Things have changed since you left home,' said Lycurgus unhappily. 'Your father—'

'I know,' Spartacus cut in harshly. 'He's dead.'

'Yes.'

He couldn't help himself. 'Died in suspicious circumstances, I hear.'

Lycurgus glanced at his companion. 'Neither of us had anything to do with it. Polles is the one you want to talk to.'

'Polles?'

'The king's chief bodyguard.' The distaste in Lycurgus' voice was clear.

'What about Getas, Seuthes and Medokos? Are they still alive?' he asked casually.

'Oh yes. They've fallen from favour, but they keep their noses clean so Kotys leaves them be.' Aware of the dangerous undercurrent to their conversation, Lycurgus licked his lips. 'Are you . . .?'

Spartacus acted as if he hadn't heard. 'I'm tired. I've been on the road for weeks. All I want is some hot food in my belly and a drink with my old friends. The king can wait until tomorrow. He doesn't need to know that I've returned until then.' *By which time, gods willing, it will be too late. Now that these two know my identity, I've got to act at once. Getas and the others will help.* 'That's not too much to ask, is it?'

'O-of course not,' stammered Lycurgus. He glared at his companion.

'We won't say a word to anyone.'

'Not a soul,' warned Spartacus. Hearing the sudden chill in his voice, the two guards nodded fearfully.

'Good.' Pulling a fold of his cloak over the lower half of his face, Spartacus walked by without another word.

'You fucking idiot,' hissed Lycurgus the instant that he had vanished from sight. 'Spartacus is one the deadliest warriors that our tribe has ever seen! Be grateful that he was in a good mood. You do *not* want to piss him off.'

'What is he planning?'

'I don't know,' snapped Lycurgus. 'I don't want to know. If anyone asks later, we didn't recognise him. Understand?'

The Forgotten Legion

A Forgotten Legion Chronicle

Three Men

Tarquinius, Etruscan warrior and soothsayer, Brennus the Gaul, one of the most feared gladiators in Rome, and Romulus, the boy slave sold to gladiator school but dreaming of vengeance for himself and for his twin sister, Fabiola.

One Woman

Fabiola, sold into prostitution at thirteen, loved by the second most powerful man in the Republic, driven by hatred for the unknown father who raped her mother.

Slaves of Rome

Their destiny is bound and interwoven in an odyssey which begins in a Rome riven by political corruption and violence, but ends far away, at the very border of the known world, where the tattered remnants of a once-huge Roman army – the Forgotten Legion – will fight against overwhelming odds, and the three men will meet their destiny.

'Bloody fast-paced, thrilling . . . a masterful debut that should not be missed.' James Rollins, author of *The Last Oracle*

'I thoroughly enjoyed *The Forgotten Legion* – so much so that I stayed up until 2 a.m. to finish it.' Manda Scott, author of the 'Boudica' novels

arrow books

ALSO BY BEN KANE

The Silver Eagle

A Forgotten Legion Chronicle

The Forgotten Legion fought against almighty odds at the very edge of the known world – and lost.

Now Brennus the Gaul, Tarquinius the Etruscan soothsayer and Romulus, bastard son of a Roman nobleman, are prisoners of Parthia. They dream of escape, but in the brutal fighting which lies ahead, only two will survive.

Meanwhile, Fabiola, Romulus's twin sister, is caught up in the vicious eddies of Roman politics. Hunted by the slave catchers, she flees, hoping to find her lover, Brutus, bound for Alexandria with Caesar.

Ben Kane's brilliant second novel plunges his characters into a cauldron of war and terror, as Caesar and the Roman Republic hurtle towards their day of reckoning.

'The Forgotten Legion marches again . . . *The Silver Eagle* is an utterly engrossing combination of historical fact and believable fiction that draws the reader in and holds his interest to the last page' Douglas Jackson, author of *Caligula*

arrow books

The Road to Rome

A Forgotten Legion Chronicle

A voyage of terror and heartache, violence and betrayal.

Betrayal
They have fought for Rome in the Forgotten Legion and been press-ganged into Caesar's legions in Alexandria, but Romulus, the ex-gladiator, and Tarquinius, the Etruscan soothsayer, are also runaway slaves – for which the punishment is crucifixion. Who can they trust not to betray them on the bloody field of battle?

Conspiracy
Meanwhile in Rome, Romulus's twin sister, Fabiola, faces great danger. Beloved mistress of Brutus, she is being wooed by his deadly enemy, Marcus Antonius – and drawn into the conspiracy to murder Caesar, the man she believes is her hated father.

Murder
As events move remorselessly towards the fateful Ides of March, a final day of reckoning awaits all three of Ben Kane's great protagonists on the lawless streets of Rome.

arrow books

THE POWER OF READING